The Kingdom of Deception

LUDEN GRAY

ISBN: 979-8-218-52643-6 (Paperback)

Cover art design by: Anze Ban V.

Printed in the United States

First Edition: October 2024

For my husband, whose unwavering belief carried me through.
For my brother, whose absence is felt every day as he traverses the
other side of the veil, and for my mother,
whom I cherish beyond words.

Content warning: Depictions of torture, sexual assault, gore, and violence. Mental health is important. Our main character goes on a journey to better hers, don't read her story at the expense of your own well-being.

Contents

"Three things can not long stay hidden: the sun, the moon, and the truth." —Buddah

Prologue

They called her *wretched. Marked. Unwanted.* Life in the gutters was all that remained for a sired child. Amara trudged through ankle high puddles and pulled her cloak over her head so as not to endure the unforgiving stares of her human neighbors. She wasn't the only one with the mark of a sired child on her chest, even if it felt like she bared the human's hatred alone.

"Your sire didn't even want you, *sireling,*" a man spat at her.

"Poor little orphan Ashenfall," one of her classmates mocked, hurling a rock at her. She wiped rain and mud from her face and kept her eyes fixated on the alley ahead. Tucked between crumbling cobblestone buildings, hidden in the shadows, her friends awaited.

"If we kill her, that's one less Nephilim to empower Hadeon," a man whispered to another as they coated her with something rancid and alcoholic from a jug. She turned from them, forcing her feet to move quicker through the mud and feces that lined the streets. Hadeon, the ruler of their land, a Fallen Angel turned tyrant. Just like the other Hallowed Fallen. She shuddered.

"Don't be ridiculous, that'll get them sniffing around here," the other man answered in disgust.

Amara swore under her breath in frustration. She was not at fault for the actions of her father, or any other Fallen Angel for that matter. She couldn't control where she came from any more than she could control the color of her hair or eyes. Did they really believe she, a child, agreed with what the fallen angels did to them?

"Amara," Laine whispered and gestured her into the dimly lit stairwell. It led beneath a tavern, into a safe space for them to converse.

She followed him into the basement and pushed her cloak off.

"No matter how you hide your face and pretend, you'll never be one of them," Thomas shook out his shaggy hair, water flinging everywhere.

"But I could be. We all could be. We can carve these marks out and hide. We don't have to transition! They can't make us," she reasoned with her pitifully small voice.

"That doesn't change who we are and who we belong to." Laine sighed.

"We should be able to decide—"

"We can't! They'll kill you for not adhering to the law. You know that," Lou asserted as she shook the dice in her pale hand.

"You want to make it to your eleventh birthday, I suggest you start accepting your fate," Laine nodded in her direction from the worn down chair.

Amara took her spot on the floor and picked at a scab on her arm. She would forever be hated by the very thing she wanted to be—human. The small group played with their dice and bet on the rolls with pebbles.

"Here's to only a decade before we earn our wings," Thomas said sarcastically. He held up his small crumbling clay cup of water and they all toasted unenthusiastically.

Amara found herself instinctively scratching at the mark over her heart, needing to tear herself free from her own body. *I won't cry, I won't cry, I won't cry.*

Later that night, as the village settled into an uneasy quiet, Amara hurried down the narrow streets toward her home. The rain had slowed to a drizzle, but the cold seeped through her cloak, chilling her to the bone. She sensed them before she saw them—three men lurking in the shadows, their eyes gleaming with malicious intent.

"Hey, sireling!" one of them called out, his voice dripping with venom.

Amara's heart pounded as she quickened her pace, her little feet not strong enough to evade them. They closed in on her, herding her like a lost lamb into a dark, narrow alley. She clung to the damp cobblestone walls, the air thick with the stench of rot and decay. She bit back bile as filthy water seeped into her shoes.

"Help me!" She screamed into an open window above.

One of the men, a burly figure with a twisted sneer, lunged at her, kicking her hard in the ribs. Pain exploded through her side, knocking the breath from her lungs. She doubled over, gasping, but there was no respite.

Unshed tears stung her eyes as another man, lean and gaunt, swung his fist into her small, round face. The force of the blow sent her sprawling into the mud, her vision swimming with stars.

As she found her place in the excrement and mud on the ground, she saw an elderly woman peek out of the window before closing it and turning the other cheek.

Their hatred for the fallen angels poured out in every strike. The third man, reeking of alcohol and desperation, raised a club and brought it down on the back of her head. Amara's world tilted and darkened, her body wracked with agony.

"Please," she begged. Mud filled her mouth, choking her words. But the men didn't stop. She was more than a child to them; she was a symbol of everything wrong in their lives. She was the spawn of their tyrants, a seed of a poison tree given life.

"I'm sorry," she whimpered, shielding her head with her arms. Her apologies were met with more blows, each one fueled by the men's grief, anger, and helplessness. Disease, poverty, and the endless struggle to survive had hardened their hearts, and now they vented their rage on her.

She clung to the sound of Laine's laugh, so high and careless. She grappled onto her friend's smiles as another blow landed and stole her breath.

Amara's vision blurred as blood and rain mingled on her face. She could feel herself slipping away, the edges of her consciousness fraying. The men's voices became distant echoes, their insults blending with the roaring in her ears. Their faces turned to smudged shadows against the dim alley walls.

"Laine," she whispered. She clung to the image of her closest friend smiling wide just minutes before.

I won't cry. I won't cry. I won't cry.

I will not die in tears.
And then, the darkness took her.

ACT
I

Chapter 1

It had been nearly two years since Amara Ashenfall was last seen. At least that was what all of the 'missing' posters reported. She pulled on her hood and ducked out of view. The poor sketch of her didn't do her justice, not that she was anything special, but honestly her aunt could have given a better account of her features. Not that she wanted to be found. She rolled her eyes and pushed through the creaky entrance of the tavern in which she occupied a room and moved toward the stairs.

"Cora!" The pudgy bearded bartender yelled. It wasn't her real name of course but she had grown used to it. "Come sit, have a drink. It's awfully slow tonight." He grinned. He didn't sound local—some northern accent, maybe Pran? She doubted he cared about who ruled what kingdom so long as the ale kept flowing. Still, he must've fled Ravenyr when the Dark One seized it, like everyone else.

She didn't understand all of the fuss, ultimately every continent was under the rule of the Hallowed Fallen anyway. Who cared if it was one of the Hallowed Fallen or a Rogue Fallen running the individual kingdoms. Same oppression, different oppressors, as far as she was concerned. The Rogue Fallen may take kingdoms but would never overthrow entire continents. The Hallowed would always maintain power, they would always control everything because they had access to some unknown source of power that no other Fallen Angel did.

She took pity on the man she'd grown used to, and gave him a few coppers in exchange for a platter of bread and chocolates. The amount of food wasn't worth the cost but she had always been overly generous.

"Thanks pumpkin!" His wife beamed. Something seemed off about her though, her smile was cut short and Amara noticed the nervous glance at the front door. *Weird.*

She decided to check the perimeter of the tavern, just to be sure. Maybe paranoia was getting to her after so long on the run. After finding nothing out of the ordinary she exhaled a quiet breath of relief. The closely stacked cobblestone buildings seemed to lean from age, as though bowing before the storm that was rolling in.

She felt strange in the humid fall air that usually brought her comfort. She had a gut feeling that something was off as she paced in front of the tavern that had become her temporary home. She had taken up many temporary homes in many small villages during her time on the run. She forever occupied beds in stranger's homes but never belonged and would never settle. She was cursed with a unique form of loneliness that would sew its way into the fabric of her soul until hope for companionship slipped further out of view.

Amara debated whether or not she should spend the night elsewhere, before deciding that she would stay one last night at the tavern and disappear the following morning. More than a few close encounters had led her to trust her instincts which, at the moment, were screaming at her to disappear again. She was more than missing, she was being hunted.

Once in her room she sat the platter on the small wooden table and began removing her cloak. She pulled daggers from her hips and tossed them on the floor with a loud clanking sound. She bent down to remove the hidden one that was strapped to her thigh when she heard the floorboards creak to her right side. *In the closet,* she thought, yanking the dagger free.

Amara straightened immediately, holding her favorite dagger in front of her. She squinted her eyes to look between the tiny planks of the door. Had someone spotted her? Turned her in? The worn handle of the dagger was familiar in her hand.

She could feel that she wasn't alone in the room, as though the closet had taken on life. She backed slowly toward the window, trying not to give away that she was aware of the other person in the room. She always kept one of the window latches undone for quick escape, no sense in fumbling with two locks when one took long enough in a life or death situation.

She glanced down at the road where pouring rain created mud. Three cloaked figures lurked below her windowsill. This was it. She had gotten so comfortable with conformity and her new identity that she had forgotten what time of year it was... or at least what it meant. Maybe she wanted to forget.

"Are you going to stand there all night?" she demanded, glancing toward the person looming in her closet. Amara knew that sneaking out was not an option, she had to confront the problem head on. She was not a step ahead this time.

She could kill him and try to run. Though, she had never killed anyone before, and would she even be able to run? Were more ominous hooded men out back?

The closet burst open in a dramatic fashion, sending fragments of wood flying. The man was much larger than she would have guessed. He was a nasty looking thing with missing teeth, a neck beard, and disproportionate body parts as though he had been stuck together by a child.

I can get out of this.

He took a heavy step in her direction, at which point she effortlessly hurled the knife in his direction. It missed his heart but struck him in his shoulder. He looked at it with a wicked smile but didn't have time to remove it before she followed it up by throwing a piece of firewood at his head. The hulking monstrosity charged at the girl with a loud shout. She ducked low out of his reach, picked up her other two daggers from the floor and spun to a standing position. He looked half impressed, as though he expected her to be easy to take.

Amara yanked her shoulder pack from the ground and bolted for the bedroom door. The sound of heavy feet slammed the ground as the man was hot on her trail, but she was faster. She had an escape route planned, if she could just make it out of the tavern. She would head to the kitchen where a side door should be unguarded. If she could do that she would make her way east into an alleyway, through the thick brush, and down into a fairly small tunnel entrance. The giant guy and most men would not fit in there so she could at least get a head start. Where the tunnel led was a later problem, she just needed to get to it.

She had come this close to capture a month earlier but narrowly avoided the guards who set up an ambush at the inn that she was renting a room from. They were getting more desperate as the annual Crucible drew closer and with it, her risk of getting caught was higher. Whatever guard or mercenary that turned her over would be paid handsomely, and that made laying low exceptionally difficult.

She made her way down the stairs, but the second her foot touched the floor she was abruptly grabbed around the waist by strong arms.

"Cora, long time no see."

"Shit." She grunted and squirmed against the man's familiar body.

"No more running," he hissed. He seized her by her forearms before roughly spinning her around to face him.

"Bastian, never pegged you for a loyal bitch to the Hallowed Fallen's plight," she spat. Bastian was a human, a guard within the kingdom, charged with maintaining order on a human level. He sneered at her, his red orange hair was tousled into a mess, he clearly had been roughing it while searching for her. She and Bastian had slept together briefly, months prior, before she left that area and made her way to this village. Leaving the kingdom of Findaria was physically impossible so she had become one with the forests and villages of the land.

"You played me for a fool...*Amara,*" he purred.. He shoved her hard against the wooden wall, and with a mere flick of his hand he shooed off two other guards who were prepared to tie her up. "Smart, not allowing me to see that mark over your heart," he mused.

A dark line in between her breasts, a line dividing all sired children from humanity, a line marking her for everything she had been running from. She spat in his face, causing him to drop her arms and grab her around the throat with one hand while he wiped her spit from his face.

Anytime she had slept with him, she was careful that he didn't see the mark. Once he started asking questions, she ghosted him and changed where she lived. He sneered at her, anger contorting his features. He tightened his grip on her throat, and the pain was almost blinding.

Amara knew Bastian would take joy in handing her in simply because she disappeared on him. He was the kind of person whose pride was fragile, his ego easily injured. It made him angry, violent. He slammed her head against the wall, tightening his grip around her throat once more until stars danced in her line of sight.

She couldn't do it; she couldn't let herself be turned in. Not after all the time she spent running. She refused to participate in the Crucible, she wouldn't make it, she wasn't cut out for it. Panic swelled in her chest and with a violent scream, she lashed out with her dagger before Bastian could react.

Time slowed, allowing the scene before her to be etched into her mind forever. A clean slice across his jugular brought him to his knees before her. In a sickening twist of fate, blood sputtered out of a mouth that she had once kissed. The spurting blood from his jugular painted her cheeks, a bare artist canvas stained forever.

Amara acted fast as the guards shouted, vaulting over Bastian's twitching body toward the tavern's back exit. His blood stained her skin like ink—guilt setting in with every step. Her vision tunneled, but she kept running, cursing herself for realizing too late that her hosts had sold her out.

Rain drenched her as she burst through the back door—only to find hooded men waiting. One grabbed her and slammed her to the ground, knocking the wind from her lungs. She coughed, scrambled into a bush, and ran. Thorns slashed her skin as she pushed through as if they were accomplices in the guards hunt. She stumbled into an alley, then dove into another thorn bush at its end, desperate to escape the pounding boots on her trail.

Blood mingled on her arms—hers and Bastian's—as she dragged herself through the brush. Voices faded, but she didn't stop until she reached the woods and collapsed. Vomiting from pain and guilt, she willed herself to focus.

Moonlight revealed her escape plan's natural land markers. She wrapped her arms with fabric to prepare for the tunnel crawl—then froze. Something rustled ahead. It couldn't be the men. Not yet.

The girl flattened herself to the ground at the base of a massive oak tree when definite footsteps signaled that someone else was in the woods with her. *Shit.*

"You can't see me but I can see you," a man's voice purred through the darkness. Chills danced up her spine and around her neck like a snake warning her of his intention. She didn't move.

"Hold your breath all you like. You can't silence the fear seeping from your skin."

She shivered, a physical response to the beings presence despite the sheen of sweat which covered her. He was no human. The silence that followed his words allowed her to hear a leaf flowing toward the ground behind her. The crickets seized their song, owls held their posts, and not even the rodents in the brush dared to move. She searched the forest frantically for her foe who already had her within his grasp.

Somewhere in the shadows before her, the endless void of night took the shape of a human with expansive wings. He sauntered through the woods toward her until he came into view. The bushes seemed to bow before him. The roots in the ground fled from him and returned to the safety of the soil. She had never seen a Nephilim before, the sight of him drawing a choked sob from her throat.

The Nephilim stood in a small clearing, his spread wings shrinking the forest itself down in size. They twitched, each feather catching moonlight as he took another step in her direction.

"Come now, don't make this difficult," he reasoned with hands folded behind his back. He added an amused skip to his walk as though to taunt her.

She stood and darted in the opposite direction. *This is NOT happening.* Her feet pounded the forest floor in tune to her drumming heart.

A rush of wind slammed into her back, sending her onto her face. Her cheek collided hard with a rock and sliced her delicate flesh open. The mighty beat of wings made her ears pop as he landed above her, one booted foot on each side of her puny form.

Amara trembled beneath him and crawled forward. He laughed maniacally and pressed his foot into the center of her back. His strong hands flipped her over so he could inspect her. He practically sniffed her like a dog. She came face to face with a man who appeared to be carved from marble. His blue and silver eyes scanned over her body as he laced his hands behind his back once more.

Silk black tendrils of hair fell into his face and she blinked in disbelief as his onyx wings threatened to consume the both of them. She was rendered speechless, motionless, frozen with terror.

"You're done running, Ashenfall." He smiled the most beautiful smile she had ever beheld.

He waved his hand in front of her face and darkness claimed her swifter than a whisper in the wind.

She was face flat on the floor of a wooden carriage when she came to. She tried to roll over with a groan before she came to the awful realization that they had hog tied her.... Actually *fucking* hog tied her. Her arms and legs burned and her lip snagged against a splintering wood board until it bled. As the wagon was pulled forward along the bumpy path, her body was tossed around agonizingly with a series of thumps.

A lump formed in her throat, her past crashing over her like a tidal wave. For twenty-five months, she had desperately avoided this exact outcome, hell for her entire life she had been dodging it. The soles of her feet were worn and aged beyond their years from all of the running throughout her life. Scars riddled her body from every attempt to escape, every encounter with guards, every beating she took as a child for simply *existing*. Memories of a lifetime spent skirting the label of 'marked' or 'sired child' flashed through her mind. Her hands trembled, her breath quickened, and she felt the crushing weight of reality settle on her shoulders.

She heard men chuckle up front—there must have been two of them on the other side of the bars who were actually handling the horses. Their gruff voices sounded nothing like the Nephilim that captured her. He had turned her over to the men who had been pursuing her.

"Bastard!"

The men stopped speaking for a moment before they burst into laughter at her expense. She tried to block it out, recalling the way humans could be so cruel to her kind.

"The Crucible awaits!" One of them guffawed.

The Crucible.

For over seven hundred years, the Crucible was a way for the Fallen to strengthen their kingdoms. Sired Children were destined to transform into full blown Nephilim but only once they competed in and survived the Crucible.

Descending from the heavens, the Hallowed Fallen came to rule within the human realm, establishing their own dominion. Their God had abandoned his little human experiment, turning the world into a dumping ground for angels that displeased him.

The Fallen bred with humans, siring warriors, healers, historians, and servants. Their desire to breed was trifold: strengthen themselves, strengthen the kingdoms, and pay their debt to Lucifer. Each successful transformation into a Nephilim not only strengthened their kingdoms in numbers but also granted the siring Fallen new power through some magic that no one seemed to understand. Usually, more children of the Fallen died in the Crucible than transitioned. The bloodshed of their children was perhaps more coveted than their survival and transition —a sacrifice to Lucifer himself. As long as the Fallen agreed to sacrifice to him, Lucifer would leave humans to their mercy.

When God abandoned the human realm, Lucifer could have risen and brought the Fallen to their knees. Instead, after a millennium of collecting human souls through his own servants, he struck a deal. Let his Fallen brethren have the human world and be guaranteed souls of the sired children. Allow the fate of humans to be decided by the Hallowed Fallen, and Lucifer would leave their realm for good.

And so, the ten Hallowed Fallen crowned themselves rulers. Gods amongst men, no army could fight them off, and eventually, humans stopped trying. As Nephilim were created to safeguard the kingdoms, there was no longer a war for the humans to fight. As long as the humans stopped resisting, they were allowed to lead 'normal' lives.

So they did, for a while.

The Dark One had been sowing discord amongst other fallen angels outside of the Hallowed ones, known as the Rogue Fallen. News of an uprising had been spreading fast in recent decades, giving humans hope for a life free of the iron fist of the Hallowed Fallen's rule.

Amara grunted in discomfort as the men paraded her toward the Crucible as though she were stolen property to be returned to a king. She scoffed to herself. The reality of her fate sunk its teeth into her and threatened to bleed her dry, her stomach turned, and a shiver washed over her. Thoughts of what transitioning into a Nephilim would look like, *feel* like, gnawed at her as she pondered her mysterious parentage and how it led her to the back of a carriage bound and gagged.

There were so many blank spaces in her memory, not enough answers, and more doors to more questions than she had the capacity to open. She was staring down the blade of a sword poised to kill her but it was dressed in the fancy garb of a year long set of trials and tests. She swallowed hard against the cloth gag in her mouth. Her obvious desire to not participate in the dreaded event would surely make her an easy target, most likely sealing her fate sooner rather than later.

"Can you at least untie me?!" She screamed through the soaked cloth. It came out mostly muffled.

"She must have come from Rase, that one. Stubborn as a rock." A deep voiced man chuckled.

Rase, one of the Hallowed Fallen. Each Fallen was different, possessing abilities and powers as unique to one as the stars in the sky. Rase had a reputation for being ruthless. Rumors said that he once leveled one of his villages because its people were whispering about hope from the Dark One. All he left was ashes. She shuddered. The thought of being likened, much less sired to him, filled her with nausea.

The wagon hit a large hole or rock, and sent Amara rolling onto her side. She winced in pain as her right arm was crushed underneath her. Her back hit something soft, hay maybe? But it didn't do much for the hard wooden floor that crushed her limbs beneath her. She let out a scream in agony before another bump made her roll back onto her face with a dizzying impact.

She supposed going to the Crucible willingly was a lot less painful. It was viewed as an honor for a majority of children of the Fallen, with celebrations to send them off while mothers watched on in excitement and worry. That was not the case for Amara who had been without a mother since she was two and left without a clue about the father who sired her.

Tears filled her eyes as her body hummed with pain, her limbs went numb, and fear consumed her. Would she have the strength and will to survive?

Chapter 2

Hours dragged on, and mercifully, Amara passed out at some point. With a kick to her ribs and clumsy work of her ropes, the men woke her up. Her limbs had been overextended for so long that she couldn't even use them. Which earned her another kick from one of the guards.

"On your feet, murderer," a grizzly older man growled and hauled her upward by the crook of her arm. Her knees were weak and shook beneath her. A smell had been stinging her nose since she roused but it wasn't until she was standing that she could see the source.

Her eyes widened. With horror she realized the soft thing she rolled into was not, in fact, hay; but a body wrapped in burlap cloth. Blood coated the cloth around the head of the body and orange red hair visible at the top struck her harshly as she realized just whose body she had been traveling with. She doubled over and vomited on the floor of the carriage. Her head spun as she realized the sticky substance on her clothes was congealed blood. *I killed someone, I killed Bastian, I really killed someone.* She examined her stained hands which brought forth more vomit from her core. She groaned and shuddered.

"Little bitch!" The burly younger one yelled and shoved her forward out of the carriage. She hit the cobblestone hard, her arms failing to catch her. She choked up some vomit and groaned before rolling onto her back. *Fuck.* Her limbs were stinging as though pins and needles had been inserted into every inch of her skin.

Airborne humanoid figures in the skies overhead confirmed their arrival at the Sanctum Metere, the hair on the back of her neck stood at attention. She sat herself up as the men hauled Bastian's body from the carriage and onto a flat cart with a single horse. The woman charged with taking his body regarding her with a look so fowl that her stomach turned.

Walls rose into the sky before her, impossibly high. Large double iron doors towered over her. She had underestimated how large the compound was, it stretched to each side of her for over a mile. Through the doors she could see buildings surrounding a massive black stone coliseum. She couldn't breath as she looked into the face of the beast she had been running from for her entire life. The place in which she would surely draw her last breath.

"Welcome to the Sanctum Metere," a familiar voice came and he flashed her a wicked smile. "The center of everything here in Findaria." He spread his arms wide. "Whether by death or honor of transition, you will not leave this place the way you are entering it now."

She zoned out, unable to respond above the roaring in her ears.

It was *him*. It was the Nephilim that caught her. She stood before him, frozen. His wings had vanished but his demeanor demanded respect. He looked like the type of person to bite the heads off of serpents for fun. She stared through him, her brain refusing to accept the reality of her situation.

"The Crowned Magister is waiting for you, Ashenfall," the Nephilim snapped as he examined her.

"Stand, *inbellis*," the older man who called her a murderer before demanded. *A new nickname, great.*

Inbellis, she knew, meant coward and she rolled her eyes but stood on her own two shaky legs. She turned to the nasty man and spat at him, narrowly missing his shoes.

He lunged for her, so easily blinded by anger that she chuckled. She really didn't care what he did to her; she was already beaten down and at the last place she ever wanted to be. The Nephilim stepped in front of her with lighting speed and grabbed the man's fist.

"You've done enough damage, she's my charge now," he growled. The giant man's eyes widened with fear as he was pushed backward. Amara looked between the two, the Nephilim bearing a certain clean cut beauty that she had never seen on any human.

He turned to face her before grabbing her arm. Despite her attempt to recoil from him, he yanked her behind him with strong hands. Again she saw those damned deep blue eyes with silver lining them—the silver confirming once more that he was a transitioned Nephilim. His short jet black hair was tousled, but not messy, and he walked with a purpose. He had nearly a foot on her, strong shoulders, an athletic build that led to a narrow waist. He was shrouded in dark clothes, leather straps, a long sword over his shoulder, and a belt with daggers hanging from it.

As he led her into the compound, something hummed inside of her, she could feel in her soul that they had entered the sacrificial grounds of the Crucible. If she died on this land, she would die a sacrifice to Lucifer. The magic which willed it so invaded her bloodstream and pulsed to life all on its own. She would be nothing more than a means to pay off Lucifer. Another sacrifice to ensure he held up his end of the bargain; the lands are to be ruled by the Hallowed Fallen without his interference. *No.* She would not be just another statistic, another sacrifice, another faceless name on the stones surrounding the cremation pit.

There weren't any people around, but since the Crucible season was still two weeks away, she wasn't surprised. She inspected the massive two-story building where all of the children of fallen lived through the duration of the Crucible and wondered how many of them there would be that year. More than that, she wondered how much death she would witness in the upcoming year.

"Can you walk faster." The man huffed.

"Can you walk slower?" She stopped and yanked her arm away. His legs were significantly longer than hers and she was doing her best to keep up with him. Especially given that her legs were still weak and shaking from being hogtied for hours... *Days actually.*

"You'll be given a tour of the grounds, don't distract yourself with it now," he snapped. He led her into a fairly boring looking building that was a little bigger than the others. She could have sworn he huffed some name under his breath but she didn't catch it nor care what these people thought of her.

She shouldn't be surprised that she had to see the Crowned Magister, given her indiscretions and avoidance of the Crucible the previous year. She didn't remember his name but he had been running the Crucible for at least a century. He was a Nephilim, born to a Hallowed Fallen by the name of Lonan over five hundred years ago. His ruthlessness had kept him in the position he held and she was not looking forward to answering to him. Maybe he would just kill her, wouldn't that be easier?

He led her to a room at the end of an arched hallway. When the doors opened, he stepped aside and allowed her to enter the room first. She got distracted, inspecting the muscles, scars, and patterns of ink on his arms, nearly missing that she was meant to face the Crowned Magister alone.

"Good luck," he whispered with a wicked taunting smile and shoved her. She stumbled, her weak legs betraying her, and landed on all fours.

She scrambled to her feet and regarded the man on the other side of the room with cold detachment. *What was she supposed to say to him?*

Against the darkness of the room, the aged man appeared as though he was emitting his own light. She didn't know what she expected, but it wasn't for him to actually *look* five centuries old. She would not have been able to imagine it if she were asked to. He had powder white hair slicked back and falling down his back. The wrinkles in his face showed that he had many years of blood on his hands and whether or not he cared, the weight of those souls aged him.

He tilted his head as though reading her, and she defiantly chose not to speak. He sat on a stone throne, clad in a fine dark red suit with golden cufflinks. The color only served to wash out his already pale aging skin.

"It's been a great many years since a sired child has killed to avoid the Crucible." His voice was deep and shaky. Could he die? How long did Nephilim live? She shifted on her feet and crossed her arms. "Do you know who your sire is?"

"No." She scowled.

"No matter, the day of transition will tell us." He sighed. "I have hopes that your stubbornness will see you through the Crucible. If only to see who it was that sired such an obstinate child." He looked bored and she felt underwhelmed. She glanced behind her at the drafty empty room. She was expecting some kind of beating with his reputation.

"You will take up residence in Oaks Hall until the Crucible. "Like all Fallen Sired," he ordered, "you'll heal then enter the Crucible through the hunt." She blinked in confusion.

"The what?" She raised her eyebrows.

"Praeceptor Cathmore will give you a better understanding of how we run things here at the Sanctum. You are annoyingly ignorant for a sired child," he grumbled.

She didn't bother to argue the point. Her need to avoid the Crucible did not come with an interest in finding information about the upcoming year, since she hadn't planned on being in attendance.

"You're annoyingly arrogant," she whispered under her breath. Doing so sent adrenaline pulsing into her head.

"Speak up child, I already know of your cowardice. Your death will be neither swift nor painless if you continue to behave this way," he threatened and she swore the room vibrated in response to the bass in his voice. She narrowed her eyes at him, bit the inside of her cheek, and thought better of saying anything else.

The doors to the massive stone room opened upon his silent command and the same man that took her there, led her back out. His hands were rough as he squeezed her forearm and dragged her behind him.

"Praeceptor," the Crowned Magister boomed. He stopped in his tracks and turned, hesitantly. "I expect you to get her in line, by whatever means necessary," the Crowned Magister demanded.

"Of course." Praeceptor Cathmore nodded his head as Amara looked between them. She swallowed hard. He dismissed them with a wave of his wrinkled hand.

He led her out of the Crowned Magister's presence, with a walk that felt as though she were being marched to the gallows. She knew better than to run, she was no match for a fully transitioned Nephilim. He would have his full powers; he would have an Imperium. She wondered what his Imperium could be, what talent or power did his bloodline grant him? She refused to think about what her Imperium could be upon transition. She didn't really expect to make it that far anyway.

The Imperium manifests upon one's transition into Nephilim, signs of it showing beforehand. The Imperium usually reflects the Fallen Angel who sired the Nephilim, imparting some of their power into their sired ones. Amara didn't want to know what kind of Imperium she would have to learn to wield, what it would feel like, or if she could survive it. When she sighed, the man looked over his shoulder as they made it to the bottom of the stone stairs.

"This tunnel will take us to Oaks Hall. The sired children dormitories connect to the underground tunnels, but you will not use these when the Crucible begins. Understood?" She looked around the small cobblestone arched tunnel.

"So why even show me that they exist?"

He shrugged. "It cuts our walk in half, and I *dare* you to disobey me." He stepped into her.

She nodded shakily, the anger flaring in his eyes shut her down completely. He turned away from her to begin down the tunnel.

"You're Praeceptor Cathmore?"

He brushed something off of his shoulder and glanced back at her.

"I am," he said stoically, without giving anything else away. The Praeceptor's were the instructors of the Sanctum Metere, though she didn't know what they taught. She knew the Praeceptor's were instructors made up of those serving time following their transformation, forced to teach the rising Nephilim. Magisters taught there as well, also Nephilim, though aged, and were the career teachers of the Sanctum Metere.

Most Nephilim were ordered to instruct during the Crucible for a few years, while others were sent off to be honed into weapons for the Hallowed. Not that teaching and serving the Crucible at the Sanctum Metere sounded pleasant, but she didn't want to be sent off to war training. She didn't have time to focus on her fate outside of the Crucible. She had to survive a year of this hell, she had to get through trials both physical and mental. If she so happened to survive them, would she survive her transition? Some didn't.

She followed him for a while down the dimly lit tunnel, passing some branching off hallways with more spiral staircases. The shuffling of their feet as they walked was the only thing filling the silence. She rubbed at the bruises forming around her wrists, her ankles throbbing from where she had been hogtied.

As luck would have it, she had been looking down at her feet when Praeceptor Cathmore stopped, and she collided with his broad back. She knocked her head on his shoulder blade, hitting the ridge of her eyebrow. The pain reverberated through her skull leaving her stunned for a second.

"Can you at least watch where you're walking?" He huffed in annoyance as he faced her.

She rolled her eyes. Her body ached and she just wanted to get to Oaks Hall so she could clean up and rest. Eating would be great too, given it had been nearly two full days since she last ate and she was feeling weak.

"Do not roll your eyes at me. You will address me with respect, as you will all of the Praeceptor's and Magister's. If you don't have the self-preservation to *at least* do that, I might as well kill you where you stand," he growled. Anger sparked behind those stark blue and silver eyes. It was as though he had a need to release some built-up tension and was just waiting for her to try him. She narrowed her eyes at him and before she could stop herself, she balled up her fist and swung. With ease he caught her by her wrist, as if she was no stronger than a child.. "Listen here, you little brat. That was your one shot at me. You try it again and you'll be on your ass before you can blink."

She blinked. *Brat?*

"Don't call me that," she snarked and jerked her aching wrist from his grip.

"Why?" He paused and leaned against the brick wall beside her. "It's what you are. You ran from your first call to the Crucible—undoubtedly because you just didn't want to do the hard thing and go through it. Then upon your second call, you killed someone to try to run." He sighed and spun a ring around his finger. "And on top of that, you are acting like a child right now," he made eye contact with her, his eyes darkening.

She narrowed her eyes at the infuriating man. Anything that she wanted to say, wanted to spit at him and hurt him, would surely only end in pain.

With a smirk, he turned down the hallway that looked exactly like all of the others and she followed him up the spiraling stairs. He unlocked the ancient looking metal door with a ring of keys she hadn't seen before and stepped aside to let her in.

The small door opened up to a massive hallway with extravagant cherry wood pillars, glass cabinets with artifacts, and at least a dozen more hallways and doors on either side. The place smelled clean, every surface looked as though dust had never laid upon it. She could make out swords and daggers displayed. Amongst them were challises, hand carved statues, and more historically significant pieces that she couldn't process quick enough as he pulled her through the expansive space.

Nearly at the end of the room, he took her down a small hallway with three doors and black wooden walls. He opened the door at the end and allowed her to walk into it. He eyed her cautiously and with disdain. She had a feeling she should expect that a lot. She was a murderer after all. Briefly, she could quite literally feel the blood on her hands but she firmly shook it off.

The room before her wasn't anything spectacular, unlike the rest of the Oak's hall, but it was still grander than any living situation she'd had. It was simple; a large four poster bed, two side tables, a wardrobe, and a small desk area. All of it was cherry wood like much of the rest of the building's furniture. Above the bed, angels wings spread wide, glowing silver amongst the dimness of the room. The green vine wallpaper tied the space together well, she thought.

"They aren't real, only art," Praeceptor Cathmore said, nodding toward the angel wings. "The washroom is through that door." He pointed to the only other door in her room.

"Where do I get the water?" she asked, her voice hoarse. Usually water in the villages was carried from nearby rivers. There were wells placed throughout the town, but still the water had to be carried from point A to point B. It was the last thing she wanted to do, and boiling water for a bath sounded exhausting but she needed it.

He tilted his head at her as though confused before understanding washed over and softened his features. He strolled past her toward the washroom and she followed.

"The Sanctum Matere has running water in every washing facility. Same way that the Hallowed Fallens homes do, and the higher paid Nephilim I suppose," he explained. He turned a brass knob that was mounted in the wall above the stone washing tub. Water poured out effortlessly and she watched with her mouth agape. "Turn right for warmer water."

She wanted to ask how it warmed itself as she looked around but found no answers. He turned the knob and the water stopped flowing.

"The hand sinks work the same way." He pointed to her small bowl shaped hand sink in the corner of the small washroom. She nodded and crossed her arms.

"I will give you an hour to attend to your needs before I bring food," he said casually before leaving her alone in the washroom. She exhaled a breath she hadn't known she was holding when she was finally alone.

Night fell on her first evening at the Sanctum Metere and she knew that the comforts provided to her were not going to last when the Crucible began. Amara had eaten her fill of lamb, potatoes, and vegetables courtesy of Praeceptor Cathmore who brought it to her room. He hadn't said anything to her and left in silence.

She sprawled on the most comfortable bed she ever laid in and watched how the stars decorated the night sky through her window. She often found herself wondering if her mother was amongst the stars somewhere watching over her. One of the stars twinkled as though winking at her, as though it knew of her longing for the mother she never knew.

She tossed and turned, cursing herself for not inquiring about the hunt. Would knowing more about it put her mind at ease? She doubted it. They were on sacrificial grounds, the only two goals were to kill or strengthen the children of the Fallen. She didn't know whether she wanted to lie down and give up, or wanted to fight to make it to transformation.

She sighed. She knew that wanting to survive would not make her strong enough to survive the hunt—much less the next year. She finally fell asleep, agonizing over the aches in her body and her unknown fate.

A banging on the door woke her abruptly, and she immediately began trembling.

"What!" She shouted when the knock came again as she rubbed her eyes. The sun wasn't even up yet, causing anger to swell within her.

"You have ten minutes to meet me in the hallway, brat," came Praeceptor Cathmore's voice. *Did he really just call her a brat again?* She couldn't believe the audacity of the Praeceptor.

"Add three hours to that," she grumbled under her breath, and flung herself back into the bed. She could not have had more than four hours of sleep and her body ached from her capture. Her dreams were drenched in Bastian's blood, which she tried to push from her mind.

Somehow she dozed back off, she was partially intending to be in the hallway to see what the Praeceptor needed but she was so tired...

Suddenly Amara was yanked by her ankle and thrown to the floor. She regained consciousness somewhere between said floor and the warmth of the bed. She recovered quickly enough to hook her leg around the ankle of the person who grabbed her, sending him backward. He didn't fall though; he just took a step back before growling something she didn't understand. It made her feel small and weak, but she jumped to her feet anyway.

"Don't touch me!" She huffed. Praeceptor Cathmore crossed his arms and scowled at her. His large frame towered over her intimidatingly, but she mirrored him by crossing her arms. He stepped toward her, making her aware of the fact that she was only wearing a night slip that was extremely thin. He wasn't clad in dark leather like before, but wearing loose-fitting pants and a more casual shirt.

"I have been charged with preparing you for the Crucible, me touching you is about to be the least of your concerns," he growled at her. His silver and blue eyes darkened. "You have five minutes to dress." He turned on his heel and strolled out of the room, slamming the door.

"Smug asshole." She grunted.

On the bench by the door was an assortment of clothing that Cathmore must have brought in at some point. She riffled through the various pants and shirts, all of which she didn't fill out even though they were small. She had no muscle mass to speak of and her reflection reminded her of a child trying on an adult's clothing—sort of. He had brought her the correct sizes but it was like the clothes were crafted for people with bigger muscles. She scoffed, as if she needed anymore reminders that she was way out of her element and underprepared for the journey ahead. She ignored the twisting ache in her abdomen that begged her to run.

"Now!" Cathmore grumbled with another beat on the door, just as she swung it open. He looked down at her disapprovingly but said nothing. She was far too thin, she knew that. But she could fight, and had fought to stay on the run. She wasn't completely helpless... *Was she?*

She found herself staring at a dirt trail that led through a wooded area which eventually consumed her line of sight. She hugged herself and rubbed her arms where the morning air sent chills over her. She turned to Praeceptor Cathmore who was tugging his leg up behind him in a stretch.

"Stretch, or don't. Either way, you're running," he said simply. He began stretching his arms across his chest one at a time, causing the muscles in his biceps to flex.

She waited for him to finish his stretching, shook her ankles to loosen them and began jogging when he did. Though she was determined not to embarrass herself, she would have no such luck.

She didn't make it more than a mile before having to slow to a walk due to a stitch in her side, earning her a side eye from the Praeceptor. Her ankles still ached from when she was captured which didn't help either.

"That's it?" He scoffed and stopped.

"What do you want from me?" She panted.

"I figured since you've been running for so long this would be an acceptable place to start." He once again stepped into her—which was beginning to annoy her. "Now run back that way." He pointed from where they came. He wasn't winded, barely sweating, and that much more infuriating.

When she walk, she was grabbed by her elbow and pulled toward him. "It was not a question, *run*," he spat. The fury behind his eyes did not leave room for her to protest, so she turned and began running. "I have two more miles to go, you better beat me to the trail head, brat." He turned and run the opposite way than he told her to go.

"Stop calling me that!" She shouted. When he ignored her she flipped her middle fingers at his back. When he ran it was as if he glided, as if it took nothing out of him to jog. He was hardly exerting any energy and it looked unnatural to be breathing so steadily while his feet pounded the gravel. She stood no chance; she was sure he could run ten miles before she made it one.

She jogged, despite the screaming in her ankles and lungs. *What was his problem?* He was so arrogant and demanding. She hadn't done anything to him. He didn't know her, yet he treated her like one treats something they stepped in. *Ugh.* She reminded herself to ask about the hunt so that she could try and prepare. Running was a start she supposed, but it felt hopeless.

She gave up, trying to inhale the morning air into her lungs and calm her beating heart. She was a murderer and labeled a coward for running. No one would ever understand her motives, but they didn't have to. She kicked a rock as she thought about how quickly the Crucible had come and how she wished she could have escaped her fate a second time. But there she was, on the sacrificial grounds of the Sanctum Metere, getting special preparation for the Crucible. Not many children of the fallen got that opportunity. She knew she should embrace it, but Cathmore was insufferable.

Cathmore's stern gaze cut through the still lingering morning fog as he watched her approach, her breath visible in the chill air. She was late, she didn't beat him. *Obviously.* Without a word, he pointed for her to turn back around and start walking. All in all, he made her cover the distance twice. Six miles of walking was just cruel, especially because she wanted nothing more than to bolt through the woods and search for a way to escape. The trail seemed endless, every step a reminder of her inadequacy in all areas that might help her survive the Crucible.

After lunch, the Praeceptor's demeanor grew even darker. His eyes narrowed and his lips pressed into a thin line as he barked orders. Her muscles burned with every push-up, each sit-up felt like climbing a mountain, and the planks and lunges seemed to stretch time itself. Sweat poured down her face, mingling with the dirt beneath her, while his brooding silhouette loomed over her, a constant reminder of her failure.

"This is tragic." He scoffed. She grunted and bared her teeth as she pushed through the exercises. "Seriously?"

By the time she made it back to her room, she and Cathmore had not exchanged more than a few sentences and her body was shaking violently. After dinner, the rest of the evening belonged to her, and she was looking forward to recovering from the day. He had instructed her to meet him in the dining area for dinner after her bath, to which she just rolled her eyes—out of his sight of course.

"The entry trial changes every year. The Hunt has not been done in about a decade, so I'm told," Praeceptor Cathmore began in response to her question.

The dimly lit dining room had about five round tables and could seat around thirty people, she thought. The space had seemed so empty with just the two of them, regarding each other cautiously in heavy silence, up until she asked her question.

"It's pretty self-explanatory I'd think." He shrugged and shoved a piece of roast beef into his mouth. She hadn't seen anyone else in the building besides the kind woman who cooked and cleaned for them. His dark curls were still wet, indicating he had showered, and they fell messily over his forehead. He glanced up at her and she gestured for him to elaborate. "The children of the Fallen are hunted. Those who survive, go on to the Crucible."

It was pretty much what she expected, but she wanted more details.

"Hunted by who?" *Where, how?* She wanted to add.

"Us." He sat back in his chair and spread his arms. "The Nephilim."

"So the Praeceptor's who have completed their transition into Nephilim," she added understandingly.

"Correct, there will be twenty of us on the grounds for the hunt," he explained between bites of food.

"How long do newly transitioned Nephilim have to be Praeceptor's?" she inquired.

"We serve for three Crucible's," he answered coldly. He seemed to go somewhere distant for a moment before blinking and focusing on her again. "I will tell you what the other sired children know; the hunt will take place in Caladrium Forest, we can not use any of our abilities, and we are hunting to kill. Your only rule is to survive." She nodded thankfully and they continued eating in silence for a moment.

"The next twelve days will look just as today did. You wake, workout, eat, sleep, and repeat. The day before the hunt, you will be at the front gates with the other conscripts as though you have just arrived," he informed her.

Footsteps approached from behind her and a stranger spoke.

"So you're the reason we were called here early, thanks for that," a woman said. She was older than her, perhaps in her thirties, and appeared to be fit. Her jet black hair was tied back into a braid and the wrinkles on her forehead showed a life of worry. She plopped down at a table on the other side of the room and put her booted feet on the table. She appeared casual but annoyed. "Murderess huh? Bastain Marlowe was a pest anyway." She took a bite of a roll.

"I didn't want to..." Amara started.

"Yeah, yeah, yeah. Worse than that you tried to desert your birthright to the Crucible. I'm impressed you escaped," the woman was indifferent toward her which was refreshing. "I'm Magister Delphine..." She regarded Amara curiously. "And your name?" *Magister, she was one of the resident instructors. Her actual career was to instruct at the Crucible. Unlike the Praeceptor's who served their time and left, she held a permanent position at the Sanctum Metere.*

"Amara Ashenfall," she introduced herself with a slight nod.

"Well, I'm only here to ensure Praeceptor Cathmore doesn't kill you before the Crucible. If you survive the hunt, I'll be seeing you in class." She smiled and swiftly left with yet another yeast roll.

"What do you mean you can't?" Cathmore demanded, glaring down at her with his arms crossed. She was on her back, staring at the bland cement ceiling of the training room they had been working in.

"It has been two days, you can't expect me to be able to do a hundred sit ups." She huffed and sat up on her elbows.

His strong arms flexed as he clenched his fists, a habit of his, she noticed, when he was thinking about something that frustrated him. His dark gray pants were made for exercising and fit him loosely...for the most part. Sometimes she wondered if his entire appearance was meant to distract her. Seriously, it was like a god had been assigned to whip her into shape.

"Legs up."

"What?" She breathed, startled because of her wandering thoughts. He crouched down and pulled her knees up and inward at ninety degree angles. Her kneecaps were touching parallel to her hips, a few seconds holding the position could be felt in her abdomen.

"Now extend your legs straight, and don't let your heels touch the ground." He gripped her calves and showed her how. She made an effort to just stare at the ceiling. "And tuck them back in," he instructed. She did so, her lower abdominal muscles shaking.

"Do that twenty times," he demanded and stood.

When she finished the set she sat up. He was on the padded floor directly across from her, in a planking position. He was looking straight ahead, in her direction, not straining at all. His arms were in the shape of a triangle, holding him up effortlessly. She could see the muscles in his shoulders and back subtly flex.

He stared past her, the picture of composure, self-discipline, and strength. He was radiating that same arrogance that aggravated her, yet somehow it worked on him in the training room. She was captivated by his confidence and the thin layer of sweat that glowed on his skin. When he moved her eyes were simply drawn to him. He was on his knees a few feet from her and wiping his face with a towel. He seemed to be allowing her to watch him while he determined what he was going to say.

"Do twenty more." He pointed at the floor behind her. *Ugh.* She didn't protest and did what she was told despite the screaming in her weak body.

"Stand up," he instructed.

When she did, he circled her thoughtfully. She felt like she was being studied. Her clothes were far too loose on her, her muscles crying, she was covered in an embarrassing amount of sweat and...

Praeceptor Cathmore swept her legs out from under her without warning, sending her to the ground. Her back landed with a sickening smack, painfully stealing the breath from her lungs.

"You're weak, you don't even have the instinct to keep yourself on your feet." He huffed a laugh and came into view above her. His raven colored hair was wild and slightly damp.

"You're an asshole," she retorted breathlessly as she got to her feet.

He smirked before placing one foot behind her right one and shoving her shoulder, sending her to the ground once more. Only this time, he was suddenly on top of her with his forearm across her throat.

"What did we say about respect?" He growled.

"Get off of me." She bucked against him, which only caused him to pin her thighs flat on the ground with his hips. *Shit.*

She clawed and shoved him with her hands. He didn't flinch; he only looked down at her as she flailed her arms helplessly.

"Are you done?"

Amara didn't respond, she just writhed harder beneath him. She felt a lump forming in her throat as her breathing became shallow. Her vision tunneled as the realization that she couldn't move finally clicked. She did, however, manage to scratch him across his cheek. Three deep welts beaded blood and he grinned sinisterly.

"Get off me," she demanded. She didn't want him to know that she was about to cry so she blinked back tears.

Get me off of you, *murderess*," he taunted in a lowered voice. She grappled at his ribs and back with her nails, which did nothing. He pressed his forearm harder into her throat which stopped her from struggling. He didn't even bother to pin her puny little arms down.

She was completely trapped beneath him, completely trapped at the Sanctum Metere, completely helpless against him, and even more helpless against her own weaknesses.

He finally removed his arm from her throat, allowing her to gasp for air beneath him. He was straddling her, regarding her with some mixture of amusement and annoyance. She was all too aware of his body on hers and despite his objective beauty, it made her sick. He made her sick. He was a bully.

"Get up, we're training through dinner tonight. Since I'm an asshole." He shrugged and pushed himself off of her. By the time he stood, the bleeding marks on his face had healed, solidifying her inadequacy to fight against him.

By the time night fell and she found her way to her bed, she was pretty sure she was dead. Her body was numb and in pain all at once. She didn't know how her legs were carrying her after the eight mile hike. Cathmore forced her to do it alone, through the woods, as the sun set. He was sick, he got off on suffering, he had to. It was the only thing that made sense.

He yelled at her for not drinking the appropriate amount of water upon her passing out after the hike. *Which was a wonderful experience.* Then he didn't even have the decency to fly her or carry her back to Oaks Hall. He just pointed her in the direction and told her to get some sleep. *Honestly he had to be insane.*

She groaned and finally got the energy to roll off of her face so that she could get herself under the blankets. She knew she should shower, but it wasn't an option. Something clattered when she moved the blanket, something she couldn't see in the darkness of the room. She turned on her oil lantern to inspect it.

It was a tray of food, and she had never been more ravenously hungry. Lunch had been twelve hours (and an endless amount of exercises) ago. She flopped onto her belly and began inhaling the creamed sweet potatoes, broccoli, and lamb. She thought it was lamb at least, but she didn't care, she ripped into it as though her life depended on it. Even her pitcher of drinking water was full so she wouldn't have to do the work of refilling it.

Amara didn't remember falling asleep, but she woke up in a world of pain. Muscles that she didn't even know existed were aching.

The sun was up but her curtains were still closed and no one had awoken her before sunrise. *Weird.*

She started to move but a muscle in her leg locked up in a massive cramp that sent her sprawling onto her face in agony. *'Don't forget to stretch, brat,'* was the advice she ignored from the Praeceptor. Once the cramp subsided, she stopped biting down on her blanket and allowed her entire body to deflate back into the bed.

She was just about to doze off when she remembered that she really needed to use the bathroom. *Ugh.* It seemed like an insurmountable task but she did it slowly. Her body felt like all of the blood had been drained from it and she was just made up of stiff hard bones.

She drank another entire cup of water before collapsing back into bed, exhaling the pain slowly.

"Fuck, fuck, fuck," she whispered when trying to pull the covers up. Her arms were giving out.

"Well this is pitiful," came a low voice from the chair in the corner of the room. Cathmore stood and strolled toward the bed before casually sitting next to her.

"Leave." She huffed and glared up at him. He stretched his legs out and leaned his head back on the wooden headboard.

"Didn't stretch, did you?" He ignored her demand. She just rolled to face the opposite way of him, leaving his question unanswered. "It's only going to get worse if you don't loosen those muscles," he warned.

"What do you care? Can't you just leave me alone," she nearly whispered. She felt defeated, broken.

She heard him stand from the bed and make his way to the washroom. The bath water was running and knew that asking him to leave her alone was pointless. She pulled the blanket over her head and hoped he would just go away, really she hoped the entire world would just fade away. She really was weak, she had no chance of surviving the hunt, much less the entirety of the Crucible.

"On your feet." He clapped as he entered her room again. She ignored him and didn't move.

"Please just go away," she pleaded.

"No," was his only response. She popped her head out from under the blanket and glared at him once more.

"You wanted to break me, congratulations I'm broken. Now get the hell out!" she exclaimed. If she wasn't so weak she'd toss something at him and his infuriating smile. He leaned against the doorframe of the washroom, smells of soap and oils drifting from the bath he was running her.

"Do you need me to carry you in there? Because I will." He shoved his hands into his pockets. *No, hell no.*

"You better fucking not," she warned.

He pushed off of the door frame into her direction, which was the only motivation she needed to force herself out of the bed.

She shoved past him and to her surprise, he didn't retaliate. She slammed the door on him and walked wobbly to the steaming bath that was beckoning to her.

Her muscles loosened up, to her relief, and by the time she emerged from the washroom, she was in significantly less pain. She tightened the towel around her when she saw that Praeceptor

Cathmore was still lounging in her bed. He didn't even look over in her direction, instead choosing to mindlessly flip through a book.

"I bathed, you can leave." She huffed.

"No, I don't think I will." He glanced over at her, unbothered. She didn't miss his eyes raking over her .

"What do you want?" She eyed him in annoyance. She finally noticed he wasn't wearing his normal exercise attire but replaced them with dark slacks and a partially opened white button-down shirt.

"I want you to stretch and recover," he shut his book and crossed his legs.

"Can I at least get dressed first?" she retorted.

"It would be preferred," he sniped and turned his back on her. She groaned and stomped over to the wardrobe to retrieve clean clothes.

He glanced over his shoulder when she slammed the wardrobe to voice her frustration.

"A little louder, brat, I don't think Hadeon heard you," he snapped. She ignored him and tugged on her pants behind him before pulling on the thick sweater. "Let's go," he swung her bedroom door open and waited for her to follow.

She didn't realize how long she slept until he led her to the small dining hall for lunch. They sat in silence, neither of them looking at each other, neither of them enjoying the other's company.

"You want to touch your toes but don't extend your lower back to the point of severe pain," he instructed. They once again were in the training room. She was bent forward barely reaching past her knees. "If you don't push yourself slightly past the point of discomfort, you will never improve," he grumbled. Her body was so tight and so unbelievably sore.

"This is as far as I can go," she whined. He was crouched in front of her, regarding her with disapproval like usual. He stood and moved behind her.

"You need to push yourself physically and mentally." His voice was low. He pressed his hand flat between her shoulder blades and pushed down. Her first instinct was to bend her knees so he used his other hand to pull her leg back toward him by her thigh.

"Fuck." She grunted. The small amount of pain that accompanied the forced stretch quickly faded into warmth and relief. She tried hard not to focus on her ass against his strong upper legs. Her fingertips approached her ankles which was shocking to her.

"Push your right leg further out," he told her. When she did he pushed her downward again, his broad hand taking up the space between her shoulder blades. She exhaled a shaky breath, she didn't know why it was so...intense.

She felt her lower back and thigh muscles stretch, becoming slowly less stiff. She finally touched her toes, and then the mat in front of her. However, when Cathmore moved his hands and stepped out from behind her, she realized she wasn't completely balancing herself and fell forward. The sigh and shake of his head that followed was meant to be seen.

"You are holding yourself back because you don't want to be here, Ashenfall. Your own stubbornness is going to get you killed," he said coldly.

"You don't know what you're talking about," anger flared in her core. She stood to face him.

"I've struck a nerve." He smiled smugly. "You're weak and you're choosing to be," he doubled down, trying to make her angrier.

"Shut up," she shouted and shoved his shoulders. He didn't even move.

"And you're a coward." He put his face in hers. "A weak, scared, little murderess," he purred. She felt his breath on her cheek.

She was shaking with anger and losing control over it, losing her grip on it. He looked her over from head to toe in disgusted annoyance. She lost it and punched him in the face with all of her strength. She followed up by shoving him again which actually caused him to stumble.

Blood dripped from his nose, coating his lips, he looked at her and smiled. He gestured her toward him, begging for her to try again. She sneered and launched into a sprint, she tackled him, her shoulder colliding hard with his abdomen. They both went to the ground but he tossed her effortlessly over his head, leaving her sprawled on her back.

"I expect more from a murderess." He was on his hands and knees in front of her. She mirrored his position. There was something in him that she was drawn to in that moment and it scared her. He looked insane, blood coating his lips, the taunting smile, the way he was ready to pounce on her...

Breaking her line of thought, he slid a dagger in her direction across the floor. *Where did that come from?*

"Come and get me," he growled and jumped to his feet. She bared her teeth, snatched the dagger, and pursued him to the other side of the large training center.

She jumped on his back, catching him around his throat. She pressed the dagger to the delicate skin at the side of his neck and wrapped her legs around his back to steady herself.

He grabbed her forearms so hard that she lost grip on the dagger before elbowing her in the ribs which caused her to drop off of him. She scrambled to the dagger, grabbing it quickly and slicing at his legs wildly. He smoothly dodged each attempt. Suddenly he kicked the dagger from her hand, sending it across the room. He grabbed her by the front of her shirt and slammed her back into the cement wall. Her feet were dangling off the ground but she still pushed against him.

"Anger can be a powerful weapon if you learn to control it," he snarled. She slapped at his arms and chest. "You're not as hopeless as I thought you were going to be." He smiled. The statement took her off guard and he dropped her.

The next few days continued exactly as Cathmore had initially instructed, and she hated every minute of it. Though she felt herself getting stronger and could jog the three mile trail, she could not shake the agonizing feeling of dread.

Terror licked up her spine at the mere thought of the Crucible. The certainty of death loomed over her, shadowed only by the harrowing prospect of discovering the identity of her sire. The very thought made her recoil. She longed for the simple, unattainable life of a human. She clung to the idea of choice, a hope cruelly snatched from her, leaving behind a seething resentment. Existing in villages, masquerading as a human for two years was so easy. No one knew who or what she was, she pretended her life didn't have some grand trial looming in the distance. She envied the humans that despised her.

Despite her yearning to live as a human, they were just as trapped as she was. Men toiled and slaved under the iron grip of Nephilim masters, while women were reduced to bearers of sires for their Hallowed Fallen. And yet, humans lived simple lives, given just enough to survive and shielded from the harshest elements. They had long since learned not to yearn for more, centuries ago. Perhaps her desire for such a reality was born from a fear of the unknown. Humans had no choice; oppression was their way of life, and rebellion was never an option. Their existence was just that—existence.

But a sired child? A turned Nephilim? They were destined to serve, to kill, to bow before their sire. She would have to swear fealty in blood and give her life to the Hallowed— she just hoped it wouldn't be an immortal one. The thought of it made her stomach churn as she tried to imagine the face of the one who had sired her.

She was throwing rapid punches at a bag to release her anger when her knuckles bruised and bled. She didn't care; she hit the bag again for the mother she lost, once more for the arrogant Fallen who sired her. She kicked the bag for Bastian's blood on her hands. All of the stealing, nearly freezing to death in the woods, bargaining for her life... It all meant nothing. She still ended up there, at the Sanctum Metere, still about to fight for her life for the benefit of the Hallowed Fallen. She had been labeled a coward and a runner, yet she couldn't even do that properly... not a second time at least.

She panted as sweat drenched her neck and arms. She pounded into the bag until the blood ran from her knuckles, giving her internal pain a physical form. She needed to feel it, to let it out. Thoughts of her abusive upbringing flooded her mind. Her aunt beat her mercilessly, told her she was 'of the devil', and that she would 'rid the world' of her all together. Before she knew it, sobs rattled her body and she hugged the bag, leaning her head against it to steady herself.

She glanced around the training room, certain she felt someone enter, but she was alone. She sighed before sliding down the wall behind her and burying her face in her battered hands. There really was no way out this time, she would simply have to go *through* it. She would need to endure.

$$Chapter\ 3$$

Amara was waiting outside of the large coliseum-like building at the center of the Sanctum Metere with the rest of the sired children. A lot of them arrived in massive carriages with four horses each, some in smaller ones with their mothers, and she noted a couple of them arriving on horseback. She imagined that that was how she would have arrived had she gone willingly. Some were murmuring amongst themselves in the small groups that they arrived with, but for the most part, most of the sired children seemed withdrawn. Fear etched their features, which made her feel less foolish for her own fear.

The obsidian stone coliseum towered over them, its age evident in the damage to the stones from the elements. Leafy vines crept up certain sections of the structure on either side of the massive entryways and barred windows. The walls must have witnessed so much horror, but their beauty lay in the evident triumph, in the way time aged the glorious stone, and in an energy that drew her closer.

Two people were shoved out of a wagon similar to the one she had arrived in. It pulled her out of her thoughts about the coliseum. They had only their hands bound behind their backs, and that's all she needed to see to know that they hadn't come willingly. The two must have been siblings, they were similar in many ways—red hair, dark eyes with bushy eyebrows, rounded faces, and appeared very boney. Dark circles beneath their eyes told stories of many sleepless nights. Given they were called to the Crucible at the same time, they were both in their twentieth year- twins. The boy helped his sister to her feet who shoved him off, flustered. Amara watched for a moment as they were untied and pushed once more toward the crowd of sired children. Amara turned her focus back toward the majority of them who were gathering at the massive entryway.

It seemed as though eyes were crawling over every inch of her skin. She was a fly trapped in a web, spiders and other insects observing her. She knew that once the others learned her name they would know who she was and what she had done, rumors traveled quickly in Findaria. A sired child that successfully avoided her first call to the Crucible, and then murdered a guard when she was caught...well, that would be the talk of the village folk for a long while. The familiar feeling of blood trickling down her hands crept its way in, stealing her breath. *No.* She shook it off and looked toward the clouded sky for anything to distract her from the hunt. The morning breeze washed over her, carrying the hunt closer and closer.

One of the Magisters had begun allowing people into the coliseum while a Praeceptor was taking down each of their names on a scroll. She sighed, it all seemed so trivial and formal for what the day was to bring.

Upon her entering of the archway, she tried not to make eye contact with the Praeceptors who were sizing them up. She could hear various conversations of similar topics.

"That one won't make it through the hunt, too scrawny," one voice whispered.

"How are we supposed to shape this lot into proper Nephilim?" A woman scoffed and was met with a chuckle.

Most of the sired children did not come from much and appeared haggard and worn down by life already. But there were some exceptions...

"That one was sired by Rase. Of course he'll make it," one of the Praeceptors said. He pointed at a dark red-haired man, not a boy, but a full-fledged ruggedly handsome man who appeared to be all muscle. *What was with the obsession over Rase?*

He appeared stoic and bored. He must have sensed her looking at him and regarded her with disgust. Well, he really was the son of one of the Hallowed Fallen called 'Rase'. Rase played a part in all of his sired children's lives, and despised 'bastard sired' children. He held the belief that because of his hand in his sired ones' lives, they would prosper as Nephilim. So he trained with them from childhood, spoiled them and their mothers, and left them with the stench of entitlement.

Some of the Hallowed Fallen were in their children's lives periodically but none left such hatred in the hearts of their sired ones the way Rase did. At least she knew for a fact she did not belong to Rase, which was a relief. Some of the Hallowed Fallen favored some of their children and abandoned others. She knew all of the sired children belonged to one of the ten Hallowed Fallen, it had been that way for centuries, but she had heard stories that every once in a while there would be a child to enter the Crucible that didn't carry the blood of any of the Hallowed but of the Rogue Fallen instead. "Most of you will be deemed unworthy of my time so I will keep this short. The Hunt will commence once you enter Caladrium Forest," the Crowned Magister said. "We have been joined by Ender and Osias for this year's entry trial." The crowd gasped. Two Hallowed Fallen were in attendance. She wondered if that was normal and looked around for them.

"They will be in the skies alongside me to oversee how you fare against our Nephilim. Your one goal is to survive. Their one goal is to ensure you don't." Amara looked around the crowd to see some with faces of excitement and some with brows furrowed in fear. "A block will be placed on their powers and Imperiums, weapons are scattered throughout the forest, and you must make it to the ocean front on the other side of the forest to be considered safe." Amara inhaled a shaky breath. Based on the maps she had examined, that was at least eight miles through the densely wooded forest. "If you are not accounted for on the beach by sunrise, if you somehow hide away in the forest, you will be retrieved and no further harm will come to you." She knew making it to the oceanfront was the best way to go. Running around the woods from armed Nephilim all night was simply not realistic if she was to survive. At least if they didn't make it to the oceanfront by sunrise it wasn't an automatic elimination like she thought it would be. Surviving the night in Caladrium Forest or making it to the oceanfront would mean successful entry into the Sanctum Metere, into the Crucible.

"However, there is no pride to be taken in cowardice, so I suggest you aim for the oceanfront." He seemed to glance in her direction. She found herself shaking her head slowly.

The Crowned Magister adjusted his gold embroidered shirt, his jewelry clanking together. He spoke so casually about everything, he was so unbothered by the bloodshed that was about to ensue.

"Are we allowed to kill them?" one of the sired children shouted. He was one of the excitable ones. The Crowned Magister laughed, it was followed by the laughs of the Praeceptors and Magisters as well. Amara's face flushed with second-hand embarrassment for him while the laughing echoed through the crowd.

"Sure, if you really want to try," the Crowned Magister belted through laughter which infuriated her. They were all just a means to an end, a means of entertainment to them. Once the laughing died out, he waved over an older-looking man with a scroll to speak next. He introduced himself as Magister Baylin.

"Seventy-eight of you have come of age for the Crucible this year, and all are accounted for," he announced proudly. He was one of those older men that must have been attractive at one point, and still was despite the wrinkles. He was tall, lean, with slicked back silver hair, and gray eyes with silver lining them—the trait of the Nephilim. "We hope to see thirty of you make it to transformation and come into your true power by the end of this Crucible year."

Transformation took place at the end of the Crucible, when the 'chosen' sired children made their transformation into Nephilim. Around that time, they gained their Imperium, the power or ability that usually had some similarities to whoever fathered them.

They expected over half of them to die, to be sacrificed in order to fulfill the literal deal with the devil himself. She seethed. She clenched her fist as hopelessness swelled in her chest. *I will not die a sacrifice, I will not. I will live.* She repeated the words to herself over and over again.

Thunder clouds loomed overhead, the breeze carrying moisture through the autumn day. Amara crouched down to secure her boot laces and slid a knife into her right one. She had taken it from a display in Oaks Hall without Cathmore noticing, just before she was taken to the dormitories. She had no doubt that she'd be killed if he knew that she had stolen it, but she was about to face death anyway, so what was another risk? Besides, she didn't know when or if she would find weapons during the hunt and she refused to die unarmed.

They had been sent into the forest at different entry points, at different times. A siren wailed to signal that the final sired child had been placed into the forest. It meant they had one hour before the Nephilim descended upon them. Only one other person was in her line of sight, a caramel-skinned boy who clearly had some level of training based on his muscle definition. But he glanced over at her, with furrowed eyebrows and the glimmer of innocence that a child possessed. She knew at that moment that she would not see him at the finish line when the hunt was over.

Her innocence was stripped away long ago, the spark in her own eyes extinguished. That was the only reason she had any hope that she would survive. She had done many things she wasn't proud of to keep herself alive and she knew she would do it again. She didn't know if that scared her or comforted her. Bastian twitching on the ground, holding his neck replayed in her mind. *How was it that the event happened so quickly but she took in every detail as though someone had slowed it down?*

They all feared what the day would bring, but she could see that his fear would shut him down in the face of death. His soul was not made to fight, not everyone's was. She let out a breath and jogged to her right, opposite of where the boy had gone.

She could not let her ability to read people, to feel their fear and their pain, cripple her. Clairvoyance was not uncommon amongst sired children and over time she gathered that she was more sensitive to emotion and the contents of one's soul rather than what the future held. Not that she could sense the Nephilim— she had already tried with Cathmore. She may as well have tried to find the soul in a brick for all she could glean from him.

A large tree came into view amongst skinnier ones, and perched in it was some kind of object. *A weapon.* She pulled her sleeves down over her hands and pulled herself into the tree. Her boots slipped on the bark from the moisture of the forest but she found enough footing to get herself onto the massive branch. Maybe she should camp in the tree, maybe the Nephilim would assume that no one would stay so close to the entry points. *That would be stupid, Amara,* she chastised herself.

She scaled up onto another branch and looked around for any sign of another conscript. They kind of were conscripts... forced into a fight for their lives against their will. She didn't see anyone else and reached to the end of the branch for what she could finally see was a rather fancy pike. It had a sturdy wooden handle that was nearly her height, with a point at the end, and two curving blades just at the base of the sharpened steel. It reminded her of a spear, though she had no experience in using one. If she shoved it into someone, their insides would be mangled beyond repair. She looked at it in awe. The blade had swirls of intricate designs that caught the sun in a breathtaking sight.

She couldn't make out much through the dense forest, but she could hear footsteps a couple of yards away from the tree. She listened harder, it was actually two sets of running feet. Did she have to watch her back for other conscripts? It was probably smart; she had a feeling that anything could happen during the hunt... During the Crucible in general really.

She didn't see the two pass but when the sound of their shuffling feet diminished, she knew she was alone again. She then noticed that the large tree branches extended into many other trees, and she could realistically crawl between the trees and make some decent distance. There was a lot of brush and thorns on the ground of the forest that would be difficult to cut through. So she opted to crawl from one tree branch to another, dropped down to a branch on another tree, climbed it, and made her way to many others.

She kept her pace steady for a while before she heard thunderous wing beats in the sky overhead. She was nowhere near the top of the trees but with it being autumn, she didn't feel as though she was completely hidden from the figure that was circling her. The leaves were not as dense as they once were, allowing her to see the massive wings of the Hallowed Fallen that seemed to know she was there.

It was Ender, renowned for his crimson wings. His golden hair cascaded in waves around his head and down his chest. She noticed a crown sitting atop his head which caused her to roll her eyes. *He wouldn't give away her position once the Nephilim descended... would he?* The Hallowed Fallen were only spectating. She sighed and decided to continue on her made up path through the trees.

All of the climbing was going to exhaust her faster, and she knew it, but she felt safer and as though she was making better time. Finally the flapping wings faded away and she was able to breathe again. Her arms shook as she lifted herself into what must have been the twentieth tree, and sweat beaded on her forehead despite the cool air. That's when the next siren sounded, the one to indicate that the Nephilim were upon them. Adrenaline spiked in her blood, sending pins and needles into her mouth and limbs.

She clambered down the tree into a small clearing, meticulously aware of the spear that she strapped to her back. She needed to run to cover more ground. She didn't know if she was running east toward the sea or further into the forest but she just needed to move. For a while it was silent and she slowed down to a walking pace as she panted for air.

The second she allowed herself to breathe, to allow the thought that she might stand a chance, the screaming echoed through the trees. It wasn't one person, not even two, but at least five different screams of agony. They were surrounding her, blinding her with terror. She heard the abrupt cut off of someone's scream, followed by a gurgling that was far too close to her. She covered her mouth to stifle a sob.

Amara crouched to the floor of the forest and gently shoved herself into some brush. She did her best to ignore the thorns that snagged on her clothes. Just on the other side of the brush-heavy boots squished in the mud. She couldn't see through the brush but she was close enough to smell the blood that had been spilled. Once again she covered her mouth, partially due to the smell, partially due to the horror of the situation. The urge to pee overwhelmed her, the same way it did when she was a child about to be found during a game 'hide n hunt' with her friends.

She had no choice but to wait for the Nephilim to move on, no doubt leaving the body in the mud to rot. Just then she heard someone else moving just outside the brush behind her. She glanced over to see a tattered leather outfit and red flowing hair tied in a ponytail. It was the girl from outside the coliseum. Her chubby cheeks were scarlet red from the cold. Amara watched as she peeked over the brush, having no clue Amara was a foot from her.

She was still very aware of the Nephilim hunter who was starting to walk away from where they were hidden. *Please don't do anything stupid, please don't get me caught.*

She could hear the girl's jagged breath; she wasn't even trying to silence it. *Idiot.* To her horror the girl did the unthinkable and bellowed out a blood-curdling scream, a singular name.

"Cade!" The cry reverberated through the space around them and Amara moved to press herself into the damp mud to make herself smaller. She was able to see through the bottom of the brush. The dark boots of the Nephilim hunter turned and he began making his way toward the girl... toward Amara too. Amara clutched the spear to her chest, laying on it, and covering her mouth for dear life. The girl was going to die.

She ran to the body in the mud, the boy's body. The one who Amara thought was her twin. *Dear God.* Amara strained to turn her neck enough to see what was happening. The girl had gathered his body into her lap and was rocking back and forth, sobbing. A mix of this girl's emotions and her own overwhelmed Amara and she pushed back against them. She didn't want to feel what the girl felt, she didn't need to. It would just get her killed along with this doomed child..

Grief crawled from the girl, across the ground, and down Amara's throat as though it were a living thing. The bitter taste of fear, the sour kick of hatred spiked on her tongue, growing stronger than the grief.

The Nephilim had gathered the girl up by the back of her shirt before Amara could even process the scene. From what Amara could see, she dangled in the hunter's grasp, fighting for her life. She screamed through sobs, begging and cursing him for taking her brother.

Amara didn't think, she simply acted on instinct because watching the girl die was not an option. She rushed out of the brush and bounded toward the massive Nephilim man. Cocking her arms back and sprinting toward the man, she threw her entire body into her thrust. To her surprise he screamed and stumbled away as he dropped the girl. The side blades of the spear dug the weapon further into his ribs like a fish hook, and she took the moment to gather the choking girl by her arm and haul her away.

"You run like hell!" she said, as quietly and as urgently as possible. The girl stared at her with wide eyes but began sprinting behind Amara. "No, don't follow me!"

The girl was mind-blowingly naive and Amara cursed herself for stepping in and risking her own life. She shoved the girl to the left and, surprisingly, the girl listened and sprinted away. *Fuck fuck fuck.* Amara's boots pounded the ground hard as she remembered the face of the Nephilim. If she lived, she for sure just made an enemy. Dark, spiked hair, scarred face, behemoth of a man.

She cut right, relieved to see the sun. High noon was over. *Rises in the east, sets in the west.* She had to run opposite of where the sun was setting in order to find the beach. She did just that when she heard a male scream somewhere in the woods behind her. *Go, go, go.* She chanted to herself.

She saw a slanted tree and took the opportunity to launch herself up into it. She climbed with a sense of urgency as well as a strength that she didn't recognize. She made it toward the top portion of the tree where the dead leaves shielded her from view enough to catch her breath. While she gasped for air, she mentally mapped out the tree branches she would take to cover more ground. This way it would appear as though her foot prints just stopped.

As she crawled across the large oak tree branch, the sky opened up and began pouring rain. *Great.* She didn't let it slow her down as the water and wind clouded her vision. She made it to the next tree, scaled down a foot, then over to the next one and so on until she was at least fifteen trees away from the one she first scaled.

She stopped to listen but was met with deafening silence apart from the rain and howling wind. There were no screams, no running, no shouting for a moment. She knew she didn't kill the Nephilim because they couldn't die...at least as far as she was aware. She was just banking on him having a hard time dislodging the spear so that they would have time to escape. She hoped he hadn't caught up to the stranger. If he had then Amara would have put herself at risk for no reason. She knew the thought was selfish, but perhaps she should have been selfish initially instead of trying to help the girl.

An arrow whizzed past her head and lodged itself in the tree just by her ear, sending her forward and she fought to cling to the branch. She tried to see who fired the arrow but couldn't make out anything through the pouring rain. Whoever shot the arrow, had to be Nephilim, only they would be able to see well enough to get that close to her. It didn't matter; it was enough to make her haul ass when she heard more than one person talking from the same direction.

She swung herself down into the next tree and hit the ground hard, her ankle rolling and protesting when she took off. The pain shot up her leg but she couldn't let it slow her down, she continued east and didn't look back. At least Praeceptor Cathmore had taught her to run fast for at least three miles. Despite the unpleasantness of the time she was stuck with him, she had to admit it was beneficial. She was running through all of the strengthening exercises mentally that he had taught her when she suddenly collided with something that had not been in front of her a moment earlier.

Not something, *someone.* It was another conscript and he hit the ground too, the reverberation of their heads colliding dizzying them both.

"Shit." He grunted and blood gushed from his nose. She grunted and got to her feet.

"We have to move, they're not far behind me." She panted. He looked up at her, still wincing in pain. His shaggy brown hair was curled all around his head, and he had friendly eyes despite the fact that they were full of concern. From the looks of his clothes, he must have come from money. He was handsome, he looked as though he were a kind person, and there was some kind of spark in his eyes. "Follow me." He stood. "I spotted a small cave just that way." He pointed further east. She nodded, his voice was gentle and she felt she could trust him, even though she knew it would probably be safer not to trust anyone.

"What were you running from?" she asked as she trailed behind the tall man. The question felt silly as she glanced behind her. The rain had let up, only a light sprinkle fell on them.

"Not sure, I was picking some berries when a dagger grazed my leg." She looked down and sure enough, there was blood trickling from his thigh. "I got the dagger though," he flipped it in his hand and flashed her a smile.

He checked out the cave first, well, cave was a generous word for the hole in the ground. It was a big hole in some bedrock that was at the base of a slanting upward rock. He made himself flat and crawled into it and when he told her that it was clear, she followed reluctantly. Some animal frolicking through the leaves startled her enough to hurry into the small space. She ignored the sensation of the rock and mud squeezing her rib cage, claustrophobia creeping its way in.

By the time they got through the narrow entrance, there was enough room for them to sit up in front of each other with a bit of space to spare. At least they didn't have to lay down. His long legs stretched from one side of the space to the other so he crossed them to give her more room.

"Sorry I broke your nose." She sighed in an effort to break the silence. It was swollen, crooked, and bloody. The spot on her forehead that was responsible was growing a knot.

"Could have been worse." He shrugged. He ripped a piece of fabric from his sweater and tied it around his thigh where the dagger struck him. It looked deeper than she originally thought, but he was right…it could have been worse. That other poor boy had been disemboweled by the Nephilim that got to him. The sight of his sister drenched in his blood… "We have a few more hours until nightfall, then I'm going for the oceanfront," he explained but there was a silent question that seemed to be asking for her grand plan.

"Sounds like a plan," she said with a weak smile. She was already exhausted, mentally and physically. "I'm Amara, by the way." She extended her hand out to his.

"Beck…" a small pause and smile, "Goldbreath." His hand lingered in hers for a beat before he dropped it. "I'm going to pull some of the brush over the entryway to better conceal us." He threw some leaves over as many of their footprints as he could before shimmying back into the hole.

"Thanks," she said genuinely.

The cave provided some warmth since it was away from the wind but with her being stationary, she was beginning to shiver from her wet clothes. She noticed that Beck was as well.

"Should we…" Beck began and a noise came from outside the cave and she shushed him.

"I don't think anyone is in there," a familiar voice said from outside of the cave.

"Well, just to be sure," another male voice spoke. Beck and Amara slid silently to the back of the cave just as a massive rock was cast into the opening. It collided directly with Beck's ankle who bit down on a scream as Amara threw her hand over his mouth. He shook from the pain but she pressed her hand tighter against his mouth, warning him to stay silent.

"See, nothing," the first voice said. *Cathmore?* She couldn't be sure. "They wouldn't be stupid enough to corner themselves in a cave." It was definitely Cathmore, she'd recognize that chastising scoff anywhere.

When the Nephilim departed the area, she released Beck. His ankle was swollen to double its size and was already turning blue. She was suddenly feeling indebted to her rolled ankle—it could have been a lot worse.

"Here." She tore the sleeve from her sweatshirt and tied it around his to try and compress it. He nodded in thanks but they were both shivering. "I think we should—" she started.

"Huddle together for warmth?" he whispered with a laugh.

"Better than freezing to death in a damp cave." She shrugged. He smiled in agreement and she leaned into the stranger. He wrapped his arm around her shoulders, her arm wrapped around his abdomen, and they remained that way for a long while.

Night fell only a couple of hours later and the time passed in silence. Both of them had stopped shivering but they knew that it had only gotten colder outside of the cave. Their body heat and breathing had warmed up the space fairly nicely. Amara had dozed off at some point and she was fairly certain that Beck had as well.

"Do you think we should hide out here instead of going to the oceanfront?" Beck asked her when she sat up. It would be less risky and they would still pass the trial if they could just wait until morning, but they would have to remain in the elements all night.

If they could make the few miles to the oceanfront, they could return to the Sanctum Metere.

"I don't know." She sighed as she mindlessly fiddled with the straps of her boot. She found herself wondering if Cathmore knew that they were in the cave. If some of the Nephilim had 'cleared' the cave, it could be safe to stay in it… right? "Maybe waiting is less risky than going out there. It's just…"

"By the time we know we're at risk, we may not be able to get out of here," Beck finished her thought with an understanding nod.

"It was a close call before."

"I wonder how many are dead," Beck mused. He looked pained, lost in thought. He had a certain charm to his features, it was the way his eyes brows furrowed, the way his smile lines framed his mouth, and his boyish grin. It was refreshing in the darkness of the situation.

"Too many I'm sure," she replied stoically. "Most of us are dead anyway, it just hasn't happened yet."

Beck stared at her for a moment but didn't speak. She always had a rather realistic view of her circumstances and the way she saw it, she was born to suffer and then die. Happiness was a stranger to her, a myth spoken about by others that she could not understand. She knew it existed…just not for her.

Right on queue with her thoughts, a man's scream reverberated through the forest. As quickly as the scream started, it was cut short. She knew he was dead by the time the sound reached their ears. The man had become nothing more than an echo in the wind of the stormy night. She hung her head in sorrow.

"We should make a break for the coast." he finally decided. He looked at her with uncertainty. "Well, I'm going anyway." *You don't have to come with me,* was the unspoken implication.

She waited a long while until she felt as though whatever killed the man was out of the area before she slowly peaked her head out of the cave. There was nothing but darkness and a gentle breeze. With a determined sigh, she pulled herself out of the cave and crouched behind some brush to further inspect her surroundings. She hadn't expected Beck to follow, but he crouched in silence behind her.

"We go together," he whispered, peering around the brush. She supposed she was lucky that Beck didn't know that she was a murderess, otherwise he would have surely abandoned her to the cold fall night.

"I'm keeping this cliffside to my left, that way there is less space we have to monitor." The bedrock had risen into a small mountain and she intended to follow it east to the sea. Beck nodded. "If something happens, you run. Do not wait for me, I will not wait for you. Understand?"

"Yeah," he replied hesitantly with a hard swallow.

The forest was far too dark; they would have to rely on feeling their way through it. Unlike the Nephilim who could see clearly in the dead of night, she couldn't see more than a few feet in front of her. She would have to rely on her other senses and her clairvoyance to know if someone was near.

"Do you get any clairvoyance from your sire?" she whispered to Beck.

"No, none." He sighed. *Great.*

She pulled the small dagger from her boot and pressed herself flat against the rocky hillside. At least they both had daggers. She tried to ignore the shortness of breath that the anxiety of the situation gave her, and scooted slowly forward. They both listened intently and were careful to make very little noise.

They made it about a mile without incident when she could start to smell the salty air blowing in from the sea. They must have only been about two miles out, hope swelled in her chest.

"Amara." Beck grunted rather loudly. When she turned to shush him, she was met with wide eyes and an arrow protruding from his shoulder blade. "Go," he breathed as he reached for the arrow, he was in shock and blood had begun soaking his back. She paused, briefly considering helping him, before he shoved her backward. "Go!"

Beck suddenly ran south, away from the cliffside. His run was weak but she didn't stay to see how it panned out. She darted east like they had planned. She heard pounding feet behind her, closing in quickly. She cut right, her shoulder hitting a tree hard but she didn't stop. She swerved through the trees clumsily and as quickly as her throbbing ankle would allow. She couldn't let it slow her down.

She saw an opportunity to scale a tree and took it when she couldn't hear the footsteps running behind her anymore. She was breathing impossibly loud but she couldn't stop herself as she hoisted herself up, up ,up. A sharp branch cut into her thigh and she bit down on a scream, the warm blood making itself known in the cold air. She realized just how deep the branch stabbed her when she jerked her leg away from it.

Still she balanced on one of the larger branches and leaped into the next tree. Her leg failed her and she slipped, catching herself with the crooks of her arms. Her face collided painfully with the branch. She struggled to swing her legs up onto it but did so successfully. A taunting whistle came through the forest from below her and she choked back a sob. *No, no, no.*

The Nephilim was taunting her, playing with its sacrifice. She briefly wondered if they were rewarded for each kill that they got. She crawled to the next tree and moved upward, struggling to control her breathing. She hoped that maybe their eyesight was dulled when their abilities and Imperiums were blocked by the Hallowed One's magic. It must have been, or she would have been dead already. *Right?*

Someone wailed in pain not far from her, a gurgling sound followed it, and then a cry for his mother. *Dear God.* Would she cry for the mother she never knew in the moment of her death? She didn't dwell on the thought but made a rather large leap to a massive branch of another tree. What if the person that just died was Beck? She knew it most likely was, given he was already in the area and injured.

She ran out of branches that connected close enough to travel by tree so she knew she had to run. She didn't hear the Nephilim that had been pursuing her but still she waited for a beat, reaching out and trying to sense him... or her.

She could in fact sense someone.... A woman but she was nervous and Amara didn't *feel* the supernatural energy of the Nephilim. She squinted hard in the direction of the strange energy but couldn't see anyone. The other girl probably assumed she was Nephilim and they were in turn just hiding from each other. Amara sighed, deciding it was worth the risk to jump from the tree and quite literally hit the ground running.

She ran hard until she could no longer sense the person that lingered in the brush below the tree. Her thigh dripped blood and the blinding pain shot up her body in waves. She needed to wrap the wound but she had to put distance between herself and where she had heard the screaming first.

In the dark she tripped over what she assumed to be a log and was hurled into the ground. The wind was knocked out of her and she gasped for air and sat up. To her dismay, it had been a body that she tripped over. She gagged at the sight of the slit throat, the tendons and muscle tissue hanging from the wound. She touched the girl's body; the limbs had already gone cold. She sighed, at least it wasn't recent.

Tears poured down her face as she scooted herself into the base of a tree. She allowed herself to sob into her hands, just to release the terror that she felt. *How was she going to survive this?*

She wiped her tears a moment later and decided to finally rip off her one remaining sleeve to tie around her thigh. She wasn't losing too much blood but she needed it to be wrapped. Maybe it would help the pain. In the brush beside her she spotted a canteen, one of the things that had been dropped in the forest for the conscripts to find. *Water.*

Tears of relief threatened to fall as she scrambled toward it. She was so impossibly thirsty. She had been on the run all day and was going to become dehydrated soon. The water was a small blessing and enough to urge her to keep going.

She found the cliff face again, it was getting bigger, and she began following it east once more. She walked as briskly as she could with her injuries. Her ribs ached from the fall that knocked the wind out of her, but she bared her teeth and kept walking despite the urge to just lay down and die.

Worthless child, her aunt's voice danced unsolicited through her mind. She grunted against the memory of the terrible woman. If she was going to die, she would not be thinking of her aunt when she did.

She sipped at the water before strapping the canteen to her belt and arming herself with her dagger. If she had to guess, she had about a mile to go. If she could run, she could cover that in less than fifteen minutes. But she couldn't run, not very quickly anyway. It would be smarter to be quiet and cautious. She was sure though, that some of the Nephilim must have been watching the woods just beyond the sand of the oceanfront. She didn't know how she would get past them.

She could hear the two Hallowed Fallen soaring above the tree line, their wings large enough to cast a gentle breeze in her direction. It could have been the Crowned Magister up there as well she supposed. She didn't like to remind herself that transitioning into Nephilim meant the agony of growing wings.

She took careful brisk steps, crouching down when she heard leaves move. Once she was sure it was an animal or the wind, she would continue on. Eventually she could hear the distant sound of waves crashing on the shore. She paused to inhale the thick salty air, welcoming the increased humidity in the freezing temperature. She had been shivering but was glad that the rain had stopped.

A stabbing pain caught her in her right arm so suddenly she didn't comprehend what happened. She screamed in agony and grappled at the object—an arrow. She tugged on it and it felt as though she were removing her own bones.

"Fuck you!" She screamed at the dark figure wielding a bow and arrow. She grunted in anguish but sprinted, leaving the arrow in her arm. If she pulled it out, she risked bleeding out faster.

Another arrow shot past her head into the path ahead of her so she zigzagged through the trees. She blocked out her bleeding leg, her throbbing ankle, the pain in her ribs, and the arrow protruding from her arm. Someone would help her once she made it to the beach, they would have medical care for the survivors, the announcer had said so that morning.

She heard the large person sprinting close behind her and she couldn't do anything but run. The arrow caught the edge of a vine and snagged, causing her to scream as her flesh tore. The arrow hung loosely out of her arm, blood began pouring down her limb at an alarming rate, causing her to become lightheaded. The Nephilim couldn't be more than two yards behind her and as the sand of the beach came into view, she made one last move to ensure that she would make it.

The ledge down to the sand was a couple of feet tall so as she approached it, she spun around and flung the dagger at the Nephilim. She watched it strike true into the center of his chest as she flung herself down the embankment to the sand. She hit the ground hard, her vision blurring from her head colliding with it. She heard the arrow snap, lodging the head of it further into her arm. She might have screamed again, she didn't know.

The Nephilim came into view above her, panting. It was Praeceptor Cathmore and he discarded the bow to the ground and began tugging the dagger from his chest. He bared his teeth at her but she just gave him a satisfied grin and flipped him off.

A woman and man had dropped down to her side and began checking out her injuries. They were older and human, which she found shocking. Human healers, it made sense if they were to heal the sired children who were pre-transition.

Amara's blood soaked the sand below her and she focused on the sound of the waves. Her limbs had started to go numb, the world spinning around her.

"I lived." She panted. The kind woman nodded, sorrow filling her eyes. "I lived," she repeated again and shook. Her body trembled as she went into shock from blood loss. *I lived,* she thought and the sky faded to black as she gave in to her body's need for the darkness. Despite the woman pleading with her to stay conscious, Amara couldn't.

Cathmore's devilish grin and anger that she made it, was the last thing she saw before the darkness consumed her.

Chapter 4

A few days later, Amara was allowed to leave the infirmary to join the other conscripts. The Crowned Magister was holding a meeting in the training cathedral to commence the start of training and celebrate those who made it through the hunt. She searched the much smaller crowd for familiar faces amongst the conscripts as they moved in unison into the massive hall.

"Amara!" A voice came from behind her. *Beck.* She turned and met his excited grin with a weak smile. "I'm so glad you made it!"

"I'm glad you did too," she answered honestly. She examined him, his ankle was in a boot, he had a gash across his face, and she imagined he was heavily bandaged and stitched on his back. "How did you get away?" She thought of the screams she heard after they got separated and how certain she was that it was him that met his fate.

"I doubled back to the cave and waited while applying pressure to the wound." He gestured to his back.

They entered the training cathedral between stone pillars and found themselves in an open space surrounded by arched windows. Everything from dummies, weapons, punching bags, and other training equipment was moved to the far walls. It was much larger than the space she had trained in during her time before the hunt.

"Oh look, the bastards are acquainted." A male voice chuffed to her right, gesturing at her and Beck. It was one of the males that she had seen before the hunt—the *man* who clearly had been honed into a weapon to pass the Crucible by whoever sired him. Based on his statement, she was confident that his sire was Rase. She shot him a look with narrowed eyes.

"Can I help you with something, *daddy's boy*?" she taunted the burly man who did not take too kindly to her bold response, but she didn't care.

She could tell that he wasn't expecting a response when he bared his teeth at her. His dark hair with a tint of scarlet undertones, confirmed further that Rase sired him. Rase was the only Hallowed Fallen with red hair. The man took a step toward her in anger before his blonde-haired companion grabbed his arm and gestured to the Praeceptor's that were watching him. She grinned but walked faster, Beck still at her side.

"You don't want to make enemies with Fallon Mournstride, are you insane?" Beck whispered. The man's name meant nothing to her, she had never heard of him. Besides, if him being the son of Rase wasn't enough for her to keep her mouth shut, nothing was. At least she had a name to put with the wretchedly offensive face, .

Amara tossed her long jet black hair over her shoulder and regarded Beck with piercing green eyes. "He will not intimidate me."

"Fair enough." He put his hands up in mock surrender.

Amara examined the Praeceptor's that they passed, who all seemed to be sizing them up. On average, Nephilim were taller in stature than humans (and sired children). She had heard that during transformation; the body can grow up to a foot taller in order to accommodate wings. The thought sent a chill up her spine. She was about five and a half feet tall; it would be strange to be six foot tall... and the pain? Growing that much that quickly... She shook her head at the thought. She hoped she wouldn't have to get any taller to accommodate her wings.

Magister Baylin cleared his throat which caused everyone in the room to stop chatting amongst themselves. She regarded the silver fox of a man in anticipation of the results he would give them about the hunt.

"Crowned Magister Bennett was called away on urgent business. As his assistant, I will deliver the results of the entry trial and give instructions for the start of this year's Crucible," he announced.

The Crucible as a whole wasn't just one bout of killing and sacrifices. It also included intense training and education of potential Nephilim for nearly an entire year. The name, though, made it sound like the former.

Amara glimpsed red flowing hair just a few people in front of her. *It was the girl she saved, she lived*. Amara sighed in relief. The girl had black ribbon intertwined in her braid in a way that Amara found gorgeous.

"Seventy-eight entered the hunt," Magister Baylin spoke again, regarding a scroll. She held her breath, preparing for the blow of knowing how many perished. The girl with the slit throat, the red-haired twin who had been disemboweled... The Nephilim had done it, they were monsters, all of them.

"Fifty-six of you remain," he said casually.

Amara expected an audible gasp from the crowd but most of them were stunned into silence. It could have been any one of them. Any one of them could have been reduced to a number on a scroll. Any one of them still could be.

The number took her breath away. Twenty-two deaths. She could not imagine seeing twenty-two dead bodies lined up together but she knew that they had been. She knew that they had been burned to ash upon the conclusion of the hunt. Bile rose in her throat, tears threatened to fall, and she bit down on her tongue to keep from puking or crying. Sadness rolled off of the crowd around her, intensifying her emotions tenfold.

Somewhere in the rush of emotions she felt joy and excitement coming from someone in the crowd. She turned in the direction of the strange aura to find Fallon Mounstride with a disgusting grin on his face, his arms crossed over his chest. She turned back toward Magister Baylin before Fallon could see her staring.

"You will be divided into four groups of fourteen. Each group will be assigned to one of the four following Praeceptor's; Sloane, Nightbane, Cathmore, and Wrathguard." He gestured to the four of them who stood evenly separated behind him. "This will be your training group. You will attend classes as a unit, you will train together, you will eat, sleep, and piss together. You will answer to your Praeceptor, and they will help guide you until the day of transition." The man spoke with such sternness that there was no room for questions.

She observed each Praeceptor; Cathmore, two women, and a stoic-looking man with nearly silver hair cropped close to his head. He was all muscle and definitely appeared as though he would be a brutal trainer given the deep scars that ran down both of his arms and around his neck. *What would have done that?*

"Praeceptor Vixon Sloane, step forward for your assignments," Baylin demanded.

The dark-haired woman had nearly white silver eyes, the blue more muted than some of the other Nephilim. Amara could see the outline of her toned muscles through her long-sleeved shirt; her hair was cropped short, and her mouth was set in a hard line. Her face, though, was rounded and soft. She looked beautiful but she had a feeling that she was equally deadly.

"Praeceptor Sloane is also teaching the Imperium course this year so all of you will be working with her at some point. When I call your name, line up behind her." He cleared his throat and began listing names.

Amara waited to hear her name. She didn't care which Praeceptor she got as long as it wasn't Cathmore. She had had about all of him she could take for one lifetime. Plus the bastard was the one that nearly caused her to lose an arm.

"Beck Goldbreath," was the last of the fourteen names in Praeceptor Sloane's group and the only name amongst the conscripts that she recognized. Beck looked over at her and nodded a farewell before going to line up behind his Praeceptor.

"Praeceptor Oryn Nightbane's unit consists of the following..." The blonde-haired man stepped forward, linked his hands behind his back, and waited. Fallon Mournstride was the only name in his group that she knew and there was relief that she wasn't in Fallon's training unit.

Unfortunately that small victory left her with a 50/50 chance of being stuck with Cathmore. *Fuck.* She hoped for Wrathguard even though she knew nothing of the blue-haired woman.

"Praeceptor Killian Cathmore's unit is as follows; Katara Verity, Molvina Hazelwood, Juliet Valentine." The third girl was the girl she had saved... Juliet. She walked with less confidence and more caution than some of the other conscripts and all that Amara could think about was that the girl had a slim chance of making it to transformation. A few more names were listed when Baylin said. "And Amara Ashenfall—our celebrity this year."

Her stomach dropped when everyone's attention turned to her. Cathmore shot her a sly grin that made her insides recoil with hatred. She had spent two weeks being taunted by him and worked to the bone. A year as his charge would surely end her.

"She's the runner," someone whispered.

"I heard she killed someone," a boy responded.

Her cheeks flamed as she pushed through the last few people to take up her spot at the back of Cathmore's line. Her legs were wobbling from the adrenaline of being stared at and judged by the crowd. Beck grabbed her arm as she walked past him.

"I didn't know you were the murderess," he whispered but it wasn't in the same judgmental tone as the other conscripts. His tone was more in awe and curiosity. She took in his soft features and kind eyes before jerking her arm away, not saying a word to him. *What could she say?*

She had genuinely hoped to lay low, but as eyes lingered on her—that hope slipped further out of reach.

Once the groups were established, training was to commence immediately according to Baylin so the group followed Cathmore to an open field outside of the training cathedral. Cathmore stopped and the group lined up in front of him.

"Sit, now," he said gruffly. The unit did as he said and sat on the ground before him. He crouched down to be closer to their level.

"First rule about working with me—if you want to stay alive, you do exactly as I say," he instructed and made eye contact with each of them.

Amara didn't miss his eyes scanning over her wrapped arm where he had shot her. He fidgeted with a bulky ring on his finger, a muscle in his jaw feathering as he thought for a moment.

"Your first session each day begins with weapons training at precisely eight in the morning," he said, rising to his feet. "Afterward, at eleven, you'll attend your educational courses: Fallen History, Clairvoyance Control, Underworld Adversaries, and Imperium Preparation." He paused as a dark-skinned girl raised her hand. "Now is not the time for questions," he dismissed her with a wave.

"Each class lasts an hour. With breaks and meal times, you'll return to the training cathedral by five in the afternoon. At that point, you'll focus on stamina with Magister Marlowe. Finally, you'll end the day with yours truly," he spread a hand across his chest, "where we'll practice hand-to-hand combat and increase your pain tolerance."

It was so much information to take in, in such a small amount of time. How were they supposed to remember that schedule and how were they to know where to go?

To her relief, he began handing out small scrolls to each of them. She didn't even see where they came from. *Had he used magic to materialize them?* She had so many questions. The scrolls contained their schedule which was twelve hours of training per day for four days, and then three days off and repeat. One thing caught her eye, .

Abyss trial; December 18th. *The next trial.* It was only six weeks away. She rolled the paper up as though she could make the looming trial date disappear.

"Now, let me make something clear. Most of you sired children will die as a sacrifice before transformation day. But those sacrifices will come on the day of trial. None of you are permitted to try and take one another out, this includes those in other units. If you have a problem, you settle it in the sparring ring or on trial day," he asserted.

He paced back and forth as he spoke, it was as though he had rehearsed everything he was going to say. His black uniform with red embroidery was pristine and tight to his body. The leather pants caused the silver buckles on his legs to stand out, he wore a black blazer over it, and black button-down shirt which had the top two buttons undone. She inspected the logo on his shoulder, it was the shape of a shield with an 'S' for the Sanctum, 'Praeceptor' was written in a dead language under it. He wore a silver chain around his neck, with a purple stone pendant in a shape she couldn't make out.

"So we can target someone during a trial?" a guy asked from beside her. Cathmore turned to him with an eyebrow raised.

"I think you'll find yourself... preoccupied during the trials," he crouched down before the guy and regarded him with cool indifference. "People die on trial day; I can't stop you from doing what you wish on the day of bloodshed but—"-" he wiped something off of his knee. "Remember that less sired children competing does not guarantee a victory for yourself. There isn't a chosen number, all of you could just as easily be killed and no one will transition."

The guy gulped and nodded in understanding which prompted Cathmore to stand before them once more.

"Today is mine to do with you what I wish." He scanned the fourteen conscripts. "Now, who knows who sired them?" he asked. "Stand if you do."

Five of the fourteen stood and regarded him curiously.

"Tell me your name and your sire," he said, crossing his arms and looking down at them. His entitled mannerisms demanding demeanor made Amara seethe.

"Katarta Verity," the dark-skinned girl started. "Sired by Arwan." She wondered if the girl shared characteristics of the

Hallowed called Arwan. Amara hadn't seen images of most of them—mostly for fear she would see herself in one of the Hallowed.

"Molvina Hazelwood," the pale dark-haired girl said. "I'm told Sylas sired me." She smiled weakly.

The other three introduced themselves—the guys called Eros Whitvale and Avren Yearwood found that they shared a sire—Osias. The last guy called Davian Axgrove was sired by Rase—of course. Their dark scarlet hair and judgmental attitude would give them away every time. He looked at the nine who didn't know their sires in disgust. Amara just rolled her eyes.

Praeceptor Cathmore saw the look Davian gave the other conscripts and stepped into him so quickly, Davian didn't have time to react. "Your entitlement and bigotry ends here. Rase can do nothing for you. I am your master now," Cathmore threatened.

Davian showed smug disregard for the Praeceptor and shook his head with a scoff. Amara jumped when Cathmore grabbed Davian by the throat and lifted him off of the ground with ease. Cathmore's bicep muscle flexed, his forearm tensing as he tightened his grip on Davian's throat.

Davian was still for a moment, likely trying to appear unphased. But he suddenly started thrashing and clawing at Cathmore's arm. Cathmore tilted his head, taking some kind of pleasure in watching the man fight for air.

"They can't kill you outside of a trial," Cathmore spat— referring to the other conscripts. He dropped Davian who landed on his knees and started gasping for air. "But I can, the minute that I deem you unworthy."

Davian looked up at his Praeceptor in anger but nodded his head understandingly. Amara couldn't help but grin, satisfied that he had been put in his place.

"The rest of you likely won't know your sire until you gain your Imperium or go through transition," Cathmore continued his instruction as he paced and the conscripts sat back down. She wondered if fallen children sired by Rase were always the troublemakers. She imagined that they most likely were.

"Your normal schedule does not begin until tomorrow. Today, I've claimed the riverfront. Our focus today is to become familiar with one another," he said and demanded that they all stand.

The girl—Katara Verity—who was next to her leaned in and whispered, "Is it just me or is he kind of hot?" Amara looked over at the girl with her eyebrows furrowed. She was staring at Cathmore's ass as he walked ahead of them.

"You must have a death wish." Amara smiled with a small laugh at the girl.

"I'd take that risk," Juliet interjected, causing Katara to giggle. Amara shook her head disapprovingly but laughed in response. It was the most normal interaction she had had in months.

She couldn't see what the girls saw, not that he wasn't attractive but...the image of him trying to kill her overshadowed any amount of attraction she could have had toward the Praeceptor. His taunting smile, throwing down his bow & arrow in defeat when it failed to take her life, and his egotistical know-it-all attitude did more to anger her than anything else.

"How'd you know your sire?" Juliet asked Katara as the three of them sat with their feet in the river, their boots were tossed haphazardly next to them.

"My mom told me. He called on her to procreate and he didn't change his form or hide his identity." Katara shrugged.

Most of the time the Hallowed Fallen would take on a normal human appearance and hook up with women across the kingdoms. A lot of times, leaving the mother clueless that they carried a sired child, until the child was born with the mark over its heart. Other times, the Hallowed would simply command a human woman into their bed and impregnate her.

Everything the Hallowed did was to sire more children in order to have a higher chance of having more Nephilim. More Nephilim born of a fallen's power meant more power for the fallen to draw on. Their entire existence was a result of a power grab so that the Hallowed could maintain control over the world.

"What if a different Fallen Angel sired one of us?" Amara asked.

"Like a Rogue Fallen?" Katara asked, turning to her.

"I heard the Hallowed placed magic which banned Rogue Fallen from procreating. They want all of the Nephilim to come from one of the ten Hallowed," Juliet said.

"So it's unlikely," Katara surmised.

"There are just so many more Rogue than Hallowed, it can't be impossible." She sighed.

"That's true. My mum told me once that a child was born to a Rogue Fallen and it burst into flames when it sat foot in the Sanctum Metere," Juliet said with wide eyes.

"Whoa." Amara shook her head.

She glanced over to Cathmore who sat on a massive rock, watching the conscripts speak amongst themselves. Davian was talking to one other guy whose name she missed. Eros, Avren, and Molvina seemed to form a clique of their own.

The other handful of conscripts were taking turns swinging from a rope into the still part of the river, some ways down the riverbank. She could hear the splashing and laughing—for the moment, their lives weren't merely a death race. Perhaps that was Praeceptor Cathmore's intention.

Chapter 5

The stench of sharing a room with fifty-six people was becoming noticeable. Amara's eyes stung with lack of sleep as she anticipated her first day of classes. The only positive thing was that the massive stone corridor was separated into four sections where each unit had their own area. Juliet smiled down at Amara from the top bunk of their shared beds as she dragged a brush through her wavy hair.

Davian and Fallon murmured in low tones, leaning against a stone pillar. Amara could feel their eyes boring into her, a prickling sensation crawling up her spine, bitter as bile on her tongue. She clenched her jaw, forcing herself to focus elsewhere, to block out their silent conversation and the discomfort it brought.

But the sharp sting at the back of her head shattered her concentration. A pen clattered to the floor beside her. She whipped around, eyes narrowed, and caught the smug, self-satisfied smirks that tugged at the corners of their lips. Their glares dared her to react to their petty deed.

Around her, the air grew tense as the other conscripts paused, watching with bated breath. They observed the situation from all around her as though gathering to watch the crescendo of a play. After all, they had heard the stories, the whispered rumors of the infamous "murderess" among them. Some of the conscripts eyed her with wariness, already believing the tales. Others looked on in ignorance, oblivious to the weight of her reputation but eager for drama, nonetheless.

Amara's eyes flickered over the crowd, assessing, calculating. She realized then that her notoriety was an open secret, something whispered in corners but never acknowledged openly. Half of them knew her name and her past. It was only time before the rest learned the truth.

She would not give them the satisfaction, but instead turned back to her bunk where Katara and Juliet were shaking their heads in annoyance. Katara stood and handed a jacket to Amara.

"This would look good with those pants." Katara attempted to turn Amara's attention from the eyes still on her.

Amara wore black pants that hugged her tight but allowed for lots of movement, and a matching long-sleeved shirt. The outfit was bland but so were all of the conscript's clothes. She shrugged on the leather halter jacket and smiled back at Katara. It really did look good and made her feel more confident going into her first day of instruction and training.

All of the conscripts wore varying shades of grays, navy blues, and blacks. It was the unofficial uniform of the Crucible. Colors and elegant fashion had no place on the sacrificial grounds of the

Sanctum Metere. The Praeceptors usually had more leather and straps in their wardrobe, but the color pallet was the same. She tugged on her boots and tried not to worry about what the day would bring.

Nobody is going to die today. She had to keep reminding herself of that fact, even if she didn't entirely believe it.

Commotion on the far end of the dormitory caught her attention where Praeceptor Sloane had just backhanded one of her charges. The sound of the slap echoed through the hall, making most of them cringe. The girl half spun and collapsed to the floor, unconscious.

"Holy shit," Juliet breathed and hugged her crossed arms tighter to her chest.

"I don't get why they feel the need to push the Praeceptors." Amara sighed. It seemed so stupid, the Nephilim could kill them with little to no effort if it pleased them to do so.

They began filing out of the dormitory, none of them brave enough to check on the girl left in a lump on the floor.

Weapons wielding took their group to a pyramid-shaped obsidian stone building opposite the dormitories. It loomed over them, casting them in shadows in response to the morning sun.

They walked through the lush greenery and sprawling ivy with blooming flowers. Amara allowed herself a moment to appreciate the colors of the gardens. As they got closer to the building, small hedges that were perfectly trimmed created a small maze-like walkway toward the entrance. The architecture and landscaping of the place was brilliant. She wondered if humans or Nephilim were charged with the smaller tasks such as landscaping and cooking. She supposed she would figure it out eventually.

Entering the weapons-wielding pyramid was like entering another world. The ceiling towered over them with massive skylights allowing sunlight to pour in. Whatever glass was used though, cast the room in dim purple shades. She stared at the way her arms seemed to glow the color as though illuminating her in false purity. Those skylights couldn't expose the blood on her hands, but it was always there. It always would be.

Stands with swords lined two different sides of the massive training room. There were staves, spears, and daggers displayed on the walls. Armor of varying styles were presented proudly upon mannequins, some fairly bland and others encrusted with crystals. They gave the illusion of soldiers preparing to march into battle.

Carved on each of the four ceilings, before meeting at the point, were Nephilim wings. One set was wide with large feathers, another narrow with razor-sharp ones, and one reminded her of butterfly wings with the extra feathers growing out of the bottom of the wings. They were all beautiful, even if it pained her to think so.

Praeceptor Wrathguard entered the center of the training floor, taking long decisive strides. Her indigo-blue hair, tied in a braid, was flowing behind her, and hanging just past her waist. She knew one of the Hallowed Fallen had blue hair like that but she couldn't remember his name.

"Hope you're all well." She stood with her feet shoulder length apart and crossed her hands in front of her. "Are there any among you who feel called to a weapon in this room?" she asked, gesturing to the far walls and standees. She had a small voice but she projected it well. The Nephilim was only about Amara's height, post transition, so she must have been much shorter when she was human.

Amara glanced around the room; there was one weapon in particular that seemed to reach out to her. Amongst all of the exquisitely crafted longswords was one mounted to the wall with a sapphire embedded in its pommel. The hilt itself had gorgeous matching blue cloth wrapping it, and had some kind of intricate swirling carvings in it which led into the blade itself.

"The longsword with the sapphire hilt," Amara blurted before she could stop herself. Juliet glanced over at her as though she had been stupid to answer the question... but no one else had.

Praeceptor Wrathguard glanced at the sword which was behind her and then back at Amara.

"You can have it," the instructor said. The group started murmuring and looking at Amara. *What...* "You just have to get through me to make it your own." She smiled. She was challenging her, Amara should have known, but she had to be the one to speak up and she wasn't going to back down even if it meant getting beat down by the Praeceptor. Amara took a step toward Wrathguard who stood between her and the longsword.

Wrathguard tilted her head as though impressed and planted her feet firmly on the ground, expecting Amara to charge her. It wasn't a bad idea but she decided to see what would happen if she simply bolted for the sword instead of head-first into a fight that she was sure to lose.

It was pointless, Wrathguard had her on her back with a knee in her chest before she even made it halfway. Amara groaned and gasped for the air that had been knocked out of her. She squirmed for a moment, anger and helplessness swirling in her chest.

"I didn't mean now," Wrathguard announced to the unit with amusement. She got off of Amara and helped her up. "You may claim a weapon of your choosing and when you can get through me to reach it, it's yours for your final trial," she explained.

Amara dusted herself off and joined her group who still stood before the Praeceptor.

"Brave, for a runner," Molvina said. It wasn't entirely a compliment or a slight against her, but an acknowledgment of what she had done.

"You're crazy, Ashenfall." Juliet laughed, exposing deep dimples that Amara hadn't noticed before.

"But you knew that." Amara nudged her.

Juliet offered her a weak smile. That event during the hunt may have saved Juliet but she still lost her twin. Amara swallowed against guilt for mentioning it and shifted on her feet.

Class proceeded with simple feet planting and balancing while holding a dull stick that weighed what a longsword would.

"You need to be rooted and centered when engaging an opponent, especially where weapons are concerned. They take more precision to wield. The last thing you want to do is miss a swing and end up on your ass because of your inability to use your body as a counterweight," Wrathguard explained as she moved between each conscript and inspected their stances.

Wrathguard was like water flowing between the conscripts. She was light on her feet, quick to make corrections, and balanced the group's needs carefully as she taught them.

Amara attended her other lessons in a fairly drab-looking building when compared to the pyramid they had been in for weapons wielding. The building had clearly been there much longer and was made of smoothed cement. Its rounded corners made her uneasy for reasons she didn't know. Even the cement floors rounded up into the walls as though it were going to melt into her and keep her there. She felt as though she were inside a clay pot.

Once she got past the odd architecture, she had to focus on getting through the propaganda that the Hallowed wanted them taught in 'Fallen History'. Magister Baylin clearly thought very highly of the ruling elites and spoke with pride as he explained The Fall.

'The Fall' or 'The Angelic Exodus', marked the largest purging of angels from the heavens. He was careful not to say why the creator chose to abandon humanity and make their home a dumping ground for his outcasts. Instead he claimed the creator had lost his control over the humans and 'gifted' them to the Hallowed Fallen.

It didn't make sense to her because the age of The Fall saw over two-hundred angels cast from the heavens. They wreaked havoc on humanity. Their landing sites were catastrophic enough to burn villages to the ground and level land for twenty miles around. She had lived in the human world. She knew their side of the story. She felt the leftover destruction of the Fallen Angel's actions in her blood and in the scars of her ancestors.

She knew how they murdered, raped, and enslaved survivors for the first century that they walked the earth. It was said to have been the end of all things. It was said that the creator must have been purging the earth, but then one day... it just stopped. Amara was fidgeting with a feather pen when all of the sudden she bent it in her hand.

"The creator left humanity in the care of our Hallowed Fallen. And what a wonderful job they've done." He smiled and she could tell that he genuinely believed it. Most humans and sired children would disagree, but no one sitting before him voiced it.

Katara looked over at her with a face that said, 'is he serious?'. At least she knew that despite their efforts, most of the sired children knew better.

The Hallowed were not in control because their God willed it so. They were in control through strategically used magic, forced breeding, and an overwhelming amount of power over the others who fell alongside them. They made great efforts to remain in control over the continent, often through decisive and violent means to put down any rebellion that stood against them.

Even if some of the Hallowed Fallen weren't as vicious or blood thirsty as Rase, they all would spill blood to stay in power. That was the only 'fallen history' lesson she needed.

She couldn't take it anymore; she didn't say a word to Magister Baylin as she walked silently out of the class.

They were attempting to indoctrinate them into some sick illusion and she despised having to sit there and listen to it. All Baylin wanted to do was praise the Hallowed and spin the truth around to make them seem like heroes. It made her sick. She may not have had the whole truth but something within her knew that whatever they were preaching was wrong.

When she made her way into the pitiful washroom, she looked at herself in the mirror. Her green eyes were bloodshot, her nostrils flaring with anger, and her skin was far too pale. She took deep breaths to try to calm her wildly pounding heart. She didn't want any part of their lessons, their world. She just wanted to run far away.

She thought about the death she had already seen, Baylin's attempts to glorify it, her near-death experience, taunting eyes from other conscripts, and Cathmore's mocking grin, until she felt as though she could explode. With a blood-curdling scream at her stupid reflection she lashed out and shattered the mirror with her fist. She would never be able to escape her situation, to crawl out of her own skin, to quiet her own mind. She didn't have the smallest hint of control over anything and it was threatening to drown her.

Amara watched her tears fall through hanging shards of glass that remained. Her knuckles had been sliced and blood dripped onto the floor below her. She didn't care, she just stood there, staring at the soulless vessel that looked back at her through a shattered mirror—which she had far too much in common with.

She didn't return to the class but instead waited for the murmuring in the hall to indicate that it was time for the next one. She was surprised that no one had gone after her. The blood had dried on her hand and between her fingers which caused Juliet to pull her to the side and question her about what happened.

"Nothing, I'm fine." She shook her head. Juliet clearly didn't believe her but also didn't push the issue.

***

The next three classes served to calm her down following the incident in history. She found that everyone placed in Cathmore's unit had clairvoyance abilities. The conscripts without the gift had no use for the clairvoyance control class. At least she knew why Beck and her had been separated. Nonetheless, the class was more introductory and gauging where everyone's threshold started out. She actually liked Magister Delpine.

Praeceptor Nightbane didn't give much away in the first lesson of 'underworld adversaries' but took a special interest in Amara's history and how she escaped her first summoning to the Crucible . He alluded to her having help and used that to speak of 'The Dark One' and how he had taken over the Kingdom of Ravenyr.

Formally controlled by the Hallowed One called Sylas, he was sent running to Findaria while the war was fought against the Dark One. Nightbane was sure he had influences over some creatures of the underworld which he intended to speak more on during future lessons.

When her last lesson—Imperium Preparation—came along, she was mentally drained. She had to listen to Katara and Eros swoon over how 'delicious' Praeceptor Nightbane was. *Honestly... didn't they have more important things to worry about than sex?*

She learned that until the Crucible progressed, there would not be a lot of Imperium training, but more of an informational session of usual Imperiums that manifest amongst the Nephilim.

Avren asked what Praeceptor Sloane's Imperium was and she made a show of sending him flying across the hall without even touching him. *Telekinesis.* Amara stared in awe at the effortless execution of the ability. *Whoa.*

Amara's head was still reeling about what Sloane had done to Avren when she finally made it to lunch with Juliet and Katara. She regarded the bland poultry and vegetables on her plate with disgust.

"They couldn't spring for bread and cheese could they?" She snarked.

"I guess I'll only dream of chocolate for the next year." Juliet sighed.

Amara regarded the girl carefully, she had plans of getting through the Crucible, of eating chocolate. Not only that, but if she was grieving her brother, she didn't let it show often. She admired her strength to simply look to the future with hope. Even before coming to the Sanctum Metere, it wasn't a quality that Amara possessed.

"Well we have to eat it, the rest of our lessons are physical feats unfortunately," she said in acceptance and ate.

The girls made idle chat about their lessons and who they thought sired whom. Amara refused to let them muse on her sire.

"I don't want to know, just keep me out of it," she snapped. No one protested.

When stamina training came around they were immediately forced to run laps.

"On the first day?" Katara whined as she jogged beside Amara who shrugged.

Marlowe was barking orders for them to speed up from the sidelines of the field. There was something about him that nagged at her, but she couldn't quite place where the unrest regarding him stemmed from.

"Maybe I'm imagining it, but the Magister keeps staring at you," Katara warned. He had been, every time she looked over at him, he was already watching her. *Weird.*

"Yeah, I get that a lot." She sighed. It was the truth. Her reputation as a runner and murderess had her under constant close watch by everyone it seemed.

Amara had begun to slow to a walk with Katara when she was abruptly pushed forward onto the ground. She grunted at the weight of the unexpected impact and tried to blink the pain away.

"What the—" Katara started as Amara turned around to see who had shoved her. Her chin had collided with a rock and throbbed as warm blood trickled from it. She had expected to see Davian.

"You do not stop running until I say you do." It was Magister Marlowe who seethed at her. Katara went to help Amara up but he stopped her. "Go," he barked. The man was much larger than either of them and much older. His silver-blue eyes blazed at Katara who obliged and continued her jog, leaving Amara alone with him.

She got to her feet and faced the Magister, who tilted his head to examine her. She wiped her chin with the sleeve of her shirt and scowled at him. The way his gray hair blew in the wind as well as the cut of his jaw was familiar...

"I'm going to take great joy in the eventuality of your death," the Magister growled and stepped into her face. "Murderess." She looked up at him and that's when it clicked.

Bastian Marlowe was a pest anyway. Fucking hell. He was related to the man she murdered.

She didn't say anything, but as a group ran by, he made a show of yelling, "You will speak to me with respect!" before rearing his fist back and punching her in her jaw so hard that she was sent to the ground once more.

Her vision was spotted with black and the world spun as she tried to sit up to face him. It was of no use. "You'll pay for killing my brother, *inbellis,*" he spat.

She held her jaw as pain shot through her face in blinding waves. He walked away without another word. Nobody said or *did* anything. She caught Juliet, Katara, and Molvina looking at her in shock as they made their way around the track and in her direction.

"What the hell happened?" Molvina asked as they helped her up.

Amara spat blood onto the ground and shook her head. Her shoulders slumped as she spoke, "They can do whatever they want to us."

That was the truth of the matter that made them so help-less. They could make it through their wicked games and still be deemed 'unworthy' and be killed by a Praeceptor or Magister. What was the point of her even trying after what she had done? She had earned death at the hands of Bastain's brother. A life for a life.

She swayed on her feet as her equilibrium tried to right itself after the impact of the Nephilim's punch. She jerked her arm free from one of the girls who tried to steady her and walked off of the field as the siren signaled the end of the lesson.

Chapter 6

As the day approached its conclusion, they had two lessons to go, Both taught by Praeceptor Cathmore, which she dreaded. She cleaned up her face in the dormitory on their break, wrapped her hand from that morning, and debated if it would be easier just to lay down and die.

They made their way to the training hall where Baylin had assigned them all to their Praeceptors. The massive hall was less tidy than it had been that morning and stunk of a day's worth of people working out. She did a double-take at the wall to her right where there was a small spattering of blood.

"What are these lessons called again?" She leaned over to Juliet who watched Cathmore stroll toward them with both his fists wrapped.

"Hand-to-hand combat and pain tolerance," she gulped. *Great.* She thought she had experienced enough pain for one day but had a feeling that Cathmore would disagree.

"All right, what Praeceptor did Ashenfall piss off?" He began, being called out so suddenly made her jump and her stomach sink. The rest of the unit looked over at her, her jaw had begun to bruise and her chin was scabbing up. He walked up to her and raised a hand, tilting her face to the side with his fingertips. She jerked her chin away from him but still allowed him to examine her.

"Magister Marlowe, but she didn't do anything—" Katara said and Amara appreciated the girl's attempt to defend her. *Was she about to be punished for having to be punished?*

"Yeah he just randomly shoved her," Juliet cut in.

Praeceptor Cathmore's nostrils flared for a moment, his jaw clenching in a way that confused Amara. He took a step away from her and paused thoughtfully before speaking.

"Your Praeceptor is the only one with authority to discipline you outside of the Crowned Magister," Amara looked over at the blood on the wall with raised eyebrows to which he acknowledged, "—combat injuries do not count as discipline."

She examined him from head to toe as he paced before them, though she wasn't sure why. He wore loose-fitting dark pants, a tighter shirt with long sleeves, and instead of boots simply wore black socks. It made sense, given the nature of the course and all of the padded mats below them. They too had been instructed to remove their shoes for training. He stretched an arm over his torso, causing his back muscles to flex in a distracting way.... *Stop, no.* She chitted herself. *She would not find him attractive. He was rude, arrogant, and had tried to kill her.*

He paired them up with a partner. She ended up with Avren, Katara with Molivina, and Juliet with Davian which made her cringe. She didn't really pay attention to whom the others were paired with. She was examining the varying training weapons and... *were those ropes hanging from the ceiling?*

"Today, we are practicing basic strikes with open hands as well as essential blocks and stances," Cathmore instructed as he strolled around them casually.

"Ow." Avren laughed when she successfully struck him in the cheek with a palm strike. She laughed too, but her humor was short-lived when he jabbed her in the rib cage with a perfect knife strike.

"What do you think the Abyss Trial will consist of?" Avren exhaled as she blocked his overhead strike and took a step backward to steady herself. His messy honey brown hair was cut close to his scalp, about finger length and he ran his head through it as though it was once longer.

"I don't know. But I've heard of the Abyss before, I think it's a terrible place," she answered. She wasn't in a rush to know what her next near-death experience would be at the hands of.

"I hope we are given an explanation so we can prepare ourselves. I don't want to be blindsided." He huffed and blocked her knife strike.

"Me too." She sighed and he gave her a hopeful smile.

After an hour of repetitive and exhausting exercises, Cathmore called them all to sit in a circle with their legs crossed.

"Pain tolerance is something that I can't make suck any less than it does. You all simply have to build your tolerance to extreme bouts of pain so that you don't go into shock or succumb to it during transformation," he spoke calmly. "Making it through the Crucible and dying during your transformation into Nephilim is unlikely but it does happen. The Crowned Magister and bureau of research has confirmed that training to increase pain tolerance does in fact decrease your chances of death." He rubbed his hands together.

Juliet looked at her with concern from the opposite side of the circle where she sat. Amara was more interested in this 'bureau of research' he spoke of. Was that one of the jobs that newly turned Nephilim were made to do during their time at the Sanctum Metere?

"Cardio exercises are going to be more the focus since the increased blood flow helps dull your pain receptors. However, there are multiple physical events that your body is going to be put through here, so please mentally prepare yourself for that. And *please*," he emphasized the word—"don't die in my class."

Amara scoffed louder than she intended. As if they had a choice on when/how they died during the course of the Crucible.

"Widen the circle," he instructed and they all scooted back.

Cathmore removed his shirt which confused most of them and left a couple of them staring far too hard at his toned stomach. It wasn't just that that caught Amara's attention . In his back, just over his shoulder blades were large piercings placed under his skin.

She could see the bars just under the surface of his skin which protruded out into large metal loops about two inches in diameter.

He also had one placed at the bottom of his spine that looked identical to the other two. Avren asked what they could possibly be for since they looked uncomfortable but Amara didn't know either.

"Hazelwood, go pull that rope." He pointed to the far wall where a series of pulleys were mounted. "Ashenfall, stand." *Oh shit.*

She had been examining his scarred and tattooed arms when Molvina lowered the ropes into the center of the circle as instructed. Davian seemed to understand what was happening and grinned wickedly, the rest of them looked on in confusion. Each rope had a steel hook at the end and she tilted her head.

Cathmore placed one of the hooks in her hand and turned around, reaching over his shoulder for the loop. "Hook it here, and do the same for the other two," Cathmore demanded. His voice was huskier than it had been, an octave lower too. The group gasped at the command and she looked around at them. "Now, Ashenfall." He looked over his shoulder. His silver eyes were blazing with a fire that she didn't know the source of.

She did as he asked and carefully hooked each one, watching his skin raise where the loop hid beneath it. It made her stomach churn but once they were placed, she stepped back.

"Go help Hazelwood," he said next and she walked over to where Molvina stood next to the ropes. *He can't actually be about to suspend himself from piercings.* "Slowly pull the red ropes, the both of you."

Molvina looked over at Amara in hesitation.

"On thee?" she asked. Amara nodded with a hard gulp and the girl slowly pulled on three.

Cathmore began being gracefully pulled upward, his skin stretching so much under the weight of holding him up that Juliet and two other girls had to look away. She expected to see blood running from the piercings but there was none. Cathmore sucked air through his teeth in a way more indicative of pleasure than pain.

"There is an art to mastering your body's reaction to pain, to understanding the way our senses perceive painful stimuli," he began. He swayed slowly as he hung from the hooks. "After the pain of transformation, I've learned how to achieve relaxation in pain that I control." He pointed to the ropes. "There's a thin line between pleasure and pain." He smiled, which caused one of the girls to blush and Molvina to nudge her with a giggle.

After a few moments he instructed them to lower the ropes and asked Amara to remove the hooks. She did so with shaky hands, momentarily distracted by the thin layer of sweat on his chiseled back.

"Are we going to get to do that?" Davian asked, in excitement.

"Yes, but not today." Praeceptor Cathmore nodded and tugged his shirt back on. She could see the rings clearly protruding through the thin material that she had not noticed before. "Today, we are going to place the piercings because they have to heal before suspension."

"You've got to be kidding me." Molvina grunted as they sat back down.

"Ah, a volunteer! Hazlewood," Cathmore responded upon overhearing her complaint.

He led them to a room that branched off of the training hall. In the small white room, there was already a set-up for placing the rings. A chair, a table with massive sterile needles, towels, and the suspension rings themselves.

He hauled Molvina by her arm and sat her in the chair, her chest leaning onto the back of it. He instructed her to remove her shirt and use it to cover her breasts while everyone looked away. She obliged nervously though Amara didn't know if it was because of Molvina's attraction to the Praeceptor, or the rings being placed into her skin. "Could we not just put hooks directly into the skin?" Katara interjected as Cathmore sanitized Molvina's back.

"We could, but because we will be exercising with these regularly, this prevents you from having to be pierced more than once. Do you want to be pierced daily?" he asked, annoyed. His eyes dug into her.

"Nope," she said and flattened her mouth into a hard line.

The group collectively winced as Cathmore pinched her skin upward and shoved the hollow needle through what must have been an inch of skin and tissue. She flinched and bit down on her shirt but he didn't hesitate and immediately followed through with shoving in the next needle above the other shoulder blade. He put the massive ring in the butt of the needle and used it to guide the ring into her skin. A small amount of blood trickled downward and he cleaned her up. The skin was inflamed around the rings, causing Amara to squirm.

There was less skin for him to work with at the middle of her spine but he was able to get it placed anyway. From Molvina's reaction, that one was far more painful.

"I'll go next," Amara blurted. She needed it over with, she didn't want to watch someone else go through it. She thought she saw a hint of a grin play on the Praeceptor's lips but he wasn't facing her so she couldn't be sure. He was probably jumping at the opportunity to make it as painful as possible for the infamous murderess.

Only a few people were in the small room watching, the rest were outside the doorway, peering in.

"Shirt off," he demanded and turned away. She faced away from everyone and pulled it forward over her head. She sat in the chair the same way Molvina had. Cathmore turned to face her and the silence hung heavy in the air, he had seen it... everyone had.

"Just do it," she barked, all too aware of the group staring at the remnants of her troubled youth.

***

She didn't understand why her aunt was always so cruel to her. She was wonderful with her own four children but when it came to Amara... She just burned with hatred. This particular day, she had found a box with her mother's name written on it, hidden below a floorboard in her aunt's room. She couldn't have been but about ten years old and already bore many scars from child-like mistakes.

She wanted to open the box in case there were more portraits of her mother. The one she had was drawn when her mother was just eighteen and it was the only one Amara had ever seen. She looked like her mother, dark hair and green eyes in the shape of almonds. A terrible sickness claimed her life when Amara was just two, and the little girl inside of her always yearned to know more about her. So she opened the box labeled; 'Josie A.' She smiled, heart swelling with hope as she broke apart the wax seal.

"How dare you!" Came the old crone of a woman's voice. Amara was yanked backward by her hair, sending the box flying.

Her aunt was furious, calling her a thief and a bastard. She dragged Amara into the living room of the small cabin where the fireplace burned.

"She was my sister; you have no right to her things!" The unreasonable woman yelled and grabbed one of the metal fireplace tools—the poker. She began rotating it in the flame, Amara started to cry.

"I'm sorry," she whimpered and tried to crawl away. The evil woman grabbed her by the back of the shirt, forced her to stand, and ripped the already threadbare fabric from her body.

She shoved Amara into the stone wall beside the fireplace, smashing her face. Her aunt placed the end of the hot poker flat in the center of her back and her skin seared. A blood-curdling scream erupted from the small girl and she thrashed as her aunt pinned her by her face into the cobblestone.

"Please!" She pleaded when her aunt stuck the poker back into the fire. "I just wanted to see Mama!"

The woman grumbled something but she couldn't hear it past the blood rushing in her ears from the pain. She pressed the poker into another part of Amara's back and held it there until her legs gave out and she dropped to the floor. She had hoped that would be it but Aunt

Grace would not stop so easily. She took far too much joy in torturing her niece.

After the sixth burn and branding with the poker, Amara was crawling away, her arms shaking and barely carrying her.

"You'll remember not to touch my things," she boomed. That's when Aunt Grace drew a ladle full of boiling water from the pot over the fire and poured it on Amara's back. She didn't remember screaming or passing out, but she remembered being disappointed that she woke up days later.

Amara's back had been left scarred from the boiling water and branded with the shape of a poker that looked like backwards 'r's in six different places. She didn't look around to see how they reacted but heard whispering amongst the other conscripts.

"Leave," Praeceptor Cathmore ordered. She heard the door shut and looked over to him when he sat back in his chair on her left side. "That scar tissue is going to cause this to be a lot more painful for you," he explained with wide eyes. *Why did he care?*

"Pain tolerance, right?" She shrugged. She didn't feel embarrassed about her scars; she had long since overcome that feeling. She just felt tired and wanted it all over with. "And what do you care anyway?. If you had it your way, you would have killed me during the hunt," she spat. He looked taken aback but thought before he spoke.

"If I wanted you dead, you'd be dead." He sneered and grabbed her skin to start the piercing.

She grunted and bit down on her arm as he fought to shove the needle through the mangled tissue. He stood and moved to her other side and repeated the excruciating action. Her screaming grew louder because the adrenaline had already come and gone on the first piercing. *Fuck.*

"Okay, one more." He sighed and reached for the next needle. Her vision was blurry so she pushed her hand against his abdomen.

"Wait, I need a second." She panted. She slightly gripped the front of his shirt until a wave of nerve pain passed, Cathmore stood frozen but she didn't care if the hesitation pissed him off.

She had always dealt with nerve damage from the incident and he just agitated it. Her vision cleared and she grounded herself after a moment. She dropped her hand, signaling for him to finish the last piercing.

He did so as quickly as possible and she was thankful that he didn't drag out the experience. She exhaled slowly and pulled her shirt back on. She stood to leave while he started cleaning the area.

"See me before going back to the dormitories this evening," he said without even looking at her. She left the room in silence and let Eros in who wanted to be next.

She couldn't think of why she had to see him after the class unless it had to do with her walking out of Baylin's course that morning. Even then, Cathmore seemed more like the humiliate in front of the class type than the talk in private type.

Chapter 7

The rest of the unit started their walk back to the dormitories while Amara stayed behind to speak to Cathmore. To her delight, Davian had cried as a result of the piercings and she didn't hide her smile from him upon seeing him wipe away his tears. She was glad that Juliet and Katara did well, Katara even saying she liked it. She heard footsteps approaching from behind her.

"Ashenfall," he said and it felt so formal when compared to him calling her 'brat' before the hunt. "I'm told you walked out of Fallen History. Why?" He was using a rag to wipe small splatters of blood from his forearms. She started to speak but he walked past her toward the door. She followed quickly.

"Because Magister Baylin is full of shit." She scoffed. She knew she probably should speak of her instructors with more respect, but she didn't care. Cathmore shook his head and sighed. She hurried behind him into the night, unsure of where he was leading her.

"Every time you do something like this I have to answer for it. I am required to punish you. It's the first day and you have already been hit by a Magister—which is strictly forbidden by the way." He turned to her and ran his hand through his jet black hair. "And now I've got the Crown Magister's bloody assistant complaining that one of my charges walked out of his class and blatantly ignored him," he snapped. "You're acting like..." he began but she cut him off.

"Like what? Like I don't want to be here? Because I don't!" She exclaimed, throwing her hands in the air.

"No one does, Ashenfall. You're acting like a brat! Like you're too good to listen to anyone," he insisted.

"You are such an ass—" she grunted before someone interrupted them.

"Praeceptor, get your charge in line!" It was the Crowned Magister. Cathmore's face shifted from frustration to wrath and she knew that he was about to make her pay for what the Crowned Magister had just heard between them. *Shit.*

The cold fall air blew between the two of them as Cathmore dragged her by the arm back into the training hall. She knew better than to attempt to flee.

"Finish that sentence, I'm a what?" he barked and spun her to face him.

Amara collided hard with his chest, he was panting from anger. She glanced up at him in nervous anticipation, close enough to smell the musk and mint coming off of him. She didn't speak, she didn't want to know what he'd do if she answered the rhetorical question.

"Do you wish to dull out the punishment, Praeceptor? Or shall I?" It was Crowned Magister Bennett who stood in the entryway. Cathmore's eyes went wide, she could tell that he knew Bennett's punishment would be far more severe.

She spun to look at the Crowned Magister, Cathmore still far too close behind her... his body touching her backside. *No.*

"She is my charge, I'll do it, sir," he said and she heard him walking away. There was some hesitation in his voice, she noticed but she was more afraid of whatever punishment Bennett would require. *Where was he going?*

Cathmore came back with some kind of whip with multiple leather tails. Her first instinct was to bolt, but Cathmore knew that and already had her by the arm. He yanked her over to a desk area in one of the corners of the massive hall and Bennett watched them.

"Twelve lashes for gross insubordination. Three more for walking out of Fallen History," the Crowned Magister demanded. Cathmore nodded at him.

She looked frantically between him and Cathmore, panicked. She knew there was no outrunning them. Her back was still burning from the piercings, how was she going to take fifteen lashes back there? What if one of the little leather whips got caught on the freshly installed ring? The thought nauseated her.

"Remove your shirt or your pants," he instructed, his arms crossed. She looked at him wide-eyed, not able to believe this was happening. "Take the lashes on your back or ass." He knew the state of her back was worse than any of the other conscripts and was clearly suggesting she take the ladder.

He tightened his hand around the leather wrapped handle of the whip and dropped his hand to his side. The long tails of the whip grazed the ground and she swallowed hard before turning around, her decision made. She tugged her pants down, rolling them just below her ass. Cathmore looked away briefly before realizing there was not a point, he'd have to see her exposed to dull out the punishment.

Amara moved to the side of the desk, before spreading her legs enough to bend over it. She made a point of choosing that side so that she could make eye contact with the Crowned Magister.

Her eyes stung not from the impending promise of pain but from the humiliation. Still she kept her eyes on Crowned Magister Bennett whose palm twitched in anticipation.

"Count out loud," Praeceptor Cathmore instructed, loud enough for Bennett to hear. He finished the sentence, though, with whispering, "Brat," and she could almost hear his grin as he pulled the whip back.

The first lash caused her to jump, slamming her pelvis into the wood of the desk. "One," she spat as she maintained eye contact with Bennett. She didn't know if Cathmore intended to punish her for walking out of class. But she knew he would not have done it this way if not for the Crowned Magister's sick need to punish the sired children.

"Two," she called as the second stinging blow heated her ass. "Three." She wouldn't cry. He would not see her broken. Bennett smiled as though to the contrary. "Four." Her voice a little hoarser. She could hear Cathmore behind her, controlling his breathing. *Why?*

She pressed her forehead into the desk, taking each lashing, fighting the tears that stung her eyes. "Ten." Her voice was a whisper. Cathmore switched sides, adjusting himself to change the point of impact. She heard Bennett leaving and watched him exit the hall with a satisfied grin.

"Eleven," she breathed. She gripped each side of the desk, her knuckles turning white as Cathmore continued the punishment. She felt her legs shaking from the position she was in and the pain that shot through them. She forgot to count the next one.

She could feel hesitation coming off of him in waves. It was thick, anger woven into it. Somewhere amongst the emotions coming off of him was something... sweeter. She couldn't place it. *Joy? Excitement?*

Cathmore usually had his emotions under tight wraps but the situation sent everything he was feeling outward, crashing into her like a wave.

"Count Ashenfall," he demanded through gritted teeth. His voice was heavier, lower again, more primal. *What the hell? Was he enjoying this?*

"Twelve," she snapped. His next hit came down harsher and faster, causing her to lurch forward and groan. "Thirteen." She heard Cathmore exhaling hard before bringing the whip down with equal force. "Fourteen," she bit out.

She pushed herself up on her toes as though she could squirm away from the last one. She was somewhere between numb and on fire both physically and mentally. She was pretty sure she was bleeding too. "Fifteen," she choked as he dealt the final blow.

He dropped the whip and she heard his footsteps descend down the hall as he walked away without a word. She laid there for a moment, calming her breathing, before standing up and slowly pulling her pants back up. The fabric stung against her raw flesh and she winced. She didn't know where the Praeceptor had gone but she walked slowly toward the door, each step sending pain over the sensitive area.

Chapter 8

The two days that followed were far more uneventful than the first day of lessons and Amara was grateful for it. She had just gotten to the point where blinding pain didn't accompany sitting down, when she and Juliet made their way onto the field for stamina training. She flexed her aching fist and became aware of the scabbing on her chin at the sight of him.

Marlowe had been there the previous day but had not paid any attention to Amara whose guilt felt heavier somehow. Seeing the grief stricken loved one of the man she killed probably should have crippled her, but it didn't. That didn't mean she didn't carry guilt and shame for her actions every day, . If she had known that killing Bastian wouldn't have set her free, of course she wouldn't have done it. She was just fighting for her freedom, for her life really. Though that didn't put her conscience at ease—it was her truth. More than that, she couldn't change it.

She and the unit were completing their mandatory stretches when Marlowe finally made his way onto the field. Multiple conscripts did a double-take though because of how unrecognizable his face had become. Amara shuddered.

He appeared to have been on the losing side of a fight, his face was swollen to twice its size. His nose was very obviously broken, both eyes black, and his lip split. She didn't even want to know why his arm was in a sling. The unit whispered amongst themselves.

"I wonder if the Crowned Magister did it for him hitting a sired child?" Eros whispered to Avren behind her.

"He did break a rule of the Crucible," Avren agreed.

"I wonder if Praeceptor Cathmore got a hold of him for putting hands on one of his charges," Katara mused, nudging Amara who just shook her head in amusement.

"Today, we are running the stairs of the arena," Magister Marlowe announced. A few people grunted which made Amara feel as though she were amongst children. *This was the Crucible, why did they expect anything but hard work?*

The coliseum style arena that was at the center of the Sanctum Metere stood tall with the same striking beauty as it had the first time she'd seen it. The lack of a roof allowed the sun to beam down on them, providing warmth from the cool day.

The 'seats' themselves inside the arena just looked like larger versions of the stairs that were placed periodically between them. She and Juliet looked upward at the section of stairs they had chosen with open mouths. There was no way they were going to run it all the way to the top.

Marlowe signaled the start, Davian and another boy he had gotten close to—Rosen Lockright—took off at full speed first. She and Juliet paced themselves as they mounted the dark stone stairs. It seemed Molvina and Katara were going at more of a brisk walk as they chatted idly.

Eros and Avren were laughing and one of them tripped the other. It was as though they were true brothers who were raised together and had a lifetime of tousling and making one another laugh. There were lots of similarities in their features as they laughed. Something about the two having child-like fun made her happy. Marlowe shouted for them to keep going once they all slowed down at the halfway point.

Amara had counted ninety-six stairs and thirty rows of stone bleachers that wrapped the entire arena. For that to be just halfway, she couldn't imagine the arena ever being full. It would seat thousands.

"Did you hear what happened?" Juliet asked. Amara looked over at the girl, perplexed. They had been to the same places that day, what would Juliet have heard that she hadn't?

"I heard some of the cooks in the washroom talking about one of the Hallowed going Rogue," she whispered.

"What?" She gasped. It was unheard of, the Hallowed had ruled for many centuries, they would never give up their position, and power to live as an outcast like the Rogue Fallen. "Who?" she asked.

"I don't know. But they think he went to join Deimos," Juliet panted and leaned forward as she moved up the stairs.

"Who?" Amara raised her eyebrows.

"The Dark One," she snarked as though she couldn't believe Amara didn't know his name.

"Oh, wow," was all Amara could say.

She didn't think it was possible that a Hallowed Fallen would join the rebellion that sought to overthrow them. Yet, it made more sense than the Hallowed One just deciding he didn't want to be royalty anymore.

Eventually, Preceptor Cathmore's classes came around. The two of them hadn't spoken the day before and she had no desire to speak to him moving forward. She hadn't told anyone what happened, the way he punished her, or the Crowned Magister demanding it. It was all far too humiliating.

In hand-to-hand combat they had also begun to use staves, in which Cathmore called Amara a 'natural' at. Davian had jumped at the opportunity to spar with her with them. She made short work of putting him on his back and hitting him in the jaw with the butt of the wooden weapon. At which point he got genuinely angry and tackled her to the ground.

"Enough, Axgrove!" Praeceptor Cathmore yelled. "She got you down, that's it."

She managed to punch him in the face as he straddled her and began choking her. She squirmed beneath him. As he reared back to punch her, he was pulled off of her by Katara and Cathmore.

"You lost, *daddies boy,*" she purred as she dusted herself off.

Davian was seething and trying to jerk out of Cathmore's grip. Cathmore just regarded her with something between amusement and cold detachment.

"Bastard-born whore!" He exclaimed and tried once more to free himself of Cathmore. She tossed her staff to the ground. Avren and Eros were patting her on the back in congratulations for winning the match.

"That'll teach you to mess with our girl," Avren laughed and threw an arm over her shoulder. She laughed too and threw her fist in the air as the rest of the unit applauded.

She didn't know how or when it happened, but she had begun to make friends amongst the conscripts—Juliet and the brothers especially. She liked Molvina and Katara but they had more in common between each other and that was okay. Juliet high-fived her and they all went to sit against the wall in preparation for the next sparring match.

She couldn't believe that Davian was still so mad, but Cathmore shoved him into the wall and restrained his arms behind his back. He warned Davian but Amara couldn't make out the words. How was he going to control someone like Davian? Davian continued to thrash against Cathmore who became increasingly annoyed as the other conscripts watched on in curiosity.

"You need to fight somebody, Axgrove? Fight me!" Cathmore roared, releasing him. "Your temper tantrum is interrupting my class." He opened his arms, welcoming Davian to throw the first punch.

To no one's surprise, his dumbass actually did it. He was so blind with anger that he actually chose to try and fight a Nephilim. He ducked down and tackled Cathmore by his abdomen which Amara was realizing was Davian's go-to move given his large frame.

Cathmore allowed Davian to tackle him but as soon as Cathmore's back hit the ground, he used his legs to launch Davian over him. It was a move that reminded her of their solo training before the Crucible began. Davian flipped and landed on his back so hard and so fast that it knocked the wind out of him.

He laid there like a fish gasping for air, Cathmore stood over him with his arms crossed. He waited for Davian to regain the ability to breath and stared at him with an 'are you done now?' attitude.

"What a *stultus*," Eros said in amusement. The word translated to *fool*, causing the group of friends to laugh. The way he spoke the words came with more of an accent than usual.

"Did you come from Ravenyr?" she whispered to him, he seemed thrown off by the question.

"I did," he said painfully. "How did you know?"

"Your accent," she whispered. She could tell that he had made a great effort to hide it. "I didn't notice it before; it just slipped up." She smiled reassuringly.

"I know, I just know that people will bombard me with questions about the kingdom being seized." He sighed. "It's not something I want to relive.""I understand. Your secret is safe with me."

Eros tied his hair up; it was so long that it fell halfway down his back. She was kind of jealous of the thick blonde waves but he seemed annoyed as he fought it into a ponytail.

"All right now that that's over with. I believe it was Eros and Judas on the mat next," Cathmore announced. Eros looked over at Amara in excitement as the dark-haired boy took to the mat and Eros followed.

Judas Bloodriver wasn't in their friend group but he wasn't a nuisance like Davian either. He seemed to keep to himself but she had seen him wrestle... Eros was in trouble. Given that the class was hand-to-hand combat training, they used very few weapons.

Either way, she wondered why Eros challenged Judas of all people, he was a great deal larger than the smaller framed guy she had come to call a friend. Eros had to be six feet tall, Judas had five inches on him, easy. But Judas stood, his hair might have been black but it was buzzed really low, still he had a sharp jawline, high cheekbones, and some small shadowing of facial hair. He always seemed to be scowling .

Lost in thought, Amara watched Cathmore position them for the start. Cathmore moved with precision and grace even in everyday tasks. He shoved his hair out of his face, exposing his chiseled jaw and sharp profile. His lips were full, his tongue darting out to moisten them before calling out the queue word for the match to start.

She recalled the punishment she had received from him—his ragged breathing, the huskiness in his voice when demanding her to count, the way the lashes became more intense as though his control was slipping... It was like the Praeceptor before her was a different person than the one who had bent her over and given her fifteen lashes—and *enjoyed* it. She was pretty sure the stranger, sweeter emotion that he felt that night was some form of joy. Whatever it was, she could still taste it.

He smiled in response to some impressive move Judas performed and she imagined the grin he must have wore when calling her a 'brat' before bringing down the whip that first time.

Amara cursed herself for the thoughts and turned her attention back to the fight. Judas pinned—more like fell on top of Eros, their faces pausing only an inch apart. The two locked eyes, both of their breathing labored, and Amara understood exactly why Eros challenged Judas. Katara gave her an 'are you seeing this?' look and she nodded in excitement.

"Not in the training room boys." Praeceptor Cathmore yanked Judas off of Eros who blushed as though remembering that they hadn't been alone. As for Cathmore, did he have to call them out like that? It seemed cruel, but they just laughed it off. "Molvina, Juliet, grab some daggers. Lets see what we've got from yesterday's practice," he called.

Amara was grateful that the practice weapons were all dulled, she couldn't imagine the bloodshed otherwise. She narrowed her eyes on the dried splatter of blood on the wall she noticed days earlier. She figured a fight got heated and sighed.

When it came time for the course in increasing pain tolerance, Praeceptor Cathmore informed them that they would be setting their starting point for pain tolerance.

"We are starting simple." He held up a small iron hammer type tool. "I will apply pressure to certain pressure points. There are four different points on your body and five different intensity levels that I will apply. I will document where everyone begins so that we can test again later on to see if your threshold increases."

"Where are the pressure points?" Avren asked.

Cathmore stood before them where they all leaned against the stone wall. He pointed to the center of his forearm just below the crook of the elbow. "I'm going to hit your radial nerve here." He slid his long fingers down his toned arm, "your median nerve here." He pointed at the center of his wrist. "I will do your thigh, where a femoral nerve is located. Lastly, your lower back is the most painful one—the sciatica."

"How do you know all of those big names?" Katara prodded.

"I trained as a doctor before I came of age for the Crucible." He gave her a nod and small smile. It was a humble gesture that they didn't see from him often. *A doctor?* No wonder he was able to do those massively deep piercings without doing serious damage. "I am not a doctor, but I have a lot of experience."

"While I work one-on-one with each of you—the rest of you can work on your jabs on the heavy bags," he instructed. "Once you finish your pain threshold test, you can go back to the dormitory."

Amara had been throwing punches at the bag for an hour before she was called. She was the last one. The girl leaving when she was called was rubbing at her lower back and grimacing. *Wonderful.*

She wiped her bloodied knuckles on her pants and shook them loose. She had reopened some of the scabs from punching the glass mirror a couple of days earlier. She found solace in the pain though, it was relieving. She had a feeling that whatever Cathmore was about to do to her, however, would not be the least bit relieving.

She followed him into a small room, similar to the one he pierced her in but on the opposite side of the training hall. *Did he have endless rooms for his little games?*

"Do you want some bandages for that?" He pointed at her bleeding knuckles casually.

"Yeah, thanks." She nodded.

He grabbed a basket of precut bandages from a wooden cabinet and told her to sit in the chair.

"Oh, you don't have to—" she began but he gently grabbed her hand and inspected it. He twisted her small wrist with his long fingers. Her eyes lingered far too long on the veins in his strong hands. When he looked down, he met her eyes and tilted his head.

"What were you thinking about that you had to draw your own blood to find peace?" He wrapped her hand carefully, the pressure from the wrap soothing the pain. She didn't want to answer the question seriously, it was far too heavy, far too much.

"I was just imagining my least favorite Praeceptor's face." She shrugged nonchalantly.

It wasn't a lie, she had been taking out unresolved anger toward him for trying to kill her and then humiliating her. Not to mention the lingering grudge for him capturing her in the first place. He exhaled a small knowing smile.

"I'll have to warn Wrathguard about your hatred toward her. I mean..." he turned and picked up more bandages. "I know she pushes you guys hard but this..." he inspected the other hand, her dominant hand that had the most damage. "Is more self-abuse than expelling anger."

He looked down into her eyes again, his own hooded. She narrowed her eyes at him in annoyance but allowed a small amount of humor to show on her face.

He finished the bandages and sat in the chair beside the one she was in. He extended her arm outward to her side and relaxed it in his lap. She ignored the rush of heat in her extremity and looked forward. He ran his fingers down her arm and stopped on her wrist.

"We're going to start here." He pushed his fingertip firmly into the pressure point. "That was a one, no pain?" She shook her head.

He added his nail and doubled the pressure in the spot. Her hand went numb and she felt some discomfort.

"That was a two, you're doing great. This is going to hurt," he said, picking up the mini iron hammer. She looked over into his blue eyes, nearly forgetting to breathe. "But you don't tell me to stop until you absolutely can't take it anymore, understand?"

"Yes." She swallowed. He still hadn't removed his finger from the area and it was starting to buzz.

He pressed the flat tip of the solid iron into the spot, replacing his finger. He pressed down and she jerked and the pain was intense but she didn't want to tap out yet.

"Okay great, here's four," he explained. He pushed with so much more pressure, this time with the pointed part of the tool. His knee pushed her wrist up which made it nearly unbearable. She couldn't help it—she grunted and pulled her arm from his grip.

He wrote something down in a small leatherbound book and moved to her right side. He splayed her arm across his lap and found the pressure point in her forearm. Pressing it made her arm tingle, the first one with the hammer made her nauseous, and again she maxed out at a four. Cathmore gave nothing away about whether or not it was a good thing. Did everyone else get fives? She doubted it.

"We're going to move to your thigh. Right or left?" he asked.

"Right's good." She sighed. It really didn't matter and he was already on her right side anyway.

Amara had her legs propped on a stool that was slightly lower than the chair. He placed his hand midway up her thigh and instructed her to move her leg toward him. The movement opened her thighs, her skin tight pants making her feel exposed all of the sudden. He tightened his grip on her thigh and pulled her leg closer to him, her breathing hitched. He didn't miss it and glanced over to her, only then was she aware that she was biting her lip. She stopped immediately.

"The pressure point is here." He pressed inward. It was at her upper thigh, inching toward the inner part. She jumped when he pressed but it was more at the shock of his touch so close to...

"That was one," he began.

"And next is two, I got it," she snapped and exhaled slowly.

He pressed in harder with his thumb. She could feel that it was going to bruise. He picked up the tool he had been using, gripping her thigh hard to keep his thumb pressed firmly into it. *Fuck.* She was a whirlwind of agitation, adrenaline, and lust. *She would be turned on by anyone touching her this way.* She told herself, only to realize she had admitted to herself that she liked his hands there. *No, no, no.*

He pressed the flat part of the tool into the space and it wasn't as abrasive as his fingertip, at least not until he slid one hand under her thigh to provide counter pressure. It was the same way he used his knee for counterpressure on her wrist. Her nerves were on fire all the way down her leg, she twitched as she subconsciously tried to get away from the source of the pain. But she was more stubborn than that.

"Here's four," he adjusted himself. He flattened his palm below her thigh and turned the tool so that the sharper part was on her skin. She nearly wanted to ask him to stop, she knew it was going to be bad.

He pressed hard with the tool, making her leg go numb, and causing her to become lightheaded. Against her will, she let out a strangled grunt.

"I don't know if that's you tapping out or..." he said in confusion.

"I'm done," she sniped at him. She hated admitting defeat.

She surmised that the mat on the ground was for the conscripts to lay on while he repeated the process on their lower backs. He allowed her a moment and then instructed her to do just that. She propped her forehead on her arms and waited as he sat down beside her in silence.

He rolled up the edge of her shirt, only exposing the lower section of her back. She inhaled sharply when his long fingers trailed seemingly mindlessly over the skin. She furrowed her eyebrows and was about to look over at him when he found the spot. He pressed down and it was a warm aching pain.

"Two," he announced and moved to sit on his knees. She grunted but she didn't need to tap out. The pain caused her legs to go numb and it felt almost like her blood was slowing. Like he was turning it to molasses.

She felt the cool iron on her skin before it was pressed painfully into her.

"Fuck," she said but didn't make him stop.

"More?" he asked. She reached with her senses, because she thought she felt that sweet emotion of his reaching for her. But it was gone as quickly as it came.

"More," she said but it came out as more of a moan.

A twinge of that feeling of his slipped out, with it was something hotter, needier. She was just about to be able to name it when the sharp part of the iron tool was pressed into her.

"Four," he told her. She found herself groaning into her arm as she bit down on it but she didn't want to get another four.

"Again," she demanded breathlessly.

"Are you sure?" he asked. The area was becoming numb, feeling in her legs long since gone. She nodded and he hesitantly applied every ounce of pressure to the spot.

Something between a scream and a moan escaped her and she reached out and shoved him away on pure instinct. The tool clattered to the ground and he wrote in the notebook again, presumably her scores.

She pulled herself up to a sitting position, and hugged her knees to her chest.

"You have a high pain tolerance, you did very well," he congratulated her and stood.

"Thanks," she breathed, exhausted. Aching pain reverberated up her spine.

He helped her to her feet, his fingertips lingering on her wrist for an extra second before he released her and looked away.

"So what are we supposed to do for the next three days?" she asked. They had reached the end of their four-day week, even if the first one was spent at the river.

"I will summon you all in the morning, the next two days are intermingled events with other units. The third day is your free day," he explained.

"Have a good night, Praeceptor," she said. He nodded a simple 'you too' as he cleaned his work area and she exited the room.

Chapter 9

T heir three days off weren't actually days off at all. It involved brutal exercises with all of the units wherein they ran obstacle courses through the woods, swam through the rushing river in the freezing cold, and sparred one-on-one with new opponents.

Fallon Mournstride and Davian Axgrove were tied at the hip, Rosen following them like a puppy. They made a game of sabotaging other conscripts that they deemed 'bastard sired', which was most of them given only about a third of the conscripts actually knew their sires. In a nauseating turn of events, by their third weekend of 'all unit training', Molvina and Fallon had been caught hooking up by Praeceptor Sloane in the woods.

Amara had to listen to her talk to Katara and Eros about how he 'actually wasn't that bad'. She didn't particularly care, so she had gone down to the river on their real day off to sit with Avren.

They were about to begin week four of training and everyone knew they would be getting the details of the Abyss Trial that would commence at the conclusion of week six. She nudged

Avren's shoulder when she sat next to him, he greeted her with a smile and tossed a rock. The sun caught his light brown hair, showing the sun-kissed strands peppered throughout as though highlighting beauty in a broken world.

Avren had become particularly close to Amara, after a private conversation brought forth that he too lost his mother very young. He had been five years old and had some memories of her. He told her that he had seen her die but didn't elaborate on how. The two of them shared a disdain for the Crucible and the Hallowed Fallen. He kept asking her to tell him how she managed to hide for almost two years but she would shoo him off or change the subject.

She came to realize that he admired her and she, him. They had begun eating together most days and seeking each other out when something particularly brutal had occurred. They found solace in one another's company on a deeper level than with Juliet, Eros, and Katara.

"Do you think we'll make it," he asked. He regarded her cautiously with hazel eyes.

"Through this trial?" she asked for clarity and fidgeted with a rock as well.

"Through the Crucible, through our transformations." He sighed.

"I don't know," she began. "I think a lot of people are going to die. We can't know who but we can try to look out for those closest to us."

Behind them Molvina had stomped off angrily in response to something Katara and Eros must have said.

"I know there's no point in dwelling on it. It's just so lonely here," he explained. She knew he missed his older sister. "It's like I don't want to get too close to anyone because I know I'm going to probably watch them die." A muscle twitched in his jaw and he tossed another rock into the river. She understood where he was coming from, as dark of a place as it was.

"I think having people gives us a reason to fight harder," she said, coming to the conclusion for the first time herself.

She didn't have anyone outside of the Crucible to fight for. Everyone she would fight for was facing the same blood sport that she was.

"I also don't feel like I've calmed down since being here. I just have all of this tension that needs to be released and I can't." He rubbed at a muscle in his neck and groaned. "I don't mean to complain. It's just that when I have time to think..." he trailed off. His voice was soft, softer than a lot of the other guys which she found endearing.

"No, it's okay, I get it." She smiled and stood up. He looked at her, perplexed, until she crouched down behind him. She began massaging his shoulder and neck muscles.

She wasn't sure why she wanted to do so, perhaps the lack of any physical contact that wasn't violent was starting to get to her. Another part of her just wanted to comfort him. The act started out innocent but slowly started to feel more sensual as he rolled his head back and his mouth fell open.

Her body responded to the groan that came from deep in his throat, causing her to become deliciously aware of her hands on his body. She let herself enjoy the lustful thoughts that watching him let go gave her. It had been so long since she had touched someone this way, since she had been touched. She trailed her hands around to the front of his chest, causing him to tilt his head to look back up at her.

Lust, arousal, desire. The sensation, the taste flooded her senses as she met his eyes. The emotions came off of him in droves, unguarded and open.

Avren's breathing was jagged, matching hers, the air between them had become charged. She knew there would be no being friends if they crossed that line. But, he looked at her lips, and she, his. She wanted so badly to just...

"Hey guys let's go, we're going to the library! We're finally allowed!" Juliet interrupted them, seemingly not picking up on what had been about to happen.

Amara jumped up and cleared her throat. Avren had a similar reaction and jogged up to talk to Eros as the unit went to meet Cathmore at the head of the trail. She took a deep breath, feeling something like excitement brew in her stomach. It was a welcomed feeling amongst the chaos of the Crucible grounds. She watched his tall legs climb the hill, noticed the way he shoved his hands in his pockets as he spoke to Eros, and mused at the way the sun caught his hair again. It was such a uniquely beautiful glow that she had never seen before.

Cathmore had granted them two hours in the magnificent library. The space was vast, with at least ten levels spiraling upward and towering around them. Dimly lit, with cherry wood bookcases trimmed in black, it was a place where one could easily lose themselves.

Amara spent many years escaping into books when they were permitted by Aunt Grace. She also used downtime while on the run to immerse herself in imaginary worlds.

"I'm going to see what they have on the other kingdoms," Eros announced.

"That sounds fun," Judas said and followed him.

"No way, fiction is where it's at!" Katara scoffed playfully. Molvina agreed with a smile and she and Avren went with her.

"I'm going to see if my family is in the kingdom's archives. Wanna come?" Juliet asked.

"They have that?" Amara asked, wide-eyed as fear pricked her scalp.

"Yeah, I mean it won't tell me my sire but all of the people in the kingdom are recorded here," she explained and pulled Amara up one staircase and down another. "I want to see if they updated it after Cade died," she said as though the words were simple. But Amara knew better, she saw the grief that weighed on her soul for her lost twin.

They followed the ornate wooden signs that led to the archived section. 'Findaria' was the section that they zoned in on but Amara ran her fingers over the carved names of the other kingdoms. 'Pran', 'Ravenyr', 'Salia', 'Tenant', 'Zithia', were all on that part of the library which extended out of view.

"Ugh, the 'V's are on the other wall," Juliet sighed and walked to the other section. *Juliet and Cade Valentine,* she reminded herself.

Amara scanned over books with different family names. Some had multiple volumes, some only on one. She was taken back to staring at that box with her mother's name on it, the promise of information, of a glimpse into her mother's life. It had been ripped from her and she buried the need so far down to know her mother, that she turned her back on the idea.

Yet, here she was staring at a wall, tracing the books with her eyes, until finally landing on 'Ashenfall'. It took her breath away, there were four volumes. All of the books were beautifully bound in varying colors of leather but her family's name was printed in silver on black leather.

She could hear whisperings in the library, people walking above her and below her, Juliet fumbling around a few shelves over, but it became drowned out as she stood on her toes and reached for the first book. Her hand shook as she traced its spine. It dated back three hundred years, the last book updated seemingly within her lifetime based on the year stamps.

She examined it closely before opening it .

The following record is for the purposes of tracking life, death, and social status within the kingdom of Findaria. All information is property of its ruler; his Hallowed Majesty—Hadeon The Fallen.

She flipped a page and ran fingers over names she had never heard. All marked 'human' every last one of them.

Morana Ashenfall —Lady of the land, non-practicing, Findaria. Died aged 49 years

Lady of the land? She read further down into Morana who lived two-hundred years earlier.

Bore one sired child for Sylas-

Forscythe Ashenfall—Killed in battle aged 57 years

It wasn't a surprise that someone had a sired child in her family, most families did at one point or another. He didn't have children though a thought entered her mind... Did Nephilim have children? She made a mental note to look into it.

More names she didn't know, addresses she had never heard of, but she kept looking as though the book drew her closer to her ancestors. She came across another sired child who lived two-hundred years before her, another sired by Osias. She found it odd that Hadeon hadn't sired children within her bloodline. There also seemed to be missing pieces within the transcript and little clarity on the 'lady of the land' title. She had no idea what 'non-practicing' meant.

She knew so little about her family or where she came from. She slammed the book closed and slid it on the shelf.]

She slowly reached for the book that was dated in her lifetime. She turned it around in her hands before it suddenly ceased to exist... like literally poofed from her hands. *What the hell?*

"Don't go looking for information you aren't ready to learn," Cathmore warned, jarring her. He stood in the entryway of the square-shaped section she was in. He leaned against the edge of the bookshelf with his arms crossed.

"How did you do that," she demanded. He reached one hand behind his back and pulled out the book, holding it up to her tauntingly.

"Part of my Imperium." He shrugged.

Amara marched up to him and tried to snatch the book from his hand. He simply held it higher, causing her to scowl. He raised his eyebrows at her when she huffed. She jumped for it a second time and he met her with a taunting smile.

"It's not yours." She pouted.

"It's not *technically* yours either," he countered before tossing the book upward and making it vanish again. She looked around frantically. It couldn't have gone *nowhere*.

"Is my sire in there? Is that why you're doing this?"

"No, I can assure you, no one knows who your sire is," he said calmly and pushed himself off of the bookcase.

"Just give it to me." She stomped in agitation.

He looked down at her foot—which was pitifully smaller than his by the way—and grinned.

"You really are a little—" he began slowly. *Brat.*

"Do not say it," she demanded, digging her finger into his chest. He looked down at her touching him as though it were some kind of challenge.

"Careful." He drew out the word.

She pulled her hand back. "You're an ass," she sniped and pushed past him. For a moment she thought for sure she'd gotten away with it unlike before. She had almost made it to where

Juliet was—when she was grabbed around her stomach and pulled backward.

"What did you do?" Juliet gasped when Cathmore walked past her, carrying a thrashing Amara against him. "She called me an ass," he barked and Juliet gave her a 'you're screwed' look.

His strong arms tightened around her abdomen the more she struggled.

"Put me down!" She demanded. This wasn't new behavior for him, he had carried Molvina away from class for punishment just the previous week.

She had told them he gave her ten slaps on the knuckles with a metal ruler. Her knuckles were swollen for days. Then again she called him a sadist for making exercises more intense so she kind of earned it, according to the Praeceptor anyway. She was gathering that he did not like to be called names.

Amara did the thing that probably worsened her situation as he walked up multiple flights of spiraling iron stairs with her. She just had to antagonize him further.

"See this right here? This is asshole behavior," she remarked as loudly as possible. She knew others heard her but she didn't care and kicked against him.

He set her down and shoved her with his large hand on her back into one of the small study rooms. He kicked the door shut behind him. She spun around to face him, humor was gone from his face. She figured it was because some of the other conscripts had witnessed her gross disrespect.

"Let me guess, back or ass, right?" she said, exasperated and crossed her arms, awaiting the Praeceptor's response.

"Whipping is not my preferred method of punishment unless the other party asks very nicely," he answered, his voice dark. "Put your arms on the table," he demanded and slid a wooden chair to her. When she didn't do it he snarked, "Don't make me do it for you."

He pulled a knife out of his belt and flipped it, the handle landing in his palm. She sat and placed her arms, palms down, on the table.

"Palms up, Ashenfall," he corrected her and circled the table as an animal would its prey. He was going to slit her wrists and let her bleed out right there, she just knew it.

"I don't subscribe to the idea of bleeding out ailments or demons," he began and made eye contact with her. "Don't be afraid, you're not dying for having a smart mouth."

"I simply find catharsis in the art of carving one's skin and watching the blood trickle out. Usually my own, admittedly. But come to find out, not many people feel the same." He pointed the knife at her. "Making this a wonderful punishment. Especially when an example needs to be set." He sighed as he shook his head.

"You're sick." She shook her head and tucked her arms under the table.

"Now, historically speaking it is healing, the old world wasn't wrong about that. But do you know the chemical reaction in the brain that occurs when opening your skin in a controlled environment?" He smiled. Of course she didn't, but he wasn't looking for an answer. She thought he looked like a psychopath from the fire in his eyes and the joy on his face as he explained it. "Arms on the table, don't make me ask again."

She gulped and slowly placed them back on the surface with her palms up.

He removed his dark jacket, exposing a white button-down and threw it over the back of the chair opposite her. He threw the knife downward forcefully; it spun and landed blade down in the wooden table just between her hands.

"Um, can I request the whipping?" She croaked.

"I'm afraid not." He smiled devilishly. He rolled up his sleeves, exposing the scars all over his arms that she had noticed once before. She swallowed hard.

"Are those from this?" she asked wide-eyed and sat back in the chair, jerking her arms from him.

"Some of them, give me your arms," he demanded. She did so hesitantly.

He pulled her right arm toward him and picked up the knife. He gently grazed the blade over her skin, sending goosebumps up her arm, he looked up at her through long lashes.

"Just get it over with," she spat. She was more annoyed at the tingles moving through her as the blade teased her skin and his hand squeezed her wrist.

He stopped just under the crook of her elbow and pressed in slowly with the blade. The skin tore with an intense burn before a warming sensation followed it. She sucked air through her teeth and opened her mouth as he continued to drag the knife through her skin, all the way down to her wrist. *What if he went too deep and bled her out by accident? Would he even get in trouble for it?*

"Ah." She winced as he finished the line. She watched. Her horror melting into awe as her blood prickled to the surface and then began running from the cut. It wasn't deep, just enough to draw blood and burn. The healing would be far worse.

He watched her, she felt the numbing adrenaline rush to the area and free her of the pain. She felt like the tension in her body had released for a moment, allowing her to take a deep breath. She looked up at him but she couldn't tell what he was thinking, couldn't feel what he felt.

"Stop trying to read my emotions," he said under his breath before lining up the knife on her opposite arm. She jerked it away, causing a small nick, and a look of frustration from Cathmore.

"How did you...?" she asked.

"You're not the only empath," he winked. *Oh shit.*

Amara started running through every instance where her body reacted to him, where she didn't want it to so she defaulted to anger. Every ounce of resentment, lust, anger, all of it, could have been picked up by him at any time. She didn't even think to shield her emotions except for in clairvoyance control, even then she was the only empath in that class. No one else could pick up on emotions the way she could.

"Don't panic." He grabbed her arm. "I don't make a habit of diving into the emotions of my charges."

He dug the knife in the same way as before, causing her to wince before the warming feeling set in. She let it take over; let it block out her emotions. The second one was more painful but she found herself wondering how it was a punishment.

She didn't know what to think about the fact that she was left feeling more relieved than punished by what had transpired. She sat for a while in the room, contemplating what could have been in the book and why he knew about it. He excused himself to tend to a matter outside of the small room, leaving her once again to dwell on the enjoyment of the 'punishment'.

"It's okay if you liked it," Cathmore said from the doorway.

"Why are you back?" she asked. She thought he had gone off to deal with another conscript.

"I wasn't needed out there." He sighed.

"Didn't answer the question," she said harshly.

"Why do you do that?" he asked.

"Do what?" She stood, turning to him.

"Make an effort to keep everyone at arm's length away." He took a step toward her, she looked up into his eyes. She could feel his breath on her face, so close that she could inhale his unique scent.

"Because most of us will die this year," she said coldly. He regarded her with sorrow.

"You can't live your life prepared to die," he nearly whispered as though seeing her for the first time.

"It's what we're born to do," she said, referring to sired children.

"Sired or not, you were born to live." He stopped her by the shoulder as she tried to leave the room. She wished she believed him, wished that she could live life with that kind of optimism and hope. It just wasn't her. "When you go through the transformation, you will taste death. You need to find a reason not to give into it," he whispered through gritted teeth.

She wasn't even sure she would make it to transformation, she wasn't thinking that far ahead. He didn't make it sound like something she wanted to rush into either.

"Amara, we're going down to the demonology section, wanna come?" Avren invited her as he and Eros walked past.

"I—"..." she began, excited to get out of the room with Cathmore.

"She can't, she has injuries that need tending to," the Preceptor cut in. Avren looked between them in concern.

"Of course, sir." He gave a slight bow and the two walked away.

"I do not." She turned to him in disbelief.

She looked down though and some of the blood had seeped through the bandages he gave her. Perhaps she was bleeding more than she had originally thought.

As she and the Praeceptor made it to the small medical room off of the dormitories, she bit her cheek to steady her temper. Anger had made itself present in response to her enjoyment of the damned punishment.

Cathmore was so confident in the way he carried himself, sure that he knew her and knew that she liked it. Regardless of if he was correct, she despised him for it. He sat before her as though preparing to re-wrap her wounds.

"I can do it myself," she jerked away from him and snatched the materials. The room couldn't have been more than six by six feet and provided very little space for her to get away from him. He stood and allowed her to manage on her own.

Perhaps she dwelled too much on him trying to kill her during the hunt. But she found it to be the driving force for her hatred, even beyond his cruelty leading up to said entry trial or capturing her. She had a million reasons to hate him.

"I really have gotten under your skin," he mused proudly. She shook her head and ignored him as she tended to her cuts.

Amara glanced over at him leaning against the wall, spinning a ring around his long finger in that distracting way of his. *How was she equally as repulsed by him as she was attracted to him?*

"You are far too easily distracted by me to hate me as much as you claim to," he dared.

"Distracted by you?" She stood. "Please." She scoffed and tossed the used bandages into the trash.

She moved to the door but didn't open it, she hesitated. She felt him behind her, his energy a living thing caressing her body.

"I don't think you actually hate me." He was trying to get into her head. *Why?*

"No, I definitely hate you," she said. *Of that she was sure.*

He placed his hand on the door in front of her, she eyed his hand. His long fingers, visible veins, scars and ink trailing up his arm. She inhaled a shaky breath.

"If you hate me as much as you claim to." He dropped his hand. "Walk out of this room right now," he demanded. She could feel his breath on her neck and it sent unsolicited chills over her body.

"Even you aren't self-sacrificing enough to risk death by involving yourself with one of us," she retorted, referring to sired children. There was a clear disparity between sired children and those who have transitioned into Nephilim. It's why the Praeceptor's always seemed to be looking down on them.

"I stand corrected. You truly believe that you hate me. That's why your need for self-destruction draws you to me," he spun her to face him. "That's why you won't leave this room," he whispered. "You're tormented trying to balance your desire for me with your resentment," he feigned sympathy with a puckered lip. It only served to piss her off more.

"You're wrong," she insisted. She didn't know who she was trying to convince.

"Am I?" He leaned down to whisper in her ear. The simple act forced her to bite back a moan, his body pressing hers into the door. "You think I don't see the way you look at me?" His lips grazed her earlobe and she couldn't move.

She held her breath in speechless anticipation. She knew she should run but she wanted nothing less. He kissed the delicate skin of her neck, propping himself on the door with his arms on either side of her.

"Do you think that I can't *feel* you craving me?" He teased in a low husky voice. *He had been picking up on her emotions, he was probably reading her better than she was reading him.*

He trailed his tongue over to her throat but she wouldn't give him the satisfaction of voicing how good it felt. She inhaled his unique scent feeling as though she could get high off of it. He moved his mouth up to her lips and she met his silver-blue eyes that had turned molten somehow.

"Kiss me like you hate me," he breathed.

She slammed her lips into his.

His lips were hot, burning with need, and his tongue invaded her mouth hungrily. She moaned into his mouth, unable to stop it as she ravenously took from him. She tasted him and he was delicious on her tongue. She felt as though she were a match that had been struck. She was alive with need everywhere. She twisted her hands into the front of his shirt pulling him closer, biting at his bottom lip hard. He groaned low in his throat and placed one of his hands on her waist.

"I fucking hate you," she whispered. He grinned; his perfect lips swollen and kissed her harder.

"Say it again," he pleaded, searching her eyes. He trailed his hand up her body, leaving her momentarily distracted once more by how perfect they were. He didn't miss it.

"You are insuffer—" she was cut off when he placed a finger over her lips. She looked at him with wide eyes because she felt like she was being shushed like a child.

He nudged her lips open slowly and pushed his middle finger into her mouth. The gesture was so intimate, so hot for some reason. He watched her mouth closely and shoved his ring finger in too. She met his eyes and sucked slowly on his long fingers, his own lips parting.

"You can be such a brat sometimes, do you know that?" He tilted his head and pulled his fingers partially out of her mouth slowly. He yanked her head back by her hair and shoved them in once more, she moaned but continued to taste him, she swirled her tongue teasingly around his fingers.

He removed them roughly and kissed her again, forcefully. His hand was still entangled in her hair when he began pushing his fingers into her waistband. She inhaled, startled and looked at him with wide eyes.

"Have you been thinking about my fingers inside of you?" he asked. She swallowed hard, not wanting to admit that she had been. He moved his fingers away from her waistband. "Tell me the truth," he warned.

"Yes." She nodded.

He pushed his hand down into her pants effortlessly and grazed her clit with the fingers that had just been in her mouth. She could feel that she was wet from their kissing and blushed hard. He noticed it too and kissed her as he slid his middle finger into her. She flinched at the delicious invasion, pressing herself harder into the door.

"If you hate me so much, why are you so fucking wet?" He moaned into her ear. He plunged a second finger into her while she bit down on her lip, trying to be quiet.

His palm was pressed against her while he continued his tortuous rhythm with his fingers. He wrapped his other hand around her throat and kissed her like she disgusted him. She loved it. She found herself grinding against his palm while he watched her. She kept her moans of pleasure quiet but he was content to watch her like that for an eternity it seemed.

"Use me, use me to make yourself come since you hate me so much." His breathing was ragged and he kissed her again.

She couldn't believe they were doing what they were doing, that his mouth was on hers, that his fingers were inside of her, and that it felt so good. She wrapped her hands around the back of his neck, interlocking her fingers. She was approaching the edge and she felt as though her legs would fail her if she didn't steady herself.

"You've done nothing but make me miserable since I met you," she antagonized him.

"Good." He smiled wickedly and fingered her harder, like he knew it's what she needed.

She was moaning, approaching her climax quickly when he suddenly stopped and threw his hand over her mouth. She was about to protest when she heard that a group of conscripts had just entered the building. *Shit.*

He pulled his hand out of her pants and motioned for her to be quiet. She was wound so tightly that it was painful. She glanced down and confirmed that he was feeling similarly. *Would it have gone further if they weren't interrupted?*

His body was pressed against hers, both of them still as they waited for the conscripts to ascend the stairs and leave the lobby. Her heart was pounding, so was his. She could feel it hammering rapidly into her hands placed on his chest.

They took a sigh of relief in unison when they were in the clear again. Amara pushed off the wall, Cathmore stepped back to allow her space. They were both still breathless from the heated encounter.

She knew if she didn't walk away, it would escalate further into something that could be dangerous for both of them.

"I have to go," she said.

"Yes, go," he said coldly, running a hand through his hair as though he had been sobered up from the moment.

<h1 style="text-align:center">Chapter 10</h1>

Lessons resumed the following day with promises of learning what the Abyss Trial would entail during Cathmore's lessons. She had learned to zone out during Fallen History but had come to know the names of all the Hallowed Fallen with a running list she made in her notepad:

Rase Ender

Hadeon Lyall

Sylas ~~Kaim~~... Kaemon

Osias Arwan

Torin Lonan

Amara was particularly distracted that day and less willing to pick a fight with Magister Baylin over his bigoted teachings. Her lips were raw from kissing her Praeceptor, a reality which she still couldn't believe wasn't a dream. She wrestled with need and disgust when it came to him. She was in no hurry to get to his classes.

She made every attempt to lay low and just get through her day. Most of the Preceptors and Magisters didn't call her out specifically, while Marlowe couldn't take his focus off of her. She obviously knew why he made her work out harder than others and seemed to love making an example of her poor form during pushups. Any chance he had to embarrass her, trip her when no one was looking, or just make her life harder...he took it.

Where everyone else would pass an obstacle in a couple of tries, she had to do it five times. Even the other conscripts in her unit were becoming fed up by Marlowe's obsession with her. Toward the end of the obstacle course for the day, Amara had gone over to the well pump behind a building to refill her canteen while the others stretched.

She had bent over to drink from the fresh flowing water when she was grabbed from behind by her hair. A knife was placed at her throat, causing her to drop the canteen.

"Did my brother have time to feel fear before you slit his throat open?" Marlowe growled. Her body started trembling as he pressed the knife to her throat. He wouldn't do it; there were too many people around... right?

"Answer the question, little bitch." He huffed and dug the knife's tip into her skin.

Amara felt the small cut and the blood trickled down her neck. She recalled that awful day when she took another man's life. He hadn't known it was coming, his throat flayed open before her so quickly that he didn't process what happened. The image of him wide-eyed and gripping at his neck as he sank to the ground crowded her vision.

"No," she whimpered and it wasn't a lie. He hadn't felt the anticipation she felt at that moment. He didn't ask himself whether or not he would survive, he wasn't given the chance. He was more in shock as he bled out than in fear.

Marlowe grunted and pulled the knife away. He shoved her forward to the ground. She turned to look up at him as she crawled away.

"Don't send your pretty boy Praeceptor this time, or you'll be bled dry in your sleep," he threatened. Marlowe disappeared around the building and she gasped for air, not realizing she hadn't been breathing. She hyperventilated for a moment and she tried to wipe away the blood from her neck that seemed to keep coming.

Amara hadn't *sent* anybody and it was Cathmore that did that damage to him? *Why?* She knew the Magisters weren't supposed to punish the conscripts but... it didn't seem *that* heavily enforced.

She used water and a ripped piece of her shirt to slow the bleed and clean the cut. It was only a couple of inches long, if it scabbed soon she would be able to explain it away in time for Cathmore's lessons.

She dodged questions from her friends when she returned from the well. Avren seemed to know that she hadn't 'accidentally done it with her knife,' but he didn't call her out on it. At least Katara and Juliet seemed to buy the excuse... *sort of.*

"The Abyss Trial involves escaping the Abyss where the kingdoms dispose of traitorous Nephlim and Rogue Fallen. The 'Abyss of Despair' as it has been named, is located in the Northern Reaches of Findaria," Cathmore began. He pointed to the map of the continent to show them where. "These Nephilim and Rogue Fallen... they're not like anything you have ever seen before. Only the immortal Nephilim and Rogue Fallen survive down there since they can't die. It guarantees an eternity of suffering," he explained. Hushed murmurs began between the conscripts in their unit. "Though I believe they wish to die." He sighed.

"That's who my mum told me the traitors are fed to," Katara whispered to Amara and Avren who were sitting next to her.

"That's correct. Traitorous humans are often thrown in there for execution, the immortals who are too far gone, feed on them," Cathmore interjected. Juliet and Eros gasped.

"I heard after decades they start to grow fangs so they can eat the animals and prisoners that are down there," Avren said to Katara.

"Like evolution," Amara mused.

"Fucking sick." Avren shuddered.

"Now, the most likely outcome of this trial is your death as most of you can guess." He glanced at Amara briefly. "But, you all have the ability to reason, you have not been reduced to primal instinct, the abyss is not made to keep intelligent beings in." He sat on the floor in front of them, mirroring their crossed-legged posture.

"But can't they fly? Why don't they just fly out?" Davian scoffed.

"Their wings are severed at the base, unable to heal, guaranteeing that they never fly again," Cathmore explained in a way that seemed to pain him.

"Doesn't that make them go insane?" Davian asked.

"To put it lightly, yes." Cathmore shoved his hands in his pockets. "Apart from that, the Abyss is up to two miles deep at certain points. Some are even chained and have been for many years."

"This trial will test your critical thinking capabilities, it will try to force you to crack under pressure, and you will be in a harrowing fight for your life until you escape," he explained.

"So that's it? We just have to... escape?" Molvina asked.

"If you think it's going to be too easy, show me some unique mark on your body so I'm able to identify it quickly," Cathmore snapped. "But no, that's not it. You are required to emerge with a feather from one of the Nephilim or Fallen."

How were they supposed to take a feather from a creature that was trying to kill them? Amara stared at Praeceptor Cathmore, half listening, half looking through him. Any hopes of sneaking through the abyss and escaping unnoticed were ripped away. Amara's mind was reeling.

"What if we make it out without a feather?" Avren asked.

"You will be dropped into the center and forced to start again which pretty much ensures your death," he narrowed his eyes at Avren before scanning the group for more questions.

"You will be armed, you will have supplies to survive on, and you will enter as a unit," he continued, listing the technicalities. "The next two weeks we will work on exercises to defend yourselves from the creatures who are so far gone. I'd prefer not to have to identify parts of you." He looked at Molvina. "So please pay attention." He gave a sarcastic smile with perfect teeth and pushed himself to a standing position. The crude words followed by that smile were cruel.

Avren nudged her leg with his knee, he gave her a small smile. It was a reassuring gesture when he knew worry for the future was setting in.

"I'm sneaking into the library tonight, interested?" He whispered to her. *Was he insane?* Ten o'clock was lights out and no one had a reason to be out after the conclusion of lessons.

"When?" She whispered. Cathmore had his back turned on the far end of the hall where he was preparing to begin their body suspension exercises. She watched for any signs that he could hear them.

"Midnight, after the book keepers are gone. I saw a section with current war records that must include what's happened with the Dark One and the Hallowed that abandoned the others," he whispered excitedly. He knew that the war and rebellion intrigued her, how could she say no?

"Okay," she agreed. Maybe that would give her the chance to learn more about her mother, or the Abyss. He smiled as though surprised and pleased.

"Meet by the shower rooms, we'll take the back exit," he directed and she nodded.

"All right, day one of body suspension. Who's first?" Cathmore turned around.

Davian raised his hand and Cathmore gestured for him to stand.

"I need another person," he instructed. When no one volunteered he called on Juliet who appeared to be the most terrified of the idea all together.

"I will start by attaching you to the hooks and just pulling gently to get you used to the sensation," he began. The two took their shirts off, Juliet left in an exercise bra but not seeming bothered by it. How could she be? They all had to shower and dress together anyway.

The ropes were already hanging down so he hooked all six to the two of them, the excitement on Davian's face in stark contrast to the fear on Juliets. He pulled gently on the two on their shoulder blades and neither exhibited any sign of extreme pain. He did the same for the ones in their lower backs. They had four weeks to heal which seemed like plenty of time and not enough all at once.

Once he was sure their suspension rings had healed properly, he asked Judas and Katara to stand behind the pair while he went over to control the pulleys that would suspend them.

"You two are just there to provide support if they need to grab someone or be bolstered to relieve pressure," Cathmore called from the other side of the hall where the control ropes were fixed. Judas and Katara nodded.

Davian was lifted first with some expression of discomfort before taking deep breaths and closing his eyes. Amara could see his body shaking so he placed his hands on Judas' shoulders to relieve some of the weight pulling on his skin. She watched his skin stretch and pull in an unnatural way.

Juliet was next and it was obvious that she hated it. She moaned from the pain and had Katara hold her legs to help. Two minutes passed before Davian was asking to get down and Juliet vomited as a result of looking at Davian's lifted skin and probably feeling hers do the same.

The group groaned in disgust as the hall became filled with the stink of vomit.

"All right," Cathmore said after unhooking them. "Valentine, clean up your mess."

Amara was the eighth to go, alongside Eros. Avren had held out for five minutes without protest which was the time that Cathmore was starting them at. She watched him intently, he seemed to forcibly relax his body so as to lean into the pain. Avren was really quite handsome, she thought, as he screwed his eyes shut and inhaled slowly. The softness of his lips were in contrast to the lines set around them—smile lines. She imagined he spent a lot of time laughing as a child. He crossed his arms behind his back, flexing his muscles inadvertently, his tan skin a distraction for her, but she welcomed it. She welcomed anything that gave her a moment of peace from reality.

Amara didn't know why watching him hang there was attractive, what it reminded her of. It certainly wasn't something she ever would have thought of as 'sexy' before. A lock of his brown hair fell into his eye, causing him to open it and blink it away. He saw her watching him closely and smiled slyly, knowingly. She looked away, blushing. *Shit.*

When it was Amara's turn, she chose to breathe into the stretching and pulling sensation, allowing the blood to flow into the space. After a minute, her head prickled in a warm calming way, so she continued to breathe deeply. She understood that fighting or struggling against it is what caused harm. It wasn't that it didn't hurt... it did, extremely so. She just somehow redirected the effect of the pain, allowing the adrenaline to numb the area and course through her body.

Amara felt also as though her head was clearing, like all of the chatter had silenced from her mind. She rolled her head back, feeling as though the experience was elevating her, freeing her in a way. She felt so in touch with every part of her mind and body that she could almost resolve herself to a purpose, a reason to fight. She reached for it, reached for something that lay dormant within her. It was a voice, a power that needed to be known. But it was so far away. *Come here, I'm here, I'm here.* She called out to it. It felt almost like a dream.

Faces that she didn't know shifted and swayed in her line of vision amongst varying shades of colors. It was like their energies were reaching for her and no matter how much she reached for them, she couldn't grasp them.

"That was eight minutes, Ashenfall," Cathmore called as he lowered the ropes. "That's good," he said. She hadn't even seen Eros be lowered nor was she paying attention how he performed.

The experience she had was so powerful, that coming off of the suspension ropes made her body feel heavy and foreign. Cathmore and Juliet said something to her but they sounded far away. She was lightheaded and she felt floaty on her feet. She began walking toward one of the rooms on the opposite side of the hall, she just wanted to sit down alone.

After a moment of grounding herself, Cathmore came into the room.

"You need to come out here and pretend like what you just experienced didn't happen," he demanded.

"What?" She turned to him. She hadn't realized she had been tearing up until a tear fell down her cheek.

"Now, Ashenfall, I will not ask again," he demanded, and tossed her shirt to her. His mouth was pressed in a hard line, his jaw clenched. *What did he know? What had happened up there?*

When she hesitated he grabbed her by the arm. "Stop being a little brat and listen to me for once," he growled and pulled her around the chair and to the door. She tried to jerk her arm free but he squeezed it harder.

"No." She pressed her feet into the ground and pulled against him. "Tell me what just happened," she whispered.

He jerked her to his chest, his breathing not the least bit changed from wrestling with her. His normally blue-silver eyes darkened a shade as though smoke filled into them. She found herself looking at his lips briefly.

"Your Imperium is developing too fast. If you come into too much power too soon, I'm supposed to kill you," he seethed. She hit him in the chest, trying to get him to release her. He grabbed both of her arms to still her. "I don't intend to kill you for it but if you don't keep this information to yourself, the choice may not be mine," he spoke in a whisper through clenched teeth. She recalled the Crowned Magister demanding Cathmore to punish her that night. She nodded in understanding.

"You have taken too long, they can't think I was in here arguing with you, turn around," he demanded.

"What?" she whispered, shaking. He released her and shoved her backward.

"We're going to talk about who cut your neck later," he growled.

He didn't break eye contact as she watched him undo his belt buckle. It was the most jarringly seductive act she had ever seen. She blinked as he yanked it free from his pants, which sent heat to her face. *Fear?* She was wearing tight shorts that exposed her from the knees down. He forced her to turn and quickly thrashed the belt across the back of her calves.

The sound of the belt echoed into the hall; she heard the conscripts fall silent in response. He hit her again, "I know this isn't much of a punishment for you but scream, brat." He huffed.

She knew he was demanding her to do so, so that the others would think he just went in there to punish her. But she didn't want to, until he hit her again with more force. It sent a stinging pain around to her shins with the impact of the leather belt. She let out a muffled scream, and another when he hit her a last time.

He pushed her out of the room, sending her stumbling into the hall before the other conscripts. They looked at her in confusion, some regarding the welts forming on her legs with a cringe.

"If I tell you to do something, you do it," he barked at her.

She watched him stroll past her and put his belt back on, he let a small grin slip that only she could see before his usual stoic face reappeared. *Ugh.*

She finally tugged her shirt on before taking a seat next to Avren and Juliet. She was so desperately tired of the punishments, she sighed.

"Why didn't you just stop walking away when he asked the first time?" Juliet asked with concern. She hadn't heard him ask her to, she had not heard anything until she got into that room. She only shrugged in defeat.

Her Imperium was developing faster, but what had she done that told him that? How could he know? It was another factor that put her closer to tongue kissing death and she didn't know how much more she would be able to take.

"I lied, we're not taking the back door," Avren whispered as the two of them crawled through the room between the other conscripts' bunk beds. Everyone should have been asleep.

"Come on, man." Avren grabbed someone's shoulder who allowed him to tug him off the bed.

"Beck?" She whispered, having barely spoken to him since the hunt.

"Hey, Amara." He smiled.

They continued in silence to the back of the building where evidently Beck had been taking a tunnel to the library for weeks. He slid an empty bookshelf to the side, revealing a doorway into the underground tunnels. *Why had she not thought the empty bookshelf was weird?*

Once they were inside, they crouched at the bottom of the staircase and listened. The tunnel was the same as when she followed it with Cathmore—cold, drafty, dark cobblestones, and spiderwebs. It wasn't that the dorm room was nice or anything but it surely wasn't ancient like the tunnels.

"How'd you find this?" she whispered to Beck.

"I knocked the bookshelf over when I was wrestling with Felix a couple of weeks ago," he said. She didn't know who Felix was but he must have been in Beck's unit. "Now I know the way to the library and a few other places in the Sanctum."

Avren's hand accidentally grazed Amara's, causing them both to awkwardly take a quick breath. He looked at her with a sincere smile, color on his high cheeks. She rolled her eyes at him and nudged him in the chest.

"I'm going to find out more about the 'Abyss of Despair,'" Amara said the Abyss' name in a mockingly haunted tone. Perhaps it would be less depressing than dredging up her family history.

"Your Praeceptor actually told you about it?" Beck asked.

"Yeah, yours didn't?" Avren asked.

"Sloane just said that it's another fight to survive trial and we'll learn more the day of," Beck told them. It was strange, why would she not want to prepare them? "Here," Beck took them through a small passageway.

The tunnel opened up under the library and led them up stone stairs to the base of it. She looked around at the desks and scattered books, and eight stairways jutted up into different parts of the library, spiraling. The lights were out amongst the endless bookcases so they each grabbed candlesticks to light their way.

"I'm going to hunt down the war archives, I'll call for you when I find them," Beck said to Avren, who nodded.

"Come on, I know where the section is with the maps and lore of the kingdoms." Avren smiled and grabbed her hand. He pulled her quickly behind him, up three different levels, and over to a section she had never been in.

Amara tripped over the corner of one of the bookshelves, causing Avren to laugh and her to shush him. She moved into the small section between two bookshelves and lit an oil lantern that was mounted on the wall, effectively lighting the small space.

She scanned over kingdoms' names, old villages, and populations. Avren moved behind her and reached up to a shelf above her head. His body pressed close to hers, not allowing much room for her to move, but she didn't want to. He paused after bringing the book down.

"Northern Reaches," he whispered against her ear, sending chills down her entire being.

"That's where the Abyss is," she whispered shakily.

He wrapped his arms around her, opening the book in front of her. His arms were strong, pulling her body closer to his, the back of her head touching his chest. She watched his nimble fingers flip through the pages; her breathing increased from the heat of his body on hers. The exhilaration of their bodies touching, of having physical touch that wasn't meant to cause pain...was so distracting.

Something hot came to life in the pit of her stomach when she recalled what the Praeceptor had done to her, how he ravenously devoured her mouth, viciously beckoned her to the edge of climax...

Avren spoke, startling her out of her impromptu fantasy.

"The Abyss formed as a result of two angels falling into the mountain side," he whispered, running his fingers over the words. She tried to focus on the book, trying not to tilt her head into the sensation of his breath on her ear. It was similar to how Cathmore teased her. "Deimos and Hadeon fell there," he said and got closer to her ear when he saw her reacting. "Is something else on your mind Amara?" He purred against her neck. A moan slipped out, she found herself pushing back against him.

He discarded the book to the side when she tilted her neck and he closed his lips around her skin, sucking sweetly. He gripped her hips, pulling her back against his chest. His hair fell around his face, the strands running over her ear and neck.

He bit down slightly, causing another small moan and removed his lips. He turned her by the hip and pushed her back against the solid bookcase. She looked up at him, his hazel eyes were wild in the candlelight, his lips moist, so she leaned up and he kissed her.

The kiss was slow and deep as he leaned into her, his body closing around hers, her fingers twisting into the front of his shirt. She pulled him closer, their tongues dancing with equal grace and need. She needed this, she needed his body, his mouth on her. She needed to feel something that wasn't worry, wasn't pain. *Wasn't Cathmore.*

He seemed to have the same thoughts—kissing her deeper to greedily take in more of her. The gesture was rough and claiming, it caused an image of someone else to temporarily take over her thoughts... *no.* Thoughts of the violent Praeceptor had no place in her mind while she kissed Avren. She didn't want Cathmore invading her mind when she was finally kissing Avren.

"You okay?" He breathed, bringing her back to him. She looked into hazel eyes, not silver and blue ones. She ran her hands through honey brown strands, not onyx waves. She nodded and smiled.

They had been dancing around their chemistry, afraid of it, not wanting to give in. But being alone... they couldn't fight it off. Neither of them had the strength to stop kissing once she pulled him closer again, so they didn't.

"Avren," she moaned as he ran his hands up the back of her shirt, splaying them on her skin. He bit at her lip, driving her mad. She had wanted to kiss him that day at the river but this was so much more intense than that could have been.

She wrapped her arms around his neck, the pain in her forearms from being cut by Cathmore, once again forced him into her mind. *What the fuck.*

He pulled away after a minute, both of them breathless. He leaned his forehead against hers and smiled, steadying himself on the bookcase behind her. She pushed away the aggravatingly intrusive thoughts of the Praeceptor that had no reason to emerge. Avren leaned down and planted soft kisses on her neck, causing her to giggle and blissfully forget the annoying and egotistical Praeceptor.

"Well, isn't this fucking adorable," someone growled from the entrance of the section they were in. No, not just someone. Praeceptor Cathmore stood there, as though summoned from the depths of her mind. *Fuck.*

Chapter 11

"Praeceptor..." Avren began.

"First, back off of her," Cathmore stared Avren down with cold disgust. Avren still had his hands in her shirt, resting on the small of her back.

Amara straightened once he was off of her and bent down to grab the book. Cathmore still gazed at Avren.

"We were just..." Amara said but Cathmore still didn't look at her.

"It was my idea, sir, I talked her into sneaking in here." Avren held his ground, but there was a glint of fear in his eye. Amara wondered where Beck was and hoped he wouldn't call out for them.

"So what was the plan, you were going to let him take you against the bookshelf?" Cathmore turned to Amara, fury evident in the set of his features. She narrowed her eyes at him but he gave her a look that dared her to answer the rhetorical question.

"Yearwood, go to study room eight. Ashenfall. Room 10," Praeceptor Cathmore demanded.

Avren looked over to her as if to silently apologize but she didn't acknowledge it. She should have known a moment of joy or distraction was too much to expect within the Sanctum Metere. It was like the walls had eyes that were intent on keeping the conscripts miserable.

Amara sat for a long time in the study room alone, she flipped through the book that mentioned the Abyss of Despair. It was wild that Deimos would come to be 'The Dark One' while Hadeon would rule Findaria as one of the Hallowed. They had been cast out together over eight hundred years ago according to the document. She was just getting lost in a paragraph about converting it to a dumping ground when a scream rang out from the other room.

Avren's deep voice screaming in agony was almost too much. He usually spoke so gently that it was jarring to hear him screaming, to know he was being hurt, punished. She covered her ears, pacing the room feeling helpless because she knew there was no way to stop whatever Cathmore was doing to him.

She distracted herself with the oil painting of an angel crying on a stone rock. She seemed so pained, so lost. *Wait...she. Why hadn't she heard of female Fallen before? Not even amongst the Rogue had any been mentioned. What the hell?* She wanted to venture out into the library to find answers when the door to the study room clicked open.

"What did you do to him," she demanded and marched straight up to Cathmore.

He rolled up his sleeves and smiled smugly at her, but he didn't answer. He looked her over from head to toe but she couldn't tell what he was thinking. She wanted to get through him, to get to Avren. She had to know that Cathmore hadn't killed him. Fear drifted through her body so she moved to shove him out of her way. He didn't budge.

"Move." She pushed against him.

He just crossed his arms, tears stung her eyes as she thought of the awful things that he could have done to Avren. She didn't even care what he was going to do to her. She slapped him hard across the face, he allowed her. He paused, clenched his jaw, a tint of red stung his cheek from the impact. She grinned at the sight. He looked back over to her before squaring his shoulders and meeting her eyes.

"I didn't kill your little distraction, brat," he growled at her.

"Don't call him that," she seethed. *And don't call me brat.* She nearly added.

"Why not?" he asked and strolled past her. He pulled out a chair before dropping down into it and kicking his feet up on the desk, crossing them at the ankles. "That's what you're looking, for right?" She looked him over in disgust, or tried to. His black shirt was tight enough to highlight his toned midsection, his jet black hair was messy, and his blazing silver-blue eyes made him look like death in a seductive wrapping. She hated it.

"You don't know what you're talking about," she retorted.

"Hmm, perhaps I should have told him what you were really thinking about while he kissed you," Cathmore challenged. He rested his thumb on his bottom lip as he waited for a reaction. His other hand fidgeted with a piece of fabric on his knee that was propped in front of him. "Did he measure up to last night?" He taunted.

She turned her back on him.

Praeceptor Cathmore was a dark cloud that brought lightning with him everywhere he went. He was destruction, light, beauty, and the vengeance of God carved into stone. He was perfection and death. He was art. She knew she should run from where lightning struck, but its beauty held her captive. He wore darkened storm clouds like a crown and drowned out her inhibitions in his ocean eyes. He was all-consuming, terrifying, and beautiful the way a storm was.

She grabbed for the door knob quickly, swinging the door open. Before she could take a step, Cathmore grabbed her by the back of her neck, stopping her in place. He kicked the door shut and pushed her down to her knees. He was so strong that her body had no choice but to obey his will.

"You are an infuriating little thing." He huffed.

He looked down at her, the sight of him from her position on her knees was... enlightening. He grabbed her chin and tilted it upward, the veins of his arm visible, her eyes followed them up to meet his eyes. She tried to push away her need that still loomed from her almost-orgasm the night before.

"You have a wickedly filthy mind, *Amara*," he purred.

"I don't know what you're talking about." She jerked her chin from his grasp.

"Mhmm, you have no idea how to control any of your abilities. You are wild and untamed," he shamed her. He crouched down behind her to whisper in her ear. "You didn't even know that you were projecting your dirty little thoughts to me," he continued. His words made her skin prickle and her body heat up.

She scrambled away from him and stood, the electricity between them boiling to an unbearable level. He stood and regarded her with amusement.

"Can't you just punish me and get it over with?" she snapped.

"No, I punished you earlier for posterity. You've paid your debt for sneaking into the library," he said.

"Then we're done here." She huffed and turned on her heel. She wanted to check on Avren, she needed to know if Beck got out unnoticed.

"I didn't dismiss you," he asserted. She inhaled in an attempt to grasp any amount of patience. "What happened to your neck before class?"

Amara was more aware of the hickey Avren probably left than the knife cut from Marlowe. She thought about his threat if she told.

"Accident with a dagger," she answered casually. "Tell me what happened during my body suspension." They got knicks and cuts when practicing with weapons all the time, why was he so concerned about her neck?

"Whatever this..." he gestured between them, "connection we have, allowed me to see what you did. You're closer to your ethereal form than you should be, it's a stronger part of you—"

"Ethereal form?"

"Your spiritual self. It's the non-physical part of you. The part of your soul that garners the power of the Fallen, the part that makes you Nephilim. It's a very delicate piece of you, and for some reason I was able to see you interacting with it."

"How?" She rubbed at her arms—a nervous habit.

"It's the part of you that allows clairvoyance, as well as other abilities that I am certain you will gain. I don't know why I can see it, it's never happened before," he explained and she believed him. "An Imperium developing this early... it's an abnormality amongst our kind. You shouldn't have any contact with your non-corporeal form until transition." He sighed. "Even then, it's not nearly to the magnitude yours is."

"So why is this happening?" she asked. She was shaking, the idea of her powers terrified her. She didn't know what to do with them, she didn't want them. "Is it because I'm older than when we were usually sent here?"

"No, it's the blessed ground, the will of the Fallen, and the transition that grant you any right to your abilities or Nephilim form. You simply would not have transitioned at all had you escaped the Crucible all together," he informed her and it broke her. That was all she wanted. All she ever wanted was a life away from the chaos of the Fallen.

She just nodded. He didn't know why it was happening so fast nor why she was projecting it onto him anymore than she did. She didn't feel like she was doing it on purpose... more like he was inside of her head when she didn't know it. Or maybe there was some line that connected their consciousness through their clairvoyance abilities? It was all so exhausting to think about.

"Why don't you fulfill your duty to kill me?" The question had been nagging at her.

"The Hallowed want those that are too powerful to be killed. Even during transition we'll have orders to kill Nephilim that develop certain abilities. Maybe I don't agree with it." He shrugged and stood.

"But they'll kill you for not obeying them."

"That's why I'm going to help you tame this. They don't have to know about anything that happens between us." His voice lowered and his meaning was two-fold. A dark promise laid in wait behind his words. She swallowed hard.

"How do you know what *this* is." She gestured at herself.

"Trust me." He smiled slyly. "You ascended today on those ropes, we'll start there."

"Ascended?" she asked.

"It just means coming into contact with your ethereal self, your ancestor spirits," he elaborated. *Oh.*

"Okay," she exhaled. "I should go, I need sleep.""If anyone asks, I punished you." He held the door open for her. She rolled her eyes at him.

"Oh wait, the book." She turned around to retrieve it from the table. "I wanna know more about the Abyss."

"You can't take it with you, the keepers will know." He stopped her. She frowned.

"The keepers?"

"They're Nephilim that run the library here. They protect the works and records of the kingdom of Findaria," he explained.

"Why haven't I seen them?" she asked, moving to stand in front of him.

"You're not supposed to, but they did see you and your little friends." He grinned and she turned red. *Damn he knew about Beck.* "They've been escorted back to the dormitories."

"We are here to face certain death and they just have to make sure there is no outlet, no joy, no distractions. Just pure suffering." She grunted and tossed the book down.

"What kind of distraction are you looking for, Amara?" His voice lowered to a whisper as he tasted her name on his tongue.

She didn't know entirely what kind of distraction she needed, just anything that made her *feel* something besides fear and dread. She suddenly recalled the moment of bliss she felt when his fingers were inside of her.

"I don't know," she breathed when he grabbed her arm to keep her in the room. She glanced over at him; he was already watching her intently. "What?"

"Let me walk you back," he offered. She nodded, not wanting to be alone in the tunnels.

She followed him through the tunnels she was familiarizing herself with. No stone was like the other, years of age wore them down in differing patterns. After a few minutes, she was sure they passed the door to the dormitories.

"Where are we going?" she asked the Praeceptor who walked with a purpose ahead of her. His long legs covered twice the space than hers did so she walked faster to keep up.

"A place that only I know about." He smiled over his shoulder at her.

Chapter 12

Amara followed him for a while, the tunnel feeling never-ending when he reached a door at the end. He pushed the heavy wooden door open, revealing spiraling stone stairs. She looked up, it just kept going, disappearing into darkness.

"What is this?" she asked in awe.

"Just come on," he said lightheartedly and tugged her up the stairs by her shirt. It was such an uncharacteristically playful act that she found herself giggling and scrambling up the stairs after him.

"How many more stairs?" She panted after five whole minutes of going around and around.

It was definitely a tower. There were no windows to speak of either as though it were a tall stone tomb.. The stale air was thick with dust, settling heavily in her lungs.

"Almost there," he promised with a boyish grin she hadn't seen from him before.

They finally reached the landing and another wooden door, which Cathmore pushed open with a grunt. The cool air from the night swept across her face. The tower was high above all of the other buildings. The landing was a fairly small open space. Pillars formed open archways all the way around it. They looked like windows but without glass, allowing for them to see the whole of the Sanctum Metere.

There was no roof, though it appeared to have one at one time. Damage to the top of the arched open windows where the roof would have once been, whispered secrets of long forgotten wars. Stone crumbled from them as though forgetting their original purpose. Despite that, the sky was clear and the stars twinkled above them.

"Wow," she scanned the horizon. The moon was directly above them, nearly full. The light from it cast shadows on Cathmore's face beneath the sharpest cuts of his features.

Caladrium Forest was to her west, she could see the dark ocean extending beyond it. Distantly, waves crashed there. Not many lights illuminated the Sanctum, some torches on buildings, some leading out to the main road. The dormitory building was to the east some distance, the view making the weapons-wielding pyramid seem so small. The apex of the pyramid only reached about three fourths of the way to the top of the tower. The Sanctum was surrounded by walls, miles of woods, and mountains to the south.

She took in the endless buildings for training, learning, and administration. Most of them were made of white or black stone. The contrasting colors promised one of two outcomes of entering the Sanctum; life or death. Wooden beams hugged the fronts of the buildings, mostly in crisscrossed patterns. Sprawling gardens and courtyards seemed so alive from her vantage point. If the entire purpose of the Sanctum Metere wasn't for suffering and death—it could almost be beautiful.

She leaned on the ledge that rose to her waist to watch the horizon.

"It used to be for keeping watch, during the war. Before the Crucible was established," he told her. "This is where Hadeon first build the kingdom of Findaria."

"Won't we get in trouble for coming here?" she asked.

"No one knows we're up here, you're with your Praeceptor so *you* won't get in any trouble." He smiled. The view was endless, it was liberating. She took a full breath of the freshest air she ever inhaled.

"Thank you." She looked at him. "For showing me this," she clarified.

"No one can know about it." He turned to her.

"I won't say anything." She shook her head. "But why bring me here?" she asked hesitantly.

"Because," he paused to weigh his response. "Maybe you're not the only one who needs an escape—a distraction."

She exhaled and turned away from him. He was so breathtaking, his words tempting her to act on fantasies she had buried deep. He was her Praeceptor... they couldn't go there. Not again. He was the snake offering her the forbidden fruit. It didn't scare her even if it should. Her life in the garden had never been fulfilling.

"And the distraction is..." she trailed off for a moment to take a breath. "This place?"

He closed the space between them, her back still turned on him as she fought a moral battle with herself. She was left unsatisfied the last time he touched her, though not of his doing. The interruption sobered both of them up, they both chose to stop. She had been coiled tight with need ever since the encounter.

"If a place to retreat is the only distraction you need." His breath fanned across the shell of her ear. The rasp in his voice sent goosebumps down her neck and arms. She swallowed hard.

Amara shouldn't do this. She despised him... most of the time. Or at least she told herself she did. He was cruel, demanding, haughty...

"Haughty?" he asked, startling her, and ran his fingers up her arm.

"Get out of my head," she sniped but didn't turn to him. *Invasive.* She continued her con list.

"Stop inviting me in," he growled. He suddenly ran his hand up the back of her scalp, twisting his fingers in her hair. He tilted her head to the side, exposing Avren's hickey. "Sloppy. I prefer them where only I can see them," he whispered, his words dripping with seduction.

He tightened his grip in her hair causing her to instinctually lean back into him, her eyes screwed closed. She felt her body come alive when he placed his other hand over her stomach. The simple hand placement made her nipples harden.

"Why do you pretend to hate me so much, Ashenfall?"

He lazily traced his fingers over her waist, her hips, down to the skin above her waistband. She was blissfully lost in the trail his fingers made over her skin.

"I'm not pretending." She sucked in a breath when he put his middle finger into her waistband. He grinned against her ear. He was thinking about being inside of her again, the taste of his desire was sweet.

"Liar," he playfully chastised her and removed his hands from her body. He stepped back, leaving her feeling heavy and reeling with need...again.

She turned to face him where he leaned against the ledge, his arms crossed.

"You like to hurt me," she said by way of answering his question.

"So?" He shrugged. She was taken aback—expecting him to deny her assertion. She scoffed and turned to the door. "You like when I hurt you," he called to her. She could not believe that he was so delusional that he actually thought she would want to be hurt and cut and whipped. She stormed over to him.

"You're insane." She had to laugh to keep from yelling. "And for the record, I *do* despise you." She felt the need to double down.

"Please! I saw you on those ropes, you were reveling in the pain." He laughed, matching her tone. "You may not even know that you like it, but you do." He straightened and towered over her. "The way you were biting your lip when I cut you, your whimpers when I whipped you, don't even get me started on your dirty little mind when I forced you to your knees downstairs."

All she could do was stare at him, enraged at how confident he was in his assertions and in shock that he may actually be right. Equally infuriated that he was playing with her, teasing her, and pushing her like he always did. Yet, the energy between them was so charged that she just wanted to feel his body on hers. She bit down on her tongue, weighing what she was about to say.

"If you want a distraction, then fuck me Praeceptor. But do NOT proclaim to know me." It was her turn to challenge him. He hadn't expected her to respond that way which caused her to give him a satisfied grin. *Checkmate.* Their molecules seemed to be drawing them together, neither of them unable to deny the offer she just put on the table. His eyes became hooded, darker as he strolled toward her. The wind swept his hair over his forehead. He looked like a God in the moonlight as he gripped her around the throat.

His eyebrows were furrowed, a wolf locking in on its prey. His eyes calculated what exactly he was about to do. She could sense that sweet flavor coming off of him. *Lust... it was lust, desire.* He wrestled with himself, weighing the consequences of giving into his desire, of giving into their desire. She tasted the strong flavor of resolve before he forcibly kissed her.

Her Praeceptor's hand stayed around her throat as he roughly claimed her mouth. He was more demanding—more sure—than Avren had been, and far less sweet about it. He released her throat and tore away his mouth. In a familiar gesture he grabbed her by the back of the head, gripping her hair. He forced her to walk over toward the ledge where she could look out into the distance.

"You want me to put you in your place don't you, brat?" He threatened.

The ledge rose to her waist and he forced her to bend over it. Her heart lurched when she registered how high up they were. She grappled at the edge of the stone to steady herself. She grunted at the roughness he displayed when he pushed her shirt up and dug his nails deep into her hips.

"What are you..." she turned to look at him when he yanked her pants down, exposing her completely to him. He took in the sight of her, pleased before undoing his belt. *Oh fuck.* He was maddeningly sexy as he prepared to take her. She watched his muscles flex beneath his shirt, his jaw clenching in anticipation, the way he ran his hand through his thick wavy hair...

"You constantly push me," he breathed. She jumped when he ran his fingers between her thighs, confirming that she was wet for him. He growled low in his throat in appreciation. He kicked her leg outward, spreading her thighs apart. "You're such a fucking brat." He slammed into her.

Amara wasn't expecting to be filled so completely, so quickly but he stretched her as she let out a scream. She didn't think she could stretch enough for his girth. Surely he would tear her apart, she screamed again. The burning turned into raw pleasure.

Cathmore reached around her and covered her mouth as he slowly pulled himself out of her. *Fuck.* He pushed into her again, slamming all the way into her. She had never heard him moan before but hearing it, from her brooding ruthless instructor... she just couldn't get enough so she pushed back against him, begging for him to go harder, faster. He wouldn't break her; this wouldn't break her. She would match him; she would see to it that he came undone as well. If they were going to go down this path, she was going to ensure it was worth it.

Tears stung her eyes as he relentlessly rutted into her. He shoved his fingers into the side of her mouth—opening it wide, cocking her neck painfully to the side. His other hand wrapped her throat; she gagged as he fucked her so hard that she couldn't think of anything else.

Amara was moaning, but she was also laughing like some kind of psychopath as he took her painfully from the back. He pulled out of her and spun her to face him, he hoisted her up on the ledge, using one hand to steady her and the other pulling her hair. He was so graceful and calculated in his movements, she could see the Nephilim grace and stamina arising for the occasion. She steadied herself on one of the pillars and wrapped her other arm around his neck.

Cathmore seemed to become fed up with the barrier of her shirt and ripped it down the middle on a particularly harsh thrust. The material fell away and he gripped her breasts, satisfied with the way they sat in her thin bra. His hands cupped them completely, drawing a moan out of her.

His mouth was open as he panted and looked down in awe where he entered her. Cathmore saw her looking too, his shirt pulled partially up—exposing his cut abdomen. He pulled her head back, pain stinging her head, more tears stinging her eyes. Without warning, he sped up his assault between her legs as she cried into the night for him. She was getting closer to her climax—watching him so intent on getting her there, seeing him angrily punishing her in such an intimate way for challenging him...

She dug her nails into his shoulders as she exploded, he grunted his approval when she tightened around him.

"Good fucking girl," he groaned as he kept taking her. She wrapped her legs around his waist, her arms around his neck. He took that as an opportunity to lift her by her ass, still inside of her and shove her against the wall.

Cathmore pinned her arms above her head with one hand and steadied her with his other hand on her hip. He never slowed his pace, he didn't tire, he wouldn't stop. Her eyes rolled back as he slammed her harder into the stone wall with every thrust.

He slapped her suddenly, causing her eyes to fly open, alarmed. "Eyes on me, brat." *Fuck.*

She found herself smiling at his words, his rough handling of her. She was actually *enjoying* it. He kissed her hard, his tongue invading her mouth, not asking for permission but telling her that he could do whatever he wanted. She let him. She tasted him on her tongue, a welcome taste, one she hadn't known she had been craving. He pulled at her bottom lip with his teeth, slowing his rhythm as though he knew she was getting close again.

"Come for me," he demanded.

Amara locked eyes with him, they mirrored each other, both wild, feral, needing. She moaned when he ripped the front of her shirt down and sucked hard on one of her breasts. She felt as though he was claiming her and she wanted it. She didn't want him to stop. Right on queue, he bit down hard sending pain shooting through her body.

"Praeceptor," she moaned and tugged his hair and she ground her hips down on him to ride out her orgasm.

"Fuck," his hand crashed into the stone wall behind her as he came undone too. She cried out as he throbbed inside of her, filling her completely.

They sat next to each other against the wall, looking up at the sky. She had gotten her pants back on but was feeling the blissful effects of the afterglow of her orgasms. She hadn't known how bad she needed that. Of all the ways she thought her evening would go... that was not on the list.

"I still hate you," she stated flatly in the comfortable silence.

"Yeah, I know." He just stared at the sky—his hair still messy from where she had gripped it.

He walked her back through the tunnel to the entrance that would let her back into the dormitory. He had given her his shirt and she took in the view of his naked back as she followed him through the tunnels. She didn't really know what to say to him, so she said nothing. She made a point not to look back at him as she took the stairs silently back to the conscript's dorms.

She flopped down on her bed in silence and threw her pillow over her head. *What the fuck had she just done?*

Guilt crept its way in... Avren. How had she gone from making out with him whom she had a genuine connection with, Avren who was sweet and caring... to being railed by her Praeceptor who was basically an animal. *Ugh.*

She became aware of the hickey on her neck. She still throbbed at the apex of her thighs, swollen from Praeceptor Cathmore. Shamefully, she enjoyed the pain between her legs as images of what he had done to her flashed through her mind. She was in way over her head and there was absolutely no one she could talk to about it. What happened between the two of them—was their dirty little secret.

Chapter 13

The next morning came with only two hours of sleep; she was particularly agitated and had very little patience for anyone.

"Where'd you get that shirt?" Juliet asked when they both stood that morning.

Shit. She looked down at the wrinkled white button-down that fell halfway down her thighs. The conscripts brought clothes which lived in their trunks. She obviously hadn't brought any but had a stocked stash of clothes courtesy of the Crowned Magister, she guessed.

"I've had it. Came in the clothing pile they gave me since I didn't bring any clothes," she answered and rolled up the sleeves.

"What is—" Juliet pointed at the hickey. Amara slammed her hand over it and cupped her neck. There was no way to make it look casual and her face heated. "Avren?"

"Why did you guess that?" She went on the defensive in a whisper as conscripts dressed around them.

"You snuck out with him last night," Juliet reasoned.

"I didn't know you knew…"

"I pay attention." She nudged her with a smirk. Amara offered her a small smile and began dressing for the day.

"Amongst the first to fall were Osias and Lyall, actually falling nearly four hundred years before the Angelic Exodus that occurred…" Professor Baylin recalled the year. " Eight hundred and thirty-one years ago."

She remembered that Hadeon and Deimos had fallen around that time, confirming for her that the two were cast out during the Exodus, not separately. She pondered how Hadeon became a Hallowed and Deimos, the Dark One. Why had they fallen together? Had they been close? She didn't know why there was such curiosity there but she made note of it.

Angelic Exodus—831 years ago

Hadeon and Deimos—831 years ago

Lyall and Osias—1200 years ago

"Did others fall before then?" Amara said while raising her hand.

"Yes, a few. Remember that Lucifer was a Fallen Angel. He wasn't cast out alone," Magister Baylin said. "Over a thousand years before that, he was the very first."

Lucifer (and friends?)—2200+ years ago

Amara tried to keep running notes of ages and significant events, but she struggled to comprehend the centuries these beings had lived.

"What did Cathmore do to you?" Avren leaned over, causing her to jump. His hands were bandaged, all of his fingers, except his thumbs in splints. The question caused her to become very *aware* of the soreness between her legs.

"Oh, uh, ten lashes on my calves," she stammered. She had been wearing pants so there was no reason for him to question it. "You?"

"Three fractured knuckles, five broken fingers." He sighed. *What the fuck.* It was such a grotesquely severe punishment for the 'crime'. It wasn't like he stole from someone.

"Are you okay?" she asked , guiltily.

"Yeah, as long as you didn't get it as bad, I'm glad to take the punishment." He smiled at her. "I think it's because I admitted that it was my idea," he added.

"Right." She nodded. She felt nauseated.

"How were the Hallowed Fallen able to come into so much power without being overthrown by the other fallen?" Amara asked Baylin.

"Well, our leaders were chosen by God himself, handpicked. They were blessed with magic beyond what the Rogue will ever be able to wield," he explained.

She didn't believe it for a second. They had come into their power through bloodshed, use of ancient magic that ran deep in the earth's soil. Somehow they had gotten control over it. It was how they were able to control their offspring and prevent their rights to their Nephilim power, stop the Rogue from breeding, turn their surviving Nephilim's power on themselves to be beneficial. Their God cast them out, he wasn't blessing them with shit.

Amara hadn't intended to scoff out loud at his response but she did, and he didn't take too kindly to it. Juliet looked at her with wide eyes.

"Ashenfall, why don't you share your disagreement with words," Magister Baylin demanded. She looked around. She wasn't going to be intimidated by him, though she knew she should keep her mouth shut.

"I just wish that what you taught in this class had just a sliver of truth to it, otherwise this is a waste of time," she remarked.

Judas, Eros, Molvina, and even Davian dropped their mouths open in shock and looked over to the Magister for a response.

"Why do you proclaim my teachings to be anything besides the truth?"

"Because I've lived, I use my eyes to observe the world around me," she said. An audible gasp came from behind her.

"Your deviant views are alarming, Ashenfall." He crossed his arms.

"If seeking truth makes me a deviant, I'll wear that title proudly before I wear your badge of ignorance." She sneered and stood. Her chair slid backwards behind here with a loud screech.

"You will mind your tongue! Sit back down!" He roared and slammed his fist on his podium. She scoffed a smile over it, and crossed her own arms defiantly.

"Mar..." Katara tried to tug her back to sitting. She jerked her arm away.

"I will summon your Praeceptor to take you before the Crowned Magister to correct these unacceptable ideals." He calmly clasped his hands together.

"Do what you need to do," she challenged the bigot of a man. She was already so far gone.

"Amara," Avren pleaded.

"It's fine," she whispered.

Some assistant to the Magister was sent to get Cathmore while Amara was forced to sit outside on the stoop like a child. She cursed herself for just having to open her big mouth...aga in.

"Praeceptor if you cannot get control of her, why is she still alive?" The Crowned Magister boomed.

"I have made great strides at keeping her in line, sir. I believe she voiced her disagreement at a poor time and should have sought clarity in a different way." Cathmore bowed his head.

The Crowned Magister had met them in one of the sprawling maze-like gardens. His hands were clasped behind his back, his suit embroidered with golden and purple thread.

"Ashenfall, let me make myself clear. You came here forcibly. You avoided your first call to the Crucible, you murdered a human, and now you've done nothing but act out. I am not under the impression you want to be here by any stretch of the imagination, child." He exhaled.

He—with alarming gentleness—touched her elbow to nudge her to walk with him. He spoke . "You don't have to like it here, but you need to address your Magisters and Praeceptors with respect. You are to take the knowledge they are giving you and use it. If you transition, you will need it."

"I understand, sir." She swallowed her pride.

"To ensure you do, two days in the pound. Maybe it will remind you to bite your tongue and open your ears."

Her eyes widened, and she looked to Cathmore who took a step toward her before Crowned Magister Bennett shot him a look.

"Don't be a fool, Praeceptor," he warned coldly.

The Pound: a deep, underground cell used to punish particularly unruly conscripts. It meant confinement—very little food, no sunlight, no room to move. Fear prickled in her mouth as adrenaline spiked through her. She knew Cathmore could do nothing. If the Crowned Magister had ordered her execution by his own hand, the Praeceptor would follow through without hesitation.

Two Nephilim came from somewhere in the maze and hauled her off under her arms. She didn't kick or scream, but went limp and allowed her feet to drag behind her.

Amara was tossed into a room that was only big enough for her to sit, or lay down in a ball, but standing was out of the question. It was made of smoothed cement, completely blacked out, and had a bucket for her to relieve herself in. No matter how she adjusted herself, the bucket was always touching her. She hugged her knees to her chest, leaned against the wall and tried to make herself warm. She shivered violently until her teeth were chattering.

Water dripped from above, each droplet echoing in the confined space. The steady *drip, drip, drip,* was enough to fray her sanity within hours. She shifted her aching body again, trying to escape the icy droplets that found her no matter where she moved. Cold seeped into her bones, and the dampness beneath her was unforgiving—her pants and shoes soaked through, submerged in the shallow puddle that had formed on the floor.

She fought to focus on anything but the relentless chill, the unyielding stone surface beneath her, or the throbbing pain that pulsed with every breath. Tears came, unbidden, streaking down her face, offering a brief, fleeting warmth as sobs shuddered through her exhausted frame.

Someone slid the stone slab away from in front of her cell bars. She scrambled to the back of the cell when the bars were opened outward and a burly Nephilim guard slid a tray of food into the small space.

"Twelve hours, sired one," he grumbled. *At least they informed them how much time passed.*

Amara didn't know what the mushy food was but the bread was definitely molded. Not that she could see it, but she could feel it so she tried to pick the bad parts off, blind. She shoveled the warm slop into her mouth for no other reason than to get warmer. It was bland and definitely had some kind of meat in it. She inhaled the water and looked out of the bars, where it was equally dark. At least they were letting fresh air into the space—albeit not very much.

The man returned after a few minutes and took her tray before closing her back inside the cell. She could hear sobbing from one of the other cells and imagined that's how she sounded earlier. Her focus turned though to the way her muscles forcibly relaxed as though she were melting. Warmth crept through her limbs, her head became fuzzy.

They had drugged her. No, no, no.

Sleep called to her, she sat up as she tried to fight it. What would they do to her if she was unconscious? She couldn't give into it. Panic spiked, causing her to hyperventilate, her eyes still getting heavier as she slumped against the wall. *Please, no. I'm so scared.* She begged some invisible deity who had never done anything for her before.

Her breathing became more of a challenge, her limbs numbing.

I don't want to die here.

They drugged me.

They poisoned me.

"Don't be scared, brat. Let it take you," Cathmore's voice in her head startled her.

What the fuck?!

It had to be her brain creating a way to cope with what they had done to her. He couldn't be talking to her through their minds.

"Trust me, sleep." His voice came through again—calming and smooth. She cried but stopped fighting it, she let sleep take her.

She jolted awake suddenly to the sound of her cell opening, her head colliding painfully with cement above her.

"Hour twenty-four," the guard said, sliding her tray to her again. She didn't hesitate to eat all of the mystery mush they served her, wanting Cathmore's magical sleep drug.

To her disappointment though, the feeling did not accompany the meal that time. She sat in silence, in a darkness that didn't even allow her to see her hand in front of her face. Her mind drifted to what the other conscripts would be doing, to what Cathmore would be doing. Fallen History would be where her unit was, meaning Cathmore was also teaching his first class of the day. She wondered if it was Pain Tolerance or Hand-to-Hand combat.

She drifted to sleep naturally after some hours of contemplating the Abyss of Despair. Her dreams were consumed with strands of raven hair and hooded silver-blue eyes. Her nails in tan skin, toned muscles, choking, slapping, his breathy grunts of pleasure... her own moan startled her awake. It took her a moment to remember where she was.

"Dirty girl, I'm teaching a class," came the Praeceptor's voice in her mind, a gentle teasing caress. Her cheeks flamed red. She needed to figure out how not to project her thoughts *about* him *onto* him.

"Get out of my head, I don't control my dreams," she snapped at him, or tried to. She didn't know if he heard her.

She mindlessly scratched at the hard stone floor, she just needed some kind of stimulation. She scratched until her nails cracked and bled. It was a welcome stinging pain, much better than the freezing that caused her bones to hurt.

The sensation took her back to one of the more painful encounters with her aunt.

"I told you not to touch my stuff, orphan!" One of Aunt Grace's four children exclaimed.

Amara was five, exactly five actually because it was her birthday. The family didn't celebrate her birthday but she was allowed to choose her food that day as well as play in the common areas of the home. Usually she was locked up in her room and fed whatever leftovers the family dumped on a tray for her.

That day she was in the living room while her cousins meddled about outside, where she was rarely allowed to go. She found a stuffed puppy under the sewing wheel. Its eyes were partially popped out, its yellow fur was dirty, and dust coated it. She knew it had been long forgotten, the sorrow in its eyes matching that in her own.

In that small beaten-up puppy she found comfort for just a moment. She examined it, petting it gently with a small smile while listening to the wind blow through the open windows. She was hugging it to her chest when she was 'caught'.

"There's no rule that I can't play with toys on my out day!" She shouted back at her cousin who was a round bitch of a girl.

"You're going to ruin him with your filthy sired blood!" The kid yelled and yanked the puppy from Amara.

Amara reeled her arm back to hit her cousin when she was picked up by her aunt.

"Do not yell at your cousins, you nuisance," she snapped. "What did she take of yours?" Her aunt asked the girl.

Her aunt's ideal punishment would have been the removal of a hand, but "people would notice."

So instead she tied Amara's little wrists to the wooden arms of a chair. The cousin that she had 'wronged' had the pleasure of watching as Aunt Grace took a metal tool and gripped a fingernail with the pincher part of it.

"No, no, no! Please!" Amara screamed.

"Quiet," her aunt sniped.

She yanked hard, freeing her fingernail from its bed, sending blood spattering. Amara screamed at the top of her lungs. Her cousin pointed and laughed. Aunt Grace did it again to her middle finger while the other child danced with the stuffed yellow puppy around the room. Everything seemed slowed down to maximize the pulsing pain that heated her fingertips.

"You're lucky I even let you live here," her aunt spat and removed a third nail which sent five-year-old Amara into her first bout of pain induced unconsciousness.

"Thirty-two, Ashenfall," a different guard said upon opening her cell. It wasn't time to eat, why had he opened it?

The man, another guard, whom she didn't recognize, tossed in a blanket. She wrapped herself in it, not caring how scratchy the material was. The simple object provided her with so much comfort that she cried as she curled into a ball. She never thought she'd long for the thin mattress of the dorms, the loud snoring of the other conscripts, the sterile and bland environment... but there she was, proof that it could always get worse and that it usually does.

"Hour 36," the familiar guard returned with her food. She greedily inhaled it, once more hoping to be taken into sleep. By her calculations, the day was over and night was approaching. She would be released in 12 hours, the following morning... if she could just sleep that away.

Sure enough and to her relief, her food had been drugged again. It relaxed her stiff and cramped muscles, forcing her into serenity, forcing her body to heat up. She drifted off to sleep, blissfully relaxed despite the situation she was in. The feeling could be addicting. She had never been so calm, so carefree, and she had never slept so deeply.

"On your feet." Someone kicked her awake. She stirred, a lantern brightening her cell to a blinding level after two days without light. The guard hauled her out of the cell by her elbow, her legs cramping.

When they made their way back to the surface of the ground, she glanced around. The guard had tied her hands behind her back. It was still dark—early morning—but dark. It hadn't been forty-eight hours yet, they had released her early.

"She's all yours." The guard shoved her backward. A fabric bag was shoved over her head by whoever she was pushed into, blinding her.

The man pulled her by her upper arm, forcing her to walk awkwardly given her hands were bound behind her back. She jerked against him but he kept tightening his grip, digging his nails into her.

He hurled her onto a horse, her stomach uncomfortably over the horse's back. He pinned her down with his hands, while she tried to work out who the hell he was.

"What do you want?" she exclaimed. Her kidnapper didn't answer, but she heard him kick the horse to speed it up.

The ride was rough and long. The horse galloped quickly through the woods, knocking the wind out of her, shaking her to the point that she became dizzy. She was starting to wonder if this was some kind of test from the Crowned Magister.

The sun was rising when they finally stopped, speckles of sunlight filtering into the cloth bag that was damp with the morning air.

"Let me go!" She grunted when the stranger pulled her off of the massive horse. She collided hard with the ground, choking on the dirt that seemed to invade her lungs.

The hood was yanked off of her head abruptly and she was pulled upward. The world spun around her, a mass of trees, thick brush, and sprawling ivy dying before the winter air. His face finally came into view

Gray hair, a jawline like his brother, deep-set wrinkles, and a bulky build confirmed what she hadn't wanted to admit she already knew. Magister Marlowe was exacting his revenge.

He looked unhinged with his eyes wide, deep bags beneath them. He smelled as though he had been drinking before the excursion to retrieve her. He looked her up and down, hatred burning in his eyes. He wore casual clothes as though trying to appear normal, abandoning the Magister's uniform along with his morals it seemed. She saw the monster that hid beneath the surface of his poor attempt at appearing human, at appearing *real*. He finally failed at taming the thing that lurked beneath his skin, the thing that he had been dying to unleash on her.

He gripped her arm and dragged her with him, toward a dilapidated building. It might have been a house many years earlier, perhaps where Magister's once lived. She tried jerking away from him as he pulled her up the rotted wooden stairs. Maggots adorned the holes in the pale wood around the door frame, giving the illusion that it was alive.

She couldn't help but wonder why wood would be chosen to build a home instead of stone and concrete. Willfully leaving your walls vulnerable felt like an idiotic choice but the thought was fleeting because Marlowe finally finished removing all four steel locks.

She waited for his grip to loosen while he pushed the door open before jerking away again, surprised it actually worked. She bolted away, only making it about five strides however. He didn't even seem bothered by her attempt but snatched her hair, stopping her abruptly and jerking her backward.

Her neck was cocked at an unnatural angle, painfully pulling something extremely important. *Fuck.* She writhed on the ground for a moment, unable to even rub the pain away because her hands were still restrained behind her back.

"Get up." He kicked her in the ribs.

"Fuck you." She grunted. He forcibly pulled her upward while she choked up the dirt she inhaled.

The house was in worse condition than she originally assumed. It was run down, moldy, and caving in on itself. Weeds grew up from between wooden floor boards, vines slinked in through the windows as though waiting to see what Marlowe would do with her. *Why had she been turned over to him?* Her time wasn't even up in the pound and she wasn't his charge. *Someone was working for him.*

"What do you want?" Amara turned to him. He was looking around the space, clearly having been in there in preparation for this little kidnapping. The horrors that were placed before her froze her in her place, her jaw on the floor, and tears pricked her eyes as fear consumed her. "Wh—"

"Be quiet, girl," he barked and struck her hard across the face with a blunt object—sending her into familiar darkness.

Chapter 14

"What do you mean? Who was she released to?" Cathmore stormed into the Serpent's Keep which was a pitiful collection of holding and solitary confinement cells beneath a scuzzy tavern.

He was seething as the guard followed behind him.

"Where is the guard that released her?" He demanded. The incompetent man before him pointed to a younger Nephilim who was perched on a stool against the bar. His eyes widened when Cathmore gripped him by the collar and hauled him backward. "Grogan," he growled.

"What the fuck, man" the guy squealed when he spilled his ale. He jerked free of Cathmore's grip.

"Who did you turn her over to?" He was so mad he was seeing red.

"Who? The fine piece of ass from this morning?" The guy whistled through chipped teeth. "She's probably getting what's coming to her by now," the drunken asshole laughed—drooling down his beard.

Cathmore reeled his arm back and landed a cracking punch into the Nephilim's jaw. He took pleasure in watching his bottom jaw disconnect from its natural place, sending the man to the floor.

"She is my charge, she should not have been released to anyone besides me." He bent down to pick the disgusting man up by his collar. He didn't give a shit that everyone watched on in amusement. He landed a punch to the man's gut, causing him to vomit out of the side of his mouth, his jaw hanging freely. "Give me a name," Cathmore growled. "Bennett did not authorize you to release her." His eyes widened, he knew what that meant. He would face the wrath of the Crowned Magister if she was killed by anyone other than her Praeceptor.

He rolled and coughed up more vomit. Cathmore stood and let him crawl into a sitting position, attempting to hold his jaw up into his face.

"Marlowe," he spat at Cathmore who kicked him hard under his chin, sending him unconscious onto his back, the crowd gasping. The amount of blood pouring from his mouth was satisfying but Cathmore fought the desire to revel in the sight of it.

He should have known that the bastard had taken her, he just hoped he wasn't so stupid. He would find her and he would deal the appropriate punishment to Marlowe. He didn't care what the Crowned Magister had to say about it.

He knew he was walking a dangerous line, but he would be equally as mad if it was another one of his students. He had been undermined; someone had taken something that was *his*.

He pushed his consciousness outward, reaching for any piece of Amara out there but he couldn't feel her. The usual ball of fire settled against the edges of his mind that which came with her presence in his head—was gone.

Darkness faded into a view of Marlowe's wicked grin. Manacles were clamped around her wrists, her knees scraping the ground as her partially limp body was pulled across the aged floor.

Shadows clouded her vision once more. She tried to make out the other voice in the room, tried to focus on the mystery tools that looked out of place mounted on the wall above an old dingy couch. Anger consumed her at her own helplessness.

"I don't want her feet on the ground, further up you idiot," Marlowe snapped at the unknown figure adjusting the chains that held her.

Her head pounded and her vision still faded in and out. She might have thrown up at some point and there was no doubt she had a concussion.

Amara awoke again to excruciating pain in her abdomen, she was definitely suspended by her arms, her feet dangling. She screamed as Marlowe carved something into her stomach with a blade. She looked between him and the dagger in her skin in shock.

"About time," he growled upon realizing she was awake.

Her torso was bare; she was exposed to the man before her. Marlowe pushed against her, pressing the blade into her again until she swayed. Stars exploded in her vision, causing bile to rise in her throat. Blood poured down her stomach, she cried out in agony when he sadistically began cutting a piece of flesh off of the side of her hip. He was going to gut her and skin her alive.

Someone appeared behind her with rough calloused hands on the exposed skin of her back. He moaned in approval of her soft skin, causing her to squirm as though she were covered in leeches. She would rather be. She screwed her eyes shut, her entire body trembling like a leaf in the wind. She tried to envision that it wasn't the stranger's hands on her back, or Magister Marlowe's fingers pulling on her pants.

She couldn't imagine Cathmore because of Marlowe's foul breath invading her nostrils. She tried to remember something happy to pull her from her reality but nothing could drown out what happened next. *Cathmore's hands, Katara's laugh, Avren's smile, Eros' dumb jokes. Please, please, give me something, anything.* She pleaded with herself.

Marlowe dropped the knife and began tugging her blood-soaked pants downward.

She raised her legs and kicked him as hard as possible. His carving of her abdomen rendered her weak, though, and she did no damage to him. He let out a taunting gut-busting laugh at her expense and she spat at him.

"Let me go!" She screamed. The sound of the chains and manacles clanking together sent a dull ache into her skull.

He ripped her pants, shredding the material. She was left completely nude with no way to cover herself up—her shoulders felt as though they would dislocate from the way she was suspended.

"I'm just taking what's mine, a life for a life." He grinned sinisterly.

He reached up, undid the chains that hung her, sending her colliding with the hard floor. Blood poured from her flayed opened abdomen; the skin of her knees split with the impact. She crawled away, her arms shaking. She was kicked onto her back, as helpless as a turtle flipped on its shell.

"This is the pathetic thing that killed Bastian?" The other man in the room burst into laughter.

"I didn't mean to!" She screamed bloody murder when the fat gapped tooth sweaty man crawled onto her. She shook violently, trying not to inhale the rancid smell coming off of his shirtless body.

"You don't accidentally slit someone's throat!" Marlowe boomed from somewhere behind her.. She was struggling beneath the whale of a man who had her pinned below his sweat covered stomach. *Stop, stop.* Panic restricted her breathing, an invisible grip on her windpipe.

Amara was naked and utterly exposed to the disgusting man on top of her who was practically drooling. Marlowe crouched above her head and tilted his head tauntingly. He wore a disgusting yellow smile, foaming at the mouth with excitement. She was hyperventilating under the stranger's crushing weight as his panting drew her attention away from Marlowe.

"You have such a sad little cry, like a baby bird," the stranger pouted his chapped lips.

The big man grabbed her arms and pinned them above her on the floor, on either side of Marlowe's feet where he was crouched and looking down on her. The ceiling above them was caving in, falling apart like the world around her. She hoped it would collapse and kill them, kill her.

The man straddled her and all she could think was that she was grateful he still had pants on, even if his torso was rubbing against her breasts and nipples.

"No one can hear you out here." The stranger laughed, drool dropping onto her face. Even Marlowe seemed briefly disgusted by it. She whimpered and squirmed beneath him.

Marlowe flipped the blade in his hand, twisted her palm upward to face him and stabbed the blade clean through her hand—pinning it to the floor. The scream that escaped her was inhuman, unnatural, and seemed to shake the building. She tried to reach for the blade with her other hand but he stepped on it, flattening it to the ground.

"Get off," Marlowe demanded of his pig-man accomplice. She tried to move, turning toward where her hand was pinned to the floor and pouring blood. She was a live butterfly pinned to a board, like the ones her cruel Aunt Grace trapped.

Marlowe dropped down on top of her while she fought the urge to pass out. She used her non-dominant hand to slap him hard. She thrashed against him but he was bigger, so much bigger than her.

"Fucking bitch." He grunted.

"Get the fuck off of me," she screamed at the top of her lungs. He shoved his entire forearm against her mouth, forcing it open so that it silenced her. She tried to bite down but he didn't care, it didn't do anything to stop him. The weight of him pulled her body agonizingly away from her hand and she could feel tissue and tendons ripping.

He shoved another knife against her throat. *Please just kill me, anything but this.* She sobbed against his arm, trying to escape as he opened the fly of his pants. She looked down, eyes wide, she was already in shock and shaking violently but she cried and cried.

"Cathmore, please." She mentally reached out for him.

Tears poured down her face as he laughed at her helplessness, the girl who killed his brother—broken in the worst way beneath him. He forced himself onto her, into her. He didn't even force himself into her vagina, but her ass. The pain was even more excruciating than she could have imagined. She felt something rip with a burning that caused her to scream.

Amara couldn't move, she couldn't think, she couldn't fight. He would slit her throat if she raised her arm to fight him further, so she froze. She closed her eyes, begging for somebody, anybody to find her in the abandoned building. She was losing too much blood, she was fading so fast.

"If she passes out or dies I'm still getting my turn," the pig-man spat. Marlowe ignored him.

Her blood from the wounds on her stomach soaked his shirt, when he saw it, he decided to carve a slice into her cheek. Her scream was muffled against his arm—the taste of sweat and dirt filling her mouth.

"Praeceptor, please." She reached out again before accepting that he could not hear her.

She didn't know how much time passed as he writhed on top of her but she was becoming weaker from blood loss, from shock, from the pain. She didn't know when, but he had removed his arm, knowing that she had lost the will to fight him. She stared uselessly at the ceiling, thinking of nothing as he ravaged her body.

Marlowe taunted her for being so weak and pathetic. He told her that his killing her was a mercy compared to embarrassing herself in the next trial. She lost sight of the pig-man but heard him fidgeting with some kind of tools out of view. Marlowe disgustingly finished onto her stomach where his seed mixed with her blood. She choked back another sob and cringed, the blade still pinning her hand to the floor.

A thunderous crash from the boarded-up window behind Marlowe signaled it had been busted in and filled the room with sunlight.

The first person through it was Cathmore, she would recognize his build and raven hair anywhere. More men came in behind him, others through the front door. Marlowe fumbled with his pants, wiping the blood off of him.

Amara heard the pig-man trying to run away. She struggled against the dagger in her hand, reaching for it but too weak to pull it out.

The men descended on Marlowe, everything happening in slow motion. Their wings crowding the room. *Their wings.* She had never seen Nephilim with their wings extended up close. Even Cathmore, who rushed to her and fell to his knees, had onyx wings towering over him, extending from his back.

He moved quickly and precisely to the blade and yanked it out without warning. She was thankful for that small mercy. He tore his long sleeve free and wrapped her hand as tight as he could.

"I've got you, I'm here," he whispered while chaos erupted between the pig-man and whoever caught up to him.

Cathmore placed a hand on her cheek, his eyes soft, concerned, but it was short-lived. Anger took him far from her, casting him from the present moment and into a blood crazed spiral. He stood and turned to Marlowe.

With the swiftness of a jungle cat, he backhanded the Magister, she could have sworn claws protruded from his hand just before impact. Magister Marlowe crumpled, blood pouring from his face. The other three Nephilim grabbed him, and chained him with silver chords.

Cathmore advanced on him but whoever the other Nephilim were, stopped him.

Amara was covering herself—her breasts with her forearm, her vagina with her other hand. She was still bleeding from her abdomen but had no way to stop it. Cathmore came back over to her and crouched down, his wings expanding outward and covering the two of them. He protected her from the view of the other men—who were dressed in the gold of the guard of the Sanctum Metere.

"Here," Cathmore used whatever his Imperium was to materialize a shirt into his hand and give it to her. He pressed some other cloth into her stomach, against the bulk of where her skin had been carved. She tried to make sense of what she saw. *He summoned items out of nowhere.*

He worked quietly and quickly. He was gentle as he bandaged her midsection, pulling materials seemingly out of thin air. Watching him work intently on her wounds was like seeing a glimpse at the man he wanted to be—a doctor.

She could feel heat coming off of him as though his blood were boiling with anger. The temperature increased as he assessed her wounds further. His breathing was shallow, she could feel the bitter taste of fury from him.

Once her midsection was wrapped, he helped her pull the shirt over her head. It was big on her and it smelled like him. There was another problem though... warm blood gathering beneath her where she sat.

"Praeceptor," she whimpered weakly. She raised her hand from between her legs where she was bleeding heavily from where Marlowe violated her.

He looked down with wide eyes, black hair sprawling wildly over his forehead. He wrapped bandages into a ball so that she could hold it against herself and absorb the blood.

Tight shorts appeared and she pulled them on, thankful for the privacy of his wings. She could hardly take a mental inventory of everything that hurt. It was too much, too overwhelming.

Once she was dressed, he lifted her in his arms, supporting her under her back and legs. He dropped his wings; they twitched as he tucked them behind him. She could only stare at them in awe.

"Torture, rape, kidnapping, attempted murder." He listed off the offenses to one of the guards who nodded. "I will meet with Bennett once my student is back on her feet."

"Yes, Captain," one of the men said.

Captain?

"I want him and Grogan taken to the old cellars while we await approval for wing removal and sentencing to the Abyss," Cathmore ordered. "The human—" he nodded to the pig-man. "-is mine, put him in the pound."

The Nephilim hauled Marlowe off who was fighting against them and trying to reason with Cathmore. The pig-man was screaming some nonsense about not having touched her.

"It's only a few minutes to fly back, can you handle it?" he asked her, looking into her eyes. He was so demanding and stern with the men but with her...

"I'm afraid of heights," she groaned. Her entire body hurt, she was exhausted, and her soul had been completely shattered. He shook his head, a small smile playing on his lips. The irony of someone designed for the sky but terrified of it seemed to amuse him.

"Just hold on tight, and don't look," he instructed and directed her hands to lace around his neck.

He showed her that he had a firm grip on her and promised not to drop her. He shot into the sky faster than she could have prepared for with a single beat from his wings. *No wonder the flight was only a few minutes.* She buried her face in his chest as the cold wind bit into her, he pulled her closer, and she focused on his breathing.

His wings pounded the air a few times and then they were soaring through the sky. Part of her wanted to open her eyes but fear forced them to stay closed. She laced her fingers tighter around his neck, determined to stay attached to him.

"You're not going anywhere," he said into her mind. His words were comfort, safety, and hope.

"I think I'm going to pass out." She pushed into his mind. Adrenaline was fading away. The blood loss and shock trying to take her.

"No, you have a concussion. Stay with me," he pleaded and dug his nails into her skin. She jumped but it helped keep her conscious.

They touched down in a large courtyard where one of the units was training. The conscripts gasped in awe when he landed gracefully, and tucked his wings back before they disappeared altogether.

"Most of you know Praeceptor Cathmore, he's just come back from a rescue," Praeceptor Sloane said to the unit.

"Amara?" Beck ran up to her. She was happy to see him and smiled weakly, still holding on to Cathmore.

"Back up, she needs a healer," he warned. Beck did so and looked at her worriedly.

Cathmore took long strides into one of the cobblestone buildings, the one she knew to have an infirmary.

Some of the healers were human and some were Nephilim. Five crowded around her as tears streamed down her face. Cathmore laid her on the cot and pushed her hair off of her face.

"Don't go," she asked through their mental bond. He looked around, his eyebrows furrowed. One of the healers shoved him out of the way.

"She's hemorrhaging," a healer said and moved in front of Cathmore. He tried to push back through to her but there were too many people working on her.

Her hand was sprawled on a flat surface where two healers assessed it to stitch it up, her abdomen was being disinfected in preparation for stitches, and they were discussing more... *invasive* stitches for the tear in her ass.

"Concussion due to blunt force trauma, complete penetration through the right hand, accompanied by two fractures in the bone. Extreme rectal tear due to forced penetration. Stitches required in hand, abdomen, face, and anus," the one who seemed to be the doctor was talking to someone. She looked over to see that it was Crowned Magister Bennet and Cathmore on the other side of the curtain. She was crying, again. She was utterly terrified and mortified.

She ended up requiring a total of thirty stitches in her abdomen, six in her ass, and ten in her face. It was an impossibly painful endeavor for them to clean the cuts and stitch them but she pushed through. It was her hand that was the worst, requiring stitches inside and outside of her skin. She lost count at forty. She knew this would put her behind in the Abyss Trial with it being less than two weeks away and that was the emotionally devastating part of it all.

She couldn't walk with the damage from the assault. Her entire body was on fire and nausea consumed her.

Cathmore had gone to speak to the Crowned Magister while the healers finished their work. He was not allowed to stay given the nature of her more intimate injuries.

They allowed her to rest for some hours, gave her some kind of concoction for the pain, and then released her back to Cathmore. The sun had set and the Crowned Magister requested to speak to her in the gardens the following morning. *Great, because that went so well last time.*

Chapter 15

"Amara!" Katara exclaimed when she limped into the dormitories for the evening. Avren, Juliet, and Eros joined her as they jogged up to greet her. The others circled around her as well as they murmured amongst themselves.

"They said Cathmore landed on the training field carrying you and you were bleeding," Avren said, inspecting her face. She raised up her shirt where the stitches dressed six differing deep slices.

"Why," Juliet gasped.

"It was Marlowe, revenge for his brother," she answered, acceptance in her tone.

"So it's true then, you murdered someone before being brought here?" Avren asked, taken aback. Katara and Eros didn't seem phased by it and Juliet appeared to solve some riddle in her head.

"I knew you were the murderess!" Juliet chimed in. "But not like in a bad way... it happens." She shrugged when the others looked at her. She almost wanted to laugh at her friend, thankful to even see her again.

219

"I have paid my debt for my crime, it's done," she said and slowly moved over to her bunk.

Her close friends wanted to talk to her more about what happened and how the pound had been but she didn't have the energy. Once lights out happened, she was able to take a deep breath as prying eyes closed for the night.

As she tried to sleep, she found herself reliving the tortures of the day. Her body ached, the literal constant pain in her ass reminding her of what Marlowe had done to her. Her abdomen was swollen and heated to the touch. Despite her desperate need to shower, she wasn't allowed to with the stitches. Nor could she eat for twenty-four hours. They wanted the wounds to start closing inside of her before she relieved herself again. Luckily she had already gone nearly a full day without eating anyway.

Phantom sweat and bodily fluids clung to her skin, the acrid scent of blood, alcohol, and aloe filled her nose. In spite of the fact that she had been cleaned by the healers, she felt filthy. The enormity of what had happened pressed down on her, yet her eyes remained dry, she had no more tears to offer herself. She had no more self-pity to wallow in, only excruciating pain. Every muscle in her body trembled with weakness, a hollow sensation in her chest signaling she was beyond repair.

Every time she closed her eyes, she felt Marlowe cutting her open, forcing himself into her. The one time she finally dozed off, she awoke screaming, Juliet and Eros by her side to comfort her. She realized that sleep was out of the question after hours ticked by. She took an extra dose of the pain relieving mixture so she could take a walk.

Eventually, she found herself mindlessly wandering through the tunnels beneath the grounds of the Sanctum Metere. She had no destination in mind, she just knew she couldn't stay in her bed for another second. The library had the keepers who would rat her out, so she ambled through the doorway that would take her to the old lookout tower. The stairs were more exhausting than before, and she had to take them slowly so as not to tear her stitches. She paused a few times, her labored breathing causing pain as her stomach expanded on each deep breath.

It wasn't until she noticed the door ajar at the top of the stairs that she remembered that the door downstairs should have been locked. Still, she pushed through it. She knew only one person could be up there besides her.

Sitting slumped against the wall, asleep, was Praeceptor Cathmore. He didn't stir when she made her way onto the landing, his head leaning back, sleep softening his features. His arms were crossed; his hands being warmed under his armpits. He looked uncharacteristically still and serene. He was usually so stiff, active, demanding, and his facial features were always hardened. All of those things weren't present as he dozed calmly beneath the stars of the cold night. It was almost entirely too cold, she didn't know how he fell asleep.

She felt suddenly as though she were looking in on a private moment that she shouldn't be, so she turned to begin the trek back downstairs.

"Come here, brat." Cathmore sighed. She turned to him cautiously, of course he sensed she was there.

Amara padded over to him and sat very carefully beside him, he leaned his head back on the wall once more and looked over at her. Heat was radiating off of his body as though he was his own heat source, maybe he was. She didn't know all of the powers the Nephilim possessed, much less what his Imperium granted him.

"You drugged me to help me sleep through my time in the pound." She sighed. It felt like a lifetime ago. "Thanks for that."

It felt so trivial a thing compared to him saving her life but she would have lost her mind in there if he hadn't done it.

"I wanted to help." He rubbed her arm gently.

"I felt your pain today. I don't know how," he admitted transparently.

"Is that not normal for empaths? I thought our connection was due to the similarities of our clairvoyant abilities." She turned to him. She winced, her butt tender.

"No, it's not normal." He sighed.

"That's how you knew what happened to me," she surmised. He nodded and looked away from her. She winced again and sat back against the wall when it seemed as though he was finished talking.

"I'm so sorry, Amara," he murmured as he fell asleep.

Time passed in comfortable silence and she found herself falling asleep, her head leaning on his shoulder. She allowed his protective nature and warmth to comfort her as she got some much needed rest.

The morning sun rose over them, awaking Amara. She was on her side, laying in Cathmore's lap, facing his body, her face nearly buried in his stomach. Her hand was curled into his dark shirt, wrinkling it. His hand was draped across her upper arm and he seemed to still be sleeping peacefully. Her entire body was warmed thanks to the heat coming from him.

He straightened suddenly, which prompted her to sit up. Her abdomen hurt far worse than the previous day and she panted from the strain it took to get up. *Fuck.*

Cathmore looked around and shot up to his feet quickly.

"What's going on?" she asked, sleepily.

"I have to take you to meet Crowned Magister Bennett," he informed her.

He was uncharacteristically patient with how slow she needed to walk. She was grateful that for once he wasn't being abrasive and demanding. They wound their way through the maze of neatly trimmed hedges before they were finally greeted by Crowned Magister Bennett.

"Ashenfall," the Crowned Magister greeted her. She said nothing. His calm demeanor and hands crossed in front of him made her skin crawl.

"A great wrong was committed against you. For that I am sorry," he offered sincerely. She couldn't wrap her head around the Crowned Magister actually apologizing to her.

"I do not tolerate gross abuse of power," he began. She fought the urge to scoff. "Marlowe broke a number of oaths that he swore in order to hold the position of Magister here at the Sanctum Metere. His bold willingness to defy my orders, torturing a sired child, kidnapping, and sexual assault are individually punishable to the highest extent."

If she had been just human the punishment wouldn't be so heavy. It's why her only punishment for Bastian's murder was to still enter the Crucible. She looked around for Cathmore who had paced away into another part of the garden.

"With that being said; Ruslan Marlowe will have his wings clipped at sunrise before the entirety of the Sanctum Metere. He will then be cast into the Abyss where he will suffer for eternity as a traitor to Hadeon and to his kingdom. He will be known as a coward for his heinous actions against you," Bennett spoke so calmly in a matter-of-fact tone. She nodded and hugged her arms to her body, careful of her stitches. Cathmore emerged behind the Crowned Magister and listened in silence. She fidgeted with a leaf on one of the hedges.

"You showed great courage in the situation, you showed a fighting spirit, and you showed that your stubbornness will not allow you to be killed so easily. So that this wrong can be righted, I hereby grant you one silent pardon from one of the two remaining trials," he offered.

Amara gasped and looked to Cathmore, who bowed his head, seemingly to hide a smile.

"What is... I..." she stammered. "Thank you." The Crowned Magister grabbed her uninjured hand, clasping it between his.

"Your Praeceptor will give you the details, but to see you standing before me after what you endured—I believe we can expect great things from you in the future, Ms. Ashenfall," he praised her. His words put her more into a state of shock than she thought she had been after the assault, though she still hadn't come down from the events either. She had a feeling that when she did, she would crumble.

"Thank you," was all she could say. She was left wondering if her impression of the Crowned Magister had been wrong.

When Cathmore led her away, Bennett called out, "Gragnor will serve time in Mistscar, three decades."

Cathmore nodded his thanks and they made their way through the gardens and back toward the dormitories. *Mistscar?*

"What's Mistcar?" she asked him.

"It's a less severe punishment than the Abyss. Nephilim in Mistcar are held and tortured but can be released after their time served," he explained.

"A prison." She nodded.

"Yes, it's just... worse than most human ones," he cringed. She wondered how he knew the details of Mistcar. "I'm going to take you back to the dormitories so you can rest. You need to limit movement. You won't be participating in the events with the other conscripts today," he instructed.

"At least the dorms will be quiet." She offered a weak smile. Cathmore resumed walking. "What are you going to do to the pig-man?" she asked. It had been nagging at her.

"The... pig-man?" He turned to her with perplexed amusement. She shot him a vicious glare, not in the mood to joke about the nickname.

"I didn't exactly catch his name." She shuddered, recalling his excitement at a turn with her.

"I'm going to find out why he was involved and then I'm going to kill him for touching you," he stated simply.

"He's not the one..." she shifted on her feet. "He's not that one that—" he interrupted her.

"I know that." He sighed. "But I saw him on top of you. I felt your terror," anger tensed his shoulder muscles.

"He's human." She sighed. "Just because he *can* die, doesn't mean he should die," her morals betrayed her anger toward the man. Cathmore tilted his head and crossed his strong arms.

"You don't want him dead?" He seemed to have trouble understanding why.

"The only reason the other two aren't dead is because they're immortal right?" She sighed.

"Marlowe is getting the closest thing to death that we can offer," he reasoned.

"Human's mortality does not make them less than us. The beings in this kingdom are far too happy to kill them," she voiced a frustration she long harbored as she paced slowly in front of him.

"But he deserves to die..." Cathmore reasoned, speaking through gritted teeth.

She cringed as she recalled him writhing on top of her and drooling on her. It made her entire body shake.

"I killed a human. This was the price I paid for that. I will not have another one killed." She resolved herself. He turned his back on her, his muscles tense.

"Do you think you deserve what happened to you?" He spoke away from her.

She didn't answer. Somewhere deep down, she felt like she did.

"That's bullshit. No one deserves that." He lost his temper, whirling back on her. The look on his face sent her heart right into the ground.

"Why do you care?" She matched his tone, getting in his face.

"You are my charge!" He roared. "This is on me." He pushed past her.

"If you kill him, you are doing it for you. I will not live with his blood on my hands too." She walked away from where he stood and resolved herself to go back to the dormitories. Her wounds were aching and she felt weak.

He let her walk away from him.

Chapter 16

Amara was jolted awake in her cot when the conscripts flooded the dormitory later that evening.

"How are you feeling?" Katara sat on the foot of her bed.

Amara grunted as she sat up.

"Healing, I guess." She offered a weak smile. "What happened to you?" She gestured at a swollen angry cut across her arm.

"Fallon got me with a sword during sparring," she told her.

"They let you spar with sharpened weapons?" She gasped.

"We wore armor but it got through." She shrugged.

"At least I have that to look forward to next weekend," she responded sarcastically.

Juliet and Eros leaned against the bunk and riddled her with questions about her condition physically and emotionally. Avren remained distant.

"I appreciate the concern, but I don't want to talk about it," she shut them down.

She was finally allowed to eat food which their Praeceptor brought to the dormitory. Eyes followed him as he walked over to hand deliver her dinner. They didn't exchange words; they barely even looked at one another. When her eyes scanned his swollen blue knuckles, he jerked his hands away and turned from her.

Her stomach was in excruciating pain both from hunger and the stitches. She shoveled the food into her mouth before accompanying it with the pain medication she was given.

Eventually she found herself in the washroom before her reflection. She stared downward, not wanting to really look at herself. She was afraid of what she would see.

Slowly she raised her head, first noticing the stitches over her cheek. She was pale and appeared utterly worn down. Her hair was matted and when she raised her hands to fix it she paused to stare at the wrapped hand that had been mutilated. Somehow it didn't hurt as bad as her abdomen but it didn't feel great. She tried to move her fingers but couldn't. She dropped her hand in defeat.

She dreaded having to relieve herself, even if just to pee. The stitches inside of her were so unbelievably painful. She found herself crying as she sat on the toilet. She was thankful that the rest of the conscripts were sleeping and that she had the shared washroom to herself.

Amara examined her stitches in her abdomen; her entire stomach was swollen and heated. She couldn't even touch the skin.

"Meet me in the watchtower," came Cathmore's voice in her mind. She sniffled and wiped her tears.

"Why am I here?" she demanded. She found him watching the horizon, his back to the entrance she just pushed through.

"Why *are* you here?" He countered, not even looking back at her.

"What happened to your hands?" She pushed. He dropped his head slightly to examine them. The knuckles were dark and bleeding.

"Nothing," he lied.

She was just about to scoff when she was briefly distracted by a shooting star dancing across the sky, he caught it too. She had never seen one and she scanned the sky for another.

"Fine," she resolved herself to his need to be broody and secretive. She turned to leave, still unclear as to why he told her to meet him.

"I need to explain the concept of a silent pardon," he spoke coldly, freezing her at the top of the stairs.

"Okay?" She turned slowly. "Tell me what you did first." She gestured at his hands.

"I went to see the pig-man. I intended to kill him," he mumbled. "I settled instead on bashing his face in and having him thrown into a human prison."

She inhaled sharply. He was impossible. Why was he so determined to avenge her?

"Thank you for not killing him,." She moved to his side and peered out at the sleeping Sanctum Metere.

Cathmore filled her in on the terms of a silent pardon, his mannerisms and tone strictly professional.

If she used it, no one could know. It would have to appear as though she had gone through the trial. In the case of the upcoming Abyss trial... where Marlowe would be... He would have her dropped in with the unit, she would separate herself, and Cathmore would fly her out with Bennett's blessing. She wasn't sure she wanted to use it for the Abyss Trial but... given the location of her stitches, she may not end up with a choice.

She was relieved to know that Marlowe's actions were being taken seriously, that he would be punished for what he did to her. She couldn't help but feel guilty though, her deed in killing Bastian Marlowe had not only taken his life, but cost his brother's life as well. She imagined that Ruslan Marlowe was once a well-kept, respected, and even sane individual.

"Do I have to use the silent pardon on this trial?" she asked, picking at the bandage on her injured hand.

"Well, no. I think you should, given the nature of your injuries..." he responded carefully.

"I'll think about it." She sighed and shook her head, pulling her sleeves over her cold hands.

"You can only use it on one of the next two trials. Everyone must compete in the conclusion of the year challenge," he informed.

"I thought there were only two more?"

"No one counts the finale. That's the day you transform. Those who transform complete one final task to earn it."

"What task?" She turned to him.

"I'm not at liberty to discuss the final challenge at this time," he responded with cool detachment.

"Fine, when are we going to work on hiding the development of my Imperium?" she asked, needing to change the subject.

"Once you're better. I'm going to have to push you and it's going to have to be very controlled," he explained and turned to her. "I'm working out the details about how we're going to keep that training a secret."

"Right, got it." She looked up at him.

"You need to focus on keeping your thoughts to yourself though." He dropped his shoulders.

"I'm trying, I just don't know how…" she trailed off.

"I'm going to teach you but I just want you to be aware of it for now." He stared into her eyes. She nodded, unable to speak beneath his glare. Everything he did was so intense, it took her breath away.

"I meant to thank you." She looked down. "For coming to get me." *And for being gentle with me, covering me when I was exposed, getting me to the healers quickly…* She had a mental list of things she wanted to thank him for.

"You're welcome." He lifted her chin so she would look at him. "For all of it," he whispered.

She didn't want to go back to the silent stuffiness of the shared dormitory. Nor did she want to walk all the way back.

"I'll stay with you," was his response when she told him. She wasn't sure how to react to this new kind Praeceptor but she took a seat next to him on the ground.

She shifted so that she wasn't sitting uncomfortably on her butt, at which point he tugged her shoulder.

"Just lay down, stubborn." He sighed. She laid her head in his lap which caused her heart to race and cheeks to inflame.

"What happened to 'brat'?" she asked, staring forward where his ankles were crossed.

"You're still a brat. I'm just feeling..."

"Like less of an ass," she finished his sentence. She heard him laugh , the sound melting over her like warm honey.

He was fidgeting with her hair and she was very aware of how much of a mess it was.

"Would it piss you off if I offered to brush your hair?" he asked after a moment. She sat up to look at him, wincing.

"No. But I don't have a brush up here." She frowned.

"Turn around." He grinned. He parted his legs so that she could sit between them, but not before he removed his coat for her to have something soft to sit on.

He pulled her long hair back behind her ears, his fingertips grazing her neck . He pulled his long fingers gently through her hair and she focused on the sound of his breathing. He materialized a brush from nowhere, something she needed to learn to expect.

"How do you—" she started.

"Shhh," he stopped her.

She stilled as he pulled the brush through her hair. To her surprise, it wasn't painful. He was tender with her in a way that was in stark contrast to the person who punished her before. She tilted her head back so that he could start at the crown of her head once he worked the tangles out at the ends.

The bristles sent chills over her body, causing her to close her eyes and enjoy it.

"Does that feel good?" He taunted, knowingly.

"Mhmm," she murmured as he pulled the brush over her scalp again.

Amara heard him drop the brush before his fingers raked over her scalp. She was afraid that after her experience she would be repulsed by another's touch. Cathmore confirmed that it wasn't the case. He pushed his fingers under her hair, starting at her neck, and massaged . It was exactly what she needed after everything she had gone through. She had never been cared for in such a simple yet intimate way as he had cared for her those two days.

She found herself leaning back against his chest as he gently rubbed the sides of her head. The motion relaxed her until her eyes grew heavy. She curled on her side against his massive leg while he rubbed her back gently. At some point she fell asleep, but not before another shooting star shot across the sky above them.

"Hey, wake up," came Cathmore's voice as he shook her shoulder. The sun had risen over them, making her feel exposed.

"They're about to take Marlowe into the arena, I didn't mean to sleep this long," he exclaimed and helped her up. They looked over the side to see people slowly moving into the massive circular building.

He thought for a moment, probably realizing that there was a good chance someone in the tunnels would see them both emerge from the old watch tower. The tunnels were a popular way of travel for the Magisters and Praeceptors.

"Shit, Amara, we have to be more careful," he grumbled, the gentle kind man from the night before was gone.

He started down the stairs, she followed after him. She almost argued that they hadn't done anything but the reality was if they were caught together in an abandoned part of the Sanctum—the consequences would be significant. Praeceptors couldn't have relationships of any kind with conscripts. She couldn't move nearly as fast as him though it was more to do with the pain in her abdomen, her ass feeling better. *Weird.*

They got to the bottom of the stairs, Amara sweating more than usual as pain coursed through her. She propped herself on the wall breathing through a more intense moment of pain that resulted from her taking the stairs too quickly. He looked back, something between annoyance and concern on his face.

"Here." He showed her a salve that he materialized from who knew where. "This will help the pain, lift your shirt."

Amara did as he asked, allowing him to gently apply the salve over the stitches. One of them was dripping a small amount of blood to which he whispered something under his breath. Her skin was raised, red, hot to the touch.

"This cut is showing signs of infection, I'll take you to the healers," he said and rolled her shirt down gently.

"No, I want to see Marlowe's wings clipped," she protested.

"You can barely stand," he argued. He touched her forehead, "and you have a fever. You're going to the healers." She wanted to argue further but she was feeling the effects of infection setting in and knew there would be no convincing him or fighting him on it.

He peeked his head out into the hallway, waited for someone to pass at the other end of the hallway and then scooped her into his arms. She winced but he took long strides down the dimly lit corridor.

The healers welcomed her quickly and began giving her all kinds of things for the fever and infection.

One of the doctors spoke quietly to Cathmore whose features became utter panic.

"Send me Praeceptor Nightbane," Cathmore demanded of a human nurse who scrambled away without question.

"Why?" she asked, fear causing nausea to overtake her.

"His Imperium is healing, none of us possess the ancient ability," the fair haired Nephilim woman told her, her voice soft.

"Can he heal me so I have a chance in the Abyss Trial." She struggled to sit up, looking at Cathmore.

"He can heal you completely, yes," he answered coldly.

After ten minutes, Nightbane stormed into the small communal infirmary, he was undoing bandages from his hands—clearly having just finished some kind of workout. He pushed his short blonde hair from his forehead as he and Cathmore spoke in hushed whispers.

"Are you sure you know what you're doing here, Killian?" Nightbane whispered, glancing at Amara. He ignored Nightbanes' concern and moved toward Amara.

"The infection has moved into your blood, this is the only way," Cathmore told her. No one had told her that it was so bad, but she nodded understandingly. "This is going to be excruciatingly painful, do you understand?" He crouched down next to her. Nightbane looked between them, eyebrows furrowed.

After a few moments, Nightbane took Cathmore's spot next to her cot. A curtain was pulled around them and one of the nurses stood by. There had only been one other person in the infirmary who seemed to only be minorly injured.

Cathmore left the small space, disappearing behind the curtain. She knew he was gone by the sound of his footsteps fading down the stone corridor. She laid her head back and stared at the wooden beams in the ceiling above her.

Nightbane placed his hands over her abdomen and closed his eyes. For a moment nothing happened. She was about to speak when it suddenly felt as though her intestines were being pulled through her skin. She looked down to see Nightbane's hands glowing silver, the stitched wounds on her stomach beginning to unravel. Blood pooled on her pale skin before spilling over the sides of her narrow hips. She let out a scream because it felt as though every nerve in her body had been lit on fire.

Nightbane was clenching his jaw, focused as he continued to heal her. She could feel her skin start to stitch itself back together, tendrils of fire reaching for one another.

"Stop!" She screamed hoarsely, squirming and unable to move. She couldn't take it, it was going to kill her, she was going to pass out from the pain.

Somewhere in the room objects clattered to the floor, the nurse that had been holding her hand was called out to tend to whatever happened. She was being held down by some invisible force. Her body shook from the pain as he sped up her body's healing process—somehow that's what it felt like he was doing.

Her hand felt like someone was ripping her fingers from it, her anal injury felt as though it was reopened.

"No!" She choked on a sob and tried to squirm again. Blood poured from her hand, her cheek, her stomach, from underneath her.

"Please," she begged as another wave of pain took over. She looked down, the wounds turning black, she could see her skin weaving together. She had never known pain so severe, it had her craving the pain of the hot poker on her back. She was sure that death was just a fingertips length away, her vision blurring.

Another scream erupted from somewhere in her throat, it tore through her against her will, needing to find some escape for the pain. Sweat poured down her face as though the fever and infection was being pulled from her veins. She became aware of each pore on the surface of her skin, it felt as though acid was being siphoned from her.

It felt as though her body had had enough when she willed herself out of his grasp... and somehow ended up on the floor, on the other side of the curtain. *It worked.* Nightbane threw the curtain back and pulled her up by her arm. She looked at him wide-eyed, just as shocked as he was by what had occurred.

"What the hell was that, Ashenfall?" He shook her, gripping her shoulders hard. Nightbane was much larger than Cathmore, much wider.

"I—I don't know," she stammered in fear. He pressed his palm to her cheek, where the stitches sat and she winced, jerking from him when he healed it.

Cathmore pushed through the curtain and looked frantically between them. He helped her back to the cot.

"What did you do!" He exclaimed, ocean eyes wide. *How did he know?*

Nightbane seemed to have the same question as he looked at Cathmore. He yanked Nightbane to the side where they argued in hushed tones, taking turns gesturing toward her. She listened hard for pieces of the conversation.

"She's your charge, her Imperium isn't my business, nor is your decision to keep her alive," Nightbane spat. "You are putting us all at risk," he whispered lower. They looked over at her, sensing her listening in. "We're even, Killian." Nightbane dropped his first name again and stomped from the infirmary. It was strange hearing him referred to by his first name but it suggested a level of acquaintanceship between the two Nephilim that she had not picked up on before.

Cathmore turned to her. "It's done; Marlowe is being taken to the Abyss now." She nodded, her body shaking violently. "I have to go," he said flatly. *Was that fresh blood on his arms?*

"Get some rest, honey." The human nurse with rosy cheeks rubbed her back—guiding her to lie down. She watched Cathmore push through the front of the infirmary before disappearing out of view altogether.

What was his problem?

Chapter 17

The next week passed with little said to her from Praeceptor Cathmore. She thought for certain that he would be trying to 'tame her Imperium' but he hadn't even mentioned it. An older lady, named Magister Seahollow, who was a lot less abrasive than the other instructors, took over Marlowe's stamina course. They were concluding their trek up the arena stairs when Amara waved to Avren and got nothing but the cold shoulder.

He had barely spoken to her either, not since finding out she was the murderess. She sighed; Eros touched her arm in an attempt to comfort her but it caused her to jump. She was a lot more sensitive to touch since she was assaulted. *Except for with Cathmore.*

"He'll get over it," Eros reassured her.

"It's fine." She shrugged and resumed her jog down the massive stone stairs. "How are things with Judas?"

"Great, actually. We found a time and place to be alone sometimes and it's been..." she glanced over at him, causing him to laugh. "Reallllyyy good," his tone was suggestive. She shook her head and laughed too.

No one knew the true nature of everything that Marlowe had done to her—save for Cathmore, Bennett, and the guards that took part in her rescue. She didn't want her friends to know about the sexual assault because then they would hold back on normal conversations like she and Eros were having.

"Did you hear?" he asked randomly.

"Hear what?"

"Molvina and Fallon Mournstride called it quits; she's with Davian now," he said judgmentally. She couldn't hide her face of disgust.

"She has a type." Amara sighed.

"Yeah, jackass." Eros laughed.

Amara was sitting against one of the buildings alone during her break before Cathmore's double class. She was taking notes from a book she chose for an assignment. She was astounded that they got a choice in what topic they wanted to study for their final Fallen History assignment.

Amara had grown particularly interested in the original fallen angels; Lucifer & Atreus.

In the annals of celestial history, the very first expulsion event from celestial heights is a claim held by two noteworthy heavenly beings – Lucifer and Atreus. Now known as the first fallen angels, their titles reverberating through the millennia. This event is hidden in the ancient narratives. For some, the fate of Lucifer and his brother is regarded as a glorious award that they earned within their celestial circle. For others, it is a regrettable fault that inevitably shaped the destiny of all of us.

While many still cling to the time-worn notion that a third of the heavenly host succumbed to the allure of rebellion and fell from divine grace, it is important to debunk the myth that surrounds this celestial diaspora. It was none other than Lucifer and his sibling who received this first descent. The souls cast out of the heavens alongside the brothers were lost souls with no place in the heavens. Never were they angels. Their God saw an opportunity, Lucifer would be charged with the stewardship of those restless souls drifting aimlessly in the vast sky, prior to the formation of hell.

Seizing the opportunity in Lucifer's betrayal, the Almighty forged a new kingdom – one created with the notion of punishment in mind. Lucifer embraced the realm bestowed at his feet, his very own kingdom.

However, amid all the grandeur and majesty of Lucifer's newfound lordship, there arose an unexpected casualty of magnificent treason of his own brother – Atreus. Possessed of mysterious virtues not unlike his brother and unshakable loyalty to him, Atreus represented the burdened twinship of blood and inevitable doom, whose legacy condemned the pair to wander the sphere of immortality for the ages yet to come. The reason Atreus himself was cast out is a subject of debate amongst historians. Most agreed that he was blindly loyal to his older brother. So, a loyal subject, Atreus descended to hell with his brother intending to prove his loyalty and to help formulate a nascent kingdom.

However, hundreds of years later, Atreus became part of the historical record once more, under the sands of the flowing time. While Lucifer's sinister influence came to Earth; historians remain stumped by the gap in time concerning Atreus's time in the underworld and his eventual ascension back to earth.

The fate of Atreus after making it back to earth is one that is unknown. While many theories circulate the kingdoms, the truth of the deity may remain unknown for centuries to come.

Amara blinked, having not heard of the brother of Lucifer until his presence in the book. *He ascended back to earth? Was that even possible?* She took notes:

See; Atreus, cross reference Deimos.

Were they the same person?

A massive bird flew overhead which drew her attention away from her book. Its dark wings took in the light and seemed to harness it as it glided away. She watched a few of the conscripts chat amongst themselves as they emerged from their break locations and drifted toward their next class. She sighed, dreading going to Cathmore's lessons. He wouldn't even look at her, he was completely shut down mentally, and he had not been on the watchtower once since the night he brushed her hair.

As though he materialized directly out of her mind, Cathmore turned the corner of the building. He took long decisive strides, daggers hanging off of his weapons belt that hugged his narrow waist. He pulled on his Praeceptor jacket which had squared shoulders and clad him in darkness. The buckles on his boots caught and reflected the sun, his hair tousled by the wind. He was achingly beautiful, his blue and silver eyes fixed straight ahead. She admired his long eyelashes, high cheekbones, and easy confidence he carried with him. He was so heartbreakingly beautiful, as though he had stepped out of a dream, perfectly formed and unreal.

He didn't seem to notice her, even though he came within about two feet of where she sat. She narrowed her eyes at him, angry at his sudden disregard for her existence.

"Killian." A woman grabbed his arm and turned him to face her. *Bold.* She said something else that Amara couldn't hear. He smiled at whatever she said, Amara able to see his perfectly sculpted face as he interacted with the woman whose back was turned to her.

She glanced down at her notepad, trying not to be nosy. After a moment, she looked back up, able to gather that the woman was a Magister and had a few years on him. The woman shifted her weight onto one foot and ran a hand down his leather jacket sleeve. Amara couldn't make out Cathmore's reaction but he didn't jerk his arm away.

Suddenly Cathmore's eyes met Amara's. Her face heated with embarrassment. Cathmore grabbed the woman's hand and led her to the side of the building, out of her view. A ping of jealousy rose in her throat and angered her.

You hate him, remember you hate him. Just go back to hating him. So what if he saved you? He's an ass.

"Less than fifty hours until you are dropped into the Abyss/" Cathmore paced in front of his unit the following day. "I'm holding out hope that at least ten of you make it back." He glanced at each of the fourteen conscripts. "We have gone over what the environment is like as well as the unpredictability of the discarded Nephilim and Fallen. You should have been practicing teamwork in your weapons wielding course, and most of your pain tolerances are about where they need to be at this point in the year. There is nothing else I can offer you right now. I encourage you to rest and prepare in any way you can for the next two days," he instructed. She noticed him clenching and releasing his fist behind his back. *Was he nervous?*

"We aren't training with the other units like usual?" Molvina asked.

"No. It is highly unlikely that you will sleep during your three-day trek through the Abyss. Rest," he instructed again with a nod. "That's all for today." He dismissed them with a wave of his hand.

Before he sat them down to brief them, they worked on sparring with each other as well as some suspension exercises. He wouldn't let Amara suspend for more than a few minutes . He probably didn't want to agitate her Imperium further after what happened with Nightbane.

"Anybody else stuck on the whole ripping a feather from one of the creatures down there?" Judas turned to the group.

"Stuck on it is an understatement, I've been having nightmares about it." Juliet shook her head and bit an apple.

"I wonder if they bleed from their wings..." Avren chimed in. Amara shuddered, recalling Cathmore's magnificent wings the first night she saw him.

"It's like 'here's this impossible journey but just to make it harder, piss off a feral being'," Eros mocked playfully.

"They're all insane." Katara giggled.

"Really? I thought the Hallowed were totally well put together in the head." Amara gestured around them and earned a touché expression from her friends who couldn't help but chuckle.

Her attention turned to Praeceptor Cathmore who was putting away sparring gear. It seemed like such a... mundane task for him.

"I'll be right back," she told her friends and stood. She slowly made her way over to him, noting how nervous she was to do so. "Praeceptor, can I speak to you for a moment." The conscripts departed.

"What do you need Ashenfall? I have a prior engagement," he asked dismissively as he unwrapped his hands. Her heart sank. *Those same hands that had been gently massaging her head the week before...*

"I decided not to use the silent pardon for the Abyss Trial," she informed him. She had spent days mulling over the decision before coming to the conclusion that the next one would probably be a lot worse. He glanced over to her and pulled his leather Praeceptor jacket on.

"Okay." He nodded, indifferently. He pushed his way through the front doors of the training hall, leaving her alone in the massive space.

She couldn't understand the change in his demeanor toward her. He was treating her the way he had the first day she arrived. It was like a whole different person had been with her on the watchtower, like a different person had rescued her. She decided that it didn't matter, she wouldn't speculate over whatever he was or wasn't feeling and thinking.

I hate him, I hate him, I hate him.

Amara used her free evening to go back to the library. She pulled fiction from the shelves and flipped through them for a while, the smell of cedar and dust in the air. Eventually the section with her family name beckoned her back as though it were a living thing calling to her.

Amara was shocked to see that the book Cathmore had taken from her had found its way back to the shelf it called home. She grabbed it quickly, determined to uncover the truth it held, not stopping to ask herself when she came to desire the truth. It was a truth she had run from for so long but... She opened the book.

Don't go looking for information you aren't ready to learn, Cathmore's warning echoed.

She scanned through the book, at the bottom of one page was her mother's name-

Kaia Ashenfall—died aged 60 years. Natural manner of death, two daughters left behind:

Amara knew that the next page would have some pivotal information on her mother, she couldn't explain the feeling. As though her entire world would change if she turned the page, but she did so anyway.

Grace Ashenfall

Her aunt.

Josie Ashenfall—Deceased Aged 28 years. Manner of death: homicide. Cause of death: decapitation.

Amara dropped the book and stumbled backward, feeling like she had just taken a blow to her ribs. *Decapitation? Homicide?* Her aunt had told her it was a sickness, an illness that took her mother from her.

Amara sank to the floor, staring at the open book. *Homicide, decapitation.* The words kept replaying in her head, an endless torturous echo. *Who could have done something like that? Why?*

After a moment of trying to ground herself, to catch her breath—she picked the book back up.

See abnormal human death in human criminal records section, file JA-986B76.

The information had been under her nose for weeks, Cathmore had known the truth. He had known that she was ignorant to the fate of her mother. He had ensured that she wouldn't find out.

Anger pulsed through her as she shoved the book back into its spot and hurried to the section where her mother's file would be.

She stumbled on shaky legs, her knees unable to bear the weight of the newfound information.

Decapitation.

She shuffled through the endless files and records for nearly an hour. Hers wasn't there; it just wasn't there. *JA-986B75, JA-986B77, were there.* She looked into them hoping that maybe there was a misprint and that the JA also stood for Josie Ashenfall but found other names instead.

One of them had been murdered by another human for stealing, one of them by an unknown assailant. She tossed the files down and sat with her head buried in her knees. Some part of her always knew that the truth would cost her the small amount of peace of mind she still had. It shattered in front of her though, as she imagined the beautiful bright-eyed woman whom she favored—lying on the floor with her head ripped from her body.

Astoundingly though, the information didn't make her feel broken, it made her feel as though she had finally found a piece of her story that had been missing. She felt like there was some resolution there, like wanting to know the truth about her mother finally gave her purpose.

It had to have been Cathmore, he must have taken the file so that she couldn't know more. It was like he was controlling how much she learned. *Why? He had no right.*

Amara wanted to hunt him down and rip his throat out but after careful consideration, she knew that's not how it would play out. She thought she could feel him briefly in her head as she considered ways to clobber him but he was gone as quickly as he peeked in.

An extremely risky idea floated to her, one that she should have let pass—but did she? *No.*

The Praeceptors usually went to the Serpents Keep at the conclusion of the work week, so her wise idea to sneak into Cathmore's chambers and find the file had no time for planning. Lights out was approaching and she knew that's when the party commenced. She hurried through the courtyard back to the dorms, catching up with Katara, Juliet, and Eros.

"Are you sneaking out with Judas tonight?" She whispered to Eros.

"Yeah, why?" He turned to her. "Sneaking out for your nightly traipse through the tunnels?" She hadn't known he saw her sneaking out.

"It's not every night," she whined.

"It's an honor system, we don't snitch on each other." He shrugged.

"But yeah, I have somewhere to go," she confirmed. They sat on his bunk; the girls lost in their own conversation left for the shower room.

"Well Avren and Beck haven't left with you in a while..." he started.

"You knew about that?" she asked in shock.

"Of course you little harlot, play the field," he joked, she gasped.

"No, no, we didn't." She choked on a laugh, horrified that he must not be the only one thinking she did both of the men that night.

"You didn't?" he asked as though she were lying. "But you had a hickey..."

"Okay, I kissed Avren but we got caught." She caved. Her cheeks flamed thinking about being enthralled with Cathmore on the roof of the watchtower.

"Ohhhh," he said as though it made sense. "Cathmore dealt your punishments that evening, that's why his fingers were broken then?" he asked.

"Yes, idiot, and I had no intention of hooking up with the both of them." She playfully popped him in the back of the head.

"So where do you run off to?" he asked. "Someone from another unit?" He prodded.

"I—" she paused thoughtfully. She didn't want to fully deny the allegation, better he think it's another conscript than... whatever the hell happened with the Praeceptor.

"I knew it!" He bounced excitedly. She just rolled her eyes.

"Are you going at eleven?" she asked. That was about an hour after lights out and usually when he and Judas would slink out of the dormitories. Eros nodded with a wide smile. R "Okay, I'll wait for a while after you go." Too many leaving at the same time would draw attention from the other units on the other side of the massive joint living dormitory.

"Don't get caught," she whispered and patted him on the back as she stood.

"You either." He smiled and kicked his legs up in the cot as he laid down.

This is so stupid. She chastised herself as she snuck through the drafty tunnels which seemed to bow inward with years of secrets. She found the entryway to Oaks Hall and hesitated. *What if it isn't even in his room, what if he didn't even take it?* Her voices of reason creep in. She decided she was already nearly there and with minimal chance of getting caught, she was going to have a quick look and leave.

Though the other side of the door was silent, she knew there was a possibility that a couple of the Nephilim stayed behind. She would need to be deathly silent and pray to whatever god was listening that they were in their chambers for the evening. To her knowledge only the library had keepers; who she had learned were Nephilim with the ability to go unseen or invisible. If they prowled the shadows of Oaks Hall too, she was done for.

The wooden door moaned in protest as she pushed gently through, nearly tripping over her own shoes as she hurried behind a magnificent weapons display case. Her time in Oaks Hall had allowed her to memorize the layout of the displays. She had full confidence in her ability to make it to Cathmore's room unseen.

She dropped into a crouch, her breathing choked to a stop, when a Praeceptor emerged from his room on the other side of the great hall. His boots announced his close proximity and then his exit as he left through the main doors. She exhaled uncomfortably and swallowed hard.

Once she confirmed she was alone, she pressed herself against a wall and took the small corridor that ended in three rooms. One of them would be Cathmore's. *Please be unlocked.* She gently clicked the door open, realizing she should have listened closer to ensure no one was in there.

The room, to her relief, was empty. It was larger than the neighboring one which she briefly occupied, but the bedroom furniture was roughly the same—his was just darker. The four poster bed had been stripped of its drapes; strips of fabric still clung to where they had been mounted. *Damn.* His bed was neatly made, a sea of black sheets and blankets. Shadows were more a part of the room than anything else, lurking in corners, alive with secrets.

He had a walk-in closet off of his room instead of a wardrobe. A massive desk with books and papers scattered amongst it promised answers to her questions. That's where she would start.

She rifled through varying notes on conscripts, ignoring the curiosity that begged her to read them, he had exercise plans for them, disciplinary records, death records from the hunt, piles of paperwork about Marlowe, and books upon books about the kingdom. *Was he not from Findaria?*

Amara laid eyes on some files with numbers on them, though none with the case number she needed. She pulled out some of the pages.

The boy was recovered from the Walstara Sea's inlet into Ravenyr. Mothers name unknown, sired child. Boy states

his mother drowned when the two of them were tossed overboard.

None of it had anything to do with her, none of them had names she recognized. She pulled open drawers. She finally found a profile on her;

Amara Ashenfall, in hiding.

Evaded first capture attempt.

Evaded second capture attempt.

Evaded third capture attempt.

Bastian Marlowe established a relationship, capture imminent.

Bastian Marlowe killed by sired child, guards successfully captured her.

Amara Ashenfall delivered to Captain Cathmore at the Sanctum Metere for the Crucible .

Nothing had anything she was looking for, nothing she didn't know. She opened a sealed envelope whose wax stamp was already broken.

> Captain, instruct others to watch the sired children of Sylas. He has joined Deimos in Ravenyr. Ensure they do not survive the Crucible; they are not worthy.

The letter was signed by a name she didn't know, presumably someone he answered to. She began trying to think of anyone who said they were sired to Sylas but drew a blank. They were going to kill them. She wanted to toss everything from his desk but resisted the urge and tried to place papers back where he had them.

He was nothing more than a puppet, he would murder on their command and he gathered intel on the sired children as they entered. Was it so they could decide who was worth keeping alive? He even hid information from her when it wasn't his place, she seethed and dug her nails into the wood of his desk.

She couldn't believe she had allowed herself to trust him even for a second. She moved over to his closet in search of any other information or her mother's file. Rows of black shirts hung on the right side. The dark purple and black Praeceptor uniform on the left, the logo of the Sanctum Metere on the shoulders. Wings erupted from a shield with an 'S' in the middle of it with intricate swirling designs, all in gold thread. She had only seen him wearing it during the hunt, the training uniforms on the other hand were more casual and the Praeceptors wore them more often.

Amara found a pile of books at the bottom of the closet and crouched down to look at them. She grabbed the bigger ones with papers hanging out of them and moved to the floor outside of the closet. She opened the first book titled 'How the Hallowed Rose to Power' and began fumbling through the pages that he stuffed into it.

Katiana Z. confirmed source, location cobalt9276redquart8. She's alive.

Amara tried to make sense of what was clearly a secret code. *Who's Katiana?* She pulled out another page.

Zalser, Katiana. Body not recovered. Murderer confessed; see statement attached.

Cathmore's handwriting accompanied the official document; *last known contact with her child; 83 years ago. False confession?*

Amara exhaled in confusion. *What did any of this mean? Who did it concern?*

She shoved those papers back into the book before examining the underlined sections of the book. He was particularly interested in the type of magic that the Hallowed used and its source. The book was spectacularly vague and unhelpful.

She flipped through more meaningless paperwork that did not concern her or her mother. *What was with all of the codes?*

Time slipped away from her and her head pounded as she tried to piece together who he was and what the hell he was up to. Perhaps she was wrong about him being a puppet, but who could tell with all of the secrets he possessed? His notes were clearly meant to be vague in the event they were ever discovered.

She jumped when she heard footsteps coming down the small corridor. *Fuck.* She threw the books into the closet which didn't have a door, and forced herself under the bed. It was a painfully tight fit but necessary because she heard him talking outside of the door.

Amara inspected a stray notebook under his bed. It was leather with a strap binding it though it was too dark to read anything in it.

She really wished she could use whatever ability she was developing to will herself out of the room. Especially when the door clicked open and Cathmore stumbled in with a giggling girl. *You have got to be kidding me.*

"I didn't know the captain got put up in such nice accommodations," the girl purred. Clearly they had been drinking. Amara watched her walk in front of him, leading him. His heavy booted feet moving gracefully behind her.

"Healers don't?" he asked, seemingly bored.

"Not human ones," she chirped.

If there were ever a moment where she wanted to evaporate from existence, she begged the god above to just do it. End her.

"Nuh uh, don't kiss me," Cathmore demanded suddenly. Amara watched the girl come down from her tiptoes. *It wasn't even the same girl that was flirting with him in the courtyard.*

"Fine." She laughed. "You're so broody," she added flirtatiously. Amara cringed, sensing that Cathmore was not having it.

"Just get on your knees." He shoved her downward and Amara could hear the girl excitedly fumbling with his pants. *Desperate,* Amara sang to herself.

Amara was making an especially tedious effort to ensure there was nothing that Cathmore could sense about her being in the room. It became harder to focus on that as the sounds of what the girl was doing to him with her mouth filled the room. Amara shoved her hands over her ears and planted her face into the wooden floor. *This is what you get, snoop,* she scoffed at herself.

It wasn't that she was particularly jealous of the girl nor that he was with someone that bothered her. It was more that she had put herself in a situation to witness it. She wasn't going to dive into the 'why' behind her nausea at what the girl was doing or the anger she felt to hear him enjoying it... she was simply in a bad situation. A situation that, come to think of it, she had no idea how she was going to get out of.

After what felt like forever, they finished their little escapade though from what she gathered... Cathmore didn't *finish* at all, but frustratingly made the girl stop.

Amara didn't have the stomach to listen to the girl ask him for another chance before she left the room and he kicked the door closed. Since he wasn't leaving the room, she would just wait for him to fall asleep. She waited for a while until he kicked off his shoes, pants, and shirt before going into the shower room. *Ugh.*

She hesitated for a long while as she tried to talk herself into sneaking out while he showered. Once the shower had been on for a few minutes and she was sure he was inside of it, she slowly crawled out from beneath his bed. She forgot the notebook, though, and turned back for it. It was at that moment that the shower turned off, of course. She pushed herself back into her hiding place. *Shit.*

She was painfully trying to adjust herself when he emerged from the room, steam bellowing out behind him, the smell of mint and soap filling the air. She could see from the distance that he had a towel wrapped around his waist. Not that she particularly cared for certain things Cathmore did, but she didn't mind the view. Especially when he dropped the towel and fumbled through his drawers for under shorts. The bed signaled to her that he had laid down so all she had to do was wait for any sign that he had fallen asleep.

The room fell dark when his bedside lantern was turned off and she exhaled slowly. *He doesn't know you're here, just stay still and quiet until he falls asleep.* She controlled her breathing very carefully, all too aware of it in the silence of his dark bedroom. Ten minutes passed, then twenty, then thirty. She still didn't hear him snoring or any kind of breathing to indicate that he was asleep or awake. She was straining painfully hard not to project any kind of thoughts into his mind.

Amara turned her focus away from thoughts of her mother, which originally placed her in the complicated situation. Instead, she found herself wondering if she would ever get to use his body to distract herself again. She had assumed that she would never want sex again after Marlowe and perhaps she wasn't ready yet, but being in Cashmore's room felt so... wrong, and so intimate. She couldn't help but be concerned as to why the 'wrongness' of it made her more excited as she remembered their bodies connecting in that way. *This is exactly the kind of thoughts to avoid, idiot.*

She unfortunately had little to do under his bed but to fight off the memories of the way he felt inside of her. It was a welcome series of memories because for the last week she could only imagine her body being taken against her will. She remembered their panting, his nails in her hips, the way it felt like he was stretching her past her body's limits...

She was able to divert her mind for a moment, forcing herself to think about the Abyss instead. She heard Cathmore take a deep breath which sparked the memory of his labored breathing during their heated make out session. She almost hated how easily she was aroused by the thought of him... *almost.*

"Dirty dirty girl," came a deep growl from the darkness of Cathmore's chambers.

Oh fuck. She had never heard his voice *that* deep and primal.

She felt a hand grab her ankle from somewhere at the head of the bed. She skittered away to the opposite side, successfully breaking her leg free. Adrenaline coursed through her veins, excitement followed, and both completely blinded her judgment. Crawling out from under the bed proved not to be the brightest way to get away from her Praeceptor.

She got to her feet only to be snatched up by him, one arm around her stomach, his hand covering her mouth. She hadn't even heard him get off of the bed.

"Why are you in my room, Amara?" he whispered into her ear, drawing out her name. He sat her down when she kicked against him and waited for an answer.

"Well, I'm not here for..." she gestured at his bed, "that." She crossed her arms. *Not that she'd turn him down,* she thought to. He stood before her, his undershorts hanging low off of his hips, his bare chest more cut than she thought it had been, heat rolling off of his body and calling to her.

Amara spotted something on his right hip bone, dark ink letters that she had never seen before. It was so low that his pants usually hid it. She wanted to reach out and run her fingers over his firm silky skin. She wanted to know what it said but it was in a different language.

"I came to search your room," she said. He was watching her examine his body and it was so sensual.

He tilted his head in curiosity, his interest piqued. She knew the punishment for the truth could be detrimental but she was already caught, maybe he would give her information.

"And did you find what you were looking for?" He crossed his arms. The muscles flexing distractingly beneath his skin. She swallowed hard.

"I know that you knew my mother was murdered. I want to know what you did with her file about the homicide," she demanded. He looked taken aback for a moment, probably from her audacity to take such a demanding tone with him.

"What makes you think I did anything with it?" He shrugged. She stood and shoved him, his skin on her fingertips, heated. His eyes darkened as he watched her stomp over to his desk.

"You have all of these other files on people and you wouldn't let me read my family's history the first day I found it." She held up a stack of three files. "It's my family Cathmore, you have no right!" She exclaimed, slamming down the files. The edge of his mouth tilted up, a small smile.

"I don't?" He stepped toward her.

"No!" She wouldn't back down.

"As long as you are my charge, I have every right in the world to you," he declared. "That includes snooping around in your past, your family, breaking your fragile little body so it's worthy of transition, and even protecting you."

"I am not *your* anything." She shoved him and stomped to the door.

Once again he gathered her up with arms around her stomach. She kicked against him and he let out a groan of annoyance.

"Yes you are *mine,*" he growled the word possessively. "You and my thirteen other conscripts. I hold the key to whether you live." He tightened his arm until he stopped breathing. "Or die." He snaked his hand up to her throat and squeezed.

Her vision blacken as his strong arm restricted her ribs while his hand choked her mercilessly. She stopped kicking against him, her heart hammering as though trying to break free for oxygen. She was all too aware of his bare skin against her body. She didn't understand the primal need that stirred between her legs for him, even while he threatened her.

Finally he released her and she dropped to her knees, gasping for air. Her lungs screamed and burned in response to the long lost oxygen and she glared up at him.

"Are you done? With this little temper tantrum?" He waved his hand in the air.

"Are you?"

"I don't have your mother's folder." He sighed. "I did have it, but it was taken. She looked at him as though he were a liar. "I thought it was Marlowe but it hasn't been recovered yet."

"What did…" she stammered. "What did it say? Did it say who…" Amara asked as she finally got back to her feet.

"No, it's unsolved," he said simply. She exhaled shakily, wiping away a tear before it fell.

"Well, not that this hasn't been fun." She straightened. "Which it hasn't by the way—I'm leaving." She turned from him.

"You know I am fully within my rights to kill you for coming in here don't you?" He growled as he appeared in front of her so fast she slammed into him. *What the…*

"But you won't," her words fell quicker than she could stop them. He took her words as a challenge and somehow just as he grabbed for her, she evaporated and appeared on the other side of the room.

Holy shit she had done it again. Cathmore looked at her in shock and fascination.

"Phasing," he breathed.

"What?" She doubled over in pain, her entire body vibrating from the exertion of power.

"That's your Imperium, or part of it…" He walked over to her and lifted her hand before letting it drop. "You basically just did to yourself what I can do to objects," he explained. *Whoa.*

"So you can do it too?" she asked, referring to how quickly he appeared in front of her a moment ago.

"No, Nephilim in general just have enhanced speed," he explained. "But you can't keep doing that, if your sire picks up on it too soon…" he trailed off. "It could be dangerous. So just try not to use it, I will keep my promise to work with you on it." He nodded.

"Okay," she agreed.

"No one can know." His voice lowered. She became aware of how close his body was to her.

"No one..."

He placed a finger over her mouth. "Now, I'd like you to tell me what you were thinking about while you were hiding under *my* bed," he whispered.

She looked up at him through long eyelashes and decided to once again be brave with him, to take what she wanted. She slid her tongue up the length of his finger before taking it into her mouth completely. His lips parted as he met her eyes, desire burning in his own.

"You're breathtaking, Ashenfall." He exhaled in awe. The words warmed her core, both turning her on and comforting her on a level she had never felt before.

He dropped his hand from her mouth before grabbing her around the waist and kissing her hard. It made her wonder why he wouldn't let the other girl kiss him. But she didn't want to stop and ask, she welcomed his greedy claiming kiss, their tongues fighting for dominance.

She ran her hands over his body and up into his hair, begging him to be closer, to kiss her harder. She shouldn't be in her Praeceptor's room, she shouldn't be kissing him, they both knew the consequences could be deadly, but just as it had been on the roof—they couldn't stop.

It was like their bodies ignited one another's, flame feeding flame, neither yielding to the other. She pushed on his chest, urging him to walk backward toward the bed, and he did. He fell backwards and she scrambled out of her pants before climbing on top of him, straddling him. She pushed against his erection, teasing as she kissed and bit at his chest. The fabric of their undergarments provided the perfect barrier for her to tease him.

"I was trying to stay away from you." He grunted. He tugged her shirt over her head, not the least bit phased by the scars on her abdomen just like he hadn't been by the ones on her back. "This is a dangerous game," he purred. She moaned her agreement, exhilarated by the possibility of getting caught.

He flipped her onto her back and began a slow tour down her body with his tongue. He ripped her panties from her skin like they were nothing before spreading her legs and placing his perfect mouth at the apex of her thighs. Amara moaned a little too loud which caused him to stop and look up at her with a warning glare.

He dipped his tongue into her and she could feel herself soaking his tongue. He groaned his pleasure when she bucked her hips so that she could ride his face. She came as he relentlessly devoured her, biting into his blanket so that she wouldn't scream.

"I could tear you apart," he threatened, crawling up her body and spreading her legs around his hips.

"Please do," she begged.

She wanted him to take away her ability to think again just like he had that night in the watchtower. She wanted the world to disappear and for it to just be the two of them. The Abyss Trial was approaching and with a strong chance of her not walking away from it, she needed to feel a moment of liberation. She scrambled for reasons to hate him, but came up short. She couldn't remember.

"If you need me to stop, I will," he said . She knew it was because of what she had gone through.

"You won't break me, Praeceptor," she wrapped her legs around his hips, urging him downward.

She gasped as he slowly pushed into her, somehow he was bigger than she remembered, stretching her more than she remembered. It was mind-blowing each time he thrusted into her; she clawed at his back as she took him. He sped up, taking her harder and faster, she had to bite into his shoulder to keep from screaming. She let out little whimpers against his skin, she focused on tightening around him each time he withdrew which earned appreciative moans.

Cathmore switched positions, rolling over so that she was on top of him. She had to slowly lower herself onto him, the position allowing him to be as deep as possible.

"Fuck," she exhaled, forcing herself down more and more until every inch of him was inside of her. He looked down in awe, biting his lip as she began riding him.

She moved from her knees to her feet so that she could ride him harder and faster. Watching him throw his head back as he gripped her breasts was enough to undo her. She exploded around him after a few minutes, collapsing onto his chest, her legs shaking. He wasn't stopping there though; he steadied her hips inches above him and began rutting deep into her. She held onto his shoulders and bit down on a scream as he ravaged her. *God.*

"Do you want me to make it hurt, brat?" He breathed, picking up the pace. She nodded eagerly. "Do you think you deserve it for sneaking into my room?" He held eye contact with her, demanding an answer.

"Yes, Praeceptor, I should be punished." She played along, excitedly.

He pulled out of her, pushing her to the side so that she sprawled onto her stomach, still panting with need. Suddenly he was gagging her with fabric... a tie maybe? He tied it around her mouth. She was just thankful she wouldn't have to focus on not screaming anymore.

He dragged her onto the hard floor, laid her on her back, and spread her legs. He looked over her hungrily before leaning down and biting the soft skin of her breast, sucking hard. She had begun to enjoy the pain when he bit down harder, causing her to squirm. The pain made her body respond to him in new ways. She bucked her hips up begging for friction when he moved his mouth down to her ribs, biting down on the soft skin below her breast.

She thrashed underneath him and clawed at his back, the burning caused her nipples to harden, he smiled when he noticed. He repeated the process a couple more times on her stomach, she had thrown her head back as she grunted, reveling in the pain that caused her clit to throb. *How was he doing this?*

She screamed loudest into the fabric when he bit her inner thigh hard and began sucking on it. She looked down at him to get a view of the raven haired god between her legs. She hadn't expected to see that the bites he made had tiny spots of blood beading from them. She could see where his teeth broke her skin.

He looked up at her, blood staining his lips pink. Her first instinct should have been to tell him to stop, to run, but she looked at him in all of his primal beauty and welcomed him inside of her once more.

Maybe she was fucked beyond belief, but she didn't care. He took her over and over again on the floor, on his desk, over his armchair, he fucked her until they were both brutalized from each other's teeth and nails.

They took out their frustrations on each other, each took their pound of flesh, moaning into the night as moonlight illuminated their naked bodies. She was healing herself by giving herself to him, by choosing who got to enjoy her body.

She knew when they were done with each other, as they lay sprawled on the floor, that for the first time in her life she had met someone as twisted and beautifully broken as she was. That realization was scarier than anything she had faced so far during the Crucible and somehow she knew that if she let it, it would cost her her life. "What does this mean?" She lazily ran her fingers over the letters on his hip.

"Evolve," was all he offered by way of explanation.

Evolve.

Chapter 18

Shadows crawled around Cathmore's unit as they latched on to one another for support while entering the Abyss. Amara accidentally kicked the back of Katara's shoe and sent them both stumbling forward into the mud.

"Come on, guys," Davian grumbled in annoyance and pulled ahead.

"Mind yourself," Erose warned him with a scowl.

"We should feed the bastard sired to a Fallen in exchange for its feathers," Davian was laughing with Molvina—who safe to say could no longer be considered a friend.

"I think your ego would be more filling for them," Eros shot back at the insufferable son of Rase.

"Big talk for someone unlikely to make it out alive, Whitvale," Davian snarked at Eros.

"Both of you shut up before they hear us," Katara snapped.

What sounded like a twig snapping about twenty yards away caused them to halt, bumping into one another. They were no better than a handful of marbles set free in a bowl. Nobody moved, everyone held their breath, and not one of them thought to put out their torches. What would be the point? If something saw them, it was too late.

She observed the dead and wilted spindly trees that had attempted to grow in the unwelcoming conditions. She supposed she'd just wither up and die if she were here for too long as well.

A small group of bats shot out of a small cave in the ceiling and upward toward the exit of the crater they were in. It wasn't exactly a crater but that wasn't far from the truth. While the Abyss had taken on a life of its own, it was formed from two fallen angels landing on Earth. The group sighed slowly and moved forward as one.

Groups of small scurrying rats pulled their attention in a million directions. She could see massive tunnels veering off in varying directions. In her mind, the impact into the earth sent shock waves outward and created tunnels connecting to the main Abyssal crater.

"How do you think the tunnels got here?" Amara asked Katara.

"Probably animals, most likely the feral angels and Nephilim that live here now," Katara mused. Also very likely.

"Ew!" Juliet gagged when her foot sank into a puddle of foul-smelling liquid.

The group paused to help her up after stepping in the deep puddle caused her to fall face forward. They began deliberating their next move. Amara was scoping out the muddy walls that towered up and over them. She was half listening to the group;

half lost in thought about the wild forty-eight hours she had spent with Cathmore. She thought about what the last thing he said to his unit;

"I know that you all can pull through this trial and come out the other side. Have each other's backs in there." He nodded at them. *"Descend."*

It was a nice sentiment but what weighed on her more was the agreement they reached during their last conversation that morning; they would have to stop sleeping together, it had to end. They both understood that as the groups of sired children grew smaller, more eyes would be upon them. If they were caught, they would be killed. Well, she would. He would be thrown into the Abyss... which loomed before her tauntingly.

"We have to get down from this ledge," Judas said. He peaked over the muddy incline, stones and sticks poking out of the mud.

The space was so expansive and unending that they had no choice but to keep moving downward which felt counterproductive. None of them had the first clue how to get out so the plan as it stood was simply; explore, don't die, get a feather, hope to find a way out.

The small group slowly slid down it into the belly of the Abyss, where it grew darker as they moved further from the summit, further from where the sun poured in. Various rocks and roots nicked at Amara's clothes. Ahead, a fraction of sunlight beckoned to them. It wasn't as much as the main chasm of the Abyss allowed in, but it lit the space to some degree.

Part of the Abyss would be tunnels of darkness, others would be opened to the sky. Amara wanted to hold off on using her candlesticks and matches as long as she could, so she kept her eyes focused on the light pouring in ahead. Rot and feces was all she could smell in the pit and it was overwhelming her senses like a thick fog surrounding her. Most of them threw their sleeves over their noses as they held onto each other and moved toward the light.

Eros jumped in response to a noise that approached from behind and Judas grabbed him to calm him. Katara and Amara whirled toward it, squinting their eyes. A small skittering noise pointed them to a rat bigger than any cat she had ever seen. It looked at her with glowing eyes before hurrying away.

"This is ridiculous, they've got us afraid of our own shadows down here," Davian scoffed.

Towering columns of rock and mud surrounded them in the dark space as he lit his torch, seemingly deciding it wasn't bright enough for him. Sharp and jagged rocks jutted from the column and they squeezed past them. Water and mud ran down the walls as though the Abyss were crying in silence. Amara swallowed hard.

She turned to look behind her to ensure everyone was still in tow when she *thunked* her head on what she assumed was a rock jutting out of one of the stone pillars. She rubbed her forehead and her eyes adjusted to the object. A rotted skull without a bottom jaw met her gaze with its Hallowed eye sockets. She yelped and jumped backward into a puddle. Davian stopped her from falling and shoved her forward in annoyance.

"What's the matter, murderess? Scared of a little ole skull?" He taunted.

She jerked away from him and in horror saw that the stone pillars towering above them were decorated like holiday trees with skulls and bones instead of jewels and carved offerings.

"It's like some kind of twisted tree offering to Hadeon like we always put up for Hallowed's day," Molvina said. Avren and the rest of the group nodded their agreement with mouths agape.

Aunt Grace never went all out with a decorated tree or altar for Hadeon for the holiday. Amara didn't have much experience with it but she had seen the black trees with glowing flowers and decorations in other people's homes.

They squeezed into a narrow tunnel to get away from the endless pillars of skulls in the massive space behind them.

Somewhere in the Abyss an awful yowling echoed and ran through them. They all froze, ducking instinctually. She didn't want to know how long the creature that made that noise had been down there and by the looks of it, her unit felt the same way. Amara, Katara, and Judas were leading the group as the cave mouth opened up once more. She was glad not to have her body pressed between someone else's and a wall again. Mud sloshed under their feet, dead trees bowed as though to welcome them into the new section of the Abyss. The trees were scabbed over and falling apart as a corpse does once life leaves it.

The new section of the Abyss was also endless, expanding outward in all directions as though they had been dropped in an underground world. She was starting to feel as though she were trapped in a paradox. Not much changed from one part of the hellscape to another. When looking up, the walls were all smooth mud and impossibly high, threatening to reach down and choke her.

Larger stone columns rose against the smooth mud walls as if they were sleeping giants. She felt small and breakable when standing next to them. Yet she found herself running a finger over the dark stone that appeared to be transparent. She was just relieved at the lack of bones within them.

Davian's torch caused a dozen sets of eyes to reflect back at them from the ceiling, just around a small opening to the sky.

"Bats," Avren whispered.

She pressed her hand to the wall, cold mud coating her palm. Maybe she hoped the walls would tell her how to get out. *Don't be ridiculous.* She had no idea how they would get out of the place but she had hope that somewhere, they would find an answer.

The Abyss isn't made to keep intelligent beings in. Cathmore had said.

She didn't realize that de-winging a Nephilim or Fallen Angel sent them into madness within minutes of the process. From her research and what Cathmore had shared, it was like they became zombified, unable to reason.

"To remove part of our wings would be to remove part of our very soul. Our life force and every ounce of power we contain is within our wings," Cathmore had said the night before as they lay entangled in his bed.

The madness only worsened with time. She couldn't help but wonder what state Marlowe would be in, if he would have the ability to reason enough to hunt her. She had no intention of finding out.

"That smell is bloody awful," Judas complained. He was right, the stench grew stronger as they traveled further into the pit.

The group made its way to where the light was pouring through a small opening nearly a thousand feet above them. They began talking—more like arguing—about the best way to go. The truth was, no one knew. All of the ways could lead out or none of them could, not to mention they couldn't solely try to avoid the creatures within the Abyss. They had to emerge with a feather pulled from one of them, leaving confrontation unavoidable.

Amara tried to focus, to think through the howling wind, arguing conscripts, and blinding stench. She put her focus on her clairvoyance, on her intuition. Another howling scream came through the tunnel up ahead to their left. She didn't know why, but she felt pulled toward it. Whatever was down there was in pain, it was stationary from the sounds of its screams. She felt like just maybe she would have a chance at pulling a feather before getting the hell out of there. They had said it took three days to cross the terrain, but she didn't see why she had to cross the Abyss to leave it. She pinned that thought for later.

"I'm going that way," she announced, pointing toward the tunnel. A gust of wind danced over her from the opening above them. She took that as confirmation from whatever god may have been watching her that she was making the right decision. Still though, chills and uncertainty danced over her.

"Leave it to the bastard one and the runner to come up with that idea," Davian scoffed.

"Fuck off, Davian," she spat.

"Make me," he bucked at her. *Was he serious?* She reeled back and kicked him in the shin.

"Listen here, Daddy's boy. I don't care what you do or where you go but I will not hesitate to shove a knife into your throat if you get in my way," she threatened after shoving him into the hard stone wall. "There's a reason they also call me the murderess," she snarled and shoved him once more, his head clunking into a rock. His eyes were wide but he nodded.

The anxiety of the situation was driving her to anger. She had less tolerance for him or for anyone.

"You want to go that way? Do you have a death wish?" Avren asked, she looked at him, surprised he cared. She ignored both him and Davian.

"I think we should go straight, keep our heads down and cover as much ground as possible," Judas said, Eros nodding in agreement.

"I don't think covering as much ground as possible is the answer. It's three days to cross the Abyss but we don't *have* to cross it to get out of it," Amara reasoned with him. He ingested the information for a moment and accepted it with a nod.

"Still, I can't in good faith go toward that screaming." Judas trembled.

A group of five decided to go ahead, so they broke off from the unit and began their hesitant track straight into the Abyss. Judas tugged Eros to follow, who stopped to talk to Amara.

"Come with us, all of you," he referred to Amara, Katara, Juliet, and even Avren whose change of heart to join her was somewhat concerning.

"I thought you were going to stay with us," Katara said to Eros and Judas.

"I'm trying, why not just go straight with us?" he pleaded.

Molvina, Davian and their small group took off to the right without saying a word to the rest of the unit. *Well fuck you guys too then.*

"I agree with Amara, left feels… correct somehow," Katara spoke up. Juliet nodded and grabbed Amara's arm. She could feel that Juliet was shaking.

"Avren?" Eros asked him as Judas waved him to follow. Amara knew that this separation may be the last time she saw some of them.

"Going straight feels too easy." He shook his head. "I'm going with them."

"All right, I'll see you guys on the other side," Eros exhaled nervously. They all exchanged hugs and Eros took Judas' hand into the darkness. Amara wanted to scream at him not to, every step he took seemed to tug at an invisible cord tethered to her organs. Still, their group was trudging forward.

"Before we go in there, you two need to figure out your shit," Katara told Avren and Amara who glanced at each other. "Avren, you've been pissed off since finding out what she did. You need to get over it because otherwise I don't trust you," Katara crossed her arms.

Katara was so headstrong and blunt, she spoke with purpose, and carried herself like a goddess. When she smiled at Amara, she couldn't help but smile back—she was just that kind of friend.

Avren and Amara looked at each other, neither of them having anything to say to the other. If he wanted to hold a grudge for something that didn't involve him, fine.

"I'm not going to stab any of you in the back over this," Avren said and motioned between him and Amara.

"Famous last words," Katara scoffed.

"Seems like she's more likely to stab one of us in the back," he pointed out. It felt like he dealt a punch straight to her stomach. Amara could sense the hurt coming off of Avren that Katara didn't believe him, the anger that she would think he was capable of hurting one of them. "Did you hear what she said to Davian?"

"You need to consider the possibility that you don't understand her or what happened with the person she killed," Katara got into Avren's face, sneering.

"And you do? She hasn't told us anything about why that shit happened Kat!" He reasoned. *He wasn't wrong.*

"She paid for her crime. That's all I need to know," Juliet jumped to her defense, tugging Katara away from Avren.

"He's not going to turn on us and now is not the time to talk this shit out, okay?" Amara sighed with an arm on Katara's armored chest. She looked at her with uncertainty. Avren just scoffed.

"Fine, let's do this," Katara unsheathed her longsword.

Wings beat overhead above the Abyss, undoubtedly the Nephilim watching over them. None of the Hallowed joined the trial which took away a certain stress factor in Amara's opinion. She couldn't help but wonder if there was something big brewing amongst the Hallowed since Sylas abandoned them. It wasn't that anyone said there was trouble afoot, more like a feeling.

They pressed on slowly into the small cave opening, having to cover their ears as the screaming became louder. Amara pushed in front to be next to Katara so that they could face whatever the cave opened up to together. The group was physically shoved backward when another scream bellowed through the chamber. After pushing against the sound waves, it took them over half an hour to reach the source of the noise. Juliet practically fell into Avren's arms when a snake slithered past them.

"Oh hell no." Katara stomped. "I can do feral angels, I can accept damn near certain death, but snakes?" She shuddered and watched it disappear into a hole.

Amara pushed forward into another blood-curdling howl, eager to see past the large boulder that blocked their path. She motioned for her group to wait while she took a look. She couldn't have prepared herself to see the state of the being before her.

He was just about to release another scream when he seemingly sensed that they were in his vicinity. The thing looked human, with rotted black wings draped onto the ground. She could make out maggots and worms wriggling within the feathered extremities. It was as though his transgressions were trying to crawl their way out of him only to be distracted by the taste of his savory rotting flesh.

It was obvious where his wings had been sliced at the base, where a dagger severed his source of life and power. Worse than any of that though, he hung by a thick chain around his neck, even stronger chains around each thigh, the skin festering and blistering where the rusted metal dug into him. Her heart ached. *How long had he been here?*

Why did she care?

Amara thought the placement of the chains was odd until further inspection revealed their purpose: to force him onto his knees. The positioning in the cave walls was extremely meticulous. His limbs tried desperately to rot out of the chains, but his stubborn immortality would let him heal just enough to keep him there, keep him suffering. He growled and lunged in Amara's direction. His eyes were bulbous, as though trying to escape his skull. They were red with dried blood around them. She swallowed the fear that was creeping its way up her throat.

He struggled against the chains, causing loud clanging to echo around them. It was as if he were begging for help, for reprieve from being forced into that position for so long. She couldn't even make out his features because of how deteriorated his skin was. *Why were his abilities taken but his immortality wasn't?* She surmised that it was because the Hallowed Fallen willed it so. A torture of such magnitude could only be orchestrated by them.

Amara took slow steps in his direction, noting his hands were bound behind his back. He was a Fallen Angel, not a Nephilim—a

"Rogue Fallen" as the Hallowed labeled them. But before the labels came into play, he was simply an angel that was cast out and did not choose to take ownership over humans. She thought that to be more noble than what the Hallowed did even though she could never voice it. Then again, the Fallen creature before her could easily have been one of the many that took joy in wreaking havoc on humans. She sighed; there was no way for her to know his story as he rotted before her.

"He's chained, we can take the feathers from him," Juliet whispered. Amara clenched her fist, it felt far too easy.

How unfortunate—he was cast to the earth among his siblings, only to be condemned by them. The Hallowed had turned their backs on their fallen kin, who were once their equals in every way—at least until the Hallowed struck that deal... or stole magic... or both. It was all so convoluted.

Was this the cost of not wanting to be a part of it? An eternity in a rotting body? She felt sick.

The thing jumped and snarled at her, trying to pitch itself forward but failing. She could see that his skin had begun decomposing from where his knees made contact with the ground, leaving the bones exposed. She took a couple more steps toward him, taking in every detail, knowing that she would recall the magnitude of his suffering for the rest of her life.

There were no feathers on the ground around him, they would have to take them off of him. It was their best shot. She knew only the most lethal of the Fallen and Nephilim had been chained, not all of them would be immobilized.

"Holy fucking shit!" Juliet screamed from behind her.

Amara whirled around to see a humanoid creature on all fours leap into the air and tackle Katara. She let out a squeal as her sword clattered to the ground, the creature that was chained seemed to become excited by the presence of the smaller being. He huffed and snorted. Foam and twitching maggots fell from his mouth.

Avren tackled the thing off of Katara, in a grandiose gesture that was entirely unlike him. Amara sent a dagger flying through the air at the creature. It was small, fast, and was murmuring something. Still, Amara's dagger landed in its chest.

"Sired..." it spat. "Children," it croaked and writhed around on the ground. It was Nephilim, not a Fallen. The creature pulled the dagger from her chest and prepared to pounce on Katara who had gotten back to her feet.

"Can the Nephilim be killed?" Katara whirled on Amara with her longsword in hand.

"Only some of them—some of us—are immortal! Remember that!" Amara exclaimed. She sprinted toward the thing and rolled it, jabbing the dagger into its gut. Amara landed on top of it, pinning it to the ground. The smell of decay and feces wafting from it. "Just try!" She screamed. The thing bit at Amara's face, narrowly missing her. Its flesh slid off of its arms as Amara fought to keep her still, the creature behind them let out another deafening scream. *Shut the fuck up.*

Katara brought down her sword into the creature's skull, its eyes widening before going vacant. Amara jumped off of her. Wiping her hands on her pants—not wanting to know what bodily fluids oozed out from the decaying skin.

"Did it work?" Juliet clung to Avren. The creature tied to the cave seemed to respond with a taunting chuckle but Amara was sure she was just making things up. Katara removed her sword, all of them cringing at the squelching noise that accompanied it.

For a moment, they were sure the creature was dead until it started squirming again. Avren charged over to it before it stopped struggling and squealing.

"Go for its heart, its brain, remove its limbs. Something will immobilize it!" He ordered and dug his curved dagger into the things chest. It grabbed and scratched at Avren's arms, Katara drove her longsword into its head again which worked to stop its movement.

"I think as long as you leave it in the brain, it keeps it down," Juliet chimed in, clearly not wanting to touch it.

"Give me the ax," Amara demanded of Juliet who did so with shaking hands.

The thing laid before them with a dagger in the heart and brain but they couldn't just leave their weapons in it, they needed them. Amara held her breath, pushed down the urge to vomit and began hacking at its neck with the ax.

"That might work," Avren breathed and pulled his dagger free from its heart. Katara steadied its head with her boot, it took three more hits to free it from its body.

Amara panted before turning around to vomit. The things blood had splattered all over them and she could see all of its bones and tendons in its neck... she vomited again.

They sighed with relief when it never regained mobility.

"We can't do that for every creature we encounter/" Katara shook her head.

"She's right, if there's more than one of them, we won't stand a chance," Amara confirmed to the other two.

"So wait, was that one immortal or not?" Juliet asked.

Katara, Avren, and Amara collectively shrugged. *Not anymore.*

"It may have been immortal but that doesn't mean invincible," Amara realized.

"You're absolutely right you fucking beautiful genius!" Katara pulled her into a hug. "Of course the Praeceptors conveniently forgot to mention that," she threw her hands in the air in amusement. Amara laughed.

"Still not easy to kill," Juliet pointed out. Katara grunted.

"We need to get the feathers from that one and then start the hike out of here/" Avren pointed to the chained one. He said it like it was easy, as if they already had a way out.

From the depths of the Abyss they heard a group of sired children scream. It was hard to know how far away they were or what unit they were a part of but whatever they were facing was horrific. Amara and her group crouched down and waited for the screams to stop. The suspended Fallen Angel just thrashed against its chains.

They laid low for a while before Amara stood and took a step in the direction of the chained Fallen, who tilted its head in acknowledgment of her bravery. Avren abruptly grabbed her arm to stop her.

"Let me go first." He nodded.

The sunlight overhead gave his brown hair that glow she liked so much. He wore a black trench coat over his trial leathers just like the rest of them. He looked handsome in a way that made her heart hurt as he departed the group to size up the creature.

"Those eyes, I've seen those eyes before." A deep wicked voice chuckled into her mind. She jumped, visibly enough for Juliet to steady her. Avren got closer to the creature, opting to crouch down and try for a feather at the end of its wing.

"Who are you?" she asked, stepping closer to the creature, to the one speaking to her. *"Why can you connect with me?"*

"Amara!" Katara snapped, trying to pull her backward. Amara tilted her head, mirroring the creature who sniffed at her. She stepped forward again, within arm's reach of the creature. She wouldn't be so brave if his hands weren't bound.

"A peculiar scent you carry," the voice chuckled. *"You are not alone within your mind,"* [

Somehow she knew what was going to happen before it did, "Avren!" She screamed.

The creature reached out with a hand from behind his back and sliced Avren down the side of his face. *His arms were never bound; it was a trick.* Avren stumbled backward, screaming and holding his face. He hadn't even gotten to touch the creature's feathers. *Fuck fuck fuck.*

Blood poured from him, even through his hand as he held it over his eye. Juliet and Katara dragged him backward, fumbling with whatever supplies they could find in their packs to help him. Avren thrashed and twisted under them.

"My eye!" He screamed a raw helpless sort of scream. Amara looked back, two of the claws had sliced straight through his eye. The deep gashes leading from his forehead, over his right eye, and down his cheek.

"Shhhh, Shhh, Avren, breathe for me." Juliet calmed him.

The creature made a laughing sound, sending Amara into a blind fit of rage. She stomped back to Katara and snatched her longsword from the ground.

"Not so fast child of…" he started probably thinking it would stop her. But it did the opposite. She pulled a dagger from her belt, inhaled a quick steadying breath, and flung it forward. It struck true, hitting him in his bulbous right eye and effectively shutting up his talking in her mind.

"You have no right!" She screamed and sprinted up to the creature, damning the consequences. She spun the sword in her grip and brought it down, severing its arm off. An image flashed in her mind of their Praeceptor teaching them a similar move. The being screamed so powerfully that it knocked her backwards.

Blood as black as night poured out of the gaping wound where its arm was, offering a pool of reflection for the creature to see itself in. She grinned; her thoughts seemed to influence him to do so.

With a glance down and the first time seeing what he had become, he let out a horrified yowl. The sound seemed to reach out and pin them all to the floor of the cave.

She recovered quickly, the thing reaching for her with its remaining arm, slicing violently, and spitting in her direction. It pulled on the chains, breaking through its bones, but it didn't care as it tried to get to her. *Oh no.*

More blood shot from his neck and thighs where bone found its way through his delicate skin. She watched with wide eyes as it destroyed itself to get to her.

"Katara! Little help here!" she exclaimed.

Her friend came running with two short swords, understanding her need to remove his other arm if they were going to get feathers. After a few failed attempts with thanks to his thrashing and screaming—Amara thrusted the longsword forward into its skull, right next to the dagger.

"That didn't work," Katara said in a panicked sing-songy voice as she danced around him, trying to grab feathers while Amara jerked her sword out. It was growing weaker though, unsuccessfully freeing himself from the chains. She watched in horror as his flesh seemed to heal *around* the rusted metal.

"Just be still!" Juliet was yelling at Avren behind them who was screaming. *For fucks sake.*

Finally after taking a number of slices on her legs and stomach, she severed his last remaining free hand. She was putting a lot of faith in the chains on his legs and neck to hold him still while they pulled feathers.

"Now!" She instructed. She and Katara yanked a handful of feathers from each of his wings.

The action resulted in a bellowing scream that shook the entirety of the cave they were in, rocks began falling from above, the ground below them vibrating violently. They turned to Juliet who was hauling Avren up, his face wrapped on one side.

"Go go go!" Katara screamed as the ground wobbled beneath their feet.

They gathered their backpacks, counting the medical supplies as a loss. The cave was coming down around them as they sprinted for the direction they had entered through.

They knew they couldn't go out of the Abyss the way they entered, that tunnel was sealed after their unit came through it. But there were more, somewhere. It would just take a hell of a lot of thought to figure out where.

It wasn't made to keep intelligent beings in.

The group darted for a massive opening to the right, turning them away from where they had entered and away from the cave that was falling inward on itself. They ran for as long as they could before they had to drop into the mud for a break. Katara and Amara still had handfuls of feathers secured in tight grips.

Juliet and Katara cleared the area they were in, not seeing anything of danger. Very little light was in the cave so Katara pulled out and lit a small lantern she packed. All of them sat panting in silence as they caught their breath.

"I have four." Katara held up the feathers.

"I grabbed three." Amara held hers up. They handed Juliet and Avren theirs. The question of what to do with the other three hung in the air between them.

"You keep two on you and I'll keep one on me," Katara said to Amara. "That way if we come across someone else on the way out and they need one, we can help."

"I think some of them would kill for our feathers... if they found us before getting one of their own," Avren said, grunting as he slouched against the muddy wall.

"We keep it secret then, for as long as we can," Amara agreed with him. "Let me look at your eye." She scooted beside him. He hesitated for a moment but allowed her to. Katara pulled Juliet to the side and they turned around to give the two some privacy.

"I can't see out of it and it hurts so bad." His voice was shaky as though he had been holding in the fear and pain. She unwrapped the bandage from around his head.

Just as she had suspected before, the eyeball was completely mutilated. When she removed the bandage, blood pulsed its way out of it. She grabbed at the canteen she had managed not to touch for the entirety of the eight hours which earned a look of horror from Avren.

"I'm going to clean it out," she whispered. He shook his head, pleading with her not to do it. She couldn't imagine the pain he was already in. "Avren, I don't want it to get infected." She shooed his hand away when he tried to block her.

"Bite down on this and try to stay quiet, okay?" She handed him a rolled up shirt from her bag. She glanced back to see Juliet and Katara conversing behind a large rock.

She tilted his head back and began letting the water trickle downward into the eye socket, washing blood and dirt out of it. Avren struggled and grunted into the cloth of her shirt. He twisted his hand into her coat, and then went limp.

"Avren." She shook him. "Hey." He had passed out. She shook him again and he slowly came to.

His eyeball had been cut nearly all the way through, revealing to her what the inside of one actually looked like. She tried not to show any fear or disgust so as not to worry him. Her insides flipped as though she needed to vomit again even if her stomach were empty.

"Okay, I need to pack the eye socket and re-wrap it," she said calmingly, giving him a sip of the water. She reached into her bag for bandages, unsure of the proper procedure for an eye that had been nearly torn out, but determined to do her best with what she had. *Clean and dress the wound. Keep moving until you are safe,* was one of Nightbane's instructions.

"There are no healers here, not even outside of the Abyss." He sighed.

"We are going to get out of here, Praeceptor Cathmore will know what to do," she reassured him, he nodded.

"Amara/" Katara jogged up to her. "There's a stream down that way but Juliet found this." She handed her a clump of bright green moss. "She said it can help prevent infection."

"How do you know that?" Avren asked Juliet who walked up behind Katara.

"I took the liberty of reading about surviving in the wild. Plants were a big part of that." Juliet smiled , a couple strands of red hair framing her round face.

Juliet helped her place the moss carefully into his eye and then they packed as much cloth into the eye socket as they could, wrapping it tightly. They repeated the steps for the deep cuts on his face as well.

"Thank you." He smiled weakly. Half of his once glorious face was torn up—not that it took away from his attractiveness per se...but it was tragic that such a beautiful person could be torn open so violently. "Amara—" Juliet and Katara told them they would be at the stream on the other side of the rocks.

"Avren, look," she interrupted.

"Just let me talk," he insisted. "I was more upset that you didn't tell me than by what you had to do. I know murders happen when sired children try to escape the Crucible... I get it. I just thought we had gotten closer than that." She sat cross-legged in front of him, their knees touching. The stench of betrayal rolled off of him, leaving a bitter taste in her mouth.

"I just didn't want it advertised, some people knew and some didn't. I didn't want it to define me," she explained. "Especially not to you." She brushed some of his hair out of the bandage, out of the blood.

"I know there's someone else." He sighed. That, she knew, was more the root of his issues than her omission of the truth. He leaned his head back against the curved wall behind him.

"What?" She breathed, not knowing what to say. The topic would have been hard to cover anyway but he was in such a fragile state.

"I saw the bites and hickeys on you in the shower room," he pointed out. Despite her efforts to keep herself turned away from everyone, the ones on her ass couldn't be hidden as well. "And after you were taken, you didn't seek me out to talk to me like usual, so I knew you had found comfort somewhere else."

His words were filled with pain—pain she hadn't realized she was causing, pain that flowed from him and back into her. That was the curse of her clairvoyance, the burden of being an empath. Whenever she hurt someone, she would feel it all: the sting, the depth, and every sharp edge of the suffering she inflicted.

"You seemed so mad to find out what I had done, I was giving you space," she pleaded. She didn't want to lose her friend. "And, I was just... distracting myself," she said by way of explaining the marks on her.

It's not like she was in some committed relationship with their Praeceptor, they weren't even in a relationship, she would barely even call it a friendship. They were just using each other's bodies for fun and that had ended. Besides that, she still had reservations about Cathmore's position within the royal guard and how committed he was to the Hallowed Fallen. For that reason alone, they would never see eye to eye, and that's why she knew it was right for them to stop fooling around.

"With who?" He shrugged, as if not understanding why she wouldn't use him for a distraction, as if he were the best and easiest option. Which he wasn't wrong about, but still.

"It doesn't matter, Avren. I care about you and I want us to be okay. I want both of us to come out of this alive." She gestured to the Abyss around them, water dripping from over-head.

"I get it." He nodded, holding the side of his face.

"It's over with the other person anyway," she admitted. She fidgeted with her fingers, a habit that he knew was a nervous one for her. He tilted his head, perplexed.

"Oh, I'm sorry?"

"Don't be, it was just a fling." She nudged his shoulder and he smiled. He had perfect teeth and those same smile lines shaped his mouth like she remembered. She found herself smiling too, she was a different person with Avren, a happier person. "You're going to be okay." She rubbed his shoulder after seeing his smile fade in response to the pain.

Amara knew that Avren was trying to make peace with the eventuality of losing that eye. She couldn't imagine the fear and uncertainty he was feeling so she scooted to sit closer to him and rested her head on his shoulder. He leaned his head on hers and exhaled, seemingly content. Another emotion was present in him then, a sweeter one. It wasn't lust, not desire. It tasted like wild flowers. *Did he feel safe? Comfortable?* She had no idea how to identify emotions even though her ability to sense them was growing stronger. *Ugh.*

Amara could tell by his soft breathing that Avren had dozed off, so she gently laid his head against the wall. She quietly moved over to where Katara and Juliet were conversing quietly.

"I expected it to get colder down here," Amara said.

"We did too, but we're deep underground." Katara shrugged.

"He fell asleep, for now," Amara informed them, dipping her canteen in the stream. She made sure to sit where she could watch Avren.

"We were talking about the best way out and this is going to sound crazy..." Katara started.

"I think we can climb out and it would be faster and safer than searching for a route out of here," Juliet chimed in.

Amara looked behind her, where just outside of their little cave, the Abyss mouth was probably five hundred feet above them. Scaling it would be deeply challenging.

"And how would we do that?" The rock faces on the inside of The Abyss were less rock and more wet mud from the moisture underground.

"We can break branches off of these trees and use them to stab into the mud to pull ourselves up," Juliet paced around the few dying trees, snatching the thicker branches. Amara knew they would not hold their weight; there was no way it would work.

"We would need something stronger, those branches are dying," Amara pointed out.

"Okay, I agree, the branches won't work but she's onto something," Katara began. "So I was thinking about what we could find that was stronger than sticks..." she paused to look at Juliet. "No offense." She smiled. "What about bones?"

"Bones?" Juliet and Avren—who had woken up—said in unison.

"I've seen them scattered here and there; they are stronger usually." Katara shrugged. She wasn't wrong but it felt so... morbid.

"Okay." Amara sighed, unable to think of a better option. "Let's start looking for strong ones. I say we follow the stream; it must be heading somewhere."

The group agreed to rest for a short while, especially Avren who was so gravely injured, and then pick up following the stream. Amara offered to keep watch first while the three of her friends dozed off. She was too wired to sleep and the faint echoes of screams from The Abyss made her wonder how anyone rested in the place.

Wind whistled incessantly through their chosen cave and she watched the slow flowing stream. The water was bright blue, nearly iridescent. She watched for tadpoles or frogs but found none. Only small insects made their presence known. She had an awful sinking feeling that just wouldn't go away, a choking fear of their environment. *Maybe she should have taken the pardon.*

Amara sat on a flat stone and cleared her mind. She reached out for something, any feeling that would tell her what to do and where to go. She could feel the warmth of sleep that usually accompanied the taste of cinnamon coming from her friends, though fear emanated from them as well. She felt a duty to them that she couldn't explain, as though she owed it to them to ensure that they survived too. Maybe it was because they were the only true friends she had ever known. She knew she would lay down her life for them, which she had never been willing to do for another person.

Amara couldn't have imagined that the Crucible would have brought her close to such good people. The thought led her down a rabbit hole of the small changes she had seen in herself since arriving there. She was stronger, both physically and mentally. Though Marlowe had taken something from her, she learned that she would not be so easily broken. She learned from him that what he took meant nothing. He took a moment of pleasure, a day of pain, and it cost him his life. He didn't take anything that mattered.

She had become more confident in her small build and the way her thick black hair fell around her heart-shaped face. She grew to like her ears that she always felt were awkwardly pointy at the top—which coincidentally Cathmore enjoyed nipping at with his teeth—and she had become more in tune with her body. She no longer felt like a bystander in her own head but as though she could take the reins and conquer anything. Something in her was changing over time and the biggest part of that was her need to survive so that she could learn what happened to her mother.

She leaned back on her palms and rolled her neck, trying to ease some of the tension. After a moment, something moved across her fingers that caused her to freeze. She could feel the scales, the slow slithery movement. She gulped hard, trying desperately not to move and startle it. It was a snake and a massive one from the feeling of it. She trembled when it moved over her hand and to her side where it started to move onto her thigh. *No.* Its tongue darted out in short inspecting hisses. She closed her eyes, stifling a scream. The thing was massive and from the looks of it, venomous. At that moment she had to agree with Katara. She would take feral angels over snakes. *Shit shit shit.*

Her arms were beginning to shake under her as she leaned back on them, her legs extended outward. *Don't move or he'll see it as a threat.* Finally after the longest time, it slithered off of her and down toward the stream. She exhaled and stood to shake off the sensation from it crawling all over her.

Time passed, perhaps an hour or two before Katara tapped her shoulder, signaling for her to try and rest. As the sun set, the distant screams grew louder, making her feel fortunate that they had only faced two encounters—three if she counted the snake. Juliet was laying in Avren's lap, her coat covering her, he slept with his head leaned back against the wall. Amara rested her head on Avren's other leg, opposite Juliet, trying to catch some sleep.

A scream jolted her awake, followed by Katara's frantic jostling of her shoulder. She, Juliet, and Avren scrambled to their feet and rushed toward the stream. Screams filled the air, mingled with snarling, growling, and more screams, while a single set of footsteps pounded toward them. Weapons drawn, they braced themselves at the entrance of the cave, prepared to defend the path they intended to follow downstream.

A tall guy with buzzed hair whom they didn't know skidded to a stop in front of them with his hands up. His eyes were wide and blood was splattered across his face and clothes.

"Who the hell are you?" Avren asked. The guy looked familiar but was in a different unit.

"Hamish, right?" Katara stepped forward.

"Uh, yes, Hamish Loclan—Sloane's unit," he panted. "We have to run, that—those things are going to find us." He pushed past them into the cave. They didn't want to know what 'things' he was referring to so they just hauled ass behind him. His lantern lit the way ahead while Juliet held theirs in the rear of the group.

The stream grew larger into more of a river, becoming deeper as well until they were climbing onto the edge and running through the rocky mud. They found a flat area of bedrock to sit and catch their breath.

"Beck Goldbreath, where is he?" Avren demanded of the other guy, who shared a unit with their friend.

"We got separated at the beginning, I don't know." He exhaled and splashed water on his face. *Fuck.*

Once they caught their breath, they decided to walk cautiously through the cave, following the way the water flowed.

"This has to lead out," Hamish said.

"Why does it have to?" Katara questioned him.

"I..." he stammered. "I don't know." Everyone was getting annoyed, tired, hungry, and no one knew of a plausible way out of the hellscape.

Hours passed wherein they walked in silence and Amara imagined the sun would be rising but she wasn't sure. The group had come in contact with two different non-immortal Nephilim who had attempted to take a bite out of them. Hamish was quick with his sword and Amara handled the other one with Juliet's ax.

"I am so tired of these mud-rock walls, they never end!" Amara squealed and kicked one. She was surely going to go insane in the labyrinth that was the Abyss.

"We should try digging our way out," Avren sniped. She narrowed her eyes at him.

"We're too far underground, not happening." Hamish shrugged.

Amara felt trapped, panicked, as though they had been buried alive and forgotten about. Especially when she couldn't see any trace of sunlight through the cracks in the cave above them. They weren't moving with any kind of speed but she had to stop to ground herself. She was hyperventilating and growing lightheaded.

"We're never getting out of here." She shook her head. Hours staring at an endless maze of walls would instill that kind of fear in someone she supposed.

"We will." Juliet comforted her but it didn't seem the least bit like she believed it.

Eventually the river ended in a massive open cave where the sky could be seen again overhead. She quite literally fell to her knees to worship the sight, finally able to breathe again.

There was no way to climb out, even if they had the equipment to do so. The group began peaking at every small cave opening and crack, trying to figure out a way to escape. The body of water branched off into three smaller streams—none of which had openings big enough to climb through. Maybe a mouse could get through those holes but nothing larger.

Amara was once more reaching for anything through her clairvoyance and receiving nothing. At least it had helped draw her closer to the Fallen Angel that provided the feathers. She sighed. They ate the bread they had been rationing and drank plenty of water while the river was at their disposal.

She was picking at her bread and talking to Katara about what time of day it must have been when she noticed something strange. The reflection of the sun in the water didn't exactly match up with what was shining in from overhead. She paced back and forth trying to figure out why it looked so strange, but couldn't figure out what was so odd about it.

The group looked at her as though she were crazy when she began throwing rocks at the water. It was like it wasn't a reflection but there was a source of light coming from somewhere under the surface, like a...

"Another cave!" she exclaimed. She began stripping off her trial uniform and piling them on the rocks.

"What?" Avren asked. His eyes scanned her body, stopping on her stomach. She looked down. *Shit.*

There were deep bite marks and hickeys from her previous traipse with the Praeceptor.

"Damn girl, who got you?" Katara inspected her, spinning her around. She swatted her friend away playfully.

"No one, I dumped his ass," she snapped. It wasn't exactly the truth but she needed Avren to know that she hadn't lied to him. She really was done with the other guy.

He looked away, not giving away what he was thinking. Katara glanced at Avren, realizing that it was a sore subject for him. She made an 'oops' face and asked what Amara was on about regarding the other cave.

"Look," she pointed down. "That light is not a reflection from up there, I think if we swim down far enough, there's a cave that looks like it opens to a river outside of the Abyss," she explained.

Once she got down to her undergarments she lowered herself into the water, aware that it dropped off and became deep very close to the riverbank. She was sure that the feathers she kept were in her bra, they had been there the entire time since she couldn't think of a closer place to put them on her body.

"Can you swim?" Katara asked.

"Yeah, can you?" She shouted over the moving water. Her friends nodded and she lowered herself into the chasm.

Amara took a deep breath and dove down toward the source of light, the water stinging her eyes. She made her way to the light source and confirmed her suspicion; it led into a body of water just outside of The Abyss. She couldn't believe it; she was so excited she nearly yelled in excitement.

She pushed her way to the surface of the water, smiling wide.

"It's a way out!" she confirmed, her friends jumped up and down. They began stripping down to make the swim easier as well.

She was just about to tell Katara to ensure Hamish had a feather when she was abruptly yanked by her leg under the water. All she could hear was the screams of her friends as the surface became more of a blur and water invaded her nostrils.

$$Chapter\ 19$$

Amara kicked against the hand around her ankle, knowing that if she inhaled, it would be the last thing she ever did. She didn't know that the body of water was so deep but the thing just kept pulling her down, down, down. She was stubborn, she insisted on going into this trial instead of using the pardon—and it was going to cost her her life. Not only would she be dead, but so would any chance of finding out who killed her mother.

She looked down at what had her, a clawed hand digging into her leg. She kicked against the humanoid creature, it let out a grotesque gurgling growl. She brought her other leg down and kicked it in its face, the grip loosened enough for her to jerk free and swim upward.

Someone, one of her friends grabbed at her arm and swam upward with her. She got a breath while Katara was just under the surface of the water stabbing at the thing that was trying to kill them. Amara coughed, Juliet tossed Amara a dagger, and she went back under to help Katara. Blood made the water cloudy. *Who's blood?*

Juliet, Avren, and Hamish jumped in as well. Seemingly they had decided to fullsend getting past the creature and escaping the cave. Chaos ensued as more blood clouded the water, all of them causing the water to splash as weapons gouged at the fanged rotted Fallen Angel. She was impressed when Hamish ripped a feather from it. She went up for air and then back down to see Avren was on the things back, sawing at its throat with his curved blade. Juliet mounted her ax in its chest while Amara searched frantically for Katara.

Once the creature's head was partially hanging off of its neck, Avren went up for air, Amara followed him. Hamish and Juliet disappeared into the cave that should take them out of the Abyss—toward the sunlight. "Your eye." She coughed up water. His bandages were soaked and coming off of the wound. The deep gouges were drenched, the eye split open in two places.

"It hurts like hell," he choked. "Where's Katara? Did she get out?"

"I don't know." She looked down frantically.

"Kat!" Avren yelled. A sense of dread flooded Amara as she reached out for her friend.

"We need to get to that cave opening. I don't know if that thing can heal." She tugged on Avren.

Avren nodded, took a deep breath, and plunged into the water. It was definitely a Fallen Angel, and though Amara couldn't fathom how anyone could survive with a partially severed head, she wouldn't be surprised at this point. When she dove in after Avren, she realized he hadn't gone into the cavern. Instead, he was struggling to free Katara's limp body, her shirt snagged on a jagged rock. Amara's heart clenched at the sight—Katara, lifeless and still, caught like prey.

She swam over, adrenaline surging, as she worked to unhook Katara as quickly as she could. Her right arm was pouring blood, making it harder to see the situation before her. She could hear Avren's muffled gasps for air beneath the surface, his strength faltering, and with one last desperate tug, she ripped Katara's shirt free. The weight of her friend's body pulled her down, her muscles burning as she kicked desperately, driving upward toward Avren, who was already struggling to the surface for air in time.

Please, Katara, please, she thought, each stroke more frantic than the last. She broke the surface, gasping, and fought to drag Katara onto the rocks where their supplies were still scattered.

"Katara!" Amara screamed, slapping her friend's pale, lifeless face. Blood was gushing from a deep gash in Katara's arm, the artery sliced clean through, staining the water and ground around them a sickening red. "Avren!" Amara cried out, her voice cracking as he tried in vain to staunch the bleeding with trembling hands.

Amara leaned in, her ear pressed to Katara's chest. A faint, fluttering pulse—the ghost of a heartbeat. She started pumping on Katara's abdomen, unsure if she was trying to expel water from her lungs or coax her heart back to life. Her mind spiraled into chaos. *No, no, no. This can't be happening.*

"It's too much—I can't stop it!" Avren's voice broke, his face streaked with water and smeared with Katara's blood as it dripped from his trembling fingers. They were both kneeling in a pool of it now, slick and warm. He was trying to stop the blood flowing out of her arm to no avail. Avren bent down, listening intently. He looked up, his eyes hollow. "There's nothing," he whispered, his head dropping in defeat.

Amara refused to accept it. She kept pushing, each compression sending more blood spilling from Katara's gaping wound. "Stop," Avren breathed, his voice choked with helplessness. Tears streamed down Amara's cheeks as she begged for someone, anyone, to help her.

"Amara, you have to stop," Avren pleaded, trying to pull her away, his voice heavy with grief.

"No!" Amara shrieked, wrenching free and collapsing back beside Katara. She cradled her friend's face in her hands, staring into those vacant, unseeing eyes that once held so much life. Her forehead fell to Katara's chest, the sobs wracking her body. Katara was too good, too bright, too alive to die like this—alone, cold, and bleeding out on these desolate rocks.

Avren gently pulled her up. "We have to go."

She could hear in his voice that the loss of Katara shattered him too. Amara wiped her tears, willing no more to fall, not until she survived.

"I'm so sorry," she whispered and closed Katara's beautiful golden eyes. She placed a feather into Katara's hand and put it over her heart. Sniffling, she squeezed her hand one last time.

She had jumped in to save Amara's life and died for it. Getting off of her knees felt like the hardest feat of her life because it meant leaving Katara in The Abyss to rot away.

When she stood she instinctively turned into Avren's arms. He welcomed her, holding her tight. The loss of Katara would be a trauma that they shared together—her life's blood at their feet, coating their arms, splattered on their faces.

He led her into the water once more, the same water that had filled Katara's lungs instead of her own. The water that her friend inhaled and bled out in to save her. They swam quickly toward the open mouth that promised them freedom, the sunlight filtering into the water above them as they emerged from the cave.

Avren was swimming faster than her as the weight of leaving Katara behind weighed her down. He grabbed her hand and pulled her upward, where they met Juliet and Hamish on the edge of the body of water. Avren pulled himself onto the rock first before helping Amara out of the water. Juliet looked between them and back to the cavern below the water.

Amara collapsed onto the rock, sobbing. Juliet looked at her quizzically but fell next to her.

Amara shook her head and Juliet covered her mouth with her palm, releasing a horrific cry into her hand. Amara looked around, they had gotten out... kind of. To their back was a massive cliffside with a waterfall trickling into the water at their feet. The body of water they had emerged from was nestled into the side of the cliff, a serene secluded and slow flowing body of water that spilled off of another cliff. *Shit.* The sky was open above them, and they were sort of out of The Abyss but they needed to get off of the cliffside.

"How were we underground and now we're above ground?" Avren looked around.

"You're right," Amara looked around. *What the hell.* Juliet and Hamish surveyed the situation as well with equal confusion.

"It's like a portal, look." Hamish pointed. The cave they swam through was closing as though it were never there. *whoa.*

So that's how they did it, the Hallowed allowed portals to open for the sake of the trial—for the intelligent beings to escape through. She was consistently in shock by what their magic allowed them to do.

"I guess we jump off of the edge and once we land below, we're done." Juliet sniffled.

Amara stared at her own feather in her hand. She knew that once Katara's body became cold, her feather would solidify as part of her. She would go into the afterlife a victor. Afterall, she had escaped the Abyss. At least her soul had.

None of them could see how high they were or how far they would fall through the waterfall to get off of the cliffside. They could make out some tree tops though over the edge as well as the sound of the water crashing down below. It might be survivable, Amara thought. She hugged her bare legs to her chest, staring blankly at where the portal-cave had been. *Katara was really gone.* Juliet sat next to her, seemingly coming to the same realization.

"She bled out, Jules, there was nothing we could do," she whispered. Juliet hugged her.

"She would want us to take that jump." Juliet rubbed her back. Amara knew that, it's why Katara died for them, to give them a chance to live.

They sat and processed the loss for a moment, Hamish less so but allowing for the silence respectfully.

"Let's go." Avren sighed and stood.

The group followed when he dropped into the water and swam to the edge where the water spilled downward. They looked over, it was about a forty foot drop into what they hoped was a deeper river which rushed quickly out of view.

"That might send us out to sea and wash us up on the coast of Findaria," Juliet said.

"Well let's just aim to hit that river and climb onto the forest's edge," Hamish interjected. Avren nodded, his mutilated eye now fully exposed to the elements. "I'll go first," Hamish added.

Guilt accompanied the relief that Amara felt from his offer, because if the drop was fatal—it wouldn't be Avren or Juliet. She shook her head at herself; she didn't want him to die either. Either way he pulled himself up and over the edge, the three close friends held their breath in anticipation as he hit the base of the waterfall.

To their relief he shot up whooping and hollering excitedly, holding up his feather. Juliet smiled, it was bittersweet without Katara.

"For Katara," they said in unison. They held hands and then pushed themselves off of the ledge.

When they emerged from the water, the reality that they had made it set in, they had *lived*. They hugged each other excitedly as

Hamish pulled himself onto the riverbank, all of them welcoming the sun on their skin. Despite the crisp coolness of the water and the winter weather, it was comfortable enough to wade in the river.

Avren swam under the base of the waterfall, laughing as he ran his arm under it. Amara followed him, not able to help her own laugh as he shoved her head into it. *This is what Katara would have wanted, to see them smiling.*

"We did it, Amara." He smiled and pulled her into him. She wrapped her arms around his neck, her legs around his bare abdomen. She tried not to look at or worry about his eye.

"For Katara," she breathed.

"For Katara," he whispered in agreement. He looked at her lips, she found herself looking at his.

She let herself get lost in the moment, in the thrill of the victory, she allowed herself to feel comfort from him as he held her. So when he kissed her, she kissed him back, his hands pressing against her back to bring her body closer. At first she wanted to stop him but he was gentle and familiar, her closest friend. She was doing nothing wrong by enjoying it.

She found herself smiling into the kiss, he returned the sentiment until Amara laughed and splashed water on him. She paused and cupped his face in her hand, careful of the gashes there. A familiar feeling sat in—that what she felt for him had the capacity to destroy her.

"Yes!" Juliet clapped. "Now let's go love birds." she waved them toward her. She pointed above them, Avren and Amara looking up at the Nephilim that were circling them after emerging from behind the waterfall.

A Nephilim for each of them landed on the riverbank. Praeceptor Sloane grabbed Hamish under the arms and took off with a praise for his accomplishment. Cathmore swooped in and grabbed Juliet who squealed in fear. Nightbane retrieved Amara while Wrathguard took Avren. The breeze of being flown through the air was startling on their wet, nearly naked bodies. Amara shivered.

The differing shape, size, and colors of their wings held her attention as they soared back to the carriages outside of The Abyss.

Sloane and Cathmore's black wings unfurled in sharp contrast: Cathmore's wings arched with razor-edged tips, giving them a menacing silhouette, while Sloane's wings swept out in soft curves, their feathers fuller and downy, reminiscent of a dark storm cloud. Nightbane's wings were vast and formidable, a sprawling expanse of gray with streaks of white feathers scattered throughout like stars on a stormy night, broader and more commanding than the rest. Soren Wrathguard's wings shimmered with hues of silver and violet, glowing like opals in the dying light of the sun. Though smaller in stature and build, her wings had a delicate, almost fairy-like grace that belied the ferocity Amara knew lurked within—small, yes, but deadly.

Wrathguard reminded her of Katara. Amara imagined that her friend's wings would have been small and mighty just like she was.

They were dropped near the carriages that had taken them to The Abyss. Wrathguard was inspecting Avren's eye, waving over Nightbane and Cathmore for assistance. Amara walked over to

Avren and rubbed his back, taking a seat in the grass next to him. Cathmore seemed to notice the gesture out of the corner of his eye but turned away, materializing supplies with his Imperium.

"Whoa," Avren breathed. Cathmore side-eyed him briefly. *Why was he so moody?*

"That eye has to come out." Cathmore huffed.

"What?" Avren jerked away from him.

"He's right, you can't see out of it, correct?" Nightbane asked. Avren shook his head in defeat.

Amara sat behind him, wrapping her arms under his, hugging him for comfort. He held her arm closer and glanced back at her. Cathmore locked eyes with her for a moment, tapping a finger on his knee.

"It's going to be okay," she whispered. Avren nodded.

"Can you do this procedure?" Nightbane asked Cathmore, who reassured him that he could.

"If we don't, his risk for infection doubles, an infection this close to the brain would be fatal," Cathmore tilted Avren's head to the side. "It's already festered too long."

"It's only been a day." Amara nudged Cathmore's hand from Avren's face. He dug his eyes into her, Nightbane and Sloane wondering what he would do to his charge for touching him.

"I know you went through a lot down there, Ashenfall, but do not touch me," he warned and tossed a bandage down. His words were ice. Amara felt like she had been slapped in the face. "The eye comes out or we prepare him for the infirmary where he will await his death." He scowled at her and then looked at Avren. "What's it gonna be Yearwood?"

"Just do it." He nodded.

"Wait! Can he heal him?" Amara gestured at Nightbane, recalling the painful experience.

"No," Nightbane said with finality. *Why?*

Cathmore shook out a handkerchief before pouring some kind of liquid on it. He didn't even acknowledge her question.

"Hold this over his mouth and nose," he handed it to Amara. *Chloroform.* She did so, it took a minute before Avren sagged against her. She kept the rag there and rubbed his hair back out of his face.

Upon Avren losing consciousness, Nightbane handed Cathmore a sharp scalpel and nodded. Juliet and Hamish were sitting next to a tree a few yards away, watching intently. She removed the rag to allow Cathmore to begin. He pulled down Avren's eyelid and began carefully severing the eyeball from the muscles of the eye socket.

Amara had to look away, unable to bear the sight of it. She chose to watch the sun setting over the trees that were wilted by the winter season. After a moment, Avren began thrashing and then screaming, Amara pinned him down.

"More!" Cathmore yelled at Nightbane who was pouring chloroform into another rag. He handed it to Amara.

"I'm here, it's okay." She shushed him as she shoved the rag over his mouth again. He screamed, his eye ball pushing outward a bit since it was severed from the socket. To her relief his body went limp against her once more.

She didn't know why but she kissed the top of his head. It may have been for him; it may have been for her own comfort.

"Just keep it there this time," Cathmore demanded, wiping the blood off of his hands.

Nightbane handed Cathmore something resembling a tiny scoop which he used to push the mangled eyeball out of the socket the rest of the way.

"Give him some oxygen," Cathmore instructed, so she dropped the rag.

Cathmore was focused, shutting out the world around him as he worked. She took in the way he sat his mouth in a hard line, the way he feathered his jaw, how meticulous his hands worked as he removed the eyeball without so much as a flinch.

Avren stirred once more and was consequently put back to sleep so that Cathmore could stitch him up. Bile rose in Amara's throat to see Avren's eye discarded in the field. She turned away. The whole thing was fucked, the entire situation.

Amara was shivering with the cold air and lack of proper clothes so she was relieved when they were allowed into the carriage. Avren's breathing was labored from the pain he had endured from the procedure; he hung his head between his legs as though he was going to puke. She rubbed his back to provide as much comfort as possible.

The Praeceptors collected each conscript's feather. The four of them were the second group out behind a group of three from

Nightbane's unit. They all needed medical attention but once they finished, they were sent back to the Sanctum Metere with Amara's group. Avren did end up vomiting before the long ride was over so she had him lay in her lap.

Hours bled into the next day, conscripts trickled into the dormitories, some taking up a bed in the infirmary instead. Juliet and Amara were going through Katara's personal effects when more conscripts entered the shared sleep space.

A heavy gloom had settled over the familiar room. Some conscripts spoke in whispers, all of them moved slowly. Every one of them carried the weight of death and anguish in their solemn movements.

Avren stood from his cot, getting Amara's attention. He hugged Eros, causing Amara and Juliet to jump up and follow.

"Judas?" she asked .

He shook his head, anguish etched in every line of his face, tears shimmering in his eyes. Amara pulled him closer, trying to hold him together as he broke.

"Kat?" he choked out, his voice barely above a whisper.

"She's gone too." Avren sighed, his words heavy and hollow. Eros slid down the wall, collapsing onto the cold floor, burying his face in his trembling hands. His skin was streaked with blood, mingling with dirt and sweat, and shallow cuts marred his arms, though none were as deep as the pain beneath.

"I watched them both die," he rasped, his voice cracking as the weight of it all came crashing down. "I couldn't... I couldn't do anything." For the first time, the dam holding his emotions back shattered. He stared at his hands, stained with blood that wasn't just his—it was Judas's, just as Amara and Avren were smeared with Katara's.

"Who else?" Amara asked gently, though her own voice wavered.

"Asher," Eros mumbled, his eyes unfocused, lost in the horror of the memory. "It had me, and I couldn't..." His words drifted off, and his gaze fell away, haunted. Asher wasn't a close friend, just another soldier in their unit—another casualty, another loss.

"It's okay," Juliet whispered, wrapping a comforting arm around him.

But it wasn't. It would never be okay. Grief clung to them, smothering the group as they huddled together on the cold stone floor, the weight of what they had lost pressing down, knowing nothing would ever be the same again. Their friends' souls would haunt the forsaken halls of the Sanctum Metere forever.

The day came to an end, the Abyss Trial concluding with it. None of them were able to doze off for more than a few hours at a time, the dormitory was a ghost town compared to how full it usually was.

To her relief, Avren was given some kind of tea to relieve the pain in his face. She laid in his cot with him, her back to his chest as he held her. The two of them faded into sleep together, comforted to have one another.

The conscripts were woken up by the Praeceptor's who stormed into the dormitory.

"Why are we in each other's beds?" Nightbane roared, banging on the metal bed frames with the hilt of a thick dagger. It reverberated through the room, jarring everyone.

Amara wasn't the only one who flopped onto the floor from someone else's bed, Eros had rolled out of Juliet's, and Molivina out of Davian's who must have come back from the trial after she fell asleep.

Eros, Molvina, and Amara were all forced to stand against the wall amongst conscripts in other units who had been caught breaking the rule. It felt so trivial to be punished for it in the shadow of the death that surrounded them.

Baylin marched into the room with a scroll alongside the Crowned Magister. The Praeceptors parted to give them the center of the floor, the conscripts turning their attention to them.

"Sired children, congratulations on surviving the second trial of the Crucible ," Crowned Magister Bennett announced. He picked at his fine tailored navy blue suit, Amara noted the silver threat around the pockets and cuffs.

"Fifty-six of you went into the Abyss Trial," Baylin began. "Forty-three of you made it out. Their sacrifices serve the Hallowed well." He closed the scroll and stepped backward behind the Crowned Magister. Silence and devastation fell over the room.

"Ten of you are still in the infirmary," the Crowned Magister added, given the scarce amount of conscripts in the dormitory.

"Read their names!" One of the conscripts Amara didn't know demanded. All six of the men in front fixated on the girl. *Oh no.*

She must have been Wrathguard's charge because she twitched her head and sent the girl flying into the stone wall behind them. She crumpled to the floor coughing and gasping for air.

"Twenty-four hours in the pound. We do not read out the names of the sired children given to Lucifer," Crowned Magister Bennett sneered. All Amara could do was shake her head and anger threatened to make her open her mouth. *Don't do it.*

Wrathguard dragged her conscript away on the Crowned Magister's orders. There was some more congratulations followed by the information that classes resumed the following day before Baylin and Bennett exited the hall. There were a total of seven of them on the wall who had been in another person's cot, three of them belonging to Cathmore. They were ordered to follow their Praeceptor's for punishment. *Fuck.*

"Bet you all are pretty exhausted, huh?" Cathmore said over his shoulder as he led them out of the dormitory. Eros, Amara, and Molvina glanced at one another nervously.

He led them to the training hall that they had all become so accustomed to. He pointed at three different places on the wall and instructed them to lean there and wait. He emerged with fountain feather pens, paper, and three books.

"'I will obey the rules of the Sanctum Metere or my Praeceptor will strip me of my life which I have fought so hard to keep,'" he said in a mocking tone. "You're going to write that over and over again. You are going to memorize it, and you are going to obey it."

He handed each of them a book to bear down on. "Additionally you will do this while in the chair sit position against this wall." He patted the stone wall they leaned on.

"For how long?" Molvina asked. Amara hated wall sits, they made her legs shake.

"An hour." He grinned wickedly.

"An hour?" Eros asked wide-eyed. A standard wall sit drill was maxed out at three minutes, five for a punishment.

"In that hour you must write the sentence one thousand times, failure to do so or hold the position will result in the breaking of your dominant hand—since you all can't seem to keep them to yourselves."

Amara exhaled, lots of things springing to mind that she could say. First of all, hypocrisy. *Seriously?* His hands and mouth had been all over her body and hers all of his, but he had the audacity to talk about keeping hands to themselves? She bit her tongue, which he noticed and gave her a sideways smirk.

"Begin," he ordered, so they did. It was an impossible task, why didn't he just go ahead and break their hands?

By the ten minute mark their legs were shaking so bad and their breathing was so labored that they could not focus on the sentences at all.

"Fuck," Eros huffed, shakily writing the next sentence. Tears ran down Molvina's reddened face as her hands shook. Amara had begun to sweat.

Cathmore was pacing in front of them, back and forth, back and forth, in an infuriatingly arrogant manner. *Jackass.* He paused and tilted his head in her direction.

Oh shit did he hear that?

He looked at her with a taunting glare. She *should* have looked away... *should* have, but no. Instead, she locked eyes with him, scowled in a way that said, 'game on,' and slammed the book onto the ground, sending her papers flying. He raised his eyebrows, seemingly impressed at how bold she had decided to be.

He marched over to her as she straightened her legs, panting as she leaned against the wall. He yanked her by the arm and hoisted her up and over his shoulder like she weighed nothing to him. Eros and Molvina watched with their jaws practically on the floor but continued writing as fast as they could.

Cathmore kicked the door shut to what she had coined the 'punishment room' at this point.

"Your little boyfriend took you back quickly." He circled her. "Desperate is he?" He picked up a hard wooden club and flipped it in his hand.

"That is none of your business," she retorted, crossing her arms. He was not about to crush the bones in her hand with that thing.

"No?" He pulled the hem of her shirt upward, exposing his bite marks and hickeys. "Are these my business?" She shoved his hand away, dropping her shirt.

"So that's what this is about? You're jealous." She huffed a small laugh. She spun on him as he circled behind her again. Something flashed behind his eyes, but she couldn't read it nor could she feel anything but rage coming off of him. He pushed her backward against the wall.

"Jealousy would imply that there's something special about you." He shook his head—his words cutting through her. She inhaled her anger and slapped him hard.

Amara saw him lose control for a moment, giving in to that primal energy that lived below the surface of every Nephilim's skin. He grabbed her hand before it left his face, twisted her arm upward, her palm inward toward her face, and cracked the bone.

Pain blinded her and she let out a scream, dropping to the floor, holding her limp hand. He had turned his back on her. He was taking deep breaths, trying to get a hold of his temper. He placed his palms on the wall and dropped his head between them, taking another breath. She writhed in pain on the floor, in disbelief not that he dealt a promised punishment, but that he had lost control and hurt her maliciously.

'You're breathtaking, Ashenfall,' he had once told her in a moment of passion. He had held her close as she slept, explored her body, ran his fingers through her hair, provided comfort in the darkness of the Crucible... *How was this the same man?*

He turned to her after a moment, his eyes wide, anger was replaced with regret. He walked quickly over to her where she was trying to control her crying because she couldn't feel or move her hand. She cowered from him, pulling herself into the corner. He shook his head and reached for her but she made herself smaller to get away from him.

Those hands that once brought excitement and pleasure had turned on her, hurt her. She never wanted those hands on her again and he knew it.

"Get the hell away from me." She grunted through tears. The words seemed to cut deep but he did, sitting on the floor and sliding to the other side of the room. He rested his forearms on his knees and dropped his head.

He stared forward, regret and fear freezing into cold detachment. He was making himself okay with what he had done. He had simply dealt a punishment. She could see he was reasoning with himself in order to erect that uncaring, egotistical, controlling facade he always wore.

She got to her feet and left the room in silence before running out of the training hall, not caring about the looks of horror from Molvina and Eros who had collapsed onto the floor.

Fuck him, fuck everything she ever gave to him, everything she ever felt for him. She was so unbelievably stupid. He would never put his hands on her again.

She made her way to the infirmary to get the hand set and wrapped with a newly reignited hatred for Praeceptor Cathmore.

Chapter 20

"It's fine, Jules, I'll make it work," she told her friend. They were in weapons wielding welding with Wrathguard, and Juliet was worried about Amara's sparring session since her wrist was broken. She would have to predominantly use her left hand.

It had been nearly three weeks since the Abyss Trial, since Cathmore lost his temper and shattered her wrist. She had been focused on getting used to using her non-dominant hand. It was a skill that she could see being beneficial long after her wrist healed. He had followed through with breaking Eros and Molvina's hands, though he used the club to shatter the bones instead of snapping the wrist.

She took her place on the mat, opposite Molivina ironically, given both of their injuries. Amara spun her sword around; it was close in size to the one she planned to earn from Wrathguard. She glanced at the blue hilted beauty on the wall. Molvina's sword was a bit smaller but still comparable to Amara's. She had been watching her opponent for days since learning that they would face each other.

Molvina was quick to anger and would swing wildly when provoked, she also talked a lot which Amara found to be exhausting. Her foot work was poor and she was terrible and counterbalanced herself. Amara had been especially sure to prepare based on her opponents' weaknesses since there was some unnamed prize to the victors of the matches.

"Fight," Wrathguard called and they began,

Right off the bat Molvina charged for her, swinging blindly over her head. Amara ducked and spun to face her, ready. Molvina was still recovering from the force that she used and sent herself stumbling. *Maybe I should just let her exhaust herself.*

"Spending so much time between Davian and Fallon that you forgot basic body control?" Amara taunted and opened her arms. Molvina narrowed her eyes, but—to her credit—blocked Amara's jab at her ribs.

Amara was quicker though and spun the sword around, striking her in the thigh. The armor didn't allow her to get cut but the force must have hurt. Molvina stumbled back with a malicious laugh before charging Amara, she missed the first wild swing but landed the second on her forearm. *That was going to bruise.*

Their dark plated armor clanged throughout the room. She was getting used to the tight fighting armor, it was separated into small pieces that allowed her body to flow and move freely.

"Let's go Amara!" Avren yelled.

He looked dashing, knelt on the mat, rooting for her. She had gotten used to his black and silver eye patch, finding it sexy. She shot him a smile before spinning low and taking Molvina's feet from under her.

She recovered quickly though and swept Amara's feet from under her with her sword. *Touchee.* Amara hit the ground next to Molvina who had discarded her sword in favor of headlocking her.

"I heard a little rumor about a Praeceptor giving special lessons to one of his students," she purred in Amara's ear. Amara had been about to flip her and end it but her words froze her. Molvina laughed before bringing out a hidden dagger and dealing a 'fatal' blow to Amara's gut.

Amara rolled out of her hold, taking her loss with dignity and nodding at her opponent. Avren and Juliet seemed dumbfounded, Amara was a much better wielder than Molvina was.

"Ashenfall, what the hell happened?" Wrathguard exclaimed. She didn't answer. "You never let an opponent that close!"

Amara said nothing.

Molvina knows, how does she know? She and Cathmore had not held a conversation since before the Abyss, why was this a rumor all of the sudden?

The rest of the unit finished their sparring matches, Molvina fighting twice since there was an uneven number of conscripts left. At least she lost to Davian.

Later that day the unit made their way to the training hall for their classes with Cathmore. He had kept his distance from Amara, effectively abandoning his intention to help with her Imperium, and she wanted nothing to do with him.

"Up!" Cathmore called to the rope handlers of the day. Amara was suspended by the rings in her back and she allowed herself to enjoy it.

How did Molvina know? What was she going to do with the information? Would she be killed? Would Cathmore be thrown into the Abyss? She exhaled her racing thoughts and gave into the tingling sensation that took over her body. She willed herself not to ascend, not to reach for those voices that called to her only when she was doing body suspension. She had gotten pretty good at it, at keeping herself present in the training room.

"You did great," Avren whispered in her ear. They were sitting next to each other watching two more go into the air.

"You did too," she responded. Avren had gone before her and he was getting really good at it. He didn't enjoy the pain, most of them didn't. But he was tolerating it better.

She didn't think Avren needed anymore pain tolerance training, not after losing a fucking eye. She shuddered remembering it being removed.

After pain tolerance concluded, Cathmore was running hand-to-hand combat sparring drills with the unit. He watched as the two guys went at it, demonstrating different techniques they had been taught. He observed every move the two made. Apart from that though, he was reading everyone in the room the way he always did.

He had a way of being able to unpack people and their motives, desires, and secrets through minimal contact and conversation. It took her a while to single it out. It was why he was so confident, why he carried himself with so little fear. There was nothing about the world or people around him that was a mystery. He seemed to have all of the answers.

She thought about the files on every single conscript laid out in his chambers. He not only watched and read people but he studied them. She scanned over his carefully cleaned and pressed training uniform, the set in his jaw, the dilation of his eyes as they scanned the room... he had a bead on everyone and everything that went on.

He was startlingly intelligent, observant, and intimidating as hell. He valued knowledge and control above everything. She swallowed hard when he spun a silver ring around his middle finger. He glanced in her direction briefly as though sensing it. *Fuck. He was good.*

"Ashenfall, Yearwood, to the mat." He stood from his crouching position. The couple looked at each other. *Well fuck.*

Really, she shouldn't be shocked that Cathmore would pit her against Avren. Honestly, she should have seen it coming. She parted her feet, squared her shoulder, and put her left hand forward instead of the right one like usual.

Avren glanced over his fist at her. He was a kind and gentle soul but she had seen him fight. He was quick, cunning, and he didn't pull punches. His smaller build allowed him to move effortlessly around his opponents. *Could she keep up? Would she want to?*

The anticipation of their bodies clashing had Amara's face heated. She and Avren had been taking it slow. Apart from heated makeout sessions and stolen kisses, they were hands off. Both of them wound tight with desire for the other. *Shit.* She recalled how intense it was when Eros and Judas took to the mat all those weeks ago.

"Winner is the one who makes the other tap out, go," Cathmore called with a bored hand wave in the air.

Both of them had similar fighting styles, they liked to tire the other out. So of course they circled each other for a moment. Avren winked at her, causing her to roll her eyes.

Amara stepped into him, he stepped back. She threw a jab; he dodged it without touching her. He threw a jab; she did the same. Someone scoffed behind them.

"Today!" Cathmore was annoyed.

Amara sighed and lunged for Avren with a fist. When he stepped backward, she dropped and swept his legs out from under him. He hit the ground hard but recovered. He grabbed her ankle and pulled her to the ground as well. She coughed from the impact but kicked him in the chest before he could get on top of her.

He smiled in that way that made her heart soar and jumped to his feet. She got to hers, taking up a fighting stance against him once more. His strong arms were accentuated in the short sleeved shirt he wore, the biceps tensing as he clenched his fists in front of him.

He stepped forward before sending a kick directly into her shoulder, and she stumbled backward. *Ouch.* Her shoulder throbbed. *It's on.*

She charged him, grabbing him around his toned midsection and pushing him to the ground. She landed sprawled on top of him, the heat of his body and his rapid breathing making her forget what to do next. He twisted his legs in hers, rolling her and sending her onto her back instead.

He grabbed her wrists and pinned them to the mat on either side of her, his hips pinning her to the ground. She stared at his lips, her heart hammering in her chest, her entire body reeling with need.

She thrashed against him, trying to wrap her legs around his thighs to flip him but he was bigger than her.

"Let's go, Avren!" Eros yelled playfully.

"Traitor!" She grunted at her friend and headbutted Avren in the chin. It was her only way out of the hold. He rolled onto his side next to her, cursing. Her forehead throbbed, signaling that maybe she headbutted him harder than she intended.

"Oh shit!" Juliet laughed.

Amara rolled her body over Avren's and adjusted herself behind him, pulling him into a headlock. She wrapped her leg around his midsection, pinning his arm to his ribs. He struggled for a minute before she tightened her grip.

"I'll help you ice that bruise later, baby," she teased and nipped at his ear. He scoffed and tapped out with a smirk.

"Ashenfall, victor," Cathmore announced. She released Avren who laughed .

"That was hot," Avren whispered with a dashing smile and helped her stand. She winked at him and the two sauntered off of the mat.

Amara had a familiar desire gathering between her legs that had her biting down on her bottom lip. Cathmore met her eyes, that cold detachment not giving anything away. Something about it though, made the throbbing between her legs increase. She broke eye contact and he turned his back on her.

"Wait wait wait, you saw what?" Avren was dumbfounded by something Juliet and Eros said. Amara took her place next to them, placing her breakfast tray in front of her.

"I swear bro, Praeceptor Cathmore is screwing Magister Copia," he whispered. Avren nearly spit out a piece of his food with a laugh. Amara froze, staring at Avren.

"Who?" she asked.

"She's one of the teachers for the library something or other." He shrugged. She had forgotten that some of the career Magisters do more than just teach.

"What did you see?" she asked Juliet, feigning careless amusement.

"We were coming back through the tunnels last night," Juliet lowered her voice.

"Y'a know how there's all of those alcoves and alleyways and tunnels that branch off?" Eros added and looked between them. Avren nodded.

"We heard something as we approached that long dark one with no door or anything." Juliet smiled. She was blushing.

"I kid you not, he was plowing her from behind. Still dressed or whatever. It was a quickie but—" Eros was cut off by Juliet.

"I'll never look at him the same," she leaned in, closer to Amara. "He's huge." She laughed with wide eyes.

"Yeah, I thought he was hot before but damnnn," Eros high-fived Juliet.

Avren was asking for more details, the three of them laughing. She tried to participate, to play it cool. Jealousy took a hold on her and lit her ablaze with fury. It was a white hot fury that she couldn't explain. She was squeezing her fork, the metal digging into her skin as she fake laughed with her friends. She hated herself for the jealousy. She didn't want it. She didn't need it, or him.

She stood quickly from the table, startling her friend group.

"I'll be right back." She offered. She headed toward the washrooms off of the dining hall to fool them before pushing out of an exit into much-needed fresh air.

I don't care.

I don't care.

I hate him.

I hate him, I hate him, I hate him.

Before she knew it, she slammed her fist into a stone pillar, so blinded by rage that she didn't even feel it.

Molvina pushed through the door behind her.

"Might want to get that anger under control," she taunted.

"What do you want," she growled. Molvina had become a nuisance, an annoyance.

"Nothing." She shrugged. She stepped closer to Amara. "I just want to know if he let you kiss him when he fucked you," Molvina smiled with fucked up teeth.

The girl was *stupid*.

"Back the fuck up," Amara threatened, seething and shaking.

"Just spill, bitch." She sighed but stepped back nonchalantly. *What does she think this is? He could be killed.* "Does he moan?" She bit her lip. Nausea rose in Amara's throat.

Molvina desperately wanted Cathmore. Amara couldn't figure out how Molvina found out about the two of them. She also didn't know why she thought pissing Amara off would get her in their Praeceptor's pants.

The thought of her getting Cathmore killed merged with the anger of him fucking that Magister. She grabbed Molvina by the throat and slammed her into the stone pillar, which she finally realized made her knuckles bleed. Molvina clawed at her arm, choking. Amara tightened her grip.

"He fucks like an animal," she growled into the bitches ear. "And you will never fucking touch him."

Molvina almost smiled. Amara reeled back her still bleeding, less dominant hand, and punched her in the jaw. She dropped her. Amara smiled as she spat blood onto the ground. For good measure, she kicked her in the ribs too.

"You stupid slut," Molvina looked up at her.

"What is going on over here?" A voice came from around the corner at the head of the alleyway between the buildings. *Shit.* It was Praeceptor Nightbane.

He charged straight toward them, Molvina on her feet by the time his large frame eclipsed the morning sun. Amara swallowed hard, looking up at him.

"Let's go." He grabbed both of them by the collars and pushed them forward.

This can't be happening.

Finding out that Cathmore was fucking someone else now was bad enough. Molvina knowing about her and Cathmore was worse. Molvina taunting her with it was just idiotic but *this...* Being taken to Cathmore for punishment while processing the rest? She couldn't imagine her day getting worse.

"What?!" Cathmore swung his bedroom door open. A toothbrush hung from his lips.

He was shirtless, his uniform pants hanging low on his hips. He hadn't done anything to his hair which was still rustled from sleep and his piercing blue eyes settled on Amara in annoyance. He seemed not to give a shit that Molvina was even there, though Amara was pretty sure she heard the girl lustfully groan in her throat.

"Found these two beating each other's asses over breakfast. They're yours, so here ya go." Nightbane shoved them into either side of his door frame. Amara's head bonked the wood, audibly. *That was deserved.*

Molvina was unabashedly sucking on the tip of her finger and scanning Cathmore's body. *Ugh.* But at least her jaw was swollen and she still had blood in her mouth.

"Back the fuck up ladies, I'll be out in a minute." He scowled at Nightbane who turned to leave Oaks Hall.

"Why do you want him so bad?" Amara demanded, turning to Molvina. She just grinned and stayed silent. Amara narrowed her eyes on the girl.

"Walk, go," Cathmore demanded in annoyance as he slung on his Praeceptor jacket. He smelled like mint but Amara tried not to focus on the ecstasy of his scent.

Amara glanced backward at him; he didn't even acknowledge her. He pushed them past the main buildings, past the training hall where she initially assumed they would be taken. His nails dug into her upper arm causing her to wince.

"Where are we going?" she demanded, trying to jerk away from his grasp.

"Who cares?" Molvina purred. She could feel the disgust that rolled over Cathmore. She had to fight the urge to grin.

Eventually Cathmore stopped them on the running field where they usually did stamina training. It was empty, most of the conscripts still eating breakfast and preparing to start their day.

"What are we fighting about?" he grumbled and turned them to face him.

He looked between them, eyebrows raised, waiting for one of them to explain. Amara dropped her head, not able to admit that he was the reason she was driven to violence. His deep blue eyes dug into her.

"You," Molvina purred. Amara's eyes darted to her, shocked. Her dark hair highlighted with streaks of blue in the sunlight.

"What did you just say to me?" He growled, closing in on the idiotic girl. She swallowed and looked up into his eyes with her black ones.

Amara took a step to the side.

"That's not exactly true," Amara cleared her throat. Cathmore ignored her, inspecting Molvina.

"Fighting over me is futile." He scoffed. "I don't want either of you." He looked both of them up and down in disgust. An actual physical pain jolted her heart, sending it to pieces. *Why?*

"How does she know about us?" Cathmore's voice was suddenly in her mind, causing her to jump.

"I don't know."

Neither of them made it obvious that they were in each other's heads. Neither of them even blinked, neither of them made eye contact.

"I don't care about your petty school girl crushes on me," he began. She knew he was trying to wind doubt into what Molvina thought she knew.

The only problem? Amara had already confirmed the affair to the girl.

"She already told me you fuck like an animal," Molvina pointed at Amara like a tattling child. *Shit.*

The Praeceptor's head snapped toward Amara, his eyes stabbing into her painfully. Something like betrayal flashed in his eyes. He must have thought Amara was lying, that she had told the girl about what they had done. Her heart squeezed in her chest.

"I only said that after she already knew. I don't know how she found out," she reasoned into his mind. He had a block up though, she didn't know if he heard it.

"Your punishments are going to be dealt right now." He exhaled a shaky breath. She saw his mind working as he came up with the appropriate punishment. "But the two of you are going to face each other on the mat, in front of your unit. I will let you make fools of yourself over someone you can never have." He smiled tauntingly, gesturing at his body.

A similar pain like a punch to the stomach took over Amara. Molvina seethed, baring her teeth. She didn't seem to remember that Cathmore was within his full rights to kill her for what she's doing, for what she knows.

Amara rubbed her still wrapped broken wrist from what he had done. She didn't want another broken bone.

"On your knees. Both of you," Cathmore boomed. Molvina jumped but got to her knees in excitement. Amara rolled her eyes, ready to get the whole thing over with. She scooted away from Molvina who was far too close to her.

"No, right next to each other." He shoved them together, their shoulders and thighs touching.

He circled them and rolled up his sleeves. Amara gulped at his exposed arms, his fingers... She looked at the ground quickly. Finally Cathmore stopped circling them and stood behind them.

He got close, way too close.

"Heads back, chins up," he demanded.

When they put their heads back, his legs were there. The crown of Amara's head rested on his right thigh, Molvina's the left. *What the fuck is this?*

She looked up at him, his short messy hair falling forward as he looked down at them. He pulled something from behind his back, something he obviously summoned from thin air.

"I don't like being talked about. I don't want to be fought over. I don't want to be the subject of your pent-up fantasies. I don't want either of you speaking to each other or me as though you have a shot," he growled.

Without warning he grabbed Molvina's head, forced her jaw open and shoved soap in her mouth. *A fucking bar of soap.*

"We're not children!" Amara protested as Molvina gagged. She tried to spit it out but he stopped her, pushing it harder into her throat.

"Keep it there." He sneered at Molvina before turning to Amara.

She tried to pitch herself forward and away from him but he snatched her by her hair.

"Fucker," she mumbled.

"What was that?" He barked, his head tilted, his teeth inches from her neck.

He forced her jaw open, painfully, causing her to grunt. She clawed at his arms but it was no use. He shoved the bitter thing into her mouth until the back of her throat stopped it. She imagined that the humiliation she felt was the main point of the punishment. He strolled around them and stood before them with his arms crossed, a wicked grin on his face. He looked proud, amused, but still annoyed.

Molvina had begun to drool foaming soap and Amara could feel that she would start very soon. The taste of the bar consumed her senses and made her eyes water. It was disgusting.

"If I find out that either of you are speaking about me sexually again, I'll kill you." He shrugged simply. "This is not the time or place. Understood?"

Amara had a plethora of things she wanted to say back but she couldn't. Both of them nodded. She accidentally inhaled a bubble which sent her sputtering foam out of the sides of her mouth. The bar fell out and she choked as she doubled over.

She expected Cathmore to retaliate but he was already walking away from the two of them. She was once again left alone with Molvina, who she wanted so desperately to stab in the throat.

Chapter 21

Amara went through the rest of the day with her head down, too many emotions running through her mind. He was so cold, so disgusted by them—*by her*. It just didn't feel right, it felt like a lie and she couldn't explain why.

Maybe it was the taste of soap that stayed with her or his venomous words but Cathmore was on her mind the entire day no matter how much she tried to change her train of thought.

"What's wrong?" Juliet asked her as they took their spots on the mat for pain tolerance.

"Nothing." She shook her head.

Her body was wound tight with anger, frustration, and need. *Why need?* She was so blindsided by the strangest mix of emotions when it came to Cathmore. She was so sick of it.

"We're doing your pressure point reevaluations today," Praeceptor Cathmore announced. *Ugh.* "Meanwhile, work on your suspension exercises."

The last thing she wanted was for Cathmore to be poking around her body again. It had been so... sensual before. Apart from that she was so angry at him for hurting her maliciously.

He had been calling them one at a time, allowing those who wanted more time suspended to do so. Molvina was practically skipping toward Amara from the room Cathmore had just conducted her evaluation in.

"Don't worry about before, I'm not going to say anything to anyone." She smiled at Amara. Her jaw had begun to bruise, Amara smirked.

"Say anything about what?" Amara opted to play dumb, in earshot of Avren. She tugged Amara to the side to speak privately.

"Cathmore and I just came to a delicious agreement to keep me quiet," she taunted her. Bile rose in Amara's throat.

"You blackmailed your Praeceptor?" she asked, astounded. Molvina smiled wickedly and skipped away.

"What's wrong?" Avren approached her, sweetly rubbing her arm.

"Nothing." She sighed. He found her hand and squeezed it reassuringly.

"Meet me in the shower room," he whispered.

The shower room was one of a few rooms branching off of the training hall. Some people showered there after more intense workouts. She inhaled a quick breath, his words playing on her need that had been building for weeks.

Avren disappeared through the door and Amara waited a few minutes before following him. She heard Cathmore announce that Davian was going after the person in the room so they had some time. Amara's heart raced with excitement as she slid into the room and locked the door.

Avren startled her which caused her to laugh, she wrapped her arms around his neck and kissed him hard. She tried to pretend it didn't bother her that Cathmore was suddenly so disgusted by her, that he was sleeping with other people, that he had apparently agreed to sleep with Molvina to shut her up. She couldn't think about any of that nor how it made her feel. She needed to focus on Avren who was kissing her hungrily.

"You're so beautiful, Mar," he whispered between kisses.

He hoisted her up, forcing her to wrap her legs around his waist. She and Avren had not slept together still, mostly due to there being very little time or places to do so. She found herself wanting him in that moment though, maybe it was the weird thrill she got out of possibly being caught, or how long she had been wanting him. It could have been the stress from the events of the day as well... she didn't know but she whispered in his ear;

"I want you now."

He paused for a moment, weighing the risks before kissing her harder.

He kissed down her breasts and feel his way around her body which caused her to moan into their kiss. She unwrapped her legs from his waist and began undoing his pants.

"We have to be quick," she whispered. The shower room was completely dark but she grabbed his erection and pushed him back against the wall. He nodded that he understood before guiding her to the cold tile floor. "I want you so bad," she breathed and pulled him between her legs.

He pushed into her, causing both of them to gasp. He thrusted into her repeatedly, she closed her eyes to enjoy every part of their bodies connecting. He was gentle and sweet with her, telling her how gorgeous she was, and she allowed him to admire her body with his.

They heard Cathmore call Davian's name, so they knew they had to hurry up. She wrapped her legs around his waist and urged him to finish. She nodded excitedly when he stilled and came inside of her, both of them breathless. It had felt amazing to share that with him so she told herself that she didn't finish because of the risk of being caught. He didn't seem to question it though but pulled on his pants and helped her up.

"I'll meet you out there," he whispered and exited the shower room.

She wrestled with herself about whether or not she truly enjoyed it. Intrusive thoughts told her that she had been avoiding sleeping with him and that's what took her so long to do so. She shooed the thought away.

She found herself drifting into thoughts about the way Cathmore ravaged her body in those secret meetings. She slid her hands into her pants and began rubbing at her clit as she remembered the way he would abruptly pull his cock out of her just to pleasure her with his mouth when she was about to come. Images of the way he threw his head back while she rode him flashed into her mind. Biting flesh, breathy moans, low groans from his chest all replayed in her mind the way they did late at night. She even found herself fantasizing about when he whipped her over the desk. She rubbed her clit harder as she chased her orgasm.

She rushed herself to finish because she heard the conscripts murmuring outside in the training hall. She pushed herself over the edge, biting into her arm as she thought about how rough he fucked her. *Shit.*

Amara left the room feeling like an awful person but put on a smile as she sat next to Juliet, Avren, and Eros. *What is wrong with me?* She swallowed hard, the taste of soap still in the back of her throat.

"Ashenfall," Cathmore called.

Of course he'd call her name right after what she had done. *Did he know?*

"She's the last one we have time for today, the other five will go tomorrow. Head back to the dorms." He dismissed them, maybe he did know. *Oh no.* Despite the dread she felt, excitement dwelled not far beneath it. *I'm insane.*

Cathmore began the pressure point test in silence, pressing the small hammer into the same pressure points as before. She would flinch at certain spots and he would take notes. She looked anywhere but the places where his fingers touched her skin. She was still so angry with him for what he had done. She was angry that he tossed her aside with a half ass excuse just to agree to start sleeping with Molvina, just to fuck with a Magister.

Was his reasoning for calling it quits even the truth?

"On your stomach," he mumbled. She rolled over and he pulled her shirt up, preparing to apply pressure to the point on her lower back. "I screwed up." He sighed suddenly.

"What?"

"Breaking your wrist in a moment of rage. I lost control," he admitted and added pressure to her sciatica.

His apology took her off guard. She rested her head on her arms and nodded. It didn't do much for the still aching bone nor did it appease the pain she felt deep down from his words to her and Molvina.

"Be careful with Molvina," Amara warned with a sigh. Cathmore froze, which prompted her to look back at him. His eyes were hooded as he stared at her. "She threw it in my face. She's going to get you killed." She gave him a look of disgust even though she didn't intend to. He thought for a moment and then sat the tool he was using on a tray next to him.

"I have to kill her," he said in a low voice. She sat up and turned to him, not surprised at all. "Not just because of this." He shook his head. "They want the known children of Sylas executed," he murmured. He was starting to resemble the person she had been entangled with, the person that she admired instead of the cruel, detached Praeceptor he had been the last few weeks.

"I know," she whispered as he resumed testing her pressure points.

"I don't want her," he explained. She knew that though, she knew about the blackmail. So she just shrugged as though it didn't matter. "You're doing great at controlling your Imperium, by the way," he offered her a small smile.

"Thanks," she returned the smile.

"You've maxed out your pain tolerance test, you're done." He sighed.

She rose from the mat on the floor, and he quickly followed, standing up to trail her out of the room and into the training hall.

"Do you have to finish yourself to thoughts of us often?" he asked suddenly as he trailed behind her. She spun around, dumbfounded by the audacity and his filthy mouth, though she really shouldn't have been.

"I fucking knew you could sense me," she groaned. Exasperation and embarrassment fought for .

"You're the one who projected your thoughts into my mind." He held up his hands feigning innocence. His arms were exposed due to the sleeveless shirt he was wearing. The veins in his forearms were particularly distracting.

"I did not!" She stomped in frustration. "Can't you teach me not to?" she asked.

"And why would I do that?" He gave her a playful sideways grin. He crossed his arms and looked her over from head to toe in the way he knew made her weak.

"Stop." She held up her hand. "I don't want you poking around in my head." She huffed.

"Or you don't want me to know that you aren't being fucked properly?" He mused and turned from her. She was momentarily distracted by his broad back before following after him.

"That's not true!" she called after him. "And you called this quits so you have no business worrying about my sex life," she added and he stopped.

"I was trying to protect you," he explained. "Do you think it's easy for me to see you with him?" His eyebrows furrowed, fear and regret in his eyes. *Where was this coming from?*

"You said you weren't jealous." She dropped her shoulders as the weight of his words settled over her.

"Like you weren't jealous when you found out about me and Magister Copia?" he retorted, leaning on the door frame, watching her.

"How did you even know that!" She was becoming more angry, more hostile. "You're the one who said there was nothing special about me. You said you didn't want *me*." Emotions swelled, causing a lump in her throat. She shoved him. "Asshole."

She stormed away from him. She would not allow him to see the tears forming in her eyes. She couldn't believe him, that he would say something like that after making her feel like she meant nothing to him.

He had been cruel and distant for weeks. He didn't get to just drop something like that on her. *Admitting jealousy? Dick move.* At least she was trying to swallow hers.

The next day Avren and Amara held hands as they made their way into the cafeteria for lunch in between their Imperium Preparation and Stamina lessons. He asked her multiple times that day what was wrong because she was lost in her own head. She cared so deeply for Avren, she needed him. She didn't want to lose him yet she felt like she was leading him on because of her desires for their Praeceptor.

No matter how many times she tried, she could not work through her messy mind. She thought about Molvina's inevitable death and despite how much she disliked the girl, she didn't want her to die. It wasn't her fault that her sire turned his back on the Hallowed Fallen. What if Amara transitioned and Sylas ended up being her sire? She had information about the death order on his children's heads and she couldn't do anything about it.

"Hey, love birds," Juliet greeted them as she took a seat across the table from them. "Who pissed Praeceptor Cathmore off?" At first she was confused until she caught his glare as he stormed out of the cafeteria.

"Who knows." She rolled her eyes. Avren squeezed her hand and took a bite of his food. "In other news, Eros kissed me."

"What?" Avren nearly choked on his food. It hadn't been a month since Judas died. "I thought he liked guys?" He added.

"He has no preference." She shrugged. The tint in Juliet's cheeks made Amara smile. Katara would be kicking her feet with excitement. "Don't tell him that I told you," she whispered as he headed their way.

Eros and Juliet? They made a cute couple.

A week later, hand-to-hand combat with Cathmore started with them finally being told the title of the next trial.

"This is going to be your most important course next to weapons wielding when it comes to the next trial," he told them. "You have three months to prepare for the Deathmatch."

"The what?" murmurs began amongst the group.

"Half of the remaining sired children will die that day," he announced. "On your feet," he demanded so that they could start their lesson. *Fuck.*

"We are sparing hand-to-hand today, no mercy, winner is whoever is still conscious," Cathmore instructed.

"Matches are as follows; Ambrose v Rosen, Juliet v Diana, Molvina v Amara, Eros v Avren, Davian v Vivianna. Isla will spar with one of the winners since we have an uneven number," he explained. *He was finally letting her and Molvina fight it out, fuck.*

Ambrose and Rosen fought hard, sweat coating them, blood dripping on the mat as blow after blow was taken by each of them. Molvina sneered at Amara across the ring, itching to get her hands on her. Amara wouldn't lose this time. Molvina switched terrifyingly between bouncy excited schoolgirl and angry manipulative bitch. It was exhausting.

Molvina had been threatening to tell Avren about her history with Cathmore all week, just for fun. Not even because she wanted anything from Amara other than to piss her off. It was grading on her to the point where she too was aching to fight the arrogant bitch.

With the sound of a jaw cracking and a thud to the floor, Rosen was down. Ambrose was the victor.

"Amara and Molvina." Cathmore motioned for them to step onto the mat. Amara's heart pounded, fueled by the searing rage that simmered beneath her skin. She could feel his eyes on them, weighing each of their movements, but the knowledge that he could easily compare them in ways that had nothing to do with fighting made her blood boil. The memory of Molvina's blackmail against him stoked her fury even more.

"Can I kill her?" Molvina asked, her voice dripping with mock sweetness, her lips curled into a smirk.

"We're not fighting to kill today," Cathmore replied coldly, his eyes narrowing as if daring her to defy him.

"Fight," he commanded.

Molvina threw a flirtatious wink at the Praeceptor, who only rolled his eyes, but Amara knew the kind of trouble Molvina's games could cause. She's going to get him thrown into the Abyss, and he's too blind to see it.

Amara charged without warning, every ounce of her anger driving her forward. She slammed into Molvina with her full weight, knocking the wind out of her. Molvina swung blindly, fists flying as she snarled, landing a few hits that stung Amara's arms and sides, but she pushed through the pain. Their screams filled the room as they wrestled on the ground, Molvina yanking Amara's hair viciously, but Amara fought back, managing to rear up and slap Molvina hard across the face. The impact sent a jolt of pain through her injured wrist, the bones still mending beneath her bandages, but she didn't care.

Molvina growled and rolled Amara, trying to trap her in a headlock. Typical, predictable Molvina. Amara twisted out of her grip, fueled by adrenaline, and scrambled to her feet. She turned just in time, delivering a brutal kick that connected with Molvina's face. A loud crack echoed through the room, and gasps erupted from the onlookers.

"Damn!" someone whistled, and the crowd's murmurs buzzed like angry bees.

Molvina staggered but forced herself up, blood trickling from her nose, her eyes wild with fury. She lunged again, this time with reckless abandon, but Amara sidestepped, watching Molvina's momentum send her crashing onto all fours. Molvina's arms trembled, one weak hand failing to keep her steady. Amara's next kick struck her square in the ribs, and Molvina crumpled to the floor with a pained gasp.

But Molvina just laughed—a ragged, choked sound—as she struggled to push herself up again, defiant even when half-broken. Amara wasted no time, leaping onto her back and wrapping her arm tightly around Molvina's throat.

"You were right, he's an animal in bed," Molvina said, her voice loud enough for everyone to hear. Amara's grip tightened as she saw the shocked faces of Davian, Eros, and Juliet turning toward Avren, who looked just as bewildered. Molvina's nails dug into Amara's skin, carving deep, stinging lines across her cheek, but Amara didn't let go.

"You don't know anything about him," Amara snarled, her voice thick with venom as she squeezed even harder, feeling the frantic throb of Molvina's pulse beneath her arm. Molvina's breaths turned to desperate wheezes, her body spasming as she fought for air. The room was drowned in chaos, but all Amara could hear was the rush of her own rage.

Molvina's face went slack, her eyes rolling back as she lost consciousness, but Amara didn't stop. She could still feel the sting of Molvina's taunts, the sting of every smirk and sly comment, and it pushed her further into her fury. She tightened her hold, watching Molvina's body twitch and shudder as the oxygen drained from her lungs. Yes.

Suddenly, hands clawed at Amara's arms, and she could faintly hear Cathmore shouting, his voice a distant roar over her own screaming. He was yelling for her to stop, to release Molvina, but she couldn't—she wouldn't. She squeezed tighter, pouring every ounce of built-up anger into the crushing hold.

Cathmore's voice cut through the haze as he finally pried her arm from around Molvina's neck, his expression stricken with shock and something like fear. Amara kicked against him, still thrashing wildly until her gaze fell on Molvina's body, now limp and unnaturally still. The girl's skin had turned a deep, dark blue, her chest barely rising as she lay there.

"What the hell!" one of the girls shrieked as Avren rushed forward, rolling Molvina onto her back, desperately checking for any signs of life.

Amara's breath came in ragged gasps, her chest heaving with the weight of what she'd done, and for a moment, the full gravity of her rage left her hollow and shaking. Nothing would ever be the same again.

"Praeceptor she's not breathing!" One of the girls screamed and chaos erupted amongst the conscripts.

"What did you do!" Avren yelled at her, Amara was staring blankly at Molvina, who was motionless. "Who was she talking about?" Avren shook her but she couldn't move.

Some of the conscripts were sent for healers to try and save her. Amara didn't move, she was simultaneously taking in the scene before her and blocking it out.

The healers called it, she was dead. The healers wrapped her body, some of the conscripts stayed with Molvina, soft cries filling the training hall.

She was a monster. She had done it again, she had killed again. The strangest form of loneliness was the kind she felt as she was trapped in her head, watching the world continue around her as she sunk into herself. The weight of her guilt crippled her and made her unresponsive to anything Cathmore might have been saying. She could see him in front of her talking and shaking her, his eyes wide, face flushed. She was pretty sure she couldn't even blink in response to him.

Cathmore yanked Amara's arm and took her out of the training hall. She knew he was taking her to the Crowned Magister by his silence.

She was dead, they couldn't kill conscripts outside of a trial and even then it wasn't common. It was all she could think about as he pulled her behind him.

The Crowned Magister made his way down the massive stairs from the building where his throne was.

"What happened, Praeceptor?" he asked. Cathmore shoved her forward. *He was going to let him kill her.*

"I ordered my student to kill one of Sylas' sired children in a one-on-one match," he answered.

What? No he hadn't...

The Crowned Magister raised his eyebrows; she made an effort to look confused as though she didn't understand why she had been instructed to do so.

"Is this true, Ashenfall?" He looked at her. She willed herself out of her catatonic state, knowing that her answers determined whether or not she lived. *Did she want to live?*

"He didn't say why, only that she was unworthy and I needed to prove that I could take orders," the lie flowed easily. She knew the Crowned Magister thought she was untamable and hard headed so maybe it would make it more believable.

"You took this order from the Praeceptor knowing it could result in your death?" he asked.

"Yes sir, I want to be deemed worthy of transformation."

"Very well, I will not sentence you to death. But it will cost you your pardon," the Crowned Magister mumbled.

"Of course sir," she bowed her head. She was still in a state of shock, trying to hold it together.

"You must make an example of her Praeceptor. This cannot happen again," he said as he turned to Cathmore.

"I intend to." He nodded respectfully, still squeezing Amara's arm.

They passed the healers carrying Molvina's body out of the training hall as they made their way back inside.

"It was only a matter of time before she killed again," one of the girls whispered to Davian as they walked past. Cathmore cleared his throat and shoved Amara forcefully to the ground before the other conscripts.

"Amara Ashenfall killed Molvina Hazelwood on my orders." He looked around the group who stared in disbelief. "However, the Crowned Magister and I have agreed on fourteen days in the pound for taking another's life." Amara looked around the room, hatred flowed off of everyone toward her. Juliet was crying, Avren hung his head as though ashamed, and Eros was trying to consol Juliet.

"I told you that your Praeceptor would kill those they deem unworthy, I did not say how. This is how Molvina paid the price for her inadequacy," Cathmore barked.

His shoulders were squared, he was steady, calm, sure of himself. He didn't leave any room for questions.

Amara stared at the very spot where she took Molvina's life, thinking that fourteen days in the pound was too much and not enough all at once.

Chapter 22

Hours passed and Amara was sitting in silence in one of the small rooms off of the training hall. Cathmore had bound her hands in front of her with rope and left her to sit on the floor, alone with her thoughts. She couldn't do anything about her throbbing broken wrist.

"Three minutes." Cathmore grunted and shoved Avren into the room with her. He scrambled to the floor, confusion dominating his usually soft features.

"What happened out there, Mar?" he asked gently.

"I'm the murderess, didn't you hear?" She shrugged, feeling empty.

"What was she talking about?" He pressed past her self-pity. "Is there someone else?" He looked like he was trying desperately to hold it together. *That's what he cares about?*

"I'm sorry, Av—" she cried and reached for his cheek. He jerked away from her.

"Who?" He got angry, which was very unusual for him.

"I can't." She shook her head, sniffling. "It's not…" She didn't have the words. She gasped for air, her world falling apart around her.

She couldn't say that she didn't cheat on him because she spent so much time longing for another, even when she wouldn't admit it to herself. She couldn't say who it was and she couldn't explain what Molvina had done. She couldn't tell him anything. She could only watch him fall to pieces in front of her and pretend like he wasn't.

"I should have known better than to trust you," Avren shook his head and stood, brushing his hair from his face. The words rang through her agonizingly.

He left the room without another word. Amara allowed her tears to fall as she stared in silence. Avren didn't deserve to be broken that way and she would have to live with what she did to him for the rest of her life.

She tried to prepare herself mentally for the pound. Cathmore hadn't spoken to Crowned Magister Bennett about it so she didn't know why he claimed that it was their agreement. She assumed though, that he would inform the Crowned Magister soon and have her transferred into the underground holding cell.

She heard the unit disperse and it wasn't long before Cathmore entered the room. He was looking less like the angry Praeceptor and more like an understanding friend. His features had softened in a way he had only seen them do for her, he stripped off his Praeceptor uniform jacket, and sat on the floor in front of her.

Not only had Avren seen and heard everything that transpired, but so had Cathmore. The only difference was that Cathmore knew that they had been fighting over him, he knew that Molvina had pushed her to kill for him. He didn't push her to talk, but waited in case she needed to.

"I don't want to talk about it." She sighed.

"Okay." He nodded. He just stared at her for a moment as though she were going to change her mind.

"When are they coming to take me?" she asked, regarding the guards that would take her to the pound. Cathmore tilted his head, one curl falling loose.

"You're not going to the pound, Ashenfall," he said , sitting back on his hands.

"What?" She whispered, finally meeting his eyes.

"You're staying in here for now. We're leaving at nightfall," he informed her. She fidgeted with the stiff ropes that bound her, the fibers burning her skin.

"Leaving? Where?" She sat forward. She didn't know whether to be excited or afraid. He was far too calm. He didn't answer her question but pulled a small knife from his pocket, stretching out one leg which grazed hers in order to reach it.

"Let me see," he asked for her hands. He gently cut the rope loose. She was left with deep red marks around her wrists. His eyes lingered on the irritated flesh there but she couldn't identify the thing that flashed in his eyes before he looked away.

"Where are you taking me?"

"I've arranged for one-on-one training on a more secluded part of the Sanctum Metere." He sighed. It felt so random, it didn't exactly sound like a punishment. *One-on-one? Just the two of them?*

"Crowned Magister Bennett approved this?" she questioned.

"What's important to him is that the students believe you are serving your time in the pound." He ran his finger down the blade of the small knife. "Let me worry about the details." He smirked.

"Why go through the trouble? Why not just lock me up?" she asked.

"Because I don't think you did anything wrong." He leaned closer to her.

"Cathmore, I murdered somebody," she snapped.

"That's part of the territory in this world. People die, you either kill or be killed. That's what the Deathmatch is about. No one transitions without blood on their hands," he reassured her.

"How many people have you killed?" She pushed, causing him to sit up and face her.

"More than you, does that make you feel better?" He retorted with a tilt of his head. She shook her head in disbelief. "I have an opportunity to help you master your Imperium before the Deathmatch. If you phase during that trial when faced with death, you're done and I can't help you."

"Maybe I need to be done," she exclaimed. She didn't know why she felt the need to get in his face to get her point across.

"No." He grabbed her chin forcefully. "I will not allow you to just give up," he vowed.

"It shouldn't matter to you," she bared her teeth. "You've made it clear I'm nothing to you." She jerked her chin free from his deliciously long fingers.

Venom laced her words. The poison of his rejection being redirected at him. She had been harboring so much hate and hurt where he was concerned.

"I made it clear? By protecting you?" He stood, scoffing in disbelief. "Do you understand that he would have executed you for what you did?" He shouted. She stood to meet him, unafraid, unyielding.

"I was prepared for that." She crossed her arms.

"You were willing to die because of your jealousy over me?" He taunted her.

"Fuck off." She shoved him.

"I mean I know you were willing to kill for it," he doubled down, curling his lip viciously.

She didn't think, she didn't even try to stop herself. She reeled back and punched him across the face.

"Egotistical asshole," she spat. He snapped his head back toward her, his eyes dilating in fury. "She is dead because of you!"

"No, she is dead because she thought she could blackmail me." He stepped onto her, causing her to stumble backward. "She is dead because of your unwillingness to accept your feelings for me." She backed into the wall, looking into his darkening ocean eyes.

"You are insane," he growled at him. He seemed to inhale her but she couldn't read his expression that was some mixture of knowing and anger.

"I'll be back at nightfall." He looked over her and stormed out of the room.

She made a strangled screaming noise in frustration and threw everything off of the cabinet in the small room. *Fuck him.*

As promised, in the dead of night, Cathmore took her out of the training hall and into the gardens.

He moved to pull her into him as he opened his massive wings before her. She stepped back.

"No, don't touch me."

"We can't walk to where we're going, brat."

"Then I don't want to go." She turned away from him.

"So you'd opt for rotting in a hole for two weeks?"

"Fine," she groaned.

He stood before her and gently pulled her against him. Her body was stiff, on edge. She didn't want to be so close to him. But still he wrapped his arms around her and shot into the sky before she could fully tighten her grip on him. She hugged him tight around his stomach and buried her face in his chest—suddenly wanting nothing more than to be within his embrace. Something between a scream and a cry erupting from her as she fought the need to pass out. She blinked through the darkness at the edge of her vision before deciding to keep her eyes closed altogether.

She was pondering his invasive need to get a bead on those around him, to understand and know exactly what they were thinking. It was probably his most annoying ability. She had been so consumed with anger and still was. It took hours alone in that room for her to realize that maybe she did have feelings for him as he proclaimed.

"Look." He tried to turn her head away from his chest. She shook her head. *Hell no.* "If you don't, I'll drop you, brat."

"That's not fair," she yelled. She glanced to the side and saw brilliant colors flowing over the mountain, decorating the sky.

Greens, purples, and blues swirled and flowed in a breathtaking display, stars peppered throughout them. Far below them, towering trees were smaller, the mountains seemingly rising to dominate them. *Wow.*

Cathmore tilted forward, making her feel like she was falling backward. She grasped his shirt; he tightened his arms around her. He began his descent toward the woods and all she could think about was how would he land amongst the trees. She looked up, curious to see the way he looked when he was flying.

He looked content with the breeze flowing through his hair, his eyes scanning the area he was aiming for, his lips were slightly parted as he focused.

"Your eyes are glowing," she said in awe. They were, the silver rings were lit up slightly, his pupils dilated as he scanned the forest below them.

"It's how we see at night," he explained and smiled down at her. "Hold on tight." He didn't have to tell her twice so she wrapped her arms around his neck, making herself smaller and closed her eyes.

He landed in a run before slowing to a stop. She heard his wings fold back and looked over his shoulder to watch them disappear.

"Where do they go?" she asked, still clinging to him, trying to catch her breath.

"Our wings are tethered to our souls and their home is in spirit. They are available to us whenever we need them but they stand by in that dimension." He paused. "I think." He laughed. She allowed herself a small laugh before uncoiling herself from his midsection.

She trailed behind him in silence, rubbing the chill from her arms. Eventually a cabin came into view as she was fixated on the crunching of leaves below their feet. The way the canopy of trees hung over it made it feel like an escape from the world around it. The logs that made up the cabin were covered in gorgeous ivy, almost giving it the illusion of having grown from the forest floor itself. The roof was coated in a thick layer of the moss, wild flowers peppered into it.

She touched a pedal of one of the glowing flowers at her feet, ivy covered the forest floor around the cabin and made the varying bright colored flowers stand out. She inhaled the clean fresh scent of the forest, excited to see what the inside of the cabin held. She ran her fingers over the delicately carved wooden handrail and took a few steps upward. Cathmore leaned against the door frame and opened the door for her.

"What does that mean?" she asked, running her fingers along words in a foreign language that was carved next to the door.

"Captain's Quarters," he answered. He was the captain of the guard, that means...

"This is yours?" she turned to him.

"Yes, kind of. I can't live here until I'm no longer a Praeceptor." He shrugged. He gently nudged her forward.

She realized that if he was going to be training her, that he would miss teaching his classes.

"What about your classes?" she asked, trying to work through the details.

"The students will learn that I mouthed off to Bennett and was thrown in the pound as well, though only for a week." He shrugged. "It was the best I could do. That second week I'll teach you in the evening after the workday is over," he explained further.

"Oh." She nodded and pushed the door open.

As she stepped inside, the vastness of the space enveloped her. The high vaulted ceiling seemed to reach for the heavens, and her footsteps sank into a gloriously soft rug that embraced a sturdy stone fireplace. She imagined her toes sinking into the cloudlike material and grinned, she had never been in a home so pleasant.

To the left of the door, a quaint kitchen came into view, complete with a wood-burning stove and pans suspended from the ceiling. Spices and fresh fruit were stored on the counter and a glass cupboard showed that the cabin had been fully stocked with dishes and food.

Cathmore moved to the fireplace on her right, striking a match and coaxing flames to life. She glanced around, noticing a massive four poster bed adorned with flowing satin drapes at the far end of the room. The bed's black sheets and dark red quilt added a touch of opulence to the rustic surroundings.

Drawn to the enormous bookshelf beside the fireplace, she ran her fingers over the spines of the books, feeling their textured and aged spines. The furniture, crafted from fine, dark wood, exuded a sense of timeless elegance. Paintings hung on the walls, depicting fallen angels, the depths of hell, and a hauntingly dark mountain landscape that seemed to whisper secrets she couldn't quite decipher.

"This feels like a reward for murder." She sighed as she stared at a stone wall.

"It's not a reward." He walked up behind her—careful not to get too close. "It's a break. It's a chance for you to breathe and train."

"How many times did you sleep with her?" She turned to him, hugging her arms to her abdomen. She needed to know, she couldn't be around him any longer without knowing the truth.

"Twice," he answered honestly and searched her eyes.

"She was going to tell Avren. She was going to get you killed." Amara shook her head, tears stinging her eyes.

"They would have killed you too." He tilted her chin so that she would look at him. "She was going to die today no matter what. I was going to do it tonight," he told her transparently. She nodded and turned away from him, unsure if it made it better or worse. *Because she was sired by Sylas, she had to die anyway.*

Did it help?

No.

"I'll be right back," Cathmore excused himself and entered a washroom opposite the fireplace.

She pulled white linens off of the couch and two armchairs in front of the fireplace. Sage green cushions had embroidered flowers growing across them in delicate patterns. It didn't seem like his taste but maybe he hadn't made it his own yet. She took a seat at the small wooden dining table off of the kitchen and inhaled deeply, resting her face in her hands. *How am I not dead yet?* Cathmore emerged from the washroom where she could hear the water still running.

"Come here." He extended his hand. She took it and he led her into a gorgeous bathing chamber.

He was running water into a clawfoot tub, the moonlight pouring through the skylight in the ceiling. She was looking up, allowing the sight above her and the smell of the bath salts to relax her, when Cathmore placed his hands on her shoulders. She turned to him with a calming exhale.

"I know you still hate me, but I thought you could use a hot bath after everything you've been through," he offered. She almost didn't know *how* to be with the version of him that wasn't sarcastic and egotistical.

"Thank you," she breathed. She began bunching her hair up to get it out of her face in preparation for the bath.

"Here," he whispered and turned her around. She waited curiously as he braided her dark hair back. It didn't take him long and she turned to him, amused.

"How?" she asked, it hardly seemed like a skill he would possess.

"I have two sisters," he stated simply. "I'll leave you to it," he exited the bathing chamber.

Amara stripped out of her training clothes, now sown with death, and lowered herself into the water, willing it to draw out every ounce of tension in her body. She allowed herself to feel the guilt of the horrors she had committed. She closed her eyes and saw Bastian Marlowe's throat slit before her, his blood painting the floor. A tear fell. She could still feel when Molvina stopped struggling for air, when her unconscious body stopped twitching, and all life faded to nothingness.

She knew what it felt like to draw life from another, to be the force that separated their soul from their body. She was disgusted with herself for how easy it had been to kill them in the moment, how fear and anger reduced her to nothing more than a blood-thirsty animal. It was a primal feeling. It was sick.

She was a sired child, she would become Nephilim. That thought didn't scare her anymore, as though the transformation could wash her hands clean of the blood that coated them. Nephilim lived with a savage beast just below the surface of their skin, which made them faster, stronger, *better* than humans. She watched the tree branches sway through the skylight, watched the branches bend to the will of the wind. It was eerily similar to the way she had begun to bend to the wrath of fate.

She was so far removed from the girl she had been, that she stumbled head-first into wanting the one thing she tried to out-run—her right to her Nephilim form and her truth. She would have both, she saw no reason not to any longer. A mediocre life of struggle amongst humans would not be her fate, she refused. Katara once told her that she needed to embrace her destiny because she couldn't change it. Maybe it just took the right amount of blood on her hands for her to accept that truth.

She felt something swell inside of her, something that had been asleep. It wasn't quite awake yet but it was making itself known. She grinned and laid back in the tub. She would fulfill her destiny, for Katara.

Chapter 23

"*A*vren?" Amara tilted her head as she padded into a startlingly empty weapons wielding pyramid.

Something wet seeped between her toes but she couldn't see what it was in the dark. She was beginning to hyperventilate as choking noises grew louder. She hesitated to turn the corner toward where the gurgling was beginning.

"Avren?" She whimpered.

Someone grabbed her arm and yanked her backwards.

"Don't worry about it, it happens." Cathmore flashed a wicked grin with a smile far too big for his face. She grimaced; he didn't look like himself.

She turned that corner, remembering that Avren was in need of help. She felt like she was moving through tar, like her steps were slowed but she didn't know why. Finally Avren came into view, standing before her. He was perfectly fine.

That was, until she stepped forward and slashed a dagger across his throat without hesitation. Crimson liquid streamed from his *flayed open skin and he gurgled again. He collapsed before her, twitching the way Bastian had.*

"No, no, no. I'm sorry!" She scrambled to the ground to help him but her body betrayed her. She pulled him into a headlock.

The substance on the floor was a pool of blood and it was flowing around them.

His blood poured over her arm and she squeezed harder as she screamed and tried to get herself to stop. She couldn't stop though and waited for him to stop struggling.

"I'm sorry."

"I'm sorry."

She kept repeating it as her body entangled with his.

"One step closer," Cathmore appeared behind her. Shadows swirled around him, his eyes bled, and his teeth protruded unnaturally from his mouth. He reached for her.

"No!" She screamed.

"Amara!" Cathmore was gathering her into his arms.

"Get off!" She thrashed against him, tears pouring down her face. He let her out of his grip and she launched herself off of the bed.

Why was he in the bed? He had slept on the couch.

"It was just a nightmare," he crouched down in front of her but was careful not to touch her. His eyebrows were drawn together, his hair ruffled, his gaze pained.

She scooted away from him to make herself smaller in the corner. She couldn't shake his distorted face from her dream.

"Amara..." he reached for her but she jumped, causing him to drop his hand. His gaze searched the room, he was trying to find any physical threat, anything to grapple with to fix her, anything to take control of the situation.

She tried to control her labored breathing. Her skin felt like it was coated in blood, her arm muscles twitching as she recalled strangling the life from Molvina. *I shouldn't know how that feels, I don't want to know how that feels. I deserve to suffer.*

Amara tried to get her bearings but she couldn't move, it seemed impossible. Cathmore brought a blanket from the bed and draped it around her shoulders but allowed her to remain in silence. She stared into the dancing flames of the fireplace, mesmerized by its beauty.

Cathmore stared at her and pulled his knees to his chest. He sat against the bed clearly not wanting to leave her alone but unsure of how to help her. Maybe he knew there wasn't anything he could say to her to comfort her. He had been sleeping in only his undershorts, his tan skin illuminated by the flames in the dark cabin. The wind howled outside as she tried to sort through her scattered thoughts.

"The events that you're being forced to endure aren't fair," he whispered into the darkness. "I never liked the thought of making sired children choose between dying or living with the guilt of murdering someone."

She didn't expect him—a Praeceptor—to have such opposing beliefs to the system. She tugged the blanket around her further, blinking back tears.

"The first time I killed someone was not because of the Crucible . Maybe I could have lived with myself if it was. The first time I spilled blood, I chose to," he confessed.

She could see him biting his cheek, his jaw fluttering. His facial features cast harsh shadows under his high cheekbones and jaw due to the fireplace. She stared at the side of his face, unsure how to take the information.

"Why did you do it?" she asked in a husky voice.

"It was him or me," was all he said.

That's how she felt with Bastian. He was turning her over to the Crucible, she thought it meant death. But with Molvina? She was blinded by rage and something deep down that wanted to drain her life from her.

She dropped her head into her knees, a lump swelling in her throat. She didn't think that a living being was supposed to take another's life—save for an animal hunting food. It felt like it was undoing her humanity and laying waste to her capacity for empathy. She felt cold and foreign within her own head.

"I think I lost a part of me in every life I took; I believe that's the price for ending a life," Cathmore said.

"Get out of my head," she snapped. His admission felt as though in direct response to her line of thinking.

"I'm not in your head. Your walls are about as solid as they could be right now," he told her.

"Great. So emotional turmoil is the only way to block you out?" She scoffed.

"No. You're in survival mode right now. Your instincts are protecting you from everything," he explained. She just nodded and wiped her tears that had been falling silently. She was so tired of crying.

The next morning, Amara awoke alone, on the floor. She had fallen asleep with her head leaning back against the wall. Cathmore must have had business to attend to back at the Sanctum Metere.

Amara spent hours rifling through the plethora of books and teachings that the cabin was stocked with. She was engaged with a book that detailed the Angelic Exodus, wanting to know more about Sylas.

Sylas had also fallen during the Exodus, nothing stood out about him really. Along with all of the Fallen, their reasons for being cast out were hidden so that didn't offer her any insight. She wondered if anyone knew the true reason their God expelled so many of his angels at once. The book alluded to him being fed up with his human creation and the way his holy creation resemble them. She knew though that it was a book and its author couldn't know for certain. She recalled other teachings that they were sent to control and watch over humans.

Sylas was described as being younger in physical appearance than most of his Hallowed counterparts, his hair was naturally blue-black, his eyes so icy blue that they were nearly white. He had pale skin, harsh features, and was generally regarded as more gentle than some of the other Hallowed Fallen.

Did his gentle nature make him an easy target for the Dark One? He originally fled Ravenyr when Deimos took over but doubled back and joined him in his fallen kingdom. *Had Sylas been working with Deimos? Did he allow his kingdom to be taken by him?* She had so many questions.

With her newfound resolve to fulfill her destiny, she started looking for any mention of 'phasing' in some of the Imperium books. She read through multiple Imperiums, followed by pages of their descriptions;

Healing—A gift from Kaemon to his sires.

Astral Projection—A gift from Arwan to his sires.

Telekinesis—A gift from Sylas to his sires.

Precognition—A gift from Lonan to his sires.

Element wielding—A gift from Rase to his sires.

Illusion manipulation-A gift from Lyall to his sires.

Dimensional Travel—A gift from Hadeon to his sires.

Energy absorption—A gift from Torin to his sires.

Shielding—A gift from Osias to his sires.

Memory manipulation—A gift from Ender to his sires.

That was how sires were learned during transition and during the development of Imperiums. *One can be sired to a Hallowed Fallen and have varying gifts though it is not common,* the book emphasized. *Ugh.*

Nowhere did it mention what she could do—what Cathmore called 'phasing'. He had also called it just the beginning, which she believed because she could feel her power waking in her core. *What else would she develop?*

She wondered who sired Cathmore, she didn't know what to call his abilities either. Telekinesis? So... Hadeon? She flipped through the Book of Hallowed Fallen to find physical characteristics of Hadeon.

He was described as having jet black hair, a thinner but toned build and deep blue eyes. If that didn't convince her, the description of his full lips and high cheekbones did. He had a short temper, ruled with an iron hand, and had superior clairvoyance abilities. Hadeon sired Cathmore. Fear coursed through her when she found similar characteristics between herself and Hadeon.

But her dark hair had come from her mother, just like her green eyes. Hadeon and Cathmore had more square faces as well, whereas hers was more heart-shaped, her lips thinner and poutier. Her face shape, lips, and body type were all mysteries. Her mother wasn't as thin as Amara was but bulkier built. Whoever sired her gave her those characteristics and those weren't exactly the same as Hadeon. Similar, but different. Plus her abilities were different from Cathmore and she didn't have telekinesis.

Just to be sure she focused on a stool across the room, trying to will it to move. To her relief, nothing happened.

What she did was kind of like teleportation, but that wasn't really mentioned as an Imperium either. Ugh. She knew she could drive herself crazy if she wanted to so she shoved the book back onto the shelf and plopped onto the bed.

Hours passed and she busied herself in the kitchen to occupy her mind away from her mother, from Avren, from the people she killed. She was chopping fresh vegitables for soup when Cathmore came in. He tossed the journal he usually carried around onto the dining table and took a seat.

"Bennett is not happy with me." He sighed.

"Because you didn't throw me in the pound?" she asked and dropped the carrots and potatoes into the broth.

"Well he thought the ploy to be an ingenious way to make the students believe you were being punished, without actually punishing you for following an order for once. He just didn't want to give me a week off and go along with the lie." He shrugged.

"So did he?" she asked

"Reluctantly, yes. I called in a favor." He smiled. "I've got to teach for the next two days, my week off will start on the three day weekend. Well my week of 'punishment,'" he used air quotes around the word.

Cathmore was particularly dashing that day. He wore a white button-down shirt with the sleeves rolled and the top few buttons open. His usual leather pants offset the shirt nicely and she didn't have to look down to know he wore his black boots with the straps and buckles. She noted that his hair was brushed back but the waves made strands still fall wildly everywhere. It was the faint hint of shadow on his face that added a new appeal, he was usually clean shaven and had obviously skipped shaving that morning.

"You seem to be owed a lot of favors." She shook her head, locking eyes with him. She recalled Nightbane saying they were 'even' after he healed her. He didn't deny it.

She turned from him and stirred the massive pot of soup, inhaling the aroma. It was nice to cook again, nice to be in a home again instead of a communal sleeping space or a tavern. Not that Aunt Grace gave her a good home, but there were some memories she could look back on fondly. Cooking being something she found comfort in.

"What is your Imperium called?" she asked curiously. He was silent for a moment.

"Why?" he asked, opening his journal.

"I was reading about them." She pointed at the bookshelf. "I didn't see one that described exactly what it is you do."

"Mine is lesser known, it's not one of the big ten, . I do have dimensional travel from my sire," he explained.

"Hadeon?" She remembered that it was the gift he often passed down to his sired children.

"Yes, the one you have seen me use kind of a mix between dimensional travel and telekinesis. They call it summoning." He walked over to her. "Bread?" He materialized a loaf out of nowhere and sat it on the wooden cutting board in front of her.

"Wow," she breathed. "Does it hurt?"

"No." He laughed. He pulled off a piece and popped it in his mouth. "What kind of soup is that?"

"Just chicken and vegetables." She shrugged. He walked away and returned to whatever he had been writing.

"Tell me about phasing." She turned to him, leaning against the counter.

"Well, it's something you can do with your body, at a cellular or atomic level," he began.

"Huh?" she asked

"Okay, you know how atoms make up the world around us and everything in it?" he askedleaned back in the chair.

"Vaguely." She nodded.

"Imagine they're kind of like beans for the sake of me explaining this. You are in touch with your spiritual self enough, that you are able to essentially break apart into a series of atoms and re-materialize elsewhere." He was talking with his hands, gesturing while he spoke as though he was passionate about the idea. She just looked at him in confusion. "Okay look," he shot up and walked into the kitchen.

He pulled a jar of dried beans from the cupboard and tossed the lid to the side. She looked at him as though he had lost his mind.

"Give me your finger," he said. She did so, hesitantly. He shoved her index finger into the jar, the beans separating around her finger. "See how the beans or the atoms go around the physical thing touching it?" She nodded. He grabbed a knife and stabbed it into the jar.

"The same thing happens here too; it forms around the shape of whatever physical thing is touching it. That's what you did when Nightbane was hurting you. You essentially evaporated from your physical to your spiritual form instantaneously. This allowed you to get out from around his touch and throw yourself elsewhere because of the pain," he clarified.

"And when you grabbed for me in your room…"

"You slipped into spirit and out of my grasp. It was miraculous," he praised. "I could see you, in between our realm and the spiritual dimension. I had never seen it happen before; I've only heard of the ability as something some of the Fallen possessed."

"So does it tell you who sired me?" She pressed. He paused as though taken aback by her sudden interest in her sire.

"No, it doesn't. I think your true tell-tale Imperium will develop at transition and that will be the answer to who sired you," he offered.

"Right." She nodded.

"I got the impression that you didn't want to know." He pushed. She stirred the soup again; it would be a while before it was ready to eat.

"I didn't, not really. I just know that I'll learn the truth eventually," she surmised. Cathmore walked back to the table to resume whatever he was doing with the book and journal.

"That you will, no outrunning it," he teased. *Yeah, yeah, I ran.*

Amara made herself comfortable on the couch and dove into a fiction book while the cabin became filled with the aroma of her simmering soup. It was such a peculiar feeling to feel safe, she wasn't sure how to accept it. She sighed.

"It is actually not bad," Cathmore mused and took another spoon-ful of her soup.

"Not bad? It's delicious," she corrected him with a laugh.

"Okay, we really need to try to work on this Imperium thing," he said more seriously. "Step one is you learning *how* to actually do it so you know how *not* to do it." They were sitting cross-legged in front of the fireplace with their soups and bread.

"I thought using it would draw the attention of my sire?" she asked.

"It could, but the second trial is over so some of the sired chil-dren are starting to feel their Imperium's development. The more time that passes, the less risky. Plus, we'll only do it a handful of times." He suddenly launched a massive piece of bread at her, it hit her square in the forehead and plopped into her bowl of soup, crumbs falling into her eyes.

"What the hell was that?!" She exclaimed.

"Well, the element of surprise didn't make it work," he mused.

"No but it did piss me off." She huffed and threw her bread at his chest. "Think of a better way."

"Fear or pain then?" he asked.

"Neither." She rolled her eyes, which flipped his mood from playful to serious.

"Didn't we talk about the eye rolling?" He tilted his head; the fireplace casting shadows over his harshly sculpted features.

"Yes, Praeceptor, I'm sorry." She held up her hands feigning innocence. Her apology was only half sincere. She pushed away the thrill she got from watching him flip into the predatory disciplinarian. "Can't we work on this whole you reading my mind thing first?"

"We can, but I don't know what or why it is," he answered, his voice low. She had put him into Praeceptor headspace and he was looking at her like she was a meal. She recalled her calling him Praeceptor in bed when she needed him to fuck her harder. *Nope stop.*

"Just tell me how to block you out," she snapped, more to get her own mind right.

"Does it happen when you think about me normally through-out the day?" he asked.

"I don't think so, usually I'm only thinking about a question to ask in class or something though," she answered. "Shouldn't you be able to tell me if I'm popping into your head during class?"

"You do sometimes it seems that it's not so much you thinking about me as much as you wanting me. I don't get bombarded with you in my head unless you are feeling—" she cut him off.

"I get it." She sighed and cringed at herself.

"I knew you were under my bed that night because I could sense you, but I didn't start hearing your thoughts really until you got all hot and bothered." He further pushed his point. "And then in the shower room..."

"Are you finished?" She crossed her arms.

"Not to mention the way you undress me with your eyes while I'm teaching." He tsked.

"Okay, so stop wanting you, easy. Done," she sassed him and stood.

"We'll see." He smirked.

"Wait." She turned. "Why could you feel me when Marlowe had me then? You saw what happened, you felt it..." she trailed off.

"And when Nightbane was healing you." He stood as if recalling something. "That was excruciating for me as well."

It was?

"And I can assure you; I was not thinking about you at that moment." She slammed her bowl onto the counter, frustrated. "This just doesn't make any sense."

"We will figure it out," he reassured her. "I'll do some more research."

"Speaking of, any word on the file about my mother?" She remembered to ask.

"No, it's still gone. But, it doesn't reveal her killer." He shook his head sympathetically.

"I know." She nodded.

"Well, we're going for a run in an hour, so prepare for that." He changed the subject. "Need to make sure your stamina stays up." He began cleaning the dishes and she sighed.

"Fine."

"Clothes for you are in the trunk in the washroom by the way," he called after her as she headed into said room.

She fumbled through the various articles of clothing from her normal training clothes, sleep gowns which she was not going to wear around him, casual pants, and even gorgeous dresses that she never would have imagined herself wearing. She had always been forced into hand-me-downs and tattered clothing, never had she seen such gorgeous dresses. There were even corsets and slips that went with them. She marched out of the room.

"You are delusional if you think I am wearing these." She held up the gowns and dresses.

"Thought you'd like some variety." He laughed. He seemed so much younger when he smiled, especially when it reached his eyes. It distracted her more often than she would ever tell him and she found herself hoping to see that smile and laugh more often.

"Ha, ha, ha," she mocked. She refused to admit that she found them beautiful and was actually curious if she could pull off the sheer looking lace dresses with beautiful forest green and blue tones.

"You can pull them off," he answered her thoughts.

"Get the hell out of my head, asshole," she chucked the nearest candlestick at him-which he dodged—and stormed into the washroom. *Ugh.*

"You're going to pay for that during training, brat!" He called.

Amara had indeed paid for the candlestick during training because he forced her to do sprints until she was sure her feet were bleeding. He worked her until her arms were practically useless.

When she awoke the next morning, she was so sore that she had to fight to drag herself out of bed. Even then it was with a limp and a wince anytime she lifted her arms. She was lifting the comforter to crawl back into bed since the sun hadn't risen yet when Cathmore had to make a smart remark.

"Try throwing something at me now." He popped his head over the back of the couch. The moonlight and soft light from the fireplace allowed him to be visible. The smart thing to do would be to ignore his taunts, but she was stubborn and refused to let him think he broke her.

She grabbed a clay trinket dish off the nightstand and chucked it as his head. When it struck true though she didn't know rather to gloat or run. She hadn't actually expected to hit him, but it had, right on the side of his head. The *thunk* noise followed by Cathmore rolling off of the couch and onto the floor in a dramatic scene made her laugh, until he was in front of her before she could blink. *Hell.*

She flung the comforter up and darted underneath it, wrapping herself as tight as possible for safety. She was put off by his silence more than anything but she could hear the faint sound of him pacing slowly around the bed. He had made himself quieter, his footsteps sounded lighter, but she could still hear him.

"You told me to!" She blurted out as anticipation swelled in her chest. *How was he going to retaliate?*

Cathmore went completely silent, the air underneath her blanket becoming thick from her ragged breathing. She waited a moment, before feeling brave enough to peek her head out. He snatched the blanket from her hands and yanked it off of her causing her to squeal. She rolled to the other side of the bed to get away from him but he grabbed her leg and wrenched her back toward him.

"What's the punishment for attacking your Praeceptor?" He questioned as she kicked against him. He grabbed both of her legs, flipped her, and pulled her to the edge of the bed where he ended up standing between her legs.

"Death." She huffed, knowing good and well he wouldn't kill her. *She hoped.* She tried to push him away when he leaned over her and pinned her arms above her head. He widened his stance, effectively spreading her legs to limit her motion.

"You're an infuriating little thing," he whispered, sending chills down her body. His hair fell messily around his head, he was shirtless because that's how he slept, so she looked anywhere but into his eyes.

"You're a jackass," she retorted. "And you're hurting my wrist." She squirmed. She knew he felt guilty for what he had done so it wasn't a surprise when he released it.

She knew if she didn't find a way out from under him she would give into the desires that were forming in the back of her mind. The man looked like a God and her body fucking came alive for him. Even at times when she didn't want it to. She was still trying to heal over Avren, still trying to make peace with what she had done to Molvina—if it was even possible.

She fought against him, when he grabbed her waist and forced her onto her stomach, she knew she was going to enjoy his retaliation far too much. *No.* Avren and Molvina flashed into her mind and before she knew it, she had phased out of his grip and onto the floor at the foot of the bed. She clattered clumsily to the floor, the stone scraping her knees. *Ow.* Not only did the landing hurt but she had phased with intention, focusing on leaving his grip which left her body humming.

Every nerve in her body vibrated as though it were one fire. She panted, allowing the pain to come and pass in short waves. She didn't recall it happening before which was odd.

"You're getting stronger, I actually had a hard time seeing you in the spiritual dimension that time," he observed and helped her up.

"It hurt that time too," she informed him. He nodded as though that were to be expected. He helped her back onto the bed, her body still reeling from the phasing and the heightened awareness of him so close, preparing to punish her. Warmth pooled between her legs. *No.*

He was leaning partially over her, watching her recover, observing the way her body reacted to the Imperium use. She watched his gorgeous eyes rake over her body, etched in concern. His jaw feathered as he thought, a tale of his when he was trying to work out a problem. *Was he trying to figure out how to help with the Imperium or punish her though?* She saw a large scar over his bare shoulder, slicing across his chest.

"What happened?" she asked and traced it with her finger. He grabbed her hand, stopping her, and shook his head.

"No." He didn't want to talk about it. She furrowed her eyebrows, frustrated but he wouldn't look in her eyes.

She reached up and touched the side of his head where the dish had struck him, there was a bump and a small bit of blood. She scooted back out from under him and he let her.

"I didn't think it would actually hit you," she said, apologizing.

She rubbed his blood between her fingers, something about it drawing her in, making her mouth water. *What the fuck.* She looked at him in confusion.

"Go ahead, if you're craving it." He bit his lip, watching her focus on his blood, craving his blood as though it were the last drop of water on earth.

"I've never... Why do I want to?" She shook her head, looking up at him in shock.

"It's complicated." He gave her a cocky grin; it reached his eyes. Any trace of what troubled him about that scar was replaced with heated amusement.

"Tell me!" she demanded.

"Try it." He sat on the bed next to her. Part of her wanted to say hell no, the other part of her was an animal that *needed it* like oxygen. She shook her head, trying to get some sense into her mind.

He touched the side of his head; a small amount of blood came off on his fingertip. He looked from his finger, to her thoughtfully. She was focused on the crimson liquid that had begun to drip down his fingertip. Her breathing was increasing. He placed the pad of his middle finger on her bottom lip, giving her a taste of his blood. The salty sweet taste took a moment for her to accept on her taste buds, but she locked eyes with him. She darted her tongue out, taking his finger slowly into her mouth.

"Good girl," he praised as he longingly watched her clean the blood from his finger. He removed it, leaving her with a feeling of disappointment. So she finally licked the blood off of hers as well. He smiled, satisfied.

"Are you going to tell me why I wanted it?" She huffed. He turned to her, his knee knocking hers as they faced each other on the bed.

"Do you think you should be punished?" He countered.

"I think you like punishing me," she retorted. He shrugged, not denying it. "But I think we can call it even after what you did to my wrist."

"Will you forgive me if I let this go?" He gestured toward his head. She didn't want to tell him she already forgave him. She nodded. She knew the broken wrist was part of the punishment that he was dealing, for them breaking a rule, but they both knew he was out of line for letting his emotions get the better of him. "Deal." He stood.

She felt a mix of relief and disappointment. She secretly enjoyed the part of him that sought to punish her, to hurt her. She felt like that meant she was fucked up, but she didn't care. Whatever she was becoming, she would do so unapologetically. She still needed time though, before letting him back in.

"Answer the question, Praeceptor," she demanded. He paused and leaned on the bed, eye level with her. His strong arms were flexing under his weight. *Fuck.*

"Every time you call me that, all I can think about is you moaning it while begging to be fucked harder," he hissed, equally pleased and annoyed by the fact. *Oh.*

"Sorry," she squeaked and made herself smaller beneath him. "Tell me, please."

"Consider what your body just went through. An Imperium of this magnitude takes a lot more to fuel," he whispered. She held her breath, frozen with the possibility that she might require blood regularly.

"Others crave it too?" she asked, still tense.

"I do." He shrugged as if it were the most normal thing in the world. "You're the only other one I've met with an uncommon Imperium," he crawled toward her, his knees stopping him on the edge of the bed. "Though, I've never craved someone the way I do you," he hummed. She took in a shaky breath, causing him to grin. He was so close to her that she could feel his slow, steady breathing.

"The bites..." she breathed recalling the night he covered her body in delicious bleeding bite marks. It had been the most erotic thing she had ever experienced. He was a master of balancing pleasure and pain.

"Mhmm," he confirmed. He, too, sensed the charged air between them and pushed himself off of the bed once more.

It seemed to take a great deal of self-control for him *not* to continue his teasing of her as he made his way back onto the couch. He sighed, reminding her to breathe. She looked over to him, the way the couch was too short for his height and his legs had to be propped up made her feel guilty.

"You can sleep in the bed you know," she informed him. *What are you doing, Amara?* She chastised herself.

"I figured you needed space." He sat up. "From me."

"I need space from myself more than anything, but since that's not possible..." She waved him over and crawled under the covers. "Besides, it's just sleeping."

After a moment he crawled into the bed as well, she was turned opposite of him. There was a certain comfort to not being in the giant bed alone, plus he was warm. Both of them made special effort not to touch one another, but she was so aware of him. It was like their energies were reaching for each other, giving a buzzing sensation of need just to scoot closer to him.

It wasn't long before she slipped comfortably into sleep to the sounds of his breathing beside her.

Chapter 24

"*I promised not to say anything!*" *A woman screamed.*

The scene was blurry, minimal details stood out. A dark-haired woman was screaming at a tall man before her.

"You can't take her from me!" She cried. "She's mine!" The woman was holding a baby who cried as it looked up at the impossibly tall man.

He had spiked black hair, silver eyes, and a skinnier build. His face was thin, with sharp angles at the back of his jaw and tip of his nose. He had high cheekbones, the shadows beneath them were harsh. His ears were pointed as well. She had never seen anyone with pointed ears but his silver eyes told her he was a Fallen Angel or Nephilim.

"I don't want the child, you fool," he growled and backhanded the blurry yet familiar woman.

"Mama!" She screamed suddenly. It was her mom, her mom.

She dropped the toddler she was holding but recovered quickly and crawled away screaming. The baby... it had green eyes and dark hair.

It was her...

The being—whose details were blurring away—grabbed her mother's head and ripped it from her body, sending blood spraying all over the cottage, all over the child. Amara screamed in horror.

Amara's scream of terror pierced the chaos. The blood rose, flooding the room in a crimson tide. The sinister laughter echoed, a cruel, mocking sound. Blood filled her lungs, choking her as her mother's lifeless body lay beside her. The younger version of herself drowned in the nightmarish deluge, gasping for breath as darkness closed in.

"Amara! Amara!" A voice sounded through the flood.

She shot straight up, drenched in sweat and panting. She looked frantically around the room and to the person beside her. *Cathmore?*

She took short shallow breaths for a moment, trying to gather where she was and why. The cabin, with her Praeceptor. He rubbed her back gently, sunlight pouring into the room. *Another nightmare.*

Against her will, sobs rattled through her body, the details of the killer slipping from her memory but the gruesome murder still very present. Cathmore pulled her unto him and laid back, she buried her face in his chest and he held her while she cried.

I shouldn't let him hold me; I should move away from him.

She found herself unwilling to move despite her better judgment.

He didn't ask for details of the nightmare but just let her lay there once she stopped crying. She knew she shouldn't, but she wrapped her arm around his waist and got closer to him. The terror in her bones seemed to be chased away by his touch, allowing her to finally take a deep breath.

"Is that the first time you dreamed of her death? Since finding out?" he asked quietly, rubbing her head gently.

"Yes, did you see it?" she asked, lifting her head to look into his deep blue eyes.

"I did, you projected it to me and it woke me up."

"But you didn't see the one from last night?"

"Only bits and pieces." He sighed.

She didn't know whether to focus on that fact or if he knew the killer.

"Did you know who he was?" she asked.

"No, it was blurry." He sighed. She laid her head on his chest again.

"I wish I knew why that happens between us." She pondered. He was silent. After a moment, she looked back at him. He was staring thoughtfully at the ceiling; his hand twisted in her hair. "Do you know?" He shook his head.

"I have to get to the training hall." He pulled his arm out from under her and got out of the bed. He was avoiding the question, she sat up.

"What do you know?" she demanded.

He pulled on a black shirt and his Praeceptor jacket. "Nothing we're talking about right now," he responded coldly.

She just scoffed at him, knowing there was no persuading him to change his mind. A few minutes later, he left the cabin, leaving her alone with her thoughts.

Amara had multiple books sprawled across the floor, trying to jog her memory of the assailant in her dream that killed her mother. She reached for anything but came back with a blur. *Ugh.*

She flipped through descriptions and painting prints of each Hallowed, no one looked familiar, infamous Rogue Fallen revolutionists that had been thrown into The Abyss didn't look familiar either.

Cathmore looked so much like Hadeon that it was startling. She couldn't see herself in any of them . She could see both Davian and Fallon in Rase, Molvina in Sylas... maybe she shared some similarities with Lonan or Kaemon but... she wasn't sure. She was born in Findaria—Hadeon's kingdom, Lonan and Kaemon ruled in some of the further away lands. Why would they have gone to Findaria to sire children? Perhaps they were there on business and it just happened. She grumbled. She had no idea.

Even then, the similarities between herself and the two Hallowed Fallen were minimal. Heart-shaped face, thinner, pouter lips, smaller frame—those were the characteristics within herself she was searching for in her sire. Both Lonan and Kaemon had dark hair, Kaemon's black, Lonan's dark brown.

Her face shape was more similar to Lonan's but her lips looked more similar to Kaemon's. Lonan was smaller in stature but, so were Sylas and Hadeon. She also showed no hint of healing or precognition which were the Imperiums the two of them bestowed. She was getting nowhere.

She had gotten too sidetracked by looking for similarities between herself and the Hallowed. That wouldn't solve her mothers murder. She racked her brain for a moment. Her dream, if she could even remember it, was just a dream. It wasn't like it was a memory of the situation, she had been far too young.

She felt like she needed to get out of the cabin. She probably had an hour or so until Cathmore got back so she found a way too large coat and pulled on a pair of pants that he had left for her.

It was far colder than she had hoped it would be but still she ventured out into the forest. She mentally marked trees and made sure she didn't take too many turns so that she could find her way back. She had just given up her side quest of finding flowers for the cabin when across a small pond, she spotted some roses blooming in a massive bush. She carefully tiptoed around the muddy pond and made her way closer to the sprawling bush.

The roses were a deep dark blue with white petals peppered throughout. She ran her fingers over them, admiring their resilience. They bloomed in the harshest weather, the weather that most flowers succumbed to. Not only did they bloom, but they thrived. They were bold and proud amongst the bare dying branches of the winter forest.

She managed to pick a dozen of them, careful of their thorns and began the trek back to the cabin. *Left at the big pine tree, right at the log, under the low hanging willow, forty paces until the clearing, and then a straight line through the canopy.* She had the way back perfectly memorized.

A roaring caused her to jump when she arrived in the clearing. She glanced around, the sound echoed for a moment, the sound was not from a source that she could identify. Not a wolf or a bear. *Weird.* She picked up her pace, especially since the sun was setting. Another roar came from behind her, closer to her, it was higher-pitched and had more of a screeching noise in it. It scratched against her soul unpleasantly and nausea rose within her. It sounded like it was running. She looked around frantically, unable to see anything gaining on her.

Suddenly she saw it, at first it looked like a man with scraggly long hair galloping on all fours toward her at mind-blowing speed. Its arms were impossibly long and it had thick feathered wings over its lion-like back. Its eyes were blood red; it snarled and roared as it closed the space between them.

"What the fuck are you!" She squealed and threw herself into the high grass of the valley

She fumbled with a dagger she had tucked into her coat, it lunged for her, she rolled, it barely missed her. She was still clinging to the roses when she flung the dagger, striking it in the front right leg. It tumbled to the ground; she bolted as fast as she could away from it and toward the cabin. Her feet pounded the forest floor as she put distance between herself and the snarling creature.

She ran through every creature she had seen in her underworld adversaries class but drew a blank on its name. They shouldn't be in the Sanctum, it was Hallowed ground, it was sacrificial ground. How did it get in?

She heard the creature's thunderous hoofbeats behind her so she hit the ground and rolled again, timing it just right so that it hit a branch. *Shit.* She could see the roof of the cabin a dozen yards away, but what would she do once she got there? It would destroy it.

And were those scales on its arms?

She grabbed a massive rock from a pile and launched it at its head. It huffed and shook it off, clawing at her leg. She screamed when its nails dug into her skin. Fire seemed to run up her veins and lace around her entire body.

When it brought down a paw toward her head with a growl, she phased. This time it was slower, she calculated her movements as though time stopped for her. The claw in her leg fell through it, the swiping paw going through her. The creature looked around frantically as though she had disappeared.

She focused during the slowed time, reaching for the dagger in its leg and yanking it out. "*When in doubt, aim for the head or the heart.*" Praeceptor Nightbane had instructed. It stumbled in confusion at the sudden absence of the dagger.

Amara willed herself onto its back, crashing into her corporal form with a painful rattling in her bones. It screamed but she stabbed the dagger down into its human-like hair which was oily and matted. The black spindly strands stuck to her hand with its black blood. *What the fuck?* It twitched and tried to sling her off, her legs holding down its wings as they flapped violently against her in protest. She removed the dagger and stabbed it again and again. It grew weaker with each strike, she didn't stop. She held on for dear life as she reared back and stabbed it repeatedly.

Finally the creature succumbed to the stab wounds in its skull, crumbling to the ground with a howling noise. She pitched herself off of its back and onto the ground where she writhed in pain from the use of her ability. It took her a while to catch her breath, the cold air stinging her lungs and stealing all sensation from her fingers.

She finally pulled herself to her feet and collected the roses that had scattered all over the ground. She kicked the creature to ensure it was dead. *What was she going to tell Cathmore?* It wasn't a huge creature but it was bigger than her and hiding it would not be easy. She could feel how weak she was and the claw she took to her leg didn't help.

She counted eight roses still intact and limped back to the cabin. She needed to clean out and wrap the bleeding wounds.

She fumbled around in the washroom thanking whatever god that was looking out for her that there were some bandages and a salve to clean out the wound. The victory was short lived though, because the middle gash that wrapped her ankle was far too deep. She held the cloth bandages against it to stop the bleeding, but she knew it needed stitches. *Fuck.* She tried elevating it to slow the blood seeping from it.

She tied bandages around the gash as tight as possible with a pained grunt. It must have been the adrenaline that she didn't notice sooner but there was blood all over the washroom floor.

Shit. She must have tracked in through the house too. She was weak and lightheaded from phasing and blood loss. She was also starting to hyperventilate, the blood pooling around her drew her back into the nightmares of the past few nights.

She had no luck finding a needle and thread in the washroom so she resolved herself to look in one of the cabinets in the main part of the house.

"What the..." she heard a gasp. "Amara!" Cathmore yelled.

"I'm in here!" She was on the floor and when she reached for the doorknob, she came up short.

He pushed through the door, his boot slipping in a small puddle of her blood. He dropped to the floor and inspected the injury. His eyes were wild, brows furrowed, he swallowed hard with shaky hands as he tried to pull the bandages back.

"What happened?" he asked in a husky voice.

"I need stitches, I tried to stop the bleeding," she said weakly.

"Who did this to you?" He was furious, frantic.

"Stitches, Cathmore!" She grunted and threw herself back on the floor.

"Okay."

She hadn't seen him so worried, so dumbfounded before.

Cathmore began unwrapping her leg. She watched him summon the tools he needed to fix the wound. He stood to scrub his hands and quickly began threading the needle.

"I phased again," she said by way of explaining why she was so weak. She had lost a lot of blood but not *that* much blood.

"Tell me what you're feeling and stay conscious," he breathed, pushing his curls from his forehead with his forearm. She could see that he was biting the inside of his cheek.

"I just feel weak, sick, I felt like I crashed into my body and now everything is rearranged half an inch to the left," she explained. He began the stitching process with a steady hand. She winced each time he shoved the needle into her skin and pulled the thread through.

"Did it feel different this time?" he asked. She jerked, he pinned her leg down with his other hand and shot her a warning glare.

"Yeah, I had more control, like time slowed, and I could think through it."

"It's getting stronger, you're not," he cautioned.

She didn't know how to respond. He clipped the string and tossed the needle to the side.

"Want to tell me what happened that you needed to phase and get sixteen stitches?" He pressed, sitting back against the sink.

"It was a..." she didn't know what to call it. "I can show you."

He tilted his head in concern. "Was?"

"I killed it." She smirked.

She got to her feet, but swayed. He steadied her, rubbing her upper arms for comfort. She felt irrevocably exhausted, unable to pull herself together. She leaned her head on his chest, inhaling deep, and trying not to put weight on her leg.

"Come on," he whispered and opened the door. She limped weakly behind him, the bed seeming impossibly far away, the front door an insurmountable feat.

Suddenly, he turned and picked her up with his arm under her knees and the other behind her back. She groaned and he laid her on the bed, she somehow missed the walk over to it. He went and got her water from the kitchen.

"Drink this," he instructed. She didn't hesitate to inhale every drop, feeling like she needed more.

"It's about twelve yards from the back right corner of the cabin," she told him. She expected him to go look for it, instead he sat next to her in the bed.

"What did it look like?" he asked as he slowly pulled off his Praeceptor jacket. Even in her weakness she found herself drawn to his powerful arms, the raw power roaring beneath his skin, his deadly beautiful body, but most of all the veins in his arms. He tossed his jacket to the foot of the bed, the buckles clinging together on it.

"Like a human but on all fours." She sighed. "It had scales and wings."

"Gray skin, red eyes?" he asked nonchalantly.

He grabbed something off of the nightstand while she looked out the window where darkness was claiming the forest. She nodded, her eyes growing heavier. She curled into a ball away from him. He slid his hand under her head, urging her to roll over toward him.

"Come here," he breathed. She did so slowly, her limbs heavy, her blood far too thick. She rested her head on his strong thigh telling herself that it was only because she was so weak that she needed his comfort.

"Sit up," he asked. She shook her head, sleep trying to claim her. "Fine." He pulled his shirt off.

He slid down in the bed, laying flat next to her, and then pulling her into the crook of his arm so she was laying on his chest. She nuzzled into his soft skin, the light dusting of hair making him softer, more comforting.

"Hey." He shook her gently until she opened her eyes. She watched him carve a straight line into his chest right near her face. "Here."

Blood began trickling from the cut, the sheer look of it waking her up. She wrapped her arm around his abdomen and licked the cut slowly, need pulsing through her. He shoved his hand into her hair pushing her closer to the source of his sweet blood that made her feel so alive. She locked her mouth over it, biting down and sucking, desperate for more.

Cathmore moaned low in his chest as she drew his blood hungrily into her mouth. *Fuck.* All of her pain and lethargy fell away, her heart rate increased, she could see clearly again. The power beneath her skin seemed to awaken once more. She told herself she needed to stop but she couldn't make herself pull off of him. She leaned up, power pulsing through her.

Cathmore threw his head back, seemingly gaining a euphoria equal to hers. She experienced a heightened state of being; her leg no longer hurt, but she was consumed by a powerful need for him.

She pulled her mouth off of the cut long enough to move on top of him, to straddle him. He dropped his head and met her gaze, his eyes burning with need. The cut was still bleeding, she leaned down and licked it slowly, not breaking eye contact with him. She settled down against him, he brought his hands up to grip her hips, digging his nails into the skin below her shirt.

Amara planted her mouth on his, the sweet taste of him mixing with the taste of his blood. It was like she didn't care what else was going on or about the reasons she needed space from him. She felt like she would rather die than to separate her body from his in that moment.

She pulled his bottom lip into her mouth, sucking slowly, enjoying the way he reacted to her. He pulled her shirt over her head and tossed it out of view.

"Fuck." He praised her breasts and grabbed them. She moaned as he pinched at her nipples and returned the torture by grinding once more against his erection. "If I get to have you again, I'm not letting you go, brat."

"Mhmm," she moaned, loving his possessiveness. He wrapped his strong arms around her and flipped her with incredible speed; she laughed as he pushed himself between her legs.

She was disappointed by the fact that they were both still wearing pants but clearly it was his turn to tease her.

He yanked her pants down, more impatient than she had thought he would be.

"What is it about you?" He planted a kiss on her inner thigh. "That makes me want to absolutely destroy you?" He forced her legs up and back, exposing her to him.

"Do it," she begged. He dipped his tongue into her, dragging it upward and circling her clit with expert skill. She rolled her eyes back as he sucked on her clit and shoved two fingers into her. She bucked her hips up, his mouth and fingers forcing her orgasm to explode fast and hard. *Fuck.*

He looked up at her from between her legs with glowing silver-blue eyes. It wasn't fair how beautiful he was. He removed his fingers and startled her when he slapped her hard between her legs. She sucked air in and bucked her hips upward again. The stinging evaporated into pulsing pleasure. She moaned.

"Tell me what you want," he demanded and slapped her again, causing her to moan and giggle.

"Make it hurt." She writhed. He kissed her clit and moved off the bed to remove his pants. He held eye contact and watched her when she ran her hand between her legs. She could make herself come just by looking at him.

He watched her in awe as she raked her eyes over his body and moaned as she circled her clit. She was soaked from his mouth and already having an orgasm. Her mouth fell open when he stroked his cock.

She was just about to orgasm again when he suddenly summoned something familiar. She stopped, excitement and adrenaline coursing through her body. It was the whip with the little leather tails on it.

"Don't stop now, brat," he demanded, his voice husky.

He placed the tails of the whip between her breasts and slid them teasingly down her body. She arched her back as it sent tingles over her. She listened to him and continued to pleasure herself while he traced her body with the whip. It felt so good that she was having a hard time focusing on making herself orgasm.

He commanded her to roll over, forced her ass in the air, and her face into the bed. He brought the whip down hard causing her to scream into the bed. She swayed her ass, begging for more, begging for him to take her.

"Beautiful," he praised and whipped her again. She shot forward onto her belly, wincing, the second one hurting a lot worse.

He gathered her by her hips and pulled her back toward him. She was expecting another whip when he shoved his cock inside of her. She bit into the sheet but pushed herself back against him.

Despite feeling like she couldn't possibly take every inch of him *and* his astounding girth, she met his thrusts and took all of him. He kept his promise to make it hurt and she loved it. He pulled her hair, forcing her head back and her ass farther up for him.

"Good, fucking, girl," he panted. She moaned and screamed as he took her relentlessly until she couldn't tell where he ended and she began.

He pulled out of her and rolled her on her back before picking her up. She giggled and wrapped her legs around him. He buried his face in her neck and pushed her down onto him. She moaned and adjusted to him in that position.

Cathmore walked her over to the wall and drilled into her. He grabbed the dagger off of the nightstand and nicked her at the base of her throat. She moaned and threw her head against the wall. He planted his mouth over the cut and sucked hard while he pounded into her. She gripped his hair and pleasure bombarded her senses.

Once he was done he kissed her before sliding her down further onto him, allowing her access to his chest so that she could take more of his blood.

They became lost within each other, neither of them yielding to the other, both meeting each other round for round. They were a mess of blood and sweat. The drapes were torn from the four poster bed, and broken trinkets littered the floor.

They laid on the floor by the fireplace, wrapped in one of the drapes, both trying to recover from what they had done. It had gone on for hours, leaving both of them panting and satiated.

Chapter 25

"Did you know that I would kill Molvina?" she asked the following morning as she sprawled across Cathmore's chest. She realized that he must have put her roses in a vase which sat silently upon the counter.

"No." He sighed. "Precognition is not one of my abilities."

She stared at the window, waiting for the morning sun to rise.

"I was going to kill her anyway but I needed to see what you would do when allowed to confront her. I needed to prove something to myself," he admitted.

"And that was?" She pulled herself up to sit and looked him in the eyes.

"That your self-proclaimed hatred of me wasn't hatred at all." He crossed his arms over his bare chest. She narrowed her eyes at him. She eyed the cut she drank from which was nothing more than a faint line but the large scar across the entirety of his chest remained.

"So you expected me to snap?" She surmised.

"I—" he started but she cut him off.

"She was going to get you sent to the Abyss!" she exclaimed.

"You don't protect someone you hate," he challenged.

"What do you want me to say?" She shook her head. "I guess I proved that I don't. Happy?" She stood, wrapping the thin fabric of the curtain around her body.

"I just wanted you to admit it to yourself."

"Do you really think I am not well aware of my feelings for you?" She threw her hands in the air. "You just wanted to break me down. You forced me to show my deepest desires," she shoved his chest. "Other people got hurt!" She threw a pillow at him. "Molvina—i-it cost her her life! You asshole!." She moved to shove him again, seething with anger.

He seized her arms and tugged her against him, the curtain falling from her body.

"If you're referring to Avren getting hurt." He turned her around and snaked a hand around her throat. She leaned her head back against his chest. "I don't give a fuck about his feelings. You were stringing him along anyway." He tightened his fingers around her throat. She groaned as she instinctively rubbed her ass against him.

"You're heartless," she spat.

"Yes, love," he whispered into her ear. "I am." He took her earlobe between his teeth. She sucked in a sharp breath. *Love?*

She jerked away from him. She was overwhelmed by her own feelings and the lengths he would go to for her to expose them. He may not care that she killed Molvina or that Avren was heartbroken, but she did.

"I need space," she announced before disappearing into the washroom.

She sat in the bathtub for nearly an hour, not emerging until he left to go teach his classes for the day.

Cathmore allowed her space and did not say a word to her before leaving for work the following day as well. He had returned to sleeping on the couch. Only the crackling of the fireplace filled the silence between them the previous evening.

She spent her day reading book after book, mostly fictional tales of kings and queens in nonexistent lands. She hated that she had to fight not to imagine her Praeceptor as the dark-haired prince in most of those stories. *Ugh.* She threw the book across the room.

He wasn't a noble prince, he was chaos incarnate, powerful beyond measure, and a force to be reckoned with that drove her mad. She flopped on the bed, thankful to be warring with thoughts of him instead of wrestling with her own guilt. She had been stuck between the two for far too long, though, and it was suffocating.

It was approaching midnight and Cathmore still hadn't returned. With the conclusion of the work week, she assumed he was at the Serpent's Keep with the other Praeceptors. *With Magister Copia.* She pushed away the invasive feeling of jealousy at the possibility.

Amara was fumbling around the cabin, looking through bookshelves and cabinets, boredom taking over. There was a wardrobe in an alcove off of the living space where Cathmore typically dressed himself behind the double doors. She got a brilliantly bad idea to ruffle his feathers.

She was so pissed at him and so annoyed with him that she wanted to hit him where it hurt. She flung the wardrobe doors open with a sideways grin. Hanging before her were multiple black and white button-downs, slacks, training leather pants and vests, simple t-shirts which were all dark in color, and his undershorts folded neatly at the bottom.

Amara had grown to realize he was anal about his appearance and his clothes. He was just egotistical and arrogant enough that what she was about to do would get under his skin. She got a thrill of excitement similar to the feeling she got before she snuck into his room that night. She recalled how that ended and it caused her to vagina to clench. She swallowed hard, shaking off the sensation. *Nope.*

She pulled all of them down, flipped a dagger in her hand and laid waste to the material. She shredded and ripped as she screamed out all of her frustrations toward him. She popped the buttons off of his jackets, stomped the crisp white shirts into the soot by the fireplace, and even stabbed the wood of the wardrobe itself until her hand was bruised. It felt great, it felt liberating. She found herself laughing as she danced around the space and chucked pieces of fabric into the air like confetti.

"Take that you asshole!" She screamed with finality as she threw one of his Praeceptor leather jackets into the fire.

Just then she heard the front door slam shut and turned to find Cathmore staring at her. He dropped the weapons belt he must have been holding with a loud clatter.

"What did you do?" he snarled, storming in her direction.

She wiped the smile off of her face and darted from the fireplace before he could reach her. His eyes were wide as he scanned the room, taking in the remains of his wardrobe. Despite the anger though, he looked breathtaking. His slacks hung low on his hips in the absence of his weapons belt, his Praeceptor jacket was open to a dark button-down, and his hair was shoved back in that neat messy look of his.

"Wait." She held up her hand as he got close to her. She bolted left and put the couch between the two of them.

He barely had to move to keep up with her clumsy attempts to skitter away but he allowed her to keep the furniture between them. He knelt down to pick up a shredded shirt and looked up at her through full eyelashes. *God, he's beautiful.* His cheeks had more color than usual, his eyes slightly bloodshot which confirmed he had been drinking at least a little bit.

"Run," he growled. The silver lining of his eyes glowed in warning which made her stomach sink.

She was grateful that she was at least wearing pants and a sweater because his tone sent her straight out the front door and into the night. Her heart hammered as she sprinted straight into the woods.

She thought she heard him descend the wooden stairs of the cabin just behind her but she couldn't hear anything from him after that.

"Keep going, brat, you're not going to like it when I catch you," he purred into her mind. His voice was husky and sent delicious throbbing between her legs. She swallowed hard.

She started to realize as she swerved through the trees that she enjoyed the anticipation of his punishments. Enticing him into doing so was erotic. *Is something wrong with me?*

She skidded to a halt at a clearing. She had two options—hide in the tall grass or scale a tree. *Fuck.*

"Not quite fast enough." He tutted and gathered her against him.

His chest rose and fell quickly as he panted against her, his scent filling her nostrils. She kicked against him but he only tightened his strong arms around her.

"I think you wanted me to catch you," he whispered into her ear. His body was solid, hot, and forcing hers to stand at attention. She would never be able to shake her need for him.

"You're insane." She grunted. *But not wrong.* She could feel the strength he possessed, the raw power he held. He could kill her without even flinching and that thought only served to excite her more. She swallowed hard.

He hauled her back to the cabin, the cold air of the night biting her face.

"You destroyed my things." He sat her down on the porch and looked her in the eyes. "What did you think that would accomplish?" He circled her.

"You pissed me off." She turned to keep watching him.

His eyes locked on her.

"Well, now I'm pissed off," he snarled. He grabbed the collar of her sweater and ripped it down her body. It split perfectly down her torso, exposing her bra. "Is this how we deal with it?" He held a piece of the torn fabric in his hand. He took her in, dragging his bottom lip between his teeth. She could fall apart beneath his gaze.

She turned her back on him, storming into the cabin, anger and desire warring within her. He didn't stop her. Anticipation hung heavy in the air. She didn't know what he was going to do, what she *wanted* him to do.

She began cleaning the mess she made. Cathmore took a seat in one of the armchairs beside the bed, leaning back. He was far too calm. He watched her, stretching out his legs while she collected scraps of fabric. She was on her knees, reaching for one under the couch when he finally spoke.

"Crawl to me," he demanded.

What? She looked up at him. He was undoing the buttons of his shirt, the sight causing her mouth to water.

"Keep your dirty little thoughts to yourself, brat."

She did as she was told, crawling toward him, aware of her breasts trying to fall from her bra. Her hair fell around her face, swaying as she crawled. He watched her intently and sat forward when she reached him. He was as cold as ice, his eyes dark and hooded, his eyebrows furrowed. She looked up at him just as he grabbed her around her throat and brought her up to meet his eyes so that she was on her knees before him.

"Tell me what you want from me. Why do you keep pushing me?" he demanded of her.

"Because I like it," she ground out through gritted teeth.

He blinked, perplexed by her response and loosened his hold on her throat. It was the truth . She had grown to love seeing him snap. It was the thing that shifted behind his eyes as his control slipped, the need to dominate was as much a part of him as his raven locks. She felt alive in his darkness.

"You like it when I hurt you?" He didn't seem surprised by her admission so much as... *relieved?* He hauled her up and over his legs and she knew where it was going.

Maybe she felt she deserved the pain he inflicted. It was easier to accept as an explanation for why she *craved* it, why she was elated every time he lit up with need to hurt her. She gasped when he tugged her pants down and she adjusted herself over his lap. He heart hammered against her ribcage as though trying to break free. Before she could look back at him he brought his hand down hard on her ass. She bit her lip and fought back the need to yelp.

Amara could hear his breathing growing shallow as he struck her again. She twisted her fist into his jacket, holding on tight as he slapped her harder. The stinging running up her body in like a forest caught fire.

"You did a very bad thing, Amara." His voice was darker. He brought his hand down a fifth and sixth time.

"Mhmm," she agreed. She had squirmed as the skin on her ass flamed red.

A smacked her again finally drawing a groan from deep in her chest as she lurched forward. He twisted one hand in her hair to keep her still as he dealt three more slaps that had her panting. She moaned against the last one and he rubbed his palm into the burning flesh to soothe it.

She found herself pushing back against his hand, need gathering between her legs. He tutted his playful disapproval. He continued to rub her sensitive skin and yanked her head upward by her hair.

"I have the capacity to tear you apart," he growled. She was all too aware of that fact and she didn't care. She was paying attention to the hand on her ass, his fingers inching downward and closer to her pussy. She tried to arch herself into his fingers but he drew them away. "Are you wet, love?" He let her look back at him and she nodded shyly.

His pupils were blown wide, his breathing ragged, his arousal evident against her abdomen. She pushed herself off of his lap before straddling him. He released a pained groan as she pressed down against his erection. She ran her fingers through his hair, meeting his eyes.

"I can't stay away from you," she admitted hoarsely.

"You weren't supposed to happen," he whispered, agony in his voice.

"Neither were you." She shook his head. He held onto her hips tightly.

She recalled the girl that just wanted to push through the Crucible unnoticed, that didn't want to get close to anybody. But she had gotten close, too close. Avren's heart was broken, Katara was dead, Judas was gone, even Molvina... She had gotten involved with and began caring about too many people and it cost her a fraction of herself.

He suddenly stood and sat her down. She could feel the agony rolling off of him, the self-control he was exercising by not burying himself into her. It drove her crazy, her arousal beginning to run down her thighs. *Shit.*

But it wasn't going to happen, they were both clearly wrestling with their feelings for each other. She sighed and pulled her pants back on as he put space between the two of them. He leaned against the far wall on the opposite side of the room. She took a deep breath to ground herself from the thrill of being spanked by him.

"Tell me about your relationship with him," he asked suddenly, pain evident in his voice.

"Avren? Why?" Amara looked over her shoulder at him, only catching a glimpse at his hardened features. She didn't understand why he was asking about Avren. It was clear that she and him were done, clear that she wanted Cathmore. They certainly had established that Avren couldn't compete with Cathmore in bed. He shook his head.

"Can't you just tell me that he's the one you want. Make this easier," he pleaded, still not looking over at her.

"Why would that be easier?" She was exasperated. She stormed over to him. She would not let him convince himself that she was better off with someone else.

"I know how we are sexually, but does he make you happy?" he asked. His shoulders gave away the tension he was holding on to. *Where was this coming from?*

"After the past few days, why would I still want him instead?" She pushed.

"You said you needed space and maybe... Maybe because he's better for you?" He remarked. *Better for me?*

"What do you mean?" *Besides the obvious risk of death if they were caught.* She placed herself between him and the wall. He let her.

"I mean that you don't know what getting close to me entails. I mean that when I look at you I have this need to destroy you, to lay waste to everything you ever were..." he leaned in to whisper in her ear. "And I want to ravage your soul until there is nothing left of you that isn't tainted by mine." She stared into the depths of his blue eyes, believing that he absolutely meant what he said. She swallowed hard before reaching up and pushing an onyx curl from his forehead. "I can assure you that the way he feels about you isn't nearly as sinister," he added but there was fire behind the agony he seemed to feel. The thought of doing those things to her, to possess her—excited him. She tried to wrap her head around the fact that he felt such strong things for her. He stepped forward, using his hips to pin her against the wall.

"Avren is one of my closest friends, he's easy to talk to, and he understands me," she began and lazily ran her fingers through his hair and sighed. "But with you..." she paused thoughtfully and laid her hands on his chest. "It's the first time I've ever been consumed wholly by someone—" she admitted before he cut her off.

"Why can't you just choose him." He furrowed his eyebrows and held her wrists against him. It pained him to hear how she felt about him, like if he stopped her from saying it, it would change the truth.

"Why do you want me to give up on you?" She pulled her wrists from his grasp and pushed him away.

"Because then I'd be free of this nagging need to risk everything for you," he locked eyes with her. "I would be able to let you go if I believed that you would be happy with him." He turned away from her. "I had done that for weeks. And then there was that day where the two of you snuck off into the shower room," he paced. "I had to fight everything inside of me not to rip him off of you, not to remove his limbs from his fucking body," he twisted his mouth in disgust and swallowed hard. "And I couldn't figure out why!" He shrugged, helplessness written all over his face.

"Cathmore..." she breathed.

"But then there you were." He sighed and threw himself onto the couch. "You were in my head, touching yourself to the thoughts of me after he failed to satisfy you." He released a small breathy laugh. She walked slowly over to him, taking in all of his words, all of the emotions he was trying to understand.

"I can't choose him even if it would be the smarter choice." She shook her head. She crawled onto his lap, straddling him, placing each arm on either side of him on the back of the couch. She became very aware that she was only in pants and a bra. Her hair fell around her face as he tried to look away from her, trying not to touch her. He was fighting with every ounce of self-restraint that he could muster. "Why won't you touch me all of the sudden?" She furrowed her eyebrows and turned his face toward her.

"When he kissed you under that waterfall, when he held you, I knew that I'd gladly go to any death to be in his place," he whispered. She placed his hand on her face and nudged her cheek into his palm, closing her eyes and inhaling . *Was this real?*

She couldn't find the words to say, so she leaned down and kissed him gently. He didn't kiss her back at first but he gave in after a moment, holding both sides of her face, kissing her like she was the oxygen he needed to breathe. It was different than when they were entangled in one another. This kiss meant something else, something more.

She pushed harder into the kiss, gripping his hair, feeling the soft strands between her fingers. He wrapped his arms around her and pulled her closer. He groaned in pleasure when she bit his lip and returned the favor by sucking her bottom lip into his mouth and biting down hard. She winced but kissed him harder, it made her ravenous for him. She forced herself to pull away from the kiss. He grabbed her ass which was still sensitive from his spanking but it only caused her to want him more.

"Are you ever going to tell me why we're in each other's heads?" she asked, referring to the question he avoided the morning before that creature attacked her. She had a feeling it was related to why they couldn't keep their hands to themselves, why they'd become addicted to one another's blood.

"It's complicated." He sighed and shook his head.

"When is it not? We could be killed for the things we've done here." She wrapped her hands in his hair the way he liked it.

"I will give you the answers to your questions, Amara." He gripped her face. "Just not yet." She leaned her forehead against his, but didn't press the issue further.

He planted a soft kiss on her lips, one that seemed to ask if she still wanted him. *Of course she did.*

"I need you." She panted between desperate kisses. He nodded and tugged his pants down.

She kicked hers off hurriedly before straddling him again. She steadied herself on the back of the couch, hovering over him. He poked at her entrance with his erection but she moved up, laughing , teasingly.

He gripped the nape of her neck, baring his perfectly straight teeth at her.

"Hold on, love." He grinned.

She didn't remember falling asleep, but it wasn't long after their messy and needy fucking. She stretched her legs, her ass still sore from his punishment. It caused her to smile. He rolled over onto her as though he had been waiting for her to wake up.

"You kept pushing your ass into me while you slept," he teased and nipped her nose. She loved when he was playful and disheveled from sleep.

"Maybe you kept grinding into my ass while I slept," she sassed. He narrowed his eyes and laughed but kissed her sweetly.

"You drive me crazy," he groaned but she pushed him off of her before sitting up. *The feeling was mutual.*

"So how long have creatures from the underworld been spilling into the Sanctum Metere?" She changed the subject, knowing that if they got lost in one another again it could be hours before she was able to ask him what she needed to—if not days. He blinked trying to prepare for a more serious conversation.

He had told her the creature was a <u>focalorum</u>, a descendant of the 'focalor' who was a duke of hell with similar characteristics. He thought for a moment before explaining.

"It's a newer occurrence," he stated vaguely.

"But why is it happening?" If the Hallowed Fallen had a deal with Satan, why are his creatures roaming their kingdoms?

"They are being summoned here. I think it has to be the doing of the Dark One but it's possible it's one of the other rebellion groups that are sprouting up," he explained.

"There are more?" she asked, shocked. He looked at her as though he couldn't believe she'd asked that.

"The Hallowed have been smiting rebellions since they took their thrones, this is nothing new." His eyebrows were furrowed. "You really detached yourself from all of this, didn't you?" he asked.

"Some elders tried to teach us that the Hallowed provided such a harmonious existence that no one ever wanted to rise up against them—not that they could anyway," she explained. "Living amongst humans though, I learned the darker side of their power and the cruelty they bestowed to maintain it. Though, it wasn't until I was on the run that I started hearing stories about the Dark One. And of course I now know of The Abyss where the traitors are sent..." she sighed. It was all so complicated.

"He's not the only one but he does pose the most significant threat to the kingdoms, to the Hallowed." He turned to her. She couldn't help but think that it was about time.

"How so?" she asked. "I mean he overthrew Ravenyr and persuaded Sylas to join him but... How is he doing it?" She elaborated. He met her eyes briefly and looked away, shaking his head.

"It doesn't matter," he stated flatly and stood from the bed, signaling the end of the conversation.

He wouldn't broach the subject again but insisted that they work out as they had been, careful of her leg after the face-down with the focalorum.

Their workout was fairly uneventful and she made sure to keep her eyes to herself. She needed to stay strong; she needed to learn from him.

He had promised to sit down with her to discuss the history of the Fallen to keep her where she needed to be knowledge wise. So following their workout, that's what they did. It was almost strange having him to herself all day but she felt like she would get used to it.

"Why aren't there any female fallen angels?" she asked him. He blinked thoughtfully.

"I believe there were some at one time," he told her. "I mean we see them in paintings and books but... I don't know. I was punished when I asked my Praeceptor about it during my Crucible year." *Punished?*

"For simply asking?" It reminded her of how she'd get in trouble, yell at, or laughed at in Baylin's class for questioning things too much. He just nodded.

They read on about the first Nephilim and how he rose into his transition, before magic halted it. There was a time when the Nephilim came of age and grew into themselves. It wasn't so easy anymore.

"We're Nephilim ever able to procreate?" She knew they couldn't now, sired children were born sterile. She had never heard of it happening.

"Yes, the Hallowed came together and put an end to it about two-hundred years ago." He flipped to a page in the book they were reading.

Virtūs et Honos;

By this solemn decree, let it be known: the sired children shall henceforth be divested of the power to reproduce, thus ensuring that no Nephilim may create life anew. The progeny begotten by the Nephilim are displeasing to the Hallowed, serving neither purpose nor benefit to them. The divine power to bring forth new Nephilim shall be reserved solely for the Hallowed.

Furthermore, by this decree, all Nephilim sired by the Hallowed are commanded to deliver their offspring unto the feet of their sire, that their blood may be spilled, thus fortifying the realms. So it is decreed, so it shall be.

Virtūs et honor semper erit iure Sanctitatis Fallen.

"It's like they were afraid of a rebellion by the Nephilim, afraid it would be a real threat," she mused.

"It all comes down to a balance of power for them," he agreed. "The Rogue Fallen were made sterile long before the Nephilim though, for the same reasons."

"Through magic?" she asked. He responded with a simple nod but didn't elaborate on the source of the magic. She knew the stories—that it was a deal with the devil or hijacked ancestral magic from the witches—but she felt that there had to be more to it than that. The Hallowed were simply too powerful, too all-consuming.

"Do you have any readings on the Fallen Angel Atreus?" she asked. "He appeared in some research I did." *The brother of the devil.*

"I'm not sure I do, what about that particular Rogue Fallen interests you?" Cathmore seemed especially taken back by the mention of him. Baylin had said he was powerful, even able to kill Hallowed Fallen.

"Baylin seemed sort of intimidated by how powerful he was..." She shrugged.

"I doubt that." He withdrew from the conversation.

Chapter 26

The following night Amara stirred awake. She was alone in the dark, Cathmore no longer in the bed. That's when she heard muffled voices just outside of the cabin. *What?*

She knew he had a keen sense of hearing so she dropped the comforter on the floor and padded to the window. He was arguing with someone she could hardly see. Someone with wings and dark hair. She squinted her eyes, trying to see clearer in the dead of night. *Nephilim sight would be great right about now.*

"You're not forcing my hand on this. I decide when," he spat at the winged figure.

"You are running out of time," he responded. "I will return. It better be done when I do," the creature shot into the sky with breathtaking speed.

What are they talking about?

She rushed back to bed and wrapped herself in the comforter, feigning sleep. Cathmore entered moments later but didn't return to bed. He sat in front of the fireplace and stared into the flames, unmoving. He stayed like that for so long that Amara fell back asleep with a million questions and suspicions.

The day that followed was her tenth day at the cabin which was the final day that Cathmore would be there for the entire day since he was to return to teaching the following day. She had to remind herself that as far as the other conscripts were concerned—she spent two weeks in the pound and Cathmore had spent a week there.

She had become pretty good at phasing on command and Cathmore thoroughly enjoyed scaring her to see if she could prevent herself from losing control and doing it randomly. She thought about the way he taught her to pause and think before reacting, to breathe, to pretend that time was slowed so that she could work out what to do in any number of situations. She could not phase during the next trial; she had to get a hold of herself.

She learned to do it on purpose fairly easily, but trying not to do it against her will was harder. She knew nothing of what the next trial entailed but the very last trial, she learned, was called the Death Match.

She was walking through the woods to get some fresh air as she pondered what the Death Match would consist of. According to Cathmore, the Crucible would make murderers of all of them, even if she hadn't killed Marlowe and Molvina... She either left the Crucible a murderer or didn't leave at all. Somehow that made her feel a little better about herself. All of the Nephilim who transitioned had to make a kill. The Hallowed wanted blood on the hands of all of their children, they saw it as a rite of passage. It nauseated her.

She didn't know what to make of Cathmore's conversation with the Nephilim in the middle of the night. *Was it a Nephilim? Could it have been a Hallowed Fallen?* She didn't get to see its eyes so she couldn't know. She was wrestling with whether or not to ask him about it.

Suddenly something swept her legs out from under her from behind. *A stick?* She hit the ground hard, knocking the wind out of her. Her eyes lost focus for a moment and a cloaked figure scrambled on top of her, wrapping their hands around her throat and closing off her windpipe. *Phase, phase, phase.* She felt the power burning to the surface as she scratched at the person's arms.

No, no, she had to find a different way out of this. This was her chance to prove to herself that she could control it. The person/creature growled but she couldn't see its face behind the massive hood.

She dug her nails into its human-like forearms and forced its hands from her throat. She bucked her hips and shoved the person off of her with a scream before quickly getting to her feet. She grabbed the massive stick the person had used to trip her and struck it hard on the back before it could get up.

It was sent flat to the ground but didn't pursue her further. A laugh came from the person as he got to his knees. *Of course.*

"You are a jackass!" She exclaimed and tossed the stick at Cathmore who pulled the hood down. He was laughing but impressed.

"You didn't phase, that's good." He had a very faint dimple on his right cheek that appeared when he genuinely laughed or smiled and she had to fight to stay mad at him because of it.

"You're lucky I don't knock you out with this." She huffed, holding up the stick.

"Try it, brat," he challenged and jumped to his feet in a single swift motion.

She narrowed her eyes at him before moving quickly, bringing the stick over her head and swinging it down at him. He threw up his arm, taking the impact on his forearm before darting right and throwing a job at her ribs. *Ow.*

She dropped low and kicked her leg out, sweeping his legs—a move he taught her. He stumbled back but didn't fall so she panicked and tackled him while he was unsteady on his feet. She got him to the ground but he rolled on his side, causing her body to roll over his which sent her face first into the dirt. She crawled forward about a foot before jumping to her feet and spinning around to prepare for whatever he was about to do next. But he wasn't there. The cloak he was wearing had been discarded . *What?* She looked around, up in the trees, and behind the biggest tree before loosing a breath.

Cathmore was a master of games, especially training games, she knew he wasn't done with her. It was just a matter of time before he caught her off guard, blatantly attacked her, or set up some trap for her to walk into. *Ugh.*

"Can't I just have a nice walk without your games!" ahe yelled into the forest.

Amara brushed herself off, still wearing normal pants and shirts because the dresses were *not* happening despite his trying to entice her into them.

"What's the fun in that, love?" He was behind her suddenly, having dropped from the tree above her. He cupped his hand over her mouth and dragged her forcefully off of the path. She thrashed against him, adrenaline beginning to spike in her veins once more.

She bit down on his palm hard until he winced and dropped it from her mouth. She used his moment of weakness to elbow him in the ribs in hope of running. It didn't work.

"You'll need to do better than that," he cooed.

He hauled her up and pinned her against a tree by her throat, she choked and pushed against him as her eyes went wide in alarm.

"Sorry, love, nothing personal. You just need to get better." He flashed her a smile.

A number of names popped into her mind to call him but she was losing oxygen quickly. She hauled her legs upward and wrapped them around his strong arm. She pushed against his face with her hands in a last-ditch effort before twisting her legs until his arm bent with a harsh *crack*. It twisted unnaturally, very obviously broken and then she was crashing into the forest floor.

Cathmore jumped back, grunting in pain but pleased.

"I'm sorry!" She stood to rush to him.

"Don't apologize, finish me!" he exclaimed. *What?* "What would you follow that up with if I were really trying to hurt you?"

She thought for a second but he advanced on her. She jumped into a flying kick which sent the entire mass of her body through a kick down onto his kneecap. She felt it dislocate with a hard snap and he crumpled with a groan.

"And?!" He spat, urging her forward.

Adrenaline was pulsing through her veins so she reeled back and punched him in the face repeatedly. Finally he went limp, feigning unconsciousness.

"Good," he panted and pulled himself to sitting. "Show no mercy." He popped his knee back into place.

"Oh God." She turned as her stomach flipped.

"You have to think fast and be ruthless." He sighed. She vomited at the sound of wherever he was doing to pop his arm back into place.

"Are you okay?" She still couldn't look at him.

He didn't answer. When she turned around, he was gone.

"Fucker!" She kicked the tree in frustration at his damned disappearing act.

She collected herself and resumed her walk back to the cabin, pulling on his cloak from the first attack.

"Have fun on your walk?" He side-eyed her with a sly smile. She threw his cloak at him, more hitting him with it than giving it to him.

"You're annoying." She grunted.

"You're getting better at controlling your Imperium." He ignored her insult. *Whatever.*

She welcomed the warmth of the cabin and decided a shower was much needed. She didn't want to leave the nice waterfall shower with actual hot water to go back to the freezing communal showers of the dorms so she wanted to enjoy it while she could.

Her shoulders were just relaxing when a roaring sound shook the entire cabin. The intensity of it made thunder seem like a gentle breeze. She braced herself against the wall as she listened.

"Cathmore!" she called.

She rushed out of the shower in a hurry, her legs shaking from what sounded like a herd of thousands of elephants rampaging through the forest.

"Cathmore!" She called again as the sound echoed into her chest.

She couldn't pull on her pants fast enough and she was pretty sure her shirt was on backwards as she hurried into the main room. Cathmore was gone.

"What the hell!" she shouted, her voice barely cutting through the thunderous pounding that reverberated through the air. Her pulse raced as she caught sight of frantic, shadowy movement outside the window. The ground quaked beneath her feet, and through the trees, she glimpsed a stampede—thousands of monstrous forms charging through the forest like a tidal wave of darkness.

She flung the front door open, and her breath caught in her throat. Her worst fears were confirmed; it was a horde of Blood Terrors, their hulking forms barreling through the night. The demons were impossibly massive, towering beasts with muscular bodies covered in scarred, leathery skin that glistened in the faint moonlight. Razor-sharp claws gouged the earth with every thunderous step, and their mouths were filled with jagged teeth that gnashed in anticipation of carnage. Their eyes were deep, empty voids—black as pitch and devoid of any soul. They moved with a terrifying, unrelenting force, their snorts echoing like a stampede of enraged rhinos as they barreled forward on all fours. She recalled that they fed on carnage and gained strength with each kill. Kingdoms fell in their wake, countless throughout history. They were every nightmare made flesh, every scary story come to life.

"Get back inside!" Cathmore's voice rang out, desperate and commanding from high above the cabin, where he hovered with wings spread wide against the sky. His arms were thrown out in front of him as he thrust his powers into something she couldn't see.

The air around them was thick and choking, stinking of sulfur and decay, a putrid stench that seemed to rise from each of the fifteen layers of hell. She gagged at the acrid, unbreathable cloud that rolled off their bodies, the foul odor clinging to her lungs like poison. Onc of the beasts veered toward her, its massive head lowering as it charged. She stumbled back, heart hammering in her chest, but it slammed into an invisible barrier inches from her face, shaking its head in frustration before snorting and rejoining the stampede. The entire cabin shook violently, wooden beams creaking as the horde continued its relentless march.

Cathmore was shielding her—his magic forming an unseen wall around the cabin, sparing her from the deadly onslaught. But the

Blood Terrors weren't alone. New horrors emerged, riding atop the demons like parasites: Plague Swarmers and Soul Reapers, their screeches and howls piercing the night.

Plague Swarmers were grotesque, skeletal creatures with eight twisted limbs and rotting flesh that hung in tattered ribbons from their skeletal frames. Their movements were jittery and insect-like, each step leaving behind the sickly scent of decay. They carried pestilence with them, a living embodiment of disease. One spewed putrid bile from its gaping, decomposing maw, the thick, greenish fluid splattering against Cathmore's shield and sizzling upon impact. Amara recoiled, horrified by the mere thought of the diseases that oozing filth carried—plagues that could kill a man in hours or rot flesh to the bone. The smell was not filtered out by the shield, causing her to dry heave violently. She stumbled backward, desperate to avoid even the faintest touch of the Swarmers' foul sputum, their very presence a threat to all life around them.

It was then that a Soul Reaper descended, its scythe glinting wickedly as it swung toward her, only to collide violently with the invisible barrier, sending a shockwave that rattled her teeth. The Reaper's skeletal arm jerked back, its hooded figure looming like death itself. Draped in a tattered black cloak, it resembled every grim folktale brought to life—a harbinger of death, its empty eye sockets burning with a cold, unfeeling light. The creature let out a bone-chilling wail, a sound that sliced through the chaos and echoed through the forest, an eerie lament that made her blood run cold. She could see the faint outline of its hollow face, gaunt and shadowed beneath the hood, its skeletal fingers clawing at the barrier with growing frustration.

She shuddered, fighting the overwhelming fear that threatened to paralyze her as she stared at the mass of reapers, their bony hands reaching, scythes swinging, and voices howling into the night. The sight of them up close, thrashing against Cathmore's magic, sent a chill raking down her spine. They were ancient, merciless beings, clawing at the barrier with a hunger that knew no end. Above, Cathmore strained, his wings flaring as he poured every ounce of his strength into keeping the shield intact, his face twisted in fierce concentration. The air around them crackled with energy, the weight of the demonic forces pressing in, testing the limits of their protection.

But for now, the barrier held—barely. And Amara, breathless and terrified, could do nothing but watch as the storm of monsters raged just beyond reach, waiting for the moment when they might break through.

How is this possible? Where are they going?

They weren't running toward the Sanctum Metere.

"Come back inside!" She pleaded with Cathmore.

"I can't protect you from in there," he answered in her mind. She panted, watching helplessly as demons ascended on mortal lands in droves.

She watched creatures from her textbook move past her as real as the beaten earth beneath their feet. It went on for over twenty minutes until she was backed into a corner covering her ears from the sheer volume of the screeching. *Who would be powerful enough to summon what appeared to be legions of demons?* It was unheard of.

A helpless sort of grief choked her and stole away her ability to breathe. Her body failed her when it came to thinking, to intaking air. So much so that she hadn't heard the commotion seize, hadn't heard Cathmore reenter the cabin. She had her head buried in her knees with her hands over her ears, trembling when he placed a hand on her shoulder.

"What the hell was that!?" she exclaimed.

"That was hell, love." He hauled her up gently.

"Where were they headed?" She tried to pull herself together.

"Ravenyr, they went North-East."

He helped her up and moved to sit her shaking form on the couch. She felt like a wildflower just barely hanging on after a tornado.

"Ravenyr has already been seized. Is this the work of the Dark One?" she asked while he chugged water greedily from a decanter.

"Yes, it would appear that Deimos is raising his army," he groaned.

A solemn look overtook him as he stared into the dancing flames of the fireplace, the glass bottle held loosely between his fingers.

"How were they here? *In Findaria?*" she asked.

"I don't know but they couldn't get any closer than this. The inner wards kept them on these outer edges of the kingdom and on the fast track to Ravenyr." He sat next to her.

"It feels like a show of power to summon them here instead of Ravenyr." She turned to him and folded a leg beneath her.

"You are correct, Deimos loves a good show."

"So now what?"

"Now we get back to the Sanctum. We finish the Crucible," he answered with cold detachment.

"How can—what? Isn't he declaring war." She stood in disbelief.

"No, he is preparing for a war that has been brewing since Ravenyr fell. The Hallowed will have the Sanctum protected and the Crucible completed at all costs."

He stood and moved toward the bookshelf, frantically searching for something.

"Why?"

"Because the sired children's transformation produces a significant amount of energy for them to draw from. It gives them the advantage." He flipped open a notebook. His movements were quick and precise, showing his growing agitation as he wrote.

"They don't need the advantage, right? I thought the Hallowed were all powerful." She pushed.

"There's more to this than you can even begin to understand, Amara." He huffed.

"Then explain it to me." She walked over and grabbed his arm.

He pulled away from her grip and gave her his back, ice chilled her core.

"Cathmo—"

"Enough," he cut her off. "We need to sleep. We return in the morning." The notebook in his hand disappeared with a snap.

"What did you just write in that? What did you do?" She turned him toward her by his shoulder.

"Listen, love. We've gotten comfortable here. But it has to go back to normal tomorrow. No one can know about this. You have to learn to trust me and stop asking questions," he bit out. He pushed her hair behind her ear and inhaled a calming breath.

His silver-blue eyes met hers and beheld her for a moment. She didn't want to let him go but she wanted to scream at him and shove him away. *Who was he to say she wouldn't understand it?*

"I will give you secrecy but I refuse to stop looking for answers." She pushed past him and moved into the bed.

"About your parents?" he asked as he turned toward her.

The fading fireplace light cast him in a warm glow and made him look taller than he was. He was a silhouette in the darkness, looming over her cautiously, unsure of her intentions.

"About everything," she promised.

"None of them are ready!" Cathmore exclaimed in a hushed tone. Though it was more the sense of intense dread coming off of him that woke her.

"It's been ordered by the Hallowed." It was Crowned Magister Bennett. "Your father insists they're needed. The northern perimeter has been breached."

Amara's breathing increased as a familiar panic enveloped her. She wanted to cover ears like a child but knew she should keep listening.

"Dawn. The two of you return to join the Death Match," the Crowned Magister said with finality before leaving. Amara heard the door slam with a swear from Cathmore.

What is going on?

"What happened?" She stepped out of the washroom. Cathmore had his hands in his hair but dropped them to look at her.

"Death Match is at dawn." He exhaled, defeated.

"What? We're supposed to have months." She covered her mouth in horror.

"It's unheard of but..." he dropped his head and turned to her.

"There's a war coming, isn't there?" She stared straight into the fireplace; it was what she gathered from what Bennett said.

"They began killing the children that Sylas sired. I was told that most of Sylas' Nephilim have joined him with the Dark One," Cathmore shook his head. "I knew this would happen when they ordered those sired children dead."

"I don't get how moving up our transitions help." She pondered in defeat, dropping onto the couch beside him.

"You'll be stronger, more untamed upon first transitioning. This year's Nephilim are going to be used as weapons. Hadeon's army can hold the North but this tells me they think there's a chance that the Sanctum is next, they want the power from the transition ritual." He turned to her, his eyebrows furrowed. "Transitioning will also call down all of the Hallowed to gather their children once they become Nephilim, they're giving them reason to fight for Findaria." He seemed to have an epiphany.

"They wouldn't fight anyway? If Hadeon asked?" she questioned.

"Most of them are more concerned with preserving their own kingdoms," he answered coldly.

"Fuck," she breathed dropped her head into her palms. *The war must be what the person was speaking to him about the night before.*

"I'm sorry," he said sincerely.

She would have to kill someone else, she would then have to transition, come into her Imperium faster, and lastly learn who sired her. She thought she had months—not days. Her newfound resolve wasn't prepared for it all to happen so fast.

Cathmore said they weren't strong enough.

"You said that transitioning kills some of us. We haven't been strengthened enough..." she shook her head as fear rattled through her. She thought of Juliet, who she knew was one of the frailest among them. *How could she lose someone else?*

He wrapped his arms around her and pulled her into him.

"You're going to make it, Amara. You're strong enough." He rubbed her head gently. "You're going to start your transition soon, probably with the full manifestation of your Imperium during the Death Match tomorrow." He shook his head and looked into her eyes. "I don't know what that's going to look like for you, but I do know that phasing isn't all you've got," he explained. He looked more wild, out of control, worried. *Worried, he looks worried.* If she wasn't panicking before, that ensured she would.

"How, but..." She stammered. *How did he know she had more than one? What would it be? How bad would it hurt?*

"Once it develops and your transition begins, I can't help you," he apologized. "Your sire will come down to greet you *when* you survive the transition. I don't have time to explain the politics of it but just bite your tongue and try to hold yourself together, do not show him fear. Do you understand?"

"I... yes." She nodded frantically. *Was she going into shock? She had to pull it together.* "I can feel that something's changed."

"The magic is lifting; they're preparing to grant transition to the victors." He sighed. He placed his hands on her shoulders. "Turn around." He guided her so that her back faced him.

"What are you doing?" She jerked away from him when he reached around her to open the towel.

"I'm removing the suspension rings," he explained. "They're not going to help you in the fight." *Oh.*

He carefully removed each one, it only felt like a small pinch but provided her something else to focus on for the moment.

"You're going to swear fealty to your sire and then you are going to fight like hell, do you understand?" He stressed his words as he removed the last ring.

"Yes." She gulped.

When he was done with the rings, he gently grazed the scars on her back with his fingers.

"Who did this to you?" Pain laced his words which came out as a whisper.

She pulled the towel over her breasts and turned to him, not prepared to see how truly saddened the sight made him.

"The person who was supposed to care for me after my mother died," she answered shyly. Something flickered in his eyes, darkening them. "It was a hot poker and boiling water. I made the mistake of wishing to know more about my mother." She wiped a tear before it fell, staring past him.

Suddenly he was a reflection of her—the furrowed eyebrows, glassy eyes, slumped shoulders. As though he felt the pain she had to relive to answer the question, as though he were entangled in her nervous system when it cried out in response to the blinding pain.

"I felt the pain when you gave it to me... but I didn't know the source." He shook his head. "I'm sorry that happened to you." He comforted. She thought she saw a glimmer of conflict play on his face but it was gone as quickly as it came. She lazily circled her thumb in his palm, his skin comforting. "There's something I need to take care of." He sighed and stood. He began pulling on a jacket.

"You're leaving?" She couldn't help but feel disappointed given it could be their last night together.

"I have to," he said regrettably. "I'll be back soon." He turned his back and left the cabin without another word, sending a wave of longing over her as well as some terrible sense that she would never see him again.

ACT II

Chapter 27

Amara had been lying awake for hours as the tree branches around the cabin gently scraped the roof. She tossed and turned, kicked the blankets off of her, retrieved them, and repeated the frustrating cycle.

Where could Cathmore have gone?

Were those demon creatures still lurking somewhere around the cabin?

Midnight came and went in silence and Amara was still wide awake. She heard a massive owl fly by the large window, despite the fact that owls were usually silent when they flew. *What?* She bolted upward.

Her hearing was heightened, more tuned into the smaller noises. She could hear the river running from half a mile away, rodents scurrying through the forest, even the breathing of deer somewhere in the distance. It freaked her out, her breathing increased, the new sensation making her keenly aware of the sound of her own heart beating. The fire crackling was even louder, painfully so.

Something was happening, she was changing. *Was she coming into another Imperium?* She stood from the bed and walked clumsily to the washroom, her own body feeling foreign. She tripped and tried to catch herself on the counter only to have the marble crumble beneath her hands as though she had doubled in size. She was the same size, her reflection proved that she hadn't gotten bigger... just stronger.

She had to do a double-take because the eyes looking back at her were no longer only emerald green, but wrapped in silver. *No no no. It couldn't be happening, how was it happening?* She hadn't gone through the final trial; this couldn't be her transition. *This has to be a dream, I have to be dreaming.*

She rubbed her eyes vigorously, convinced it was a glare, sure she could uncover her true eye color again. It never faded though and she frantically moved backward from the mirror. She moved faster than she intended to though, and just as she crashed into the wall—phased through it against her will. *She was losing her mind.*

She lay sprawled in the dirt, gasping for breath, her chest heaving as she fought to make sense of her surroundings. Panic clawed at her mind, disorienting her further. The world around her seemed to tilt and blur, every sound amplified to a deafening roar in her ears. Above, she heard the rush of wings, heavy and purposeful, followed by a thundering crash as something massive landed just yards away. She scrambled backward, her instincts screaming at her to get away, her hands clawing desperately at the dirt. She felt her nails cracking and tearing against the sediment in the dirt.

It moved slowly, its heavy footsteps crushing dead leaves beneath its feet. The sound of each crunch was unbearable, slicing through her newly heightened senses like jagged glass.

Stop!

Stop!

Please stop!

She clamped her hands over her ears, but it did nothing to dull the torturous noise, each step driving needles of pain through her skull. Her vision blurred as tears welled up, the dark forest around her coming into a harsh, painful focus. She could see every detail of the shadows creeping between the trees, the rough texture of bark, the sharp edges of leaves—everything felt excruciatingly vivid, overwhelming her senses. She could hear the creature's low, ragged breathing, the cautious scrape of its feet dragging through the underbrush. Her heart pounded in her chest as she pressed herself behind a large, rotting log, its mossy surface cold and damp against her skin. The texture was unbearable; it felt like her nerves were exposed, every sensation raw and abrasive. She bit down on her tongue to keep from crying out, her breaths shallow and frantic.

Further away, the unmistakable sound of more wingbeats cut through the night, another creature landing with a heavy thud that made the ground vibrate beneath her. Panic seized her—what the hell was going on?

The figure closest to her finally came into view as she dared to peek over the log, and her stomach twisted at the sight. He was enormous, towering over the forest floor at nearly seven feet tall, draped in crimson and black armor that glistened like the scales of a dragon, each piece reflecting the moonlight in a menacing shimmer. His wings were vast and inky, jet black and absorbing the faint light that touched them, as if the night itself had come alive, sprouting from his lean back in a cascade of shadow.

His skin was pale, a stark contrast to the darkness surrounding him, and his hair was wild, dark spikes that jutted out in every direction. He moved with a deliberate slowness, stalking the area like a predator on the hunt, his gaze sharp and searching. There was something off about him, something that didn't fit with anything she'd seen before. His ears—long and pointed—were an anomaly she couldn't place, not a trait of any Nephilim, Hallowed Fallen, or any being she'd ever known. The sight nagged at her, tugging at a distant, buried memory, but she couldn't put her finger on why.

Suddenly, he snapped his head in her direction, and she slammed herself into the ground behind the log. A sudden, searing pain shot through her entire body, forcing her to writhe onto her stomach. She thrashed in agony, every nerve set ablaze, as if her very bones were being scorched. She bit down hard on her arm, trying to stifle the pained whimpers escaping her lips. Tears flowed freely from her eyes, but something was wrong—these weren't tears. They burned as they trickled down her face, searing a path in her skin like molten metal. She wiped at them frantically, only to find her hands smeared with a thick, glowing substance—like lava pouring from a volcano, hot and alive, threatening to consume her.

What the fuck?

Her body convulsed, and she was hit with a violent, uncontrollable cough that wracked her entire frame. She coughed up the same fiery substance, each retch sending fresh waves of blistering pain through her throat and chest. She tried to silence herself, but the choking sounds were too loud, echoing through the stillness of the forest. She was exposed—vulnerable—and there was nothing she could do to stop it.

The being moved closer, its footsteps slow and deliberate, the low rumble of its laughter cutting through the night like a sinister lullaby. She could feel its presence bearing down on her, the ground seeming to tremble under its weight as it drew nearer. Fear gripped her throat, squeezing tight, as she realized she was trapped with no way out, and no one to save her from whatever monstrous fate awaited.

"Hello, sireling," he purred. She looked up at him with his crooked smile and black eyes.

She spewed more magma from her throat and dug her nails into the ground, feeling her entire body heating. It burned so bad that she was certain her organs were melting. More and more poured from every orifice of her body, she writhed and tried to get away from it, phasing through the log. The man laughed as though impressed by her and strolled in her direction, observingly.

She felt like she was going to pass out from the pain, her eyes losing focus on the person before her.

Who are you?

She sensed another presence suddenly enter the area, joining the man who was watching her. A powerful flap of wings sliced through the air, and with a single thunderous beat, the pointed-eared figure was slammed to the ground by another being with dark wings. Amara struggled to make out the details, her vision wavering between moments of perfect clarity and blinding pain.

Someone was pulling her up from under her arms as she pushed more magma out of her mouth and nose.

"Stop please stop," she sobbed incoherently at the source of the pain.

"Amara, I'm here." It was Cathmore and he was gathering her into his arms. He saw her eyes and his breathing hitched in shock.

"What's happening?" She choked.

She heard commotion from behind her along with the sounds of grunts and punches landing. Someone shot into the sky above them, the other winged one following to meet them in combat.

"I tried to get back in time," he breathed and frantically ran in the opposite direction with her in his arms.

"Who are they?" she asked, trying to focus on anything but the pain in her body.

Cathmore shot into the sky without warning. To her horror she could hear screaming coming from the Sanctum Metere. Explosions echoed there as well as the roars of various creatures. She clung to him, coughing up chunks of the same substance she had been before.

"They fooled us, the North was just a distraction," he explained breathlessly. "He's here now, he's forcing your transition," he elaborated.

"Who?" she asked, wide-eyed.

Cathmore didn't answer but flew faster, away from the Sanctum. She watched in terror as chaos engulfed the Sanctum. She never thought it would fill her with sadness to see the Crucible grounds burn, but her friends were there.

"Stop, go back." She pushed against him. He looked down at her cradled in his arms but didn't do so. "Turn around!" She screamed as a splintering pain shot down her spine.

"No, Amara," he growled in frustration.

Another wave of agony came over her, bending her spine inward, draping her over his arm in an unnatural way. He fumbled for a moment but gripped her tight.

"Shit." He huffed and faltered but kept flying.

She screamed and gurgled on the fluid in her throat and lungs, she could see a reflection of herself in his wide eyes. Her eyes poured orange lava and it bubbled out of her mouth. Something in her back snapped and blood began pouring from her now broken skin. *She was going to die in pain as nothing more than a sacrifice. She couldn't survive this transition. It was too agonizing.*

Cathmore descended from the sky and toward a cluster of trees outside of a small village. Her stomach flipped, adding nausea to the agony. They had been flying for a long while, her body going through waves of pain which she passed out in between.

He descended with care, lowering her gently to the ground. Kneeling beside her, his expression was etched with concern. She was just grateful that her body stopped producing the lava stuff but her entire being felt as though it was breaking apart. Cathmore rolled her onto her stomach as she felt skin in her back begin to tear itself open.

"Please!" She begged for him to make it stop and pulled herself to her knees. She was hunched over, feeling like her skeleton was trying to crawl out through her back.

She vomited blood before phasing against her will once more, landing painfully on the open wounds on her back. Cathmore sped toward her, watching cautiously.

"You have to give in to it, you're transitioning," he coached her. She didn't want to; it hurt so bad.

Who was '*he*'? The one forcing her transition.

"Why is it happening?" She pleaded and thrashed onto her stomach, feeling like an invisible force was pulling her spine toward the sky.

"After the Hallowed lifted the magic... Your sire forced your transition," he explained carefully and moved over to her to comfort her. "Since you've spilled blood..." He shook his head. *There was nothing else stopping it.*

But who? Who was her sire?

"Who?" She grunted as something slithered... *actually slithered* out of her back. It was wet, forcing blood to pour over her back and abdomen. The sensation of snakes crawling from her back caused her to vomit stomach acid.

She was sent to her face in the dirt once more as the thing that she could only guess was a wing moved on its own, trying to expand outwards. Cathmore was breathing and grunting as though physically feeling her pain. *How?*

A being landed next to Cathmore who stumbled to his feet.

"Destroy her," the Hallowed boomed. Hadeon, it was his father.

She pulled herself to her knees again and crawled into the base of a large tree. She screamed as something else slithered from her other shoulder blade, the first wing still twitching painfully.

Cathmore and Hadeon argued incoherently over the sound of blood rushing in her ears before Hadeon backhanded him and sent him flying backward as though he were weightless. He turned his attention to her and smiled wickedly—looking far too similar to Cathmore—to the man she could only now admit she was falling for.

"Get away!" She screamed as he got closer. She tried to phase but couldn't get up the strength. She felt so weak and broken; she was so confused. *What had she done? Why did a Hallowed Fallen want her dead?*

"Don't!" She heard Cathmore demand from behind his father. *No, no, no. Hadeon would kill him for his defiance.*

The other being from before landed nearby, Cathmore rushed to him, shoving him backward and trying to reason with him. She regarded the entire situation that seemed to evolve around her in intense confusion.

Hadeon grabbed her by her hair and hauled her across the ground—her nails cracked off of their nail beds as she grabbed at the roots of trees. Her wings draped sadly over her body, pain causing her to fade in and out of consciousness. *Just let me die.*

"You behead her, or die with her." Hadeon threw her to Cathmore's feet. *No, no, no.*

The threat was the push she needed to finally phase and she focused everything on getting out of the forest they were in. She doubted her ability to phase far enough away. Phasing through an entire forest felt more like teleportation.

She didn't have time to think before she was falling into a river that she didn't know was nearby. She coughed and spewed water, kicking to keep herself afloat as it swept her downstream. She didn't know if the water was soothing the open wounds in her back or making them worse. It was certainly a welcome relief to her raw windpipe in lieu of fucking lava. Her wings twitched and stretched as though trying to grow accustomed to her.

She finally got herself onto a riverbank, too weak to even think about moving. She was sprawled on her stomach, writhing, as pain continued to course through her body. She became inundated with thoughts of blood, Cathmore's blood more specifically. She needed the strength it provided her, needed to feel the warmth coursing through her freezing limbs.

She listened for any sound that would indicate that Cathmore and the Fallen were nearby but couldn't hear anything. *How far had she gone?*

None of this could be happening. She hadn't finished the Crucible. She wasn't ready to transition. *Was she?* Her entire body was revolting against her, telling her no. She couldn't survive it.

After a while, the pain subsided, but she knew another wave would come eventually. She needed to put more distance between herself and the others, but she didn't know where they were anymore. *Fuck.*

Her face was pressed into the cold mud; she alternated between choking and vomiting. Eventually she pulled herself to her feet, her legs wobbling beneath her. She swore her wings made her twice as heavy.

She limped through the darkness of the woods, shivering, stopping periodically to rest against a tree, and then continuing on. She had been on the run before, she would get through this. *Though she wasn't running from a Hallowed Fallen who wanted her beheaded back then.*

She was in shock about everything her body was going through, she could see clearly in the pitch black of night, she could seemingly hear for miles, her wings were drying and gaining shape... The thought made her throw up again but she was just glad it wasn't more lava.

She just wanted to be curled into Cathmore in front of the fireplace. She thought they had more time. They needed more time, they didn't had enough time. Dread consumed her as she wondered if he could hold his own against Hadeon. Of course he couldn't, Naphilim was no match for a Hallowed Fallen.

Eventually she made her way to what appeared to be the edge of a small village. It wasn't one she immediately recognized, but she knew she needed to stay hidden within it regardless. She wasn't safe in any part of Findaria, given its Hallowed Royalty was not so lovingly nipping at her heels.

A wooden sign indicated the village was 'Marrens Eve'. She knew it was the Easternmost village on the continent. It meant she must have put a good few miles between herself and the ones pursuing her. Astoundingly, it meant that she also wasn't within the border of the Sanctum Metere anymore either.

She could feel her body still trying to transition, she needed to get somewhere and lay low—she needed to ride it out. Maybe she would be strong enough to fight them off and escape Hadeon's continent. She was lucky that it was the middle of the night as she stumbled between small stone houses and businesses, mud coating her ankles. Every now and then she spat up blood and the magma-like substance.

How long had Cathmore been under orders to destroy her? She choked down the bitter taste of betrayal and tried to avoid the ache in her chest. Wind blew through the alley where she leaned against a cobblestone wall, shivering. She was still wearing the clothes she had worn to bed—which were far too thin, soaked, and sticking uncomfortably to her skin. Not to mention the useless wings hanging from her shoulder blades, making failed twitchy attempts to fan out. They were weak. She was weak. She was as good as dead.

She stumbled around pathetically for a while before locating a small shed a fair way from a small house. It was a gardening shed and was poorly insulated but it was better than still being completely exposed to the elements. She pulled on a foul-smelling coat, reeking of dirt, and shrank into the far corner of the small space, like a wounded animal retreating to its den.

Despite the sting of betrayal she yearned to be in Cathmore's arms, to taste his blood. His blood. Her mouth watered.

She groaned at the aching in her bones. *How long would the transition take?* She hoped the worst of it was over. Her body kept overheating and cooling to alarming levels. Did that have something to do with her Imperium? That and the magma she had been... producing. She sighed, staring at her palms as though they were foreign objects. Her sire had initiated her transition before the Death Match, but who the hell was he?

The harder she tried to undo the puzzle of her life, of the last few hours, the more she burned with rage. Hadeon wanted her dead—she didn't know why. He sent his son to do it, which made her question every moment they spent together. Even if Cathmore had refused to do it—it was still his entire reason for getting close to her. Tears streamed down her face; she had been so stupid. Who was the other Fallen Angel in the equation though? Why was he familiar? She twisted her hands into her hair, unable to come up with any answers.

Her own screaming pierced the air before the pain even registered—a searing agony that began in her palms and blazed through her skull, igniting every nerve as if her entire body were being consumed by flames. The fire within her raged uncontrollably, a torrent of heat that exploded outward, scorching everything in its path. Desperation clawed at her mind; she needed it to stop, to cease burning her alive from the inside out. Her vision wavered, fading to black, and when it returned, the place she'd sought for refuge was engulfed in flames, collapsing around her in a fiery inferno.

Damn it. The sight was sickeningly familiar, a cruel mirror of Cathmore's false sanctuary—a place that promised safety only to betray her in the end. For a fleeting moment, she considered surrendering, letting the flames consume her until she was nothing more than ash, crumbling with the structure around her.

Her scream tore through the chaos as her wings erupted to life, their sudden emergence accompanied by a sickening crack that shot pain through her spine. She had no control; they thrashed wildly, propelling her with a blinding speed through the roof. Wood splintered and shattered as she burst through, chunks of debris and embers raining down, glowing like falling stars. The embers tried to cling to her skin, but they fizzled out, dying before they could claim her, scattered like fireflies against the night sky.

A few humans had gathered around the shed, watching in horror. She paused, suspended high above them, looking down on them. *She needed to go.* She was frozen, unable to use the newly developed wings. Instead, she willed herself to be elsewhere—pleased when it worked.

She landed harshly on the ground of the forest again, the plume of smoke from the burning shed in the far distance. She crawled herself a few feet so that she could lay against a tree. *Phasing, teleportation, some kind of fire wielding.* She made a mental list of all of the abilities she had developed.

Her wings wrapped around her as she shivered. *Wow.* She looked down at them, inspecting her feathers. *Her feathers, she had feathers.*

She gently touched them, shocked at the chills it sent over her body. Violet feathers shone through the black ones which were the majority, she could make out some twinges of dark blue in them too. There seemed to be an iridescent effect from the gentle moonlight above her, it was beautiful. *Wow.* She was equally amazed by the warmth and comfort that they provided.

She buried her head within them, hoping that her transition was complete. Her body was finally relaxed, no more waves of pain taking over her... for the moment. She dreaded having to learn to control her abilities, having to get accustomed to her new body, and learning to fly. She pulled her knees to her chest, her massive wings consuming her until she was swallowed by them completely.

"Amara," someone whispered. She had been cradled within her wings for a long while before the crunching of leaves below feet signaled someone was nearby. "Come out love, I can sense you're here." It was Cathmore, she stopped breathing.

He was so close to her, but why couldn't he see her? Was it the wings? She listened to him circle the tree that she was leaning against. *He really couldn't see her.* She needed to get away from him, she wanted to throw herself at him. She didn't know what to do or where to go.

If I stay here, she can't get me, she can't fit under the bed. Amara pulled her small frame toward the wall, shoved uncomfortably under her Aunt Grace's bed, her face smashed into the stone floor.

"You can't stay under there you ungrateful child," her aunt bellowed and kicked the wooden frame of the old bed.

She had made the mistake of taking too much food at dinner, Aunt Grace couldn't get seconds. She barely felt Amara was worth feeding at all, much less worthy of more than just the bare minimum. But Amara was eleven and going through a growth spurt, her hunger was seemingly insatiable. She knew she'd be beaten for it if she got caught, and even as she hid—her stomach still growled.

As Cathmore circled her apparently invisible form, she felt the same way she had when her aunt would circle that bed, waiting for her. *Was he going to kill her for Hadeon?* She felt impossibly weak and helpless. All of her limbs felt soggy and useless as a result of transitioning. At least her wings were keeping her hidden.

A hand rubbed her wings, causing them to separate and reveal her. Her eyes were wide in horror; she regarded him with fear. Once again she was a cornered animal. His eyes were wide too, something between shock and amazement in them. Once more they mirrored each other, though their matching reflections held different emotions.

"Please, just let me go," she whimpered. She hoped that there was some small part of him that cared for her, some small part within him that would spare her.

She begged whatever God was watching, that she wouldn't be slain at the hands of the one she'd come to love. It was too cruel, even for her, who knew just how cruel life could really be. *Love, she loved him.*

He towered above her, draped in shadows and unknown intentions. His wings were spread wide, his chest heaving as though he had been running.

"I'm not going to hurt you." His voice softened and he kneeled in front of her. "Can you fly? We have to go." He looked her over, realizing how truly broken she was from her transition.

"Who...who is my sire?" She pleaded. He dropped his head in shame. "Cathmore, please." She pushedHis eyes softened, pain coursing within them. She could feel the misery and conflict radiating off of him as though the emotions came from deep within her own soul.

"Before this all ends." He wiped one of her tears. "Before you can't stand to look at me for the wrongs I've done," he paused and sank lower, closer to her. "I want to hear my real name on your lips, just this once."

Real name? Killian? She had never called him Killian... why did he need to hear it? What else had he done?

"I can't." She shook her head. It would be too painful, because they both knew that the stolen kisses, entangled limbs, and heated moments were gone. They both knew that everything was changing, speaking his name that way...it was too intimate for a love that needed to be buried. "I'm sorry, Cathmore."

He clenched his jaw, the reality sinking in that his final plea would go unanswered—a consequence of every manipulation, every secret, and every lie that had built the chasm between them. Desperation flickered in his eyes as he stretched out a trembling hand toward her, a silent yearning for one last touch. She leaned in, craving the warmth of his palm against her cheek, but it never came. In an instant, he was ripped away, tackled with such brutal force that it barely registered until he was already on the ground, struggling beneath the weight of his attacker.

She sprang to her feet, her breath hitching as instinct took over—protect him. The drive to shield him blazed stronger than any flicker of self-preservation, eclipsing even the primal fear she felt toward the Hallowed Fallen that had him pinned. Her heart pounded as she stumbled forward, wild and reckless, ready to tear herself apart all over again if it meant keeping him alive. She would face every agony, every wound, without hesitation if it meant saving him from the darkness closing in.

Chapter 28

S he watched Hadeon force his son to his feet only to punch him over and over again, sending him to the ground. He wasn't fighting back. *Why?*

"You had orders!" He boomed before kicking him in the ribs, the cracking echoed through the forest.

Anger and heat blinded her, sending her running in the direction of the Hallowed. She allowed that heat to explode from her, she willed it toward the beings back. It was flame given life, brilliant hues of violet and emerald dancing within the fire. He screamed, took off guard, and fell to his knees. *She had brought a Hallowed to his knees.* Cathmore scrambled away from him as the flames engulfed his father.

For a moment she was filled with hope as he squirmed. But soon the screaming became laughing, before he just stopped the flames with a snap of his fingers. He turned to her, Cathmore taking up the space between the two of them. Blood poured from his clearly broken nose but he sneered at his father.

Someone else landed somewhere behind them. Neither she nor Cathmore took their eyes off of Hadeon to see. They both knew it was the other Fallen Angel from before. Amara shook with uncertainty, her limbs still weak.

Hadeon materialized a sword that she thought she had read about. It was massive and glowing. She could feel the magic roiling off of it in waves, the promise of death singing at a tenor so high—she didn't know if anyone else could hear it. If they could hear it, they didn't react.

"You do not get to end my child's life," the unknown man growled before flinging a dagger from somewhere behind them, where it struck Hadeon in the throat. She saw herself within him at that moment, from the way he held the dagger to the way his fingers paused in the air as it struck true. *My child.*

Hadeon laughed and pulled the dagger out as the man charged him with impossible speed. Cathmore turned, pushing her to the ground to shield her from the impact of the two beings. The ground shook and she found herself clinging to him as her head vibrated with the earth beneath her. It made her dizzy and nauseous.

"Who..." she pleaded.

He didn't answer, he only summoned a knife to cut his wrist open. "Here." He began feeding her his blood. It felt like an out of place gesture because it was normally such a sensual act for them... but it was helping her. It was strengthening her as the two Fallen brutalized one another.

Blood and chunks of flesh rained over them as the Fallen soared just above them, fighting. The clang of swords rang through the air, the unnamed Fallen holding his own against Hadeon who suddenly crashed into the ground beside them, forming a small crater. *What the fuck.*

"That's not Sylas, who is he?" She wiped the blood from her mouth. Only the Hallowed could mate, if that being was her father... it had to be the one that rebelled if he was fighting against Hadeon in his own kingdom. But Sylas didn't look like the pointy eared Fallen who was giving Hadeon a solid fight...

Cathmore sneered, annoyed at her questions and forced her to drink more of his blood. It was like swallowing silk, sweeter than her favorite chocolate.

Amara's vision was clearing, her pain subsiding and becoming tolerable as her body started piecing itself together after feeling like it had been shattered. She thought she had been better before, but after feeding... she realized how weak she really had been.

"Come on," he urged her to her feet but her legs were shaking from fear of what she had witnessed.

"No, no." She shook her head. "Here." She pricked her wrist on his exposed blade and forced him to drink. He was weak too; he needed to heal.

She was briefly distracted by his darkened eye contact as he wrapped his soft lips around her wrist. The suctioning of the blood made her insides twist with desire. He was so breathtaking that the chaos in the sky above them was overshadowed.

Hadeon landed abruptly and froze, his jaw dropping as he watched his son feed on her. It seemed to stop him from breathing as though it was so far outside of the realm of possibility that he couldn't believe what he was seeing. Hadeon froze as Cathmore continued to drink, lost in her.

The other Fallen—her father, she gathered, landed beside them, he was inspecting them too with a sniff. Hadeon rose to his feet, with wrath in his eyes that could only be imparted from a being cast from the heavens. It froze her, it brought down God's very own form of wrath and instilled fear within her that settled like lead.

"You mated her?" He boomed. She looked over at Cathmore who tore away from her wrist and licked his lips, tauntingly. He turned to his father, ready for however the cruel Hallowed Fallen was going to retaliate.

"What?" She inhaled.

He regarded his father, prepared for his punishment. All bets were off, there were no illusions, no secrets. They had been found out. He would die for her and he was about to.

The other Fallen Angel put himself between them and Hadeon who seemed a bit amused by the act. Cathmore looked conflicted, angry, unsure what to do.

"You align yourself with me now, child of Hadeon or die by your father's hand. I'm not protecting what isn't mine," the Fallen Angel growled, looking back at them. He smirked at Cathmore though, knowingly, as if there were some kind of inside joke that she didn't understand. She narrowed her eyes on him.

She wanted to run far far away, confusion drowning her once more. *Mate?* She got to her feet, the raw power between the fallen angels overwhelming her.

"Deimos!" Hadeon warned before seemingly calling down thunder into himself. A lightning bolt shooting directly into his raised hand as though calling forth another weapon.

Deimos?

"D—Deimos?" She whimpered, a new wave of shock engulfing her.

The Dark One?

He was her sire?

Cathmore was staring in horror at his father, weighing the ultimatum that Deimos just gave him. Rain poured from the skies, soaking them all instantaneously as though their God were crying to see the Fallen brothers turned on one another.

"I will not beg for her life, *Father*." Cathmore snarled at Hadeon. "But you will have to end me first."

Hadeon appeared taken aback by the assertion but he couldn't have been more shocked than Amara was.

How did she end up in the middle of a forest cast between a Nephilim, a Rogue Fallen, and a Hallowed Fallen?

"Easy enough." Hadeon charged for Cathmore who ducked and rolled out of the way. Amara jumped backward with a start.

"I, Killian Cathmore, swear fealty to you, Deimos," he met eyes with the pointy eared Fallen Angel and nodded with a sly smirk.

Cathmore materialized some kind of dark bladed weapon and tossed it to Deimos who smiled wickedly before freeing more weapons from his belt and engaging with Hadeon again.

It was a signal, so Cathmore grabbed Amara and shot into the sky. She couldn't process everything that had happened, her head was spinning, how had this happened?

"You knew who my father was? You mated yourself to me?" She struggled against him. "How long have you been under orders to kill me?" She hurled questions at him repeatedly and tried to wriggle free of his grasp. She didn't care if it meant falling to her death because her own pathetic wings were untrained.

Below them, where they left the fallen angels, flame swallowed the forest, lightning striking repeatedly.

"What did you do?" She screamed hoarsely and punched his chest. He bit down on his tongue, trying to not give in to his frustration. "Let me go! You're just a liar!" She pushed herself out of his grasp... or maybe he let her. She didn't know.

They had been extremely high in the air because she fell for what felt like forever. She was screaming and covering her eyes before her wings finally caught the wind and slowed her plummet. She didn't know how to fly, she was just coasting clumsily through the air. She panted, her fear of heights still very real. She knew she had to stay conscious if she had any chance of surviving.

Still, she lost consciousness for a second and when she came to, she was plummeting to earth like a rock tossed into the ocean. She screamed in horror as the ground and trees grew closer, reaching up as though prepared to swallow her up.

She tried everything, she tried flapping her wings, she tried to stretch them out, but they were not obeying her. They just draped down her back uselessly.

She was preparing for impact when Cathmore darted into her, seemingly absorbing her as he pulled her into him. The collision with his chest knocked the wind out of her. They were both plummeting for a moment before he slowed them by spreading his brilliant wings. Her wings were mangled uncomfortably due to the way he held her. She found herself unable to move them to ease the pain of his strong arms around her. She winced and squirmed to no avail.

"I will tell you everything," he breathed. His chest heaved as he put distance between the Fallen who were laying waste to the forest and village behind them.

"People are going to die because of them! We have to go back!" She cried as the realization hit her, screams echoing toward the atmosphere from below.

"We can't do anything about it, Amara!" he snapped as he leaned forward to pick up speed, soaring with a gust of wind. He carried her as though she were weightless.

"Where the hell are you taking me?" she demanded, squirming again in his grip.

She wished she knew how to put her wings away. She pushed away the faces of her friends back at the Sanctum Metere who were undoubtedly facing horrors of their own if the walls were breached.

He didn't answer.

"We have to go help with the fighting at the Sanctum," she protested.

"They will kill us; we are aligned with Deimos. If we touch down at the Sanctum, we will be perceived as a threat."

She had never seen him more disheveled, more out of sorts than he was. It was never his intention to swear fealty to Deimos. He did it to save her.

"I'm not aligned with him!" She countered.

"You are his daughter." His eyes pierced hers. The words allowed what she already knew to settle on her like a led weight. *His daughter, she was sired by the Dark One.* "Besides, let's not pretend you don't share some of his rebellious ideals."

He wasn't wrong, she hated everything about the Hallowed and how they ran the kingdoms. She hated the way they bred for power, monopolized every resource that humans needed to survive, the way they forced labor and sacrifice. But Deimos... He was starting a war. War meant death, war meant suffering, especially for the humans who could not defend themselves.

"Well, son of Hadeon, why don't you just let me go and return to your perfect Hallowed father. You enjoy enforcing his ideals anyway," she spat. She couldn't help but feel it would hold more weight coming from her if she wasn't being cradled in his arms like a small child. She felt ridiculous.

"You assume you know so much about me, brat. Did I not just turn on him? Did I not just give up everything I've worked for, for you?" Anger laced his words in poison, in resentment.

"I didn't ask you to!" She launched herself out of his arms before tears could fall. She spread her wings and soared downward, away from him, away from his past intentions, his lies, everything she ever felt for him.

Her wings finally obeyed her.

"Stop doing that!" he yelled at her in frustration.

She wasn't satisfied with soaring, she needed speed, she needed to get away from him. Her wings thundered behind her, doubling her pace from before. She thought Cathmore was flying somewhere behind her, but every time she looked over her shoulders, her own wings blocked her view. *Shit.*

At least they were working this time.

Amara didn't anticipate the amount of energy it took to fly, so before long she was heading clumsily for the ground. She had made it over the mountains in the North and she could sense that Cathmore was nearby, even if she couldn't see him.

"Amara," Cathmore demanded as he landed in front of her. He landed with grace and ease whereas her knees were bleeding from the impact. "We need to get off of this continent..."

"I'm not leaving them." She shook her head.

"He's not going to hurt the sired children," he said cautiously, holding his hands up. She was clearly ready to attack him, ready to put up a fight if he tried to force her to go.

"You don't know that!" she exclaimed. Her eyes burned as her temper ignited, Cathmore stumbled back.

"What the—" he stared at her in concern. She wiped at her face, burning magma had begun to pour from her eyes. *Fuck.*

"It's part of my Imperium." She rolled her eyes and stepped toward him, expecting him to move away from her. He didn't though, he squared his shoulders and regarded her with curiosity.

"He has no interest in hurting them. He came for you. He came to keep Hadeon from ending you before transition," Cathmore explained. He took a step closer to her, pleaded for her to listen to reason and join him in leaving the continent. She shook her head, unsure if she believed him.

"How do you know that?" She screamed.

"It doesn't matter. It's the truth," he insisted with another step in her direction.

"You'll say anything to keep me from turning back," she challenged.

"I will, because I won't let you die," he agreed. "But I am not lying about this."

"Why should I trust you?" she asked and glanced down at his hands where he was summoning something... clothes?

"Here." He handed her a sweater and long pants. She welcomed them in lieu of the nightclothes she had been wearing. She pulled the pants on but when it came to the sweater... *How was she supposed to get it on over her wings?*

Cathmore walked over to her, his boots sloshing in the water puddles on gravel beneath them.

"Will them away." He placed his hands on her shoulders.

"What?" she asked.

"You control them, not the other way around," he instructed. It was familiar, comforting. Her wings twitched as though alive. She closed her eyes and breathed .

She imagined they weren't there, that they closed up inside of her. She didn't even feel it happen but she felt lighter all of the sudden. Her body felt less foreign, except for...

"You're taller," Cathmore smiled. It was true, she no longer only reached his chest but his shoulders now. *whoa.* That was a few inches of height in just a couple of hours.

She was able to shrug on the sweater, actually relieved that the wings were no longer behind her. It was a strange feeling.

"You have no reason to trust me," he started and pushed her hair out of her face.

"I don't trust you," she agreed and took a step away from him.

"Keeping you safe is all I care about," he reasoned. She didn't necessarily doubt that.

"You mated yourself to me. What the hell does that even mean?" she demanded and crossed her arms. He dropped his head and twitched his fingers at his side.

"It wasn't my choice or my doing," he said, defeated. "I would have told you..."

"But you didn't tell me, *Killian.*" Her voice cracked from the weight of his betrayal, she let it accentuate his first name.

"Do not call me that." It seemed to pinch a nerve all of a sudden.

"What?" she asked, exasperated. "You asked me to call you that before, now's just not the time?" She retorted.

"It's not my real name." He looked to the ground then back up to her. He searched her eyes for a reaction, a rejection maybe.

"What?" She was lost in a sea of confusion, weathering the storm that was him.

The shadows under his eyes and cheekbones were darker than usual. He was agony incarnate, a mass of secrets and regret but as beautiful as he had always been.

"You want the truth? We can start with my name," he barked.

Something inside of her jolted with fear, the realization that she had no idea who he was strengthened. She was looking at a stranger before her. Was he the Praeceptor she hated and then fell for? Her mate? Was he her hunter or her savior? She didn't even know his real name... She found herself stepping away from him.

"You can try to run, but I will stop at nothing to keep you safe. Even if it's from your own stupidity," he growled the threat. She knew that running defenseless into the woods was stupid but that didn't make his words hurt less.

"I don't want to know your real name," she spat and turned from him. "*I want to destroy you. I want to lay waste to everything you ever were.*" His words echoed somewhere in her mind.

"Atreus," he whispered, and as the weight of recognition crashed over her, he snapped his fingers. In an instant, darkness swallowed her whole.

Chapter 29

"*A*treus was one of the first angels cast into Hell alongside Lucifer. Though he didn't stay there," Baylin chuckled and shook his head. "There are whisperings that he walks somewhere on Earth amongst the other Rogue Fallen—an advisory of evil, the bringer of the end, the dealer of death—even to the Hallowed," the class gasped. "Some don't believe he exists. That if he did, he would have shown himself centuries ago, some say he's in the Abyss... which is my professional opinion," Baylin surmised.

"Why didn't he stay in Hell?" Eros asked.

"He didn't want to!" Davian said in excitement, in praise.

"No one knows how or why he left, he just did," Baylin answered.

"Why is he rumored to be able to kill Hallowed?" Amara asked.

"Because during the war all those centuries ago... There were two other Hallowed—Einar and Rook. They were hunted to the ends of the earth until they were ripped apart limb from limb and misted out of existence. It was Atreus' show of power, his demand to be left alone."

"Why wasn't he left alone to begin with?" Molvina asked in her perky high voice.

"They wanted him to take one of the Thrones as a Hallowed—they wanted to share in his power," Baylin answered.

"And he didn't want that?" Davian asked as though he couldn't believe anyone would turn down the chance to be a Hallowed One.

"Apparently not." Katara rolled her eyes at his ignorance.

Amara remembered being intrigued by the rebelliousness of the being. She even looked into him a few times in the library. There wasn't a lot to be said though, past what Baylin had already taught them.

He served as an idea of opposition to the Hallowed so of course there wouldn't be extensive knowledge on him. But Amara tucked him away in the back of her mind, looking up to everything he stood for—freedom, strength, rebellion, hope, and independence.

Amara awoke on her back on a concrete floor. It took a moment for her eyes to adjust to the darkness of the drafty space. The room couldn't be more than ten by ten feet. There was a small pathetic window above her—about eight feet—that was long and rectangular.

There was a blanket balled up at her feet and a small lantern that had burned out by the massive steel door. She was still wearing the clothes that Cathmore had given her, her hair was knotted and dirty, her wings still tucked...wherever they went. *You've got to be kidding me.* Was all she could think when she saw the bucket in the corner. She knew what it was for from her experience in the pound back at the Sanctum Metere.

How had she been rendered unconscious? Her head didn't hurt so she wasn't knocked out. She thought of the last place she was...

Cathmore. He made her sleep when she was in so much pain that day. It was part of his abilities. Anger caused her nose to flare and her hands to begin trembling. He wasn't even actually named Cathmore, she hit the stone wall beside her.

"Atreus."

Cathmore had claimed to be Atreus... the Fallen Angel... the mind-numbingly powerful Fallen Angel... The *brother* of Lucifer. The one she was studying, the one he said he knew nothing about. Anger caused her to breathe entirely too audibly in the silence of the cell.

Her back and neck were painfully stiff so she stretched out, peering at the moonlight flooding the space. When she lost consciousness it had nearly been time for sunrise so she must have been out for at least twelve hours. She grunted, feeling helpless and lost.

She had been mated to him, whomever he was. Would he really lock her up? Or had someone else captured her when she lost consciousness?

She tried to think of the person who seemed to care deeply for her, the Cathmore she was falling for. *He would never lock her up.* Cathmore wouldn't, would Atreus? Bile rose in her throat.

She laid in silence in the cell, listening for anything outside of it that would indicate where exactly she was. The occasional metal door would open and then close. She thought she heard murmuring in the distance but the thickness of the cement walls dulled even her sharp hearing abilities. *Were the cells intended to house Nephilim?*

Hadeon referred to Cathmore as his son, he was a renowned Praeceptor at the Sanctum, she had heard about the day of his transformation... How could he be Atreus? It didn't make sense. He was Killian Cathmore, son of Hadeon, Praeceptor at the Sanctum Metere, and captain of the guard.. He was her trainer, her punisher, her lover. He was sent to kill her by his father. How would he have everyone, including Hadeon, fooled? It didn't add up.

She tossed and turned on the hard floor for hours, the sun finally rising. She tried to deduce everything that had occurred from Deimos being her father to being mated to Cathmore/Atreus.

She was trapped in a perpetual storm of deceit, where truth was a flickering mirage that vanished the moment she reached for it. Every time she found the courage to stand on her own, the ground was ripped out from beneath her feet, leaving her spiraling in a chasm of uncertainty. It was like the very God who had abandoned his creation was still pulling strings at her expense just to get a laugh. He was playing a cruel game, shifting the rules just when she thought she understood them. She cursed the wretched being in silence, her lips unwilling to form words.

Every fucking illusion of escape was a lie, a carefully tailored game being played around her. Whenever she became accustomed to the chains that held her, they tightened until she choked on a reality that was out to get her.

She had become a prisoner of shifting fears, each more suffocating than the one before. It began with witnessing her mother's decapitation before she could remember it, being tossed into Aunt Grace's abusive home, and continued from there. Really the horrors of the Crucible were just par for the course. She was always looking over her shoulder, trying to catch a glimpse at death which she felt breathing down her neck.

Death.

The weight of guilt pressed down on her chest, heavy and suffocating, as if the walls themselves were closing in. In the silence, she could almost feel the blood on her hands—sticky, warm, and impossible to wash away. The emptiness of the room amplified every haunting memory, every mistake, every ounce of rage that had once blinded her.

Molvina's lifeless eyes flashed in her mind, a stark reminder of the moment she lost herself. She'd killed in a jealous fury, over something that was never even real. A lifeless, unamused laugh escaped her lips, tinged with bitterness. What did it say about her that she'd been willing to spill blood over a lie? The shame twisted in her gut, burning like acid, and she wished she could claw the memories out of her mind, tear them from her soul. But they were seared into her, a brand of her own making, forever marking her as something broken, something lost.

Somewhere in the torment, sleep found her, though it was probably the worst sleep of her life. She dreamed of Cathmore, of all the good moments they shared. She awoke in tears some hours later.

"He wasn't real," she whispered to herself. "None of it was real."

She repeated the mantra, rocking back and forth as she hugged her knees. He had been inserted into her life to kill her for Hadeon.

Yet, she could feel the warmth of his lips on hers when she closed her eyes. Those lips she had memorized every curve of were full of deceit and lies. She had been entangled with a snake for months. The thought made her sick... and yet she worried about what had happened to him in those woods. Though her instincts told her he was her captor, part of her hoped he was also a prisoner. Because then maybe, just maybe. She meant something to him after all.

She was pathetic.

She felt in her core that his heart was still beating, she knew he was still alive. As much as she despised the connection that they shared, he was a small ember burning in the far reaches of her soul.

"He wasn't real," she told herself when she began reminiscing on the fun they had together.

An endless day gave way to the darkness of night and she started to wonder if her captors were going to simply allow her to starve to death in the dreary old place. She briefly pondered mustering up her flame wielding abilities to try and escape... but to what end? She sank into herself, utterly defeated, unwilling to even fight for her freedom.

She didn't know where she was or where she would go. She had a feeling that her father would hunt her down no matter where she ran, if Atreus—*Cathmore*—didn't do it first. She couldn't deduce her role in it all, what her purpose was. She figured Hadeon wanting her dead had to do with her being sired by Deimos but she couldn't even fathom *how* he procreated. She groaned and clunked her forehead on the floor.

The heavy door to her cell was pulled open slowly, causing her to jump to her feet. Someone shorter than her strolled in. He was young, in a tailored dark blue suit with a tailcoat and a thick fluffy white collar around his throat. She blinked, finding someone in a suit felt odd, he looked out of place.

He pulled the door closed behind him and she pushed herself to the back wall of the cell. She wouldn't let her guard down because of how young he looked. He was scruffy-looking, fit, and fairly handsome. He lit the lantern that refused to come alive for her and she could see that his hair was short, the strands on top curly, and dark blue. *Like Sylas.*

He extended a bundled-up cloth in her direction. She looked at it but didn't take it.

"It's just bread," he said.

"You eat some first," she demanded despite her stomach begging for it.

"Very well." He pulled a piece of the bread free and popped it between his plump lips. She snatched it from him.

He inspected her from head to toe, pacing in the front of her cell with his hands clutched behind his back. She had been there for over thirty-six hours and this was the first person she had come into contact with.

"You're magnificent," he concluded, as though that were the answer to some equation. She tilted her head at him in confusion. She scanned his silver tipped pointed shoes, once again seemingly out of place in a prisoner's cell.

"Can I help you with something?" She crossed her arms, annoyed by his presence.

"Nope," he said.

He brushed dirt off of his shoulder as though the filth of the place were an inconvenience to him. He watched her in silence until she felt uncomfortable.

"Where's Cathmore?" she asked finally.

"Who?" He scoffed.

"Atreus," she said reluctantly.

He grinned and then he exited the cell without a single word.

"What the fuck!" She screamed and launched the bread roll at the door which slammed closed behind him. It bounced and rolled across the floor. It seemed to silently shame her for such an infantile act.

She finished the bread, grateful to have something to absorb the stomach acid that seemed to have turned on her.

Seven. There were seven cracks in the wall in front of her. They all spread out and ran in opposing directions. It made her think of her friends who she hoped had escaped whatever war Deimos had waged on the Sanctum.

But she thought she knew what the war was really about—freedom. It was about breaking free from the Hallowed's control and, more importantly, stripping them of the stolen magic that made them so powerful. Yet, the unsettling truth lingered: she might know nothing at all. She was piecing together fragments of what she believed to be true, but even she wasn't naive enough to assume she understood the motives of the Hallowed Fallen's greatest adversary.

Sounds of feet shuffling approached her door before a loud click of a lock and the massive steel thing was swinging open. She hurried to her feet, tucking herself in the corner cautiously.

An overly large man crowded her small space, grabbing her arms. Behind him stood the man who entered the cell the night before, he leaned on the doorframe casually. She tried to jerk free of the big one to no avail.

"No reason to fight, love. You've been upgraded," came the voice of the guy she met the evening before. *Upgraded?* The bigger gray-haired one gave nothing away.

They led her past at least a dozen other cell doors, all seemingly occupied given the various sounds and lantern light trickling under the cracks. The stone corridor was dark though, some torches spread out to light their way—barely. The bluish-haired one led her up some skinny winding stairs, the bigger one behind her.

"Can I at least know where the hell I am?" she demanded. The one in front of her tightened his grip on her wrist where it rested at the small of his back.

"Neither here nor there," the one in front of her said in a sing-song type voice that threw her off. He turned and flashed her a sharp toothed smile that caused her to stumble. Sharpened teeth weren't a trait of the Nephilim, not that she knew of.

She followed them through towering corridors with marble statues of fallen angels, endless branching off hallways, and massive entryways that allowed the breeze from the nearby ocean to roll in.

She watched the waves crashing for a while, no more than ten yards from the small foot path they took between the buildings. There was so much smooth white stone and marble, cobblestone of gold and ivory... *Where the hell was she?*

They entered an unassuming building that blended in with the rest of the others in the unnamed palace. The guy in front of her brushed off his tailored suit, which fit his slim figure perfectly. He had silver thread down his sleeves and some symbol she didn't recognize on his shoulder. She didn't miss the daggers handing off of a leather belt under the jacket either.

The men opened the double doors, allowing her to enter before they took up their place behind her. The first thing she noticed was the glass tile floor, where the ocean ran under it. *Or maybe an inlet?* The crisp blue waters were alive with varying sea creatures. *Wow.* She could get lost in watching the world below her feet but she was shoved forward.

She narrowed her eyes when she realized a throne sat at the far end of the room. A wing backed throne of silver and ivory to be exact, massive in its build. A deep royal blue rug led directly to the altar upon which it sat and even though the throne was empty, it was intimidating.

There were eight rising stone columns hugged by black braziers. They lit up the lower levels of the throne hall. Everything was cast in a soft glimmer from the flickering flames. Depictions of angels and demons looked down upon the stone floor of the ostentatious hall from a vaulted dome ceiling. The sheer size of the space threatened to steal her breath.

Two forked banner flags hung from the high ceiling on either side of the throne. Each black with blue and silver details adorning the kingdom's crest. She squinted her eyes to make out the details; there was a profile view of a horned goat standing on its back legs, it was blue though its horns were gold. Silver wings adorned the sides of the crest, and a knight's helmet with flowing designs crowned the top of it. The crest itself was black, the 'V' shape behind the goat was silver. She tried to deduce its meaning but had no luck.

The royal blue rug running from the throne to the doors was matched by smaller ones on either side of the hall. Simple forked banners of the kingdom's colors with elegant silver threaded floral designs decorated the walls. Between each banner hung a torch, all of them lit and in turn illuminating the murals of angels in varying stages of their falls.

Curtains were tied back to reveal the sprawling clear glass windows with the ocean view. The curtains were adorned with emblazoned edges and jewels that Amara couldn't name if she tried. She swallowed hard. She didn't know where she was but she knew whoever sat on that throne, held a position of enough power to end her puny existence.

She squinted her eyes at the empty throne, searching for clues as to who ruled the sprawling palace...*Kingdom?*

The broad pillows were that same shade of blue and had been sewn with gilded ridges. Those wishing to listen to or speak with their ruler could do so from the long and rather bulky onyx benches, all of which were diagonally facing the throne. Additional elegant throne-like seats were on either side of the main throne, she wondered who they were for. They were smaller but clearly meant for people of great importance.

Amara couldn't wrap her head around anything she was seeing. "What—" she began.

"This way," the blue-black-haired one said. He had an excited bounce to his walk that both put her at ease and on edge all at once. He grabbed her arm and led her down the hall to the right of the massive entry way.

After a few minutes of walking she was growing irritated at the needless size of the nearly empty palace. *I mean seriously,* she scoffed in her head. A smaller hall ended in two doors on either side. Cherrywood and ivory trimmed the space with etchings of different historical scenes from the Fallens' history.

"To the left, this is where I leave you, my lady." The blue-haired one nodded, where the gray-haired one rolled his eyes.

The heavy wooden door opened as if sensing her presence. She was prepared to take in the dark, dimly lit beauty of the room, but the person standing in the center of it ignited her rage.

"You!" She stomped over to him, pulling off her shoe and flinging it hard before following it up with the second one. The first bounced off his shoulder while the other overshot him entirely. She pounced on him before he could fully react, driving her knee into his groin, making him double over with a grunt. "You filthy liar!" she screamed as she slapped him hard across the face.

Cathmore looked nothing like the man she'd last seen. He was cleaned up, his hair neatly trimmed, dressed in sleek leather and silver. And was that—"A cape?" she spat, disgusted. She could hardly believe the sight of him, looking every bit like royalty, while she was filthy, starved, and stinking of sewer filth.

"Actually, brat, the term is mantle," he corrected with a smug grin that only stoked her fury.

"You arrogant asshole!" she shouted, grabbing the cape and yanking it off him. The rich blue velvet crumpled to the floor, and she set it ablaze with a touch of her fingertips, watching it smolder and turn to ash. He stood there, making no move to stop her, not even as she tore books from the shelves and hurled them at him, tossing artifacts like worthless trinkets.

"I can't believe I was actually worried about you!" She screamed again, and shoved at his chest. "I was trapped in some cell while you were up here? Pretending to live a life of royalty!" She laughed and pushed him again, he took it, biting down on the inside of his cheek.

He stomped out the dying fire of the cape-robe thing with a booted foot before gesturing for her to continue as though he were bored. *Asshole.*

"If you're finished, I'd like to explain," he said calmly.

She couldn't believe she had been held captive down there, for any amount of time, worried for him.

"You are a coward," she spat. She could see that it finally struck a nerve. He left her down there for days. Left her to think something terrible had happened to him.

She stared into his eyes, no longer bearing a silver ring around them as hers now did. His eyes were still deep blue, most of his features the same, but he was a stranger.

"I don't care what you have to say, Cathmore." She sighed and shrugged with cold detachment.

"I deceived you," he began. "It was necessary, Amara."

"Necessary?" she scoffed, her laughter brittle and sharp. "I don't want to hear it." She shook her head, unwilling to let him weave his excuses. Questions raced through her mind faster than she could catch them, but she didn't want his answers. He stood there, willing to explain, but all she could see was a beautiful snake—charming and deadly, and she had been too mesmerized by the sunlight glinting off his scales to notice the poison beneath. She swallowed hard, forcing down the bile of her own foolishness.

"There's so much you don't know, don't understand. I want to make it right," he said , stepping toward her, but she backed away, signaling him to keep his distance. "I am Atreus. I did seek you out, and I am your mate."

"What... what does that even mean?" she demanded, her voice trembling with a mix of anger and despair. "Where are we?"

"Constantine, my home," he replied simply. She had never seen it on a map, and she doubted she ever would.

"I want to be left alone. Am I allowed that privilege, or am I still your prisoner?" she sneered, her words laced with all the bitterness she felt.

"I want to be left alone. Am I allowed that privilege or am I still a prisoner here?" She snarked.

"As you wish." He sighed. She watched him leave the room, the most familiar stranger she had ever encountered.

She allowed the panic to wash over her, allowing the helplessness she felt to envelope her. Waves and waves of agony and betrayal froze her in the center of the massive bedroom. She was a block of ice in the ever expansive frozen Sea of Icarus. Her limbs were as heavy and cold as Molvinas's when her body was removed from the training hall.

She had the eerie feeling that this is what death felt like; utterly empty, alone, numbingly painful, and darker than shadows cast by her own despair. She felt so out of place as though cast into a different realm entirely.

She wouldn't even do herself the decency of lying in the far too soft-looking bed or bathing in the massive washroom. The floor-to-ceiling archway windows to her right were threatening to swallow her up. Far too much sunlight poured in, the ebb and flow of the waves made her feel unsteady on her feet.

I have to get out of here.

I have to go.

The door was locked, the windows didn't open. *What kind of windows faced the sea but weren't made to open?*

She was pacing back and forth in the room, unable to find a plausible escape. If she got out, where would she go? She didn't even know where in the world she was.

"My love you're not a prisoner here," came Cathm—Atreus' voice in her mind.

My love.

"Then why am I locked up!" she shouted into the open space and threw a small figurine at one of the window panes.

A sensation overcame here, making the air thicker for a moment. Then all of the windows swung open along with the bedroom door. Wind drifted into the room from the ocean front, sprinkling the wooden floor in white sand. She inhaled the cleanest air she thought she had ever breathed and padded toward the beach. Her mind reeled with endless possibilities of how he had done that but it only had one plausible answer; magic. She could taste it lingering in the air and coating her skin like oil.

The sand sank between her toes; it was uncharacteristically cool despite the sun high in the sky. She allowed it to cool the rage burning within her. She stared into the crystal clear blue water as she approached it. She wondered what drowning was like, she wondered if it was worse than the way she already felt. She had been drowning in dread and nothingness for so many years, perhaps she could find out if the metaphor of her lifelong mantra was accurate.

Her feet met the water, the waves lapping at her toes hungrily. She was entranced in the call of the sea before her, the promise of being taken out with the tide and away from every ounce of uncertainty, every ounce of fear.

She glanced from side to side; the private beach was empty. No one would know, no one would stop her. Would anyone even blame her if she just decided to be done? She didn't know if any of her friends were alive, she had been controlled and lied to for her entire life. Even when she finally found someone she trusted, it was all a lie. She swallowed hard. The inescapable feeling of being trapped both physically and within her own mind was the thing that made her step forward.

Another step.

Water pooled around her ankles, her calves, the chill doing nothing to talk her out of it. She was focused on one thing; the end of her suffering.

All of the things she endured to escape the Crucible, everything she faced to get through it, failing to discover who killed her mother, learning that she was far worse than a bastard sired—that she had been sired by a Rogue Fallen...it was all a weight attached to her core that caused her to crave reprieve at the bottom of the sea.

It was the one act that she felt she could choose for herself apart from the one that left her heartbroken. Cathmore was a choice she had made to feel joy unapologetically. It cost her everything. She had nothing else to lose as she dove beneath the waves and swam as far and as hard as she could.

No matter how many times she tried to force herself to inhale the water, her body refused. She floated to the surface on her back and laid there weightlessly.

She had the sense that she was being watched, though she didn't know by whom or from where. She glanced back at the white marble building, the daunting bedroom she exited was such a small portion of it.

After some time in the water she realized she didn't want to die. It was a conclusion she was tired of coming to, truthfully. She was just so tired of being pushed around without a say. She was so tired of just trying to survive. She wanted quite the opposite of what originally called her into the sea; she wanted to live.

She was approaching the shore, her sweater drenched and heavy when Atreus came into view.

"Can you hear me out now? Please," he implored.

He did not replace the cape/mantle thing that she found ridiculous but he was still dressed extravagantly. He wore a finely tailored suit with sharp edges, accents of red sewn into the black blazer. A white undershirt with a ruffled neck, black vest, red tie, and golden cufflinks completed the look. His dark hair was fixed again; strands of crow feathers slicked back where not even the wind touched it.

She had to take in the other details of him though, the parts of him that were no longer there. He no longer appeared Nephilim. Most notably the silver ring around his eyes were gone. She knew it had disappeared that day. Something in his facial features were harsher, more beautiful, and cast deeper shadows. He had no wrinkles and his porcelain skin remained perfect.

She stepped out of the water, feeling absurd to be emerging from the sea fully dressed but still filthy while he looked...like that.

"So what, you're like a prince of this place?" She shoved past him, not truly caring of his position after all of the lies and manipulation.

"King actually." The blue-haired guy that had been in her cell was standing in the room when she entered. She gasped and whirled on Cath... Atreus.

"King?" She was exasperated.

"Leave us," Atreus demanded and he left. She found herself laughing.

"This is insane." She laughed harder. "You're a ruler... a king?" She made a disbelieving gesture in the air.

"I told you it was a lot to take in," he answered. He sounded like him but also didn't.

"So you're responsible for throwing me in a cell for days?" She seethed.

"It's protocol, you were transitioning, Amara," he reasoned.

"I fucking hate you." She was close enough to feel his breath on her face. She hoped he understood that she meant it. Her nails dug into her palms as she clenched her fist.

"I've heard that before." He smirked. *Wrong thing to say.* She reeled back and smacked him hard across the face. She heard two sets of feet rush into the room behind her, Atreus' eyes met them.

"Sir?" they asked, watching her.

"You will not lay a hand on Ms. Ashenfall. No matter her actions against me," he commanded. "Leave." His voice was almost deeper, darker. The two armed guards obeyed.

His eyes found hers, pink staining his cheek where she slapped him. She had the familiar feeling of being picked apart and examined under his gaze.

"What does it mean to be mated to you?" she demanded, her voice edged with both curiosity and defiance. She needed answers, even if she dreaded what they might be.

"It means our souls are bound together, Amara," he said, his tone softening, almost reverent. "I know you've felt it too—the pull, the way our blood strengthens each other, the connection in our minds. It's why you hear me when no one else can, why you feel me even when I'm not there." He paused, tilting his head as he studied her face, searching for a hint of understanding. "We are destined, but you haven't fully accepted it. Until you do, we are only partially bonded. You aren't truly mated to me... not yet."

"I don't want that." She swore and crossed her arms. Did she?

"Right." He shook his head as though he didn't believe her.

"I don't know you. I am not accepting you as my mate no matter..." she trailed off.

"No matter what?" He was close to her, achingly close.

She was going to say no matter how she felt, what it was like to taste his blood. She was going to say no matter how good he made her feel. She didn't have to say it though, something registered in his eyes and she knew that he knew what she was thinking.

"It doesn't matter." She turned from him. A shiver ran through her, her dripping clothes leaving water on the floor below her.

She padded over to the bed, yanked the comforter off and wrapped herself in it. He just watched her. For a moment she thought he would protest but he didn't.

"Deimos continues his war on Findaria. He will be away for some time," he explained. She recalled that night in the woods. *I Killian Cathmore, swear fealty to you, Deimos.*

"So you were never Hadeon's son? You never swore fealty to Deimos?" she asked for clarity.

"Correct, I assist Deimos in his... quarrel with the Hallowed Fallen." He shrugged. He grabbed some kind of nut from a bowl on the bar and popped it in his mouth.

"Why come after me? Why did you seek me out?" She decided to let the questions pour out as she fumbled around his rather extensive mini bar with varying liquors. He was on the other side of it, watching her curiously.

"You were something that he started many years ago, I was always supposed to see you through the Crucible," he explained coolly.

"Why?" she asked.

"Some part of his bigger plan, more of a question for him, really." He sat in one of the large arm chairs. She just rolled her eyes at him. She felt like he was holding some part of that truth back.

"What was in it for you?"

"Maybe a question for another day." He stared past her. She narrowed her eyes at him.

"So you don't give a shit about any of the students you taught? You'll let them die a casualty of a war that isn't theirs?" she asked, slamming a clear glass bottle of liquor on the wooden bar in frustration. Some of it sloshed out of the top, not making a big enough mess in her opinion.

"That's really very expensive, love." He pointed to the bottle. She bore her eyes into his, lifted the bottle, and slowly poured it onto the bar.

"Don't call me that," she demanded and threw the bottle to the floor, allowing it to shatter. He didn't flinch.

"Many of the sired children began their transitions after their first kill in the battle. We flew most of them here," he informed her as he stood in frustration at her destroying the room. "Some of them are still going through the rough part. We'll give them a few more days."

Relief flooded over her that Avren, Juliet, Beck, and Eros could be there, could be safe. She didn't know what to say. He crouched down and began picking up the broken glass, she didn't care.

"They'll join the fight only if Deimos calls for backup. I personally think the creatures he summoned will be more than enough, now that Hadeon is... indisposed." He grinned up at her and once more she was faced with a stranger.

"You're the only reason his rebellion wasn't stopped," she realized.

"Well." He shrugged proudly. She took a shot of a random dark liquor though she wasn't sure why. It burned all the way down but settled in her core with warmth. He stood and discarded the large chunks of glass in a bin.

"This is too much." She sighed and sat on the bed, dropping her face into her hands. She should be happy to see him, happy he's alive and that they're together, but the distrust sent a wave of nausea through her that she couldn't shake. She made her way back to the bed, sitting quietly in the comforter.

"I know," he said genuinely. She felt the bed dip as he took a spot next to her on the onyx sheets. "It wasn't supposed to happen this way." *How was it supposed to happen? What was 'it'?*

She just couldn't wrap her head around the fact that everything had changed so drastically in only half a year. She should have still been on the run from the Crucible. She never wanted anything to do with any of it. Of course she would end up sired by the 'the Dark One,' and somehow mated to Atreus—one of the deadliest fallen angels to set foot on the planet. *How did her role in anything make sense?* She felt so lost and so small compared to the weight of the world bearing down on her shoulders.

Even when she had to face the Crucible—she started to have hope for survival, started making peace with what that future could hold. Even that was ripped away from her. She examined the man before her, trying to piece him together with her Praeceptor, her lover. It didn't match; it wasn't right.

"I have been away from home for years. I went through the Crucible; I did become a Praeceptor and a captain for the Sanctum. All of that is true, Amara," he pleaded and turned to her.

"How did you fool them? The Hallowed?" She sniffled and rubbed her arms under the blanket—feeling weak and fragile.

"The abilities I possess are unique, untraceable. After I faked my transition into Nephilim, Hadeon approached me about a sired child on the run..." he explained.

"He wanted to kill me." She nodded.

"Not at first." He shook his head. "He wanted to know who sired you. He grew suspicious of your origin," he chuckled. "He was cleverer than I gave him credit for." He shook his head as though appreciating some inside joke she didn't understand.

"What was the point of Deimos siring me at all? Why do any of it?"

"Power, obviously." He laid back on the bed and put his arms behind his head. She narrowed her eyes at him. She became overwhelmingly annoyed by him and his cockiness.

"Get out," she demanded and pointed out the door. He leaned up on his elbows and looked at her quizzically. *I am not a pawn.*

"You're kicking me out of *our* room again?" he asked with a raised eyebrow.

"Our room?" She scoffed. "No, no, no, I'm getting my own room or I want my cell back." She stood and crossed her arms. "Now go away." She pointed at the door. Something like pain played on his face but it was gone as soon as it showed.

"You'll change your mind." He sneered, all humor leaving him, and left the room swiftly.

Once she was sure that he wasn't lingering in the hall, she shredded off the wet clothes and flopped onto the bed. She placed a pillow over her face and pressed it down hard, effectively muffling a scream that needed to be let out.

Once she felt lighter, she stepped into the expansive bathing chamber connected to the room. It was a stunning blend of ivory, gold, and black accents, radiating a refined beauty. To her left, an enormous window spanned almost the entire wall, offering an unbroken view of the ocean beyond. She watched the waves rise and fall, lonely drifters guided by a greater force, just as she was. But unlike the waves, she didn't answer to the moon, and she knew she would never find the peace it offered.

She eyed herself in the mirror, she was tattered and disgusting. Her hair was tangled and matted with dirt, blood from growing her wings, and probably magma that was coming out of her ears. Even her time in the ocean didn't clean her up, she needed to *scrub*. Stains adorned her face and arms, her eyes were foreign, her facial features more angular… more beautiful. She was taller and looking down her body felt strange. *Were her feet bigger?* She couldn't tell.

She leaned on the marble counter, digging her nails into it until her knuckles turned white. Deimos was her sire, her father. She hadn't given herself the opportunity to taste that information, much less swallow it. She looked up at herself and compared the features to what she had seen in him. Same high cheekbones, similar nose and eyebrow ridge, thinner build, and -she moved her hair back—her ears were pointier than they had been. She jolted back from the mirror.

Pointed ears were not a noted change that Nephilim received and Deimos was the only Fallen Angel she heard of having the trait. *Wow.* She touched them. They weren't too noticeable and not nearly as pointed as her father's… *her father, her father.*

She had gone her entire life without a clue as to who she took after, who she resembled apart from her mother. Now, she knew who he was and she didn't know how to deal with it. He was known to lay waste to villages and summon demons from hell for his own gain, he was ruthless. But he was also powerful, driven, seemingly intelligent, and unrelenting. She glanced back up at her reflection. *Did she have anything in common with his personality?* She didn't know if she wanted the answer, especially not while he tore through the Sanctum Metere.

Then again, why did she care about the Sanctum? She never wanted to be there. It was a sacrificial killing ground for sired children, a place that most who entered never left. It was a symbol of power and control for the Hallowed Fallen to take anything they wanted. She would have been another nameless corpse somewhere on those grounds if it weren't for Cathmore-*Atreus*.

The thought hit her hard, she wasn't prepared for it. He really had played a huge role in her continued survival. If not for him, Marlowe would have...she recalled the assault she endured from him. How disgusting she felt afterward. She couldn't help but draw similarities between what Marlowe did and when Cathmore tied her up in the woods. She didn't feel violated or disgusted after Cathmore's dominating of her. Consent made a world of difference.

She also refused to give him all of the credit for her survival of the Crucible. She survived the hunt, she survived The Abyss, she survived Marlowe's torture... She recalled him pursuing her during the hunt. He wasn't *actually* trying to kill her then. *Ugh.* She was so sick of feeling like she was being tossed around in the world instead of dominating her life. She felt like a pawn throughout every stage of her life except for when she was on the run. Even then, that wasn't living.

Cathmore had expertly guided her and protected her at the Sanctum, her aunt only took her in to collect her sister's money, her sire placed her in Findaria to begin with as part of a power play. What was her purpose in the world? How could she be anything if she was nothing to herself? She had spent so many years broken and tortured and on the run. She was done surviving; she was done being a puppet.

She sneered at her reflection in disgust.

"You're done being a pawn," she declared and shattered the mirror before her without even touching it.

In the fractured glass she could see her eyes the color of burning embers, the edges of the glass charred. *Whoa.*

Chapter 30

"Time for breakfast." A knock came at her door the following morning.

"Go away!" she yelled at the male stranger on the other side. She buried herself under a heap of pillows. The bed felt like a cloud hugging her body, she had no plans on leaving it. She was relieved when the person could be heard walking away so she dozed back off, content to rot there if it kept her away from Cath—Atreus.

She awoke at eleven in the morning with a body aching from hours of stillness. Thanks to her shower the night before, the soft scent of cherry blossoms lingering around her.

Amara turned to a window that allowed sunlight to pour in, dressed with dark curtains and gold trim. On either side, a wardrobe. She padded to the one on the right and rifled through it—leather jackets, black pants, suits, button-downs, another cape thing... she narrowed her eyes. *He really intended for them to share the room.*

The other wardrobe was clearly stocked for her; she was pleased to see only two dresses amongst the heaps of varying dark shirts and pants. Amara tugged on a pair of tight leather pants that fit perfectly. The shirt she chose was made of straps and clear mesh, only covering her breasts and crossing some of her abdomen. She was satisfied with the creamy pale skin showing through the thin lacey material. The back of it dipped into the shape of a V, leaving most of her backside exposed.

The clothes felt so right, so her. She wondered who chose them. She pulled on a pair of heeled boots, snagged some dangling scarlet colored earrings from a jewelry box, and searched for the inevitable weapon stash in the room.

Under the massive four poster bed, sure enough was a flat chest. The key was already sitting in the lock. She opened it, expecting to find some daggers but the true contents took her breath away. In the box was a longsword, wrapped in blue cloth. It called to her, it was familiar. It was the same sword from Wrathguard's class, the one that stuck out to her, the one she was going to earn if it killed her.

She reached out and touched the sword, her fingertips grazing the cold metal. The sapphire embedded in the hilt flickered to life at her touch, glowing with a sudden, vibrant light that pulsed like a heartbeat. Startled, she jerked her hand back, and the gem dulled to a muted blue, lifeless once more. Rocking back on her heels, she studied the blade with a newfound intensity. Strange, cryptic symbols she had never seen before were etched along the steel—small, dark, and unassuming, yet humming with an ancient, untold power. The hilt was pure silver, polished to a mirror-like sheen, its intricate design both fierce and breathtaking.

She picked it up and stood, and the moment the sword settled into her grip, a surge of energy flooded her veins, electric and intoxicating. It was as if the blade awakened something dormant inside her, something she hadn't even known was missing. Power thrummed through her, harmonizing with her very being, singing in her blood. She felt whole, exhilarated, and inexplicably complete. She knew in that moment she would never part with this sword—it was no longer just a weapon; it was a part of her, an extension of her soul.

Bending down, she grabbed the strap that had been stored with it and secured the sword to her back. It fit against her newly transformed body with a natural ease, resting perfectly between where her wings would unfurl. Her wings. She moved swiftly to the wardrobe and swung open the door, revealing a tall mirror inside.

Amara stared at her reflection, her breath hitching. Taking a step back, she closed her eyes and focused. Inhale. Exhale. She tried to will her wings into existence, imagining them bursting free. But... nothing. She tried again, pushing harder, willing them with every ounce of her determination. Still, they refused to appear. Frustration bubbled up as her face flushed red with effort, her muscles straining as she fought against an invisible barrier.

What the...

She knew there was more training at the Sanctum Metere after transition, she was starting to realize exactly the reason why. She had no real control over her new form and next to none over her abilities.

She sighed, slammed the door shut and left the massive room. She briefly wondered if she was *allowed* to do so before deciding she didn't care one way or the other. Just outside of the hall in which her room was, there were a few people in the foyer walking wherever, one person dusting the statues, and a woman with a small child walking out to the beach. One of the men looked at her for far too long but when she met his eyes, hurried away.

"Yes, it will be arranged. My apologies for the delay Ms. Constance," came Atreus' voice from the great room with that damned throne. Amara slinked into the shadows on the edge of it and watched.

He sat with an arm on each armrest, a well-fitted dark suit, and his feet planted firmly on the ground. He signaled another person up to address him, the woman from before smiled as she left the throne hall. *Humans, they were humans.*

"This is for you," the man said and held up some hand carved trinket she couldn't make out. "Welcome home, your Highness." He bowed. Amara just watched on in shock, not quite believing what she was seeing.

"Thank you, Winiston, it will go in the gallery with the others." He smiled sincerely.

There were only a few more people waiting to see him. The next in line was a woman clutching a newborn, her face lined with exhaustion and grief. The child grunted , squirming in her trembling arms as she stepped forward. She was not trembling out of any kind of obvious fear of her king, but because of a darker and heavier emotion that she carried with her.

"King Atreus," the woman began, her voice breaking as she struggled to keep her composure. "His father died at sea before he was born, leaving him nameless." She looked up, tears streaming down her cheeks, her desperation palpable. "He is a child of your kingdom. Please, I beg you—bless him with a name."

Atreus rose from his throne, his regal demeanor softened by a rare tenderness which was usually only pointed toward Amara. He descended the three steps, each footfall heavy with the weight of his responsibility. As he reached the woman, he met her tearful gaze, a silent exchange passing between them—one of shared sorrow and unspoken promises. Gently, he pulled back the blanket from the infant's face, revealing a small, delicate child with eyes shut tight against the world.

Atreus leaned in, whispering quietly into the woman's ear. Whatever he said was meant for her alone, a private moment in a room filled with watchful eyes. The woman's breath hitched, and she clutched the baby tighter, weeping with a mixture of grief and relief. "Thank you," she sobbed, her words thick with gratitude.

Turning to the woman beside her, likely her sister given their shared features, she held her head high and announced to the small gathering, her voice resonating with newfound pride. "Roman of Constantine," she declared, wiping away her tears with still trembling hands.

Atreus's expression hardened with resolve as he addressed the room, his voice echoing with a quiet authority. "This child may be fatherless, but he will not grow without guidance. He will have a place in my court when he reaches his tenth year." His words were a solemn vow, binding and final, and the room murmured in response, ripples of awe and approval passing among the dozen or so onlookers.

"Roman means strong," one woman whispered to her companion, her eyes glistening.

"It's beautiful," the other replied , marveling at the gesture.

The room fell quiet, each person deeply moved by the king's act of compassion. Atreus returned to his throne, his heart heavy yet resolved, knowing that this small moment—a name, a promise—could change the course of a life. The weight of his crown was never more apparent, but neither was the purpose it gave him.

The smaller thrones next to his were empty initially but a woman ascended the dais and whispered something to him. He nodded and she took the seat on the end, two thrones from his. She watched the red-haired woman; her hair pulled back in two tight braids over the top of her head. She adjusted her extravagant purple dress which seemed to have layers upon layers. It pooled around her and threatened to consume her when she sat.

"I will see the prisoners now," Atreus called. *Prisoners?*

Two men in shackles entered the opposite side of the throne hall from where Amara slinked in the shadows. Holding on to a massive chain that joined them was a large, winged man with some kind of metal mask over his mouth. She tried to squint her eyes to see the *why* behind the mask but couldn't tell what it was for.

Neither of the prisoners looked particularly dangerous but they were forced to their knees to bow before their king. Atreus was lounging with an air of indifference and annoyance coming off of him.

Atreus asked the one on the left to stand, his blonde hair matted and she could see more of his bones than she cared for.

"James Windolen, human. Your Highness, he stands accused of theft after many witnesses complained of him pocketing items from their shops," the jailer spoke.

"How long has he been held?" Atreus asked.

"Prince Elichai dismissed his sentencing last month, he's been in holding for six months with his friend here," the jailer kicked the other one. The blonde one looked particularly offended at the title of 'friend' given to the other one.

"And what are the charges for this one?" Atreus gestured at the dark-haired one.

"Chay Brackenridge, Nephilim. We found him forcing himself on a young girl," the jailer swallowed in disgust. This seemed to cause Atreus significant distress. He sat up straight in his throne and stared at the offender.

"Who was the victim?" Atreus asked, standing. The prisoner—Chay—was shaking under his king's gaze, staring at the floor.

She recognized his anger, his need for retribution. It burned the same way it always had in his eyes. He held it together though as he waited for the jailer and red-headed woman to look through scrolls. He was a leader, that was the similarity. Rather king or Praeceptor, he was meant to lead and he was good at it. Amara on the other hand wanted to rip the man apart.

"Macy, daughter of Oceana Greyvault. She is seven years old," the red-haired woman informed her Atreus. The crowd gasped.

The amount of citizens in the throne hall grew, filling quickly. They were more interested in punishments than favors, it seemed.

"Thief, stand," he demanded. "We will break your dominant hand for your transgressions. If you are stealing for survival, you may have an audience with me to discuss your needs." His punishment was fair. But it was his offer to help the thief that stirred emotion in Amara that she didn't want.

"Yes, your majesty." He bowed his head.

Atreus stood then, as the thief was removed. Murmurs came over the crowd.

"Is Macy Greyvault here?" He called and scanned the faces of the crows.

"Yes," a woman cried. She carried her young daughter through the crowd, people parting for them.

Macy, the child, was looking around the room but when she saw the criminal who assaulted her, cried. She buried her face into her mother's shoulder and wailed. Her cheeks were red, her blonde curls fell around her face, and tears streaked her face. It took everything inside of Amara not to destroy the Nephilim who assaulted her. *Who could do such a thing?*

Upon glancing at her king, the little girl reached for him, whimpering. He grabbed her from her mother and held her tight against him. He stroked her hair and whispered something in her ear. A sense of calm seemed to overcome the child before she whispered something back.

Amara had never seen him that way. She wasn't sure how to take the sympathetic and caring king who cradled children and wiped their tears.

"Oceana?" The woman approached and he spoke in a whisper to her. The child was handed back and they were escorted from the throne hall.

Atreus paced for a moment in front of the thrones, trying to calm his temper. His hands were locked behind his back. He crouched down to speak to the red-haired woman on the far throne, both of them nodding.

"Chay Brackenridge. Stand," he commanded. The prisoner complied, the jailer's grip on his chains firm and unyielding. "Few crimes are as abhorrent as those committed against children. I will tolerate neither rapists nor anyone who harms innocents within my realm." Atreus took a step closer, his voice low and menacing. "Exile is too lenient for the suffering you've inflicted on that child." The prisoner, a pitiful figure, quaked under the weight of the king's gaze.

Atreus backhanded him, claws extending so quickly that she almost missed it. Chay Brackenridge was sent to the floor, blood splattered Atreus' face. He spat on the lowlife. The crowd was completely silent.

"I sentence you to execution at sunrise." His words were final. The red-haired woman wrote in a scroll. Amara gasped but covered her mouth. Not that it wasn't a fair punishment, it was shocking to see him in such a role.

The prisoner wailed but no one had a shred of sympathy for him. Amara swallowed bile because she was so disgusted by his actions.

Atreus was making it harder to hate him so she turned on her heel and made for the other exit at the end of the long hallway.

Chapter 31

S he followed a group of people down from the building with the throne. She spent time winding through sprawling gardens, fountains, two-story homes stacked together with varying paint colors, some with shops on the bottom floor, and even a couple of bookstores.

She watched a few ladies move into one of the shops but Amara kept going, passing many people in the street who seemed concerned by the longsword on her back.

At the foot of and surrounding the palace was a community, a thriving village of humans. They seemed healthy and fed. She didn't see beggars or people brawling every ten feet. It was strange, it was... nice. Nephilim were even spotted in the crowd, coexisting amongst the humans. It was nothing like Findaria.

She passed a hanging sign that said 'Mel's flowers,' another shop that was called 'Sixth Scents Bakery & More.' She paused to watch children playing marbles in a small alleyway, giggling and laughing.

She spent hours lost in streets of shops and galleries, listening to people murmur that their king was home. She didn't know if she would ever be able to swallow who he really was. She sipped a coffee and tried a croissant from Sixth Scents Bakery on her way back to the heart of the kingdom, to where she just so happened to be *living*. Both the items were on the house for the 'new Lady of the Kingdom'. Which she mentally jotted down to yell at Atreus for later.

"Can I touch your sword?" A small boy startled her. She turned to see a shaggy-haired child no more than six at her heels. He smiled with a gapped tooth smile and regarded her with pleading eyes.

"Sure." She crouched down and pulled the sword from her back.

His eyes were wide with astonishment and curiosity. He ran his tiny fingers over the hilt and blade. Before she knew it, his friends joined and there were seven children gathered around her, touching the weapon.

One of the boys' shirts was open at the top buttons and she saw something all too familiar. He was a sired child, her breathing hitched.

"Hey, what's your name?" she asked the boy.

"Nicholas Tarrenglade," he announced proudly. He couldn't have been more than six. They weren't in any of the Hallowed's kingdoms. *Who sired the child?*

"I'm Amara," she said to the group who smiled. "It was wonderful to meet you, but I have to get going now." She frowned. All of them had introduced themselves, but she would keep her eye on the sired one.

Amara found her way to the library not far from the throne building. It was not nearly as expansive as the one at the Sanctum Metere, but impressive, nonetheless. There were enough books to keep her occupied for months... years even.

People were hunched over varying tables with dim shaded lamps; some regarded her with human eyes while others observed her with thoughtful Nephilim glares. The space was quiet save for the sound of crashing waves from the open windows. *That explains why the shelves are behind the glass wall.* The ocean air would destroy books if exposed for too long. She thought it nice that there were reading areas where one could enjoy the waves without the books being at risk.

She pushed her way into the glass door and ran her fingers over the spines of the books. The section was all educational material, histories, and 'how to's'. Mostly she was looking for a map because she had no idea where she was in the world... literally.

'Constantine' had its own smaller section in the history aisle. She grabbed one and flipped it open. There were no maps in it but it did say that it was established nine hundred years earlier by Atreus. *Before the Angelic Exodus.* The book claimed the land to be isolated and thriving, spanning over a hundred miles. It seemed the palace and villages claimed most of that land, with some space left for farming—thousands of acres apparently.

It was shielded from the rest of the world—warded with magic. It was a pure magic, one that was wielded willingly, not stolen. Her interest was piqued on the source of the magic but she kept reading about the kingdom.

"Need help finding anything, my lady?"

She spun around, startled. "Wha-." She looked down at the book and closed it. "No." It was the young blue-haired guy that removed her from her cell. *How old was he? He looked so young.*

"I've been asked to retrieve you for dinner." He smiled—her eyes darted to those sharp teeth. He had the silver ring around his eyes so he was definitely Nephilim...

"So you're an errand boy?" she asked and slid the book back onto the shelf.

"Oh, no." He blushed. "A guard, actually." He showed his daggers. "I've just been assigned to you." He smiled. *Of course he'd assign her a guard.*

"And what is your name?" She crossed her arms and leaned against the wooden bookshelf.

"Kit." He smiled. "Uh, Zalser." He fumbled over his words nervously.

Zalser. Why was that name familiar?

"All right, Kit. I don't *want* to have dinner with Atreus. So where does that leave you?" She challenged; he blanched.

"Well, he gave me an order to retrieve you for him..." he started.

"I'm not an object. Tell him I refused." She shooed him off.

"My lady, I can't..."

"Stop calling me that! My name is Amara!" she said far too loudly, causing Kit to jump. She wondered how he could possibly be a guard.

"A-apologies," he stuttered. She could see the worry in his face, the fear of letting his king down. *Would he be hurt?*

"Fine, I'll go." She huffed for no other reason than not wanting him to get in trouble. She knew Cath—Atreus had a temper. She had seen it. She snatched two books on Constantine from the shelf and followed him out.

Kit deposited her at the entryway of a small dining room not far from her bedroom. *Her bedroom, not 'their' bedroom.* She was expecting some ridiculous dining hall, perhaps there was one around there somewhere... she glanced back and Kit was gone.

She entered the room where Atreus sat alone, jotting something down in a notebook like he always did. He looked like the Cathmore she knew at the cabin, but only for a moment. He glanced up upon her entry to the room and stopped breathing when he took in her appearance. He stood as though he were nervous, the chair scraping clumsily back from him.

"You look..." He couldn't think of a word for a moment. "Ravishing." She ignored how her body responded to the compliment. He was still wearing the suit from earlier that day, only the buttons were opened and he looked more exhausted.

"What are we eating?" She stomped in and dropped into the chair opposite him, discarding the books on the table. She crossed her arms, a defense mechanism. His eyes followed her every movement, taking her in as though she were oxygen. "Stop looking at me like that."

He said nothing but took his seat once more and pushed the platter of meat and vegetables over to her. She served herself, neither of them speaking while they ate.

"Why am I here?" she asked him after having had enough silence. He dropped his utensil in frustration.

"Because I want you here," he answered as if it were so simple.

"Liar," she spat. *He didn't want her, he used her.*

"You think I don't want you?" He stood and moved over to her with astonishing speed. "I've never wanted someone more in my life." His eyes were dark as he looked down into hers.

"You used me." She looked away from him. She tried to ignore the charged air between them; his hips were at eye level... mouthwateringly close.

"No, I protected you." He jerked her chin up to face him. "I wasn't supposed to bring you here. You were supposed to be given to Deimos." Anger contorted his features. His skin on hers was a match waiting to strike. She pulled away from him.

"I have no reason to believe anything you say." She slammed her hand on the table and stood to face him. "You won't get another chance to betray me."

She stormed out of the dining room with her books while she could hold herself together, while she could still fight her body's need for him. Her reaction to him was truly unnatural, more than physical. It was chemical and they were destined to ignite.

Later that night she grew bored and couldn't focus on reading any of the books. She was burning with need still from the simple touch of Atreus' fingers. She could sense that he was in the same building, she knew his energy anywhere. It was maddening.

She tried to get comfortable, tried laying on the floor, then took a shower. She knew if she pleasured herself, he would know it. She knew she would think about his body on hers, him inside of her...stretching her. She bit her lip. *Fuck.*

When she couldn't fight the urge and it grew later and later, she spread her legs and ran her fingers over her clitoris. She was swollen and wet with need already. *Don't think about him, don't think about him.* The chanting would have worked except it only made her think about him more.

She slipped a finger inside of herself anyway, massaging gentle and deep.

"A little harder, don't be ashamed," Atreus spoke into her mind, causing her to jump. She stopped for a minute; her cheeks flaming with embarrassment and need. She wanted to tell him to go away but instead she pushed in further, harder.

"I hate you, leave me alone," she shot back. Her body betrayed her though and she pushed against her hand. He chuckled , the sweet sensual sound echoing through her mind.

"Another finger, you can take it," he guided her in a deep husky voice, his accent dripping from his tongue like honey. She slipped another finger in and bit down a moan as she screwed her eyes shut, imaging it was his fingers inside of her. *Wrong, this is so wrong.* Her nipples hardened at the thought.

"Dirty girl, you want me more when I'm off limits," he chortled, she could hear him grinning. She ground into her palm, biting her lip with a shudder. She pushed in further and faster, remembering him taking her the first time in the watchtower. *Fuck.*

"There you go, just like that," he coached as she imagined his hard body during fighting lessons. The way his muscles rippled and pulled under his creamy skin. She whimpered as her insides tightened. He groaned, pleased at her thoughts, it was enough to finish her.

"Cathmore," she whimpered as she finally came undone.

She felt him dissipate at the mention of the name she once knew him by. He was no longer in her head; she was alone again.

She felt a twinge of guilt, but it was a habit at that point. It's what she had grown used to calling him. She then felt angry at the possibility of him being upset when he had been lying to her the entire time. She then kicked herself for doing it at all, for him being a part of her pleasure. She sighed; she was back to being mad at him but at least she was satisfied.

Chapter 32

"Time to get up!" Someone was shaking her awake. He was far too chipper and excited. She shot up in the bed just as Kit flung the drapes open. The room was cast in sunlight that caused her head to pound.

"Why are you here? What if I was naked?" She snapped at him. He dusted off the top of a table by one of the massive windows and inspected his fingers.

"I'm working on getting you a lady's maid. She'll be the one to tend to you moving forward. She'll also keep your chambers clean." He glanced around disapprovingly. She didn't think it was all that messy but the clothes on the floor and dust was probably too much in such an extravagant palace.

"I don't want a servant," she insisted.

"She's meant to be your assistant and companion." He frowned.

"Is she forced against her will? Or doing it as a punishment?" She pushed and stood from the bed. She pulled a brush through her tangled hair.

"I—"

"I don't want a lady's maid," she interrupted with finality.

"Fine, but I don't think you quite understand how Atreus runs things here," he said incredulously. He wasn't wrong, she didn't understand anything really. "You'll need to wear something red for the execution." He swung her wardrobe open. It explained his dark red slacks and matching jacket with high collar.

"Why?" She pulled down her oversized shirt that she slept in. He seemed totally disinterested in looking at her but she didn't want him to see her in her underwear.

"It's a tradition here. When a life is ended under instruction of the crown, we dress in red to commemorate 'die pluit sanguine'," he informed her.

"Commemorate what now?" She shook her head as she fumbled through the ancient Latin variations she'd studied. *Blood of the day?* No.

"It means the day it rained blood." He handed her a pair of black pants and a frilly red top. He said it like it was normal. *Did it rain blood here?*

She inspected the puffy sleeves and high neck on the blouse.

"This is ugly." She tossed it to the side.

"I agree, what about this one?" He spun with raised bushy eyebrows. It was a lot more her style, it was a dark red leather thing with black mesh down the sides. It would show some skin but not a lot. The neck was 'V' shaped with black gems lining it. "But put it with the dark leather pants, you'll look like a fighter." His eyes scanned her. "Which is exactly the energy you give off."

She took it as a compliment.

"Thank you." She smiled and took the clothes to the washroom.

Kit was right, the outfit made her look like some kind of trained warrior, like a Praeceptor even. She liked it. *What was it about leather?* She decided to braid her hair back so that it fell down to the middle of her back. She fumbled around the drawers in the vanity and found silver clips which she added to her braid. She noted the way the silver matched that new ring around her stark green eyes.

"Perfect!" Kit jumped from the chair he was lounging in. He had been picking at the blade of one of his daggers but resheathed it when she moved closer to him.

"So how is this going to work? The execution?" she asked.

"You'll see." He smiled wickedly. She didn't know how Nephilim were executed in Atreus' kingdom.

Not all Nephilim were immortal, and immortal didn't mean invincible. She thought of the immortal Nephilim cast into the Abyss in Findaria to rot away slowly. Did he have something similar? She had an endless plethora of questions. The first one though; *what the hell am I doing here?*

Kit led Amara to the heart of the palace, guiding her into a vast courtyard encircled by six imposing stone buildings. Hundreds of humans and Nephilim gathered in clusters, their hushed conversations mixing with the wind, creating a tense, anticipatory hum. The air was thick with the scent of incense and gardenia flowers, drifting down from balconies above as part of the day's ritual. Kit escorted her to the edge of a raised stone platform guarded by Atreus' men; each dressed in ceremonial black armor which was somehow polished to a mirror-like sheen. They were as still as the roaring gargoyles that lined the palace rooftops.

Amara glanced around, searching for the dark silhouette of Atreus, but his raven hair was nowhere in sight. The platform itself was unassuming—a cold, flat dais with no visible instruments of death. No guillotine loomed ominously, no noose swung in the breeze, and there was no executioner sharpening his blade. Instead, only the four guards held their post, their eyes fixed on the horizon, as if waiting for something more profound than a mere execution.

As the sun continued to rise, Atreus emerged behind her, his presence magnetic and commanding. He met Amara's gaze with a brief nod before ascending the steps with a deliberate, regal grace. His crown, wrought of black iron and embedded with dark rubies, shimmered in the dying light, stealing her breath. His hair fell messily beneath the crown, disheveled in his signature style. A single red earring shaped like a jagged spike hung from his earlobe, catching the light with every movement, a symbol of both royalty and bloodshed. Rings adorned his fingers, heavy and bold, each bearing the crest of his lineage. A chain hung around his neck, its pendant hidden beneath his dark tunic, which contrasted sharply against the rich crimson mantle draped across his shoulders.

From the opposite side, the jailer ascended, dragging Chay Brackenridge—a wretched, struggling figure—by a heavy chain. Even the jailer, a grim sentinel of punishment, wore a red sash over his armor, paying homage to the ancient tradition. The crowd before them, a sea of red and black, stood in reverent silence, their garments reflecting the bloody memory they all honored. One that

Amara had no idea about. As Atreus took his place, the entire assembly bowed in unison, a ripple of respect that swept through the courtyard like a wave of dark water. Kit nudged Amara sharply, urging her to follow suit, but she remained defiant, her eyes fixed on the king. *I'm not bowing to him.*

Atreus noticed her defiance, the briefest flicker of a smirk crossing his features before he addressed his people. The crowd straightened, some stealing curious glances at Amara.

"Chay Brackenridge, you stand condemned," Atreus proclaimed, his voice resonating with the weight of his crown and the anger of his kingdom. "For the violation of Macy Greyvault, you have committed a crime against the very soul of our realm. You have taken something that can never be restored, and for that, your life is forfeit. As long as your heart beats, that child will never know peace. She will live in fear, haunted by your shadow." His voice darkened, each word laced with righteous fury as he shook his head in disgust.

The chains were thrust into Atreus' grasp, and with a violent jerk, he pulled the prisoner closer. Brackenridge stumbled, his knees hitting the stone as he pleaded. "P-please, my king, show mercy!" he sobbed, his voice trembling with desperation. But his cries only stoked Atreus' anger. The king's jaw tightened, his palm twitching as if barely restraining the urge to strike. The crowd held its breath, the tension palpable, waiting for the final act in this grim pageant of justice.

"Sectatores ad genua," Atreus called over the crowd. *Followers to your knees.* That one was easy enough to translate.

"You're going to want to do it this time," Kit warned and pulled her to the ground, her knees clashing painfully with the stone.

She scoffed but did so. Everyone was looking at the ground, some subjects were shaking, some smiling in excitement. None of them looked up, except for Amara.

"Look away," Kit growled. She didn't listen to him of course, she wanted to watch.

Atreus seized the prisoner by the chains crossing his chest, hoisting him effortlessly into the air with one hand. The man's feet kicked uselessly, scrabbling against the emptiness below. Amara's eyes darted around, still searching for the means of execution—no sword, no ax, no visible weapon at all. The guards and jailer had hurried from the dais, leaving Atreus alone with his prey to writhe in his clutches.

The condemned man was sobbing—his cries a pitiful, high-pitched wail. Tears streamed down his cheeks, but Amara felt no pity. Atreus showed even less; his expression was carved from stone, cold and unyielding. The moment of judgment came swiftly, violently—a blur of motion that left Amara reeling.

With terrifying ease, Atreus clenched a fistful of the man's spindly hair and, in one savage movement, tore his head clean from his shoulders. The sound was wet and sickening, a grotesque rip of flesh and separating of bone that echoed through the courtyard. Blood erupted in a geyser, spraying in a violent arc, but before the first drop could stain the king's mantle, Atreus' eyes darkened—pits of black that swallowed light—and the prisoner's body disintegrated. The severed head, still wearing the man's final expression of terror, crumbled into ash before it even hit the ground.

Grey ash drifted between Atreus' fingers, like the remnants of a burned parchment, carried away on a calm wind toward the ocean. The ashes swirled, spiraled, and vanished, leaving only the faintest traces of death in the air.

Amara's scream tore from her throat, raw and unyielding, but Kit's hand clamped over her mouth, muffling her cries. He wrestled her to the ground, pinning her beneath his slight frame as she thrashed in blind terror. The world blurred around her, her vision swimming with tears and horror as she struggled against the weight of her own fear. Kit pressed her down, shielding her from the gaze of the crowd until her screams died away into ragged sobs.

She had never known fear so profound, so raw, so consuming. Terror clawed at her insides and left her trembling. She had just witnessed the impossible: an immortal reduced to dust with barely a flicker of effort. No one saw her unraveling; Kit had made sure of that. No one except Atreus, who watched her from the dais, his distant gaze fixed on her with an unreadable expression, as if he alone understood the weight of what had just transpired.

The crowd erupted into cheers and celebration. Somewhere someone played music which moved through the courtyard. The subjects began a choreographed dance together—full of stomping and clapping in rhythm to the music. Amara felt as though time was slowed. She was lifted from the ground but stared at Atreus in shock. His eyes locked on hers and held her as tears painted her face.

She couldn't reason with herself, she knew the prisoner deserved it. She just couldn't understand the magnitude of the power that Atreus' held. Her mind couldn't make sense of it. As he was escorted from the dais, she could see the man's ashes scattered up his arms. It seemed ridiculous that he would need a guard or an escort anywhere if that's what he was capable of.

She was finally on her feet, Kit holding on to her arm to steady her. She jerked it out of his grip and pushed through the crowd.

"Where are you going?" he asked, following her.

"I just have to go." She was frantic. Of course she had no idea where she would go. She just needed to get away from the celebration.

"Atreus is holding court but he requested your presence at dinner," Kit pleaded. *That was hours away.*

"No," she snapped. "I do not want to see him; I don't care if he doesn't like that and I don't care if you get in trouble. I will not see him."

"Have it your way." He finally stopped following her when she pushed out of the crowd.

She headed toward the east of the palace, to a village she hadn't explored yet. It was much further than the main village at the foot of the palace but she needed to get away for a while. It was pretty much empty, most of the subjects still celebrating the execution of the rapist.

The village of Everton wasn't all that dissimilar from the first one she visited, the one she forgot to read the name of. Most of the shops were closed for the day save for a small clothing store that she peeked into.

"Come on in!" A pink-haired older woman beamed.

Amara smiled politely and began shuffling through racks and racks of clothes. She held up an elegantly made piece of lingerie, unsure of what she would use it for. She imagined the deep blue lace hugging her breasts. When her cheeks heated she thought of the length allowing her ass to hang out just enough to tease someone. *Not Atreus.*

She briefly wondered what he would do if she seduced someone else. The image of the prisoner turning to ash played in her mind, causing her to jump. She shook the thought out of her head.

There was another set her size that came with hand stitched underwear which would expose her butt completely. The top was more of a gown but it appeared as though the backless design was meant for Nephilim to have their wings erected in the set. She adored the deep green color and lacey material.

"Excellent for those interested in having their wings teased." The pink-haired woman winked. Amara swallowed hard, not really sure if that would feel good.

"You made these?" she asked her.

"I did. Madame Tate, Everton's favorite seamstress," she introduced herself,

"They're beautiful." Amara returned her warm smile. "Do you have any tight-fitting pants?"

"Right over here." She pulled out three separate pairs of denim material pants.

"I've never had denim," she told her. It wasn't a common fabric used or made in Findaria.

"It's going to change your life, dearie These two are skin tight." She held up two black pairs that looked similar. "These are stretchy and allow for movement," she showed a deep violet pair.

"I want them all." Amara beamed. She also handed over the lingerie.

"Of course. I'll charge it to the palace, my lady." She began writing things down. Amara nearly jumped at the opportunity to spend Atreus' money. She hoped it would piss him off. "Will this be to your personal account?" she asked which wiped the smile off of Amara's face. She didn't know she had her own account.

"Uhm no, Atreus' account," she batted her eyelashes.

"Great." She smiled and folded the clothes. She wrapped twine around them so they would be easy to carry.

"Thank you, Madame Tate," she said sincerely and exited the shop.

As she walked down the street she realized something strange about the woman; she had sharp teeth. She didn't have Nephilim eyes . *What did sharp teeth mean?*

She eventually found a tavern which was convenient because she really needed a drink to drown out thoughts of the eviscerated prisoner from that morning.

She tucked her purchased clothes under her arm and took a seat in the smoke filled bar. She watched patrons enter, most of them seeming like normal people. She was relieved when no one moved out of her way or referred to her as 'my lady'.

"What can I get for ya, dearie?" An older Nephilim man asked as he dried out the inside of a cup. "Wraith's Drought and Warlock's Nectar mixed drinks are half off today."

"What is the most expensive stuff you have?" She sighed and took a seat at the booth near the bar.

"Why, that would be the Blood of the Fallen." He gestured to a blackboard menu behind him where it was five times the usual price for one drink. Decanters decorated the shelves with differing colored liquors and flavorings below it. One among them was dark crimson.

"What's in it?"

She recalled the taste of Atreus' blood but was certain the drink wouldn't contain real blood.

"Dark cherry base with bloodroot brandy, garnished with coagulated blood pearls of Atreus which has been aged for many decades," he answered simply.

"That stuff will have you waking up next week with your head and your ass sewn on backwards," a drunkard slurred.

"I'll take one. Keep the tab open." She sighed.

She sat in silence and sipped the odd concoction which was rich and sweet. It tasted like bliss going down and the crunchy blood pearls caused her skin to vibrate. Colors appeared brighter and her acute sense of hearing weakened significantly.

She inspected the two drunks who appeared to live on their respective barstools and reeked of booze and sweat. One of the nice waitresses brought her a second drink.

"Reaper's kiss." The kind woman sat the dark mixed drink before her.

"Bring out a third, surprise me." Her finger swirled around the rim of the glass as she pondered the truth of her situation. Her entire body had relaxed and softened like sap in the sun and she was blissfully uncaring of those around her.

"Whatever you need, honey, next one is on him." She pointed at someone she hadn't seen enter.

Blonde hair was cropped close to the younger man's head. He wore a tunic with rolled up sleeves, a cotton low collar jacket and loose-fitting pants. What was most strange though, was the mask he wore over his eyes. His two friends had them on too. She thought it odd but maybe it wasn't in Constantine.

He nodded at her in a gentlemanly manner to which she smiled shyly. She accepted the drink and then a fourth one which was apparently on him as well. Once she was feeling light on her feet and less self-loathing, she decided it was probably time to wrap it up.

"Heading out?" The blonde-haired stranger grabbed her arm gently. He flashed her a flawless smile. The silver ring around his eyes told her he was Nephilim, just like her.

"I have somewhere to be," she lied because she was not going to dinner with Atreus.

"I'll walk with you." He placed his mug of Blackrose Ale on a table and then held the door for her.

She nearly protested but his charming demeanor made him hard to say no to. They were walking down the main street but she didn't want the stranger to know she lived in the palace. He had not referred to her as 'my lady' yet so he clearly didn't know who she was. She turned down an ally, stalling.

"I've never seen you before, are you new to Constantine?" She was about to answer when she tripped. He caught her and they both fell against the wall.

She was pinned against it with his lean frame and he laughed . The alcohol in her system made it sound heavenly. He placed a hand on her cheek which caused them to heat. She looked up into his eyes and he searched hers hungrily. Her heart hammered and she watched his tongue dart out to moisten his lips. She swore marvelous colors danced around him as though his aura had come to life before her.

He leaned down slowly, as though asking permission. *I've never done anything like this before.* She wanted to say. She pulled at strings for reasons not to kiss the stranger but had nothing despite the fact there were a million reasons not to.

She was flooded with need as well as anger at the one she really wanted. So she threw caution to the wind and slammed her lips to his. His lips were foreign and slightly cold but soft. He pressed her into the wall harder, his hands exploring her hips, her lower back, the sound of their heavy breathing filled the air between them. She gripped his shirt and tasted the beer and tobacco on his lips.

He grunted and lifted her so that her legs were wrapped around his waist, she didn't mind it. His tongue invaded her mouth in a sweet, delicious torture. She savored the thrill of making out with someone she didn't know, of taking what she wanted, of choosing who to kiss instead of feeling the suffocating *need* for someone.

That need led to thoughts of Atreus, of Cathmore. As she continued to inhale the stranger, she found herself imagining it was Atreus instead. *No, stop.* She glanced at his blonde hair and tried to use that to drown out thoughts of Atreus' raven locks.

"Everything okay?" He sensed her hesitation.

"I uhm—" she climbed off of him. "I have to go."

"Right." He cleared his throat. She bent down to grab her bundle of clothes and ensured that no one else was in the ally.

"Bye." She waved and hurried away.

Guilt ate way at her. It was ridiculous, she and Atreus weren't together. They were barely even talking. Her lips were swollen from the encounter.

She fumbled up the impossibly endless steps to the palace and found her way to the throne hall with heavy limbs and swimming vision. Atreus was lounging in his throne, listening to someone speak so she slinked into the hallway. She took a deep breath once in her bed chambers and threw the bundle of clothes down. It was approaching dinner time and she knew Kit was going to try and talk her into dinner with Atreus again.

Amara threw herself into bed with a book, hoping to distract herself from the day. Instead, the alcohol beckoned her to unconsciousness. Still she wrestled with guilt as she fought sleep. The last thing she needed was more guilt. She chastised herself for doing something so reckless. *What if someone else saw? What if someone reported it to Atreus?* She dozed in the bed, awaking in the dark. She felt as though someone was watching her, as though she weren't alone in the room.

She rubbed her eyes so that they'd adjust to the dark. Sure enough, sitting in the large armarmchair across from the bed was Atreus.

"Hello, brat," he growled.

Oh no, he knows.

"What do you want?" She put up her defenses.

"You don't get to speak to me that way," he retorted. *He really is mad.* She didn't respond. He rose and crossed the room, his steps slow and deliberate. She remained still; her eyes fixed on the ceiling.

He climbed onto the bed, moving over her with a quiet, predatory grace. The comforter lay between them as he hovered above, close enough that she could feel the heat radiating from his skin. He leaned in, his breath ghosting over her neck as he seemed to inhale her scent, his movements deliberate and unhurried. It was an act of inspection, both unsettling and electrifying, his presence a blend of danger and desire.

"Who touched you?" He sneered. His eyes burned a brighter shade of their usual blue.

"Wha-what?" She opted to play stupid. *Sure that'll work.*

"You think I didn't know it the moment it happened?" He tilted his head.

"You're exhausting," she snapped at him.

He pushed his legs between hers and rested his hips against her. She was grateful for the comforter and layers of clothes between them. His strong arms flexed as he held himself above her, dirty thoughts floated to her.

"You're maddening," he retorted.

She pushed against his chest but he didn't move. He just smiled wickedly down at her.

"Who are these for?" He materialized the lingerie she had purchased and dangled them above her. "Me? Or your new boyfriend?" He taunted. She tried to speak but her mouth had gone dry, blood rushed to her cheeks and ears.

"I don't know who he was," she finally choked out. He threw the lingerie on the bed before gathering up her arms and trapping them above her head in one of his hands.

"Why didn't you let him fuck you?" he whispered in her ear, sending chills down her body. *Because he wasn't you.*

She chose silence. She was at his mercy; she had seen him turn someone to ashes and all that power lived just below his skin. She could feel that power, that rage rolling off of him.

"What are you going to do? Punish me?" She decided, like always apparently, to make matters worse for herself. "Throw me in a cell again?"

"Who was he?" His face was nearly touching hers, anger raging beneath the surface of his skin.

"I told you I don't know. He had a mask on." She bucked her hips to try to get him to move but he didn't budge. She noticed at the same time he did that she was visibly shaking, trembling at her core.

He released her and sat back on his knees between her legs, staring at her. Uncertainty glazed his eyes and she scooted herself up to the headboard. She pulled her knees to her chest, the same way she did as a child, to comfort herself. All she kept seeing was what he did to that Nephilim.

"What are you, Atreus?" She stared through him blankly. She recalled the way his eyes were completely black when he eviscerated the criminal. He reached a hand toward her but she jerked away.

"You know what I am." He furrowed his eyebrows in pained confusion.

"Fallen Angels can't do what you did today." She shook her head. Her voice was shakier than she wanted it to be. She didn't like showing fear but he made her vulnerable.

"You're afraid of me." He came to the realization as though it stopped his heart.

She couldn't deny it; this beautiful man was lethal. He was everything she wanted and needed but everything she should run from. He could end her with a touch. What if he did it by accident? She didn't know how it worked.

"I don't understand you. You're unpredictable," she reasoned. She didn't understand anything.

"I would never hurt you."

She wanted to believe him.

"You already have." Her voice cracked. "Atreus, you're a stranger to me." He glanced up at her, a broken man. Every bit of the confident King of Constantine had given way to someone afraid, unsure.

He pushed himself from the bed and paced at the foot of it. His tight-fitting shirt accentuated his toned body when he ran his hands through his hair.

"How did you know?" she asked him after moments dragged on in silence. "How did you know that I kissed someone? Can you smell it on me?"

"I checked in on you through our mental connection but I couldn't feel you. You were blocking me out, or trying to." He sighed and dropped into the armchair. "Then your defenses slipped and I saw what you were doing. You were trying to push out thoughts of me so that you could kiss *him*." Pain was clear in his voice; his nails dug into the fabric of the chair arms.

"I should apologize for last night." She cleared her throat. She took a steadying breath as she watched him. He was too far away and way too close all at once.

"For which part?" his eyes darkened as he glanced up at her across the lit room. *What was she sorry for? Involving him in her self-pleasure? Calling him the 'wrong' name? Leading him on? Was she leading him on?* She looked away from his intense gaze, nervous and unsure. "Tell me." He was angrier, impatient. She didn't respond, she wouldn't.

She stood from the bed and stomped over to him, damned if he was going to try and be angry.

"You don't get to be angry and impatient. You lied to me." She sneered. He stood, his height swallowing her.

"I never lied about my feelings for you," he retorted. "Every laugh was genuine, every kiss and every time I *needed* you was real."

He scanned over her body, carefully controlling his breathing, and making her feel small.

The heat rolling off of him called to her, his soul seemingly ensnaring her and drawing her to him. Her intuition told her that he was being truthful. *A lot of good her intuition did her before.*

"I deserve your hatred, but must you torture me?" He sighed and leaned down to rest his forehead on hers.

"You're destroying me," Amara whimpered. He looked into her eyes, sorrow darkening them a shade. She inhaled him and she swore she could hear his heart hammering against his chest just as hers was. "You said it yourself, you wanted to break me, to lay waste to everything I ever was." She paused. "Congratulations. You did it." Her voice broke as a tear fell.

"I only ever craved your destruction because I fell for you with no choice in the matter," he whispered. He pulled his forehead from hers and rested a hand on her cheek. "No matter how long it takes, I will fix this. I will earn the right to hold your heart." He swallowed slowly and dropped his hand from her cheek. The absence of his touch was almost painful.

He stalked out of the room without another word, leaving her standing there with endless thoughts trampling over one another.

Chapter 33

A few days passed and she wasn't sure if she was avoiding Atreus or if he was avoiding her. Either way, they hadn't spoken, she hadn't been summoned for dinner, and she hadn't run into him. She awoke alone the morning after they fell asleep together, which was a mixed signal if she ever received one.

She spent a lot of time with Kit who informed her that it was finally the day to start letting the freshly changed Nephilim out of the holding cells.

"Wait, like today?" She bounded off the bed in excitement. Kit smiled to see her smiling.

"Yes well, tonight." He nodded. He had mentioned that he was the son of Sylas, which explained his blue hair. He resembled his father sometimes when he spoke. It still didn't explain the sharpened teeth .

"How many were taken from the Sanctum?" she asked. Last she remembered there were forty-three students remaining. *What of the Nephilim Praeceptors?*

"Looks like." He flipped through a tiny notepad while she held her breath. "Twenty," he informed her.

She sat back down on the bed. "Wow."

"What's wrong?" he asked.

"That means twenty-three didn't make it out." She sighed as faces flashed through her mind.

"Oh." He was sympathetic but he didn't say more than that.

"Do you have names?" She looked at his notebook.

"No, most of them were unconscious or unable to speak because of their transition," he responded.

"That makes sense." She nodded.

"But as for today, I am taking you flying," he told her.

"I hate flying." She frowned.

"Atreus mentioned that. You're going to have to get over it." He laughed.

"Kit!" She screamed, her voice hoarse from hours of screaming in terror.

His method was to fly her as high as he could and drop her. By the fifth time she had landed in a canopy of trees, the ocean, and a small lake. She was covered in dirt, mud, and blood. The good news though was that she was getting used to getting her wings to come out on command.

"Flap!" He soared down next to her. Her wings were getting beaten by the wind, feathers poofing up and flying out into the air.

The ground was getting closer and she really didn't want to take another impact as her heart lurched in her chest. She learned he would let her land in water and trees but if she was going to hit the ground or rocky cliffs, he would stop her.

"I don't have it! Catch me!" She squealed.

"Not this time, kid." He crossed his arms. His wings carried him effortlessly beside her.

"What?" She looked from the ground to him.

She focused like he had taught her and the wings straightened out, slowing her for a moment. She lost it and her plummet to the ground resumed. She did it again and veered right. She was only able to get them to flap once which sent her straight into a massive tree.

With a deafening *crack* she smacked the tree trunk and slid down onto a branch, hitting her ribs. She knew the second crack was a rib breaking. She slid off of that branch though, her hands failing to grip at anything.

"Shit!" She huffed when she landed on another branch. She was draped over it on her stomach, her wings tangled in the branches. She sputtered and coughed painfully.

Kit was standing below the tree laughing.

"We've got work to do." He shook his head.

"Shut up. I'm done for the day!" she exclaimed.

She spent the rest of the day sleeping and nursing her cracked rib. She felt utterly useless. *What kind of Nephilim can't even fly?*

She was becoming disheartened by Atreus' absence and the lack of requests to see her. Later that night, a knock came at her bedroom door and Kit retrieved her to visit the Nephilim from the Sanctum Metere.

"Okay, let's go." She dusted off her tank top and black pants before taking his arm and exiting the room. It was a playful gesture between them, despite her annoyance with him from flying lessons. His bouncy and chipper personality was refreshing. She could see herself getting close to him.

A collection of far bigger guards opened the cell doors to check on the Nephilim, most of whom were *not* happy. Amara glanced in behind each door that opened for familiar faces. No, familiar, no, no, never seen her, familiar...

"Wait," she breathed. Long cascading golden hair—nearly white—made her heart sink. He looked up upon hearing her voice, silver around his iris.

"Eros," she breathed shakily. She darted into the cell and fell to her knees before him. She touched his face, his matted hair...

"Amara," he coughed. His wings were draped behind him, still slimy and soaked down, still having not fanned out. "It's so bloody painful." He grunted and lurched forward.

He coughed again except this time an invisible force sent her flying backwards into the wall outside of the cell, along with Kit and two other guards. The impact made her ears ring and stole her breath. *Fuck.*

"He's not ready, close it!" a guard shouted.

"Eros! I'll be back for you," she promised and the steel door closed him in. She saw agony in his eyes.

He was sired by Osias, his Imperium was shielding, that's what that was. He put up a shield on accident, that's why it felt like they were hit with a brick wall.

They moved down the cells, Fallon Mournstride still alive and well. *Of course.* His red hair would give him away anywhere. His wings matched his hair perfectly in color and were fanned out and massive. He smiled at her, mockingly.

"Imperium?" a guard asked him.

"Whatever this is." He threw a hand out toward Amara. Pain echoed through her first followed by numbing cold, she looked down. She was frozen in place by a thick layer of ice around her torso. *Rase, element wielding.* She had remembered what each Hallowed gifted their children.

She tilted her head at his cocky smile before she grunted and heated her entire body, the ice melted from her like it was nothing. Her eyes turned red and it sent Fallon stumbling back.

"I wouldn't try that again." She stepped closer to him. "And my wings are bigger." She looked him up and down. She remembered every time he tried to make her life harder during training, every time he tripped her, every nasty remark.

"Escort him to sector B, second floor," one guard said to another. *To where?* She looked at Kit but he just shook his head in an 'I'll tell you later' way.

"That's half of the cells." One of the guards turned to their leader. *Ten cells, only three were ready.*

"Give them three more days," the leader instructed.

"Wait!" She placed her hand on the guard with the keys. "I need to know if my friends are in the other ten," she begged.

"Sorry." He shook his head after glancing at his superior. *Fuck. Eros was alive, he was going to make it, he was going to be okay.*

The fact that they were taking so much longer to transition than she did was curious. She couldn't help but wonder why hers happened so quickly.

***

"The sectors he was referring to are a part of the training zone, the second floor has the medical wing in it," Kit shrugged as they stuffed their faces with cheese and crackers.

"Wait, so do newly turned Nephilim show up here a lot?" she asked.

"More like they're sent here." He shrugged.

"Do you know why I'm here?" She leaned in and whispered to him.

"Because you're mated to King Atreus..." he responded slowly, confused by the question. *Ugh.* "Trouble in paradise?" He grinned.

"It was never paradise," she groaned and dropped the cracker she was about to eat.

"Never is," he offered with a smile. Kit's hair was tied back, he wore a long blazer that seemed to fly behind him at the tails, and he propped his legs on the table, crossed at the ankle.

"Does Deimos come here?" she asked.

He straightened and took his legs off of the table. "Oh you mean 'the Dark One'—" he put the title in air quotes with a chuckle. "Not unless he has dealings with the king, even then he's not allowed out of his sight." He shrugged.

"Oh," she thought better about saying anything else. At least it confirmed they weren't living or ruling together.

"Why do you ask?" He seemed intrigued.

"He was all the rave in Findaria, figured I'd see what the rumors were here." She played it casually. No one could know that he was her sire.

She thought about what Atreus said. How he was supposed to leave her with Deimos, not take her away.

"So, how long have you been a guard here?" She popped some cheese into her mouth.

"Only a couple of decades," he told her. *Decades?*

"When did you come to Constantine?" She prodded; he froze momentarily and glanced at her.

"When I was a child." He cleared his throat.

"Oh," she said, assuming he didn't want to talk about it.

"Did you live your entire life in Findaria?" he asked.

"Yes, I was born there," she shifted in her seat. Kit's chambers in the guard's wing of the palace were extravagant. It was all bright colors and shining accents. It suited him.

"That must have been awful." He shook his head, a glint of amusement on his face.

"It wasn't great." She smiled lightly. Findaria was a horrendous place to live unless you were rich.

Most people toiled endlessly in the farmlands, labor camps, or factories, their hands blistered and bodies bent under the weight of their unending servitude. The air was thick with the stench of sweat and despair, and the fields seemed to stretch on like yawning graves, swallowing up those who worked them. Health was a fleeting luxury; the life expectancy for humans barely scraped forty years, their bodies worn down by malnutrition, disease, and relentless labor.

Taverns lined the cobblestone streets like tombstones, their dim interiors reeking of stale ale and hopelessness, where the broken lurked to drown their sorrows in murky cups. But no amount of drink could wash away the misery that clung to the villagers, seeping into their bones. A suffocating sense of dread hung over the villages like a heavy fog, creeping into every corner of their lives. There was no reprieve, especially for the women forced to carry the Hallowed's children, their bodies commandeered for a twisted purpose.

She had once longed to be human, to feel the simplicity of their lives, but that dream was now a bitter pill. She would never bow to the Hallowed Fallen's whims, she refused to carry their children just to cast them into a hopeless existence.

"I hear you ran from the Crucible." Kit leaned forward, excited to know more.

"I did; I was on the run for nearly two years. I almost escaped the second one too." She smiled. Though part of her was glad she didn't... because then she wouldn't have met Atreus, or her friends.

"You're a badass, that kingdom is crawling with Nephilim and human bitches graveling for Hadeon's affection." He laughed and she couldn't help but laugh too. She tossed a piece of cheese at his well-tailored navy blue suit.

"You wouldn't make it a day in Findaria with that attitude." She laughed again; he burst out laughing as well—covering his mouth so he didn't spit his food out.

It had been so long since she laughed genuinely, she was grateful for Kit. He was kind and easy to talk to. It reminded her that she needed to speak to Atreus, that she had questions for him.

"Do you know where Atreus is?" she askedShe had questions.

"I can take you to him in about an hour. I'm afraid he's occupied until then." Kit nodded.

"Thanks." She smiled. *Why was he occupied at this late hour?*

He took her to a bed chamber off of the throne room, not far from hers. He knocked gently before being instructed to enter. She followed in behind him, cautiously, his shorter stature not providing her with the option to stay out of view.

"Zalser." He nodded by way of greeting Kit.

"The lady asked to see you, apologies it was unannounced." He bowed his head. Atreus was hunched over a desk, the room dark except for the small lantern beside him. He was more casually dressed, his white button-down untucked and unbuttoned, his pants loose-fitting.

"Very well, leave us." He stood and placed his fountain pen down. The room was adorned in shades of maroon and dark wood; gorgeous pieces of furniture decorated the space. He moved to the front of his desk and leaned against it, waiting for her to speak.

"Wh—" she stammered and shifted on her feet under his blank stare. "What are you doing?" She nodded at the scattered papers behind him.

"Lots of matters need my attention, my fill in couldn't do certain things while I was away," he responded coolly.

"I have some questions for you." She sighed, clearly needing to explain her presence.

"Please, ask anything." He gestured.

"First, why have you been avoiding me since that night..."

"I haven't exactly been avoiding you," he interrupted her with a hand held up. "You clearly needed space and I took the opportunity to get some things in order in the kingdom."

"Oh."

"What did you want to ask?" He crossed his toned arms; there was a smudge of ink on his long fingers.

"Do you still want to kiss me after I kissed that stranger?" She blurted out what was really bothering her. She knew he felt betrayed by the action and the guilt ate away at her. He didn't kiss her that night in her room. *Was he disgusted?*

His eyes settled on hers and he prowled in her direction. She swallowed hard, unable to move.

"There is not a moment that I do not wish to have the taste of you on my tongue." He tilted her chin up. He leaned in as though he was going to kiss her but he paused just short of her lips. "But I'd like to watch you squirm." He grinned sinisterly and dropped his hand. He was so close that she could almost taste him.

"You once told me that I wasn't supposed to happen." She tugged his hair so he couldn't move. "What did that mean?"

"It meant..." he searched her eyes, glanced elsewhere, and then found her eyes again. He took a step back from her, still wrestling with the words to say. "You weren't supposed to make me fall in love with you. You changed everything." He released a small helpless sort of ironic laugh. He widened his arms as though gesturing to his kingdom, his life plan having been flipped on its head. "You were a deal that I made with Deimos, that was supposed to be it." She walked toward him. *Love, he said he loved her. Something she had never known, never thought she needed. Love.*

"But you took me instead of turning me over to him?" She recalled. He turned from her, rubbing at the back of his neck where onyx hair met tan skin.

"I couldn't stand the thought of him using you. You were a power move for him that I was willing to help with. Until I met you." He turned to her, looking her up and down with wild eyes.

"Why did he attack Findaria before my transition?" She pressed for more information, fighting the swelling emotions in her chest.

"You were getting too powerful too quickly, you were turning heads. I couldn't stop it, especially after you killed Molvina..." The statement was weightless, simple for him. But for her, it drew the air from her lungs and choked her. "He meant to claim you, he knew that attacking would force them to speed up the Crucible, to move up the Death Match. I didn't anticipate he would force you to transition as soon as the magic lifted though." He shook his head, "He gave up on keeping appearances and became dangerous." He turned and leaned on his desk with his palms, glancing at the mess of paper and books.

"He became power hungry. I still don't understand how I was ever a power move. I'm just a Nephilim, his first sired child. The Hallowed have hundreds, how would channeling me provide him with enough power for anything?" She faltered.

"You are so much more than just a Nephilim, Amara," he breathed and dropped his head. She padded gently over to him where his back was still to her.

"Tell me." She placed a hand on his strong back which caused his breathing to hitch.

"I intend to." He turned to her. He looked exhausted, sad, as though he hadn't slept in days.

"You don't have to explain everything right now." She yielded and touched his cheek gently. Relief flooded his features; a weight visually lifted from his shoulders. He was half sitting, half leaning on his desk, she stepped between his legs, and rested her forehead on his. They seemed to sigh at the same time.

She could feel her heart racing because of how close he was, she could sense that his was too. Atreus closed his eyes and inhaled her scent. He placed his hands on her hips, squeezing as though needing to prove to himself that she was real, that she was there, allowing him to touch her.

Amara knew she should bat his hands away because she was still so mad at him, still felt dazed by the sudden shift in her reality and who he was. She couldn't stop thinking about what he had done by selfishly stealing her away from her father. It was because he fell in love with her and suddenly she couldn't think of anything else.

The beautiful, complicated man before her whom she fell for as 'Cathmore' could be loved as Atreus, as himself. He nuzzled his face into her neck, pulling her closer as they savored the quiet intimacy between them. His hand found her hips, drawing her nearer, and she responded by wrapping one arm around his neck while her other hand tangled in his hair.

He was different in so many ways, but so much was the same. The scent of him, her fingers were the same in his hair, her body the same against his, the pattern of his breathing that had lulled her to sleep so many nights...

Her body burned with need for him as his moist lips rested against her neck, his soft breathing caressed her ear.

"The last thing I ever wanted to do was hurt you," he whispered. She believed him, she could feel the desperate sincerity behind his words. She pulled his head up to look into his eyes.

"You're going to have to explain what it means for us to be mated and how it happened."

"I—It's—" She placed a finger over his mouth.

"Not yet," she murmured, stopping him before leaning in to press her lips to his.

He was familiar, warm, but hesitant. She stopped and looked at him, his eyes fluttering open.

"If I give into this, Amara, I can't promise that I'll have the self-control to stop," he breathed, clinging harshly to her shirt that was bunched at her waist.

"So don't." She curled her hands into his hair.

He groaned low in his chest, the last shred of his restraint snapping. In one swift movement he stood and hoisted her up, her legs wrapping around his waist. His muscles tensed and flexed under his skin where she ran her hands over his exposed chest. He fell onto the bed with her, slamming his lips into hers as he sprawled on top of her. His hands explored her body slowly, teasingly. He pulled her arms above her head and pinned them in place with one of his hands as he nipped at her throat.

"What happened to making me squirm?" she teased and bit at his lip.

"You know I can, love." He grinned and took her bottom lip into his mouth.

She writhed beneath him, a breathless moan escaping her lips as he tore her shirt off with a single, effortless motion, the fabric shredding beneath them. His grip on her wrists loosened, and he began his descent down her body, his mouth exploring every inch, leaving trails of heat with every flick of his tongue. Freed at last, she hastily pulled his shirt over his head, revealing the hard lines of his sculpted form, but he didn't give her a moment to admire him. His gaze was heavy with lust, his need palpable, and before she could catch her breath, his mouth found the sensitive spot between her legs.

Her pants, now in tatters, lay forgotten; she didn't care. She needed him—needed this—more than her next breath.

"Fuck," she moaned and bucked her hips into his face. He alternated between circling her clit and dipping his tongue into her while digging his nails into her thighs, spreading them wide. It was a maddening, perfect combination that had her coming undone for him over and over again.

"I missed you." He smiled.

"I like when you do that." She touched his cheek. He tilted his head, questioningly. "When you smile," she whispered. He was beautiful in every possible way but his wide smile gave way to small dimples and deep smile lines that framed his mouth.

He nuzzled his face into her stomach, kissing sweetly. She couldn't help but wonder if he had ever been loved before. She was sure someone loved him, the people in his kingdom adored him, but what of this kind of love? She sensed in his soul that he had been alone for a long long time. He made his way back up to her mouth and kissed her deep.

Hours passed of them taking from one another like their lives depended on it. She was laying across his stomach, tracing circles mindlessly as she listened to his breathing. Moonlight painted his skin a color she couldn't name but it had grown to be her most favorite color in the world.

"I didn't choose to mate myself to you," he whispered into the dimly lit room.

"When did you discover it?" she askedlifted her head to look at him.

"The first time I bit you." He looked at her. She recalled returning to the dormitories covered in shallow bites and bruises. "The taste of your blood, it..." he paused as though he was trying to turn an impossible feeling into tangible words. "At first it was maddening, it was overwhelming. A drop of your life had been poured into me and it completed me. I craved you always, I needed to be close to you, I needed to possess you. I had never been so out of control."

"Oh," she breathed.

"I suspected it before then, but that was when I knew for certain." He stared at the ceiling.

"What does it mean, going forward... for our lives?" she asked hesitantly. He sat up against the wooden headboard, she pulled herself to sit next to him and wrapped herself in a blanket.

"Well, I think that depends on you accepting me as your mate." He glanced over at her. "Which is not something I would ever force on you." She recalled when he stepped back to let her be with Avren if it gave her a chance at happiness.

"If I don't?" She stared into the distance.

"I will ensure your safety wherever you wish to go, I will not force you to stay here," he said simply.

"What of my father then, in that scenario?"

"He won't touch you." He sneered.

"Will there be war if I accept?" she asked. He paused for a moment and turned to her.

"There's war anyway, darling. It just changes what I'm fighting for." He grinned.

"That's fair."

"More than that though, as my mate, you inherit this." He gestured to the kingdom around him. "You will have the option to rule alongside me," he informed her. She stared at him with her mouth wide.

My lady. It made sense as to why she was called that. *On the house for the new Lady of the Kingdom.*

She was astonished, probably in shock. *She couldn't be a queen, she didn't know anything about ruling a kingdom.*

"Essentially," he said cautiously.

"Someone called me the 'new Lady of the Kingdom,' has there been one before?" She could tell that he had not seen the question coming.

"You would not be the first," he said transparently.

She became inundated with jealousy, that she felt was misplaced but it consumed her, nonetheless. *So he had loved someone before, he had ruled with someone before, was she his mate as well? Was that possible?* For some reason the information didn't sit well with her. She went from feeling as though she were his one true love, to feeling like one of many who warmed his bed.

"I..." She stood from the bed. "Need to go."

"Wait," he pleaded. "She wasn't my mate, it was a political move." He moved in front of her.

"I just need more time." She sighed and walked past him. She pulled a shirt and pair of shorts from his wardrobe.

"I am trying to be honest and open with you," he said, distantly as though he were withdrawing.

"No, I know." She nodded, pulling on his clothes as he looked through her. "It's just a lot."

She made her way to the door, reminding herself that he was over nine centuries old, that she had a lot to learn about him.

"Goodnight, Atreus." She smiled weakly and left the room. She allowed his name to settle on her tongue and found it to taste sweet.

Chapter 34

This is a stupid idea, she chastised herself as she tiptoed down the winding stairs to the cells where the other sired children were being held.

"I really think we should wait the suggested few days," Kit whispered from behind her.

"I'm not taking anyone out, I just need an inventory of who's alive," she sniped at him.

"Fine." Kit moved in front of her and greeted the guards at the bottom of the stairs.

"Atreus has asked that I escort the lady down here to see who amongst the changelings she knows, to see how she can help with their transition," Kit informed them smoothly.

They knew he was her personal guard, technically in a position higher than them so they didn't question his authority.

He provided her with a fountain pen and paper while he operated the slots in the doors so she could figure out who was who.

'Fallon Mournstride' had already been removed from the cells so she took his name down first.

Fallon Mournstride

Eros Whitevale

Amara moved through the cells asking their names, adding them to her list. She recognized Rosen from her unit, which gave her hope. Ambrose appeared to still be mid-transition in the cell next door.

Rosen Lockright

Ambrose

Five more names and faces she didn't know, then a familiar face.

Diana

"Okay, go ahead," she breathed. She was shaking. She was looking for at least three more people and there were only two cells left.

Kit pulled the metal door open with a screeching sound that seemed to go on forever. She peered in, the sired child already done with his transformation, having fanned out enormous pearl colored wings. He looked familiar, the dark hair...

"Beck!" she whispered in excitement and relief. He still seemed dazed and confused but scrambled to his feet when he recognized her through the slot.

"Amara?" He squinted. "Why are you out there, where are we? What's going on?" he asked frantically, sweat coating his body.

"You're safe, I'll explain everything, you're going to be released once they know you're done transitioning," she explained and placed her hands on the bars.

He touched her hands.

"So many of them are gone…" tears pooled in his brown eyes, now hugged by silver. "Those things they just…" he shook his head. A pulsing sort of pain echoed through her chest, loss, so much loss.

"I know, I'm so sorry," she teared up too. She looked for any clue as to his Imperium or sire but couldn't find anything. It didn't matter. She just wanted to help him, to be there for him. He had aged so much since she first met him during the hunt, he had seen so much. She had too. "I'll see you soon, okay?" She squeezed his hand reassuringly and added his name to the list.

Beck Goldbreath

"Are you all right?" Kit rubbed her back. It wasn't a strange gesture from him; he always seemed the comforting type but it was a new interaction. She nodded and he jerked his hand away.

He pulled the last door open and she almost didn't want to look. Avren or Juliet, it had to be one of them but it couldn't be both. Either way heartbreak would follow for one of her lost friends. She didn't know how much loss one person could take, but she was going to crumble under the weight of it.

Messy brown hair and a silver and black eye patch greeted her on the other side.

"Avren," she exhaled in relief while she choked back grief all at once.

"Why are you on that side," he spat, hatred heavy in his voice. He was bigger, bulkier in his build, the green in his eyes was deeper when mixed with silver and his wings… Split into four sections, two of them moving downward, they were brown in color—similar to his hair. *Wow.* He reminded her of a falcon that had been caged.

"I came to check on you, you're getting out soon," she said . He crashed into the cage angrily to get closer to her.

"Why are you out there, and we're in here?" He slammed his hand against the steel door, sending a loud bang echoing through the tunnel. It caused her to jump.

"It's a precaution. I was put in a cell too." She tried to explain.

He grunted and shoved himself into the door, trying to get to her in anger.

"Avren..." She tried to stay calm but she truly didn't recognize him. He wasn't acting like himself at all. "I'm sorry." She shook her head.

"I bet you are." He shook his head in disgust at her.

He was still angry at her for killing Molvina, for there being someone besides him. She wanted to explain to him where he was and why, she wanted to explain it to all of them. Only, she wasn't entirely sure either. Apart from bits and pieces she gathered, she only really knew that they were in Atreus' kingdom. But Kit had made it clear that they were not to be briefed on Constantine until they're moved to the training sector.

"Where are we?" he shouted and threw himself into the door again, causing her to jump backward into Kit.

"Avren..." she murmured. She couldn't answer his questions. She was more perplexed that no one had informed them on what was going on.

"Were they all knocked out for the journey here like I was?" She turned to Kit and whispered. He nodded in confirmation. *Ugh.*

Kit yanked the small viewing door shut.

She added him to the list.

Avren Yearwood

"Let's go." She sighed.

Kit led her out of the tunnels and back above ground, it was just past midnight. She wiped her tears that were falling silently. *Juliet, something happened to Juliet.*

"Amara?" Kit asked and tried to look at her face.

"She wasn't down there," she whispered. "Juliet didn't make it," she screamed and threw the papers, the wind catching them.

Kit took a step back from her. *Juliet was good, she was too good, too pure for this world and it destroyed her.*

Amara watched the papers dance in a circle as though mocking her before the wind picked them up again. With a scream she lit them ablaze, watching them burst into flames and fall to ash. It took no effort on her part to do it; Kit had his hands up toward her.

"Amara..." it was a warning to calm herself, to control her Imperium.

All she could think about was how unfair it all was. Why did she get to live and Juliet didn't? Just because she wouldn't kill? It was the only thing she could think of. They had to kill another being to begin their transition. Juliet wouldn't be able to do that, yet Amara had taken two lives. Three if she counted sending Ruslan Marlowe to the Abyss for an eternity.

Kits fingers twitched in her direction; it was almost unnoticeable. She tilted her head in his direction, feeling threatened, feeling devastated, like a rabid animal. He moved his fingers again, this time an invisible force seemed to bring her to her knees. *Son of Sylas... Telekinesis.*

"Your eyes are heated like the sun, I need you to breathe," he warned, circling her cautiously while his hands were held straight out. Kit was pinning her to her knees in the gravel.

"Let me go." She grunted, pushing against the force.

"I can't do that," Kit reasoned.

Amara tried to turn her focus to the ocean behind her, the small village in the distance, the towering ivory palace in front of her. Nothing took her mind off of the overwhelming loss of another friend, another piece of her heart. She felt as though she were going to burn alive from the inside out if she didn't release the energy. Kit was whispering something beside her, she couldn't make it out.

She released the tension within her, the raging beast. First she phased out of his telekinetic grip, seemingly slowing time. She could take in the shock and confusion on his face as she disappeared.

Amara slammed into some kind of pointy-looking statue a few yards from where she had been. The entire structure burst into flames around her, she couldn't feel it. She could hear herself screaming into the air, heating the flames hotter around her. Sobs tore through her, wild and unrestrained. She couldn't stop. *Why couldn't she stop.*

Before she knew it, the grass around the structure had caught fire, Kit watched on in horror as a few other guards sprinted to his sides.

"Fire, retrieve the hoses!" a man yelled. *She had to go.*

"Amara!" Kit screamed just as she made eye contact with him through the violet and orange flames.

She phased, far away from her path of destruction. In fact, she somehow phased so far away that it took her a minute to orientate herself. She was probably a mile away from the burning structure, easy, atop a hill. Tall grass flowed around her ankles and she could see the palace to her right about half a mile.

Amara was hyperventilating, exhaustion digging into her bones and turning them to sludge. She allowed herself to fall onto her back. The sky above greeted her with twinkling stars and slow rolling clouds. Her entire body vibrated as the energy dissipated—well as the energy burned down the structure in the village square below her. *Oops.*

So much for sneaking out and into the cells unnoticed.

Amara watched the sky for a long while, until she was convinced she could feel the earth rotating below her. She thought about Atreus, what he wanted from her. She saw faces of those she knew who didn't make it to Constantine. Juliet's was the most prominent but she remembered the others... Isla, Vivianna, even Davian. What came of them? Was death the only other possibility? *No, but it was the most likely.*

Amara decided she needed to know how the battle was panning out at the Sanctum Metere, if Deimos took any prisoners. She was even worried about her Praeceptors who were probably among the main Nephilim tasked with fighting the war. She couldn't say she was too worried about Crowned Magister Bennet or Magister Baylin but she wasn't going to waste energy on wishing them dead either.

She closed her eyes for some undetermined amount of time before the sound of wings alerted her to someone landing nearby. She didn't have to open her eyes to know exactly who it was.

"Let's go, brat." He stood standing over her with his arms crossed, clearly annoyed.

"It was one statue," she was immediately defensive.

"And the fountain it sat in along with the grass and landscaping around it," he pointed out.

"Whatever, just go away," she groaned.

A moment passed and he sat down in the grass next to her, before lounging back, mirroring the way she was laying.

"Didn't find who you were looking for down there?" he asked, suddenly sounding more like a friend than an instructor, king, or lover.

"Not all of them." Her voice cracked.

"The Valentine girl... she may not be dead," he informed her.

"But it's likely," she reasoned realistically. He didn't object.

"I'll send two soldiers in to search for her, I don't think the battle is going to last much longer," he offered.

"She probably won't kill anyone, she won't transition." She turned to him. Surely it wouldn't be worth it to go all the way there for someone as weak as a sired child.

"So? Humans thrive here." He turned on his side and propped himself up on his elbow. "If she's alive, she'll have sanctuary here." She nodded with a smile, and held onto the small bit of hope that blossomed in her heart.

"Let me get you back, you're shaking," he said and stood. Amara took his hand and allowed him to lift her into his arms. He shot into the sky and flew them back to the heart of the palace.

"I'll never get used to that." She shuddered once they landed. He sat her down but she had to lean on him, her body giving out after the power she exerted.

"You will, you have a lot of training to do, if you decide to stay." He smiled.

He helped her inside and into the room she had claimed as hers. She had become especially fond of the massive archway over the open window to the ocean. She didn't know if she would ever get enough of it.

He laid her in the massive bed, gently removing her shoes and pants. He was careful not to linger too long or look at her in any way that would make her uncomfortable. She found herself wishing he would.

"Goodnight, brat," he teased with a small touch on her cheek before turning to leave.

"Wait," she whispered. He stopped and turned slowly. "Stay with me tonight?" She couldn't make out his reaction in the dark but he moved to the other side of the bed and slid in beside her.

He was on his back, under the same blankets, his clean scent enveloping the space between them. She turned and scooted into him, resting her head on his chest. He traced the pad of his thumb gently on her shoulder. A familiar urge crept its way in, one that at first she mistook for needing him sexually.

She nuzzled into his chest; the shirt he wore created an annoying barrier. He froze when she moved up his body and planted her lips to his neck. She was craving his blood, the need for it was stronger and more intense than she had ever felt it. It was the first time she needed it since her full transition. He was still frozen, her hand twisted into his thin shirt, pulling it up to expose his chest.

She didn't know whether she wanted her mouth there or on his throat. She groaned, darting her tongue out to trace a line down his neck. His intake of breath was audible.

"Amara…" he warned.

"Just a taste," she whimpered and bit down, hard. He was on top of her in a flash, before she could finish breaking his skin.

All she could focus on with her sharper hearing was the sound of his heart pounding, his blood pulsing just below the surface…

"It's different this time." He looked into her eyes. She believed him, her need for it was different, stronger. She nodded.

"Please." She squirmed but her arms were pinned down, her hips pinned down by his. She also found herself bucking her hips upward, needing friction between her legs. She didn't care if they had spent hours earlier, she couldn't get enough.

"I fucking *love* to hear you beg," he growled into her ear.

She could feel his hard cock straining in his pants. She didn't know if she wanted that or the blood more. She *needed* both. He knew it.

He pushed her underwear aside quickly, freed himself and pushed into her. She stretched around him as he thrusted deeper. She moaned and reached for him, needing him to be closer. She needed his blood on her tongue, in her body.

"Please," she moaned and tightened around him. He propped himself above her, his throat just out of reach and smiled tauntingly. She dug her nails into his back while he slowly moved in and out of her in the most sinful way.

"I thought you needed space?" he whispered breathlessly, pulling himself out slowly and waiting for an answer. *Cruel.* She tried to buck against him, needing to feel him against every nerve within her.

"I need you." She sneered and gripped his throat. She dug her nails into him, her need driving her to anger. He smiled lazily, blinking slowly as he eased back into her.

Amara dropped her hand, a small amount of blood beading where she dug into him. He leaned down and allowed her to taste him. It was insanity, the way her throat constricted and begged for more. But there was no more, she had barely scratched him and he healed too quickly. When she groaned in frustration at his healed skin he smiled down at her.

"Greedy girl." He tutted.

She took his bottom lip between her teeth, silencing him and wiping that stupid smile off of his face. He pressed further into her, hitting her at her deepest spot. It caused her to scream and release his mouth. She had already broken skin though and the smear of blood on his mouth was glorious, his plump lips glowing crimson.

She pushed the pad of her thumb over his lip admiringly; he took it into his mouth and met her eyes as he continued his slow thrusts into her.

It was too much and not enough all at once. He was honey and poison, sweet and deadly. She felt removed from her body but pleasure coursed through every part of her.

He pushed her legs higher, spreading her wide to allow him deeper, earning an appreciative moan. He tilted his head back, exposing the strong column of his throat as he increased his rhythm. She curled her fingers into the sheets, screaming his name. He reached for something she couldn't see. He brought it to his throat and she could smell the blood begin to drip out when he cut his flesh open. The perfection of his skin and his elegantly sculpted throat dripping blood looked as though a marble statue wept.

He collapsed onto her; she pulled him closer while he thrusted his hips. She latched onto him, sucking desperately at her mate's lifeblood.

Her mate, her mate. He was hers; she was his and that's all there is.

It's all she knew as she drank from him, moaning in pleasure.

I need more.

"I know, baby," he breathed. His words washed over her like honey, as she indulged in his sweet warm blood. He knotted his fingers in her hair, telling her it was okay to take more. His rhythm never stopped; he rolled his hips into her over and over again. She could feel his ragged breathing on the side of her head, her nails in his skin spurning him on.

"Do you like to taste me while I fuck you?" he questioned and pulled his throat free; he kissed her hard as she nodded and finally released around him. Her orgasm came in a violent symphony of her moans and his low whimpers as she tightened around him. They were a symphony of moans, tearing flesh, and screams.

She loved it.

He turned her onto her stomach and brought her ass up in the air before slamming into her. He leaned over her and bit down on her shoulder, successfully breaking skin and tasting her in return. One hand pulled her hair while the other gripped her ass.

She began pushing back against him, begging for him to be rougher and harder. He tore his teeth from her flesh and obliged until she was screaming into the massive bedroom. She didn't care who heard them.

He was hers.

She was his.

She didn't care who knew it.

Everyone would know it.

He was her mate.

"Atreus!" She screamed and came apart again, allowing his old name to die in her mind.

"There's my girl," he praised, yanking her head back and drilling into her harder.

She took him for as long as he would give it to her. She couldn't get over the stamina he had, even now. She couldn't get enough and neither could he and when bloodlust came into play, they could indulge forever.

The sun rose on them before they finally fell asleep, Atreus holding her close.

Chapter 35

Amara sat and contemplated her interaction with Avren, contemplating why it stung so much when he slammed his fist into the wall. Maybe it was the pain she could see burning behind his eyes, the remnants of the way they left things. Perhaps she was worried that once he was released he would be faced with the truth of who Cathmore was... more than that; what she had been doing with Cathmore. He would get the answer to the question she knew had been nagging at him—who was the other guy? The guy that left bite marks on her and complicated her heart. She sighed.

Amara fumbled with the napkin on the small wooden table that she occupied inside the Sixth Scents Bakery. Finances weren't an issue since she found out that Atreus had an account for her. He assured her that she didn't want to know the amount that was in it. *What's mine is yours.* He had told her.

Amara ttried to distract herself with the hushed conversations within the shop, the people of the village strolling along outside.

Yet her mind was on the two stealth warriors that were sent to Findaria to find the last of the sired children. They were given special orders to learn what came of the red-haired girl specifically. If she wasn't alive, Amara needed to know what happened.

Hatred grew and festered in her heart for Deimos. It wasn't because she didn't agree with his intention to overthrow the Hallowed. No, it was his willingness to kill the sired children that made him no better. Her feelings had not changed; the sired children of fallen angels should not be forced to compete in barbaric sacrificial games to earn their Nephilim form. Beyond that, they should have a choice in the matter. The culture that the Hallowed forged, created a sort of devaluing of sired children, at least until they transitioned.

The minutes ticked into an hour there as she tried to compartmentalize her thoughts. She had been faced with many moral dilemmas in her life, many philosophical questions she had to ask herself as well. She stretched her legs and crossed her ankles as we weighed her most recent question. *What had Atreus done to dispose of Hadeon? Did she care if he killed him?*

He had not specifically said he was dead, seemingly he was trapped or overpowered somehow. She realized she had no true idea of the magnitude of Atreus' abilities. He could arguably be the most powerful Fallen Angel on the planet. She weighed the 'truths' she learned from Cathmore... When he was Cathmore.

He told her that he had two little sisters... How could that be true? Why tell such a random lie? He was such an enigma. He was not something she could compartmentalize because he was too much, too intense, too many things to her. He was her teacher, at one point her punisher, her lover, he savior, captor, lover again, and now her king. There was no unraveling that mess of titles nor compartmentalizing him.

"My lady, a refill?" The kind barista offered. It was the same one that referred to her as the 'new Lady of the Kingdom' the last time she was there. Amara nodded, trying to get up the courage to ask the Nephilim woman a burning question.

"What's your name?" Was a good place to start. The young woman regarded her with wide brown eyes—save for the silver around them. Her brown hair was tied back in a pair of braids with flowers decorated throughout.

"Dahlia." She smiled nervously.

"Can I ask you something, Dahlia?" She leaned forward, which seemed to intimidate her. It was the opposite of her intention.

"Of course, anything," she said.

"When was the last time there was a lady ruling beside Atreus?" She seemed taken aback by the weight of the question.

"Oh, I—really don't think it's my place—" she stuttered and took the seat across from her. "I assumed you knew..." The girl blushed.

"Please." She placed a hand gently on her shaky one. "Atreus won't know it came from you." She didn't know if that was a concern for her but the girl was shaking. *Why was she so afraid?*

She glanced around nervously before leaning close to Amara.

"It's been nearly three hundred years," she imparted. *Three hundred?* Amara's brain could hardly wrap around that time frame and it was only a fraction of what Atreus had lived.

"Who was she?" Amara sipped her coffee.

"Lady Jane Cyperian, she was wonderful, everything the people needed. She was kind and compassionate..." Something like fear flashed in her eyes. "Until she wasn't. One day something changed... She became a cruel wicked tyrant," she stuttered.

"Where was Atreus?" Dahlia's eyes widened, she clearly had said too much. *How could she have been a tyrant if she ruled with Atreus?*

"You don't know?" She looked down at the table and scratched at something Amara couldn't see, a nervous habit she presumed.

"Were you there?" *Was she immortal?*

"I was," she spoke . "How could you not know the story..." she looked past Amara.

"I didn't know this place existed until last week." Amara shook her head, concern enveloping her.

"I'm sorry, I really, I can't..." she stood hurriedly. "Forgive me," she half bowed at the waist and rushed away.

How was it that every answer she found led to five more questions? She didn't know how she would decide whether or not to stand beside him. Something in her heart fluttered. She needed to focus on getting the sired children out of the cells and settled. If there was even the slightest possibility that the war was going to involve them, they needed to be prepared.

She needed to be prepared.

"When can I start training?" She stood with her arms crossed in front of Atreus who sat stiffly in his throne. It felt both ridiculous and intimidating. There was a severe lack of people in the throne room. "And why are you sitting here right now?"

"I had an assembly with my soldiers, they only just departed," he said and stood. He appeared more tense than usual, more distracted.

"I want to train, I'm going crazy doing nothing all day." She pushed and followed behind him.

"I instructed Zalser to show you how to fly," he reasoned.

"I need more than that," she ordered.

"So come to the ball this evening." He sighed.

"I didn't know there was a..." she shook her head. "You're hosting a *ball?*" She was astounded.

"It's being thrown in celebration of my return, I am not hosting it." He held up his finger by way of correcting her.

"I'll think about it, I still want to begin training." She pushed.

"I told you I would train you if you decide to stay." He sighed.

"And what if we have to go to war before I decide?" she asked.

"I'm hoping you decide soon." He was being short with her. "Because this—" he gestured between them—"is agonizing, you are torturing me, Amara," pain present in his voice and he stopped walking. She nearly bumped into him.

"How?" She was genuinely confused. She was also angry that he would make such an assertion when she accused him of the very same thing days earlier.

"You keep seeking me out when you want me to fuck you, you act like this connection we have is consuming you the way it is me... you—" he lowered his voice. "—you take my blood like you'll die without it. Yet, you hesitate to commit." He shook his head.

"Because I don't trust you." Unresolved anger burst out of her.

It wasn't like the situation wasn't destroying her too, he knew that. She was driving herself crazy. She wouldn't just be accepting him but his kingdom, his world, his nine hundred plus years of life that she knew nothing about.

"I will tell you anything you need to know. I don't know how many more ways I can explain the depth of my affection for you!" He shrugged, his piercing blue eyes wild. "I rescued you from an impossible fate with Deimos, I am trying to rescue the people you care about, I've been investigating your mother's death—" she cut him off.

"You what..." she inhaled in shock. They were standing outside of the throne building now, his back on the stone wall. She could see his perfectly tailored suit hugging his body in all the right ways...

"It's important to you..." he whispered, not meeting her eyes.

She felt herself melting for him, for this puzzle of a man before her, this mystery whom she was hopelessly in love with, whose secrets were trying to reach up and stop her plumpent into him.

"I've learned the truth, Amara," he whispered, looking up at her through hooded eyes. It felt like the oxygen was sucked from her lungs. *Her mother... he knew who killed her mother.*

She felt like her legs were going to melt out from under her, as though she were going to cease to exist completely. She had been so wrapped up in everything else that finding the truth about her mother's murder had slipped her mind. She had been selfish, so unbelievably selfish... how could she have...

"You're not selfish," he interrupted her racing thoughts. "She has been dead a long time; the truth of who murdered her was not going to change with time. You have been going through a lot." He stepped closer to her. "I want to tell you the truth, about everything. But if you're waiting to know it all before you accept me... I'm afraid we don't have that kind of time."

"What do you mean?" She looked up at him.

"Deimos is losing the battle in Findaria, Sylas is done." He exhaled a shaky breath. "It won't be long before he retreats here for help, effectively leading the Hallowed back to Constantine, we only have about a week to prepare our defenses." He swallowed hard.

"What... how... why?" She might have gone into a state of shock as she envisioned the small children in the kingdom whose lives were about to be devastated. How could such a peaceful place be subjected to such destruction? There had to be another way. "Why is he coming to you for help?" She was trying not to fumble over her words.

"He and I worked together to see you through the Crucible, he knows I'm the only being powerful enough to save his ass when he pisses off the Hallowed, and I'm pretty sure he is not aware that I have no intention of returning you to him." He held out a finger as though piecing his thoughts together in the air between them as if it were a mathematical equation.

"What do we do..." She trembled.

"We are going to intercept them before they ever make it to my home." He placed his hands on her shoulders. "Follow me."

She trailed behind him to a massive conference room off of the library, where she thought they would continue the conversation. Until he moved some random book and pressed a button and a wall of books slid into the wall, revealing a passageway. A draft entered the room, unannounced and haunting. He glanced over his shoulder and grabbed her hand.

A small passageway opened up to a larger room with a plethora of bookshelves that met the ceiling just a few feet above her head. A desk, a small round table with six chairs, no windows, a few swords in display cases, and on the wall opposite her was a massive map. Pins stuck out of it in random positions that she couldn't see from the distance.

She hurried over to it, desperate to know exactly where she was in the world. She had seen maps before—Findaria at the heart of course—the sea separating it from one continent on the right and another on the left, making it look like the sea was an upside-down 'Y'. The lands and kingdoms under the rule of the Hallowed were always listed. As far as she knew, that was the whole world. But *this...*

She couldn't hardly take it all in. The three continents that she always knew were at the left of the massive 'World Map', but there was more, so much more. There were four other continents, oceans, rivers, mountain ranges, villages, kingdoms she had never heard of. She ran her fingers over the cloth-like fabric. Atreus observed her.

"There's more... more than the Hallowed's land?" Her lip quivered. It was like an answer to a nagging feeling she always had, it was a lie. Everything they had been taught was a lie. She knew it to some extent; it's why she stayed in trouble in school and at the Sanctum ... but this...

"The world is much bigger than they would have you think," he answered.

"How do you hide the rest of the world from three continents of people?"

"Indoctrination, education mostly. When the Nephilim transition, the truth remains hidden. There are only a select few that the Hallowed trust with the truth of the world. Nephilim, like the Crowned Magister and Magister Baylin, are tasked with keeping the illusion as their number one goal, to keep the Hallowed holy. It's their main job, any of them who stray, die at their father's hand, along with anyone they reveal the truth to." Atreus cringed as though he was going to be sick.

"I'm sure the magic they're manipulating helps." She shook her head. She found Constantine at the center of a small continent, its villages mapped all around it. "What about when people try to leave?" She gestured at the sea.

"Usually some unfortunate storms ensure they don't make it off of Hallowed land." He sighed. "The only way out of their circle of power is by sea, so they use magic to control the tides."

"But the Nephilim fly," she stated, staring at nothing.

"Only when their sire allows them to or orders them to, just like the Crowned Magister had to allow us use of our wings to rescue you from Marlowe. It's all very..."

"Needlessly complicated and sick?"

"Precisely."

"Now." He walked over to the map. "This is the kingdom and its villages, pretty much taking up most of this small island, right?" He was pointing at Constantine on the map, his chest touching her back.

"Right," she breathed.

"I have wards protecting the outer part of the island, and stronger wards around the main kingdom and its villages." He traced lines on the map. "They're going to fly into the first set of wards, weakening them."

"How?" she asked.

"The magic is... from a restricted source. I'll explain that another time. "I will strengthen the outer wards so that they believe it's the main frame, so that when it goes down it takes some of them with it," he explained.

"Do you know what Hallowed Fallen are coming? Are they bringing soldiers?" she asked, turning to him and he was so close she could feel his breath on her cheek.

"Yes, and yes," he said simply. "It is in this ten-mile gap that we engage with them. They will not get close to my home or my people."

She swallowed hard and nodded understandingly. He placed both of his arms on the wall, on either side of her.

"I know you have a lot of questions," he whispered. *That's an understatement.*

She couldn't think of them, not really. Her thoughts fell out of her head as she glanced at the muscles in his arms, the veins, scars, and tattoos that decorated them. It was so easy for the atmosphere to charge between them. It was painful and deliciously distracting.

"Are there more like you?"

"There's no one like me, darling." His voice was sultry, seductive.

Amara turned to him, trying to regain some part of the conversation that was dying in the longing between them. Though it was no use, because when he looked into her eyes, all rational thought abandoned her.

"Have you sired any children," she blurted out one of a million questions in her mind. He furrowed his brows, dropped his arms, and exhaled a laugh.

"No, I genuinely cannot procreate." He moved to sit at the desk behind him.

"Why not? The Hallowed's magic?" she asked.

"No, that really only affects their..." he searched for a word. "Realm."

"Wait..." her brain skidded to a halt.

"So can Nephilim have children here?" she asked in awe.

"Yes." He nodded.

"Fallen Angels... well *Rogue Fallen." He put* air quotes around the name, "can as well, and there is no magic restricting the sired children from entering their true form." He kicked his legs up on the desk. She took a seat in front of it. *That meant she could have children.*

"Why can't you procreate?" she asked again.

"I don't know really." He shrugged. She had a feeling it wasn't from lack of trying.

"Does it bother you?" she asked slowly. She thought of the baby whom he'd named—Roman, the affection in his eyes.

"No, I have taken in and raised many children over the centuries. It's a part of me that I've had time to accept."

"Oh." She looked at her hands in her lap.

"Does it bother you?" He scanned over her.

Up until two minutes ago, she never thought she could have children, so she didn't allow herself the heartache of longing for them.

"I don't think so," she said. He nodded, a simple sympathetic and understanding nod. "Where do the marked children here come from?" she asked

"Well, some of the Nephilim's children are born with a mark. Most of them are a result of rescue operations I have operated over the years." He sighed.

"Rescue operations?" she asked for clarity.

"The rest of the world does not exactly support what that gang of fallen angels subject their people to. I was working behind the scenes during my time in Findaria to send as many children both human and sired back to my kingdom," he explained.

"So why don't the other leaders fight them?" she asked.

"It would be a suicide mission, the Hallowed's dealing with the devil himself really does grant them immense power. Most of the other world leaders sway in the direction of minding their own land, protecting it when need be, and allowing others to run their kingdoms how they see fit."

"But you don't take that approach?"

"No, my love." He smiled to himself. " I do not fear them and as such I see no reason not to help as many people as I can. I do of course consult my court and my advisors on the appropriate time to step in." He was twirling a pen in his hand, the lighting in the room casting harsh shadows on his face. He was beautiful. *My love.* He'd never called her that, it sent a frenzy of butterflies into her abdomen.

"How come I've not met the other members of your court? Your soldiers?" She leaned back in the chair, content to berate him with questions for the rest of the day.

"You've met Kit." He raised his eyebrows.

"Someone besides my personal guard," she sassed and crossed her arms.

"Fine." He exhaled as he sorted through papers on the desk. "I didn't see it as necessary, after all you are a visitor here right now. If you become part of my court, my family, you will be drowned in conversation with more people than you probably care for. I see no reason to rush that; I do not wish to overwhelm you."

He was speaking calmly, in a tone of absolute fact that left no room for questions. He was every bit the leader, the strategist, the kind-hearted rescuer of sired children in that moment. She was still looking for that harsh side of him, the part of him she had seen in the Praeceptor she once knew. There had to be a firmness about him, how could he rule an army, a kingdom without it? She thought of the execution. That was all the show of power he'd ever need.

"Is the devil really your brother?" she asked, referring to the legends written about him.

"Lucifer," he corrected. "He is."

"That's why you're not afraid of Deimos drawing help from him. Do you have similar powers?" she asked. *It would explain the black eyes.*

"We are different in more ways than we are similar. We are both far more powerful than the others though, yes." He was schooling his features into cool indifference. She couldn't draw any amount of emotion about the subject. She changed the topic of conversation.

"Where is Kit?" She had not seen him since he was literally putting out the fire she created.

"He was burned pretty badly. He's needed time to heal," he informed her. She felt like she had swallowed lead.

The cold realization that she injured him felt like being stabbed in the throat.

"What? How did he get burned?" she asked, horrified. He shouldn't have gone near the fire she created.

"He tried to reach in for you, he thought you were going to kill yourself." He was stifling his anger.

Amara tried to remember what she saw, what she felt. She remembered seeing him through the flames. *He was holding his arm, his sleeve burned.* She didn't notice it at the moment but her memory held the information. All she remembered was the fear in his eyes. *Was it a concern for her? Fear of failing his king?*

"I-I didn't mean for anyone to get hurt." She dropped her head in shame. She was so emotional, so out of control. "Why didn't you tell me sooner?"

"It wouldn't have changed anything," he stated coldly. "The healers have done their job and he's recovering."

"Thank you," she croaked and stared at her hands in her lap.

"Would you like me to tell you the truth about your mother?" His eyes flashed, alternating empathy and anger. She only ever saw that dance of emotion in his eyes when it came to her pain.

There it was, the opportunity for the truth. A truth she only recently knew she needed to learn. She could know who it was that looked her mother in the eye as the life was drained from her. She would know whose face it was and saw her into the afterlife.

"I don't know." She shook her head as tears poked at the back of her eyes.

Amara wished she had more memories of her mother, she wished she had more to be angry about because startlingly—she wasn't angry enough. Her mother carried her and gave her life, but she had no memories of her and that was something that crept into her mind when the night was darkest and threatened to choke her to death.

"It was easier when I thought she died due to a sickness, I could make peace with not remembering her, I could make peace that maybe she wasn't in pain... but this. All I dream about is her beheading, her headless body on the floor..." She stood and paced. "What good would it do to know the identity of her killer? Doesn't that give them power?" She was breathing heavily, her thoughts a jumbled mess of panic and grief and anger and...

"Amara." Atreus was behind her, turning her gently to him. "The power is in your hands. You decide if you want the name, you decide what to do with it, and you will have the opportunity to decide their fate. I promise you that."

She turned to him, trying to take in what it was he was saying.

"Would you be okay with me wanting revenge?" she asked through tears, looking up at his soft face

"Darling, I will drop him at your feet and then dance with you in the downpour of his blood." He touched her cheek, wiping a tear. "All you have to do is ask." He smiled a wicked smile that sent heat burning through her.

She pushed herself up onto her toes and crashed her lips into his with reckless abandon. He tasted like fresh air, sea salt, and him... just like he always had. He stumbled forward into her, shoving her roughly into the wall, the hanging items vibrating as though to make their presence known. He pulled her hair and tilted her head back, exploring her mouth with his tongue as though his life depended on it.

She returned the same need, the same hunger because despite her fears... she couldn't imagine walking away from him. Doing so would surely drive her mad, it would destroy her. As his hands snaked up and down her body, pulling her closer, kissing her harder, she knew her choice had been made. She would not be able to walk away from him. She pulled back from his mouth, just for a moment.

"I want you; I've always wanted you." She tugged him close, kissing him hard. "I will stand beside you." She panted, looking into his eyes. "I will fight with you." She pressed her hands hard against his chest, if for no other reason to ensure he was real. He looked stunned at her words for a moment, blinking once, twice, trying to process them.

"Amara." He fell to his knees in front of her, wrapping his arms around her legs and resting his head against her stomach. "I was so afraid you were going to walk away from me." He exhaled in relief. She ran her fingers through his raven strands of hair, tugging gently and reassuringly. She couldn't believe he was on his knees in front of her, holding her so tight that maybe, just maybe he could put her broken pieces back together.

"I can't, I won't." She shook her head and sank to the floor in front of him. He looked desperate, his eyebrows furrowed, his eyes wide. His jaw tightened as though he were clenching it. She placed her hand over his heart, which beat wild under his skin. "I thought I didn't know you. I don't know all of you, but I know your heart. Everything I have seen here—" she gestured to the kingdom around her. "Your words, your selfless actions, and your strong will... It's still you. I feel like I've known you for an eternity. I'd sooner die than walk away from you now, Atreus." She sighed, feeling like she was rambling while he listened intently. He squeezed her wrists in his hands, holding her tight.

"To hear my name on your lips." His voice was sultry, husky. He ran the pad of his thumb over her bottom lip.

"Atreus," she whispered, he smiled in awe. "Tell me how to accept you as my mate."

Chapter 36

"You're here!" Amara exclaimed when Kit appeared in the entryway to her bedroom. His arm was wrapped, and draped over the other one were varying dresses. She hugged him hard, "I never meant to hurt you, Kit," she choked.

"I know." He laughed a light breathy laugh. "I'm really okay," he reassured her and she unwrapped herself from his small frame.

"Can you come with me to the ball tonight? I've never been to something like this." She swallowed hard as he made his way over to her bed and began laying the dresses across it.

"I'll be there, but I'm afraid you already have a date," he joked.

"Are you rejecting me, Zalser?" She prodded playfully with narrowed eyes.

"Yes, respectfully, high treason is not my style," he pressed her nose. "I adore you, though." He smiled.

"Even though I nearly burned you to death?" She smirked.

"Especially so." He smiled wide. She turned her attention to the dresses.

"Where did you get these?" She ran her fingers over lace, sequins, thick cotton, beautiful shades of velvet, blue, gold, and red. *Wow.*

"I had them made, Atreus wanted you to have options," he told her. "I think this one is the most you." He held up the dark blue one. It had a deep v-neck, thin material that looked like it would hug her skin. She inspected the flowing bottom, lace sleeves made to hang off of her shoulders, sapphires on thin see-through lace that would decorate her chest...

"It's, wow..." She was breathless. The blue was lighter at the bottom as though dusted with snow; it was beautiful. "Are these real?" She touched the sapphires.

"Of course, pulled from Atreus' personal treasury," he informed her proudly. "I thought it went with your sword." He smiled. *Treasury?*

"It's perfect."

"Have you named your sword yet?" he asked her and hung the dress on a hook by her wardrobe.

"I have to name it?" she asked, confused.

"It's kind of a tradition here, but you don't have to. It's supposed to strengthen the bond between the sword and its master," he sank into the oversized armchair by the towering archway windows.

"I would love to do that." She smiled.

Something was magical about accepting Atreus and his kingdom, his people. A sense of excitement and purpose was growing inside of her. Amara had agreed to accept the mating bond to

Atreus following the ball, leaving her a ball of nerves and excitement.

"Where is it?" he asked. She moved to the trunk under her bed and retrieved the massive longsword that always seemed to be a part of her. He stood, noticing the way it came to life and lit up in her grip.

"Whoa." He looked between her and the sword in awe.

She focused on it, intent to learn its name, its purpose, looking at it through the same lens she was always watching herself through. It felt as though it had a life of its own, as though its intention was to strengthen her and her alone. She inhaled a shaky breath as the inanimate object's personality take shape in the palm of her hand. Kit stood and circled her once, watching her interacting with it.

"Amara..." he started.

"Quiet," she demanded, enthralled in the piece of weaponry.

She sank to the floor onto her knees, finally listening to it, feeling the magic exchanging between them. She didn't think anything so extraordinary was possible. She caught a glimpse of her reflection in its shining steel blade, it startled her. Her normally emerald green eyes were glowing a similar sapphire blue as the hilt of the sword. She swallowed hard, ignoring the twinge of fear and reveling in the raw power it gave her.

"Eversor," she whispered. Kit stilled before her, his hand over his mouth.

"Destroyer, overthrower..." he translated its meaning.

"Yes." She nodded, unable to break eye contact with her reflection.

It felt like an eternity passed before she could put the blade down, it both terrified and thrilled her.

"We have three hours until the ball, Prince Elichai is impossibly particular about people being on time, so do NOT be late." He pointed at her and turned to leave.

"Prince?" She gasped.

"The king's brother." He looked genuinely concerned at her lack of knowledge, but sauntered back over to her. "He ruled in Atreus' sted the last five years..."

"Back up." Amata stood and motioned for him to sit. "How does one of the oldest fallen angels on the planet have a brother?" He stumbled into the small couch as she towered over him demanding answers.

"Well, there is Lucifer..." he quipped.

"I know that, you dote." She flicked his forehead. "I doubt he was watching over Constantine in Atreus' absence."

Kit regarded her with amusement and propped his head on his hand, fumbling his bottom lip between his fingers with thoughtful amusement.

"Not brothers in the conventional sense, but they've been close for a very very long time. There is no separating them," he explained. "The fact that you have not met him is only because he is occupied with the trouble Deimos has stirred up in the west," he assured her. She took Kit in for a long moment, his smaller frame, poutier lips, his thick eyebrows, and dark blue hair that could be mistaken for black. Somehow she had never really noticed his beauty before.

"How come your teeth are sharp?" She blurted out, even though it had nothing to do with the conversation at hand. She wondered if he was aware that he was running his tongue across them. She wondered if it hurt at all but it seemed to be a mindless habit of his.

Every single perfect tooth was pointed, looking sharp as razors. It perplexed her about who and what he was. It reminded her of Madame Tate whose teeth were sharp in the same manner.

"Uhm, my mother's a witch." He cleared his throat.

Zalser, Zalser... Finally she remembered why that name was familiar. She was mentioned in the paperwork she discovered in Atreus' chambers at the Sanctum. *Katiana Zalser, body not recovered, false confession, alive.*

"Wait, really?" She flopped into the seat next to him.

"Yeah, though I've never met her," he informed her and wrapped an arm around her. She leaned her head on his chest. Talking to him was easy, his presence relaxing. "I'm pretty sure she died."

"I never met mine either," she exhaled.

"Seriously?" He looked down at her.

"Nope, she was murdered when I was two." She tried to make it sound simple, as though she had time to process it and move on, but she failed.

"Wow, I'm sorry, kid, I didn't know." He sighed. She leaned up to look at him.

"Kid? Aren't you younger than me?" she asked.

"On the contrary, I'm approaching my eighty-fourth birthday." He raised his eyebrows and pressed her nose in that fun playfully way of his.

"Liar." She laughed. *Last contact with her child was eighty-three years ago.*

"Nope, honest." He held up his hand in an 'I swear it' motion. He didn't look a day over nineteen, it was amazing.

"Wow, you look great for your age," she laid in his lap and looked up at him. She crossed her legs over the armrest of the couch.

"Thanks, it's the immortality." He smiled, stretching his arms behind his head.

She felt like she should tell him about the notes she found in Findaria about his mother. She wasn't really sure what it meant and she definitely didn't know how to decipher the code of her location. She would have to bring it up to Atreus. If his mother is alive, he needs to know.

"I wonder if I'm an immortal Nephilim." She sighed, changing the subject. She stared at the ceiling. She didn't know if she wanted-ed to be.

"Only time will tell." He shrugged. "If you haven't started aging in a few years or developed some human ailment, you're golden."

"Thanks, helpful as ever," she hit him in the stomach with her knuckles.

"It's what I live for," he snorted.

"Are you going to fight when we go to intercept them outside of the border?" she asked, turning the tone more serious.

"Yes, I suppose I will, unless King Atreus asks me to do something else." He twirled a strand of her hair in his fingers.

"Have you fought in a war before?" she asked curiously.

"Yes, occasionally smaller kingdoms seek to overthrow us. I've seen death and I've dealt it." He swallowed, staring forward. "Definitely not my favorite thing to do." He tried to smile but it didn't meet his eyes.

"How many people have you killed?" she asked, staring up at his chest and chin from his lap.

"A few," he recounted painfully. She couldn't help but feel like he held an awful lot of grief in his modest frame.

"I've killed two people," she whispered. She didn't know why, but she felt like she needed to say it, like it needed to be heard. He didn't react as though it surprised him nor did it disgust him.

""It's a grim truth in the wake of God's abandonment—everyone is forced to kill to survive." He shook his head. "I have faith that it would have been you or them." He looked down at her. "And I'm glad it wasn't you."

"Yeah." She tried to smile.

She wished it was the case. Bastian Marlowe was trying to turn her in for a reward, he wasn't trying to kill her. Though at the time she didn't see a difference. And Molvina... Well, she would live with that guilt for the rest of her life. Anger and jealousy pushed her to kill. No matter the excuse that she would expose them and get them killed, it was jealousy that wrapped her hands around the girl's throat and squeezed until the life left her.

"None of this depressing shit, we'll be here all night," he snapped her out of her trance. "I'll send in a stylist in an hour,." She moved out of his lap to let him leave.

"Thank you." She smiled at him.

"Chin up, kid, a magical night awaits you," he sang in a taunting-joke type manner and bounced out of the room. She found herself giggling at him before going to inspect her dress of choice for the evening.

"Prince Elichai has arrived in the ballroom, it's nearly time!" a woman whispered excitedly into Amara's room, speaking to the woman who was styling her.

"Oh dear, you're going to just adore him!" The plump kind woman smiled and she smoothed out Amara's dress around her waist.

The woman had a motherly aura about her. She was overly nurturing, had a soft voice, and seemed to genuinely care about her work. She had come to know her as Brenda, she was the tailor and stylist for the kingdom, a human woman aged about fifty years. Her brownish-red hair was graying in parts, but it suited her. Amara sensed that she had lived a full life and had much more to look forward to.

She had all kinds of clumpy jewelry, a bright intricately designed blouse, and small platform shoes that clicked when she walked. Her green eyes had some wrinkling around them, the kind that comes with many years of smiling too wide or laughing too hard. She alternated between pushing her thick rimmed glasses onto her nose and pulling them down to find a makeup item or hairpin she needed.

"All right, now." Brenda exhaled, satisfied with her work. She opened up the wardrobe to allow Amara a look at herself.

Her black hair was braided back, hanging down to the center of her partially exposed back. Her pale skin was bright, only lightly touched up by makeup. The sapphires seemed to be part of her chest and twinkled in the light, the straps of the dress pooled around her arms just under her shoulders, exposing the delicate skin there.

She wore elegant white silk gloves that flowed nearly all the way up to her elbows. The long gown of the dress dropped to the floor, the dark blue fading lighter, and then down into a dusty white color. *Wow.* She nearly didn't recognize herself, especially because the dress made the silver around her eyes pop.

"Thank you." Amara smiled, touching the sapphire pins decorating her braid.

"Oh, Atreus left this for you." She pulled out a box.

Within the dark velvet box sat two dangling teardrop earrings, each with a sapphire set in diamonds. It was as if he knew she'd pick the sapphire dress.

"Whoa." She inhaled a shaky breath.

Brenda stood behind her as she admired herself once more.

"I'll tell Kit you're ready to be escorted to the ball." She rubbed Amara's arms, giving them a small reassuring squeeze.

As the sun set and the stars claimed the sky, Amara took Kit's arm and descended the stairs into the ballroom. People chatted amongst themselves as the small orchestra played. In the center of the dance floor, many couples danced together in unison as though the choreography was memorized from birth and mastered with their first steps.

Kit and Amara descended golden and ivory marble spiraling stairs. She clung tight to her friend; afraid she would fall. Kit was adorned in all black, down to his tie, a violet handkerchief in his chest pocket. *Don't trip, don't trip, don't trip.*

Backs melted into faces and eyes found her, nearly everyone glanced toward the stairs. Easily a few hundred people, both human and Nephilim seemed to pause to take her in. On a platform on the other side of the massive hall stood a group of well-dressed Nephilim—she thought—conversing, seemingly about her from their glances in her direction. One amongst them was the red-haired woman who seemed to advise Atreus during the sentencing of the prisoners. Amara was suddenly very self-conscious about her pointed ears and how they gave away exactly who fathered her.

And there stood Atreus, grinning up at her from the foot of the staircase, his presence impossible to ignore even among the most extravagant. His attire shimmered with an otherworldly elegance, a far cry from the simple suits worn by the other men. He was dressed to ensure no soul would miss the sight of their king, though such a thing was unthinkable.

His usual dark slacks and buttoned shirt had been transformed by a flowing sapphire sash that draped across his chest, starting from his right shoulder. Silver pins, gleaming like stars, adorned the fabric, their intricate shapes too distant to discern. Draped over his left shoulder, a leather half-cape, understated yet regal, whispered of his character—a subtle blend of grace and command.

Upon his brow rested what could only be his crown, though it defied expectation. Slender and wrought of silver, it bore no gemstones, only a pair of wing-like adornments that rose near his temples. The feathered details caught the light, scattering it outward like the gleam of a celestial bird in flight.

Stray strands of onyx hair fell across his forehead, framing the dimples that deepened with his smile. His silver rings gleamed in the ballroom's light as he extended his hand toward her. When she met his gaze, those deep blue eyes made the bustling crowd fade into nothing—they were alone. She no longer had to concentrate on keeping her balance; his presence steadied her, soothing the chaos in her mind and bringing peace to her soul.

She released Kit's arm, who murmured a greeting to his king before Atreus held out his hand for her to grab. His touch grounded her and made her feel as though she were floating all at once. The crowd separated for them in such a surreal moment as the music swelled. His subjects bowed and greeted him... no *them*. She smiled at each of them, unsure of how to handle the attention.

"Your beauty never ceases to amaze me." He leaned down and whispered in her ear. Her cheeks heated and she hoped it wasn't too obvious.

She took in the massive crystal chandeliers, each with more candles than she could count. *Who lit those?* Stone pillars were carved with intricate designs, dark wallpaper with maroon and gold floral patterns decorated the walls between them. The towering ceilings rose so high that she had to stretch her neck painfully to see the gold beams that seemed to be holding them up. Below her, marble floors were hushed below her feet, the clicking heels silenced by the music and murmur of the guests. Floor-to-ceiling windows overlooked the sea, the stars twinkling as though perfectly placed to add magic to the evening. She could spend the entire night just marveling at the beauty of the space.

Women wore varying colors of ball gowns, each with their own touch, no one dress was like the other. Pearls, diamonds, gemstones of all cuts and sizes decorated the women of his court. She wondered who had the privilege of being styled by Brenda.

The gentlemen were dressed in suits, some with tails, some too big for their owner, others tailored just right. Most in dark shades, but a few stood out in the crowd. She met eyes with Nephilim and humans, none seemingly harboring hatred for the other the way they might have in Findaria. The atmosphere was calm, excitement peppered throughout.

She thought she caught a scowl or two from some young women leaning against the wall to her right but she couldn't be certain.

They stood between golden statues of fallen angels that seemed to be reaching toward the arched golden ceiling.

"Amara/" Atreus squeezed her forearm to get her attention.

They made it to the raised platform where the six unnamed people were still conversing. three of them were beautiful women who seemed to be sculpted by hand, their beauty stopping her in her tracks.

"Ms. Ashenfall, what a privilege to finally lay eyes on the snatcher of my brother's heart." A tall blond headed man stepped down from the platform.

"It's nice to meet you, Prince Elichai," she guessed. He bowed half with a dashing smile. He was nearly Atreus' height, appeared younger in years, and looked... tired. It was one of his most noticeable features... the dark bags below his eyes, bloodshot around his silver iris', his grip far too tight on his glass as though he were trying to ground himself. His white button-down shirt had the top few buttons open, his bowtie undone and hanging around his neck. He was beautiful, from his gray eyes and chiseled face, to his lean frame and messy golden hair.

"Elichai," Atreus greeted and hugged him, patting his back.

"Brother." Elichai held him at arm's length and examined him closely. "You and I have much to discuss."

"Yes of course." He laughed lightly.

A woman on the platform behind them stepped down while the others resumed their conversation.

"Amara, this is my royal council." He gestured to all of them. The woman who was red-headed, doe-eyed, and drop dead gorgeous laced an arm into Elichai's as though claiming him. He looked down at their arms linking and seemed to clear his throat uncomfortably. "This is Helena Hart, she is the Lady of the Witches, she tends to all magic wielders in my kingdom. She often acts as my advisor as well."

"Pleasure." She gave a weak smile. Amara returned the sentiment. At least she had a name to put with a face.

"You will have the privilege of acquainting yourself with them all soon but that—" he pointed to a blond haired chubby woman—"is Peony Langston, she oversees diplomatic concerns, the gentleman beside her is Anders Hale who is the commander of our army." He pointed to a handsome dark-haired gentlemen who was enormous. She was compartmentalizing the people before her as he spoke. Helena and Elichai had disappeared out of sight.

There was something familiar in the way Elichai sauntered through the crowd and the way those blonde locks flowed from his head.

"The last two, the twins." He pointed to a male and female set of Nephilim who both had harsh features and abnormally silver hair. "Are Wren and Hawk Undergrove, they tend to public safety and finances for my people. Oh, and of course Kit is part of the council as the head of the royal guard."

"This is so..." she paused. "So much more complicated than I could have imagined," she exhaled slowly.

"Running a kingdom?" He smirked at her. She nodded. "Yes love, it's very involved," he joked and extended his hand. "But it's nothing for you to fret over. Tonight, we dance." His smile melted away all of her concerns.

She found that despite her lack of experience when it came to dancing, she could effortlessly follow Atreus' lead. His expressive gaze met her emerald eyes, locking her in as he whirled them around the room. Whispers of adoration about the king and the new Lady of the Kingdom were peppered throughout the great hall. She was lost in the dark blue ocean that were the windows to his soul. She so desperately wanted to dive into them, to learn every aspect of his immeasurable existence. He swung her outward on the music's queue and spun her twice, the room fading into a blur of colors.

She landed against his firm chest, a glimmer of heat pulsing between them, both of them recognized the fire in the other's eyes. She swore she saw a splash of color reach his cheeks. She wrapped her arms tightly around him, sneakily digging her nails into his back. He smiled a small, knowing smile, before biting his lip and sending her spinning again.

"I am not above leaving my own royal ball to take you on the floor of one of the many rooms in this building," he whispered huskily into her ear once she collided with him again. She looked around at all of the people who would surely notice their absence. "And I don't care who notices it," he hissed, answering her thoughts. She swallowed hard, anticipation and need rising within her where fear and hesitation should have.

Minutes melted into hours as they danced, chatted with strangers, danced more until her feet hurt, sipped wine, and finally listened to a speech from Prince Elichai.

"As you know, it has been an honor of mine to guide everyone in my brother's stead for the last five years." He shoved a hand into his slacks, nervous. "But I am relieved to be handing the reins back to a more capable leader." He laughed low in his throat, more laughing echoed through the crowd.

"You didn't do that bad!" A wasted Kit whooped from the front of the crowd, a few people seemed to second the notion.

"Thank you, Zalser." He lifted his glass. "Welcome home, King Atreus. And welcome to Constantine Lady Amara." He dipped his head and cheering erupted through the crowd. She felt as though she was floating from excitement, fear, uncertainty... she didn't know. She wrapped her arms around Atreus' neck as more slow dancing music began.

"Are you sure I can do this?" she asked, referring to the whole inherited kingdom and helping him rule and such.

"I can't think of anyone better suited to rule by my side," he reassured her as he swayed her gently.

His hands wrapped around her waist, making her heart pound wildly. She tugged on a few strands of his hair as she buried her head in the crook of his neck, inhaling his familiar scent. The heels she wore made her just tall enough to do so. She moved her hands down his body and locked them around him tightly.

Her heart beat wildly as she nuzzled his neck. Most of the crowd were wine drunk and lost in their own partners, and she thought about the fun little threat he made earlier in the night. To ensure he cashed in on it, she tilted her head slightly and nipped at the soft skin of his neck. He faltered a moment in swaying her before a low groan escaped his throat and his grip on her waist tightened.

He trailed his hand slowly up her back, scanning the room around them. He gripped the back of her neck, allowing his nails to dig in just enough to send sweet stinging prickles over her skin.

"Dirty girl," he praised, staring into her eyes, his own wild with need. He spun her away from him, grabbed her hand, and led her smoothly to the back of the ballroom.

Three sets of double doors were there, none of them had seemingly been used that evening. He unlocked the one on the right and ushered her in quickly.

Before them was a massive dining hall, at least thirty round tables with white table cloths and simple centerpieces. The room was completely dark, completely isolated. She was just about to glance out of one of the windows with flowing drapes when he appeared behind her.

He grabbed her hips and walked her forward roughly, urgently. She could feel his swollen erection against her and excitement spiked in her blood. He forced her forward, over one of the many tables, causing her to giggle. He kicked her right leg outward with his and she assisted him in pulling the bottom of her ball gown upward.

"Fucking hell." She heard him drop to his knees behind her at the discovery of her lack of undergarments.

He grabbed her ass, spreading her wide, and slid his tongue against her. She moaned as he tasted her, still in earshot of the party on the other side of the door.

"You're perfect," he told her. He paused to nip at her inner thigh, causing her to jump. It sent the centerpiece toppling over and caused her to laugh. "You taste so goddamn good..."

She moaned and pushed back against his face as his nails dug into her ass. Before she knew it, the feeling of his mouth there, his expert rhythm, his torturous fingers sliding in and out of her, and the thrill of getting caught culminated into an orgasm that had her biting down on her arm to silence her screams.

"There's my girl," he whispered.

He forced himself into her violently before she could ride out her orgasm completely. The sensation was overwhelming in the most delicious way, tearing a scream from her chest and allowing her to finish against him.

He was rough and unforgiving. He needed his climax desperately before anyone noticed their absence. He grabbed her braid and forced every inch of himself into her, her hip bones digging into the table, adding a twinge of pain to the pleasure. It was everything she loved, and he knew it, he thrived on it.

"Harder, Atreus." She squealed just to drive him crazy. A husky noise in his throat confirmed that it worked. He obliged and pounded into her until her eyes were rolling back in her head and she lost all focus of where they were.

She exploded around him as he orgasmed, pulsing heat into her. He collapsed for a moment over her back, panting before planting kisses on her shoulders.

"I'll never tire of you, brat." He grinned and pulled out of her.

He had just finished pulling her dress down when they heard someone enter the room.

"Amar—" Kit inhaled a shocked breath. "Oh fuck, oh shit," he stammered upon seeing Atreus zipping up his pants and her still bent over the table. "I'm so sorry." He drunkenly backed out of the door he came in from.

Amara burst into laughter, Atreus following suit. She stood and he pulled her into his arms.

"Well, at least he was being a good guard. He didn't let you out of his sight for very long." He comforted her as she wrestled with absolute horror and embarrassment. All she could do was laugh.

They made their way, discreetly back out to the ball room where bodies were still dancing and people were still chattering. She spotted Kit at one of the tables, his suit disheveled, and his head buried in his hands. *He was probably more embarrassed than they were.*

"One last dance?" he asked. She nodded and grabbed his hand. He held her close, held her tight.

Amara never wanted to leave his arms, never wanted to know the absence of him, of that moment. She didn't care about all of the details that came with it. She knew that as they had each other, they would thrive.

So she watched the people of his kingdom and court enjoying themselves, glanced at her friend still mortified at the table, watched Prince Elichai dance with Helena, and listened to the music swimming through the room.

Somehow she had found a place and a life to embrace, one worth running head-first into, not away from. She was not a pawn, she was a leader, a lover, a friend, and she would work hard to be the best version of all of those things that she could be. Apart from that, she was Nephilim, and she would embrace that part of her wholeheartedly.

Chapter 37

ATREUS

Within his heart of hearts, he knew she deserved the truth before she accepted him as her mate. He watched her close her mouth around his palm where she carved her name, and he didn't even flinch. He didn't think twice about stopping her from tying herself to him. Perhaps he was selfish but he couldn't bear the thought of *not* having her.

Fear can be a surprisingly effective motivator and he could not have her backing down under the weight of it. Amara would learn the truth; she would learn how to handle it alongside him. Of that he was sure. He's the only one that could ensure her safety, her continued existence.

The magnitude of Amara's power and abilities was unknown to her. She didn't know the half of her lineage or who her mother really was. Amara—his mate, his angel, his eternity given meaning—was sound asleep in his bed on the other side of the room with no idea about the truths he wrestled against.

Deimos would arrive on the continent seeking his assistance in a matter of days, with a war hot on his trail. It plagued him, truly, that he forged that cursed alliance with Deimos all those years ago. Deimos was foolish, reckless, and weak. He put Atreus' entire kingdom at risk. It was still recovering from his absence, his soldiers grew lazy, legal matters were so far behind he would never catch up, requests from other kingdoms demanded his attention all of the time... He had much to correct amongst the members of his council. He adored his brother but he was very lenient, a lot younger, lazy, and far less responsible. At least there was peace amongst his people, he had to give him that.

Additionally, he had twenty newly transitioned Nephilim preparing to train just as a war approached his land, his mate was a ticking time bomb that would detonate if he didn't handle her with the love and care she deserved, and he was... Well, he was just trying to do right by her and right by his people.

Hyde and Rowan, his master spies, reported no luck on finding Juliet Valentine nor did they discover what happened to her. Atreus didn't know how much Amara was going to be able to handle. He knew she was strong, stronger than anyone he ever had the privilege of knowing, but there was only so much heartbreak one person could take.

He brushed her hair from her beautiful sleeping face. Her skin was soft, pale, and silky below his fingertips. She breathed as she slept, it reminded him of the sound of a bird's wings gliding in the wind. She was on her stomach, shirtless from their celebration just hours earlier, and she was so breathtakingly perfect that he could fall apart at the sight of her. He traced the lines on her back, the odd scars from a viscous woman that should be disemboweled for her cruelty. Especially to a child.

Amara's palm was open, facing up because her arm was under her head. *'Atreus'* carved deep into her skin. He could still taste her blood in his mouth from the sweet sinful commitment they had made. He never wanted to hide things from her, never wanted to hurt her. He was holding on to so much knowledge that he wished he didn't have, that he wished he didn't have to be responsible for telling her. He sat on the bed beside her, listening to her calm restful breathing, taking in her softened features. She always seemed to him as though she had come alive out of a dream and he still couldn't fathom how she was real or how she loved him so deeply.

She was a shining sapphire in a broken world, hope amongst the ruins, truth within the lies, elegance given life, peace within his eternity, an exquisitely sculpted sapphire sat amongst the hardened diamonds within his heart. He had coated his sapphire in crimson and she only shined brighter for him.

He had to compartmentalize facts so that he could tell her exactly what she needed to know at the correct time; Deimos would turn on Atreus quickly upon learning he would not turn over Amara for his own power gain. That was the truth easier to swallow.

Deimos turning on him could be fixed, would have to be fixed really, once Amara learned what he had done. He shuddered at the thought of her wrath turned on her father in light of the earth shattering truth that was beating down the door to be heard.

"I'm so sorry my love," he whispered as he ran the backs of his knuckles across her ribs. He watched the small bumps form on her skin, amazed at how her body came to life for him.

"For what?" She whispered, startling him. He didn't mean to wake her, but she was looking at him with big sleepy eyes, worried. He shook his head, unable to face her, what he needed to say was threatening to rush out of him. *Knock, knock, knock,* the truth was demanding to be let in. She sat up and pulled the blanket to her chest, concerned, sensing his agony.

"Deimos is flying toward Constantine," he began, his voice cracking like a brittle branch underfoot.

Her eyes widened, a flicker of disbelief dancing across her features. "Okay…" she replied, though her tone trembled, half a question, half a plea for clarity. She already knew they were meant to intercept him outside the kingdom's borders…

"He expects me to turn you over to him so that he can…" His words faltered, his gaze dropping as if the very sky had fallen upon him, suffocating him with its oppressive weight. His shoulders slumped, and the air seemed to grow heavy, as though the earth itself was mourning the truth he was about to reveal. The metaphorical door within him groaned and splintered, its edges fraying and cracking, the ancient wood giving way to the relentless pressure of his guilt.

"So he can do what?" She gently squeezed his forearm, her touch like a cool breeze against his burning skin.

He felt the fresh scarring from their bond pulse beneath her fingers, each mark a reminder of their shared burden. The door inside him gave way completely under her touch, shards of secrecy exploding outward.

"So he can drain the life from you, and complete the ritual he started when he sacrificed your mother," he confessed. The words spilled out of him with a rush of torment, as though they were dragging him down with them. He slumped forward, his head bowed, eyes meeting hers with an expression of deep-seated dread and sorrow. Each breath he took seemed labored, as if the weight of his admission was a physical force pressing down on him. He watched her with a pained urgency, desperate to convey the gravity of the impending doom that now loomed over them.

Chapter 38

Amara backed up, putting space between herself and Atreus. He stared at her with wide eyes, waiting for his world to fall away from him. She winced at the weight on her palm where his name was carved to complete their mating ceremony. She suddenly felt as though all of the oxygen had been removed from the room. She gasped for air against her tightening throat.

"You knew..." she fell onto the floor, still regarding him in horror. "You knew the whole time?" She was shaking. She tried to focus so that the world wouldn't begin spinning around her. He shook his head.

"I didn't. I swear I didn't know the entire time." The cool, calm and collected composure of King Atreus was gone. He was frantic, afraid.

She stood on wobbly legs, holding on to the side table for support. She imagined her mother's beheaded body the same way she saw it in her dream. Then the face cleared from the blur of the dream... Deimos. She recalled the spiked black hair, the pointed ears like her own. She shook her head as though she could reset her reality.

"You said you weren't ready to know her killer's identity yet but..."

"I didn't think it would be my own father! You should have told me, Atreus!" She paced in the room, grabbing clothes.

"I wanted to, I didn't know how." He approached her slowly, cautiously.

She hurriedly pulled on leather pants and a dark sweater.

"Amara..." he grabbed her elbow pleadingly.

"You said sacrifice. For what gain?" Tears were streaming down her face. "My mother was human, I'm just Nephilim." She shook her head. "It doesn't make any sense." She sniffled.

"I..." he looked at the ground in shame.

"You need to tell me everything you are keeping from me. If you don't, I'm done. We are done," she screamed and shoved him backward.

She underestimated her own strength, her own scream shaking the room. Her wings erupted before Atreus hit the ground. The pain of them tearing free from her skin sent shockwaves through her which felt like needles on every inch of her skin.

He shot to his feet, his eyes wide. His nostrils flared and she could feel him trying to reign in his temper.

"I have not kept this from you maliciously. I am trying to protect you. I have always tried to protect you." His own wings showed themselves. He was preparing for whatever she would do next whether it was fighting or running.

"To what end? Huh?" She laughed half. "I don't believe for a second that you got involved with Deimos out of the kindness of your own heart."

When she looked at him she saw her mate and the man she fell in love with. But she also saw a king who aligned himself with her wicked father and had a hand in controlling her life from the moment she was born.

"I never claimed there was no gain for me," he reasoned. "I just don't care about that part of the deal anymore. I care about you." He looked utterly defeated, broken down, scared. She had that kind of power over him. It was terrifying. Then, something occurred to her.

"How do I know that mating yourself to me wasn't a power move? I don't know what it is about me that Deimos wants, but how can I know that you don't want it to?" She wasn't crying any longer. She was petrified, angry, and defensive.

"You have no idea what you're talking about," he growled. He lost the grip on his anger and closed the space between them. "I will prove it to you." He gripped her wrist and dragged her behind him.

"Let me go," she demanded through clenched teeth and tried to jerk away. He ignored her and pulled her through some kind of secret passageway off of the bedchamber. "How did you..." she glanced around to see where it came from.

Magic tickled her senses; torches came to life in the king's presence. She withdrew her wings for fear of fire catching them, Atreus did the same. Though she might expect the stone passageway to be drafty or musty, it smelled of fresh sea air. The corridor was fairly narrow but they didn't have to make themselves smaller to traverse it. She begrudgingly trailed behind him down a few stairs and the corridor opened up to an underground chamber.

He finally released her wrist and strode over to the massive table in the center of the room. Above it hung two circular chandeliers with soft flickering candles. Sprawled out on the table was a map of the Hallowed Realm, scattered scrolls, fountain pens, stone sculpted pieces meant for strategy planning, and ancient looking books. She picked up a portrait, one she had never seen before—of her mother. Another sat beside it, Deimos.

The portraits did little to distract her though, from what looked like a stone circular structure that took up the back wall of the chamber.

"What is all of this?" She fought back an emotion that tasted similar to betrayal.

"Deimos sought me out many years ago," he started. "He heard whispers that Constantine was responsible for missing sired children in Findaria and its adjoining kingdoms."

"You rescue them?" she asked. She kind of gathered that information beforehand.

"I always have," he answered, sorrow in his eyes.

"Why?" She rolled a piece of charcoal between her fingers.

"I have experienced captivity firsthand," he stated simply.

"Lady Jane Cyperian," she whispered. He jolted, clearly not prepared for her to know that name.

"Do not ever speak that name again," he roared and slammed his hand on the table. Stone warriors sent sprawling over the cloth map.

"I want to know what she did." Amara leaned over the table. She flat out refused to be intimidated by him now. Even if she could feel the power roiling off of him and flicking against her senses tauntingly.

"Do you want that information or the information that pertains to you?" He sneered.

"What did Deimos seek you out for?" She redirected her conversation.

"To put it simply, he wanted to destroy them. He wanted the Hallowed Realm for himself or destroyed. He knew that I learned of ways to infiltrate their kingdoms and steal their children right out from under their noses," she saw the anger melting from him.

"Did he know who you were?" she asked.

"Yes." He nodded. "As such, he knew I was the only one with the power to help him."

"How?" She pushed. He took the seat at the head of the table.

"He managed to impregnate one of Findaria's subjects. At the time I didn't know how. He should not have been able to do so with the wards placed around their lands; with the magic they choked their citizens beneath." Before she could ask how he did it, Atreus continued, "He asked me to do something I never thought to do before—place myself in the heart of Findaria. Do so and protect his child to ensure they transitioned."

"To what end?"

"He found a way to drain their source of magic, through you. He would bring war upon them and while they were defending their lands, he would use you as a siphon. The same way the Hallowed use their children to draw on their source of magic, he wanted to use his child, except he would drain everything they had." "They claim their magic came from the devil..." *from your brother.* Though she always knew better deep down.

"Not completely." He scoffed. "Their magic comes from the enslavement of witches kept beneath the Cobalt Mountains."

The information made her flinch and stole her breath.

"Kit's mother?" she whispered.

"Yes." He raised his eyebrows. He was clearly taken aback by what she did know. "She is one of hundreds trapped there."

"Why would he be able to siphon all of their magic through me?" None of it made sense, she couldn't put the pieces of the puzzle together. He picked up the portrait of her mother.

"Josie and Grace Ashenfall were born to Kaia Ashenfall. Though they did not have the same father. Josie—your mother's father was an extremely powerful warlock named Orick. Making her part witch," he informed her simply.

"What?" She gasped.

"Where is Orick now?" She didn't know why that was the first question.

"I would imagine he is under the Cobalt Mountains." He sighed.

"I'm part witch?" She blinked.

"Orick was *THE* warlock of the land of Findaria long before it was seized by the Hallowed. You're the daughter of the soil, just as your mother was," he said cautiously. *Daughter of the soil.*

She stared at him, mouth agape.

"You are Daughter of the Soil *and*—" he emphasized the word dramatically—"Nephilim. It is unheard of."

"I... but how—" coherent words were lost to her. She paused for a moment, thinking. "But Kit is..."

"Kit was born of a witch and Sylas, not so unlike yourself. What makes you so remarkable is the fact that you did not come from an ordinary magic bloodline. You came from Oricks, you are the last of his descendants. In you and through you lives all of the magic of Findaria," he twirled a toy soldier between his deft fingers.

"It's not possible." She shook her head and turned her attention away from him.

"Deimos sought to breed into that line so he could use you to siphon everything from the land, from the Hallowed. Or Hadeon at least. He suspected he could drain the entire realm this way, but he would settle just for Findaria."

"I still don't understand why my lineage would allow him or anyone to use me to just siphon all of the magic. It can't be that simple," she reasoned.

"Clever girl. It's not that simple." He grinned half-heartedly. He slid a book in her direction.

It was a history of the witches and warlocks.

"Are there witches and warlocks here?" she asked.

"Of course, as I said Helena Hart is my emissary for the magic folk here. She is the Lady of the Witches. This is her land, magically speaking. I do all I can to respect that."

"You don't enslave them?" she asked.

"No." He laughed . "I've been searching for a way to free those under the Cobalt Mountains." She nodded, knowing it would be no simple task. "What I didn't know about his plan was that it meant ending Orick's bloodline. I didn't know he would kill your mother and I didn't know he was organizing a ritual that would cost your life as well."

"What did you think happened when she turned up dead?" Amara spat.

"Your mother had dealings with all manner of people. I simply thought it caught up with her or that Hadeon grew suspicious of who fathered her child. I did not lie to you when I said I was investigating it."

"I still don't understand what was in it for you. Why did you agree to help him see me through transition? Why place yourself into the heart of enemy land? Surely your royal court would have advised against it."

"Of course they advised against it. But I had the opportunity to free a record number of sired children during my time there, I was able to get close to information that even my master spies couldn't touch, I could disguise myself and walk amongst the enemy. I even managed to become one of Hadeon's most trusted sons."

"What else? I know he offered you something besides opportunity. You could have taken that idea and not helped him." She crossed her arms and leaned against the wall. He narrowed his eyes.

"He threatened to free an enemy that I imprisoned in their Abyss if I didn't assist. Happy?" He tilted his head. She knew it was no small thing for a king to lay out all of his secrets and motives to someone.

"Who?" She pressed.

"No." He shook his head. "I am happy to give you the information pertaining to you, but my secrets need to be mine." The response felt like a punch to the gut.

"Why would you imprison someone in your enemy's land?" She redirected.

"It's a brilliant form of torture." He shrugged. "Besides, anyone who escapes the Abyss is still stuck in Findaria."

"Why bring me in here to tell me any of this?" she asked. He stood, something weighing heavy in his features.

"I needed you to see this," he motioned toward the circular stone structure on the opposite side of the room. "Place your hand here," he guided her hand over a diamond-shaped part of it.

"What is it..." She glanced up at him.

Within the center of the stone a blue light flickered to life, stealing her breath away. She jumped back and it died out.

"No, keep your hand there," he instructed calmly. She placed it back. A graying man came into view within the swimming blue light. Amara shook, he was facing a woman.

"Josie, my child," he greeted her. She smiled, it was nearly identical to Amara's, and hugged him around his neck. She looked back at Atreus who nodded for her to watch.

"Father," she cried as though not having seen him in years.

"I do not have long, they will know I'm gone. I have come to give you a prophecy regarding the child that you carry," he spoke slowly. Amara's mother rubbed her swollen belly.

"A prophecy?" she asked through tears. He nodded.

Orick's words echoed with dark gravity. "Mark my words: the child of flame shall ascend and lay waste to all that is entrenched. From deceitful origins, her father will unleash a torrent of blood, eradicating the bloodline that rules this land."

"What?" Her mother whimpered.

Amara reached out to touch the woman, wanting more than anything to fall through the portal thing and into her arms. There was no physical form there though, and the blue light died out along with the only interaction she ever had with her mother.

She found herself on her knees sobbing. What was she supposed to do?

Atreus was on the floor behind her, pulling her into his arms. She let him and curled into his lap. She let the emotions swallow her. She was absolutely no one and nothing yet the fate of an entirely bloodline rested in her hands.

"I'm here, I'm so sorry, Amara." He ran his hand over her hair.

"Why not just let him go through with it? Why not let him defeat the Hallowed by sacrificing me. I'm just one person." She looked up at him through tears. "Kingdoms of people could be freed."

"I don't trust him to care for them any better than the Hallowed," he said, shaking his head with a mixture of sorrow and frustration. "But beyond that, my heart is consumed with love for you. I am overwhelmed, adrift in a sea of affection for you. My love for you is so profound that I would risk everything, abandon all caution, just to keep you close." He pulled her closer. "You've had my heart from the moment you mocked me after the hunt," he let out a helpless sort of laugh. "You wicked beautiful thing, you've taken me to my knees for the first time in my life."

He drew her hand to his lips and pressed a tender kiss to the spot where his name was etched. She rested her head in his palm where she had carved her own. The mark remained, and she gazed at it, unhealed and enduring. Curious.

"It's still there." It was more of a question.

"It's our mating bond; it will always be there so long as my heart beats for you. Just as yours will be so long as your heart beats for me." He smiled lazily. He seemed half drunk off of the notion and as though his shoulders were lighter from the truth he had revealed to her.

He leaned down and kissed away her tears until his mouth trailed down to hers.

"I love you," she whispered to him. "Even when I hate you, I love you," she breathed.

"We will survive this," he whispered. "I will not let you go. Ever." He pulled her closer. "That prophecy will not be. You will live, Amara. I promise you this."

"We have nearly a week. Tell me how we fight this war and win," she implored.

Chapter 39

The morning came quickly and she awoke alone. She took to the skies to get ahead in training. She was going to show Kit that he could toss her out of the sky all he wanted; she was going to catch herself.

It came easier than she remembered. She thought it might be because of her newfound resolve after Atreus revealed the truth to her. She was the grandchild of Orick, a Child of the Soil. Something in that truth gave her power, gave her a sense of control. She no longer felt so wild and untamed.

It only took about an hour before she got the feel of soaring without sending herself straight into trees. She beat her wings against the sky to speed up and found that she was smiling wide when it worked. She tucked her arms to her side and sent herself over the western village of the kingdom. Some kids pointed and waved at her. She waved back before pushing herself higher into the sky. The sun caught the shades of blue and purple in her feathers. Her wings were finally starting to feel like part of her body.

Amara flew for a long while, inhaling fresh air as she approached the western coast of the continent. It's where they would intercept Deimos, where they intended to stomp out whatever war trailed behind him.

She looked to the west where the sprawling field seemed to drop off of a cliff. She pressed through the grass, forging her own path. Sure enough, at the end she was met with a cliff that seemed bottomless except for the waves crashing violently into the rocks at the base.

"You're fast for a newly transitioned Nephilim," an unfamiliar voice came from behind her.

Strolling toward her with a cigar in hand was Prince Elichai. One of his hands was in the pocket of his slacks. He wore a loose-fitting long-sleeved shirt with untied laces that created a 'V' on his chest. His mess of golden hair seemed to catch the sunlight and his wings... Enormous, four sectioned, and dark red like blood. *Whoa.* The blonde hair and crimson wings reminded her of Ender.

"Why did you follow me?" she demanded.

"I saw someone flying quickly and clumsily out of the palace. I was curious." He shrugged casually before exhaling a cloud of smoke. "My brother is searching for you," he informed her.

"I'll go see him later," she said.

Just as he spoke, a cold realization flooded over her, she knew why he was familiar.

"It was you." She narrowed her eyes and stepped toward him. He tilted his head curiously.

"What was me?" He moved toward her cautiously, humor in his eyes. *Those eyes.*

"You wore a mask, but it was you…" she shuddered. She stared at his lips and could feel them sliding over her mouth, his tongue fighting with hers.

"Forgive me, I didn't know who you were, my lady," he offered sincerely.

"Then it never happened." She stared into his eyes.

"Never happened." He held up one hand and placed the other over his heart.

"Can Atreus overpower the Hallowed Fallen?" She saw an opportunity to garner information from the prince and took it.

"Yes."

"How?" She prodded.

"That's not a simple question and as such does not come with a simple answer."

"Fine." She scoffed.

"It's my understanding that you'll be attending strategy meetings moving forward?" he asked.

She nodded and turned to look out to the horizon.

"You bear a certain resemblance to Deimos." His voice was darker. "You're the child aren't you?" She turned back to him.

"Yes," she saw no reason to lie.

"Do you have any allegiance to him?" She realized this was an interrogation. He circled her like a jungle cat.

"Absolutely not," she growled. "I want him dead."

"My brother declared the same just this morning." He tilted his head. It was becoming clear that Prince Elichai didn't have all of the information. "Why?"

"Why not ask him?" she countered, turning so she was still facing him.

"He is filling in the war council this evening. Maybe I want to know your motivations alongside his."

"The dutiful prince." She smiled sarcastically.

"Always, my lady." He gave a playful bow.

"He killed my mother," she blurted. Realization danced across his features.

"That explains my brother's call for a very public execution of him." He sighed.

"Wait what?" She gasped.

"He wants him taken alive while we defend the borders. He intends to execute him before the kingdom. Actually I believe his exact words were 'I want him delivered to the feet of my queen.' Or something to that effect," he mused. *His queen.*

"I don't want him delivered to me, I intend to look him in the eyes and cut him down myself," she informed. "I have to do this myself."

Elichai took a step back and she recognized it was due to her eyes changing colors. "Let me help you ensure you have your chance," he implored.

"Why?" She was suspicious of him.

"I've wanted him dead for decades. I was there when he informed Atreus that he impregnated someone of great importance. And now you stand before me, refusing to bend to his will." He grinned. "I quite like to ruffle feathers."

"I don't believe it's that simple for you. You would disobey your king for a bit of mischief? No." She realized they were slowly circling one another now, feeling each other out.

"It's not exactly disobeying as much as taking orders from his equal," he corrected.

"Oh." The statement took her breath away. *How was she ever going to adjust to her position in his kingdom?* She sighed and rubbed her arms to comfort herself.

"I ask for one thing." He raised a gloved finger. *Of course.*

"Upon the middle finger of his right hand, Deimos wears a golden serpent ring. I want it," he declared.

"Why?" dhe asked.

"Does it matter?" He crossed his arms and shifted his weight to one hip.

"Get me the ring and I'll ensure you have your chance to end him before we set upon him," he insisted.

"Fine," she agreed.

It wasn't that she didn't appreciate the sentiment of Atreus delivering him to her feet. She did. She loved him for it. It's just that she needed to take back control. She couldn't do that if Deimos was rendered helpless for her. She would either die battling him or she would destroy him. But she would not be his sacrifice and she would not kill him while he couldn't defend himself.

Elichai turned to leave.

"Wait." She put a hand on his shoulder. He glanced at where her fingers touched him but turned his attention to her. "Would you tell Kit I won't be flying with him today? I'm going to stay out here for a while."

"Of course. I'll let my brother know you are taking some time alone," he informed.

"Thanks." She smiled. He took off in a blur of gold and crimson.

Amara spent hours strolling through the rolling fields of flowing tall grass and wildflowers. She sat for a while on the cliff's edge and watched the ocean come and go. She thought long and hard about what the fields would look like scattered with bodies and pouring blood. It seemed impossible, unnatural. She knew it wasn't.

She wished she knew what the numbers were going to look like. How many soldiers would the Hallowed send after Deimos? How would they answer his attack on the Sanctum Metere? She hated that Deimos' actions resulted in war for Constantine, all because of her.

"Hey, kid." Kit landed suddenly behind her. "Strategy meeting is starting soon. Your presence is required."

"Have the sired children been released yet?" she asked, following her train of thought.

"Some of them, there's a few still in transition," he informed her. "They've begun training and preparing to stand with Commander Hale."

"Oh." She nodded.

"Once this is over, they'll have the opportunity to exit the army," he reassured her. He had a way of knowing what was bothering her and making her feel better.

"I want to know what Atreus did to Hadeon," she asked when he sat on the cliffside beside her.

"Why?" He cringed.

"Is he alive?" She pushed. She recalled Atreus referring to him as 'indisposed'.

"Unfortunately."

"Do you know where he's being kept?" She turned to him, a terrible idea forming.

"Nope." He stood. "No, no, no." She stood as well. "I learned my lesson about sneaking you in places. If you want to see Hadeon, Atreus will need to take you." He threw his hands up. He was serious, no humor in his eyes.

"Kit," she whined.

"No way." He crossed his arms.

Deimos and Hadeon fell from the heavens together. If anyone was aware of a weakness that she could exploit, it was Hadeon. Atreus insisted on putting himself at risk, on delivering Deimos to her. If she wanted to do it herself, she needed information from Hadeon without Atreus knowing about it.

"What if I get permission from Atreus?" She bounced, holding his hands in hers. She begged him, blinking rapidly.

"I'll think about it," he groaned.

With that, he flew alongside her back to the palace.

"You two are late," Atreus said by way of welcoming them into the strategy room. It seemed to have infinite entrances besides the one off of Atreus' chambers. She wondered what the smaller one in the library was for.

"She was scoping out the battlefield," Kit informed.

She scanned the room. Commander Hale, Master Spies Rowan and Hyde, Prince Elichai, Wren and Hawk Undergrove, and two unknown people took up seats at the massive table. She tried to think of who *wasn't* there; Peony Langston was absent despite the fact that she was overseer diplomatic concerns. Helena Hart wasn't there either, as Lady of the Witches, though perhaps she had other concerns to attend to. p

"What did you learn?" Commander Hale asked in a gruff voice.

"We'll have the high ground if they come by sea," she started.

"But they fly," Hawk chimed in.

"They do, but they won't fly first and they aren't trained to fly for long." She stared at him.

"She's right/" Atreus guided her to take the seat next to him. "They keep them on tight ropes. Even the soldiers are limited to an hour of flight a week."

"Did you guys have any luck searching out their elemental weakness?" Kit asked the spies.

"If the bulk of the soldiers are from Findaria..." Rowan started.

"Which it appears that they are," Hyde interjected which earned a sideways glance from Rowan.

"Their elemental magic is based in fire, they pull from the heated core of the earth," Rowan continued.

"Making their elemental weakness water?" Prince Elichai chimed in. "Convenient of them to come by sea." He scoffed.

"Does it matter what their source of power is?" Amara glanced around the room. "It's not like they're coming draped in flames."

"She has a point, we can't exactly shoot water arrows at them." Hawk looked at his comrades.

"I can spell arrows not against their source of power but to weaken their wings," Kit answered. Amara's eyes shot to her friend. She nearly asked out loud if he could do magic but it sounded stupid.

"We can place a few hundred on the cliffside and in the caves and glamor them to be invisible." Commander Hale nodded.

"I think we should send a few dozen with the arrows into the air as well, just to double down and hit as many as possible," Wren recommended.

"Very good, we hit them where it hurts before they even realize we've done it. We're already intercepting them miles before they will ever get to Constantine," Atreus started. "What of their numbers?" He turned to his master spies.

"Our eyes on the continent say they're gathering their entire army, lots of Ravenyr's soldiers have been forced into serving Findaria," Rowan said.

"Who's making these calls without Hadeon?" Amara asked.

"Rase and Ender," Atreus informed her.

"They aren't employing their own armies. They're mobilizing Hadeon's army primarily. Right now we are looking at about two-hundred Nephilim and two-hundred human men," Hyde nodded. Elichai and Atreus were standing over the map, writing various numbers, and moving stone pieces.

"Humans are being forced into this?" Amara was horrified. She knew there were human guards and soldiers but she always assumed with the power of the Nephilim that they were tasked with smaller feats, not full-scale wars. Kit elbowed her.

"Where did we land on using Deimos' abilities?" Prince Elichai turned to his brother.

"We allow him to believe we are fighting alongside him. We do not restrain him until my order. We take him alive," Atreus answered. Elichai glanced over at her, confirming their plan would remain the same.

"His abilities?" Wren asked for clarity.

"Summoning creatures from the underworld. We'll call that plan B." Prince Elichai grinned.

"I'd prefer not to call creatures of hell to my kingdom if at all possible," Atreus said. "Findaria is now crawling with them, I have no doubt."

"Helena is working with the witches now to raise wards around the outer border of the continent. They will also be strengthening our inner wards," Hawk informed the group.

"Amara, I have a task for you specifically." Atreus turned to her, his crown allowing only a few strands of his hair to tumble toward his forehead. She felt the room's attention follow and swallowed hard.

"You're going to set fire to their ships before they can reach the coastline." Her mate grinned proudly. A few of the council gasped, clearly not aware of her abilities.

"But I—" she started.

"Lessons start tomorrow." Kit stopped her. *How would she head for Deimos if she needed to be in the air taking down ships?*

"They seek to free Hadeon, your majesty. Shouldn't we consider killing him before they get the chance?" Commander Hale asked. *He had a point.*

"I mean to make an example out of him. I will ensure they do not set foot on this side of the map again," Atreus growled his promise. Even Amara froze, not usually so easily intimidated by him. Silence swallowed the room before he spoke again. "Commander Hale, do you have an update on the release of the newly transitioned Nephilim?"

"They've all been moved to the training sector. I hope you will come speak to them. They are not adjusting well." He shook his head. "Two of them are restrained as we speak. They are annoyingly combative/"

"They don't understand where they are or why," Amara snapped at him. "They were taught that nothing outside of the Hallowed's realm even exists and you expect them to begin training for a war against everything they've ever known?"

Commander Hale stared at her, clearly furious at her assertion. Or maybe angry that her statement undermined him in a way. His fist clenched as he wrestled with what she assumed were feelings of indignation. She didn't break eye contact with him, she wouldn't be intimidated.

"Are you suggesting that I have not tried to explain it to them?" He sneered at her. "You only just got here, do not pretend to be one of us! Do not claim to know how I handle my army!"

Atreus began to speak but was cut off.

"I don't care what she was suggesting. You will mind your tongue when you speak to her." It was Kit who stood with a fist slamming on the table. Wren and Hawk looked between the men. "But she doesn't know the half of..." Hale stood.

"Sit down," Atreus roared at him, sitting him immediately. Kit remained standing, he knew his king wasn't speaking to him.

"She is King Atreus' mate and she will be treated with the same respect that he is," Kit demanded. She had never seen anger flare so bright in his eyes. She was starting to see why he was tasked as her personal guard.

"Yes, Captain." Hale smiled sarcastically.

It was only then that Amara understood that Kit's title as Captain of the Royal Guard placed him above the commander of Atreus' entire army

"I will not tolerate another instance where you speak to her in such a way," Atreus spoke to Hale. He turned to Kit. "Thank you, take your seat, Zalser."

"When will she be crowned our queen? Her position here needs to be established," Prince Elichai said. "Quickly."

She glanced over at Atreus.

"I already consider her my equal in every way," Atreus informed his brother.

"As do I, but she must make the official ascent before the kingdom," Prince Elichai insisted.

"I am aware of the necessity and have begun the preparations." Atreus turned to Amara. "My love, we have much to discuss about this in private." She nodded, unsure of what accepting that role would entail. She had assumed that accepting him as her mate and being titled 'Lady of the Kingdom' was essentially being his queen.

"Since we're here, brother, I have a slightly smaller issue to bring to the table." Prince Elichai kicked a leg up onto the table. He sipped some kind of liquor from the bar.

"Does it pertain to the war?" he asked. Elichai paused to think.

"I'd argue that it does." He grinned.

"Proceed." Atreus gestured.

"Well, you've dismissed the royal court's consorts." He held his hands up as if appalled. "Every last mistress and paramour have been relieved of their positions. I find myself..." Elichai trailed off. "Bored."

Atreus let out a breathy laugh. "What exactly does your lack of sexual pleasure have to do with the upcoming battle?"

"I have to agree with the prince," Hawk spoke up. "Helena has been especially agitated. We have grown used to their services."

It took a moment but Amara finally gathered what it was exactly that the paramours and mistresses were responsible for.

"I find that I am better able to focus when I am satisfied." Elichai shrugged lazily.

"Brother, I do not doubt your abilities to lure people into your bed chambers." He laughed to himself. Elichai smiled but shook his head as though enjoying some private joke.

"I believe I share in the royal court's joy that you have found your mate, but we miss our companions very much. My lady, what is your opinion on the court's consorts?" Prince Elichai turned to her.

"I..." she trailed off. Not exactly loving or hating the thought of various people warming Elichai or Atreus' bed. She would address *those* feelings later. She felt her cheeks heat. "If they held that position willingly, I see no issue with it," she concluded.

"See." Elichai smiled smugly. "The Lady understands."

"I will revisit the matter of the royal court's consorts after the battle." Atreus sighed.

Amara's thoughts were drifting into sexual fantasy and she didn't like that she was intrigued by the thoughts of other people in bed with her and Atreus. Elichai stretched his long legs out on the tabletop and rolled up his sleeves. He was nearly as attractive as his brother. She wondered if he and Atreus ever pleasured someone together. *No, stop.*

"Greedy girl, would you have me invite the prince into our bed?" Atreus' voice came in her mind. She jumped, the muscles in the pit of her stomach tightening. She met his burning sapphire eyes; she knew her entire face was red.

"I want to see the newly transitioned Nephilim," she informed the council by way of breaking the sexual tension between herself and the king. He grinned, knowingly.

"You will see them in the morning. I intend for us to visit them at the training sector," Atreus reassured her though there was an underlying promise of what would occur for the remainder of the evening.

"All right, if no one else has anything to add, we can conclude this meeting," Prince Elichai spoke. Everyone glanced at each other from across the aged 0wooden table but no one had anything to add.

She grabbed Kit's arm to get him to stay while the others left through two separate exits. Atreus waited to see what they needed.

"You did well, Zalser, but you pissed off Hale," Atreus told him. He was taking notes presumably from the meeting. Though she picked up on the shift of his leg, the tapping of his fingers. Her daydreaming had him distracted with need.

"I can take him. I don't care if he's pissed off. Just as long as he doesn't touch her." He pointed at Amara.

"I want to see Hadeon," Amara blurted. Atreus seemed as though that might be the last thing he expected her to ask.

"Absolutely not. No one sees him." He shook his head. Kit gave her an 'I told you so' look.

"Even if Kit takes me?" She batted her eyelashes at him. He wasn't having it.

"Kit doesn't know where he is. No one does," he disputed.

"Can you take me?" she asked.

"No," he answered far too quickly. Kit was making a face that said it physically pained him to hear the conversation.

"Well, I'm going to get to work on those arrows." Kit dismissed himself.

"Why do you want to see him?" Atreus stood and pulled a book from the shelf behind him.

"Why wouldn't I?" She chose to be vague instead of outright lying.

"It's not safe," he said disapprovingly.

"It will be if I go with you," she reasoned.

"I will consider it. I'll need to ensure he is properly restrained."

He took his seat again and began searching for something in the book he retrieved. She moved behind him, feeling the need to touch him. She would never tire of watching him control a room. The way he carried himself as the Praeceptor was similar to how he carried himself as King Atreus. He was confident, demanding, and intelligent.

She rubbed at his shoulders, which were more squared off in the suit style jacket he was wearing. She kneaded into his strong muscles, pushing the tension out of them with slow circular motions. He exhaled and slouched into her touch.

She moved her fingers to graze the skin on either side of his neck, watching the small goosebumps form beneath her touch. He rolled his head back slightly and she used her nails to massage his scalp. Her fingers found the intricately designed crown and she started to remove it with a mischievous grin.

"Brat." He drew out the word in a warning. She knew that no one was supposed to touch the crown, much less remove it.

"Your majesty," she whispered a mockingly similar warning in his ear as she adjusted the crown on his head.

He gripped her hands, stopping her. He abruptly pulled her into his lap. She found herself laughing as he regarded her with a wide smile.

"So why don't you tell me about the little fantasy you were having during the strategy meeting?" His gaze turned hungry, curious. He pushed the hair from her face and held her cheek.

"I have no idea what you're talking about," she said shyly.

"No?" He bit his lip and ran a hand up her thigh. He kept going until he pushed his hand up her shirt. "I'm not against sharing your body for the purposes of worshiping it." She met his eyes, not quite able to believe what he was saying. "As long as I have your heart," he whispered. His hand moved up until it rested between her breasts before he leaned down to kiss her .

"But what if I don't want to share you?" She sucked on her bottom lip and gripped his hair. She thought of Molvina who she killed purely out of jealousy.

"Then you don't have to." He brought her hand down from his hair and kissed it. "Sex with others is purely for fun, not affection. No one else will ever have my heart and I'm content to never touch another person as long as I have you."

"I might have to think about it," she said shyly. She didn't know how she would ever be able to adjust to having his love.

"You make the calls, my love." He kissed her until they were both breathless. His hands explored her body and she moved to straddle him. "I only wish to indulge your every fantasy."

"Even if that fantasy includes this carefully organized strategy table?" She glanced back where models of soldiers were scattered on a map and plans were written out.

He slid his chair backward and stood, forcing her to her feet. "As long as you don't mess anything up," he growled and spun her around.

He bent her forward over the table, knocking over two of the strategy pieces.

"Pick them up." He huffed and dropped down behind her. He pulled down her pants while she fumbled to put the pieces back on the map.

He started kissing her calves, her thighs, gripping her ass. She grabbed both sides of the table while he bit and sucked at the delicate skin of her ass. She grunted and groaned as he drew blood but he reveled in making her squirm. She tried to push herself back against him, begging for friction where she pulsed with need.

She stared forward and tried to control her moaning as he bit and nipped at her again and again. He slid his fingers into her slowly. She watched the door near the circular portal on the opposite side of the room. He added another finger and licked at her clit, pulling moans from deep within her. The thrill of having the king on his knees devouring her in his strategy room was all-consuming.

He played her body with the skilled precision of someone who had been doing it for centuries. He twisted his fingers and began pulling at that spot deep within her. His experience was endless, his abilities infinite. He controlled when, if, and how she orgasmed and she loved it. He pulled her closer and closer to that edge until her insides twisted painfully. Her orgasm kept winding tighter and tighter as he curled his fingers inside of her and bit down on her ass.

She could feel him freeing himself from his pants and her mouth watered in anticipation. She bit down on her arm to silence her screams as her orgasm seized her violently. He didn't stop hitting that spot, spurring her on for what felt like forever. She didn't know where she ended and he began; her orgasm left her shaking as he worked her quickly. It was nearly becoming painful when he ripped his fingers from her tender flesh and pushed his massive cock into her.

"Ah fuck, Atreus." She winced. She shot her arms out to try and steady herself but ended up sending strategy pieces, pens, and compasses sprawling onto the floor.

"You're making a mess, brat," he growled. He sprawled his hand on her back. She could feel how wet his fingers were from being inside of her. "Fix it."

She tried to grapple for the pieces that were still on the table but he started fucking her harder. She tried to put her head down on the table as she took each thrust but he pulled her hair so that she was forced to look at the strategy map she laid waste to.

She was becoming lost in him when her keen sense of hearing alerted both of them to someone approaching the door to the room. It could only be someone on the royal council that knew about the secret entrances.

"Come here." He pulled out of her, grabbed her around her throat and sat in the chair. He brought her down onto him quickly and roughly. His hand shot up to her mouth as she groaned, stretching all too quickly to his girth.

The table came up to her waist and if the person didn't enter the room completely they might be fooled. *Right?* He tensed his cocked inside of her and gripped her hips. He slid her back and forth, drawing whining sounds from her throat. It felt good, way too good. She grabbed the armrests of the wooden chair. *Fuck.*

"Brother, I..." Prince Elichai entered the room with various pages. He knew. He knew immediately. She stopped moving. Prince Elichai stopped moving. The room fell into a knowing silence as wide eyes met wide eyes.

Chapter 40

Atreus' hand snaked around her throat, the other around her stomach and pulled her closer to him, further *onto* him.

Elichai swallowed hard, his eyebrows darting up as he met his brother's stare.

"I should go," Elichai finally choked out. His golden locks fell untamed around his forehead, his gray eyes were blown wide, and she could sense his arousal. She shifted; Atreus pulsed his cock inside of her. Elichai's throat bobbed as he searched the room, waiting for Atreus to dismiss him.

"Unfair," she said to him mentally.

"Elichai, how long were you going to hide the fact that you kissed Lady Amara?" Atreus taunted and tensed his cock inside of her. Elichai froze, shock evident on his face.

"My king, I didn't know..." He shook his head. There was significantly little fear from Elichai but it was clear he meant no disrespect to his king.

"I know." He rolled his hips, not hiding it. Amara cleared her throat and tried to shift upward. He only tightened his grip on her throat and around her midsection.

"Tell me you want him gone and I will dismiss him," Atreus growled into her mind. It was a test, he could sense the thrill she felt of Elichai being in the room.

"She didn't tell me after she found out it was you." He tutted and rolled his hips again. Elichai backed up a step, trying to find a way to witness what they were doing in the utmost respectful manner. "She seems to forget about our pesky little mental bond," he breathed.

"I never would have kissed her if I knew, I swear it," Elichai assured him. Atreus knew that. Even Amara knew that.

Atreus moved his hands to her hips. He pushed them forward and pulled them back. She moaned involuntarily. Elichai's eyes shot to her at the release of the sound. She could nearly see his rapid breathing, his heart hammering. His jaw was tense but she held his eyes and did as Atreus was instructing her to. She rode him slowly, biting down on her lip. The prince turned and exhaled through his teeth. He was wild, wound tight with need, and he was trying to get a grip on it for the sake of his king.

"She doesn't want you to go, brother," Atreus informed him. Elichai had his palms on the wall, the papers hanging pointlessly there. He dropped his head and shook it, a small chuckle escaping.

Prince Elichai was alluring, charming, secretive... something about him drew her in. It was wrong, so very wrong but as Atreus pulled her down onto him, she felt greedy. She could see the muscles tensing in his back, between his strong shoulder blades, and down to his thin waist. The white tunic hung loose on him, his dark pants accentuating his strong legs.

What was so sensual about having sex in front of someone else?

"My king, my lady, I do not wish to do anything disrespectful," he spoke slowly.

Amara felt so powerful as she took control of riding Atreus, Prince Elichai unable to even look at them. She raised up slowly and lowered herself all the way down his length. It was mind-blowing, it somehow felt *better*. She knew it was the thrill of someone else in the room, the power being placed in her hands over the two gorgeous men.

"Fuck," Atreus hissed and laid his head back against the chair.

"Prince Elichai," she breathed, pleasure and venom in her voice. He looked over his shoulder slowly. "Do you wish to leave?" She tilted her head at him and moved back down onto Atreus who was wrapping her hair in his hand.

He thought for a moment, carefully crafting his answer.

"I'd like to do whatever you wish of me," he answered. *Clever.*

She would not have both of them unless it's what she absolutely wanted. Atreus stilled her and began thrusting.

"What do you want him to do, love?" Atreus hissed into her ear. She didn't know, she had never been with two people at once.

"I want you to decide," she whispered to her mate who grinned wickedly.

"Elichai." Atreus gestured for him to approach them. "She's beautiful, is she not?"

Elichai took a cautious step forward.

"Exceptionally so, my king." He exhaled shakily. Another step. Her eyes scanned his body, he clocked it.

"Kneel," Atreus demanded while she rocked back and forth on him. Amara couldn't take in the magnitude of the situation fast enough. The prince was kneeling before her while Atreus allowed her to use his body for her own pleasure.

Atreus snaked his hands up her torso, removing her shirt quickly. Prince Elichai's gray eyes scanned over her body, seemingly unbothered by her riding his brother. *Not really brothers*, she reminded herself.

Her nipples were hard and poking through the lace of her bra. Elichai seemed almost pained by the sight.

"Worship her," Atreus breathed.

Elichai's hands started on her hips and moved up over her ribs. He licked his plump, pouty lips. He squeezed her ribs and swallowed hard before taking her breasts in his hands. She moaned and rolled her head back onto Atreus' shoulder. Elichai's lips parted, he was captivated.

Amara gripped his head and pulled him up toward her breasts where he started to nip at one of her nipples through her bra. The light stubble forming on his face was darker than his blonde hair and she could feel it prickling her skin. He pulled her other breast free of the bra and rolled her nipple between his fingers.

Atreus groaned as it forced her to tighten around his cock. She rolled her hips hungrily while Elichai's other hand rested on her hip.

"You deserve to be worshiped endlessly," came Atreus in her head. She reached her hand back and twisted it into his hair.

Elichai's hand traced over her stomach until he found her clit at the apex of her thighs, just above where Atreus was thrusting into her. She leaned forward, changing her angel so that Atreus could take her harder and deeper.

Elichai tilted his head up to watch her, his mouth agape as he rubbed her clit. She screamed for them, Atreus' nails digging into her hips. Elichai seemed to pick up on her likes fairly quickly and seized her throat with his other hand. He squeezed hard, not showing nearly as much mercy as her mate.

She was lost in pleasure, consumed by so many different sensations that the only way her body could respond was through a mind-blowing orgasm. Elichai raised up on his knees and sucked hard on her nipple as she came, his fingers working her while Atreus pounded into her. She screamed into the strategy room; her vision spotted with black from Elichai choking her.

"I fucking love you," was all she could think, all she could send to Atreus as the orgasm rattled her.

"That's sweet love, but we're just getting started," he purred back through the bond.

Elichai stood as if Atreus' gave a silent queue. The way they seemed to understand how to work around each other showed her they had shared someone *or someones* before.

Elichai moved through one of the secret doors but her mind was reeling still after her orgasm. She stood off of Atreus but he picked her up under her legs and carried her through the door to their bed chambers. It was Elichai who opened the door for them. He nodded at Amara with a wicked smile and kicked the door closed behind them.

They're fucking perfect, too perfect. Far too beautiful. How was she supposed to handle both of them?

Atreus laid her on the bed. Only her bra remained so she tugged the blanket over her. He leaned on the bed frame, watching her for a moment. His eyes were nearly glowing that deep blue of his. He was breathtaking, though she didn't recall when he pulled his pants back on. His hard cock fought against the cotton material. He seemed to be calculating his next move when Elichai appeared beside him. The men stood before her, like marble sculptures given life. They were cut, toned, powerful creatures and her mind whirled at the sight before her.

Atreus whispered in his brother's ear whose eyes darkened as he fixated on Amara. She tugged the blanket to her chest tighter, moisture building between her legs in anticipation.

"I've instructed Elichai to fuck you," Atreus informed her with crossed arms. "Would you like that?"

"Wha—" she glanced between them. "What about you?"

"We have all night." He smirked.

"You shouldn't hide yourself," Prince Elichai tugged his shirt over his head and crawled up the length of her body. He was thin, lean. His pale chest was inked in spiraling designs that she hardly had time to inspect.

"There's no part of you that will go untouched tonight," Atreus promised. She thought she saw him materialize something into his hand but was distracted by Elichai.

He pulled the blanket off of her and she watched his shoulder muscles flex as he leaned down into her neck. His tongue was warm and foreign but he traced it up to her jaw where he nipped her skin. He propped himself with one arm but pulled one of her legs upward, her other one following it.

She looked around for Atreus but didn't find him. The thought that she was doing something wrong left as soon as it appeared. Elichai reached down and slid a finger into her, moaning in approval at how wet she was. She whimpered when he pushed a second finger in.

"Would you like me to be gentle with you, my lady?" he asked playfully.

"No," she whimpered and rolled her hips to feel his fingers deeper.

She sprawled a hand on his chest, needing to feel his sculpted body. She used her other hand to tug at his pants. He removed his fingers and pinned her hands above her head. His face was close to hers and she wanted to kiss him again, to taste his lips again. She leaned up but he backed up slightly with a teasing grin.

"I told you she's greedy." Atreus finally appeared near the head of the bed. Elichai moaned his approval.

"I want her begging for us to stop by the end of the night," Elichai growled. His words pulled at something dark within her.

She wanted to beg him to hurt her, she wanted them to use her until she was nothing.

"I look forward to it," she teased. Elichai nodded at Atreus who grabbed one of her wrists.

"Hey, what the hell are you—" she started. He skillfully tied a rope around her wrist before pulling it taught and fastening it to a hook in the bed post.

She was watching Atreus' long fingers work the rope, lost in how swiftly they finished the job. She didn't even notice that Elichai had moved down her body until his tongue teasingly circle around her clit, not fully giving her the respite she needed. His tongue harassed her as he danced around her entrance and never plunged into her. It was maddening.

Atreus was tying up her other arm and she was squirming in frustration beneath his brother. She watched him take pleasure in her frustration, the dull candlelight of the room casting his hair a brighter shade of gold. She looked at Atreus pleadingly, he only smirked.

Assholes.

It was then that she remembered that technically she had power over him. She decided to try and use it.

"Damn it, Elichai, if you don't fuck me with your tongue or your cock I'm going to—" he cut her off by pushing his tongue into her. He lapped at her and flicked it up and down her entrance. She rested her ankles on his shoulder as he tasted her clit, flicking it in a way that made her twitch.

"You're going to what?" His breath sent chills through her but he shoved his tongue deep into her. She was panting, her eyes wide, and she was gripping the ropes.

"You're fucking beautiful." Atreus crawled to one side of her. He brought his lips down and kissed her hard.

She moaned into his mouth as Elichai devoured her hungrily. Atreus' tongue fought with hers, Elichai's circled her clit. She was a panting mess of moans when Atreus bit down on her neck. He bit until she bled, until she was screaming his name. She kissed her mate again, tasting her own blood on his lips.

Elichai removed his mouth and pulled her down closer to him by her hips. Atreus smiled at her, knowingly. He pushed her legs open, Atreus holding one knee back and sucking on her nipple.

Prince Elichai pushed himself into her with a breathy groan. She found herself being stretched with a similar painful pleasure she got from Atreus. He steadied himself as though trying not to come apart immediately. She tightened herself around him, drawing a whimper from deep in his chest.

"Play nice, brat. I took away his playthings, remember?" Atreus warned and bit down on the swell of her breast. That time it wasn't her fault when she clamped down on the prince's cock.

Elichai moved. He didn't hold back. He took no prisoners as he drilled into her. He gripped her around her hips, pinning them to the mattress as he shoved every inch of himself into her. Their breathing filled the room; Amara shifted between screaming and moaning into Atreus' mouth. She couldn't touch either of them, she was at their mercy.

Atreus suddenly had a dagger which caused her to smile in excitement. She had grown to adore their blood play. Elichai's eyes flickered open and met hers when Atreus shoved his bleeding wrist into her mouth. The blood heightened her senses and made her nerves spark to life. She could feel every inch of Elichai striking every nerve inside of her.

She exploded, screaming through the blood lust and mind-numbing sensation of the men using her body.

"Fuck." Elichai panted. She looked down and could see that she had soaked him all the way up to his stomach. *Shit.*

"Good girl," Atreus praised and kissed her. Elichai pulled himself from her, leaving her confused because he hadn't finished.

They flipped her onto her stomach, the ropes having enough give that her arms were forced to be crossed in front of her. They burned more in that position but it was a welcome sensation with her throbbing pussy. Her hips were brought up, her ass in the air. They forced her onto her elbows which caused her wrist to cross even more painfully. She glanced back to try and anticipate what or who was going to happen next.

Elichai moved so that he was in front of her at the head of the bed, kneeling between the ropes that held her. He pushed her hair back and forced her head up to look at him. His cock was not inches from her mouth, her tongue darted out to moisten her lips in anticipation.

"You better hold on, little nymph," he taunted and glanced at Atreus who she felt appear between her legs. *Little nymph.*

Oh fuck. She knew what was coming.

Elichai tightened his grip on her hair and shoved his cock into her mouth. He pushed to the back of her throat until she choked and gagged. He pulled out teasingly before burying himself in her throat again, stretching in painfully. She was a mess of saliva before long. Atreus teased her entrance before finally pushing his entire cock into her.

Atreus took her at maddening speed but she couldn't move, her mouth was around Elichai's cock, his hands steadying her head. She drooled and choked which he seemed to love, earning groans and swears periodically.

She didn't know how much time passed before Elichai tore his cock from her mouth so that she could catch her breath while Atreus continued his assault on her pussy. He scratched at her sides until they bled and she screamed empty threats at him. He laughed a breathy laugh.

"Ask nicely for my cum, my lady," Elichai ordered with amusement as he stroked his cock. She shook her head with a cocky grin. She wanted to see what he would do. He clearly wanted to cum, but she wouldn't let him so easily.

"Don't be a vrat," Atreus warned. She could sense the amusement in his voice.

"Why not?" She looked back at him and tightened herself around him as he withdrew. He sneered at her and removed himself completely.

She didn't know where the item came from and it took her a moment to figure out what *it* was. But Atreus brought a wooden cane down across her ass. Elichai had moved so when she jumped forward she was on her face, painfully entangled in the ropes.

He hit her again, causing her to groan. Elichai was cutting the ropes as she got angrier. Her arms were freed so she lurched off of the bed away from the men with a laugh. She was satisfied that she had come so many times and neither of them had yet. Atreus spun the cane in his hand and approached her; she grinned and bolted before he got to her.

Elichai grabbed her around the waist and wrestled her onto the bar. She thought she heard him laugh but she wasn't sure. It was cold and she giggled when he held her down until Atreus retrieved some other toy. It was her favorite one, the one with the leather tails that hurt like a bitch.

He handed it to his brother who winked at her before bringing it across her breasts. She screamed and thrashed but Atreus was pinning her across the bar. Elichai hit her again across the front of her thighs and she groaned but laughed hysterically leaving both the men intrigued.

"She likes pissing us off," Elichai surmised. Atreus nodded, eyes hooded.

Elichai discarded the whip thing and stood between her legs. The bar was the perfect height for him to grip her legs and thrust into her quickly. Her head hung off of the other side of the bar. She was so overcome with whatever mixture of bliss, excitement, and pain that all she could do was let out little breathy laughs as he fucked her.

"Do you like it when I watch you get fucked by someone else?" Atreus came into view with a satisfied smile.

"Mhmm." She closed her eyes as her orgasm built once more to a blinding level.

"Do you have any protests to being filled with cum now little nymph?" Elichai asked. His voice was sultry, husky. She couldn't respond though because Atreus forced her jaw open and shoved his cock into her mouth.

She was upside-down, allowing his cock to stretch her throat to a painful degree. Though it was painful, she wouldn't tap out. She wanted both of them to finish in her, she was blind with need to have them both come undone because of her. She gripped Atreus' hips and moaned around him, drawing out groans as he approached his climax. Meanwhile Elichai was pounding into her, chasing his own release. She wasn't going to be able to hold off her own orgasm for much longer. She was determined not to orgasm without them .

Atreus' hips stilled and he moaned her name as he came down her throat. She was dizzy from being upside-down but swallowed all of him. When he removed his cock from her mouth she lifted her head to look at Elichai who was about to finish too.

"Fuck." He rolled his hips into her again. He threw his head back and bit his lip which was enough for her to come apart again. Her orgasm drew his out and he roared as he thrusted viciously into her, giving her every ounce of his seed.

Atreus was holding her head up and gently massaging her scalp. Elichai steadied himself on the bar and removed his cock from her.

She adjusted so that she was laying longways on the bar instead of across it and panted.

"You never cease to amaze me," Atreus praised into her mind. She blinked over at her beautiful mate who was running his fingers through his hair.

"I love you," she said aloud to him, though she meant to say it mentally.

"Aw I'm flattered, my lady, but—" Elichai turned with a glass of liquor from the bar.

"Not you," she cut him off and shoved him.

"I love you too." Atreus kissed her. "I'm going to run you a bath." He stood and disappeared into the washroom. Elichai was retrieving his clothes from random parts of the room.

She was absolutely spent and partially in disbelief at what just happened. She was so tired that she didn't even care that she was bare naked on a wooden bar. Elichai brought her a blanket and she sat up, wrapping herself in it. She made a mental note to clean it after her bath.

"What was in the papers you were bringing Atreus before..." she trailed off, cheeks heating.

"Correspondence about the current location of the warships from Findaria." He pulled his shirt over his head. She nodded.

"We'll take a look at them." She smiled shyly.

"Am I free to go?" he asked Atreus when he emerged from the washroom.

"Amara? Will you be needing his services anymore this evening?" Atreus teased her, she scowled at him. He gave her a cocky grin.

"No, Prince Elichai. Thank you," she answered awkwardly. He smiled as though he was going to make a joke but spared her.

"Goodnight, my lady," he half bowed. "Brother." He nodded his greeting and exited.

Atreus carried her into the washroom upon the prince's exit. He took a spot on the floor next to the clawfoot tub and began pouring water over her back. They sat in silence for a moment as he cared for her. She met his eyes and sighed, satisfied.

"Oh, you'll need this," he summoned something and handed it to her. It was a vile of clear liquid, corked shut.

"What is it?" She inspected it, glancing over at him.

"Contraceptive." He gestured for her to take it. *Of course.*

She could procreate outside of the Hallowed's realm, Elichai could too. She may be safe from pregnancy with Atreus but not anyone else. She threw it back without hesitation. *Babies? Not happening. No way.*

After she washed her hair, he braided it back into a long braid that fell down her back.

"You once told me you learned to braid because you had two sisters," she started.

"Not exactly sisters." He cleared his throat. "It's a part of after-care that I learned many years ago."

"Oh," she was once again reminded of his limitless experience. "Have you and Elichai." She glanced at him nervously. "Shared someone before?" She felt like it was obvious that they had but she wanted to know.

"We have." He nodded. "It's okay if you enjoyed it, you know?" He tilted her chin so she turned to look at him.

"I just never thought that I would do something like that." She laughed lightly.

"It's more taboo amongst humans. You'll find that life amongst immortals has a lot more sexual promiscuity," he gently rubbed a washcloth under her eye.

"Perhaps now Elichai will have an easier time focusing on the upcoming battle." She laughed again, referring to his complaints on the release of the royal court's consorts. Atreus laughed too, nodding in a 'touché' manner.

When Elichai threatened that no part of her would be left untouched, she expected that one of them would take her ass. But they didn't. Atreus knew what had happened to her with Marlowe. Perhaps he told Elichai it was a no-go. She was thankful for that, at least for the time being.

Atreus showered and stumbled into bed beside her where she was fighting sleep so she could fall asleep in his arms.

"I know you've never had a mate before. Was it different to see someone else with me versus other people you've been with?" She had been wanting to ask. She was trying to figure out if the roles were reversed if she would feel jealous to have someone pleasuring him alongside her.

"I feel extremely protective and territorial over you but I trust Elichai. I know his intentions. It was different to see you with

Avren. He wanted you all to himself even though I knew within my soul that you were mine," he explained. He was lazily running his fingers over her shoulder and down her arm. "Your sexual pleasure is separate from our mating bond."

"You're more a part of me than I am," she reached up and brushed his cheek. "I guess I feel guilty as though what happened should make you angry."

He held her palm open so she could see where his name was carved and kissed it gently.

"This shows that we are eternally joined, that your heart beats for me just as mine does for you. I believe it is only death that could separate us." He laced his fingers into hers. "Not sexual experimentation." He kissed her forehead. "As long as we both agree on who enters our bed chamber, I see no problem with it."

"And if I only want you from here on out?" she asked.

"Then I would honor that and my body will only be available to you." He shrugged lazily.

"We'll take it as it comes. I think we have bigger things to focus on this week." She kissed him hard.

"Bigger?" He glanced down at his erection beneath the comforter. "Really?" He smiled wickedly. She slapped his chest with a laugh and he rolled on top of her. "I'll never tire of you," he moaned.

She could never have enough of him, not emotionally or physically. She pulled him into her and they were lost within each other once more.

Chapter 41

A treus and Amara entered the training sector the following morning hand in hand, ready to face the surviving sired children from the Sanctum Metere. All twenty of them had been released and began adjusting to the massive training compound in which they were being housed. The facilities were far nicer than those at the Sanctum. The newly transitioned Nephilim were given their own rooms, which must have been a relief after the communal living they were used to or the cells following that.

Eyes followed them through the well-equipped training hall. Familiar faces filled the bleachers, anger and confusion contorting their features. Beck and Eros were the only ones who seemed happy to see Amara, though their mouths agape showed that they weren't prepared for who Cathmore turned out to be.

He was clad in the colors of the kingdom; silver, black, and royal blue. His hair neatly pushed from his head to accentuate his crown. He moved through the room, nearly floating, with an easy sort of confidence that Amara found herself trying to mimic.

Brenda could not talk her into wearing a dress. Though she did agree to the black corset and paired it with leather pants. She strapped daggers to her chest and thighs. She agreed to the clunky silver jewelry and a royal blue blazer-style jacket that hung off of her shoulders and over her arms. She fiddled with the rings on Atreus' fingers while they were entangled with hers.

Kit trailed behind them along with two other members of the royal guard who were only assigned to the king. She hadn't asked for their names but reminded herself to do so later.

"Please stand for King Atreus and Lady Amara," Commander Hale called to them. They stood sporadically and hesitantly as they glanced at each other. Amara was just glad they had all figured out how to put their wings away.

"Today I am not addressing you all as King Atreus. I understand that most of you are pissed off and confused. As such I will allow the expression of these emotions. I have asked my guards to stand down. You will not be punished for speaking your mind nor throwing insults my way." He glanced over at Commander Hale with a warning scowl. Amara felt tiny under her classmates' glares.

"So you were fucking your Praeceptor!" Fallon Mournstride exclaimed. She turned her head slowly and narrowed her eyes on him. The few that laughed quieted down quickly upon her eyes burning red.

"I didn't say my lady would tolerate such disrespect," Atreus quipped.

"Yes, I was sleeping with our Praeceptor. I am sure that comes as a shock to most of you," she stepped closer to the group seated on the stone bleachers.

"Slept her way to the throne," Avren whispered to Fallon. Both of them shook their heads.

"A throne that none of us knew existed," she snapped at him. "We are here now and he is my mate. However I came across that truth is of no importance."

"You killed Movlina! He's who she was talking about that day wasn't she?" Avren stood, sneering at her. He really was larger in build after his transition, the silver ring around his remaining eye was startling briefly.

"She was the murderess," Ambrose interjected with a shrug.

"You'll find that killing for him is the least of what I'm willing to do." She had it with Avren. He was becoming more incessant than Fallon and Davian combined.

"I'd advise you to get over yourself. She didn't choose you. Now sit down," Atreus roared at him. Avren hesitated but did so, sneering at Amara.

"So this place is really a sanctuary for sired children?" Diana spoke up.

"I run rescue missions to save sired children from the Hallowed's realm." Atreus nodded. "I was working under an alias when the war started. I tried to pull as many of you as possible."

"So we can fight your war?" Fallon asked.

"No. To save your lives. You will not be expected to fight with us. You are only training to learn to control your Imperiums before being offered a home here in my kingdom," he announced.

"Though I argue that you should fight to show where your loyalties lie," Amara turned to Atreus. It was part of the conversation they had prior to arriving at the training sector.

"I am content to have them swear fealty to prove their loyalties," Atreus said.

"What if we don't want to be here?" Avren snarled.

"Then you're free to go back to Findaria." Atreus shrugged. He seemed equally annoyed by Avren.

"So are you the queen?" Beck spoke for the first time.

"I am the Lady of the Kingdom as his mate." She gestured to Atreus. "I will accept the title of queen following the battle at the Western Cliffs," she announced. She thought she heard Kit clap with excitement behind her.

"Taking a queen is not something that has ever been done within my kingdom," Atreus explained over breakfast in bed that morning. "As you know, there was a Lady of the Kingdom in the past. That was her title and it looked a little different than it does now."

"How is it different?" she asked as he tore a bite off an apple.

"You're Lady of the Kingdom. That affords you a great deal of freedom and respect. You technically serve me as it stands now and you have very little power unless I were to leave or vanish. Even then

it has been arranged that Prince Elichai rules before a lady in that instance. Following how horribly wrong things went with the previous lady, I ensured that unless I took a queen, I would not hand power over again. The Lady of the Kingdom is a smaller role than it once was," he paused to take a bite of bread.

"Will you ever tell me what happened with her?" she asked .

"I will." He nodded. "I am not prepared to broach the subject yet."

"Anyway," he continued. "I never wanted another Lady of the Kingdom, so I didn't take one again. Not until you." He glanced at her longingly. "The role of my queen is never one I intended to fill," he chuckled to himself. "I molded the role in a similar fashion that other kingdoms do. Except I needed to be sure that my queen would not turn on me, that she was not out for her own personal gain."

The things he said were starting to fill in the puzzle of Lady Jane Cyperian.

"Okay..." Ahe didn't know where he was going with the explanation. She tried to imagine what the catch was.

"Through carefully crafted magic, a ritual will take place which ensures that you cannot turn on me or attempt to harm me in any way." His eyes were hooded. "You would bind yourself to me and become my equal. You will have every ounce of power and control that I do. You will make decisions with me instead of serving as an advisor."

"How does it ensure that I won't turn on you?" she asked.

"Any ill will you attempt to bestow upon me will also happen to you. You try to imprison me? Your body shuts down, making you a prisoner inside your own flesh. You attempt to kill me, you die in the

same manner." He was speaking rapidly. There was definitely anger in his voice. She couldn't help but wonder what she had done to him to create such an elaborate set of rules.

"But couldn't a Lady of the Kingdom just try to do those 958+things to you and get off scot free?" she asked.

"She could try, but without the ritual she would be nowhere near powerful enough to overpower me. Not to mention that as it stands now, she... well you have nothing to gain from harming me. For example, if you killed me now, Elichai would take over. What would be the point?" He shrugged but seemed amused at the thought.

"So I would grow in power? Again?" She was breathless, almost afraid.

"I don't believe it's quite as painful as transitioning to Nephilim," he offered. "We would be one, my love." "You are already my mate, my other half. This ritual to place you on the throne just puts us on an even playing field."

She wasn't sure if she could undergo another transition, if she could contain more power. She didn't even have control over the power she held presently.

"I already consider you my equal in every way, my Queen. This just makes it official. I have sat on that throne alone for hundreds of years. Even when she was here? I was empty, detached, my life felt it had no purpose. I'd never known true love— but I am so desperately in love with you, Amara, that I can't even think when you aren't by my side." He was pacing in the room. She was just wondering what benefit it gave him to share in his power when he spoke again. "You were part human; you existed in the human world as a sired child.

You know what I do here. I know that you are passionate about saving them the same way that I am."

She thought about Nicholas, the little boy in the street with the mark of the sired children over his heart. The joy she felt that he was free from what that mark meant in the Hallowed Realm was incredible.

"You are unbelievably strong and intelligent, my love. I know you have much to offer my home and my people. I have come to the realization that I don't want to do this without you. Your anger and passion sets me ablaze, you make me want to bring down the Cobalt Mountains to free the witches, you make me feel as though I can tear down the Hallowed, like I can end the slavery of humans in the northern continents... You wreck me and you complete me," he knelt before her and placed his hands on her legs. He wasn't pleading with her; no he was making sure she knew everything he felt for her.

"You aren't responsible for saving everyone." She took his face in her hands. His eyes were wild.

"You and I can make this world a better place my love," he breathed. She nodded and leaned her forehead against his. She felt as though if Katara were party to the conversation, she would be giddy with excitement.

"Then I'll do it," she decided. He jerked his head up to meet her eyes; he searched them frantically. "Following the battle."

"It ensures your immortality; you understand that, right?" He seemed worried, as though that would change her mind.

"So I tie myself to you forever?" she asked. "I've made worse decisions." She laughed .

He laughed with her and stood and planted a soft kiss on her lips. He pushed her backwards onto the bed and kissed every inch of her skin.

"Your education is to begin today. It is meant to deconstruct the indoctrination you've all undergone during your time in the Hallowed Realm," Atreus instructed the newly transitioned Nephilim.

"You will be taught the truth of the world which is vastly different from what you were taught to believe," Amara scanned the group.

"What about those of us who aren't here? Are they dead?" Eros asked, slouching. She realized that he lost Judas, Katara, and Juliet. Not to mention he didn't seem to be on good terms with Avren who shared a sire with him.

"We continue to search the Sanctum for them. We have their names, as well as the confirmed casualties. There are quite a few unaccounted for," Atreus answered. "I expect they are being forced to fight in the impending battle."

She knew there was a good chance that she would see some familiar faces on the other side. She couldn't imagine seeing Juliet fighting alongside the Hallowed. It made her skin crawl.

"What is the benefit in staying here?" another Nephilim asked.

"Sanctuary, safety. You will be given a home and work as well," Atreus told them. "You will not be forced into death games, nor will your children."

"We can't breed." Fallon scoffed.

"You can. Magic prevented it there, but you can in the rest of the world," Amara announced. The group looked dumbfounded, shocked.

"There is much more for you to learn but I thought it critical that we introduce ourselves and our purpose here. If you decide to stay upon the conclusion of that education, you may swear fealty and build a life in Constantine. If you choose otherwise, I will not keep you here. But once you leave, you do not get to come back," Atreus stated with finality. He brushed something off of his tailored suit and nodded to Commander Hale.

"Remain seated until the Royal Guards see them out," he instructed.

She stood by while he made arrangements with Commander Hale to release them for their lessons. He still would have to train them in flying and combat but he was relieved to hear he didn't have to make warriors out of them in a matter of days.

"Zalser," Atreus called for Kit who hurried to his side. "You may begin training with Lady Amara for her task in the battle."

"Wait." She turned to Atreus. "I need to talk to him." She nodded her head in Avren's direction. He exhaled slowly but nodded his understanding. He held out a hand, signaling Kit to wait.

He spoke with Commander Hale who retrieved Avren. As he was guided in Amara's direction, he became more tense and agitated.

"We'll leave you two alone," Atreus said as they removed themselves from the situation.

"Avren." She sighed longingly.

He looked her up and down, disgust carefully camouflaging hurt. "I don't have anything to say to you, *my lady,*" he said sarcastically.

"But I have something to say to you," she asserted. "I cared about you, deeply," at this he scoffed. He pushed rolled up his sleeves over his larger arms and crossed them. "I still do," she insisted through gritted teeth.

"But not romantically? Is that it? Wanna patch things up and be the best of friends again?" he asked as he shook his head.

"I never cheated on you," she felt it needed to be said.

"Wow, thanks for that I guess," he sniped.

"What do you want me to say? I can't help that I fell in love with someone else, Avren!" She gestured dramatically.

"I was there for you." He stepped toward her. "It was me in the Abyss with you, it was me you clung to when it all became too much, I'm the one you stayed up talking to into the early morning..." he trailed off.

"I—" she was trying to say that those things still meant the world to her.

"He broke my fingers because I kissed you in the library, didn't he?" He slumped his shoulders.

"That's not fair, he dealt punishments to everyone. He even broke my wrist!" She was half shouting to get him to listen to reason.

"I never laid a hand on you, yet you call what you feel for him to be love? It is nothing more than blind infatuation because your souls are mated. Your choices are not even your own, Amara. They're his." He turned away from her.

"You're wrong." She sighed. She wouldn't argue the point. Those that didn't understand being mated couldn't be made to understand it. He didn't say anything, he only dropped his head. "So that's it then?"

"That's it." He turned to her and regarded her with familiar doe eyes. "I'm done. I can't just be your friend after falling in love with you."

His words felt like being punched in the lungs. She couldn't speak, couldn't think. He walked away, allowing Commander Hale to guide him back to the group.

"I'm ready," she told Atreus and Kit when she made her way back to where they retreated to give her privacy.

"Let's go, kid." Kit wrapped his arm in hers with a sharp toothed smile. Atreus regarded them with amusement but they skipped from the training facility, Kit humming some tune.

Chapter 42

K it led her down through the palace and into a smaller one of
the ivory colored buildings. She felt that there was a small
hole within her heart that had Avren's name on it. He was the kind
of person whose absence was heavier than others.

They came to a halt on the stoop of a massive house. Kit looked
around and then led her into the foyer while she wandered whose
home they had just entered unannounced. Massive marble staircases wound upward on her left and her right. Between them, the
centerpiece of the foyer was a statue of a Nephilim with a crown
atop his head. *That looks like...*

"My lady, Zalser!" Prince Elichai exclaimed from the balcony
above them. He wore his crown, nearly identical to the one on his
statue. "Give me a moment to dismiss my guests." He disappeared
again, padding away on bare feet, wearing loose-fitting pants and
an open button-down shirt.

Her mouth was dry, her face heated. How was she supposed to
interact with him after the night they had? She didn't realize she

had been staring at the balcony where the prince stood a moment earlier until Kit spoke.

"Amara?" Kit was waving his hand in front of her face. "Everything okay?"

"Mhmm." She swallowed hard and turned her attention to him.

"He's training with us?" she asked.

"He can wield the elements, fire being one of those." He nodded as though she was supposed to know that.

"Wait." She held up her hand. "What's your Imperium?" she asked, realizing she had never learned it. "I know you have telekinesis. Is that it?" She recalled him bringing her to her knees that night with the simple twitch of his fingers.

"Telekinesis is a very small part of my abilities." He smiled proudly.

"Tell me." She shoved his shoulder.

She followed him into a massive sitting room. Elichai's tastes were clearly extravagant. Everything seemed to be accented with gold, sprawling black sofas, a full sized bar with crystal bottles containing various liquors. Custom paintings adorned the walls. Each signed by artists whom she'd never heard of. There was a portrait of Atreus, of Elichai himself, and the rest of the royal court. The portrait of Kit showed him adorned in the colors of the kingdom and scowling at the artist who must have painted him.

"You look so cute!" she teased him.

"That was a long time ago, I did not want to sit for Elichai's portraits but he insisted." He rolled his eyes. She kicked her legs over him on the couch. He adjusted them on his lap and tilted his head back.

"You're going to burn me again. I just know it." He sighed.

"This time it'll be on purpose if you don't tell me more about your Imperium," she threatened.

"You've guessed that I was sired by Sylas so obviously that's where the telekinesis comes from," he started. She nodded. His blue hair was the first sign of his sire. "But I'm also a magic wielder because of my mother. It's not something that's common but I can do many things by drawing on the magic within me."

"So you can technically summon fire?" she asked.

"I can, it takes practice but it doesn't work the same as a true element wielder which is going to be more similar to what you do." He tightened a hand around her ankle to offer comfort. He could sense she was unsure of herself.

Amara thought about how she had magic in her bloodline too. She had learned that the fire and magma production of hers was nearly identical to Deimos' abilities. She sighed. Would she ever be able to tap into her ancestors magic? She realized then that her grandfather Orick was most likely under the Cobalt Mountains just like Katiana Zalser, like Kit's mother. He had no idea she was still alive. Guilt settled in her core.

"Kit, I think I need to tell you something." She sat up and turned to him. He furrowed his eyebrows, amused curiosity on his beautiful face.

"Absolutely not my love. There is a reason he is protected from that knowledge," came Atreus' voice in her mind.

"Get out of my head," she snapped.

He was right though and it wasn't her place to break that news. Atreus needed to. She heard Elichai speaking upstairs with whomever his guests were.

"Need to tell me..." Kit pushed. She was fumbling for something, anything else to say instead of the truth about his mother.

"I slept with Elichai," she blurted out. His mouth dropped open and he stood, pushing her legs off of his lap with a loud thud.

"You did what!" he exclaimed in shock. "Are you insane!"

"What did she do?" Elichai appeared in the doorway to the room, leaning against it with a cigar in hand. His crown was tilted, his hair messy. At least his shirt was partially buttoned this time.

What she didn't expect though, was the information to enrage her guard. Kit stormed over to Elichai.

"You touched the Lady of the Kingdom?" Kit slung his hand forward, an invisible force taking Elichai's leg out from under him.

"Kit, wait!" she exclaimed, sprinting across the room to her guard. He was just protecting her but what of his alliance to Prince Elichai?

"My lady, I beseech you to clarify the situation for your guard before I retaliate," Prince Elichai growled as he was taken to his knees. He gripped the door frame, his nails digging into the wood.

"Atreus knows! He was there," she squeaked and gripped Kit's shoulder.

"What?" Kit whirled on her in confusion. She saw the moment it clicked for him. "Oh." He looked between them. "Oh!" Color flooded his cheeks. "Lead with that!" He snapped at her before helping the prince to his feet.

"I am so sorry my prince." Kit bowed apologetically.

"You were doing your job." He shook his head.

Just then two men descended the stairs, one was clearly human, the other Nephilim, both young.

"Amara," Prince Elichai called her attention. "This is Ansel and Kenzo, two of the Paramours that Atreus dismissed."

They were both very handsome and looked thoroughly exhausted. They greeted her with polite nods and smiles. Both of them were redheads. *Does the prince have a type?*

"I believe your positions will be reinstated soon provided you still want them," she reassured them. They both nodded excitedly.

"Yes, of course. Thank you my lady." The Nephilim—Kenzo smiled. Elichai dismissed them.

She couldn't fathom how he had participated in a threesome the previous night and woke up needing another one. *Wow.* Then again she and Atreus indulged in one another after the threesome too...

"They showed up asking for work." Elichai shrugged lazily. "They were paid handsomely for their services." He grinned.

"Okay!" Kit clapped his hands. "There is entirely too much sexual tension in this room. We are training in fire wielding today so dress for that." He pointed to the Prince. "She and I will wait outside." He grabbed Amara's arm. She and Elichai were both laughing at him but she allowed him to usher her outside.

"What did you… how did you even?" Kit was pacing in front of her, dumbfounded yet delighted. She liked that about him, he made things feel exciting, feel juvenile and fun.

"Atreus and I were… you know." She blushed. "In the strategy room and he walked in." She glanced at him nervously, guiltily. He burst out laughing.

"So it was like 'hey, guys, oh let me get in on that,'?" he asked.

"Not exactly…" she whined, embarrassed.

"This is gold, I want to know more." He beamed. "I thought Atreus would kill someone for touching you." He took a seat on the stoop to Elichai's house.

"Me too." She laughed.

"Well, remind me not to touch that strategy table ever again." He wrinkled his nose.

"We had it cleaned! It's our bed chambers you should steer clear of," she joked. "Oh and the bar in there."

"You little freak! I knew it!" He was practically bouncing with laughter.

"Shut up! You are never going to hear the end of it when I learn about your sex life." She punched his arm.

"Good luck with that," he teased with a wink. Kit never gave much away about his sex life or romantic life. She took it as a challenge.

"All right, let's go." Elichai sighed behind them.

He appeared in leather and mesh fighting gear though there was no armor attached to it. He wore a weapons belt across his chest with various shining daggers and knives. He extended his blood red wings and they followed.

"No, no, no," Elichai huffed. She had burned down the wrong tree. "You're not focusing!"

Kit was hovering in the air next to her, not saying a word while Elichai tried for the seventh time to get her to hit the small sapling in the small forest.

"You are sending it from your palm; you need to send it from your fingertips. If you envision it coming from your fingertips, you will hit your target with more accuracy."

"A boat is bigger than a tree so I think I would have hit my target!" she snapped at him.

"You have had no training. You can't aim much less control the amount of flames you put out." Elicahi was frustrated. She wasn't arguing that point.

"Kit, can you go retrieve my brother? I think she needs some motivation," Elichai ordered.

"Motivation?" She raised her eyebrows.

Kit shook his head, signaling to her that she wouldn't like whatever Elichai was planning.

"Land and gather your strength," Elichai instructed.

She rolled her eyes at him. He was right though, flying and drawing on her Imperium left her feeling drained. She became excited that Atreus would be coming to the secluded side of the kingdom where they were training. She could use some of his blood. She found it to be the only thing she could focus on. She wasn't even paying attention to whatever Elichai was doing in the clearing to her right.

She dropped her head into her shaking hands. A lot was dependent on her ability to burn down those ships. Even if she hit them, Elichai was right, if she didn't hit them with enough power—it wouldn't do enough damage.

"You are trying to get me to will the flames from within me. I don't think that's how this works for me. I have an easy time with that concept when it comes to my wings and to phasing. This feels different," she explained to Elichai when he wandered back over to the log she was sitting on.

"But you are using your ability by force of will, you're just doing a bad job," he quipped.

"I just mean I feel like I need to do something else to access it." She sighed. She felt like something was pushing back against her every time she tried. It felt similar to when she was suspended from ropes the first time. Like she was just about to touch something powerful but couldn't quite grasp it.

Amara recalled what her transition felt like, where she got closer to that source of power. Atreus had once told her that transitioning put her closer to her ethereal form. What if she needed to get closer? What if the voices she heard were from the part of her that possessed magic? What if it was her ancestors? She didn't know why but that felt like the answer. It felt like tapping into that part of herself would give her more control over her Imperium.

"If you aren't having success through concentration and visualization or focus of will then I'm not sure what else will work. That's where my element wielding expertise ends." Elichai crossed his arms and put his weight on one leg.

"She has to channel it." Atreus landed alongside Kit. She hadn't even heard them flying in.

"Channel it?" she asked.

"Wait, do you come from a magical bloodline?" Kit asked.

"She only just learned that her grandfather is Orick," Atreus explained.

"As in The Warlock of the Land? Of what is now the Hallowed's Findaria?" Elichai pushed. She nodded to them. "Brother." He clapped Atreus on the back. "You have to stop keeping secrets about this one."

"It was her truth to tell," he said simply.

"Okay, so how do I channel this? What do I channel?" She huffed and stood. She became lightheaded immediately and swayed on her feet.

"Kit can explain channeling." Atreus sat her down gently.

I need blood, she informed Atreus through their bond. He nodded and tugged a dagger from her weapons belt. Elichai tilted his head in confusion when his king cut his own wrist, Kit jumped to stop him.

"Wha—" they both realized it wasn't a deep cut and froze when he placed it to Amara's mouth.

She latched onto her mate's wrist and took from him hungrily. She glanced up at Kit and Elichai who were dumbfounded by the sight. His warm blood went down like honey and began working on strengthening her.

"I could have brought some meat or bread..." Kit said with opened palms, awkwardly and shoved them into his pocket.

"She is my mate. Siphoning my blood strengthens her. Just as her blood does for me," he explained to the prince and her royal guard. They glanced at each other.

"Whoa," they said in unison.

She came to the understanding that mates were extremely rare, nearly a myth in most of the world. As such the practices and truths about them were blurred overtime. Not all mates could share blood but it was one of Amara's favorite things about being mated to Atreus. She pulled her mouth free and licked her lips. She felt as though she was ready to take on more hours of training. She was just relieved that she could put out so much energy before becoming drained. It made her realize just how weak she was when they began training.

"You're a child of the soil. That soil's primary elemental energy is fire... obviously," Kit started.

"I thought I could wield fire because of my sire?" She stopped him.

"Deimos can wield fire but he's more of a shadow and entity wielder," he corrected her. "You don't wield like your father does so this must come from or at least be strengthened by the magic in your blood."

"Why am I not even shocked that Deimos is your father?" Elichai threw up his hands and sauntered away playfully. "No one tells me anything," the prince and Atreus went after him. Amara laughed at the brothers.

She could hear them speaking in whispers in the distance but Kit continued.

"With channeling you can either draw on the elemental energy around you, which would be best on your home soil. Or you can channel the magic within you. It's more difficult but if you can contact your source of power at your core and strengthen that connection, that would be the best way to go," he explained as he spun a stick in his hand.

"When I was transitioning there were voices that I could almost touch..."she whispered, more to herself.

"Yes! Good! Your magic is a living breathing thing, it originates from those who lived before you,. Kit was excited and crouched down in front of her. "This is amazing!"

"I don't think we have time for me to master this before the battle. We have three or four days max." She sighed. Kit pursed his lips thoughtfully.

"You may be right. Bu..." He lifted a finger, an idea coming to mind. "You can phase right?" he asked.

"Yes?" She answered slowly.

"If we can practice phasing while flying, maybe you can get close enough to start small fires on the ships." He grinned. It was smart, brilliant even, but dangerous.

"I exhaust myself too quickly when I phase." She frowned. "But if we practice, I can realistically phase onto a few of their vessels and set fire where it'll hurt most."

"Brilliant!" His eyes lit up.

"You told Kit about last night?" Atreus stormed back to the stump she was sitting on, a smiling Elichai in tow.

"You know sometimes I think you guys can be a tad bit immature." She deflected and crossed her arms. "Don't we have bigger things to worry about?"

"I thought it went without saying that what we do in our bedroom stays with the parties involved!" he snapped.

"Not to mention *who* you do," Elichai instigated. They both scowled at him, wiping the smirk off of his proud face.

"I won't tell anybody." Kit squirmed.

"It just slipped out," she argued back at Atreus. He took a grounding breath.

"We will discuss this later," he promised. He had that threatening tone in his voice that pissed her off. She wasn't scared of him. Hadn't he learned that by now?

"What are you going to do? Punish me? *Praeceptor*," she purred tauntingly at him.

Elichai smiled at the audacity of her, his eyebrows raising as though impressed. Kit took a cautionary step away from the two. For all the talk of war, the conversation felt small, adolescent. Given her very little experience in the realm of having friends and engaging in gossip and drama though, she liked it.

"Zalser, leave," Atreus growled.

"Okay, wait," Amara held up her hand. She did not want whatever punishment came with him and Elichai alone with her in the woods. *Did she?* Kit paused, his wings still extended as he was preparing to take off.

"Leave, Zalser. I won't ask again," Atreus demanded. *Damn it.*

"Sorry, kid." He shrugged and disappeared into the sky.

"Well, this was fun, really," she backed up away from Atreus and extended her own wings. "But I have some practice runs to do."

Chapter 43

The punishment in question was in fact a punishment. Not the exciting kind oor the kind that might involve the two men taking her in the woods. No.

They thought it entertaining, given her previous fear of flying, to play a little game. They began by hauling her impossibly high into the sky. She didn't even know anyone could fly that high. The altitude alone seemed to weigh down her own wings. The king and the prince had to work hard against it themselves.

It was Elichai who suggested that a little harmless plummet to earth would encourage her to remember discretion. It was also Elichai whose face she clawed when they pitched her forward from the highest possible altitude with her wings tied down. It was triple as high as Kit had taught her to fly from and flying was out of the question. She couldn't even see through the clouds to the ground and she was pretty sure she passed out at one point.

She felt heavier and was falling faster than she ever had. Her flying lessons with Kit were nothing compared to it. Her wings were being wind whipped behind her, twirling painfully in the ropes. She couldn't get them to forcefully expand enough to break the ropes so that she could catch herself. She was too high up and it was too windy and her wings were too weak.

The brothers soared not far from her to ensure she wouldn't hit the ground if her wings failed her. They bantered with each other in amusement at her struggle, but she wasn't laughing. She was pissed off at the little game they made out of punishing her.

She thought of what Kit had said about phasing onto the boats and phased herself far away from them. It may have been stupid, especially with her wings bound. She didn't care. *Time to find out if I'm immortal.* She braced herself for the very high chance she had of landing within the canopy of trees. Luckily, she was able to direct herself over a large lake which she plummeted painfully into.

A storm of fury and humiliation crashed over her, violent and unrelenting. It yanked her back into the past, where memories twisted like jagged shards of glass. She was ten again, small and defenseless, her body aching from being shoved and beaten, the dull thud of fists echoing in her bones. The cold, unforgiving walls of her room seemed to close in on her as she curled up, choking on her sobs while the mocking laughter of her family sliced through the air like knives. Then she was fourteen, the wind biting at her bare skin as she wailed into the night, helplessly bound to a tree trunk by her peers.

She emerged from the lake, still far from Atreus and Elichai, blocking out Atreus from contacting her through their bond. She freed herself from the ropes and shot into the sky. Her thoughts moved faster than she could process them, hurt, betrayal, fury all molded together until the need for a friend seized her so deeply that she only had one place to go.

It's how she ended up sitting across from Eros in his room in the training sector. He pulled his long white-gold hair back into a ponytail. He was slouched against the wall and sitting on his single bed. She needed to talk to someone comforting and familiar about anything besides what she had just endured.

"I'm not mad at you," he reassured her. "Avren is losing it. I don't share his anger about all of this."

He had explained to her what occurred the night of the attack. There had been demon creatures pouring into the Sanctum and tearing down the guards. Nephilim were fighting in the air and on the ground, even Hadeon had joined in the battle.

Eventually some other soldiers showed up and found the sired children hiding in the tunnels under the Sanctum. Most of them had begun transitioning or died in the initial attack. They used magic to render them unconscious and then they awoke in those cells.

Amara and Eros talked the entire night, distracting her from what Prince Elichai and Atreus had done to her.

"We are trying to find Juliet." She placed a hand on his. He and Juliet seemed to have sparked a romantic relationship before everything happened. He had already lost his previous partner, Judas.

"I know." He nodded. "I know you won't give up on her."

"I'm sorry." She sighed. "For not telling you about Cathmore...well Atreus."

"You couldn't have. I understand," her friend smiled.

His smile wasn't as innocent and hopeful as it once was . The weight of the things he witnessed and the losses he endured weighed on him and creased his face.

"Is something else bothering you? You seem... upset. Like there's something you want to talk about," Eros spoke again.

"No." She inhaled and smiled . "I'm good."

Once the time dragged on past midnight, she figured it was time to leave him. Atreus had been pushing to speak to her through their mental bond but she kept shutting him down. She was, thankfully, getting better at that.

Resting while speaking to Eros didn't rejuvenate her the way Atreus' blood did but it did just enough that she took to the skies to teach herself to phase and sling fire in unison.

She was panting after about an hour, eight different Phases, and eight different trees lit ablaze. She was proud of herself though; she hit every mark she set for herself.

Amara knew she should have stopped; she really should have. But the seething anger that bubbled inside her, fueled by the cruelty of Atreus and Elichai, was impossible to ignore. Atreus was acutely aware of her deep-seated fear of heights; the panic she felt every time she tried to adjust to her wings and the anxiety of flying. He knew the depths of her past suffering, the raw edges of her pain. To exploit her fears so cruelly was not only a betrayal but a violation of the deepest kind.

Fueled by a tempest of rage, she shot herself skyward, the air whipping past her like a frenzied storm. Her ascent was brutal, a defiant push against the world that had wronged her. But as gravity reclaim her, she plummeted down with a fierce, reckless abandon. Just before she struck the ground, she phased through it, a split-second of liberation. She aimed herself at a towering tree, its bark gnarled and imposing, and with a furious burst of energy, she ignited it. The tree erupted in a blaze of fierce, unrelenting fire, turning to ash in a matter of moments.

The charred remains fell away as she soared through the space where the tree had stood. The ashes fluttered around her like the remnants of her frustration. She wasn't picturing Atreus directly, but the searing, destructive energy she unleashed was a cathartic expression of her rage against him, her need to channel her anger into something tangible.

Amara sprawled in the grass, staring at the night sky as she tried to catch her breath. She felt as though she passed over some threshold. A new level of exhaustion crawled over her body, making it harder to breathe. She needed to get home.

She wasn't far from the village at the foot of the palace so she settled for a long and slow walk home.

I need to get home.

I need to find Atreus.

Something is wrong.

"Fucking hell kid, there you are!" Kit exclaimed, landing behind her.

"Not now, Kit." She sighed. She was completely drained, utterly defeated, and pretty sure her legs would give out any minute.

She wiped her nose, confused at why it was running and was shocked to see blood. She paused as she started to choke up something. It was that same lava-like substance she had been choking up during her transition. More blood poured from her nose, splotches of black clouding her vision.

She had gone too far.

She pushed her body too far.

"Kit?" She turned to him. She registered his look of terror before collapsing onto her knees.

Chapter 44

ATREUS

"Where is he? Get me the king!" a voice shouted from the throne room.

Atreus bolted down the corridor and slid to a stop at the entrance. Zalser was panting, frantic. Atreus' heart nearly stopped to see Amara's limp frame in his arms, blood and liquid flame pouring from her face.

"What the hell happened?" He roared.

Zalser placed her onto the floor, shaking his head, tears filling his eyes.

"I don't know!" He exclaimed.

Atreus grappled at her neck, searching for her pulse. It was there but it was weak. She can't die; she would not die.

"She was setting stuff on fire at the base of the village," Zalser breathed.

"Healers! Go wake the healers! All of them!" He shoved Kit away and gathered her into his arms.

"Come on baby, wake up." He pushed her hair from her face.

He rushed her into their bedroom and laid her on the bed. He sliced his wrist and forced her mouth open. The blood poured into her mouth, filling it, and then spilled over the edges.

"Swallow it," he screamed. She couldn't hear him; she wasn't doing it. He massaged and rubbed her throat, only managing to get a little bit of the blood to go down. "Please,"

They hadn't learned if she were immortal or not. If she wasn't and she pushed herself too far, he knew he may lose her. He couldn't have that; he would not lose her. He didn't care what he had to do, it would not happen.

Guards had come into the room, checking on him, his screams echoing through the throne hall. Her heart was slowing, her pulse hardly detectable.

"My blood! She needs my blood," he shouted at the healers who were scrambling around the bed. He couldn't breathe, his world was closing in around him, he could feel her heart stopping.

Some of the healers were placing massive needles into her arms and another one took his already bleeding wrist. Both needles in both of her arms connected to a small funnel which he bled himself into. He watched the blood move through the clear tubing and into her. Everything was a blur. People were speaking to him, Zalser was trying his best to answer for him but he couldn't hear over the roaring in his ears.

Her features were still, soft. He had hurt her, scared her to prove a point and it may be the last interaction they ever had. It brought him to his knees. He had only ever gone to his knees for her.

"Please my love," he choked out.

Elichai found his way into the room, one of the healers begging him and the guards to get Atreus out.

"No! I will not leave! This is my kingdom and she is my mate! I will not leave this room without her!" He fought against his brother.

Madame Tate had entered on Zalser's request with a dozen witches in tow. They floated into the room in their robes of varying colors.

"She is the last of Orick's bloodline," he explained to the coven in which he belonged.

"Her heart stopped," one of the healers whispered to the other, their words brittle in the suffocating stillness.

The sound that tore from him was monstrous, a raw, primal howl that transcended anything known to this world—or any other. It was an unearthly wail, not of man, beast, or demon. The very air around him trembled, as if recoiling from the agony he unleashed. The walls shuddered violently, dust raining down as he slammed his fists into the ground, fingers clawing deep into crumbling marble tile. His bond with her throbbed painfully, like a string pulled too tight, and he could feel her slipping further, her essence drifting toward the cold, unreachable abyss of the ethereal realm. It was as though the world itself was breaking with her—dragging them both toward a place where nothing could follow.

"Pull her back!" Zalser screamed and he and his coven began chanting.

Elichai was on the floor, trying desperately to console him.

"Can the king spare more blood?" Madame Tate asked one of the healers who said 'no'.

"Yes!" He jumped up. "Bleed me dry, take it all. End me if it saves her." He allowed her to slice open his other wrist

"Brother?" Elichai grabbed his arm. He jerked it away, not caring for anyone's concern. He would not let her die, he would not continue living if she did.

He braced himself on the bed frame as they alternated slitting each wrist to take more blood. He healed too fast, requiring one of the healers to continue tearing open his skin as their primary duty.

He didn't know how much time passed, he nodded in and out of consciousness from blood loss. He reached for her through their bond, reaching and finding no answer. He was trapped in a paradox of endless misery and unknowing as he literally bled out for her.

"We have a pulse," the healer announced. They were propping her feet and head up, he didn't know why.

The witches were all touching her, their hands glowing the colors of their auras as they called on Amara's ancestors to help. Magic and blood poured into her while healing hands tried to stitch together the fabric of her soul which had been torn open.

Atreus exhaled roughly, the effects of blood loss becoming more evident. He was healing and regenerating it quickly but it was taking a toll on him. If it killed him, he would die knowing he left a gift for this world. She would save it, she would heal it, she was the answer. He would die for her and the salvation she would bring.

Though her heart beat resumed, she felt a world away. She was still so far away as though she were wandering the ethereal realm.

"Amara, my love. Come back to me," he pleaded to her.

He didn't know how much time passed before they stopped draining his blood. He was on his knees beside the bed, fighting to stay conscious, still searching for her in spirit.

He could hear her heart, he could hear her breathing, but he couldn't *feel* her. She was far away. Both of their palms were still carved with the mating bond. It had not broken. Why did she feel so distant?

"She is stabilized." A healer crouched down beside him. He was staring at the floor, unmoving.

"Why can't I feel her? Where is she?" He growled. The healer looked over to the witches.

"She is engaging with her ancestors," Madame Tate informed. Her eyes were closed, flickering. "She said to tell you and I quote; 'I'm not a big enough brat to die on you.'"

Atreus laughed in relief. Of course she fucking dies and uses that time to figure out channeling and connecting with her ancestors. She was going to be the death of him.

"What do we do until then? How long will she be gone?" he asked, still frantic when looking at her unmoving body.

"She's searching for her mother. I don't think she's going to return until she finds her," Zalser answered. He looked at her longingly, holding her hand.

"The Lady of the Kingdom is walking in spirit," an older witch by the name of Morgana turned to Atreus. "She will rise with the answers you seek."

He leaned back on his heels, trying to understand what exactly that meant.

"We will tend to her and keep her body alive until she returns to it," a doe-eyed healer spoke .

"Thank you." He nodded. He was trying to regain some of his composure. He was shaking though, his heart feeling as though it had been ripped away from him.

He spent the next several hours pacing around the room. Elichai would not leave him despite his demands. The prince knew he wouldn't have him forced out . One of the healers entered in silence and notified him that Amara should be bathed.

"Very well. Do it," he instructed her to bring in another healer to assist.

He couldn't watch. Her unmoving body and heavy limbs were too much. Her eyelids weren't fluttering like butterfly wings as they usually did when she slept. Her breathing was hushed and shallow. It was like she was asleep except he couldn't feel her.

The sun was rising over the horizon as his brother led him from the room to give the healers privacy with Amara. Her heart had stopped, the weight of the truth growing heavier as he left her. He couldn't accept how close he had come to losing her. It solidified his desire to go through with making her his queen. He wanted her to have his immortality, he needed her forever, he needed to allow her to become everything she was destined to be.

He watched that sun rise over that exact horizon for many centuries, somehow that morning its beauty was gone. His love was wandering the ethereal realm. It was the one place he couldn't access her. He found himself wishing he actually possessed the ability to dimension travel.

"She doesn't want you to deliver Deimos to her," Elichai said, seemingly out of nowhere.

"What?" He responded.

"She wants to take him down and kill him herself." He sighed.

"Why didn't she tell me?" Atreus asked, his heart sinking.

"I don't know. She asked for me to ensure he wasn't captured before she was able to fight him herself," his brother informed. He tugged his bottom lip between his fingers as he always had when he was nervous and thoughtful.

Amara was always peculiar to him, behaving in ways that he hadn't prepared for. She had to know the risks of facing her father herself. It would be a suicide mission. She had to know that he hadn't ordered him captured in an attempt to control her but for her own safety.

"He murdered her mother." Elichai met his eyes.

He knew that Elichai understood where Amara was coming from. Elichai endured a similar heartbreak and a similar thirst for revenge. Atreus couldn't stop him from seeking retribution. He couldn't help his brother; it had to be done on his own. He saw the same spark of pain in his brother's eyes that he had seen many times in Amara's and he understood. He wasn't angry that she asked for Elichai's help.

"I won't let him take her life," Atreus decided.

"Don't, but let her try. She is searching for a way."

"I can help her." Atreus shook his head. Why did she insist on doing this without him? "That's why she wanted to see Hadeon," he realized. Elichai nodded as though the conclusion made sense.

His mate had been subject to extreme control for her entire life in the Hallowed Realm. She had been lied to. She had been used and tortured. He was no stranger to pain but she had endured more pain than anyone should in two short decades of life.

"How was she planning to burn down the ships and fight her father one-on-one." Atreus stopped walking and leaned against one of the walls outside the great garden.

"I'm not sure she had a solid plan. I think she was pushing herself as hard as she was so that she could do both," Elichai offered.

"She's insane." He had to laugh away the anger. *Beautiful infuriating thing.*

Hours later he found himself lying beside her, apologizing for punishing her so harshly. His heart ached at the possibility of that being their last moment together.

"Ships are forty-eight hours out, Deimos' arrival imminent," Hyde reported that evening.

"How long?" Atreus asked. He was slouched over the planning table of the strategy room, his council giving updates.

"He's about a day ahead of them, estimated arrival is tomorrow evening," Rowan informed.

"Sir, Kit continues to forge arrows with the coven," Helena Hart spoke . "They are also attempting to gather their strength after the events with Lady Amara."

Atreus didn't miss her scowl at Prince Elichai with the mention of her name. *This again?*

Helena had been pining after the prince for years. It was tediously annoying. He tried with her but he wasn't interested in committing to her. If he would stop sleeping with her she would probably have an easier time buying that he wasn't interested.

Evidently she knew of the... duties he fulfilled to Lady Amara a few nights prior. Honestly he was starting to think the walls could talk in his palace.

"A few of the Nephilim from Findaria have asked for positions on the field," Commander Hale said.

"How many?" Atreus asked.

"About fifteen sir," he answered. That meant about five of them were not willing to fight for Constantine, which was fine. He hadn't expected anyone to ask to join their war efforts.

"Give them bows and place them with the archers," he directed with a dismissive wave.

They could never have too many soldiers shooting down invading Nephilim. Their newly heightened senses would make them better shooters than fighters with such little training. At least he knew he taught them to shoot during weapons wielding.

Atreus hadn't slept that day, but instead sat on the bed next to Amara. He read to her. He read her stories about his kingdom, of wars waged on it and lost. He told her about the horses he bred a century ago and how he wanted to start it again.

He drifted into his own story. A story of many years of isolation, of a king who never understood love and had no use for it. The king who finally took a lady into his kingdom only for her to attempt to destroy him.

He spoke briefly of Lady Jane Cyperian who was the reason he swore never to share power all those years ago. Lady Jane Cyperian who called blood from the skies to rain down on his kingdom when he could no longer be contained. Lady Jane Cyperian who was very much still alive and wandering the Abyss. The very same prisoner who Amara's sire threatened to release.

Now, he was bent over the planning table, his eyes bloodshot, as he mulled over the war plans.

"Sir?" Wren interrupted his thoughts. He snapped his head over to her; he was so tired that he was in and out of it. "Are we clear to move forward with Ocean's Embrace?" she asked him.

'Ocean's Embrace' was a plan that had been in the vault for many years. It only works if the enemy is coming by sea. Without Amara to attack and burn the ships down, they would destroy the vessels from the ocean floor.

"Yes, go, raise the traps." He dismissed them all.

The steel traps were laid flat in the sea bed. When raised, massive spikes would sit just below the surface and out of eyesight. Raising them where the captains believed they still were in deep enough waters, would be critically damaging to the ships.

He stumbled through the door into his chamber where Amara lay motionless. He crawled into bed and curled himself around her small frame. He listened to her heart and her soft breathing. He inhaled her and was transported to the top of the watchtower where she curled into his lap. He had been terrified of her even in her weakened state after being kidnapped. Somewhere in all her stomping around, pouting, and talking back—he learned what love was.

He imagined she were with him, awake, and within her body. They would be laughing over a few too many shots and those skimpy little outfits she bought. He thought she was breathtaking, she thought they were ridiculous. If she were really there, he would pull fresh flowers from the garden and spread the petals over her until she giggled as they tickled her skin. He would ask her endless questions about her time on the run and why she was so obsessed with the way the waves looked on the beach at night. She hated when he asked that, like it was obvious. Maybe it was.

He tightened his grip and rested his head on the soft creamy skin of her stomach.

"Please come back to me, my love," he whispered.

He nuzzled into her soft midriff and finally slept for a short time. He only had twenty-four hours until Deimos arrived.

Chapter 45

ATREUS

"You will not enter the palace!" Atreus shouted, his voice a command as the wards flared, trapping Deimos just outside their reach.

"Since when am I not allowed in?" Deimos sneered, pacing back and forth in front of the shimmering barrier, his movements dripping with that familiar swagger. His dark, predatory gaze never left Atreus, the shadow of a smirk playing on his lips.

"Since you brought war to my doorstep," Atreus retorted, his voice steady but laced with a simmering fury.

Deimos's expression hardened, his voice dropping to a low, gravelly growl that seemed to rise from the very shadows trailing him. "I came to retrieve my child."

"She died," Atreus said flatly, his tone cold, unyielding. It wasn't a lie—Amara had technically died. Whether or not they revived her was irrelevant to this conversation. He wouldn't let Deimos know more than he needed.

Deimos's eyes flared, molten and dangerous, a burning red orange that mirrored Amara's own. "Do not lie to me," he roared, the raw power in his voice shaking the air. With a swift, furious motion, he unsheathed the massive broadsword strapped to his back, stepping one pace too close to Atreus.

Before Deimos could blink, Zalser had him on his knees, not with brute force but a power that wrapped around him like invisible chains. Deimos struggled, his defiance blazing through his eyes even as his body remained pinned.

"Drawing your sword is a direct threat to my king," growled Vincent, Atreus' other guard, his voice dark with promise.

With a flick of his wrist, Deimos sent the broadsword vanishing into some unknown dimension without even touching it. Dimensional travel. Impressive, even for him. Atreus couldn't help but feel a grudging admiration for the maneuver, though he didn't let it show.

"Let's try this again." Atreus sighed, his patience fraying. "You brought war to my home. Now, you will help defend it. Only then will we discuss your child."

Deimos glared up at him, teeth clenched in frustration. Zalser, sensing the shift, released him, and Deimos stood, shaking the dirt from his legs as though shaking off a blow.

"Fine," Deimos spat the word like it burned his tongue. "But don't think for a second that you'll get away with bailing on your end of the bargain. I have men waiting at the Abyss, ready to release your precious Jane."

In an instant, Atreus's hand shot out, seizing Deimos by the throat. The air crackled with deadly intent as he held the other man in his iron grip. "You release her, and Hadeon meets his end," Atreus growled, his eyes gleaming with a lethal promise.

Zalser and Vincent exchanged quick glances, their confusion palpable. Why would Deimos care so much?

Deimos wrenched free, disbelief flashing across his face. "You would sink so low as to kill my mate?"

Zalser's eyes widened in realization, the pieces clicking together. Deimos's motives made sense now.

"You seek to kill mine," Atreus spat, his voice colder than the depths of the Abyss itself. He opened his palm, revealing the mark of Amara's name etched into his skin. He had known they were bound as mates, but until now, he hadn't known if she accepted. "Besides," he added, "Hadeon hasn't wanted you in decades. Why do you care?"

Deimos's face darkened, his body trembling with barely contained fury. "You have no idea what you're talking about," he hissed, taking a threatening step toward Atreus.

Atreus raised a hand, stopping him in his tracks.

He did know . He knew that Hadeon and Deimos were cast out together for lust when they had fallen for one another in the heavens. He knew they solidified their mating bond years after falling into and creating the Abyss.

Some need for power on Hadeon's end separated them and they've been on and off ever since. Deimos became the 'Dark One' to his 'Hallowed One' and the scandal has continued.

"I don't particularly care. This will go my way," Atreus demanded. "I have your child and I have your mate. I would strongly advise against any tricks you think you have up your sleeve."

Deimos didn't know that Hadeon would die anyway, that he would never sacrifice Amara, nor did he know that Amara had every intention of destroying him herself. He smiled at Deimos.

"There's a cozy little cave on that mountainside. Don't freeze to death." Atreus' blew him a fake kiss. Deimos was trying not to lash out in anger; Atreus could see him squirming.

Atreus and his guards moved through the ward, becoming invisible to Deimos who was cursing the sky and making obscene gestures.

"We can anticipate that Ender and Rase will go straight for King Atreus," Prince Elichai advised in the meeting later that night.

"I'm counting on it." Atreus smiled. He was winding up the leather and steel whips after inspecting them.

"Finally the day has come to break those out," Langston sighed longingly. It was about time she joined the meeting. Though there wasn't much for her to do regarding diplomatic concerns in this particular war.

"I don't like the idea of three Hallowed on this continent at once. I need to guarantee that I have them contained as soon as possible," Atreus told them. The whips could be used to capture, ground, and sedate any Fallen Angel.

"What of their... abilities?" Wren asked.

"They will be able to enter the outer ward, I've spelled it to stun them long enough for Atreus to ensnare them," Zalser said proudly.

Sitting amongst his royal council, he felt a sense of pride to have them on his side. Many years of battles fought, long nights, and royal balls had turned them into a family. He took in each of their faces as he often did before facing a threat to their home. He would sacrifice himself for each of them and for every subject in Constantine.

He was about to say something to them when shouts erupted from his bedchamber. *Amara.* His heart raced, it was her. He could feel here again. A louder set of screams came from the healers.

His eyes couldn't adjust to the scene in the room. Flames engulfed it, roaring and consuming everything. A healer was thrown to the floor beside him where she screamed and thrashed as flames lapped at her skin.

"Amara!" He screamed, trying to shield his eyes.

He heard her then, roaring in agony. Her flames weren't touching her, shadows from her body pushing them outward in all directions. They danced around and caressed her floating form. A symphony of red, orange, and yellow hues ate away at the bed she once laid upon.

He still couldn't make out what was happening. He pushed his shield outward, allowing him to walk through her flames.

It was only then that he understood what exactly had occurred. She had awoken in her father's clutches.

Chapter 46

Amara was yanked violently back into her body, her lungs burning as she gasped for air. A faceless ancestor's scream echoed through her mind, tearing at her consciousness: "*Danger!*"

"I'm not ready! I need to see my mother!" she screamed into the void, her voice desperate and raw, pleading with the ethereal realm to give her more time.

She had spent what felt like years trapped in the liminal space between life and death, drifting through endless darkness, unraveling truths buried deep in her soul. Answers she didn't know she had been searching for surged through her, each revelation a painful, exhilarating jolt. She had finally uncovered the secret—how to break free from the chains that had bound her, how to ensure no one would ever control her again.

Honing her power was the key, her only guarantee of the freedom she craved, the quiet life she had longed for.

"*If you have no control over yourself, others will control you,*" a voice whispered, low and commanding.

"Forge your own path," another urged, its tone fierce and resolute.

"Free your coven."

"Perfect your craft."

The voices cascaded over her, a flood of ancestral wisdom and power surging through her veins, filling every corner of her being until she thought she might explode. Power, raw and violent, was woven into the fabric of her soul, stretching her to the brink of breaking. It twisted inside her, burning with the intensity of a thousand lifetimes, threatening to tear her apart—and yet, it fortified her.

You will emerge with the power to end this war and free your coven.

"I'm Nephilim!" she had protested, her voice trembling with defiance. But the chorus of ancestors snapped back, their voices rising as one, commanding her attention.

"You are both! A gift from Orick, who prophesied your purpose!"

No single voice spoke to her. They were all speaking—her bloodline calling her to fulfill the destiny written in her very bones.

"Show me how!" she screamed into the endless black, her voice echoing through the heavy, energy-laden abyss. "Give me the tools!"

And they did. They gave her more than she could have imagined—more power than she had ever dreamed of wielding.

Deimos had no idea what he had unleashed. The moment he sought to awaken her, he had stirred the fury of thousands of witches, each one bound to her bloodline, each one crying out for vengeance. Her Nephilim form was now a conduit—an endless reservoir of power. She alone could harness this raw, primal energy. She alone had the strength to tear Deimos from existence.

He had murdered her mother. He intended to eradicate their entire lineage from the world.

The ancestors demanded blood.

And now, Amara was sent back to deliver it. She had returned with the power to end him, to avenge them all—and she would.

She was sent back to avenge the ancestors who died enslaved to the Hallowed. They were dead, all of them. They just didn't know it yet.

The first breath after reuniting her body was excruciating. Though she realized quickly that the flowing shadows crawling into her throat were responsible. Healers scrambled to her when she began choking. Even though she wanted to warn them away, she was unable to.

"Hello, my child," they whispered at her and she howled. She sent forward flames to consume everything around her.

Her newfound power surged through her, wild and untamed, flickering like a storm of flames beyond her control. The fire lashed out in every direction, devouring anything in its path—yet Amara could not command where it landed or what it consumed. Deimos hovered in the top corner of the room, his long, spindly nails digging into the wall like some grotesque spider. His blazing red eyes gleamed with sinister amusement, lips curled into a wicked grin as shadows enveloped him, slipping between the cracks of the room.

He was untouchable, a shifting web of darkness beyond her flames' reach. With sickening grace, he slithered down the wall and crawled across the floor, his movements insect-like and repulsive, his elongated limbs twisting in ways no creature should move. The flames parted before him, bowing to the shadows that wrapped around his gaunt frame like a shroud.

Amara's body still felt foreign, heavy, and disconnected from her will, but she was regaining control, the awareness of her limbs returning in slow, agonizing waves. She just needed him to come closer, just a little bit closer...

Deimos reached her, his disgustingly long claws tracing the curve of her cheek with a mockery of tenderness. Revulsion churned in her gut. *What manner of Fallen Angel was he?* His touch felt like death itself, cold and crawling beneath her skin.

She remained utterly still, her breath shallow as she watched his shadows tighten around her, lifting her limp body into his arms. He dug his claws into the side of her throat, and Amara winced as they broke the skin, blood trickling down her neck. The pain should have terrified her, but instead, something darker stirred inside—a plan, a reckoning.

From the corner of her eye, she noticed a sudden commotion on her left, but her head refused to move. Instead, a dark laugh bubbled up from her throat. Deimos's smile faltered, his brows furrowing as he tilted his head, the claws pressing deeper to make her bleed more.

Let him closer.

"Father," she whispered, the laughter dying on her lips as her eyes blazed.

Before he could react, she unleashed a torrent of force, sending him hurtling across the room with a skill granted by her ancestors. He crashed into the far wall with a sickening thud, splintering the wooden beams as he hit. Amara tumbled to the floor, landing in a low crouch, her body vibrating with the raw power she was finally beginning to control. Her wings erupted behind her, massive and fierce, absorbing the flames that danced wildly around the room, pulling them into her being like they belonged to her all along.

"Amara!" Atreus's voice broke through the chaos, but she didn't turn to face him. She couldn't stop. Not now.

Deimos lay sprawled on the floor, choking from the impact, his body writhing in pain as broken beams rained down around him. Amara rose slowly, her hair falling like a dark curtain around her face, her eyes blazing with the same unholy fire as her sires. Her wings, glowing with the embers of the room, stretched wide, radiating an intensity that filled the space with her presence.

Everything she had once feared becoming, everything that had haunted her nightmares, was the very thing now setting her free. She no longer trembled at the thought of it. She *welcomed* it.

With nothing more than a thought, she flung Deimos again, sending him crashing into the stone fireplace. His body hit with such force that the stones cracked beneath him. Struggling to his feet, he pulled himself onto all fours, his body contorting in agony.

"Get up!" Amara's voice thundered through the room, her wings blazing with fiery light, rising high above her like the fury of an avenging goddess. The flames danced in her wake, twisting and writhing with her anger, and for the first time, Deimos looked up with something resembling fear.

She sent just a small amount of liquid flame toward him, scorching one of his wings. It was useful when it wasn't pouring from her nose and she wasn't throwing it up.

She did it again, hitting his dominant arm. He screamed as the lava-like substance crawled up his arm and coated it, melting flesh. He healed but it kept burning the skin away before repeating the process.

With his other hand he threw forward shadows that crashed into her. They didn't feel like anything and she grinned at him.

She heard those shadows were lethal, poison, dealing death to any being they touched.

Not her . He chose the worst time to make his move. She was bursting with raw power with no other goal than to keep herself alive and end him.

She eyed Eversor which was on the mantle above him. She stomped over to him, barefoot. She didn't care that she wore only her mate's pants and oversized shirt. She dealt a powerful kick to her sire's face, sending his head cracking against the stone of the fireplace.

"Amara!" Atreus tried to get closer. She threw her hand out, stopping him and his royal council in place.

"Do not!" She roared at them. She could see the reflections of her flaming wings in their eyes. Fear and uncertainty playing across their faces.

Eversor came to life in her hand, the hilt inhaling some of her power and making her feel lighter.

Destroyer.

Overthrower.

She became one with her blade, choosing it as the weapon that would end her sire. She bestowed upon it the power needed to stop his heart.

Deimos got to his feet, blood pouring from his head, lava still eating away at his arm and wing. He slung daggers at her with blinding speed and precision. She ducked and flipped out of the way. She dodged two more as she covered the space of the room where he had retreated to his original spot in the corner.

She flipped Eversor in her hand, flame and sparks dancing from its silver blade.

End him. The call of her ancestors demanded.

"I thought you would put up more of a fight, Father." She tutted.

"What are you?" He trembled in horror.

"I am your end." She shrugged. She brought him down from the rafters of the room where he tried to crawl away like a roach.

Amara felt Atreus trying to speak to her through their bond but she was blocking him out. It was effortless with her newfound power.

"On your feet, coward!" She forced him to stand. He winced in pain.

Amara set upon him quickly and viscously. She swung and spun her sword with foreign precision and unwavering accuracy. His screams flooded the room as she flayed his skin and sliced at his limbs, wings, and neck.

She made sure to take in the look of sheer terror in the moment he realized that he was going to die. It was the same look Bastian Marlowe had. He could do nothing against her. She lashed out with deafening screams, shaking the room.

He was cut down exactly like she wanted. He was a mass of blood, missing limbs, unrecognizable features, and flayed flesh. She drove the sword into exposed bone and brought it down repeatedly on his neck while he squirmed and attempted to drag what remained of himself away. At some point he stopped screaming, at some point he stopped gurgling on blood, but she didn't stop. She hacked away at what had become a pile of twitching muscles, flesh, and bone. His head had been removed just as he did to her mother.

She slung Eversor to the floor where it clattered against the stone. The beautiful stone of the room was now covered in blood and ash. She grabbed her father's head by the short spiky hair.

"That's for my mother," she growled. His wide lifeless eyes didn't answer.

She released the hold on Atreus and his royal council before bringing the ceiling of the room down. It shook and protested for a moment and then wooden beams tumbled.

She forced her way through the shattered glass windows, emerging onto the beach as the salty ocean air stung her lungs. The cool night breeze clung to her skin as she moved slowly through the sand, her steps heavy, her body still humming with raw power.

She felt like a stranger in her own skin, every muscle rippling with energy she hadn't yet learned to control. Her clothes were soaked in blood, and behind her, the distant sound of the throne hall collapsing echoed through the night. She hadn't destroyed it entirely—just the chamber where part of Deimos's body lay—but the damage was significant, and she knew it.

She stared into nothingness as she walked, her brain still trying to process the time she spent in spirit searching for her mother. Everything she learned, every ounce of power she gained... it was entirely too much yet not enough all at once.

"*A year with us was just two days here,*" a voice answered for her.

"My Lady!" Prince Elichai called. She didn't answer.

Amara moved toward the large rocks that jutted out to the ocean which separated their small section of beach from others. She retracted her wings, the flames disappearing with them. She could feel them underneath her skin swirling like snakes.

Amara took careful barefoot steps over the slippery rocks where waves crashed sporadically. Her hands were twisted in the blood-soaked strands of Deimos' hair. It worked. The magic worked, it killed an immortal Fallen Angel. Without it, he could have recovered from any of the blows she'd dealt him.

She reached the end where she was a few yards out from where the waves crashed onto the sand. Amara stared into the dark endless night. There was no separation between the night sky and jet black unlit ocean. She watched stars fall and shoot across the sky. Distantly shades of green and purple painted the sky, she inhaled, allowing it to ground her.

She heard that Atreus was slowly approaching her, following the lone rock path. He didn't say anything . She would face any repercussions for her actions with pride.

She held up the decapitated head and stared into the empty black eyes. They were the last eyes her mother's met before she died. The eyes that denied her her life as she begged for it in the presence of her child, of *his* child.

She allowed herself to accept the similarities she saw of herself within him. She vowed she would never kill innocent people for power. She would make the world better with her presence, not worse. If nothing else, she would do it in spite of him.

She burned his head to ash in her hand and allowed the wind to carry the ashes out to sea. He wouldn't hurt anyone ever again. She would see to it that the Hallowed met their end even if it was similar to his vision. She just wouldn't slay humans and destroy villages to accomplish it. She would save the people first. The death toll from his attacks were last estimated at three thousand casualties with over half of those being innocent bystanders.

He deserved what he got. Not taking into account her mother's death and her own life of suffering, he deserved his fate for his other schemes alone.

"My love," came Atreus' breathless plea behind her.

She turned to him, finally allowing herself to see him. She feared that meeting his eyes before would stop her. Her heart ached and longed for him. Her time away felt like an eternity to be separated from her mate as she traversed the veil between worlds.

She collapsed onto her knees, into his arms. Atreus pulled her into his lap and held her close to his chest. Ocean water sprayed over them with a gust of wind which seemed to be in response to their reunion. He was her entire world. He had become woven into her mind, her body, her spirit. Being apart from him was a death all on its own.

"I love you." He exhaled and kissed her hair. "I love you." he pulled her closer. "Don't leave me again."

His words broke her; she could hear the magnitude of suffering that he endured in her absence just as she had his.

"I love you," she answered and kissed him . He wiped a tear from her cheek and caressed it gently.

He looked into her eyes; unsure she was truly there. The moonlight bathed him in silver and highlighted his raven hair. She made it back to him. *She made it back to her mate.*

"What time is it? How long have I been out?" she asked him for confirmation.

"A few days and it's nearly three in the morning," he answered and kissed her forehead. "I need to know what just happened, Brat. How did you kill him with a simple blade?"

"It's kind of a long story." She smiled up at him. Truthfully, she didn't know if she'd be able to put into words what she saw. She experienced truths that most people die never having known. How could she put them into words?

"Guys! Problem!" Wren yelled from the beach, waving them over.

Atreus stood and carried Amara back over the rocks and to the sand. The royal council were all present. All six of them watched her curiously.

"Welcome back, kid." Kit hugged her.

She looked over his shoulder to see Prince Elichai. He winked at her and snatched a gold serpent ring from one of Deimos' severed fingers. She had forgotten to retrieve it. *Oops.* He slid it on his own middle finger and she found herself wondering what it was for.

"A fleet of eight ships were spotted about two hours out. Nephilim flying overhead," Commander Hale announced.

"They're early." Atreus grinned at Amara who couldn't figure out why.

"Ocean's Embrace is a go, they should collide in about an hour and a half," Hawk informed the king.

"Ocean's Embrace?" Amara asked.

"It's our back up plan for the ships since you were out of commission," Kit told her. "Giant spikes raised from the seafloor to shred them."

"That should have been the first plan before trying to get me to burn them down! And for that matter, why wasn't Elichai tasked with that? He actually has control over his fire welding!" She was dumbfounded.

"The prince has his own task," Helena narrowed her eyes on Amara.

Amara looked over both shoulders dramatically to ensure she had actually given her such a look.

"Do we have a problem?" She stepped into Helena who barely said anything to her until giving her that look.

"Nope," Elichai exhaled a breathy laugh. He held Helena's shoulders and pulled her backward. "No problem at all." He glanced at Atreus.

"She's jealous that we took Elichai to bed," Atreus informed her through their mental bond. *Oh.*

"Here." Kit handed Atreus a set of lengthy whips and handed Amara her sword.

"What are those for?" she whispered to her mate.

"They're spelled so I can capture the Hallowed." He grinned. "But, come with me. There's something we must do before we head to the Western Cliffs." He placed a hand on her back.

"Hale, begin moving the soldiers west. Zalser, ensure all of the archers have the arrows your coven forged," he told them. "Elichai and Helena, come with us. We will meet on the battle-field." He nodded at the rest of them.

"Where are we going?" she asked Atreus.

"I'm making you my Queen, now," he insisted.

"Now?" She glanced back at Elichai and Helena.

"Now. I lost you once, I will not lose you again," he said unwaveringly. She shared the sentiment but she wasn't sure if they had time to complete the ritual.

"Do we have time?" she asked.

"Yes, it doesn't take long. We're already mated and we already share blood."

"Which is weird, by the way," Elichai poked his head between them. She rolled her eyes at him.

They made their way into a small gazebo which stood at the end of a small pier over the water.

"Wait, let me change first!" She looked down at Atreus' oversized clothes on her small frame which were covered in blood.

"Here." Atreus summoned a simple pair of her pants and hooded sweater. "Go behind that tree, no one is looking."

"Fine," she did so. She used some of the ocean water and sand to scrub her hands and face free of blood until she felt somewhat refreshed.

"Okay, I'm ready," she jogged to the gazebo where the other three stood. "How does this work?"

"It's fairly simple," Helena started. She and Elichai stood between them. "You proclaim her your Queen, and you." She turned to Amara, "accept him as your king."

"That's it?" Amara asked, looking at all of them.

"You swear oaths of fealty to one another, drink from the scars of the mating bond, and then consummate the joining." *Oh, that makes more sense.*

Atreus summoned something and Elichai grabbed it from behind his back, keeping it out of her view. She grunted in annoyance.

"Atreus, King of Constantine," Prince Elichai started. "Who do you take as your Queen?"

"I chose Amara Ashenfall, Daughter of the Soil of Findaria, Nephilim, and Lady of Constantine, to be my queen." He looked into her eyes and took her hands. Elichai placed Atreus' crown on his head.

"Do you acknowledge that this joining shall only be shattered by death?" Helena asked him.

"Yes," he answered.

"Amara Ashenfall, Lady of Constantine, and the other titles he said..." Elicha trailed off sheepishly. "Do you accept King Atreus' bid for you to be his queen?"

"Yes." She smiled shyly at him. She suddenly cared about the casual clothing she wore.

"Do you accept his immortality and the duties required of you as Queen of Constantine?" Helena asked.

"Yes," she answered.

"Swear your oaths," Elichai instructed with a wave of his hand.

"Amara," Atreus started. He seemed short of breath, nervous. "I swear myself to you wholly. In every way I will be your partner. I will love you always. I will worship you for eternity and when my time runs out, I swear even then that every star in the sky will bow down to worship you in my stead." He pushed her hair back behind her ear. She had never known him to cry but she could see his eyes flooding.

"Atreus, I swear my mind, body, soul, and heart to you. I never wish to be parted from you. I will be your other half and your partner in all that you do. I understand that should I ever turn on you that I accept the end of my life as well. I swear to love you completely and endlessly as I always have." Her voice cracked at the end and she sniffled. Looking up at him as the waves crashed beneath them was perfect.

"As prince of Constantine," Elichai said.

"As Lady of the Witches of Constantine," Helena added.

"We bear witness and confirm the crowning of Queen Amara of Constantine," they said in unison.

Atreus took a small silver circlet from Elichai, a crown. It was fashioned after his own, with two winged feathers rising upward. He placed it on her head and finally let one tear fall.

"Palms out," Elichai instructed.

He dug a knife into the center of the palm where Atreus' name was carved and did the same to Atreus'.

"Drink," he waved them on.

They placed one another's palms against each other's mouths and took the blood. It wasn't a lot of blood but it invaded her system with a spark, nonetheless. Her eyes flickered open to see his already on her. His gaze was heated, hungry.

They pulled away, Atreus pulled her in and kissed her hard. The salty and sweet flavors of their blood mixed. She could get lost in his embrace, in his kiss forever and now she would.

"Lastly, consummate to finalize it." Helena sighed. "We'll be on the beach, bearing witness." She slumped her shoulders and Elichai followed her off the pier.

"They have to watch?" She pulled from the kiss and looked up at him, her hands entangled in his hair.

"I modeled the joining ritual after traditions of other kingdoms." He shrugged. "Witness to the consummation seemed to be very important."

"Elichai has already seen us consummate." She grunted.

"We can hear you!" Elicha called from the beach. "Just putting that out there!" He looked at Helena nervously. *They definitely had a past.*

"Fine." She kissed him hard. "Let's do this, we have a battle to fight."

"Better bite your tongue and stay quiet," he teased and nipped at her earlobe.

At least their witnesses were fairly far away and hard to see in the dark.

They became entangled with one another, already so familiar with their bodies. She did everything she could to remain quiet as she reveled in the deeper meaning behind this night, this joining. His strong arms held her as he rutted into her like it was the last thing he'd ever do.

She cried out for him and held him desperately, lovingly, pouring every ounce over herself into him.

They came apart together, both panting each other's names into the horizon. The two became one beneath the night sky as the ocean sprayed them from crashing waves. She felt the shift within her, the exchange of power between them, and lastly Atreus' understanding of exactly the sort of power she now held.

"Mine," he whispered and kissed her greedily once it was done. She couldn't stop smiling as he adjusted her crown. "You destroyed our bed chambers but I intend to fuck you properly once all of this is over."

"Promise?" She moaned into his kiss and he nodded, biting her lip.

They had done it. They had been fully joined. She was the Queen of Constantine. She kept chanting it to herself as they approached Helena and Elichai on the beach.

They both dropped to one knee and placed a fist hand over their chest.

"I swear fealty to you, my queen," they said in unison. She urged them to get up, unsure how to deal with *that.*

Chapter 47

Atreus, Amara, Helena, and Elichai made it to the Western Cliffs an hour later and on the tail end of the soldiers.

She could smell the stench of the Hallowed and their children riding on the wind that blew across her face. She sneered before leaping and flying upward to get a better view of the ships approaching. They charged ahead with remarkable speed for the wind to be bellowing into them.

Still though, the ships were headed straight for the spikes that lurked beneath the surface of the water. She smirked and circled around the enormous battlefield on the edge of the cliff. Their enemies couldn't see anything, and would not expect them to be waiting for them at the cliffside.

She observed Constantine's soldiers who were more in number. There had to be five hundred there. All of them dressed in smooth black and violet armor that fit close to their bodies. It wasn't clunky and allowed for easy movement as well as wing use. She had observed the soldiers training, their styles of combat less stiff and more flowing. It involved all limbs and all manner of weapons. They were cats in the training ring moving with stealth and speed around one another. It was nothing compared to the training style of Findaria where it was mostly based on how much power you could put behind your hit. Her soldiers were jungle cats ready to pounce on the wild boars of Findaria. *Her soldiers.*

She circled back around and landed after exchanging a few words with Beck and Eros who were nervous but prepared for battle in light of the truth. After pulling back the veil that had been draped over their eyes for their entire life, it wasn't hard to convince them to fight for Constantine. Avren on the other hand still refused to participate along with a few others of the group that had been rescued. She expected they would need to be cast out of Constantine eventually.

"Here." Prince Elichai tossed her a bundle of armor. "You're going to need these."

The small dark plates ran up her legs, abdomen, arms, and even her neck. She pulled on the small helmet that left her eyes exposed. All of their helmets mimicked their king's crown—two feathers rising out of the forehead like horns. She and Atreus had left their crowns in the palace. In the sun everyone's armor had an iridescent effect, glowing shades of violet and indigo.

She pulled on the gloves made of chain and leather before sighing.

"Are you going to tell me what that ring is for?" she asked Elichai, glancing down at the golden serpent on his middle finger.

"No." He smirked.

"You would if I forced you to." She frowned.

"I would," he admitted. "But you wouldn't compel me in such a cruel way, my queen."

He was right, she wouldn't use her power to get information unless it was absolutely necessary. She knew Elichai would obey her if she truly wished to know and that was enough.

Commander Hale glided a few feet off of the ground, causing the rolling crowd of soldiers to quiet down. He demanded respect from his massive build to his stoic and scarred face.

"This morning a war approaches from the western part of our world. We were led to believe this would be a simple battle, but that is incorrect. This will go down as the most brutal yet necessary fight in Constantine's history." He looked over his soldiers. "The threat we are facing is one like no other. They do not seek to take over our kingdom, no. They intend to lay waste to this continent and its inhabitants." The crowd gasped in unison. "The Hallowed Fallen Ender and Rase lead this battle and they seek vengeance for something Deimos did. Because of his actions, he is dead."

"I ask you to think of the children, the humans, and those in the Hallowed Ones' realm that still need liberation. We have been hope for the children of those continents for centuries. Most of you were rescued just as I was. Today we face the merciless tyrants who wish to claim you once more," he spoke clearly, boldly, and with more conviction than she had ever heard from anyone. Amara searched the crowd of archers, able to see both Beck and Eros amongst them.

"Immortality does not equal invincibility—for any of us. We will arise victorious on this field today and we will stop them from reaching the innocents which we have sworn to protect. Think not of mercy for the enemy. For they will not spare us. Do not take your eyes off of what we are fighting for." He raised his voice and threw a closed fist into the air.

"If not for kingdoms such as Constantine, if not for kings like Atreus, if not for warriors like you, we would be slaves to them as well. We will die free before we swear fealty to them!" He shouted and the soldiers erupted into a battle cry with fists and weapons in the air.

"Lastly, I leave you with this," Commander Hale called. "Lady Amara has completed the ritual and is now Queen Amara Ashenfall of Constantine!"

She was nearly knocked back by the announcement, especially when helmets were lifted into the air and the crowd roared with joy.

"She is fighting alongside you today and alongside your king." Hale smiled proudly.

"I've decided I want to light some shit on fire, care to join?" Elichai smiled wickedly, pulling her attention from Commander Hale.

"What about your task?" she asked.

"My task was Deimos." He shrugged.

She laughed at him. "Fine, let's do it." She was determined to use her new supply of power.

With that Elichai took a running leap off of the cliff and expanded his wings. He fell out of view for a moment before rising on the wind with varying colored wings. They were beautiful. She took a deep breath before looking behind her, needing to see him once more.

Atreus sensed her and met eyes with her. He nodded and she took off in a sprint toward the cliff.

"Fly my love," came his voice in her mind as he took up his place where Ender and Rase could see him clearly once they broke through the first wards.

She hated that he was using himself as bait but she knew he was the only one with the ability to subdue them. The magic she used to end Deimos was specifically crafted for Deimos; she didn't know if she had anything for the Hallowed Fallen.

Her heart dropped just as she jumped from the cliffside before her wings shot out as if on instinct and carried her high into the sky. She trailed Elichai, Kit coming up behind her.

"Are we still doing this?" Kit asked.

"Let them hit the spikes first, we'll light 'em up when panic ensues!" Amara shouted at him. Elichai nodded.

They leaned forward and sent themselves over the sea with mighty wing beats, flying as one. They purposely flew high in the sky, Kit shielding them from view as they observed Findaria's army taking up the decks of the ships.

"It's a spell, not part of my Imperium," Kit answered the question she was about to ask.

She spotted the two Hallowed Fallen on the bow of the massive warship at the head of their fleet. Rase was much taller than Ender, he was characterized by his deep red hair, scarred face, and broad shoulders. Ender's wings were extended, sitting higher on his back and smaller than others she had seen. It was the red tint to the wings though and the unique golden blonde hair that reminded her who she suspected Elichai's father to be. He looked so much like their prince, from the shape of his eyes to the way he paced on the deck of the ship.

She turned to Elichai.

"Now is probably not the time to ask but is Ender your sire?"

"Yes he is my queen," he answered as the all veered right in unison to circle the fleet of ships. "No, I will not hesitate to put down my father, just as you didn't."

"I had to ask." She sighed. Bloodlines were so complicated and fickle in their world.

She inspected the massive sails of the wooden vessels. There seemed to be endless ropes, countless men wrestling them into submission to keep the ships moving in the proper direction. The wind was sending the ships toward the cliffs at a higher speed than its passengers would like.

Section leaders were shouting things at their soldiers to get them in whatever formation they needed to be in for their attack.

"30 seconds until that first one makes contact with the spikes, they're still moving at full speed," Kit voiced as they watched over their enemy.

Amara was searching for Juliet's red hair but their clunky silver helmets hid the Nephilim's features. She had underestimated how many soldiers eight warships could carry.

They were rounding the ships again when the chaos began with a loud scraping and wood splintering noise as the ships collided with the traps. Screams erupted from the barges, wings erupting into a cloud of chaos as the Nephilim took to the skies. Amara, Elichai, and Kit remained shielded and invisible.

They just needed them to fly toward the cliffside which appeared empty and barren because of the wards. They had no idea what awaited them on the other side. Amara watched the humans scrambling around on the decks, readying their weapons, and begging the last two ships to turn quickly enough to avoid the trap. With the help of the Nephilim they were able to slow to a stop, nearly capsizing their ship.

"We go for the Nephilim on the still standing ships first," she ordered Kit and Elichai which felt strange.

They dove downward, Kit removing his shield to redirect his power for whatever he was about to attack with. They came into view, a few of the soldiers pointed at them. They didn't have time to raise their spears or their bows . Elichai began his barrage of rapid firing small balls of flame. Some of the Nephilim returned with ice and fire of their own but couldn't reach them. They had the advantage of coming from above.

Amara aimed for the linen sails, the fire catching quickly and forcing the Nephilim into the air. Most of them took off toward their comrades who barreled toward the cliffside just as they intended. About a dozen engaged with them, Elichai wielding a set of swords and effortlessly chopping them down alongside Amara with Eversor. Kit had a bow now and was firing at them as they flew toward the group, even taking down a few with wing shredding arrows as they tried to retreat.

War was dirty, if you showed mercy it could cost your life. That's what she told herself as a Nephilim soldier rushed her, sending her backward and knocking the wind for her due to the clash of their armor. She brought her sword upward, attempting to remove his head but only removing his helmet instead.

"Davian!" She screamed in shock as he hissed at her with black and silver eyes. She heated up, ready to char him alive when he brought waves up from the ocean and sent them crashing over her.

The cold stunned her and extinguished her flames. She tumbled for a moment, toward the ocean, when Elichai intercepted her and allowed her to get her equilibrium. Kit turned and fired an arrow straight through Davian's head. He was sent into the ocean immediately, sinking like a stone.

"No!" She screamed, he might have known where Juliet was.

"Wha—" Kit was grabbed by his foot by an older Nephilim without a helmet.

"Take the ships!" She screamed at Elichai and fired lava over the Nephilim's face. He screamed as it ate away at his flesh, revealing bone, and teeth beneath. He didn't heal as quickly as Deimos did though so Kit drove a dagger through his heart and dropped him into the sea.

She finally realized that the Nephilim had made it to shore, arrows rained down on them, sending many of them into the ocean like rocks. She joined Elichai in setting fire to the ships, humans jumping overboard in panic.

Kit cracked the necks of human soldiers with the twitch of his fingers. It would never cease to amaze Amara. They dropped in pairs until one of the ships was just a mass of bodies. She set fire to it before she could grieve the humans who shouldn't have been involved in the Hallowed's war. It wasn't theirs to fight. They suffered enough under the Hallowed Fallen's thumbs.

"To the cliffside!" Elichai yelled at her and Kit. He followed them as the ships burned and humans screamed in their wake.

Nephilim warriors of Findaria were engaging in violent one-on-one sword fights with the Nephilim of Constantine. Some were airborne, some on their feet. Blood soaked the grass just as it stained the ocean and painted the cliffside. She landed in the grass, nearly stumbling backward when one of the enemy Nephilim cut down one of her soldiers. He fixated on her and then teleported behind her. He kicked her in the back, sending her embarrassingly to the ground. She recovered quickly though and swung Eversor wildly.

The soldier teleported skillfully away from each swing until she phased directly into where he teleported for the last time, effectively sending Eversor through the eye slit in his armor. *Poorly designed.* Blood poured from his head, his eyes frozen wide as he fell. Something was familiar in his eyes.

She jerked her sword from his skull as the battle raged on around her. She kicked his helmet off, her heart lurching because this was somebody she knew. Her breathing increased, the world tilted for a moment as blood soaked his features. He had helped her; he had saved her life. Oryn Nightbane, struck down by her own hand. She turned from him and jerked the base of her helmet up just in time to vomit.

Battle, war, and bloodshed weren't meant for everyone, and they should never be waged between those who once shared bonds. No one should have to kill a friend, a brother, or an instructor. The air was thick with the sounds of dying breaths and strained grunts, haunting her ears and searing into her mind. She knew those sounds would never leave her. Trembling, her stomach churned, on the verge of heaving again, when a sword slashed toward her, aimed directly at her exposed mouth.

She was quick though, jumping backward and allowing the helmet to drop back down. She was so startled that she dropped her own sword. Her opponent had caught her in a moment of weakness and taken it. The other soldier was fast; she brought the sword over her head and toward Amara's. Which forced Amara to throw her forearm upward to block the hit, it ricocheted off of the armor painfully, vibrating into her bone.

She twirled her sword, bringing it against the armor on Amara's ribs. It would leave a bruise. Amara was getting pissed off. While her opponent growled at the impenetrable armor and brought her sword down again, Amara seized the opportunity to phase into the girl. She grabbed her face plate where the breathing and eye slits were far too large. She brought the girl forward, meeting her eyes, and slinging her to the ground with a helmet full of magma. Amara panted and shook out the heat from her hand. The other soldier screamed and wailed as she thrashed, trying to remove the helmet which was turning to liquid metal and melting into her face. The smell and sight overwhelmed Amara so she gathered her sword from the ground and hurried away, leaving her opponent to die an excruciating death alone.

She found Rase engaging with Commander Hale while Atreus seemed to have successfully leashed Ender who was being pulled violently across the ground by his throat with the whip.

Hale was going to die, Rase was getting the upper hand and using his Imperium to flood his mouth with water. *Element wielding, like Davian.* He was going to drown him.

She speared Rase, who didn't bother to wear armor, through the ribs with Eversor and tackled him to the ground. Kit wasn't in her line of sight anymore, neither was Elichai. *Shit.* Rase got to his feet far too quickly, pulled the sword free and discarded it. He sneered at Amara and held on to his bleeding rib while it healed.

"Well well well, if it isn't the bastard sire turned queen." He spat blood on her boots. "A tragedy really that this insignificant kingdom will be mine by nightfall."

She growled at him, the threat burning to her core. *He wouldn't get the chance.* She charged him.

The smell of death and blood filled the air as they sprinted toward one another. Time slowed, impact was imminent. Amara leaped into the air, flipped over him and sent raw flame into his spine. She followed it up with lava which poured from her hands and over him while he sank to his knees. It didn't last long though; he was able to extinguish it all with ice and water which seemed to come from within him.

Amara's eyes found Elichai under someone's sword across the field. The man was on top of him and had him pinned to the ground with the sword against his throat. *No.*

"I need your whip thing over here," she spoke to Atreus but couldn't find him.

She offered a fake apologetic smile at Rase who had been stabbed in the back by Commander Hale. She knew it wouldn't kill him but freed up a moment for her to help Elichai. She hoped Atreus would intervene soon. She sprinted across the blood soaked filled, jumped bodies, and slid under someone swinging a sword to get to her prince. He had the blade between his hands now, fighting with everything he had to keep it out of his throat.

Amara barreled into the man with every ounce of strength she could muster. She grabbed at the white and gold wings, clawing at them as he struggled. She found herself underneath him. She pulled a dagger free from her leg and stabbed upward at the exposed skin of his throat under his helmet. She missed the first time, allowing him to deal a devastating punch to her own helmet. Her ears rang from the impact. She lashed out again, blood pouring down onto her from his throat as Elichai pulled him off of her.

"Where the hell is your helmet and neck guard?" She scolded him. She laid there for a moment, trying to catch her breath.

"Lost it." He grinned. He helped her up with a thankful nod and they turned to take in the scene before them.

Constantine was winning, more soldiers remained on their end than the other. Though there were many of their own soldiers lying motionless on the battlefield. Elichai tugged at her arm.

"Be a little more obvious this is your first battle, my *queen*," he emphasized the word to get his point across. He was right, she needed to pull herself together.

They found Kit wrestling the whip leash that held Ender. He pulled against it but his power had been stifled by the magic of the whip.

"Help the king!" Kit roared.

They found him engaging with Rase, Hale's lifeless body not far from where Amara left him to fight Rase alone. She froze for a moment, swallowing hard. *She left him to die, to save the prince.*

Atreus took a devastating blow to the head from the base of Rase' sword, sending him stumbling backward. She and Prince Elichai glanced at each other with the same heated determination of someone ready to destroy another for touching something they love.

She and Elichai came down on Rase in a storm of fire, they needed to distract him. Atreus shielded himself from another blow that Rase threw his way. He slung out the whip but it wouldn't catch Rase. He was too quick. Atreus regained control of the fight, dealing a brutal kick to Rase' abdomen and sending him to the ground. His crown of red hair fell wildly around his head as he sneered at Atreus and spat blood.

Rase stood and the two engaged in a brutal sword fight, meeting each other blow for blow. Elichai had flown off somewhere but she couldn't be bothered to watch him leave. She jumped forward, ready to help Atreus when Hawk grabbed her arms and held her back from helping Atreus.

"They have to do this one-on-one," Peony told her. "It's about honor, about their kingdoms."

That may be the case but the minute he got the upper hand on Atreus; nothing would stop her from interfering.

Elichai was hauling Ender over by the throat, Kit in tow with Hadeon. *There are far too many Hallowed here.*

Elichai said something to Ender with a sinister smile. He forced him to his knees, relishing in the fact that his limitlessly powerful father had been rendered powerless. Clashing and clanking continued between Rase and Atreus along with the last of the Nephilim.

Elichai held up his hand, the one with the golden serpent ring on it. Ender's face went blank, humor gone. Elichai closed his fingers before dropping his fist and opening it. What must have been a hundred snake looking creatures dropped from his hand and slithered up Ender's body who screamed and thrashed, Amara was running to the scene.

"What did you just do." She panted in fear. More snakes came from his hand, dropped to the ground, and crawled up Ender who was on his knees. He struggled against his son who gripped his hair violently and forced his jaw open.

"You worthless being," Elichai growled before spitting on Ender. Amara was breathless at the sight, at the hatred in Elichai's eyes. It reminded her of her own hatred for her sire. More snakes consumed Ender.

Ender attempted to speak through blood, failing to find the words as pain consumed him.

"You are..." Ender grunted. "Nothing."

The snakes were part shadow part scale and didn't look like anything bred on earth. They slithered into his mouth, down his throat, and invaded his lungs. She saw snakes crawling within his skin as he choked and fought for air against them. They were devouring him from the inside out. She turned away as he was consumed wholly.

You are nothing. A fathers dying words to his estranged son.

The crowd whooped and cheered at the death of one of the Hallowed. Hadeon thrashed against Kit but was bound and gagged.

Constantine's soldiers had begun bringing human prisoners from the ships and dropping them on the shore, all hogtied. It must have been ordered by Atreus to take humans alive if possible.

Rase bellowed a scream at the death of Ender and momentarily had enough anger to overpower Atreus. Amara felt it happened but she couldn't get to him fast enough.

Chapter 48

She had heard many years before that to love is to die, that to love is to suffer death twice. She didn't know what it meant, not until that moment.

Rase slashed Atreus across the face hard enough to spin him around from the impact. Rase brought his sword upward and severed the base of one of Atreus' great wings. Their king roared in pain, shaking the ground beneath them hard enough to take many of them off of their feet.

Amara was discarding her helmet as she ran to him, unable to breathe as her mate was cast forward onto his face. Rase moved swiftly and quickly, tearing his beautiful wing from him. The sound of tearing flesh devastated the crowd who shouted and charged for Rase. Anyone who wasn't engaged in the battle, were going to their king.

"No!" She screamed as his pain laced through her.

It was excruciating, it brought her to her knees as Atreus wailed into the sky. Amara's throat closed, she couldn't move. She felt the absolute and definitive snap of something inside of him.

"To remove part of our wings would be to remove part of our very soul. Our life force and every ounce of power we contain is within our wings," he once told her.

She got to her feet, Elichai was already upon Rase with a sword wedged in the back of his neck. He couldn't be decapitated. "Stand down!" Amara screamed at the soldiers, making it to her mate before they did.

She retrieved the whip from Atreus who was writhing on the ground. Blood was pouring from the wound, his healing abilities diminished. She couldn't soothe him; she couldn't go to him yet. She had to end this. She could feel madness creeping into him, through their bond. It was a dark entity, slithering around his consciousness and constricting.

He was trying to calm her and tell her it would be okay through their bond.

"I'm okay, it's okay, my love."

"It doesn't hurt that bad."

She wiped a lone tear and slung the whip forward, it snapped around Rase waste who was speaking something in another language, spitting insults at her and Elichai.

Kit was at Atreus' side with his council.

"The coven! Bring my coven! Now!" He was screaming. "And the healers! And the Coven of the Western Village! All of them!"

Rase was laughing and horrible evil laugh.

"Poor rebel king," he taunted Amara.

She yanked the whip forward, sneering at him. He fell forward to his knees. Elichai was shaking and staring forward, he was shutting himself down. She couldn't do that, she had to finish what they started.

She drove her boot into Rase's mouth, cutting off his smug grin, then followed it with a punch that shattered his jaw with a sickening crack, sending him crumpling to the ground. A storm of violent thoughts swirled in her mind, each more brutal than the last. She would make him suffer, starting with his wings—the same way he harmed her mate. Rase struggled, his limbs weak as he tried to push himself back to his knees.

"Now you bow before the rebel queen," she snarled through gritted teeth. Without hesitation, she delivered another blow to his broken, barely healing jaw, feeling her own knuckles split open on impact. Blood dripped from her hand, but the pain was meaningless. Elichai's boot connected with Rase's spine, and Amara heard the unmistakable sound of bones snapping beneath the force.

She planted her foot on his head, forcing him down, and raised her sword high. With a swift, decisive movement, she drove the blade between his wings, his body writhing beneath her as he desperately tried to retract them. But it was too late—he was pinned. She tore into his wings with her bare hands, ripping at the feathers first. Blood sprayed into the air, staining the ground and sky with crimson as feathers flew around her like grotesque confetti. His wings tried to heal, regrowing feathers as fast as she could tear them out, but she was relentless.

Finally, Amara reached the base of his wings. She dropped to her knees, breathing heavily, her heart pounding with fury. Unsheathing her dagger, she carved into the flesh at the root of his wings, her movements brutal and deliberate. This wasn't just a punishment—it was an execution of his pride, his identity. She would rip them from him, every last shred of what made him soar, made him sane.

She wasn't just removing his wings. She would hang them for all to see, a grim display of her victory over him.

Amara looked up, her hands slick with blood, and met Elichai's distant, hollow gaze. He stood there, whip in hand, his eyes locked on his brother, empty and broken as if his soul had already left him.

"You bitch!" Rase screamed once she jerked the meaty base of the wing from his shoulder blade. His blood splattered upward and all over her.

She lashed out and stabbed him repeatedly in the face and head when Atreus screamed in pain at whatever Kit was doing. She caught her breath, not caring if the soldiers were watching her. She carved out his other wing, plucking it free from his body. He was twitching and mouthing non-words by the time she was done.

She set fire to him. He burned and burned and burned. He healed and burned more. His screams echoed over the battlefield. She was on her knees continuing to burn him until she finally had enough. She let the flames die, leaving him there bound in the whip and groaning. Hadeon was watching on in horror.

"Barbarians! Animals!" Hadeon declared.

Amara got to the ground beside her mate. The mind-numbing pain rolling off of him and into her was too much.

"Elichai, delay Hadeon's execution. Have him returned to his cave." She leveled out her mind and began giving orders. "I want Rase hung by his throat in the same cave, using the whip as a noose."

"Yes, my queen," he said distantly. The battle itself was concluding, most of the enemy Nephilim dead or captured with the humans.

Fog roll over the battlefield as though the land were grieving all of the death, weeping for what had been done to its king. She pulled him into her arms and took to the sky with Kit who had his severed wing. Atreus grinned weakly.

"You're carrying me this time," he whispered.

"Don't get used to it," she quipped half-heartedly. She wondered how long he had until he lost his mind. Minutes? Days?

She pushed her hand into his hair, feeling the strands between her fingers. She couldn't lose him. She wouldn't be able to endure it. She inhaled his familiar scent, now laced with foreign blood, dirt, and sweat.

"Get me to the throne room, I must address my kingdom." He grunted.

"Atreus..." she protested. He needed to get to the healers.

She felt him then, waging war against that darkness which was creeping into him. It was violent, constant, unyielding. He was fighting it with everything he had. She felt his energy being drained.

"I have to address them before—" she cut him off.

"Before nothing, you're going to be okay," it came out as more of a whimper.

He made a small scoffing sound which caused him to wince, his blood still seeping from his wound.

"Get the witches and healers to the throne hall!" She instructed Kit, who glanced at her in confusion. He didn't question it.

They landed; Atreus' heavy breathing filled the empty hall but he stood. He leaned into one of the pillars and groaned but walked to his throne. He crashed into it violently, hanging his hand and he huffed through the pain. She approached him and held his face in her hands, pulling his weary eyes up to hers.

She planted a soft kiss on his lips which were far too cold, too foreign. *No.* He pulled her into his lip but she hesitated.

"Please, my love," he pleaded. So she did, ever so gently. "To hold you is the greatest gift."

"You can't say stuff like that," she nestled into his chest.

"Like what?" he whispered and hugged her close.

"Like you're saying goodbye." She sniffled.

"Goodbyes are for mortals, my love. We are not mortals. We are eternity," he said into her hair and kissed the top of her forehead. He inhaled her scent as though trying to memorize it.

She realized when she prodded into his mind that he was using her to keep himself together, to tether himself to reality. She was his anchor in the storm that insanity waged on him. His breathing became jagged and his eyes glazed over for a moment, his entire body rigid. He shook it off quickly and she straightened up in his lap.

"Here." She straddled him and offered him her neck. *Blood would help, right?*

He didn't hesitate like she expected, he didn't even use one of her daggers to cut her. He bared his teeth and bit down onto her jugular roughly. She grunted and jumped but didn't tear free. He clamped down harder and she felt him drawing her blood from her. She wrapped her arms around his head and held him there with her eyes closed.

She knew it was probably the last time she would ever hold him that way, the last time he would drink from her. She cried silently into his hair, his beautiful crown of hair. *Don't go. Please don't go.*

"I have to, baby." His voice came down their mental bond. She didn't realize her silent pleading could be heard. *Please no.*

Upon people entering the throne hall, he finally tore himself free. His pupils were blown wide, the black nearly overtaking his ocean eyes completely. Blood coated his mouth and ran down his chin. He looked feral, animalistic. He was shuddering but leveled out his breathing. He wiped his mouth and she stood from his lap with a kiss on his forehead.

The healers urged him to turn so they could work on the wound itself where the wing was removed. He cooperated but she could sense that he felt it was unnecessary.

"The people are coming," Kit informed them.

Kit knew when she told him to come to the throne hall exactly what his king needed. He needed to address his people. She placed a hand over her mouth and turned from her mate. Kit was at her side.

"He is fighting it off, I fear he won't last much longer," he whispered. She nodded. She already knew that. The fact that he wasn't reduced to a spitting snapping animal already was miraculous. "We will find a way to restore him."

She appreciated Kit's attempt to comfort her but it felt like empty hope. She looked at Atreus, who had lost consciousness, bent forward while the healers stitched him together. He came to a moment later, hyperventilating and looking around frantically. He was losing it; she could sense it.

The throne hall filled quickly with murmuring citizens. Witches, Nephilim, and humans all regarding their king in concern. Surely they'd heard the news.

"My people." He didn't stand but he regarded them with affection. "Once again a time has come where I must leave you."

Once again? Was he referring to his time in Findaria or his absence during whatever Lady Jane did?

"No victory is without its risks, without its losses. I have faith that I will return to you. I have faith that my queen and my court will care for you as I have. I only ask that you embrace her and that you do not waste more than a day mourning me." He was speaking loudly, confidently. His nails were digging into the stone though as he fought off whatever was causing him to twitch.

The hall was silent, only small weeping sounds could be heard.

"Mommy, what's wrong with the king?" A small child near the front asked her mother, who shushed her.

Amara stood by Atreus' side, watching him. The blue faded completely and gave way to shadows which threatened to take the whites of his eyes too. Fear spiked from him, flying into her and crashing like a deadly wave as the insanity overtook him further.

Madame Tate placed a hand on his shoulder and nodded to Kit. Amara watched as Kit removed some kind of shackles from his belt. Atreus stood on shaky legs and held his hands out to his Guard Captain. He regarded him with a thankful nod, sorrow behind his eyes. Kit's own eyes filled with tears.

The entire kingdom dropped to their knees in unison, a wave of hundreds gathered outside the throne hall and along the stone steps. Each placed a fist over their heart, heads bowed in reverence. Their gazes fixed on the torn wing with horror and dread, the air heavy with the weight of what had transpired. A somber silence enveloped the kingdom, thick with sorrow. Amara could no longer contain her tears as they spilled down her face, carving paths through the grief that clung to her.

He faced her, shaking from the pain that was coursing through his body. She touched his shackled hands, his fingers grazing hers.

"It seems the stars will bow before you sooner than I had hoped." He was growing weaker. He was fighting to stay conscious; to stay mentally sound, she could feel it.

"I love you," she choked out in a whisper. "I will bring you back from this."

His eyes turned foreign and he was staring through her at that. He dropped to his knees suddenly and she could hear his kneecaps shatter against the stone.

"I love you," was the last thing he sent down their mental connection. Atreus had lost consciousness, slumped in Madame Tate's arms before his people— who couldn't find the strength to rise from their knees.

Elichai entered then, staring from the back of the throne hall at his brother. His gray eyes found Amara's, his own flooded with tears too. He seemed to be moving in slow motion as he approached the dais to retrieve his brother.

"Kit, I can't," she cried and turned to him. She collapsed then, Kit dropping to the ground with her.

"I know." He rocked back and forth with her in his lap. "I know."

"He's strong, the witches can help him. They will help him," Kit offered. "Our king will live."

She didn't doubt he would live—after all, he was truly immortal—but the thought brought her no comfort. What she feared was the madness that would consume him. If they couldn't heal him, he would descend into a darkness from which there was no return. His mind would break, leaving him a shell of the being he once was. She had seen what became of fallen angels when their wings were severed, the hollow shells they became, lost within their own minds, prisoners of their mutilated bodies. A fate worse than death awaited him.

Amara's gaze drifted to Elichai as he quietly slipped through a hidden passage, Atreus limp in his arms. Behind him, witches and healers followed, their faces etched with urgency and concern. The sight of Atreus, the king who had once commanded such strength, now broken and vulnerable, sent a pang through her chest. When he was finally gone from the dais, the people filtered out of the throne hall in stunned silence, their faces a reflection of the kingdom's sorrow.

She knew she should rise, address them as their queen, offer some semblance of strength in this moment of despair—but her body refused to move. She was rooted to the ground, weighed down by the enormity of what had just transpired, her limbs heavy with grief. All she could do was sit there, staring at the spot where Atreus had once stood, her heart torn between fear and the unrelenting ache of loss.

Amara didn't leave his side for over a month. Only then, it took Prince Elichai and three guards to pull her out for her own well-being. Once he awoke after about twelve hours of silence, she had been faced with new horrors.

His ocean blue eyes melted into pools of black, his teeth elongated, and he lost the ability to speak. He viciously and continuously bit at anyone who approached him. To her horror, they were feeding him raw animal meat to satiate his bloodlust and newfound cannibalistic nature.

She found herself curled into a ball in a corner of his cave crying while he snarled and thrashed against the chains. She watched the skin she loved to kiss decay and heal just to repeat the cycle. He bit into his bottom lip until it was shredded, the chains flayed his skin from the pressure he put on them despite the efforts everyone made to prevent it. He vomited blood and defecated on himself and made it impossible for the healers to try to clean and dress him.

The few times she tried to speak to him in hopes he could hear her, he only grew more violent. It was easier the first week when she couldn't access his mind. It was when his mind opened up to her that she was truly inconsolable.

He screamed constantly, a deep blood-curdling scream that echoed off of the inside of her head. He bellowed and cried her name into nothingness while his body and mind wasted away. She tried to speak to him but he couldn't hear her, she couldn't reach him. What remained of his consciousness was hidden deep in the back of his mind where she couldn't access him. He never stopped screaming. The screams just didn't stop. Eventually she had to put a block on her own mind just to silence the agony which she couldn't free him from. Even then, she would never forget the sound of her mate in pain.

To love someone is to suffer death twice. To watch someone you love become a stranger though, was to die over and over again every day.

Epilogue

Amara had suffered only one literal death where her heart stopped. Since then, she has suffered exactly two hundred and seventeen deaths. Every single day that Atreus suffered, a part of her died again.

"My queen." Prince Elichai found her on the beach watching the stars.

"Elichai." She smiled; he sat beside her.

Elichai spent a lot of time blaming himself for what happened to Atreus. Thinking that his need to kill his father led to Atreus' fate. She tried to argue with him that it didn't but maybe there was part of her that believed if he hadn't killed Ender, Atreus might not have been overpowered by Rase' anger. She didn't see a point though, in blaming anybody. She spent enough time blaming herself for Hale's death.

If she hadn't helped Elichai, would things have ended differently? If she was going to blame anyone, it was going to be herself. She tossed a seashell into the ocean.

"What is the next punishment for Rase?" Elichai asked.

She had spent much time orchestrating elaborate ways to ensure Rase's suffering while he fell into insanity. She'd left him engulfed in flames for a week, hanging for two, in a pit of snakes for a short time. He couldn't die. There were a lot of ways to torture him and she had infinite time. Mental agony wasn't enough; she needed him to suffer physically.

"Hang him from the cliff's edge, allow him to be submerged. I want him to die of drowning repeatedly," she instructed. She wanted him to suffer even a fraction of what she and Atreus were suffering.

"And Hadeon?"

"The same." She grinned sinisterly. Hadeon was still sane, his wings intact.

"Absolutely," Elichai smiled in excitement. "Such a merciless queen." He seemed genuinely proud of her.

"To our enemies anyway." She shrugged. She had actually been relatively kind to the human prisoners, even allowing some of them to have homes and build lives in Constantine once they swore fealty to her.

"And I appreciate that." He grinned playfully.

"Any word from the Hallowed's realm?"

"Discourse, the remaining are fighting over Ender, Hadeon, and Rase's kingdoms," he answered.

"Just as I expected, they won't come snooping around here."

"They're just biding their time." He sighed.

"How is Juliet adjusting?"

They found her cowering on a broken piece of one of the ships. Amara knew she wasn't meant for war but was far beyond relieved that she was alive.

"She seems to be doing well, I believe she and Eros intend to ask for a home of their own soon," he informed her. She smiled and nodded. She would take care of that later.

"The witches...they believe they have found something," he informed her.

The witches would not stop until Atreus was healed and restored. She had ordered it to be.

"I will go down there when they have made progress for certain," she told him as she had many times before. She could not bear to see him.

"The answer was in the riddle given by your ancestors," he told her. She still couldn't figure out what that riddle meant and it took months for the witches to learn.

"I doubt that, I'm pretty sure they were just trying to get rid of me."

He sat next to her, hesitating to tell her what he learned.

"Caius' blood is the answer," he said.

She turned to him, her eyes wide.

No.

The most heartbreaking truth of Atreus' story was that only when he descended into madness, did he finally become a father. Despite his claims that he didn't long for a child, his journals detailed hundreds of years of asking why he couldn't procreate.

She didn't know how but they had conceived a child on the night she became queen. He had never been able to have a child in nearly a thousand years of life. It was never a possibility for him and he had no idea now that he had a son. That *they* had a son.

Elichai placed Caius into her arms, aged only a week. She brushed his onyx strands of hair from his forehead. He squirmed but remained sleeping. His eyes were the same deep blue as his father's, a truth that caused her to weep on many occasions.

Caius was the answer to saving his father. For the first time she had hope that Atreus would know his son. Though she would not sacrifice one for the other. Elichai met her eyes and they regarded each other with some mixture of hopeful concern as Caius cooed at a shooting star.

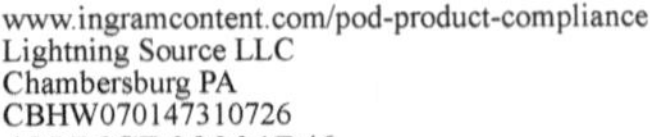
www.ingramcontent.com/pod-product-compliance
Lightning Source LLC
Chambersburg PA
CBHW070147310726
48976CB00001B/6